KEEPER

OF

DREAMS

ALSO BY ORSON SCOTT CARD
FROM TOM DOHERTY ASSOCIATES

FROM OTHER PUBLISHERS

Orson Scott Card's InterGalactic Medicine Show at oscigms.com

KEEPER
OF
DREAMS

ORSON SCOTT CARD

A TOM DOHERTY ASSOCIATES BOOK
NEW YORK

KEEPER OF DREAMS

Copyright © 2008 by Orson Scott Card

A Tor Book
Published by Tom Doherty Associates, LLC
175 Fifth Avenue
New York, NY 10010

www.tor-forge.com

Tor® is a registered trademark of Tom Doherty Associates, LLC.

The Library of Congress has catalogued the hardcover edition as follows:

Card, Orson Scott.
    Keeper of dreams / Orson Scott Card.—1st ed.
        p. cm.
    "A Tom Doherty Associates book."
    ISBN 978-0-7653-0497-1
    1. Science fiction, American. 2. Fantasy fiction, American. I. Title.
PS3553.A655K44   2008
813'.54—dc22

2007046720

ISBN 978-0-7653-2414-6

First Hardcover Edition: April 2008
First Trade Paperback Edition: April 2010

Printed in the United States of America

0 9 8 7 6 5 4 3 2 1

FIRST PUBLICATION

SCIENCE FICTION

"The Elephants of Poznan"—*Fantastyka* (Poland)

"Atlantis"—*Grails: Quests, Visitations and Other Occurrences,* ed. Richard Gilliam, Martin H. Greenberg, and Edward E. Kramer

"Geriatric Ward"—Written for *Last Dangerous Visions,* ed. Harlan Ellison, but never published

"Heal Thyself"—*Amazing Stories,* Summer 1999

"Space Boy"—*Escape from Earth: New Adventures in Space,* ed. Gardner Dozois and Jack Dann

"Angles"—*Destination 3001,* ed. Robert Silverberg and Jacques Chambon (France)

FANTASY

"Vessel"—*BEM Magazine* (Spanish); *The Magazine of Fantasy and Science Fiction,* December 1999 (English)

"Dust"—*Doorways*

"Homeless in Hell"—http://www.hatrack.com/osc/stories/homeless-in-hell.shtml

"In the Dragon's House"—*The Dragon Quintet,* ed. Marvin Kaye

"Inventing Lovers on the Phone"—*Stars: Original Stories Based on the Songs of Janis Ian,* ed. Janis Ian and Mike Resnick

"Waterbaby"—*Galaxy Online*

"Keeper of Lost Dreams"—*Flights: Visions of Extreme Fantasy,* ed. Al Sarrantonio

"Missed"—*Greensboro News & Record*

To Andy and Debbie Lindsay.
The play's the thing . . .

Contents

III LITERARY

IV HATRACK RIVER

V MORMON STORIES

PREFACE

When I was just starting out as a writer, one of the reasons I chose to work in the science-fiction genre was because there was a viable short-story market—one that paid, but not enough to live on.

This was and remains vitally important to science fiction's success as a genre of literature. Short stories give writers a place to try out their ideas and find their voices, with an audience to goad them on, through either their jeers or their applause. A new writer's short story is published in the company of other people's work, rubbing shoulders with fiction that appeals to different people and uses different techniques.

It's like being invited to a crowded party, where you don't know anybody but you're pressed by the crowd right into the middle and rather forced to be part of the conversation whether you like it or not.

But because short stories don't pay well, anyone trying to make a career in science fiction has to move to novels as quickly as possible. Novels are a different form from the short story and not everyone learns how to make the transition. However, most do.

This means that the "stars" who might dominate the party are always being drawn out another door, and the new short-story writer has a chance to become something of a hit at the party. Short-story writers get *noticed*. And that is more important to a young writer than the money.

Truly.

If you got three thousand bucks for a short story but never heard the slightest feedback, the money would be gone and you would feel empty. But get three hundred bucks for the story and a lot of comment, with (perhaps) a Nebula recommendation or two, and you are much encouraged. Or even if somebody absolutely *savages* your story, then—unless you're so fragile you can't stand the slightest jostling—you buckle down to show *them* what you can do.

At the same time, if you got only *thirty* dollars, then it would feel like a hobby instead of a profession.

That's the situation I found when I entered the science-fiction field—a handful of magazines, paying not too much, not too little: *Analog, Fantasy and Science Fiction, Galaxy,* and, at that precise moment, *Amazing* and *Fantastic.* Soon the last three would disappear, but a new one—*Isaac Asimov's Science Fiction Magazine*—arose and quickly outsold them all.

And then *Omni* came along and for a short while dosed the field with payments in the thousands of dollars.

It was a heady time, with *Asimov's* and *Analog* selling upwards of 100,000 copies per issue and *F&SF* not far behind at a steady 80,000.

It's a different world today. The numbers for the magazines are wincingly smaller. I think the main reason is that the newsstands are gone. Now, if you see a sci-fi magazine at all, it's at the back of the bottom shelf at Barnes & Noble or Borders; a tall person has to kneel to even know that shelf exists.

Or it might be a decline in the science-fiction field as a whole. Or a decline in the quality of the editing. Or the rise of fantasy as the dominant form of speculative fiction. Or the movement of science fiction to television and the movies instead of print. I'm not pretending to know why the circulation numbers are now in the 8,000–20,000 range, less than a fifth of what they used to be.

But the need for short stories hasn't abated. It's still where new writers get discovered.

There have been quite a few excellent anthologies to take up the slack. The trouble is that most anthologies—and certainly the ones that sell best—put together known writers, each of whom brings some portion of his audience to the book. So new writers need not apply.

The only exception is the outstanding *Writers of the Future* series, which has, for decades now, devoted itself to discovering new writers and introducing them to the public. Many a fine career has begun in the pages of that anthology series.

And I'm not the only one who has tried to find a way to use the net to reinvent the sci-fi magazine. My modestly titled *Orson Scott Card's InterGalactic Medicine Show* (at http://www.oscigms.com) is my effort to try to keep alive for a new generation of writers something like the situation I found when I was starting out. With occasional print anthologies drawn from the online zine to help draw people from the bookstore to the net, I hope we—and others as well—can succeed.

But what about *my* short stories? I'm not starting out anymore. I came to the short-story party, I jostled around for a while, and then I went on to write novels, which is where my career is firmly settled.

A story collection called *Maps in a Mirror* brought together most of my short fiction from that early formative stage of my career. Only a few of the early stories were excluded—the ones that belonged in story cycles, like *The Worthing Saga* and *The Folk of the Fringe,* or the stories that were always fragments of novels, like the Hatrack River stories that ended up in *Seventh Son, Red Prophet,* and *Prentice Alvin.*

I was done with short stories, wasn't I? And yet here we are with another big fat book of short fiction by Orson Scott Card. Where did all *this* stuff come from?

What's the inducement for an established writer to return to the short-story market? While it's true that short stories require less typing than novels, they don't take much less in the way of development. That is, to get a story ready to be written, to bring it to ripeness, takes about as much time and effort no matter how long the finished fiction turns out to be.

So why would I devote any time to writing short stories, for a few hundred or, sometimes, a few thousand dollars, when I can get many times more if I turn that idea into a book?

Believe me, that's not a rhetorical question. Sometimes, when I'm late on a book which will actually pay the bills, and I stop to write a short story that I promised to an anthology editor, my wife looks at me and says (only more nicely), "What were you *thinking*?"

Good question.

How does a serious novelist end up with more than 200,000 words of short stories, novelets, and novellas?

One answer is: I'm one of the writers who gets invited to take part in some really cool anthologies. Robert Silverberg tells me about a series of big-name-only science-fiction and fantasy anthologies he's editing, and invites me to contribute a story to the sci-fi volume. Sure, I say—are you kidding? He's not just a friend, he's a legend in the field, and it's going to be a great book.

Or a total stranger says, We're doing an anthology of stories about the Vietnam War, and I say, I didn't fight in that war, and I didn't fight against it, I don't see what I could contribute . . . but then my mind starts ticking over the problem and I realize there *is* a story for somebody like me to write and so I write it.

Or they're putting together a book for the World Fantasy Convention just at the time that I'm developing this cool concept of the source of all the stories of the Flood, and so instead of waiting till I'm ready to write the novel, I write a very long story that gets it down on paper. It's a trial run. I'm still going to write the novel . . . someday.

Or I go to another country and see a plaza that is so fascinating I have to set a story there, and just at that moment I'm reading a fascinating book about elephants, and those two things come together and I have to write the story.

Or Christmas is coming, and on a lark I decide to whip out a whimsical little Christmas story.

So it comes to four things driving this novelist, at least, to write short stories:

1. The irresistible anthology.
2. Stories for a particular occasion.
3. The big idea that has to get down on paper so I might as well try it out as a short story first and see if it's good enough to grow into a book.
4. The jewel of an idea that is fully formed and simply *has* to exist as a short story, even if it doesn't make me any money.

Story by story, I'll tell you in afterwords just how each of these tales arose. Right here, though, I'll simply tell you how surprised I was to realize just how much short fiction I had written over the years. Some of my best work is here, I think.

I appreciate your being willing to look at my shorter pieces, and I hope you find them worth the time you devote to them.

But I hope you'll also remember that there are new writers out there, trying to be part of the conversation. Look for the magazines—online or in print—and the anthologies and collections. Give them a try. I can promise you that now and then—more often than you might suppose—you'll find something and somebody wonderful.

Because if sci fi is to survive as a genre, it won't be because readers stick to books with familiar names on the cover. I grew up in the era when the great triumvirate of Heinlein, Asimov, and Clarke ruled the field. But they aren't producing much anymore. They moved on. So will the next generation, and the one after that. If there is no *new* generation to take their place, then the genre becomes a part of literary history, no longer able to produce great new work. And if a new generation is to take flight, it will fledge in the nest of short fiction.

I

SCIENCE FICTION

THE ELEPHANTS OF POZNAN

In the heart of old Poznan, the capital of Great Poland since ancient times, there is a public square called Rynek Glowny. The houses around it aren't as lovely as those of Krakow, but they have been charmingly painted and there is a faded graciousness that wins the heart. The plaza came through World War II more or less intact, but the Communist government apparently could not bear the thought of so much wasted space. What use did it have? Public squares were for public demonstrations, and once the Communists had seized control on behalf of the people, public demonstrations would never be needed again. So out in the middle of the square they built a squat, ugly building in a brutally modern style. It sucked the life out of the place. You had to stand with your back to it in order to truly enjoy the square.

But we'd all seen the ugly building for so many years that we hardly noticed it anymore, except to apologize to visitors, ruefully remember the bad old days of Communism, and appreciate the irony that the occupants of such a tasteless building should include a restaurant, a bookshop, and an art gallery. And when the plague came and the city was so cruelly and suddenly emptied, those of us who could not let go of Poznan, who could not bear to eke out the last of our lives in the countryside, drifted to the old heart of the city and took up residence in the houses surrounding the square. As time passed, even the ugly building became part of the beauty of the place, for it had been part of the old crowded city now lost forever. Just as the toilets with little altars for the perusal of one's excrement reminded us of the many decades of German overlordship, so this building was also a part of our past, and now, by its sheer persistence among us, a part of ourselves. If we could venerate the bones and other bodily parts of dead saints, couldn't we also find holiness of a kind even in this vile thing? It was a relic of a time when we thought we were suffering, but to which we now would gladly return, just to hear schoolchildren again in the streets, just to see the flower shop once more selling the bright excesses of overcopious nature, spots of vivid color to show us that Poland was not, by nature, grey.

Into this square came the elephants, a group of males, making their way in what seemed a relentless silence, except that a trembling of the windows told us that they *were* speaking to each other in infrasound, low notes that the human ear could not hear, but the human hand could feel on glass. Of course we had all seen elephants for years on our forays out into the gardens of suburban Poznan—clans of females and their children following a matriarch, gangs of mature males hanging out to kill time until one of them went into musth and set off in search of the nearest estrous female. We speculated at first about where they came from, whether their forebears had escaped from a zoo or a circus during the plague. But soon we realized that their numbers were far too great to be accounted for that way. Too many different clans had been seen. On Radio Day we learned, from those few stations that still bothered, that the elephants had come down the Nile, swum the Suez, swarmed through Palestine and Syria and Armenia, crossed the Caucasus, and now fed in the lush wheat pastures of Ukraine, bathed in the streams of Belarus, and stood trumpeting on the shores of Estonia and Pomerania, calling out to some god of the sea, demanding passage to lands as yet unpossessed by the great stumpy feet, the probing noses, the piercing ivory, and the deep thrumming music of the new rulers of the world.

Why should they not rule it? We were only relics ourselves, we who had had the misfortune of surviving the plague. Out of every hundred thousand, only fifty or a hundred had survived. And as we scavenged in the ruins, as we bulldozed earth over the corpses we dragged from the areas where we meant to live, as we struggled to learn how to keep a generator or two running, a truck here and there, the radios we used only once a week, then once a month, then once a year, we gradually came to realize that there would be no more children. No one conceived. No one bore.

The disease had sterilized us, almost all. There would be no recovery from this plague. Our extinction had not required a celestial missile to shatter the earth and darken the sky for a year; no other species shared our doom with us. We had been taken out surgically, precisely, thoroughly, a tumor removed with a delicate viral hand.

So we did not begrudge the elephants their possession of the fields and the forests. The males could knock down trees to show their strength; there was no owner to demand that animal control officers come and dispose of the rampaging beasts. The females could gather their children into barns and stables against the winter blast, and no owner would evict them; only the crumbling bones and strands of hairy flesh showed where horses and cattle had starved to death when their masters died too quickly to think of setting them free from their stalls and pens.

Why, though, had these males come into the city? There was nothing for them to eat. There was nothing for *us* to eat; when our bicycles gave out and we could cobble together no more makeshift carts, we would have to leave the city ourselves and live closer to the food that we gathered from untended fields. Why would the elephants bother with such a ruin? Curiosity, perhaps. Soon they would see that there was nothing here for them, and move on.

We found ourselves growing impatient as the hours passed, and the days, and still we kept encountering them on the city streets. Didn't they understand that we lived in the heart of Poznan specifically because we wanted a human place? Didn't they feel our resentment of their trespass? All the rest of Earth is yours; can you not leave undesecrated these crypts we built for ourselves in the days of our glory?

Gradually it dawned on us—dawned on me, actually, but the others realized I was right—that the elephants had come not to explore Poznan, but to observe *us*. I would pedal my bicycle and glance down a cross street to see an elephant lumbering along on a parallel path; I would turn, and see him behind me, and feel that shuddering in my breastbone, in my forehead, that told me they were speaking to each other, and soon another elephant would be shadowing me, seeing where I went, watching what I did, following me home.

Why were they interested in us? Humans were no longer killing them for their ivory. The world was theirs. We were going to die—I, who was only seven years old when the plague came, am now past thirty, and many of the older survivors are already, if not at death's door, then studying the travel brochures and making reservations, their Bibles open and their rosaries in hand. Were these males here as scientists, to watch the last of the humans, to study our deathways, to record the moment of our extinction so that the elephants would remember how we died with only a whimper, or less than that, a whisper, a sigh, a sidelong glance at God?

I had to know. For myself, for my own satisfaction. If I found the truth, whom else would I tell it to, and for what purpose? they would only die as I would die, taking memory with them into the fire, into the ash, into the dust. I couldn't get any of the others to care about the questions that preyed upon me. What do the elephants want from us? Why do they follow us?

Leave it alone, Lukasz, they said to me. Isn't it enough that they don't bother us?

And I answered with the most perplexing question of all, to me at least. Why elephants? The other wild animals that roamed the open country were the ones one might expect to see: the packs of dogs gone wild, interbreeding back to mongrel wolfhood; the herds of cattle, breeding back to hardiness; and of horses, quick and free and uninterested in being tamed. The companions of man, the servants and slaves of man, now masterless, now free. Unshorn sheep. Unmilked goats. Sudden-leaping housecats. Scrawny wild chickens hiding from ever-vigilant hawks. Ill-tempered pigs rooting in the woods, the boars making short work of dogs that grew too bold. That was the wildlife of Europe. No other animals from Africa had made the journey north. Only the elephants, and not just from Africa—the elephants of India were roaming the orient, and on the most recent Radio Day we learned, through messages relayed many times, that they had somehow crossed the Bering Strait and were now, in ever greater numbers, grazing the prairies of America, small-eared cousins to the great-canopied beasts that now shadowed us on the streets of Poz-nan. I pictured them swimming, or piling onto boats that some last human pilot guided for them onto the stygian shore.

They had inherited the Earth, and were bent on surveying their new domain.

So I took to spending my days in the library, reading all I could about elephants, and then about all the processes of life, all the passages of history, trying to understand not only them but ourselves, and what had happened to us, and what our cities might mean to them, our houses, our streets, our rusting cars, our collapsing bridges, our sorry cemetery mounds where winter brought fresh crops of human bone to the surface, white stubble on a fallow field. I write this now because I think I know the answers, or at least have found guesses that ring true to me, though I also know they might be nothing more than a man hungry for meanings inventing them where they don't exist. Arguably, all meanings are invented anyway; and since I have no one to please but myself, and no one to read this who will care, except perhaps one, then I may write as I please, and think as I please, and reread this whenever I can bear it.

They made no effort to follow me inside the library. What good would it do them? Clever as they were with their inquisitive trunks, I could imagine them being deft enough to turn pages without tearing them. But what would the markings on the pages mean to them? Elephants sang their literature to each other in octaves we humans could not hear. Their science was the science of the temporal gland, the probing nose. They observed, but—or so I thought—did not experiment.

I did learn enough to warn the others before the first of the males went into musth. When you see one of them acting agitated, when his temporal glands pour out a steady black streak down his cheeks, when the other males are shy of him and give him room, then we must do the same, staying out of his way, not meeting his gaze. Let him pass. The city is his, wherever he wants to go. He won't stay here long, in musth. He must go and find a female then, and they were all outside in the open fields. He would give his deep rumbling call and pour out his lusty scent into the air and dribble musky fluid onto the ground where every other elephant could smell it and know: This way passed a male bent on making babies. This way passed God, looking for the Holy Virgin.

So we studied each other, and avoided offending each other, and grew used to each other's ways, the elephants and the fifty remaining residents of Poznan.

And then one day they began to push.

The males all gathered in the public square. We, too, gossiping to each other that something important was going to happen, gathered in our houses and leaned at our windows to watch.

They wandered aimlessly through the square, eleven of them—the twelve apostles, I thought, sans Iscariot—until noon made the smallest shadows. Then, as if of one mind, they surrounded the ugly old Communist building, facing it. When all were in place, they moved forward, slowly, each bull resting his massive brow against the miserable façade. Then, slowly, each began to tense his muscles, to shift his weight, to make little adjustments, to plant his feet, and then to push with greater and greater strength against the wall.

They're trying to push it down, I realized. And so did the others, all of us calling out to each other in our high-pitched human voices.

They're critics of architecture!

They've come to beautify Poznan!

We began to address the elephants with our calls, as if they were our football team, as if the plaza were a playing field. We cheered them, laughed in approval, shouted encouragement, placed meaningless bets about whether they could actually break through the walls.

Then, abruptly, I was no longer part of the playfulness. For without meaning to, I changed perspective suddenly, and saw us as the elephants must have seen us. This was Africa after all, and we were the primates perched in the trees, hooting and screeching at the giants, unaware of our own insignificance, or at least unbothered by it.

When I pulled my head back inside my window, I was filled with grief, though at that moment I could not have told you why. I thought at first it was because we humans were so diminished, reduced to chattering from safe perches. But then I realized that the human race had always been the same, had never risen, really, from our primate ways. No, what I was grieving for was that ugly old building, that relic of noble dreams gone sour. I had never lived under Communism, had only heard the stories of the Russian overlords and the Polish Communists who claimed to be fulfilling the will of the masses and perhaps, sometimes, believed their own propaganda—so my father told me, and I had no reason to doubt him. When the Communists decided what was good and what was bad, they acted as rigidly as any Puritan. Aesthetic concerns in architecture led to wasteful overspending of the labor of the working class; therefore, the ugliness of all new buildings was a badge of virtue. We human beings had reinvented ourselves, *Homo sovieticus, Homo coprofabricus,* or whatever the scientific name would be. A new species that never guessed how quickly it would be extinct.

The elephants would keep pushing until the walls came down—I knew that. Intransigence was built into the elephants' shoulders the way screeching and chattering were built into the primate mouth. And even though the other humans were cheering them, egging them on, I was sad. No, wistful. If we had really wanted that ugly building taken down, we knew where the dynamite was kept, we could have blown it out of existence. Elephants are mighty and strong, as beasts go, but when it comes to destruction, their foreheads are no match for the explosives in the locked sheds at the construction sites of buildings that will never be finished.

We don't need you to take it down, you meddlers, I wanted to say. We built it, we humans. It's ours. What right have you to decide which artifacts should stand, and which should fall?

The fascination of it was irresistible, though. I couldn't stay away from the window for long. I had to check, again, again, to see if they were making any progress, to see if some crack had appeared. The beasts had enormous patience, pushing and pushing until their shadows were swallowed up in the shade of the buildings as the sun headed out past Germany, past France, out to the Atlantic to be plunged steaming into the sea of night. That was the clock they lived by, these elephants; they had put in their day's work, and now they wandered off, heading out of the city as they did most nights, to eat and drink and sleep in some more hospitable place.

The next morning they were back, earlier this time, and formed their circle much more quickly, and pushed again. The betting among us began in earnest, then. Would they succeed? Would they give up? How long till the first crack? How long till a wall fell? We had nothing of value to bet; or rather, we had everything, we had inherited the city from the dead, so that we could bet enormous sums of money and pay in cash or diamonds if we wanted to, but when we wagered we never bothered to carry such useless objects from one house to another. Enough to say who won and who lost. The only reason we had such wealth was because the dead had left it all behind. If they didn't value it any more than that, what was it worth to us, except as counters in games of chance?

There was unguessed-at meaning in their pushing after all. For on the third day of the elephants' pushing—still to no visible effect—Arek came home to Poznan. Arek, whom I had named for my father. Arek, who dashed my last hope. Arek, who killed my wife.

For years after the plague, no children were conceived. From Berlin, where one of the survivors was a doctor, we learned that when the plague was new and they were still trying to study it, the medical researchers determined that the virus rooted in the reproductive systems of men and women, specifically attacking their bodies where the human seed was made. This was not how the plague did its slaughtering, but it guaranteed that the few survivors would be sterile. The message left us in despair.

But I was young, and though I had seen more death before I turned ten than I would ordinarily have seen even if I devoted my whole life to watching American movies, my hope was still undashable. Or rather, my body's hope, which in my teens was much stronger than my reason. As the people from the hinterlands and smaller towns came seeking human company, Poznan became a gathering place. In those days we lived on the outskirts of the city, in a place where we could actively farm, before we realized that farming was redundant with miles and miles of fields and gardens reseeding themselves faster than we could harvest them. So I was hoeing the turnips—the kind of task the adults gratefully left to my strong and flexible young arms and legs—when Hilde and her family came to town in a horse-drawn wagon.

It wasn't Hilde herself that I saw at first, it was the miracle of seeing a family. At first, of course, we assumed they were a nonce family, clinging to each other because no one else in their area survived. But no, no, they *looked* like each other, that miracle of resemblance that told us all that they were genetically connected. And soon we learned that yes, they were a mother, a father, a daughter, all of whom had survived the plague. They knew it was wrong of them to grieve for the two sons and three daughters who died, for they had not lost everyone they loved, as all the rest of us had done. There was something in them that was stronger than the disease. And Hilde, a plump nordic blonde, soon became beautiful to all of us, because we knew that if any woman had a viable ovum left, it would be her.

She and her parents understood that her womb, if it was not barren, could not belong to her alone, and that her only hope of continuing our poor, weak species was to find a mate whose body still could spew forth living sperm. She had been sexually immature when the plague came, but now was womanly, ready to bear if bear she could. One man at a time would husband her, for three months; then a month of solitude, and then the next man's turn to try. That way there would be no doubt of fatherhood if she conceived; he would be her husband, to father more children on her. She agreed to this because there was no other hope.

I was third to try, at fifteen a frightened child myself, approaching her like the temple priestess that she was, begging the god to choose me, to let life come into her from me. She was sweet and patient, and told no one how clumsy I was. I liked her, but did not yet love her, for she was still a stranger to me. I could mate with her, but not speak to her—or at least not be understood, for she came from a German-speaking area in the westernmost mountains, and had but little Polish—though more of Polish than I had of German.

The second month she had no period, and the third, and the fourth. She was kept away from me, from all men, until in the fifth month she asked for me. "You are half of this miracle," she said in halting Polish, and from then on I was her companion. No more fieldwork for me—what if I was injured? What if I caught cold? Instead I stayed with her, taught her to speak Polish and learned to read German, more or less.

In the eighth month the doctor finally came from Berlin. He had never worked in obstetrics, but he was the best hope we had, and since no one in Berlin was pregnant, they understood what was at stake; even a half-Polish baby in Poznan was better than no more babies anywhere at all. We made him welcome; he taught us how to make beer.

The ninth month. Nothing happened. He spoke of inducing labor. We worked to get a room in the hospital powered up, the old equipment working, and he gave Hilde an ultrasound examination. He could not face us after that. "You counted wrong?" he offered, as a possibility.

No, we did not count wrong. We knew the last time she had sex with anyone—with me—and it was nine months and two weeks ago.

"The baby is not ready yet," he said. "Weeks to go. Maybe many weeks. The limb-length tells me this. The development of the face and hands."

And then the worst news. "But the head—it is very large. And strangely shaped. Not a known condition, though. I looked in the books. Not seen before, not exactly this. If it is still growing—and how can I tell, since it is already as big as an adult human head—this does not look happy for her. She cannot bear this child normally. I will have to cut the baby out."

Cut it out now, her parents said. It has been nine months.

"No," the doctor said. "If I cut now, I think that it will die. I think it has the lungs of a fetus of five months. I did not come here to abort a fetus. I came to deliver a baby."

But our daughter. . . .

Hilde agreed with the doctor. "If he has to cut me open anyway, there is no hurry. Wait until the baby himself thinks that he is ready."

We knew now it would be a boy, and were not glad of it. A daughter would have been better, everyone knew that. Everyone but me—I was not ready to play Lot with a daughter of mine, and I was the only man proven to have viable sperm, so I thought it was better that I would have a son and then could wander with Hilde and the boy, through all the world if need be, searching for a place where another mating had happened, where there might be a girl for him. I could imagine that future happily.

Ten months. Eleven. No woman had carried a child for so long. She could not sit up in bed now, for still it grew, and the ultrasound looked stranger and stranger. Wide hips, and eyes far apart on a face appallingly broad. The ultrasound, with its grainy, black-and-white image, made it look like a monster. This was no baby. It would never live.

Worse, it was draining the life out of Hilde. Most of what she ate went across the placenta to feed this cancerous growth inside her. She grew wan of face, weak of muscle even as her belly grew more and more mountainous. I would sit beside her and when she was tired of the book I read, I would hold her hand and talk to her of walks along the streets of the city, of my visit to Krakow when I was six, before the plague; how my father took me along as he escorted a foreign author through the city; how we ate at a country restaurant and the foreigner could not eat the floury bread and the chewy noodles and the thick lard spread. She laughed. Or, as she grew weaker, smiled. And finally, near the end, just clung to my hand and let me babble. I wanted nothing more than to have Hilde. Forget the baby. It's already dead to me, this monster. Just let me have Hilde, the time with her that a man should have with his wife, the life together in a little house, the coming home at night to her embrace, the going forth in the morning with her kiss on my lips and her blessing in my ears.

"I will take it now," said the doctor. "Perhaps the next child will be normal. But she grows too weak to delay any longer."

Her parents agreed. Hilde, also, gave consent at last. The doctor had taught me to be his nurse, and trained me by making me watch the bloody surgeries he did on hares and once on a sheep, so I would not faint at the blood when the time came to cut into my wife. For wife she was, at her insistence, married to me in a little ceremony just before she went under the anesthetic. She knew, as did I, that the marriage was not permanent. Perhaps the community would give me one more try to make a normal child with her, but if that one, too, should fail, the rotation would begin again, three months of mating, a month fallow, until a father with truer seed was found.

What we did not understand was how very weak she had become. The human body was not designed to give itself so completely to the care of such a baby as this one. Somehow the baby was sending hormonal messages to her, the doctor said, telling her body not to bear, not to present; the cervix not to efface and open. Somehow it caused her body to drain itself, to make the muscles atrophy, the fat to disappear.

The doctor's incision was not large enough at first. Nor with the second cut. Finally, with the third, her womb lay open like the belly of a dissected frog, and at last he lifted the little monster out. He handed it to me. Almost I tossed it aside. But it opened its eyes. Babies aren't supposed to be able to do that, I know now. But it opened its eyes and looked at me. And I felt a powerful trembling, a vibration in my chest and arms. It was alive, whatever it was, and it was not in me, its father, to kill it. So I set it aside, where a couple of women washed it, and did the rituals that the doctor had prescribed—the drops into the eyes, the blood samples. I did not watch. I returned to Hilde.

I thought she was unconscious. But then the baby made a sound, and even though it was lower than a baby's mewling ought to be, she knew it was his voice, and her eyes fluttered open. "Let me see," she whispered. So I ran and took the baby from the women and brought it to her.

It was as large as a toddler, and I was loath to lay such a heavy burden on her chest. But Hilde insisted, reaching with her fingers because she could not raise her arms. I leaned over her, bearing as much of the baby's weight as I could. He sought her breast and, when she found the strength to raise a hand and guide a nipple into his mouth, he sucked mightily. It hurt her, but her face spoke of ecstasy as well as pain. "Mama loves the baby," her lips said silently.

She died as the doctor was still stitching her. He left the wound and tried to revive her, shoving the baby and me out of the way and pumping at her heart. Later, after the autopsy, he told me that her heart had been used up like all her other muscles. The child had ruled the mother, had demanded her life from her, and she had given it.

My Hilde. Till death parted us.

There was some debate on whether to feed the child, and then on whether to baptize it. In both cases, mercy and hope triumphed over fear and loathing. I wanted to oppose them, but Hilde had tried to feed the baby, and even after she was dead I did not wish to contradict her. They made me choose a name. I gave it my father's name because I could not bear to give it mine. Arkadiusz. Arek.

He weighed nearly ten kilograms at birth.

At two months he walked.

At five months his babbling noises became speech. They taught him to call me papa. And I came to him because he was, after all, my own.

Hilde's parents were gone by then. They blamed me—my bad seed—for their daughter's death. In vain did the doctor tell them that what the plague had done to me it no doubt also did to her; they knew, in their hearts, that Hilde was normal, and I was the one with the seed of monstrosity. They could not bear to look at me or at Arek, either, the killers of their last child, their beautiful little girl.

Arek walked early because his wideset legs gave him such a sturdy platform, while crawling was near impossible for him. His massive neck was strong enough to hold his wide-faced, deep-skulled head. His hands were clever, his arms long and probing. He was a font of questions. He made me teach him how to read when he was not yet two.

The two strange apertures in his head, behind the eyes, before the ears, seeped with fluid now and then. He stank sometimes, and the stench came from there. At the time we did not know what to call these things, or what they meant, for the elephants had not yet come. The whole community liked Arek, as they must always like children; they played with him, answered his questions, watched over him. But beneath the love there was a constant gnawing pain. He was our hope, but he was no hope at all. Whatever his strange condition was, it might have made him quicker than a normal child, but we knew that it could not be healthy, that like most strange children he would no doubt die before his time. And definitely, mutant that he was, he must surely be as sterile as a mule.

And then the elephants came, great shadowy shapes out in the distant fields. We marveled. We wondered. They came nearer, day by day. And Arek became quite agitated. "I hear them," he said.

Hear what? We heard nothing. They were too far off for us to hear.

"I hear them," he said again. He touched his forehead. "I hear them here." He touched his chest. "And here."

The flow from the apertures in his head increased.

He took to wandering off. We had to watch him closely. In the middle of a reading lesson, he would stand up and face the distant elephants—or face the empty horizon where they might be—and listen, rapt. "I think I understand them," Arek said. "Here's a place with good water."

All of Poland has good water now, I pointed out.

"No," he said impatiently. "It's what they said. And now they talk of one who died. They have the scent of him. The one who died." He listened more; I still heard nothing. "And me," he said. "They have the scent of me."

Elephants care nothing for you, I said.

He turned to me, his eyes awash with tears. "Take that back," he said.

Sit and do your lessons, Arek.

"What do I care what dead people say? I have no need of what they said!"

You're five years old, Arek. I know better than you what you need to know.

"Your father had to know all this," he said. "But what is it to me? What good has reading done for you?"

I tried to hold him, but at five years old he was too strong. He ran from the room. He ran out into the field. He ran toward the elephants.

I followed him as best I could. Others joined me, calling out Arek's name. He was not swift, and we could have caught him if we were willing to tackle him like rugby players. But our goal was only to keep him safe, and so we jogged alongside him, his short and heavy legs lumbering forward, ever closer to the elephants. A matriarch and her clan, with several babies of varying sizes. We tried to stop him then, to hold him back, but by then the matriarch had noticed us, and as she approached, Arek screamed and tried more violently to get away, to run to her. She trumpeted at us, and finally, tentatively, in fear of her we set him down.

She let him embrace her trunk; he clambered upward, over her great impassive brow, and sprawled his body across the top of her head. Her trunk reached up to him; I feared that she would sweep him from her head like lint. Instead she touched the leaking aperture on his right cheek, then brought the tip of her trunk down to her mouth. To smell and taste it.

That was when I realized: The matriarch, too, had an aperture between eye and ear, a leaking stinkhole. When I did my reading, I learned that it was the temporal gland. The elephants had it, and so did my son.

Neither Hilde nor I was elephantine. Nor was there any logical way, given the little science that I knew, for me to explain how a gland that only elephants had should suddenly show up on a human child. It wasn't just the temporal glands, either. As he sat perched atop the matriarch, I could see how closely his brow resembled hers. No great flapping ears, no abnormality of nose, and his eyes were still binocular, not side-aimed like the elephant's. Yet there was no mistaking how his forehead was a smaller echo of her own.

He has been waiting for them, I murmured.

And then I thought, but did not say: They came in search of him.

He would not go home with me. One by one the others drifted back to our village, some returning to bring me food and offer food to Arek. But he was busy riding on the matriarch, and playing with the babies, always under the watchful gaze of the mothers, so that no harm would come to him. He made a game of running up the trunks and turning somersaults onto an elephant's back. He swung on tusks. He rode them like horses, he climbed them like trees, and he listened to them like gods.

After two days they moved on. I tried to follow. The matriarch picked me up and put me back. Three times she did it before I finally acquiesced. Arek was their child now. They had adopted him, he had adopted them. Whatever music they were making, he heard it and loved it. The pied piper had come to lead away our only son, our strange inhuman child, the only hope we had.

From that day I did not see him, until the twelfth bull elephant arrived with Arek astride his neck.

Full-grown Arek—just a little taller, I estimated, than his father, but built like a tractor, with massive legs and arms, and a neck that made his enormous head look almost natural. "Father!" he cried. "Father!" He had not seen me at the window. I wanted to hide from him. He must be fifteen now. The age I was when I met Hilde. I had put him from my mind and heart, as I had already done with my parents, my baby sister, whom I had left behind unburied when I was too hungry to wait any longer for them to wake again, for God to raise them up from their sickbeds. Of all those I had lost, why was he the one that could return? For a moment I hated him, though I knew that it was not his fault.

He was their child anyway, not mine. I could see that now. Anyone could see it. His skin was even filthy grey like theirs.

He didn't see me. He slid down the brow and trunk of the bull he was riding and watched as his steed—his companion? his master?—took its place in the circle that pushed against the walls of the ugly building. He walked around them, a wide circle, looking up at the windows on the opposite side of the square. But it was not by sight that he found me. It was when he was directly under my window, looking the other way, that he stopped, and turned, and looked up at me, and smiled. "Father," he said. "I have seen the world!"

I did not want him to call me father. Those were his fathers, those bull elephants. Not me. I was the bearer of the seed, its depositor, but the seed itself had been planted in both Hilde and me by the plague. Born in Africa and carried to the world on airplanes, virulent and devastating, the plague was no accident of nature. Paranoid as it sounded even to myself, I had the evidence of Arek's elephantinism to bolster what I knew but could not prove. Somehow in the kettle of the temporal gland, the elephants created this new version of man, and sent the seed out into the world, carried by a virus. They had judged us, these beasts, and found us wanting. Perhaps the decision was born as grieving elephants gathered around the corpses of their kinfolk, slain and shorn of their tusks. Perhaps the decision came from the shrinking land and the drying earth. Perhaps it was their plan all along, from the time they made us until they finally were done with us.

For in the darkness of the library, as I moved along the table, keeping my yellowing books always in the slant of light from the window, I had conjured up a picture of the world. The elephants, the true gods of antiquity. They had reached the limit of what they could do with their prehensile noses. What was needed now was hands, so virus by virus, seed by seed, they swept away one species and replaced it with another, building and improving and correcting their mistakes. There was plenty of the primate left in us, the baboon, the chimpanzee. But more and more of the elephant as well, the kindness, the utter lack of warfare, the benevolent society of women, the lonely wandering harmless helpful men, and the absolute sanctity of the children of the tribe. Primate and elephant, always at war within us. We could see the kinship between us and the apes, but failed to see how the high-breasted elephant could possibly also be our kind.

Only now, with Arek, could the convergence at last be seen. They had made at last an elephant with hands, a clever toolmaker who could hear the voices of the gods.

I thought of the bulldancers of Crete, and then of Arek running up the trunks of elephants and somersaulting on their heads. The mastodons and mammoths were all gone, and the elephants were south of the Mediterranean; but they were not forgotten. In human memory, we were supposed to dance with joy upon the horns and head of a great loving beast, our father, our maker. Our prophets were the ones who heard the voice of God, not in the tempest, but in the silent thrumming, the still small voice of infrasound, carried through stone and earth as easily as through the air. On the mountain they heard the voice of God, teaching us how to subdue the primate and become the sons of God, the giants in the earth. For the sons of God did marry the daughters of men. We remembered that God was above us, but thought that meant he was above the sky. And so my speculation and imagining led me to this mad twisting of the scripture of my childhood; and no less of the science and history in the library. What were the neanderthals? Why did they disappear? Was there a plague one day, carried wherever the new-made Cro-Magnon wandered? And did the neanderthals understand what their woolly mammoth deities had done to them? Here was their ironic vengeance: It was the new, godmade men, the chosen people, who hunted the mammoths and the mastodons to extinction, who bowed the elephants of India to slavery and turned the elephants of Africa into a vast wandering ivory orchard. We men of Cro-Magnon descent, we thought we were the pinnacle. But when God told us to be perfect, as he was perfect, we failed him, and he had to try again. This time it was no flood that swept our souls away. And any rainbow we might see would be a lie.

I spoke of this to no one—I needed human company too much to give them reason to think me mad. Elephants as gods? As God himself? Sacrilege. Heresy. Madness. Evil. Nor was I sure of it myself; indeed, most days, most hours of the day, I mocked my own ideas. But I write them here, because they might be true, and if someday these words are read, and I was right, then you'll hear my warning: You who read this, you are not the last and best, any more than we were. There is always another step higher up the ladder, and a helpful trunk to lift you upward on your way, or dash you to the ground if you should fail.

Arek called me father, and I was not his father. But he came from Hilde's body; she gave her life to give him breath, and loved him, ugly and misshapen as he was, as she held him to her empty breasts while her heart pushed the last few liters of blood through her worn-out body. Not a drop of pap came from her into his mouth. He had already sucked her dry. But for that moment she loved him. And for her sake—and for his, at first, I will be honest here—I tried to treat him well, to teach him and provide for him and protect him as best I could. But at five years of age they took him and he was raised by elephants. In what sense now was he my son?

"Father," he said to me again. "Don't be afraid. It's only me, your boy Arek."

I'm not afraid, I almost said.

But he would know it was a lie. He could smell a lie on me. Silence was my refuge.

I left my room and went down the stairs to the level of the street. I came blinking into the sunlight. He held out a hand to me. His legs were even stockier now; whenever he stood still, he looked as planted as a pair of old trees. He was taller than I am, and I am tall. "Father," he said. "I want them to meet you. I told them all the things you taught me."

They already know me, I wanted to say. They've been following me for years. They know when and where I eat and sleep and pee. They know all they want to know of me, and I want nothing at all from them, so . . .

So I followed him anyway, feeling my hand in his, the firm kind grasp, the springy rolling rhythm of his walk. I knew that he could keep walking forever on those legs. He led me to the new elephant, the one he had arrived with. He bade me stand there as the trunk took samples of my scent for tasting, as one great eye looked down on me, the all-seeing eye. Not a word did I say. Not a question did I ask.

Until I felt the thrumming, strong now, so powerful that it took my breath away, it shook my chest so strongly.

"Did you hear him, Father?" asked my son.

I nodded.

"But did you understand?"

I shook my head.

"He says you understand," said Arek, puzzled. "But you say that you don't."

At last I spoke: I understand nothing.

The elephant thrummed out again.

"You understand but do not know you understand," said Arek. "You're not a prophet."

The elephant had made me tremble, but it was Arek's word that made me stumble. Not a prophet. And you *are,* my son?

"I am," said Arek, "because I hear what he says and can turn it into language for the rest of you. I thought you could understand him, too, because he said you could."

The elephant was right. I did understand. My mad guesses were right, or somewhat right, or at least not utterly wrong. But I said nothing of this to Arek.

"But now I see you do understand," said Arek, nodding, content.

His temporal glands were dripping, the fluid falling onto his naked chest. He wore trousers, though. Old polyester ones, the kind that cannot rot or fade, the kind that will outlast the end of the universe. He saw me looking, and again supposed that I had understood something.

"You're right," he said. "I've had it before. Only lightly, though. And it did me no good." He smiled ruefully. "I've seen the world, but none like me."

Had *what* before?

"The dripping time. The madness."

Musth, I said.

"Yes," he answered. He touched the stream of fluid on his cheek, then streaked it on my cheek. "It takes a special woman to bear my child."

What if there isn't one?

"There is," he said. "That's why I came here."

There's no one here like you.

"Not yet," he said. "And besides, I had this gift to give you."

What gift?

He gestured, as if I should have understood all along. The building that the elephants were pushing at. "You always told me how much you hated this building. How ugly it was. I wanted to give you something when I came again, but I couldn't think of anything I could do for you. Except for this."

At his words, the elephants grunted and bellowed, and now it was clear that all their pushing before had been preliminary to this, as they braced themselves and rammed, all at once, again and again. Now the building shuddered. Now the façade cracked. Now the walls buckled.

Quickly Arek drew me back, out of danger. The elephants, too, retreated, as the walls caved in, the roof collapsed. Dust blew out of the place like smoke, blinding me for a moment, till tears could clear my vision.

No silence now, no infrasound. The bulls gave voice, a great triumphant fanfare.

And now the families came: the matriarch, the other females, their

babies, their children. Into the square, now unobstructed except for the
rubble pile, they came by the dozens. There must be three clans here, I
thought. Four. Five. Trumpeting. Triumphant.

All this, because they knocked down a building?

No. The fall of the building was the gift to the father. It was the signal for the real festivities to begin.

"I made them bring her here," said Arek. "You're my family, and
these are my friends." He indicated the people leaning out of the windows over the square. "Isn't that what weddings are for?"

The elephants made way for one last arrival. An Indian elephant lum-
bered into the square, trunk upraised, trumpeting. It progressed in stately
fashion to the place where Arek and I were standing. On its back sat
Arek's bride-to-be. At first glance she was human, boldly and charmingly
nude. But under the shock of thick, straight hair her head was, if anything, larger than Arek's, and her legs were set so wide that she seemed to
straddle the elephant's neck the way a woman of my species might be-
stride a horse. Down the forehead and the trunk of the beast she slid,
pausing only to stand playfully upon the tusks, then jump lightly to the
ground. Those legs, those hips—she clearly had the strength to carry a
baby as large as Arek had been for the entire year. But wide as her body
was, could such a head pass through the birth canal?

Because she was naked, the answer was before my eyes. The entrance
to her birth canal was not between her thighs, but in a pouch of skin that
drooped from the base of her abdomen; the opening was in front of the
pubis. No longer would the pelvic circle limit the size of a baby's head.
She would not have to be cut open to give birth.

Arek held out his hand. She smiled at him. And in that smile, she became almost human to me. It was the shy smile of the bride, the smile that
Hilde had given me when she was pregnant, before we knew it was no
human child she carried.

"She's in heat," said Arek. "And I'm . . . in musth. You have no idea
how crazy it makes me."

He didn't sound crazy, or act it, either. Instead he had the poise of a
king, the easy confidence of an elephant. At the touch of her hand, his
temporal glands gave forth such a flow that I could hear the fluid dripping
onto the stones of the plaza. But otherwise he betrayed no eagerness.

"I don't know how it's done," said Arek. "Marriage, I mean. They said I should marry as humans do. With words."

I remembered the words that had been said for me and Hilde. As best I could, I said them now. The girl did not understand. Her eyes, I saw now, had the epicanthic fold—how far had they brought her? Was she the only one? Were there only these two in all the world? Is that how close they came to the edge of killing us all, of ending the whole experiment?

I said the words, and she shaped the answers. But I could tell that it didn't matter to her, or to him, either, that she understood not a bit of the Polish words she had to say. Below the level of audible speech, they had another kind of language. For I could see how her forehead thrummed with a tone too low for my ears to hear. But he could hear. Not words, I assumed. But communication nonetheless. The thing with speech, they'd work that out. It would still be useful to them, when communication needed to be precise. But for matters of the heart, they had the language of the elephants. The language of the gods. The adamic tongue. The idiom God had used one time to say, Multiply and replenish the earth, and subdue it. We did the first; we did the last. Now, perhaps, this new couple in their new garden, would learn the replenishing part as well. Only a few of us lingering beasts, of us the dust of the earth, would remain, and not for long. Then the whole world would be their garden.

Today they're gone. Out of Poznan, the elephants and their new creatures, the son and daughter of the gods. My Arek and his wife, whose name he never spoke aloud to us. No doubt he has some deep and rumbling name for her that I could never hear. They will have many children. They must watch them carefully. Or perhaps this time it will be different. No stone crashed against a brother's head this time. No murder in the world. Only the peace of the elephants.

They're gone, and the rejoicing is over—for we did rejoice, because even though we know, we all know, that Arek and his bride are not of our kind, they still carry the only portion of our seed that will remain alive in the earth; better to live on in them than to die utterly, without casting seed at all.

They're gone, and now each day I go out into the square and work amid the wreckage of the building. Propping up the old façade, leaning it against a makeshift wall. Before I die, I'll have it standing again, or at least enough of it so that the square looks right. Already I have much of one wall restored, and sometimes the others come and help me, when they see I'm struggling with a section of wall too heavy or awkward for a man to raise alone.

It may have been an ugly thing, that Communist monstrosity, but it was built by humans, in a human place, and they had no right to knock it down.

NOTES ON "THE ELEPHANTS OF POZNAN"

I was thrilled when my Polish publisher offered to pay my way to a science-fiction convention in Katowice. Mieczyslaw Proszynski had first read my fiction when he was working as an engineer in the United States, and when the strictures of Communism ended and he started up a publishing company in the newly-free Poland, he not only specialized in science fiction, but also the first American novel he published was *Ender's Game.* He was continuing to publish more of my titles, and he believed it was worth the cost of bringing me there.

Guided by editor Arek Nakoniecznik, who quickly became a friend, I traveled to Łodz, Warszawa, Krakow, and Poznan. Each city was fascinating, with very different histories and different meanings within Polish culture as a whole.

In Poznan, though, I was particularly struck by something Arek pointed out to me—some ugly modern buildings from the Communist era that utterly defaced a beautiful old square at the heart of the old city. That picture stayed in my head and I had to write about it. But what? Since when does thoughtless, ugly architecture become a story?

It happened that at the same time I was reading a book about elephants, full of the kinds of information that lead sci-fi writers to think up cool possibilities. So I conjured up a world where elephants are actually running the show, and since the human race is grossly out of hand, it was time to rein us in. The human race too often treats the world the way the Communist overlords of Poland treated the public square of Poznan—we feel free to put anything we want wherever we want, without regard to what it defaces and destroys.

So I told my elephants-controlling-our-evolution story and set it in

Poznan because I could. This is about as close as I ever come to having a symbol-dominated story, but I feel like I took the curse off because the elephants themselves regarded it as a symbol. It wasn't just an author-symbol, imposed on the text; it was part of the story. And if you can't see the difference, and you think it's hypocritical of me to decry the ac-lit world's obsession with symbols and then go ahead and use one myself, what can I say? I got my M.A. in English. I know how to do ac-lit stuff. And sometimes it's fun. So sue me.

I'm happy to say that the story's first publication was in Polish, in the magazine *Fantastyka*—published by Prosynski i Ska.

ATLANTIS

Kemal Akyazi grew up within a few miles of the ruins of Troy; from his boyhood home above Kumkale he could see the waters of the Dardanelles, the narrow strait that connects the waters of the Black Sea with the Aegean. Many a war had been fought on both sides of that strait, one of which had produced the great epic of Homer's *Iliad*.

This pressure of history had a strange influence on Kemal as a child. He learned all the tales of the place, of course, but he also knew that the tales were Greek, and the place was of the Greek Aegean world. Kemal was a Turk; his own ancestors had not come to the Dardanelles until the fifteenth century. He felt that it was a powerful place, but it did not belong to him. So the *Iliad* was not the story that spoke to Kemal's soul. Rather it was the story of Heinrich Schliemann, the German explorer who, in an era when Troy had been regarded as a mere legend, a myth, a fiction, had been sure not only that Troy was real but also where it was. Despite all scoffers, he mounted an expedition and found it and unburied it. The old stories turned out to be true.

In his teens Kemal thought it was the greatest tragedy of his life that Pastwatch had to use machines to look through the millennia of human history. There would be no more Schliemanns, studying and pondering and guessing until they found some artifact, some ruin of a long-lost city, some remnant of a legend made true again. Thus Kemal had no interest in joining Pastwatch. It was not history that he hungered for—it was exploration and discovery that he wanted, and what was the glory in finding the truth through a machine?

So, after an abortive try at physics, he studied to become a meteorologist. At the age of eighteen, heavily immersed in the study of climate and weather, he touched again on the findings of Pastwatch. No longer did meteorologists have to depend on only a few centuries of weather measurements and fragmentary fossil evidence to determine long-range patterns. Now they had accurate accounts of storm patterns for millions of years. Indeed, in the earliest years of Pastwatch, the machinery had been so coarse that individual humans could not be seen. It was like time-lapse photography in which people don't remain in place long enough to be on more than a single frame of the film, making them invisible. So in those days Pastwatch recorded the weather of the past, erosion patterns, volcanic eruptions, ice ages, climatic shifts.

All that data was the bedrock on which modern weather prediction and control rested. Meteorologists could see developing patterns and, without disrupting the overall pattern, could make tiny changes that prevented any one area from going completely rainless during a time of drought, or sunless during a wet growing season. They had taken the sharp edge off the relentless scythe of climate, and now the great project was to determine how they might make a more serious change, to bring a steady pattern of light rain to the desert regions of the world, to restore the prairies and savannahs that they once had been. That was the work that Kemal wanted to be a part of.

Yet he could not bring himself out from the shadow of Troy, the memory of Schliemann. Even as he studied the climatic shifts involved with the waxing and waning of the ice ages, his mind contained fleeting images of lost civilizations, legendary places that waited for a Schliemann to uncover them.

His project for his degree in meteorology was part of the effort to determine how the Red Sea might be exploited to develop dependable rains for either the Sudan or central Arabia; Kemal's immediate target was to study the difference between weather patterns during the last ice age, when the Red Sea had all but disappeared, and the present, with the Red Sea at its fullest. Back and forth he went through the coarse old Pastwatch recordings, gathering data on sea level and on precipitation at selected points inland. The old TruSite I had been imprecise at best, but good enough for counting rainstorms.

Time after time Kemal would cycle through the up-and-down fluc-
tuations of the Red Sea, watching as the average sea level gradually rose
toward the end of the Ice Age. He always stopped, of course, at the abrupt
jump in sea level that marked the rejoining of the Red Sea and the Indian
Ocean. After that, the Red Sea was useless for his purposes, since its sea
level was tied to that of the great world ocean.

But the echo of Schliemann inside Kemal's mind made him think:
What a flood that must have been.

What a flood. The Ice Age had locked up so much water in glaciers
and ice sheets that the sea level of the whole world fell. It eventually
reached a low enough point that land bridges arose out of the sea. In the
north Pacific, the Bering land bridge allowed the ancestors of the Indies
to cross on foot into their great empty homeland. Britain and Flanders
were joined. The Dardanelles were closed and the Black Sea became a
salty lake. The Persian Gulf disappeared and became a great plain cut by
the Euphrates. And the Bab al Mandab, the strait at the mouth of the Red
Sea, became a land bridge.

But a land bridge is also a dam. As the world climate warmed and the
glaciers began to release their pent-up water, the rains fell heavily everywhere; rivers swelled and the seas rose. The great south-flowing rivers of
Europe, which had been mostly dry during the peak of glaciation, now
were massive torrents. The Rhone, the Po, the Strimon, the Danube
poured so much water into the Mediterranean and the Black Sea that
their water levels rose at about the same rate as that of the great world
ocean.

The Red Sea had no great rivers, however. It was a new sea, formed
by rifting between the new Arabian plate and the African, which meant it
had uplift ridges on both coasts. Many rivers and streams flowed from
those ridges down into the Red Sea, but none of them carried much water compared to the rivers that drained vast basins and carried the melt-
off of the glaciers of the north. So, while the Red Sea gradually rose
during this time, it lagged far, far behind the great world ocean. Its water
level responded to the immediate local weather patterns rather than to
worldwide weather.

Then one day the Indian Ocean rose so high that tides began to spill
over the Bab al Mandab. The water cut new channels in the grassland

there. Over a period of several years, the leakage grew, creating a series of large new tidal lakes on the Hanish Plain. And then one day, some fourteen thousand years ago, the flow cut a channel so deep that it didn't dry up at low tide, and the water kept flowing, cutting the channel deeper and deeper, until those tidal lakes were full, and brimmed over. With the weight of the Indian Ocean behind it the water gushed into the basin of the Red Sea in a vast flood that in a few days brought the Red Sea up to the level of the world ocean.

This isn't just the boundary marker between useful and useless water-level data, thought Kemal. This is a cataclysm, one of the rare times when a single event changes vast reaches of land in a period of time short enough that human beings could notice it. And, for once, this cataclysm happened in an era when human beings were there. It was not only possible but likely that someone saw this flood—indeed, that it killed many, for the southern end of the Red Sea basin was rich savannah and marshes up to the moment when the ocean broke through, and surely the humans of fourteen thousand years ago would have hunted there. Would have gathered seeds and fruits and berries there. Some hunting party must have seen, from the peaks of the Dehalak mountains, the great walls of water that roared up the plain, breaking and parting around the slopes of the Dehalaks, making islands of them.

Such a hunting party would have known that their families had been killed by this water. What would they have thought? Surely that some god was angry with them. That the world had been done away, buried under the sea. And if they survived, if they found a way to the Eritrean shore after the great turbulent waves settled down to the more placid waters of the new, deeper sea, they would tell the tale to anyone who would listen. And for a few years they could take their hearers to the water's edge, show them the treetops barely rising above the surface of the sea, and tell them tales of all that had been buried under the waves.

Noah, thought Kemal. Gilgamesh. Atlantis. The stories were believed. The stories were remembered. Of course they forgot where it happened—the civilizations that learned to write their stories naturally transposed the events to locations that they knew. But they remembered the things that mattered. What did the flood story of Noah say? Not just rain, no, it wasn't a flood caused by rain alone. The "fountains of the great deep" broke open. No local flood on the Mesopotamian plain would cause that image to be part of the story. But the great wall of water from the Indian Ocean, coming on the heels of years of steadily increasing rain—*that* would bring those words to the storytellers' lips, generation after generation, for ten thousand years until they could be written down.

As for Atlantis, everyone was so sure they had found it years ago. Santorini—Thios—the Aegean island that blew up. But the oldest stories of Atlantis said nothing of blowing up in a volcano. They spoke only of the great civilization sinking into the sea. The supposition was that later visitors came to Santorini and, seeing water where an island city used to be, assumed that it had sunk, knowing nothing of the volcanic eruption. To Kemal, however, this now seemed farfetched indeed, compared to the way it would have looked to the people of Atlantis themselves, somewhere on the Mits'iwa Plain, when the Red Sea seemed to leap up in its bed, engulfing the city. *That* would be sinking into the sea! No explosion, just water. And if the city were in the marshes of what was now the Mits'iwa Channel, the water would have come, not just from the southeast, but from the northeast and the north as well, flowing among and around the Dehalak mountains, making islands of them and swallowing up the marshes and the city with them.

Atlantis. Not beyond the pillars of Hercules, but Plato was right to associate the city with a strait. He, or whoever told the tale to him, simply replaced the Bab al Mandab with the greatest strait that he had heard of. The story might well have reached him by way of Phoenicia, where Mediterranean sailors would have made the story fit the sea they knew. They learned it from Egyptians, perhaps, or nomad wanderers from the hinterlands of Arabia, and "within the straits of Mandab" would quickly have become "within the pillars of Hercules," and then, because the Mediterranean itself was not strange and exotic enough, the locale was moved outside the pillars of Hercules.

All these suppositions came to Kemal with absolute certainty that they were true, or nearly true. He rejoiced at the thought of it: There was still an ancient civilization left to discover.

Everyone knew that Naog of the Derku People was going to be a tall man when he grew up, because his father and mother were

both tall and he was an unusually large baby. He was born in floodwater season, when all the Engu clan lived on reed boats. Their food supply, including the precious seed for next year's planting, was kept dry in
the seedboats, which were like floating huts of plaited reeds. The people themselves, though, rode out the flood on the open dragonboats,
bundles of reeds which they straddled as if they were riding a crocodile—
which, according to legend, was how the dragonboats began, when the
first Derku woman, Gweia, saved herself and her baby from the flood by
climbing onto the back of a huge crocodile. The crocodile—the first
Great Derku, or dragon—endured their weight until they reached a
tree they could climb, whereupon the dragon swam away. So when the
Derku people plaited reeds into long thick bundles and climbed
aboard, they believed that the secret of the dragonboats had been given
to them by the Great Derku, and in a sense they were riding on his
back.

During the raiding season, other nearby tribes had soon learned to
fear the coming of the dragonboats, for they always carried off captives
who, in those early days, were never seen again. In other tribes when
someone was said to have been carried off by the crocodiles, it was the
Derku people they meant, for it was well known that all the clans of
the Derku worshipped the crocodile as their savior and god, and fed their
captives to a dragon that lived in the center of their city.

At Naog's birthtime, the Engu clan were nestled among their tether
trees as the flooding Selud River flowed mudbrown underneath them. If
Naog had pushed his way out of the womb a few weeks later, as the waters were receding, his mother would have given birth in one of the seedboats. But Naog came early, before highwater, and so the seedboats were
still full of grain. During floodwater, they could neither grind the grain
into flour nor build cooking fires, and thus had to eat the seeds in raw
handfuls. Thus it was forbidden to spill blood on the grain, even birth-
blood; no one would touch grain that had human blood on it, for that was
the juice of the forbidden fruit.

This was why Naog's mother, Lewik, could not hide alone in an enclosed seedboat for the birthing. Instead she had to give birth out in the
open, on one of the dragonboats. She clung to a branch of a tether tree
as two women on their own dragonboats held hers steady. From a near

distance Naog's father, Twerk, could not hide his mortification that his new young wife was giving birth in full view, not only of the women, but of the men and boys of the tribe. Not that any but the youngest and stupidest of the men was overtly looking. Partly because of respect for the event of birth itself, and partly because of a keen awareness that Twerk could cripple any man of the Engu that he wanted to, the men paddled their boats toward the farthest tether trees, herding the boys along with them. There they busied themselves with the work of floodwater season—twining ropes and weaving baskets.

Twerk himself, however, could not keep from looking. He finally left his dragonboat and climbed his tree and watched. The women had brought their dragonboats in a large circle around the woman in travail. Those with children clinging to them or bound to them kept their boats on the fringes—they would be little help, with their hands full already. It was the older women and the young girls who were in close, the older women to help, the younger ones to learn.

But Twerk had no eyes for the other women today. It was his wide-eyed, sweating wife that he watched. It frightened him to see her in such pain, for Lewik was usually the healer, giving herbs and ground-up roots to others to take away pain or cure a sickness. It also bothered him to see that as she squatted on her dragonboat, clinging with both hands to the branch above her head, neither she nor any of the other women was in position to catch the baby when it dropped out. It would fall into the water, he knew, and it would die, and then he and everyone else would know that it had been wrong of him to marry this woman who should have been a servant of the crocodile god, the Great Derku.

When he could not contain himself a moment longer, Twerk shouted to the women: "Who will catch the baby?"

Oh, how they laughed at him, when at last they understood what he was saying. "Derku will catch him!" they retorted, jeering, and the men around him also laughed, for that could mean several things. It could mean that the god would provide for the child's safety, or it could mean that the flood would catch the child, for the flood was also called derkuwed, or dragonwater, partly because it was aswarm with crocodiles swept away from their usual lairs, and partly because the floodwater slithered down from the mountains like a crocodile sliding down into the water, quick and powerful and strong, ready to sweep away and swallow up the unwary. Derku will catch him indeed!

The men began predicting what the child would be named. "He will be Rogogu, because we all laughed," said one. Another said, "It will be a girl and she will be named Mehug, because she will be spilled into the water as she plops out!" They guessed that the child would be named for the fact that Twerk watched the birth; for the branch that Lewik clung to or the tree that Twerk climbed; or for the dragonwater itself, into which they imagined the child spilling and then being drawn out with the embrace of the god still dripping from him. Indeed, because of this notion Derkuwed became a childhood nickname for Lewik's and Twerk's baby, and later it was one of the names by which his story was told over and over again in faraway lands that had never heard of dragonwater or seen a crocodile, but it was not his real name, not what his father gave him to be his man-name when he came of age.

After much pushing, Lewik's baby finally emerged. First came the head, dangling between her ankles like the fruit of a tree—that was why the word for *head* was the same as the word for *fruit* in the language of the Derku people. Then as the newborn's head touched the bound reeds of the dragonboat, Lewik rolled her eyes in pain and waddled slowly backward, so that the baby flopped out of her body stretched along the length of the boat. He did not fall into the water, because his mother had made sure of it.

"Little man!" cried all the women as soon as they saw the sex of the child.

Lewik grunted out her firstborn's baby-name. "Glogmeriss," she said. *Glog* meant "thorn" and *meriss* meant "trouble"; together, they made the term that the Derku used for annoyances that turned out all right in the end, but which were quite painful at the time. There were some who thought that she wasn't naming the baby at all, but simply commenting on the situation, but it was the first thing she said and so it would be his name until he left the company of women and joined the men.

As soon as the afterbirth dropped onto the dragonboat, all the other women paddled nearer—like a swarm of gnats, thought Twerk, still watching. Some helped Lewik pry her hands loose from the tree branch and lie down on her dragonboat. Others took the baby and passed it from hand to hand, each one washing a bit of the blood from the baby. The afterbirth got passed with the baby at first, often dropping into the floodwater, until at last it reached the cutting woman, who severed the umbilical cord with a flint blade. Twerk, seeing this for the first time, realized that this might be how he got his name, which meant "cutting" or "breaking." Had his father seen this remarkable thing, too, the women cutting a baby off from this strange belly-tail? No wonder he named him for it.

But the thing that Twerk could not get out of his mind was the fact that his Lewik had taken off her napron in full view of the clan, and all the men had seen her nakedness, despite their efforts to pretend that they had not. Twerk knew that this would become a joke among the men, a story talked about whenever he was not with them, and this would weaken him and mean that he would never be the clan leader, for one can never give such respect to a man that one laughs about behind his back.

Twerk could think of only one way to keep this from having the power to hurt him, and that was to confront it openly so that no one would laugh behind his back. "His name is Naog!" cried Twerk decisively, almost as soon as the baby was fully washed in river water and the placenta set loose to float away on the flood.

"You are such a stupid man!" cried Lewik from her dragonboat. Everyone laughed, but in this case it was all right. Everyone knew Lewik was a bold woman who said whatever she liked to any man. That was why it was such a mark of honor that Twerk had chosen to take her as wife and she had taken him for husband—it took a strong man to laugh when his wife said disrespectful things to him. "Of course he's naog," she said. "All babies are born naked."

"I call him Naog because *you* were naked in front of all the clan," answered Twerk. "Yes, I know you all looked when you thought I couldn't see," he chided the men. "I don't mind a bit. You all saw my Lewik naked when the baby came out of her—but what matters is that only I saw her naked when I put the baby in!"

That made them all laugh, even Lewik, and the story was often repeated. Even before he became a man and gave up the baby-name Glogmeriss, Naog had often heard the tale of why he would have such a silly name—so often, in fact, that he determined that one day he would do such great deeds that when the people heard the word *naog* they would think first of him and his accomplishments, before they remembered that the name was also the word for the tabu condition of taking the napron off one's secret parts in public.

As he grew up, he knew that the water of derkuwed on him as a baby had touched him with greatness. It seemed he was always taller than the other boys, and he reached puberty first, his young body powerfully muscled by the labor of dredging the canals right among the slaves of the dragon during mudwater season. He wasn't much more than twelve floodwaters old when the grown men began clamoring for him to be given his manhood journey early so that he could join them in slave raids—his sheer size would dishearten many an enemy, making them despair and throw down club or spear. But Twerk was adamant. He would not tempt Great Derku to devour his son by letting the boy get ahead of himself. Naog might be large of body, but that didn't mean that he could get away with taking a man's role before he had learned all the skills and lore that a man had to acquire in order to survive.

This was all fine with Naog. He knew that he would have his place in the clan in due time. He worked hard to learn all the skills of manhood— how to fight with any weapon; how to paddle his dragonboat straight on course, yet silently; how to recognize the signs of the seasons and the directions of the stars at different hours of the night and times of the year; which wild herbs were good to eat, and which deadly; how to kill an animal and dress it so it would keep long enough to bring home for a wife to eat. Twerk often said that his son was as quick to learn things requiring wit and memory as to learn skills that depended only on size and strength and quickness.

What Twerk did not know, what no one even guessed, was that these tasks barely occupied Naog's mind. What he dreamed of, what he thought of constantly, was how to become a great man so that his name could be spoken with solemn honor instead of a smile or laughter.

One of Naog's strongest memories was a visit to the Great Derku in the holy pond at the very center of the great circular canals that linked all the Derku people together. Every year during the mud season, the first dredging was the holy pond, and no slaves were used for *that*. No, the Derku men and women, the great and the obscure, dredged the mud out of the holy pond, carried it away in baskets, and heaped it up in piles that formed a round lumpen wall around the pond. As the dry season came, crocodiles a-wandering in search of water would smell the pond and come through the gaps in the wall to drink it and bathe in it. The crocodiles knew nothing of danger from coming within walls. Why would they have learned to fear the works of humans? What other people in all the world had ever built such a thing? So the crocodiles came and wallowed in the water, heedless of the men watching from trees. At the first full moon of the dry season, as the crocodiles lay stupidly in the water during the cool of night, the men dropped from the trees and quietly filled the gaps in the walls with earth. At dawn, the largest crocodile in the pond was hailed as Great Derku for the year. The rest were killed with spears in the bloodiest most wonderful festival of the year.

The year that Naog turned six, the Great Derku was the largest crocodile that anyone could remember ever seeing. It was a dragon indeed, and after the men of raiding age came home from the blood moon festival full of stories about this extraordinary Great Derku, all the families in all the clans began bringing their children to see it.

"They say it's a crocodile who was Great Derku many years ago," said Naog's mother. "He has returned to our pond in hopes of the offerings of manfruit that we used to give to the dragon. But some say he's the very one who was Great Derku the year of the forbidding, when he refused to eat any of the captives we offered him."

"And how would they know?" said Twerk, ridiculing the idea. "Is there anyone alive now who was alive then, to recognize him? And how could a crocodile live so long?"

"The Great Derku lives forever," said Lewik.

"Yes, but the true dragon is the derkuwed, the water in flood," said Twerk, "and the crocodiles are only its children."

To the child, Naog, these words had another meaning, for he had heard the word *derkuwed* far more often in reference to himself, as his nickname, than in reference to the great annual flood. So to him it sounded as though his father was saying that *he* was the true dragon, and the crocodiles were his children. Almost at once he realized what was actually meant, but the impression lingered in the back of his mind.

"And couldn't the derkuwed preserve one of its children to come back to us to be our god a second time?" said Lewik. "Or are you suddenly a holy man who knows what the dragon is saying?"

"All this talk about this Great Derku being one of the ancient ones brought back to us is dangerous," said Twerk. "Do you want us to return to the terrible days when we fed manfruit to the Great Derku? When our captives were all torn to pieces by the god, while *we,* men and women alike, had to dig out all the canals without slaves?"

"There weren't so many canals then," said Lewik. "Father said."

"Then it must be true," said Twerk, "if your old father said it. So think about it. Why are there so many canals now, and why are they so long and deep? Because we put our captives to work dredging our canals and making our boats. What if the Great Derku had never refused to eat manfruit? We would not have such a great city here, and other tribes would not bring us gifts and even their own children as slaves. They can come and visit our captives, and even buy them back from us. That's why we're not hated and feared, but rather *loved* and feared in all the lands from the Nile to the Salty Sea."

Naog knew that his father's manhood journey had been from the Salty Sea all the way up the mountains and across endless grasslands to the great river of the west. It was a legendary journey, fitting for such a large man. So Naog knew that he would have to undertake an even greater journey. But of that he said nothing.

"But these people talking stupidly about this being that same Great Derku returned to us again—don't you realize that they will want to put it to the test again, and offer it manfruit? And what if the Great Derku *eats* it this time? What do we do then, go back to doing all the dredging ourselves? Or let the canals fill in so we can't float the seedboats from village to village during the dry season, and so we have no defense from our enemies and no way to ride our dragonboats all year?"

Others in the clan were listening to this argument, since there was little enough privacy under normal circumstances, and none at all when you spoke with a raised voice. So it was no surprise when they chimed in. One offered the opinion that the reason no manfruit should be offered to this Great Derku was because the eating of manfruit would give the Great Derku knowledge of all the thoughts of the people they ate. Another was afraid that the sight of a powerful creature eating the flesh of men would lead some of the young people to want to commit the unpardonable sin of eating that forbidden fruit themselves, and in that case all the Derku people would be destroyed.

What no one pointed out was that in the old days, when they fed manfruit to the Great Derku, it wasn't *just* captives that were offered. During years of little rain or too much rain, the leader of each clan always offered his own eldest son as the first fruit, or, if he could not bear to see his son devoured, he would offer himself in his son's place—though some said that in the earliest times it was always the leader himself who was eaten, and they only started offering their sons as a cowardly substitute. By now everyone expected Twerk to be the next clan leader, and everyone knew that he doted on his Glogmeriss, his Naog-to-be, his Derkuwed, and that he would never throw his son to the crocodile god. Nor did any of them wish him to do so. A few people in the other clans might urge the test of offering manfruit to the Great Derku, but most of the people in all of the tribes, and all of the people in Engu clan, would oppose it, and so it would not happen.

So it was with an assurance of personal safety that Twerk brought his firstborn son with him to see the Great Derku in the holy pond. But six-year-old Glogmeriss, oblivious to the personal danger that would come from the return of human sacrifice, was terrified at the sight of the holy pond itself. It was surrounded by a low wall of dried mud, for once the crocodile had found its way to the water inside, the gaps in the wall were closed. But what kept the Great Derku inside was not just the mud wall. It was the row on row of sharpened horizontal stakes pointing straight inward, set into the mud and lashed to sharp vertical stakes about a handsbreadth back from the point. The captive dragon could neither push the stakes out of the way nor break them off. Only when the floodwater came and the river spilled over the top of the mud wall and swept it away, stakes and all, would that year's Great Derku be set free. Only rarely did the Great Derku get caught on the stakes and die, and when it happened it was regarded as a very bad omen.

This year, though, the wall of stakes was not widely regarded as enough assurance that the dragon could not force his way out, he was so huge and clever and strong. So men stood guard constantly, spears in hand, ready to prod the Great Derku and herd it back into place, should it come dangerously close to escaping.

The sight of spikes and spears was alarming enough, for it looked like war to young Glogmeriss. But he soon forgot those puny sticks when he caught sight of the Great Derku himself, as he shambled up on the muddy, grassy shore of the pond. Of course Glogmeriss had seen crocodiles all his life; one of the first skills any child, male or female, had to learn was how to use a spear to poke a crocodile so it would leave one's dragonboat—and therefore one's arms and legs—in peace. This crocodile, though, this dragon, this god, was so huge that Glogmeriss could easily imagine it swallowing him whole without having to bite him in half or even chew. Glogmeriss gasped and clung to his father's hand.

"A giant indeed," said his father. "Look at those legs, that powerful tail. But remember that the Great Derku is but a weak child compared to the power of the flood."

Perhaps because human sacrifice was still on his mind, Twerk then told his son how it had been in the old days. "When it was a captive we offered as manfruit, there was always a chance that the god would let him live. Of course, if he clung to the stakes and refused to go into the pond, we would never let him out alive—we poked him with our spears. But if he went boldly into the water so far that it covered his head completely, and then came back out alive and made it back to the stakes without the Great Derku taking him and eating him, well, then, we brought him out in great honor. We said that his old life ended in that water, that the man we had captured had been buried in the holy pond, and now he was born again out of the flood. He was a full member of the tribe then, of the same clan as the man who had captured him. But of course the Great Derku almost never let anyone out alive, because we always kept him hungry."

"*You* poked him with your spear?" asked Glogmeriss.

"Well, not me personally. When I said that *we* did it, I meant of course the men of the Derku. But it was long before I was born. It was in my grandfather's time, when he was a young man, that there came a Great Derku who wouldn't eat any of the captives who were offered to him. No one knew what it meant, of course, but all the captives were coming out and expecting to be adopted into the tribe. But if *that* had happened, the captives would have been the largest clan of all, and where would we have found wives for them all? So the holy men and the clan leaders realized that the old way was over, that the god no longer wanted manfruit, and therefore those who survived after being buried in the water of the holy pond were *not* adopted into the Derku people. But we did keep them alive and set them to work on the canals. That year, with the captives working alongside us, we dredged the canals deeper than ever, and we were able to draw twice the water from the canals into the fields of grain during the dry season, and when we had a bigger harvest than ever before, we had hands enough to weave more seedboats to contain it. Then we realized what the god had meant by refusing to eat the manfruit. Instead of swallowing our captives into the belly of the water where the god lives, the god was giving them all back to us, to make us rich and strong. So from that day on we have fed no captives to the Great Derku. Instead we hunt for meat and bring it back, while the women and old men make the captives do the labor of the city. In those days we had one large canal. Now we have three great canals encircling each other, and several other canals cutting across them, so that even in the driest season a Derku man can glide on his dragonboat like a crocodile from any part of our land to any other, and never have to drag it across dry earth. This is the greatest gift of the dragon to us, that we can have the labor of our captives instead of the Great Derku devouring them himself."

"It's not a bad gift to the captives, either," said Glogmeriss. "Not to die."

Twerk laughed and rubbed his son's hair. "Not a bad gift at that," he said.

"Of course, if the Great Derku really loved the captives he would let them go home to their families."

Twerk laughed even louder. "They have no families, foolish boy," he said. "When a man is captured, he is dead as far as his family is concerned. His woman marries someone else, his children forget him and call another man father. He has no more home to return to."

"Don't some of the ugly-noise people buy captives back?"

"The weak and foolish ones do. The gold ring on my arm was the price of a captive. The father-of-all priest wears a cape of bright feathers that was the ransom of a boy not much older than you, not long after you were born. But most captives know better than to hope for ransom. What does *their* tribe have that we want?"

"I would hate to be a captive, then," said Glogmeriss. "Or would *you* be weak and foolish enough to ransom me?"

"You?" Twerk laughed out loud. "You're a Derku man, or will be. We take captives wherever we want, but where is the tribe so bold that it dares to take one of *us*? No, we are never captives. And the captives we take are lucky to be brought out of their poor, miserable tribes of wandering hunters or berry-pickers and allowed to live here among wall-building men, among canal-digging people, where they don't have to wander in search of food every day, where they get plenty to eat all year long, twice as much as they ever ate before."

"I would still hate to be one of them," said Glogmeriss. "Because how could you ever do great things that everyone will talk about and tell stories about and remember, if you're a captive?"

All this time that they stood on the wall and talked, Glogmeriss never took his eyes off the Great Derku. It was a terrible creature, and when it yawned it seemed its mouth was large enough to swallow a tree. Ten grown men could ride on its back like a dragonboat. Worst of all were the eyes, which seemed to stare into a man's heart. It was probably the eyes of the dragon that gave it its name, for *derku* could easily have originated as a shortened form of *derk-unt,* which meant "one who sees." When the ancient ancestors of the Derku people first came to this floodplain, the crocodiles floating like logs on the water must have fooled them. They must have learned to look for eyes on the logs. "Look!" the watcher would cry. "There's one with eyes! Derk-unt!" They said that if you looked in the dragon's eyes, he would draw you toward him, within reach of his huge jaws, within reach of his curling tail, and you would never even notice your danger, because his eyes held you. Even when the jaws opened to show the pink mouth, the teeth like rows of bright flame ready to burn you, you would look at that steady, all-knowing, wise, amused, and coolly angry eye.

That was the fear that filled Glogmeriss the whole time he stood on the wall beside his father. For a moment, though, just after he spoke of doing great things, a curious change came over him. For a moment Glogmeriss stopped fearing the Great Derku, and instead imagined that he *was* the giant crocodile. Didn't a man paddle his dragonboat by lying on his belly straddling the bundled reeds, paddling with his hands and kicking with his feet just as a crocodile did under the water? So all men became dragons, in a way. And Glogmeriss would grow up to be a large man, everyone said so. Among men he would be as extraordinary as the Great Derku was among crocodiles. Like the god, he would seem dangerous and strike fear into the hearts of smaller people. And, again like the god, he would actually be kind, and not destroy them, but instead help them and do good for them.

Like the river in flood. A frightening thing, to have the water rise so high, sweeping away the mud hills on which they had built the seedboats, smearing the outsides of them with sun-heated tar so they would be watertight when the flood came. Like the Great Derku, the flood seemed to be a destroyer. And yet when the water receded, the land was wet and rich, ready to receive the seed and give back huge harvests. The land farther up the slopes of the mountains was salty and stony and all that could grow on it was grass. It was here in the flatlands where the flood tore through like a mad dragon that the soil was rich and trees could grow.

I will *be* the Derkuwed. Not as a destroyer, but as a lifebringer. The real Derku, the true dragon, could never be trapped in a cage as this poor crocodile has been. The true dragon comes like the flood and tears away the walls and sets the Great Derku crocodile free and makes the soil wet and black and rich. Like the river, I will be another tool of the god, another manifestation of the power of the god in the world. If that was not what the dragon of the deep heaven of the sea intended, why would he have made Glogmeriss so tall and strong?

This was still the belief in his heart when Glogmeriss set out on his manhood journey at the age of fourteen. He was already the tallest man in his clan and one of the tallest among all the Derku people. He was a giant, and yet well-liked because he never used his strength and size to frighten other people into doing what he wanted; on the contrary, he seemed always to protect the weaker boys. Many people felt that it was a shame that when he returned from his manhood journey, the name he would be given was a silly one like Naog. But when they said as much in Glogmeriss's hearing, he only laughed at them and said, "The name will only be silly if it is borne by a silly man. I hope not to be a silly man."

Glogmeriss's father had made his fame by taking his manhood journey from the Salty Sea to the Nile. Glogmeriss's journey therefore had to be even more challenging and more glorious. He would go south and east, along the crest of the plateau until he reached the legendary place called the Heaving Sea, where the gods that dwelt in its deep heaven were so restless that the water splashed onto the shore in great waves all the time, even when there was no wind. If there was such a sea, Glogmeriss would find it. When he came back as a man with such a tale, they would call him Naog and none of them would laugh.

Kemal Akyazi knew that Atlantis had to be there under the waters of the Red Sea; but why hadn't Pastwatch found it? The answer was simple enough. The past was huge, and while the TruSite I had been used to collect climatological information, the new machines that were precise enough to track individual human beings would never have been used to look at oceans where nobody lived. Yes, the Tempoview had explored the Bering Strait and the English Channel, but that was to track long-known-of migrations. There was no such migration in the Red Sea. Pastwatch had simply never looked through their precise new machines to see what was under the water of the Red Sea in the waning centuries of the last ice age. And they never *would* look, either, unless someone gave them a compelling reason.

Kemal understood bureaucracy enough to know that he, a student meteorologist, would hardly be taken seriously if he brought an Atlantis theory to Pastwatch—particularly a theory that put Atlantis in the Red Sea of all places, and fourteen thousand years ago, no less, long before civilizations arose in Sumeria or Egypt, let alone China or the Indus Valley or among the swamps of Tehuantepec.

Yet Kemal also knew that the setting would have been right for a civilization to grow in the marshy land of the Mits'iwa Channel. Though there weren't enough rivers flowing into the Red Sea to fill it at the same rate as the world ocean, there were still rivers. For instance, the Zula, which still had enough water to flow even today, watered the whole length of the Mits'iwa Plain and flowed down into the rump of the Red Sea near Mersa Mubarek. And, because of the different rainfall patterns of that time, there was a large and dependable river flowing out of the Assahara basin. Assahara was now a dry valley below sea level, but then would have been a freshwater lake fed by many rivers and spilling over the lowest point into the Mits'iwa Channel. The river meandered along the nearly level Mits'iwa Plain, with some branches of it joining the Zula River, and some wandering east and north to form several mouths in the Red Sea.

Thus dependable sources of fresh water fed the area, and in rainy season the Zula, at least, would have brought new silt to freshen the soil, and in all seasons the wandering flatwater rivers would have provided a means of transportation through the marshes. The climate was also dependably warm, with plenty of sunlight and a long growing season. There was no early civilization that did not grow up in such a setting. There was no reason such a civilization might not have grown up then.

Yes, it was six or seven thousand years too early. But couldn't it be that it was the very destruction of Atlantis that convinced the survivors that the gods did not want human beings to gather together in cities? Weren't there hints of that anti-civilization bias lingering in many of the ancient religions of the Middle East? What was the story of Cain and Abel, if not a metaphorical expression of the evil of the city-dweller, the farmer, the brother-killer who is judged unworthy by the gods because he does not wander with his sheep? Couldn't such stories have circulated widely in those ancient times? That would explain why the survivors of Atlantis hadn't immediately begun to rebuild their civilization at another site: They knew that the gods forbade it, that if they built again their city would be destroyed again. So they remembered the stories of their glorious past, and at the same time condemned their ancestors and warned everyone they met against people gathering together to build a city, making people yearn for such a place and fear it, both at once.

Not until a Nimrod came, a tower-builder, a Babel-maker who defied the old religion, would the ancient proscription be overcome at last and another city rise up, in another river valley far in time and space from Atlantis, but remembering the old ways that had been memorialized in the stories of warning and, as far as possible, replicating them. We will build a tower so high that it *can't* be immersed. Didn't Genesis link the flood with Babel in just that way, complete with the nomad's stern disapproval of the city? This was the story that survived in Mesopotamia—the tale of the beginning of city life there, but with clear memories of a more ancient civilization that had been destroyed in a flood.

A more ancient civilization. The golden age. The giants who once walked the earth. Why couldn't all these stories be remembering the first human civilization, the place where the city was invented? Atlantis, the city of the Mits'iwa Plain.

But how could he prove it without using the Tempoview? And how could he get access to one of those machines without first convincing Pastwatch that Atlantis was really in the Red Sea? It was circular, with no way out.

Until he thought: Why do large cities form in the first place? Because there are public works to do that require more than a few people to accomplish them. Kemal wasn't sure what form the public works might take, but surely they would have been something that would change the face of the land obviously enough that the old TruSite I recordings would show it, though it wouldn't be noticeable unless someone was looking for it.

So, putting his degree at risk, Kemal set aside the work he was assigned to do and began poring over the old TruSite I recordings. He concentrated on the last few centuries before the Red Sea flood—there was no reason to suppose that the civilization had lasted very long before it was destroyed. And within a few months he had collected data that was irrefutable. There were no dikes and dams to prevent flooding—that kind of structure would have been large enough that no one would have missed it. Instead there were seemingly random heaps of mud and earth that grew between rainy seasons, especially in the drier years when the rivers were lower than usual. To people looking only for weather patterns, these unstructured, random piles would mean nothing. But to Kemal they were obvious: In the shallowing water, the Atlanteans were dredging channels so that their boats could continue to traffic from place to place. The piles of earth were simply the dumping-places for the muck they dredged from the water. None of the boats showed up on the TruSite I, but now that Kemal knew where to look, he began to catch fleeting glimpses of houses. Every year when the floods came, the houses disappeared, so they were only visible for a moment or two in the Trusite I: flimsy mud-and-reed structures that must have been swept away in every flood season and rebuilt again when the waters receded. But they were there, close by the hillocks that marked the channels. Plato was right again—Atlantis grew up around its canals. But Atlantis was the people and their boats; the buildings were washed away and built again every year.

When Kemal presented his findings to Pastwatch he was not yet twenty years old, but his evidence was impressive enough that Pastwatch immediately turned, not one of the Tempoviews, but the still-newer TruSite II machine to look under the waters of the Red Sea in the Mits'iwa Channel during the hundred years before the Red Sea flood. They found that Kemal was gloriously, spectacularly right. In an era when other humans were still following game animals and gathering berries, the Atlanteans were planting amaranth and ryegrass, melons and beans in the rich wet silt of the receding rivers, and carrying food in baskets and on reed boats from place to place. The only thing that Kemal had missed was that the reed buildings weren't houses at all. They were silos for the storage of grain, built watertight so that they would float during the flood season. The Atlanteans slept under the open air during the dry season, and in the flood season they slept on their tiny reed boats.

Kemal was brought into Pastwatch and made head of the vast new Atlantis project. This was the seminal culture of all cultures in the old world, and a hundred researchers examined every stage of its development. This methodical work, however, was not for Kemal. As always, it was the grand legend that drew him. He spent every moment he could spare away from the management of the project and devoted it to the search for Noah, for Gilgamesh, for the great man who rode out the flood and whose story lived in memory for thousands of years. There had to be a real original, and Kemal would find him.

The flood season was almost due when Glogmeriss took the journey that would make him into a man named Naog. It was a little early for him, since he was born during the peak of the flood, but everyone in the clan agreed with Twerk that it was better for a manling so well-favored to be early than late, and if he wasn't already up and out of the floodplain before the rains came, then he'd have to wait months before he could safely go. And besides, as Twerk pointed out, why have a big eater like Glogmeriss waiting out the flood season, eating huge handfuls of grain. People listened happily to Twerk's argument, because he was known to be a generous, wise, good-humored man, and everyone expected him to be named clan leader when sweet old ailing Dheub finally died.

Getting above the flood meant walking up the series of slight inclines leading to the last sandy shoulder, where the land began to rise more steeply. Glogmeriss had no intention of climbing any higher than that. His father's journey had taken him over those ridges and on to the great river Nile, but there was no reason for Glogmeriss to clamber through rocks when he could follow the edge of the smooth, grassy savannah. He was high enough to see the vast plain of the Derku lands stretching out before him, and the land was open enough that no cat or pack of dogs could creep up on him unnoticed, let alone some hunter of another tribe.

How far to the Heaving Sea? Far enough that no one of the Derku tribe had ever seen it. But they knew it existed, because when they brought home captives from tribes to the south, they heard tales of such a place, and the farther south the captives came from, the more vivid and convincing the tales became. Still, none of them had ever seen it with their own eyes. So it would be a long journey, Glogmeriss knew that. And all the longer because it would be on foot, and not on his dragonboat. Not that Derku men were any weaker or slower afoot than men who lived above the flood—on the contrary, they had to be fleet indeed, as well as stealthy, to bring home either captives or meat. So the boys' games included footracing, and while Glogmeriss was not the fastest sprinter, no one could match his long-legged stride for sheer endurance, for covering ground quickly, on and on, hour after hour.

What set the bodies of the Derku people apart from other tribes, what made them recognizable in an instant, was the massive development of their upper bodies from paddling dragonboats hour after hour along the canals or through the floods. It wasn't just paddling, either. It was the heavy armwork of cutting reeds and binding them into great sheaves to be floated home for making boats and ropes and baskets. And in older times, they would also have developed strong arms and backs from dredging the canals that surrounded and connected all the villages of the great Derku city. Slaves did most of that now, but the Derku took great pride in never letting their slaves be stronger than they were. Their shoulders and chests and arms and backs were almost monstrous compared to those of the men and women of other tribes. And since the Derku ate better all year round than people of other tribes, they tended to be taller, too. Many tribes called them giants, and others called them the sons and daughters of the gods, they looked so healthy and strong. And of all the young Derku men, there was none so tall and strong and healthy as Glogmeriss, the boy they called Derkuwed, the man who would be Naog.

So as Glogmeriss loped along the grassy rim of the great plain, he knew he was in little danger from human enemies. Anyone who saw him would think: There is one of the giants, one of the sons of the crocodile god. Hide, for he might be with a party of raiders. Don't let him see you, or he'll take a report back to his people. Perhaps one man in a pack of hunters might say, "He's alone, we can kill him," but the other hunters would jeer at the one who spoke so rashly. "Look, fool, he has a javelin in his hands and three tied to his back. Look at his arms, his shoulders—do you think he can't put his javelin through your heart before you got close enough to throw a rock at him? Let him be. Pray for a great cat to find him in the night."

That was Glogmeriss's only real danger. He was too high into the dry lands for crocodiles, and he could run fast enough to climb a tree before any pack of dogs or wolves could bring him down. But there was no tree that would give a moment's pause to one of the big cats. No, if one of *them* took after him, it would be a fight. But Glogmeriss had fought cats before, on guard duty. They were not the giants that could knock a man's head off with one blow of a paw, or take his whole belly with one bite of their jaws, but still, they were big enough, prowling around the outside of the clan lands, and Glogmeriss had fought them with a hand javelin and brought them down alone. He knew something of the way they moved and thought, and he had no doubt that in a contest with one of the big cats, he would at least cause it grave injury before it killed him.

Better not to meet one of them, though. Which meant staying well clear of any of the herds of bison or oxen, antelope or horses that the big cats stalked. Those cats would never have got so big waiting around for lone humans—it was herds they needed, and so it was herds that Glogmeriss did *not* need.

To his annoyance, though, one came to *him*. He had climbed a tree to

sleep the night, tying himself to the trunk so he wouldn't fall out in his
sleep. He awoke to the sound of nervous lowing and a few higher-
pitched, anxious moos. Below him, milling around in the first grey light
of the coming dawn, he could make out the shadowy shapes of oxen. He
knew at once what had happened. They caught scent of a cat and began
to move away in the darkness, shambling in fear and confusion in the near
darkness. They had not run because the cat wasn't close enough to cause
a panic in the herd. With luck it would be one of the smaller cats, and
when it saw that they knew it was there, it would give up and go away.

But the cat had not given up and gone away, or they wouldn't still be
so frightened. Soon the herd would have enough light to see the cat that
must be stalking them, and then they *would* run, leaving Glogmeriss behind in a tree. Maybe the cat would go in full pursuit of the running
oxen, or maybe it would notice the lone man trapped in a tree and decide
to go for the easier, smaller meal.

I wish I were part of this herd, thought Glogmeriss. Then there'd be
a chance. I would be one of many, and even if the cat brought one of us
down, it might not be me. As a man alone, it's me or the cat. Kill or die. I
will fight bravely, but in this light I might not get a clear sight of the cat,
might not be able to see in the rippling of its muscles where it will move
next. And what if it isn't alone? What if the reason these oxen are so
frightened yet unwilling to move is that they know there's more than one
cat and they have no idea in which direction safety can be found?

Again he thought, I wish I were part of this herd. And then he
thought, Why should I think such a foolish thought twice, unless the god
is telling me what to do? Isn't that what this journey is for, to find out if
there is a god who will lead me, who will protect me, who will make me
great? There's no greatness in having a cat eviscerate you in one bite.
Only if you live do you become a man of stories. Like Gweia—if she had
mounted the crocodile and it had thrown her off and devoured her, who
would ever have heard her name?

There was no time to form a plan, except the plan that formed so
quickly that it might have been the god putting it there. He would ride
one of these oxen as Gweia rode the crocodile. It would be easy enough
to drop out of the tree onto an ox's back—hadn't he played with the
other boys, year after year, jumping from higher and higher branches to

land on a dragonboat that was drifting under the tree? An ox was scarcely less predictable than a dragonboat on a current. The only difference was that when he landed on the ox's back, it would not bear him as willingly as a dragonboat. Glogmeriss had to hope that, like Gweia's crocodile frightened of the flood, the ox he landed on would be more frightened of the cat than of the sudden burden on his back.

He tried to pick well among the oxen within reach of the branches of the tree. He didn't want a cow with a calf running alongside—that would be like begging the cats to come after him, since such cows were already the most tempting targets. But he didn't want a bull, either, for he doubted it would have the patience to bear him.

And there was his target, a full-size cow but with no calf leaning against it, under a fairly sturdy branch. Slowly, methodically, Glogmeriss untied himself from the tree, cinched the bindings of his javelins and his flintsack and his grainsack, and drew his loincloth up to hold his genitals tight against his body, and then crept out along the branch until he was as nearly over the back of the cow he had chosen as possible. The cow was stamping and snorting now—they all were, and in a moment they would bolt, he knew it—but it held still as well as a bobbing dragonboat, and so Glogmeriss took aim and jumped, spreading his legs to embrace the animal's back, but not *so* wide that he would slam his crotch against the bony ridge of its spine.

He landed with a grunt and immediately lunged forward to get his arms around the ox's neck, just like gripping the stem of the dragonboat. The beast immediately snorted and bucked, but its bobbing was no worse than the dragonboat ducking under the water at the impact of a boy on its back. Of course, the dragonboat stopped bobbing after a moment, while this ox would no doubt keep trying to be rid of him until he was gone, bucking and turning, bashing its sides into other oxen.

But the other animals were already so nervous that the sudden panic of Glogmeriss's mount was the trigger that set off the stampede. Almost at once the herd mentality took over, and the oxen set out in a headlong rush all in the same direction. Glogmeriss's cow didn't forget the burden on her back, but now she responded to her fear by staying with the herd. It came as a great relief to Glogmeriss when she leapt out and ran among the other oxen, in part because it meant that she was no longer trying to get him off her back, and in part because she was a good runner and he knew that unless she swerved to the edge of the herd where a cat could pick her off, both she and he would be safe.

Until the panic stopped, of course, and then Glogmeriss would have to figure out a way to get *off* the cow and move away without being gored or trampled to death. Well, one danger at a time. And as they ran, he couldn't help but feel the sensations of the moment: the prickly hair of the ox's back against his belly and legs, the way her muscles rippled between his legs and within the embrace of his arms, and above all the sheer exhilaration of moving through the air at such a speed. Has any man ever moved as fast over the ground as I am moving now? he wondered. No dragonboat has ever found a current so swift.

It seemed that they ran for hours and hours, though when they finally came to a stop the sun was still only a palm's height above the mountains far across the plain to the east. As the running slowed to a jolting jog, and then to a walk, Glogmeriss kept waiting for his mount to remember that he was on her back and to start trying to get him off. But if she remembered, she must have decided she didn't mind, because when she finally came to a stop, still in the midst of the herd, she simply dropped her head and began to graze, making no effort to get Glogmeriss off her back.

She was so calm—or perhaps like the others was simply so exhausted—that Glogmeriss decided that as long as he moved slowly and calmly he might be able to walk on out of the herd, or at least climb a tree and wait for them to move on. He knew from the roaring and screaming sounds he had heard near the beginning of the stampede that the cats—more than one—had found their meal, so the survivors were safe enough for now.

Glogmeriss carefully let one leg slide down until he touched the ground. Then, smoothly as possible, he slipped off the cow's back until he was crouched beside her. She turned her head slightly, chewing a mouthful of grass. Her great brown eye regarded him calmly.

"Thank you for carrying me," said Glogmeriss softly.

She moved her head away, as if to deny that she had done anything special for him.

"You carried me like a dragonboat through the flood," he said, and he realized that this was exactly right, for hadn't the stampede of oxen been as dangerous and powerful as any flood of water? And she had borne him up, smooth and safe, carrying him safely to the far shore. "The best of dragonboats."

She lowed softly, and for a moment Glogmeriss began to think of her as being somehow the embodiment of the god—though it could not be the crocodile god that took this form, could it? But all thoughts of the animal's godhood were shattered when it started to urinate. The thick stream of ropy piss splashed into the grass not a span away from Glogmeriss's shoulder, and as the urine spattered him he could not help but jump away. Other nearby oxen mooed complainingly about his sudden movement, but his own cow seemed not to notice. The urine stank hotly, and Glogmeriss was annoyed that the stink would stay with him for days, probably.

Then he realized that no *cow* could put a stream of urine between her forelegs. This animal was a bull after all. Yet it was scarcely larger than the normal cow, not bull-like at all. Squatting down, he looked closely, and realized that the animal had lost its testicles somehow. Was it a freak, born without them? No, there was a scar, a ragged sign of old injury. While still a calf, this animal had had its bullhood torn away. Then it grew to adulthood, neither cow nor bull. What purpose was there in life for such a creature as that? And yet if it had not lived, it could not have carried him through the stampede. A cow would have had a calf to slow it down; a bull would have flung him off easily. The god had prepared this creature to save him. It was not itself a god, of course, for such an imperfect animal could hardly be divine. But it was a god's tool.

"Thank you," said Glogmeriss, to whatever god it was. "I hope to know you and serve you," he said. Whoever the god was must have known him for a long time, must have planned this moment for years. There was a plan, a destiny for him. Glogmeriss felt himself thrill inside with the certainty of this.

I could turn back now, he thought, and I would have had the greatest manhood journey of anyone in the tribe for generations. They would regard me as a holy man, when they learned that a god had prepared such a beast as this to be my dragonboat on dry land. No one would say I was unworthy to be Naog, and no more Glogmeriss.

But even as he thought this, Glogmeriss knew that it would be wrong to go back. The god had prepared this animal, not to make his manhood journey easy and short, but to make his long journey possible. Hadn't the ox carried him southeast, the direction he was already heading? Hadn't it brought him right along the very shelf of smooth grassland that he had already been running on? No, the god meant to speed him on his way, not to end his journey. When he came back, the story of the unmanned ox that carried him like a boat would be merely the first part of his story. They would laugh when he told them about the beast peeing on him. They would nod and murmur in awe as he told them that he realized that the god was helping him to go on, that the god had chosen him years before in order to prepare the calf that would be his mount. Yet this would all be the opening, leading to the main point of the story, the climax. And what that climax would be, what he would accomplish that would let him take on his manly name, Glogmeriss could hardly bear to wait to find out.

Unless, of course, the god was preparing him to be a sacrifice. But the god could have killed him at any time. It could have killed him when he was born, dropping him into the water as everyone said his father had feared might happen. It could have let him die there at the tree, taken by a cat or trampled under the feet of the oxen. No, the god was keeping him alive for a purpose, for a great task. His triumph lay ahead, and whatever it was, it would be greater than his ride on the back of an ox.

The rains came the next day, but Glogmeriss pressed on. The rain made it hard to see far ahead, but most of the animals stopped moving in the rain and so there wasn't as much danger to look out for. Sometimes the rain came down so thick and hard that Glogmeriss could hardly see a dozen steps ahead. But he ran on, unhindered. The shelf of land that he ran along was perfectly flat, neither uphill nor downhill, as level as water, and so he could lope along without wearying. Even when the thunder roared in the sky and lightning seemed to flash all around him, Glogmeriss did not stop, for he knew that the god that watched over him was powerful indeed. He had nothing to fear. And since he passed two burning trees, he knew that lightning could have struck him at any time, and yet did not, and so it was a second sign that a great god was with him.

During the rains he crossed many swollen streams, just by walking. Only once did he have to cross a river that was far too wide and deep and swift in flood for him to cross. But he plunged right in, for the god was with him. Almost at once he was swept off his feet, but he swam strongly across the current. Yet even a strong Derku man cannot swim forever, and it began to seem to Glogmeriss that he would never reach the other side, but rather would be swept down to the salt sea, where one day his body would wash to shore near a party of Derku raiders who would recognize from the size of his body that it was him. So, this is what happened to Twerk's son Glogmeriss. The flood took him after all.

Then he bumped against a log that was also floating on the current, and took hold of it, and rolled up onto the top of it like a dragonboat. Now he could use all his strength for paddling, and soon he was across the current. He drew the log from the water and embraced it like a brother, lying beside it, holding it in the wet grass until the rising water began to lick at his feet again. Then he dragged the log with him to higher ground and placed it up in the notch of a tree where no flood would dislodge it. One does not abandon a brother to the flood.

Three times the god has saved me, he thought as he climbed back up to the level shelf that was his path. From the tooth of the cat, from the fire of heaven, from the water of the flood. Each time a tree was part of it: the tree around which the herd of oxen gathered and from which I dropped onto the ox's back; the trees that died in flames from taking to themselves the bolts of lightning meant for me; and finally this log of a fallen tree that died in its home far up in the mountains in order to be my brother in the water of the flood. Is it a god of trees, then, that leads me on? But how can a god of trees be more powerful than the god of lightning or the god of the floods or even the god of sharp-toothed cats? No, trees are simply tools the god has used. The god flings trees about as easily as I fling a javelin.

Gradually, over many days, the rains eased a bit, falling in steady showers instead of sheets. Off to his left, he could see that the plain was rising up closer and closer to the smooth shelf along which he ran. On the first clear morning he saw that there was no more distant shining on the still waters of the Salty Sea—the plain was now higher than the level of that water; he had left behind the only sea that the Derku people had ever seen. The Heaving Sea lay yet ahead, and so he ran on.

The plain was quite high, but he was still far enough above it that he could see the shining when it came again on a clear morning. He had left one sea behind, and now, with the ground much higher, there was another sea. Could this be it, the Heaving Sea?

He left the shelf and headed across the savannah toward the water. He did not reach it that day, but on the next afternoon he stood on the shore and knew that this was not the place he had been looking for. The water was far smaller than the Salty Sea, smaller even than the Sweetwater Sea up in the mountains from which the Selud River flowed. And yet when he dipped his finger into the water and tasted it, it *was* a little salty. Almost sweet, but salty nonetheless. Not good for drinking. That was obvious from the lack of animal tracks around the water. It must usually be saltier than this, thought Glogmeriss. It must have been freshened somewhat by the rains.

Instead of returning to his path along the shelf by the route he had followed to get to this small sea, Glogmeriss struck out due south. He could see the shelf in the distance, and could see that by running south he would rejoin the level path a good way farther along.

As he crossed a small stream, he saw animal prints again, and among them the prints of human feet. Many feet, and they were fresher than any of the animal prints. So fresh, in fact, that for all Glogmeriss knew they could be watching him right now. If he stumbled on them suddenly, they might panic, seeing a man as large as he was. And in this place what would they know of the Derku people? No raiders had ever come this far in search of captives, he was sure. That meant that they wouldn't necessarily hate him—but they wouldn't fear retribution from his tribe, either. No, the best course was for him to turn back and avoid them.

But a god was protecting him, and besides, he had been without the sound of a human voice for so many days. If he did not carry any of his javelins, but left them all slung on his back, they would know he meant no harm and they would not fear him. So there at the stream, he bent over, slipped off the rope holding his javelins, and untied them to bind them all together.

As he was working, he heard a sound and knew without looking that he had been found. Perhaps they *had* been watching him all along. His first thought was to pick up his javelins and prepare for battle. But he did not know how many they were, or whether they were all around him, and in the dense brush near the river he might be surrounded by so many that they could overwhelm him easily, even if he killed one or two. For a moment he thought, The god protects me, I could kill them all. But then he rejected that idea. He had killed nothing on this journey, not even for meat, eating only the grain he carried with him and such berries and fruits and roots and greens and mushrooms as he found along the way. Should he begin now, killing when he knew nothing about these people? Perhaps meeting them was what the god had brought him here to do.

So he slowly, carefully finished binding the javelins and then slung them up onto his shoulder, being careful never to hold the javelins in a way that might make his watcher or watchers think that he was making them ready for battle. Then, his hands empty and his weapons bound to his back, he splashed through the stream and followed the many footprints on the far side.

He could hear feet padding along behind him—more than one person, too, from the sound. They might be coming up behind him to kill him, but it didn't sound as if they were trying to overtake him, or to be stealthy, either. They must know that he could hear them. But perhaps they thought he was very stupid. He had to show them that he did not turn to fight them because he did not want to fight, and not because he was stupid or afraid.

To show them he was not afraid, he began to sing the song of the dog who danced with a man, which was funny and had a jaunty tune. And to show them he knew they were there, he bent over as he walked, scooped up a handful of damp soil, and flung it lightly over his shoulder.

The sound of sputtering outrage told him that the god had guided his lump of mud right to its target. He stopped and turned to find four men following him, one of whom was brushing dirt out of his face, cursing loudly. The others looked uncertain whether to be angry at Glogmeriss for flinging dirt at them or afraid of him because he was so large and strange and unafraid.

Glogmeriss didn't want them to be either afraid or angry. So he let a slow smile come to his face, not a smile of derision, but rather a friendly smile that said, I mean no harm. To reinforce this idea, he held his hands out wide, palms facing the strangers.

They understood him, and perhaps because of his smile began to see the humor in the situation. They smiled, too, and then, because the one who was hit with dirt was still complaining and trying to get it out of his eyes, they began to laugh at him. Glogmeriss laughed with them, but then walked slowly toward his victim and, carefully letting them all see what he was doing, took his waterbag from his waist and untied it a little, showing them that water dropped from it. They uttered something in an ugly-sounding language and the one with dirt in his eyes stopped, leaned his head back, and stoically allowed Glogmeriss to bathe his eyes with water.

When at last, dripping and chagrined, the man could see again, Glogmeriss flung an arm across his shoulder like a comrade, and then reached out for the man who seemed to be the leader. After a moment's hesitation, the man allowed Glogmeriss the easy embrace, and together they walked toward the main body of the tribe, the other two walking as closely as possible, behind and ahead, talking to Glogmeriss even though he made it plain that he did not understand.

When they reached the others they were busy building a cookfire. All who could, left their tasks and came to gawk at the giant stranger. While the men who had found him recounted the tale, others came and touched Glogmeriss, especially his strong arms and chest, and his loincloth as well, since none of the men wore any kind of clothing. Glogmeriss viewed this with disgust. It was one thing for little boys to run around naked, but he knew that men should keep their privates covered so they wouldn't get dirty. What woman would let her husband couple with her, if he let any kind of filth get on his javelin?

Of course, these men were all so ugly that no woman would want them anyway, and the women were so ugly that the only men who would want them would be these. Perhaps ugly people don't care about keeping themselves clean, thought Glogmeriss. But the women wore naprons made of woven grass, which looked softer than the beaten reeds that the Derku wove. So it wasn't that these people didn't know how to make cloth, or that the idea of wearing clothing had never occurred to them. The men were simply filthy and stupid, Glogmeriss decided. And the women, while not as filthy, must be just as stupid or they wouldn't let the men come near them.

Glogmeriss tried to explain to them that he was looking for the Heaving Sea, and ask them where it was. But they couldn't understand any of the gestures and handsigns he tried, and his best efforts merely left them laughing to the point of helplessness. He gave up and made as if to leave, which immediately brought protests and an obvious invitation to dinner.

It was a welcome thought, and their chief seemed quite anxious for him to stay. A meal would only make him stronger for the rest of his journey.

He stayed for the meal, which was strange but good. And then, wooed by more pleas from the chief and many others, he agreed to sleep the night with them, though he halfway feared that in his sleep they planned to kill him or at least rob him. In the event, it turned out that they *did* have plans for him, but it had nothing to do with killing. By morning the chief's prettiest daughter was Glogmeriss's bride, and even though she was as ugly as any of the others, she had done a good enough job of initiating him into the pleasures of men and women that he could overlook her thin lips and beakish nose.

This was not supposed to happen on a manhood journey. He was expected to come home and marry one of the pretty girls from one of the other clans of the Derku people. Many a father had already been negotiating with Twerk or old Dheub with an eye toward getting Glogmeriss as a son-in-law. But what harm would it do if Glogmeriss had a bride for a few days with these people, and then slipped away and went home? No one among the Derku would ever meet any of these ugly people, and even if they did, who would care? You could do what you wanted with strangers. It wasn't as if they were people, like the Derku.

But the days came and went, and Glogmeriss could not bring himself to leave. He was still enjoying his nights with Zawada—as near as he could come to pronouncing her name, which had a strange click in the middle of it. And as he began to learn to understand something of their language, he harbored a hope that they could tell him about the Heaving Sea and, in the long run, save him time.

Days became weeks, and weeks became months, and Zawada's blood-days didn't come and so they knew she was pregnant, and then Glogmeriss didn't want to leave, because he had to see the child he had put into her. So he stayed, and learned to help with the work of this tribe. They found his size and prodigious strength very helpful, and Zawada was comically boastful about her husband's prowess—marrying him had brought her great prestige, even more than being the chief's daughter. And it gradually came to Glogmeriss's mind that if he stayed he would probably be chief of these people himself someday. At times when he thought of that, he felt a strange sadness, for what did it mean to be chief of these miserable ugly people, compared to the honor of being the most ordinary of the Derku people? How could being chief of these grub-eaters and gatherers compare to eating the common bread of the Derku and riding on a drag-onboat through the flood or on raids? He enjoyed Zawada, he enjoyed the people of this tribe, but they were not his people, and he knew that he would leave. Eventually.

Zawada's belly was beginning to swell when the tribe suddenly gath-ered their tools and baskets and formed up to begin another trek. They didn't move back north, however, the direction they had come from when Glogmeriss found them. Rather their migration was due south, and soon, to his surprise, he found that they were hiking along the very shelf of land that had been his path in coming to this place.

It occurred to him that perhaps the god had spoken to the chief in the night, warning him to get Glogmeriss back on his abandoned journey. But no, the chief denied any dream. Rather he pointed to the sky and said it was time to go get—something. A word Glogmeriss had never heard before. But it was clearly some kind of food, because the adults nearby be-gan laughing with anticipatory delight and pantomiming eating copious amounts of—something.

Off to the northeast, they passed along the shores of another small sea. Glogmeriss asked if the water was sweet and if it had fish in it, but Zawada told him, sadly, that the sea was spoiled. "It used to be good," she said. "The people drank from it and swam in it and trapped fish in it, but it got poisoned."

"How?" asked Glogmeriss.

"The god vomited into it."

"What god did that?"

"The great god," she said, looking mysterious and amused.

"How do you know he did?" asked Glogmeriss.

"We saw," she said. "There was a terrible storm, with winds so strong they tore babies from their mothers' arms and carried them away and they were never seen again. My own mother and father held me between them and I wasn't carried off—I was scarcely more than a baby then, and I remember how scared I was, to have my parents crushing me between them while the wind screamed through the trees."

"But a rainstorm would sweeten the water," said Glogmeriss. "Not make it salty."

"I told you," said Zawada. "The god vomited into it."

"But if you don't mean the rain, then what do you mean?"

To which her only answer was a mysterious smile and a giggle. "You'll see," she said.

And in the end, he did. Two days after leaving this second small sea behind, they rounded a bend and some of the men began to shinny up trees, looking off to the east as if they knew exactly what they'd see. "There it is!" they cried. "We can see it!"

Glogmeriss lost no time in climbing up after them, but it took a while for him to know what it was they had seen. It wasn't till he climbed another tree the next morning, when they were closer and when the sun was shining in the east, that he realized that the vast plain opening out before them to the east wasn't a plain at all. It was water, shimmering strangely in the sunlight of morning. More water than Glogmeriss had ever imagined. And the reason the light shimmered that way was because the water was moving. It was the Heaving Sea.

He came down from the tree in awe, only to find the whole tribe watching him. When they saw his face, they burst into hysterical laughter, including even Zawada. Only now did it occur to him that they had understood him perfectly well on his first day with them, when he described the Heaving Sea. They had known where he was headed, but they hadn't told him.

"There's the joke back on you!" cried the man in whose face Glogmeriss had thrown dirt on that first day. And now it seemed like perfect justice to Glogmeriss. He had played a joke, and they had played one back, an elaborate jest that required even his wife to keep the secret of the Heaving Sea from him.

Zawada's father, the chief, now explained that it was more than a joke. "Waiting to show you the Heaving Sea meant that you would stay and marry Zawada and give her giant babies. A dozen giants like you!"

Zawada grinned cheerfully. "If they don't kill me coming out, it'll be fine to have sons like yours will be!"

Next day's journey took them far enough that they didn't have to climb trees to see the Heaving Sea, and it was larger than Glogmeriss had ever imagined. He couldn't see the end of it. And it moved all the time. There were more surprises when they got to the shore that night, however. For the sea was noisy, a great roaring, and it kept throwing itself at the shore and then retreating, heaving up and down. Yet the children were fearless—they ran right into the water and let the waves chase them to shore. The men and women soon joined them, for a little while, and Glogmeriss himself finally worked up the courage to let the water touch him, let the waves chase him. He tasted the water, and while it was saltier than the small seas to the northwest, it was nowhere near as salty as the Salty Sea.

"This is the god that poisoned the little seas," Zawada explained to him. "This is the god that vomited into them."

But Glogmeriss looked at how far the waves came onto the shore and laughed at her. "How could these heavings of the sea reach all the way to those small seas? It took days to get here from there."

She grimaced at him. "What do you know, giant man? These waves are not the reason why this is called the Heaving Sea by those who call it that. These are like little butterfly flutters compared to the true heaving of the sea."

Glogmeriss didn't understand until later in the day, as he realized that the waves weren't reaching as high as they had earlier. The beach sand was wet much higher up the shore than the waves could get to now. Zawada was delighted to explain the tides to him, how the sea heaved upward and downward, twice a day or so. "The sea is calling to the moon," she said, but could not explain what that meant, except that the tides were linked to the passages of the moon rather than the passages of the sun.

As the tide ebbed, the tribe stopped playing and ran out onto the sand. With digging stones they began scooping madly at the sand. Now and then one of them would shout in triumph and hold up some ugly, stony, dripping object for admiration before dropping it into a basket. Glogmeriss examined them and knew at once that these things could not be stones—they were too regular, too symmetrical. It wasn't till one of the men showed him the knack of prying them open by hammering on a sharp wedgestone that he really understood, for inside the hard stony surface there was a soft, pliable animal that could draw its shell closed around it.

"That's how it lives under the water," explained the man. "It's watertight as a mud-covered basket, only all the way around. Tight all the way around. So it keeps the water out!"

Like the perfect seedboat, thought Glogmeriss. Only no boat of reeds could ever be made *that* watertight, not so it could be plunged underwater and stay dry inside.

That night they built a fire and roasted the clams and mussels and oysters on the ends of sticks. They were tough and rubbery and they tasted salty—but Glogmeriss soon discovered that the very saltiness was the reason this was such a treat, that and the juices they released when you first chewed on them. Zawada laughed at him for chewing his first bite so long. "Cut it off in smaller bits," she said, "and then chew it till it stops tasting good and then swallow it whole." The first time he tried, it took a bit of doing to swallow it without gagging, but he soon got used to it and it *was* delicious.

"Don't drink so much of your water," said Zawada.

"I'm thirsty," said Glogmeriss.

"Of course you are," she said. "But when we run out of fresh water, we have to leave. There's nothing to drink in this place. So drink only a little at a time, so we can stay another day."

The next morning he helped with the clam-digging, and his powerful shoulders and arms allowed him to excel at this task, just as with so many others. But he didn't have the appetite for roasting them, and wandered off alone while the others feasted on the shore. They did their digging in a narrow inlet of the sea, where a long thin finger of water surged inward at high tide and then retreated almost completely at low tide. The finger of the sea seemed to point straight toward the land of the Derku, and it made Glogmeriss think of home.

Why did I come here? Why did the god go to so much trouble to bring me? Why was I saved from the cats and the lightning and the flood? Was it just to see this great water and taste the salty meat of the clams? These are marvels, it's true, but no greater than the marvel of the castrated bull-ox that I rode, or the lightning fires, or the log that was my brother in the flood. Why would it please the god to bring me here?

He heard footsteps and knew at once that it was Zawada. He did not look up. Soon he felt her arms come around him from behind, her swelling breasts pressed against his back.

"Why do you look toward your home?" she asked softly. "Haven't I made you happy?"

"You've made me happy," he said.

"But you look sad."

He nodded.

"The gods trouble you," she said. "I know that look on your face. You never speak of it, but I know at such times you are thinking of the god who brought you here and wondering if she loved you or hated you."

He laughed aloud. "Do you see inside my skin, Zawada?"

"Not your skin," she said. "But I could see inside your loincloth when you first arrived, which is why I told my father to let me be the one to marry you. I had to beat up my sister before she would let me be the one to share your sleeping mat that night. She has never forgiven me. But I wanted your babies."

Glogmeriss grunted. He had known about the sister's jealousy, but since she was ugly and he had never slept with her, her jealousy was never important to him.

"Maybe the god brought you here to see where she vomited."

That again.

"It was in a terrible storm."

"You told me about the storm," said Glogmeriss, not wanting to hear it all again.

"When the storms are strong, the sea rises higher than usual. It heaved its way far up this channel. Much farther than this tongue of the sea reaches now. It flowed so far that it reached the first of the small seas and made it flow over and then it reached the second one and that, too, flowed over. But then the storm ceased and the water flowed back to where it was before, only so much saltwater had gone into the small seas that they were poisoned."

"So long ago, and yet the salt remains?"

"Oh, I think the sea has vomited into them a couple more times since then. Never as strongly as that first time, though. You can see this channel—so much of the seawater flowed through here that it cut a channel in the sand. This finger of the sea is all that's left of it, but you can see the banks of it—like a dried-up river, you see? That was cut then, the ground used to be at the level of the rest of the valley there. The sea still reaches into that new channel, as if it remembered. Before, the shore used to be clear out there, where the waves are high. It's much better for clam-digging now, though, because this whole channel gets filled with clams and we can get them easily."

Glogmeriss felt something stirring inside him. Something in what she had just said was very, very important, but he didn't know what it was.

He cast his gaze off to the left, to the shelf of land that he had walked along all the way on his manhood journey, that this tribe had followed in coming here. The absolutely level path.

Absolutely level. And yet the path was not more than three or four man-heights above the level of the Heaving Sea, while back in the lands of the Derku, the shelf was so far above the level of the Salty Sea that it felt as though you were looking down from a mountain. The whole plain was enormously wide, and yet it went so deep before reaching the water of the Salty Sea that you could see for miles and miles, all the way across. It was deep, that plain, a valley, really. A deep gouge cut into the earth. And if this shelf of land was truly level, the Heaving Sea was far, far higher.

He thought of the floods. Thought of the powerful current of the flooding river that had snagged him and swept him downward. And then he thought of a storm that lifted the water of the Heaving Sea and sent it crashing along this valley floor, cutting a new channel until it reached those smaller seas, filling them with saltwater, causing *them* to flood and spill over. Spill over where? Where did their water flow? He already knew—they emptied down into the Salty Sea. Down and down and down.

It will happen again, thought Glogmeriss. There will be another storm, and this time the channel will be cut deeper, and when the storm subsides the water will still flow, because now the channel will be below the level of the Heaving Sea at high tide. And at each high tide, more water will flow and the channel will get deeper and deeper, till it's deep enough that even at low tide the water will still flow through it, cutting the channel more and more, and the water will come faster and faster, and then the Heaving Sea will spill over into the great valley, faster and faster and faster.

All this water then will spill out of the Heaving Sea and go down into the plain until the two seas are the same level. And once that happens, it will never go back.

The lands of the Derku are far below the level of the new sea, even if it's only half as high as the waters of the Heaving Sea are now. Our city will be covered. The whole land. And it won't be a trickle. It will be a great bursting of water, a huge wave of water, like the first gush of the floodwater down the Selud River from the Sweetwater Sea. Just like that, only the Heaving Sea is far larger than the Sweetwater Sea, and its water is angry and poisonous.

"Yes," said Glogmeriss. "I see what you brought me here to show me."

"Don't be silly," said Zawada. "I brought you here to have you eat clams!"

"I wasn't talking to you," said Glogmeriss. He stood up and left her, walking down the finger of the sea, where the tide was rising again, bringing the water lunging back up the channel, pointing like a javelin toward the heart of the Derku people. Zawada followed behind him. He didn't mind.

Glogmeriss reached the waves of the rising tide and plunged in. He knelt down in the water and let a wave crash over him. The force of the water toppled him, twisted him until he couldn't tell which way was up and he thought he would drown under the water. But then the wave retreated again, leaving him in the shallow water on the shore. He crawled back out and stayed there, the taste of salt on his lips, gasping for air, and then cried out, "Why are you doing this! Why are you doing this to my people!"

Zawada stood watching him, and others of the tribe came to join her, to find out what the strange giant man was doing in the sea.

Angry, thought Glogmeriss. The god is angry with my people. And I have been brought here to see just what terrible punishment the god has prepared for them. "Why?" he cried again. "Why not just break through this channel and send the flood and bury the Derku people in poisonous water? Why must I be shown this first? So I can save myself by staying high out of the flood's way? Why should I be saved alive, and all my family, all my friends be destroyed? What is their crime that I am not also guilty of? If you brought me here to save me, then you failed, God, because I refuse to stay, I will go back to my people and warn them all, I'll tell them what you're planning. You can't save me alone. When the flood comes I'll be right there with the rest of them. So to save me, you must save them all. If you don't like *that,* then you should have drowned me just now when you had the chance!"

Glogmeriss rose dripping from the beach and began to walk, past the people, up toward the shelf of land that made the level highway back home to the Derku people. The tribe understood at once that he was leaving, and they began calling out to him, begging him to stay.

"I can't," he said. "Don't try to stop me. Even the god can't stop me."

They didn't try to stop him, not by force. But the chief ran after him, walked beside him—ran beside him, really, for that was the only way he could keep up with Glogmeriss's long-legged stride. "Friend, Son," said the chief. "Don't you know that you will be king of these people after me?"

"A people should have a king who is one of their own."

"But you *are* one of us now," said the chief. "The mightiest of us. You will make us a great people! The god has chosen you, do you think we can't see that? This is why the god brought you here, to lead us and make us great!"

"No," said Glogmeriss. "I'm a man of the Derku people."

"Where are they? Far from here. And there is my daughter with your first child in her womb. What do they have in Derku lands that can compare to that?"

"They have the womb where I was formed," said Glogmeriss. "They have the man who put me there. They have the others who came from that woman and that man. They are my people."

"Then go back, but not today! Wait till you see your child born. Decide then!"

Glogmeriss stopped so abruptly that the chief almost fell over, trying to stop running and stay with him. "Listen to me, father of my wife. If you were up in the mountain hunting, and you looked down and saw a dozen huge cats heading toward the place where your people were living, would you say to yourself, Oh, I suppose the god brought me here to save me? Or would you run down the mountain and warn them, and do all you could to fight off the cats and save your people?"

"What is this story?" asked the chief. "There are no cats. You've seen no cats."

"I've seen the god heaving in his anger," said Glogmeriss. "I've seen how he looms over my people, ready to destroy them all. A flood that will tear their flimsy reed boats to pieces. A flood that will come in a single great wave and then will never go away. Do you think I shouldn't warn my mother and father, my brothers and sisters, the friends of my childhood?"

"I think you have new brothers and sisters, a new father and mother. The god isn't angry with *us*. The god isn't angry with you. We should stay together. Don't you *want* to stay with us and live and rule over us? You can be our king now, today. You can be king over me, I give you my place!"

"Keep your place," said Glogmeriss. "Yes, a part of me wants to stay. A part of me is afraid. But that is the part of me that is Glogmeriss, and still a boy. If I don't go home and warn my people and show them how to save themselves from the god, then I will always be a boy, nothing but a boy, call me a king if you want, but I will be a boy-king, a coward, a child until the day I die. So I tell you now, it is the child who dies in this place, not the man. It was the child Glogmeriss who married Zawada. Tell her that a strange man named Naog killed her husband. Let her marry someone else, someone of her own tribe, and never think of Glogmeriss again." Glogmeriss kissed his father-in-law and embraced him. Then he turned away, and with his first step along the path leading back to the Derku people, he knew that he was truly Naog now, the man who would save the Derku people from the fury of the god.

Kemal watched the lone man of the Engu clan as he walked away from the beach, as he conversed with his father-in-law, as he turned his face again away from the Gulf of Aden, toward the land of the doomed crocodile-worshippers whose god was no match for the forces about to be unleashed on them. This was the one, Kemal knew, for he had seen the wooden boat—more of a watertight cabin on a raft, actually, with none of this nonsense about taking animals two by two. This was the man of legends, but seeing his face, hearing his voice, Kemal was no closer to understanding him than he had been before. What can we see, using the TruSite II? Only what is visible. We may be able to range through time, to see the most intimate, the most terrible, the most horrifying, the most inspiring moments of human history, but we only see them, we only hear them, we are witnesses but we know nothing of the thing that matters most: motive.

Why didn't you stay with your new tribe, Naog? They heeded your warning, and camped always on higher ground during the monsoon season. They lived through the flood, all of them. And when you went home and no one listened to your warnings, why did you stay? What was it that made you remain among them, enduring their ridicule as you built your watertight seedboat? You could have left at any time—there were others who cut themselves loose from their birth tribe and wandered through the world until they found a new home. The Nile was waiting for you. The grasslands of Arabia. They were already there, calling to you, even as your own homeland became poisonous to you. Yet you remained among the Engu, and by doing so, you not only gave the world an unforgettable story, you also changed the course of history. What kind of being is it who can change the course of history, just because he follows his own unbending will?

It was on his third morning that Naog realized that he was not alone on his return journey. He awoke in his tree because he heard shuffling footsteps through the grass nearby. Or perhaps it was something else that woke him—some unhearable yearning that he nevertheless heard. He looked, and saw in the faint light of the thinnest crescent moon that a lone baboon was shambling along, lazy, staggering. No doubt an old male, thought Naog, who will soon be meat for some predator.

Then his eyes adjusted and he realized that this lone baboon was not as close as he had thought, that in fact it was much bigger, much *taller* than he had thought. It was not male, either, but female, and far from being a baboon, it was a human, a pregnant woman, and he knew her now and shuddered at his own thought of her becoming the meal for some cat, some crocodile, some pack of dogs.

Silently he unfastened himself from his sleeping tree and dropped to the ground. In moments he was beside her.

"Zawada," he said.

She didn't turn to look at him.

"Zawada, what are you doing?"

Now she stopped. "Walking," she said.

"You're asleep," he said. "You're in a dream."

"No, *you're* asleep," she said, giggling madly in her weariness.

"Why have you come? I left you."

"I know," she said.

"I'm returning to my own people. You have to stay with yours." But he knew even as he said it that she could not go back there, not unless he went with her. Physically she was unable to go on by herself—clearly she had eaten nothing and slept little in three days. Why she had not died already, taken by some beast, he could not guess. But if she was to return to her people, he would have to take her, and he did not want to go back there. It made him very angry, and so his voice burned when he spoke to her.

"I wanted to," she said. "I wanted to weep for a year and then make an image of you out of sticks and burn it."

"You should have," he said.

"Your son wouldn't let me." As she spoke, she touched her belly.

"Son? Has some god told you who he is?"

"He came to me himself in a dream, and he said, 'Don't let my father go without me.' So I brought him to you."

"I don't want him, son *or* daughter." But he knew even as he said it that it wasn't true.

She didn't know it, though. Her eyes welled with tears and she sank down into the grass. "Good, then," she said. "Go on with your journey. I'm sorry the god led me near you, so you had to be bothered." She sank back in the grass. Seeing the faint gleam of light reflected from her skin awoke feelings that Naog was now ashamed of, memories of how she had taught him the easing of a man's passion.

"I can't walk off and leave you."

"You already did," she said. "So do it again. I need to sleep now."

"You'll be torn by animals and eaten."

"Let them," she said. "You never chose me, Derku man, I chose *you*. I invited this baby into my body. Now if we die here in the grass, what is that to you? All you care about is not having to watch. So don't watch. Go. The sky is getting light. Run on ahead. If we die, we die. We're nothing to you anyway."

Her words made him ashamed. "I left you knowing you and the baby would be safe, at home. Now you're here and you aren't safe, and I can't walk away from you."

"So run," she said. "I was your wife, and this was your son, but in your heart we're already dead anyway."

"I didn't bring you because you'd have to learn the Derku language. It's much harder than your language."

"I would have had to learn it anyway, you fool," she said. "The baby inside me is a Derku man like you. How would I get him to understand me, if I didn't learn Derku talk?"

Naog wanted to laugh aloud at her hopeless ignorance. But then, how would she know? Naog had seen the children of captives and knew that in Derku lands they grew up speaking the Derku language, even when both parents were from another tribe that had not one word of Derku language in it. But Zawada had never seen the babies of strangers; her tribe captured no one, went on no raids, but rather lived at peace, moving from place to place, gathering whatever the earth or the sea had to offer them. How could she match even a small part of the great knowledge of the Derku, who brought the whole world within their city?

He wanted to laugh, but he did not laugh. Instead he watched over her as she slept, as the day waxed and waned. As the sun rose he carried her to the tree to sleep in the shade. Keeping his eye open for animals prowling near her, he gathered such leaves and seeds and roots as the ground offered the traveler at this time of year. Twice he came back and found her breath rasping and noisy; then he made her wake enough to drink a little of his water, but she was soon asleep, water glistening on her chin.

At last in the late afternoon, with the air hot and still, he squatted down in the grass beside her and woke her for good, showing her the food. She ate ravenously, and when she was done, she embraced him and called him the best of the gods because he didn't leave her to die after all.

"I'm not a god," he said, baffled.

"All my people know you are a god, from a land of gods. So large, so powerful, so good. You came to us so you could have a human baby. But this baby is only half human. How will he ever be happy, living among *us*, never knowing the gods?"

"You've seen the Heaving Sea, and you call *me* a god?"

"Take me with you to the land of the Derku. Let me give birth to your baby there. I will leave it with your mother and your sisters, and I will go home. I know I don't belong among the gods, but my baby does."

In his heart, Naog wanted to say yes, you'll stay only till the baby is born, and then you'll go home. But he remembered her patience as he learned the language of her people. He remembered the sweet language of the night, and the way he had to laugh at how she tried to act like a grown woman when she was only a child, and yet she couldn't act like a child because she was, after all, now a woman. Because of me she is a woman, thought Naog, and because of her and her people I will come home a man. Do I tell her she must go away, even though I know that the others will think she's ugly as I thought she was ugly?

And she *is* ugly, thought Naog. Our son, if he *is* a son, will be ugly like her people, too. I will be ashamed of him. I will be ashamed of her.

Is a man ashamed of his firstborn son?

"Come home with me to the land of the Derku," said Naog. "We will tell them together about the Heaving Sea, and how one day soon it will leap over the low walls of sand and pour into this great plain in a flood that will cover the Derku lands forever. There will be a great migration. We will move, all of us, to the land my father found. The crocodiles live there also, along the banks of the Nile."

"Then you will truly be the greatest among the gods," she said, and the worship in her eyes made him proud and ill-at-ease, both at once. Yet how could he deny that the Derku were gods? Compared to her poor tribe, they would seem so. Thousands of people living in the midst of their own canals; the great fields of planted grain stretching far in every direction; the great wall of earth surrounding the Great Derku; the seedboats scattered like strange soft boulders; the children riding their dragonboats through the canals; a land of miracles to her. Where else in all the world had so many people learned to live together, making great wealth where once there had been only savannah and floodplain?

We live like gods, compared to other people. We come like gods out of nowhere, to carry off captives the way death carries people off. Perhaps that is what the life after death is like—the *real* gods using us to dredge their canals. Perhaps that is what all of human life is for, to create slaves for the gods. And what if the gods themselves are also raided by some greater beings yet, carrying *them* off to raise grain in some unimaginable garden? Is there no end to the capturing?

There are many strange and ugly captives in Derku, thought Naog. Who will doubt me if I say that this woman is my captive? She doesn't speak the language, and soon enough she would be used to the life. I would be kind to her, and would treat her son well—I would hardly be the first man to father a child on a captive woman.

The thought made him blush with shame.

"Zawada, when you come to the Derku lands, you will come as my wife," he said. "And you will not have to leave. Our son will know his mother as well as his father."

Her eyes glowed. "You are the greatest and kindest of the gods."

"No," he said, angry now, because he knew very well just exactly how far from "great" and "kind" he really was, having just imagined bringing this sweet, stubborn, brave girl into captivity. "You must never call me a god again. Ever. There is only one god, do you understand me? And it is that god that lives inside the Heaving Sea, the one that brought me to see him and sent me back here to warn my people. Call no one else a god, or you can't stay with me."

Her eyes went wide. "Is there room in the world for only one god?"

"When did a crocodile ever bury a whole land under water forever?" Naog laughed scornfully. "All my life I have thought of the Great Derku as a terrible god, worthy of the worship of brave and terrible men. But the Great Derku is just a crocodile. It can be killed with a spear. Imagine stabbing the Heaving Sea. We can't even touch it. And yet the god can lift up that whole sea and pour it over the wall into this plain. *That* isn't just a god. That is *God*."

She looked at him in awe; he wondered whether she understood. And then realized that she could not possibly have understood, because half of what he said was in the Derku language, since he didn't even know enough words in *her* language to think of these thoughts, let alone say them.

Her body was young and strong, even with a baby inside it, and the next morning she was ready to travel. He did not run now, but even so they covered ground quickly, for she was a sturdy walker. He began teaching her the Derku language as they walked, and she learned well, though she made the words sound funny, as so many captives did, never able to let go of the sounds of their native tongue, never able to pronounce the new ones.

Finally he saw the mountains that separated the Derku lands from the Salty Sea, rising from the plain. "Those will be islands," said Naog, realizing it for the first time. "The highest ones. See? They're higher than the shelf of land we're walking on."

Zawada nodded wisely, but he knew that she didn't really understand what he was talking about.

"Those are the Derku lands," said Naog. "See the canals and the fields?"

She looked, but seemed to see nothing unusual at all. "Forgive me," she said, "but all I see are streams and grassland."

"But that's what I meant," said Naog. "Except that the grasses grow where we plant them, and all we plant is the grass whose seed we grind into meal. And the streams you see—they go where we want them to go. Vast circles surrounding the heart of the Derku lands. And there in the middle, do you see that hill?"

"I think so," she said.

"We build that hill every year, after the floodwater."

She laughed. "You tell me that you aren't gods, and yet you make hills and streams and meadows wherever you want them!"

Naog set his face toward the Engu portion of the great city. "Come home with me," he said.

Since Zawada's people were so small, Naog had not realized that he had grown even taller during his manhood journey, but now as he led his ugly wife through the outskirts of the city, he realized that he was taller than everyone. It took him by surprise, and at first he was disturbed because it seemed to him that everyone had grown smaller. He even said as much to Zawada—"They're all so small"—but she laughed as if it were a joke. Nothing about the place or the people seemed small to *her*.

At the edge of the Engu lands, Naog hailed the boys who were on watch. "Hai!"

"Hai!" they called back.

"I've come back from my journey!" he called.

It took a moment for them to answer. "What journey was this, tall man?"

"My manhood journey. Don't you know me? Can't you see that I'm Naog?"

The boys hooted at that. "How can you be naked when you have your napron on?"

"Naog is my manhood name," said Naog, quite annoyed now, for he had not expected to be treated with such disrespect on his return. "You probably know of me by my baby-name. They called me Glogmeriss."

They hooted again. "You used to be trouble, and now you're naked!" cried the bold one. "And your wife is ugly, too!"

But now Naog was close enough that the boys could see how very tall he was. Their faces grew solemn.

"My father is Twerk," said Naog. "I return from my manhood journey with the greatest tale ever told. But more important than that, I have a message from the god who lives in the Heaving Sea. When I have given my message, people will include you in my story. They will say, 'Who were the five fools who joked about Naog's name, when he came to save us from the angry god?'"

"Twerk is dead," said one of the boys.

"The Dragon took him," said another.

"He was head of the clan, and then the Great Derku began eating human flesh again, and your father gave himself to the Dragon for the clan's sake."

"Are you truly his son?"

Naog felt a gnawing pain that he did not recognize. He would soon learn to call it grief, but it was not too different from rage. "Is this another jest of yours? I'll break your heads if it is."

"By the blood of your father in the mouth of the beast, I swear that it's true!" said the boy who had earlier been the boldest in his teasing. "If you're his son, then you're the son of a great man!"

The emotion welled up inside him. "What does this mean?" cried Naog. "The Great Derku does not eat the flesh of men! Someone has murdered my father! He would never allow such a thing!" Whether he meant it was his father or the Great Derku who would never allow it even Naog did not know.

The boys ran off then, before he could strike out at them for being the tellers of such an unbearable tale. Zawada was the only one left, to pat at him, embrace him, try to soothe him with her voice. She abandoned the language of the Derku and spoke to him soothingly in her own language. But all Naog could hear was the news that his father had been fed to the Great Derku as a sacrifice for the clan. The old days were back again, and they had killed his father. His father, and not even a captive!

Others of the Engu, hearing what the boys were shouting about, brought him to his mother. Then he began to calm down, hearing her voice, the gentle reassurance of the old sound. She, at least, was unchanged. Except that she looked older, yes, and tired. "It was your father's own choice," she explained to him. "After floodwater this year the Great Derku came into the pen with a human baby in its jaws. It was a two-year-old boy of the Ko clan, and it happened he was the firstborn of his parents."

"This means only that Ko clan wasn't watchful enough," said Naog.

"Perhaps," said his mother. "But the holy men saw it as a sign from the god. Just as we stopped giving human flesh to the Great Derku when he refused it, so now when he claimed a human victim, what else were we to think?"

"Captives, then. Why not captives?"

"It was your own father who said that if the Great Derku had taken a child from the families of the captives, then we would sacrifice captives. But he took a child from one of our clans. What kind of sacrifice is it, to offer strangers when the Great Derku demanded the meat of the Derku people?"

"Don't you see, Mother? Father was trying to keep them from sacrificing anybody at all, by making them choose something so painful that no one would do it."

She shook her head. "How do you know what my Twerk was trying to do? He was trying to save *you*."

"Me?"

"Your father was clan leader by then. The holy men said, 'Let each clan give the firstborn son of the clan leader.'"

"But I was gone."

"Your father insisted on the ancient privilege, that a father may go in place of his son."

"So he died in my place, because I was gone."

"If you had been here, Glogmeriss, he would have done the same."

He thought about this for a few moments, and then answered only, "My name is Naog now."

"We thought you were dead, Naked One, Stirrer of Troubles," said Mother.

"I found a wife."

"I saw her. Ugly."

"Brave and strong and smart," said Naog.

"Born to be a captive. I chose a different wife for you."

"Zawada is my wife."

Even though Naog had returned from his journey as a man and not a boy, he soon learned that even a man can be bent by the pressure of others. This far he did *not* bend: Zawada remained his wife. But he also took the wife his mother had chosen for him, a beautiful girl named Kormo. Naog was not sure what was worse about the new arrangement—that everyone else treated Kormo as Naog's real wife and Zawada as barely a wife at all, or that when Naog was hungry with passion, it was always Kormo he thought of. But he remembered Zawada at such times, how she bore him his first child, the boy Moiro; how she followed him with such fierce courage; how good she was to him when he was a stranger. And when he remembered, he followed his duty to her rather than his natural desire. This happened so often that Kormo complained about it. This made Naog feel somehow righteous, for the truth was that his first inclination had been right. Zawada should have stayed with her own tribe. She was unhappy most of the time, and kept to herself and her baby, and as years passed, her babies. She was never accepted by the other women of the Derku. Only the captive women became friends with her, which caused even more talk and criticism.

Years passed, yes, and where was Naog's great message, the one the god had gone to such great trouble to give him? He tried to tell it. First to the leaders of the Engu clan, the whole story of his journey, and how the Heaving Sea was far higher than the Salty Sea and would soon break through and cover all the land with water. They listened to him gravely, and then one by one they counseled with him that when the gods wish to speak to the Derku people, they will do as they did when the Great Derku ate a human baby. "Why would a god who wished to send a message to the Derku people choose a mere *boy* as messenger?"

"Because I was the one who was taking the journey," he said.

"What will you have us do? Abandon our lands? Leave our canals behind, and our boats?"

"The Nile has fresh water and a flood season, my father saw it."

"But the Nile also has strong tribes living up and down its shores. Here we are masters of the world. No, we're not leaving on the word of a boy."

They insisted that he tell no one else, but he didn't obey them. In fact he told anyone who would listen, but the result was the same. For his father's memory or for his mother's sake, or perhaps just because he was so tall and strong, people listened politely—but Naog knew at the end of each telling of his tale that nothing had changed. No one believed him. And when he wasn't there, they repeated his stories as if they were jokes, laughing about riding a castrated bull-ox, about calling a tree branch his brother, and most of all about the idea of a great flood that would never go away. Poor Naog, they said. He clearly lost his mind on his manhood journey, coming home with impossible stories that he obviously believes and an ugly woman that he dotes on.

Zawada urged him to leave. "You know that the flood is coming," she said. "Why not take your family up and out of here? Go to the Nile ourselves, or return to my father's tribe."

But he wouldn't hear of it. "I would go if I could bring my people with me. But what kind of man am I, to leave behind my mother and my brothers and sisters, my clan and all my kin?"

"You would have left me behind," she said once. He didn't answer her. He also didn't go.

In the third year after his return, when he had three sons to take riding on his dragonboat, he began the strangest project anyone had ever seen. No one was surprised, though, that crazy Naog would do something like this. He began to take several captives with him upriver to a place where tall, heavy trees grew. There they would wear out stone axes cutting down trees, then shape them into logs and ride them down the river. Some people complained that the captives belonged to everybody and it was wrong for Naog to have their exclusive use for so many days, but Naog was such a large and strange man that no one wanted to push the matter.

One or two at a time, they came to see what Naog was doing with the logs. They found that he had taught his captives to notch them and lash them together into a huge square platform, a dozen strides on a side. Then they made a second platform crossways to the first and on top of it, lashing every log to every other log, or so it seemed. Between the two layers he smeared pitch, and then on the top of the raft he built a dozen reed structures like the tops of seedboats. Before floodwater he urged his neighbors to bring him their grain, and he would keep it all dry. A few of them did, and when the rivers rose during floodwater, everyone saw that his huge seedboat floated, and no water seeped up from below into the seedhouses. More to the point, Naog's wives and children also lived on the raft, dry all the time, sleeping easily through the night instead of having to remain constantly wakeful, watching to make sure the children didn't fall into the water.

The next year, the Engu clan built several more platforms following Naog's pattern. They didn't always lash them as well as he had, and during the next flood several of their rafts came apart—but gradually, so they had time to move the seeds. The Engu clan had far more seed make it through to planting season than any of the other tribes, and soon the men had to range farther and farther upriver, because all the nearer trees of suitable size had been harvested.

Naog himself, though, wasn't satisfied. It was Zawada who pointed out that when the great flood came, the water wouldn't rise gradually as it did in the river floods. "It'll be like the waves against the shore, crashing with such force . . . and these reed shelters will never hold against such a wave."

For several years Naog experimented with logs until at last he had the largest movable structure ever built by human hands. The raft was as long as ever, but somewhat narrower. Rising from notches between logs in the upper platform were sturdy vertical posts, and these were bridged and roofed with wood. But instead of using logs for the planking and the roofing, Naog and the captives who served him split the logs carefully into planks, and these were smeared inside and out with pitch, and then another wall and ceiling were built inside, sandwiching the tar between them. People were amused to see Naog's captives hoisting dripping baskets of water to the roof of this giant seedboat and pouring them out onto it. "What, does he think that if he waters these trees, they'll grow like grass?" Naog heard them, but he cared not at all, for when they spoke he was inside his boat, seeing that not a drop of water made it inside.

The doorway was the hardest part, because it, too, had to be able to be sealed against the flood. Many nights Naog lay awake worrying about it before building this last and largest and tightest seedboat. The answer came to him in a dream. It was a memory of the little crabs that lived in the sand on the shore of the Heaving Sea. They dug holes in the sand and then when the water washed over them, their holes filled in above their heads, keeping out the water. Naog awoke knowing that he must put the door in the roof of his seedboat, and arrange a way to lash it from the inside.

"How will you see to lash it?" said Zawada. "There's no light inside."

So Naog and his three captives learned to lash the door in place in utter darkness.

When they tested it, water leaked through the edges of the door. The solution was to smear more pitch, fresh pitch, around the edges of the opening and lay the door into it so that when they lashed it the seal was tight. It was very hard to open the door again after that, but they got it open from the inside—and when they could see again they found that not a drop of water had got inside. "No more trials," said Naog.

Their work then was to gather seeds—and more than seeds this time. Water, too. The seeds went into baskets with lids that were lashed down, and the water went into many, many flasks. Naog and his captives and their wives worked hard during every moment of daylight to make the waterbags and seedbaskets and fill them. The Engu didn't mind at all

storing more and more of their grain in Naog's boat—after all, it was lu-
dicrously watertight, so that it was sure to make it through the flood season in fine form. They didn't have to believe in his nonsense about a god
in the Heaving Sea that was angry with the Derku people in order to recognize a good seedboat when they saw it.

His boat was nearly full when word spread that a group of new captives from the southeast were telling tales of a new river of saltwater that
had flowed into the Salty Sea from the direction of the Heaving Sea.
When Naog heard the news, he immediately climbed a tree so he could
look toward the southeast. "Don't be silly," they said to him. "You can't
see the Salty Shore from here, even if you climb the tallest tree."

"I was looking for the flood," said Naog. "Don't you see that the
Heaving Sea must have broken through again, when a storm whipped the
water into madness. Then the storm subsided, and the sea stopped flowing
over the top. But the channel must be wider and longer and deeper now.
Next time it won't end when the storm ends. Next time it will be the
great flood."

"How do you know these things, Naog? You're a man like the rest of
us. Just because you're taller doesn't mean you can see the future."

"The god is angry," said Naog. "The true god, not this silly crocodile
god that you feed on human flesh." And now, in the urgency of knowing
the imminence of the flood, he said what he had said to no one but Zawada. "Why do you think the true god is so angry with us? Because of
the crocodile! Because we feed human flesh to the Dragon! The true god
doesn't want offerings of human flesh. It's an abomination. It's as forbidden as the forbidden fruit. The crocodile god is not a god at all, it's just a
wild animal, one that crawls on its belly, and yet we bow down to it. We
bow down to the enemy of the true god!"

Hearing him say this made the people angry. Some were so furious
they wanted to feed him to the Great Derku at once, but Naog only
laughed at them. "If the Great Derku is such a wonderful god, let *him*
come and get me, instead of you taking me! But no, you don't believe for
a moment that he *can* do it. Yet the *true* god had the power to send me a
castrated bull to ride, and a log to save me from a flood, and trees to catch
the lightning so it wouldn't strike me. When has the Dragon ever had the
power to do *that*?"

His ridicule of the Great Derku infuriated them, and violence might have resulted, had Naog not had such physical presence, and had his father not been a noble sacrifice to the Dragon. Over the next weeks, though, it became clear that Naog was now regarded by all as something between an enemy and a stranger. No one came to speak to him, or to Zawada, either. Only Kormo continued to have contact with the rest of the Derku people.

"They want me to leave you," she told him. "They want me to come back to my family, because you are the enemy of the god."

"And will you go?" he said.

She fixed her sternest gaze on him. "You are my family now," she said. "Even when you prefer this ugly woman to me, you are still my husband."

Naog's mother came to him once, to warn him. "They have decided to kill you. They're simply biding their time, waiting for the right moment."

"Waiting for the courage to fight me, you mean," said Naog.

"Tell them that a madness came upon you, but it's over," she said. "Tell them that it was the influence of this ugly foreign wife of yours, and then they'll kill her and not you."

Naog didn't bother to answer her.

His mother burst into tears. "Was this what I bore you for? I named you very well, Glogmeriss, my son of trouble and anguish!"

"Listen to me, Mother. The flood is coming. We may have very little warning when it actually comes, very little time to get into my seedboat. Stay near, and when you hear us calling—"

"I'm glad your father is dead rather than to see his firstborn son so gone in madness."

"Tell all the others, too, Mother. I'll take as many into my seedboat as will fit. But once the door in the roof is closed, I can't open it again. Anyone who isn't inside when we close it will never get inside, and they will die."

She burst into tears and left.

Not far from the seedboat was a high hill. As the rainy season neared, Naog took to sending one of his servants to the top of the hill several times a day, to watch toward the southeast. "What should we look for?"

they asked. "I don't know," he answered. "A new river. A wall of water. A dark streak in the distance. It will be something that you've never seen before."

The sky filled with clouds, dark and threatening. The heart of the storm was to the south and east. Naog made sure that his wives and children and the wives and children of his servants didn't stray far from the seedboat. They freshened the water in the waterbags, to stay busy. A few raindrops fell, and then the rain stopped, and then a few more raindrops. But far to the south and east it was raining heavily. And the wind—the wind kept rising higher and higher, and it was out of the east. Naog could imagine it whipping the waves higher and farther into the deep channel that the last storm had opened. He imagined the water spilling over into the salty riverbed. He imagined it tearing deeper and deeper into the sand, more and more of it tearing away under the force of the torrent. Until finally it was no longer the force of the storm driving the water through the channel, but the weight of the whole sea, because at last it had been cut down below the level of low tide. And then the sea tearing deeper and deeper.

"Naog." It was the head of the Engu clan, and a dozen men with him. "The god is ready for you."

Naog looked at them as if they were foolish children. "This is the storm," he said. "Go home and bring your families to my seedboat, so they can come through the flood alive."

"This is no storm," said the head of the clan. "Hardly any rain has fallen."

The servant who was on watch came running, out of breath, his arms bleeding where he had skidded on the ground as he fell more than once in his haste. "Naog, master!" he cried. "It's plain to see—the Salty Shore is nearer. The Salty Sea is rising, and fast."

What a torrent of water it would take, to make the Salty Sea rise in its bed. Naog covered his face with his hands. "You're right," said Naog. "The god is ready for me. The true god. It was for this hour that I was born. As for *your* god—the true god will drown him as surely as he will drown anyone who doesn't come to my seedboat."

"Come with us now," said the head of the clan. But his voice was not so certain now.

To his servants and his wives, Naog said, "Inside the seedboat. When all are in, smear on the pitch, leaving only one side where I can slide down."

"You come too, husband," said Zawada.

"I can't," he said. "I have to give warning one last time."

"Too late!" cried the servant with the bleeding arms. "Come now."

"You go now," said Naog. "I'll be back soon. But if I'm not back, seal the door and open it for no man, not even me."

"When will I know to do that?" he asked in anguish.

"Zawada will tell you," said Naog. "She'll know." Then he turned to the head of the clan. "Come with me," he said. "Let's give the warning." Then Naog strode off toward the bank of the canal where his mother and brothers and sisters kept their dragonboats. The men who had come to capture him followed him, unsure who had captured whom.

It was raining again, a steady rainfall whipped by an ever-stronger wind. Naog stood on the bank of the canal and shouted against the wind, crying out for his family to join him. "There's not much time!" he cried. "Hurry, come to my seedboat!"

"Don't listen to the enemy of the god!" cried the head of the clan.

Naog looked down into the water of the canal. "Look, you fools! Can't you see that the canal is rising?"

"The canal always rises in a storm."

Naog knelt down and dipped his hand into the canal and tasted the water. "Salt," he said. "Salt!" he shouted. "This isn't rising because of rain in the mountains! The water is rising because the Salty Sea is filling with the water of the Heaving Sea. It's rising to cover us! Come with me now, or not at all! When the door of my seedboat closes, we'll open it for no one." Then he turned and loped off toward the seedboat.

By the time he got there, the water was spilling over the banks of the canals, and he had to splash through several shallow streams where there had been no streams before. Zawada was standing on top of the roof, and screamed at him to hurry as he clambered onto the top of it. He looked in the direction she had been watching, and saw what she had seen. In the distance, but not so very far away, a dark wall rushing toward them. A plug of earth must have broken loose, and a fist of the sea hundreds of feet high was slamming through the gap. It spread at once, of course, and as it spread the wave dropped until it was only fifteen or twenty feet high. But that was high enough. It would do.

"You fool!" cried Zawada. "Do you want to watch it or be saved from it?"

Naog followed Zawada down into the boat. Two of the servants smeared on a thick swatch of tar on the fourth side of the doorway. Then Naog, who was the only one tall enough to reach outside the hole, drew the door into place, snugging it down tight. At once it became perfectly dark inside the seedboat, and silent, too, except for the breathing. "This time for real," said Naog softly. He could hear the other men working at the lashings. They could feel the floor moving under them—the canals had spilled over so far now that the raft was rising and floating.

Suddenly they heard a noise. Someone was pounding on the wall of the seedboat. And there was shouting. They couldn't hear the words, the walls were too thick. But they knew what was being said all the same. Save us. Let us in. Save us.

Kormo's voice was filled with anguish. "Naog, can't we—"

"If we open it now we'll never close it again in time. We'd all die. They had every chance and every warning. My lashing is done."

"Mine, too," answered one of the servants.

The silence of the others said they were still working hard.

"Everyone hold on to the side posts," said Naog. "There's so much room here. We could have taken on so many more."

The pounding outside was in earnest now. They were using axes to hack at the wood. Or at the lashings. And someone was on top of the seedboat now, many someones, trying to pry at the door.

"Now, O God, if you mean to save us at all, send the water now."

"Done," said another of the servants. So three of the four corners were fully lashed.

Suddenly the boat lurched and rocked upward, then spun crazily in every direction at once. Everyone screamed, and few were able to keep their handhold, such was the force of the flood. They plunged to one side of the seedboat, a jumble of humans and spilling baskets and water bottles. Then they struck something—a tree? the side of a mountain?—and lurched in another direction entirely, and in the darkness it was impossible to tell anymore whether they were on the floor or the roof or one of the walls.

Did it go on for days, or merely hours? Finally the awful turbulence gave way to a spinning all in one plane. The flood was still rising; they were still caught in the twisting currents; but they were no longer caught in that wall of water, in the great wave that the god had sent. They were on top of the flood.

Gradually they sorted themselves out. Mothers found their children, husbands found their wives. Many were crying, but as the fear subsided they were able to find the ones who were genuinely in pain. But what could they do in the darkness to deal with bleeding injuries, or possible broken bones? They could only plead with the god to be merciful and let them know when it was safe to open the door.

After a while, though, it became plain that it wasn't safe *not* to open it. The air was musty and hot and they were beginning to pant. "I can't breathe," said Zawada. "Open the door," said Kormo.

Naog spoke aloud to the god. "We have no air in here," he said. "I have to open the door. Make it safe. Let no other wave wash over us with the door open."

But when he went to open the door, he couldn't find it in the darkness. For a sickening moment he thought: What if we turned completely upside down, and the door is now under us? I never thought of that. We'll die in here.

Then he found it, and began fussing with the lashings. But it was hard in the darkness. They had tied so hurriedly, and he wasn't thinking all that well. But soon he heard the servants also at work, muttering softly, and one by one they got their lashings loose and Naog shoved upward on the door.

It took forever before the door budged, or so it seemed, but when at last it rocked upward, a bit of faint light and a rush of air came into the boat and everyone cried out at once in relief and gratitude. Naog pushed the door upward and then maneuvered it to lie across the opening at an angle, so that the heavy rain outside wouldn't inundate them. He stood there holding the door in place, even though the wind wanted to pick it up and blow it away—a slab of wood as heavy as that one was!—while in twos and threes they came to the opening and breathed, or lifted children to catch a breath of air. There was enough light to bind up some bleeding injuries, and to realize that no bones were broken after all.

The rain went on forever, or so it seemed, the rain and the wind. And then it stopped, and they were able to come out onto the roof of the seed-boat and look at the sunlight and stare at the distant horizon. There was no land at all, just water. "The whole earth is gone," said Kormo. "Just as you said."

"The Heaving Sea has taken over this place," said Naog. "But we'll come to dry land. The current will take us there."

There was much debris floating on the water—torn-up trees and bushes, for the flood had scraped the whole face of the land. A few rotting bodies of animals. If anyone saw a human body floating by, they said nothing about it.

After days, a week, perhaps longer of floating without sight of land, they finally began skirting a shoreline. Once they saw the smoke of some-one's fire—people who lived high above the great valley of the Salty Sea had been untouched by the flood. But there was no way to steer the boat toward shore. Like a true seedboat, it drifted unless something drew it an-other way. Naog cursed himself for his foolishness in not including drag-onboats in the cargo of the boat. He and the other men and women might have tied lines to the seedboat and to themselves and paddled the boat to shore. As it was, they would last only as long as their water lasted.

It was long enough. The boat fetched up against a grassy shore. Naog sent several of the servants ashore and they used a rope to tie the boat to a tree. But it was useless—the current was still too strong, and the boat tore free. They almost lost the servants, stranding them on the shore, forever separated from their families, but they had the presence of mind to swim for the end of the rope.

The next day they did better—more lines, all the men on shore, draw-ing the boat further into a cove that protected it from the current. They lost no time in unloading the precious cargo of seeds, and searching for a source of fresh water. Then they began the unaccustomed task of hauling all the baskets of grain by hand. There were no canals to ease the labor.

"Perhaps we can find a place to dig canals again," said Kormo.

"No!" said Zawada vehemently. "We will never build such a place again. Do you want the god to send another flood?"

"There will be no other flood," said Naog. "The Heaving Sea has had its victory. But we will also build no canals. We will keep no crocodile, or any other animal as our god. We will never sacrifice forbidden fruit to any god, because the true god hates those who do that. And we will tell our story to anyone who will listen to it, so that others will learn how to avoid the wrath of the true god, the god of power."

Kemal watched as Naog and his people came to shore not far from Gibeil and set up farming in the El Qa' Valley in the shadows of the mountains of Sinai. The fact of the flood was well known, and many travelers came to see this vast new sea where once there had been dry land. More and more of them also came to the new village that Naog and his people built, and word of his story also spread.

Kemal's work was done. He had found Atlantis. He had found Noah, and Gilgamesh. Many of the stories that had collected around those names came from other cultures and other times, but the core was true, and Kemal had found them and brought them back to the knowledge of humankind.

But what did it mean? Naog gave warning, but no one listened. His story remained in people's minds, but what difference did it make?

As far as Kemal was concerned, all old-world civilizations after Atlantis were dependent on that first civilization. The *idea* of the city was already with the Egyptians and the Sumerians and the people of the Indus and even the Chinese, because the story of the Derku people, under one name or another, had spread far and wide—the Golden Age. People remembered well that once there was a great land that was blessed by the gods until the sea rose up and swallowed their land. People who lived in different landscapes tried to make sense of the story. To the island-hopping Greeks Atlantis became an island that sank into the sea. To the plains-dwelling Sumerians the flood was caused by rain, not by the sea leaping out of its bed to swallow the earth. Someone wondered how, if all the land was covered, the animals survived, and thus the account of animals two by two was added to the story of Naog. At some point, when people still remembered that the name meant "naked," a story was added about his sons covering his nakedness as he lay in a drunken stupor. All of this was decoration, however. People remembered both the Derku people and the one man who led his family through the flood.

But they would have remembered Atlantis with or without Naog,

Kemal knew that. What difference did his saga make, to anyone but himself and his household? As others studied the culture of the Derku, Kemal remained focused on Naog himself. If anything, Naog's life was proof that one person makes no difference at all in history. He saw the flood coming, he warned his people about it when there was plenty of time, he showed them how to save themselves, and yet nothing changed outside his own immediate family group. That was the way history worked. Great forces sweep people along, and now and then somebody floats to the surface and becomes famous but it means nothing, it amounts to nothing.

Yet Kemal could not believe it. Naog may not have accomplished what he *thought* his goal was—to save his people—but he did accomplish something. He never lived to see the result of it, but because of his survival the Atlantis stories were tinged with something else. It was not just a golden age, not just a time of greatness and wealth and leisure and city life, a land of giants and gods. Naog's version of the story also penetrated the public consciousness and remained. The people were destroyed because the greatest of gods was offended by their sins. The list of sins shifted and changed over time, but certain ideas remained: That it was wrong to live in a city, where people get lifted up in the pride of their hearts and think that they are too powerful for the gods to destroy. That the one who seems to be crazy may in fact be the only one who sees the truth. That the greatest of gods is the one you can't see, the one who has power over the earth and the sea and the sky, all at once. And, above all, this: That it was wrong to sacrifice human beings to the gods.

It took thousands of years, and there were places where Naog's passionate doctrine did not penetrate until modern times, but the root of it was there in the day he came home and found that his father had been fed to the Dragon. Those who thought that it was right to offer human beings to the Dragon were all dead, and the one who had long proclaimed that it was wrong was still alive. The god had preserved him and killed all of them. Wherever the idea of Atlantis spread, some version of this story came with it, and in the end all the great civilizations that were descended from Atlantis learned not to offer the forbidden fruit to the gods.

In the Americas, though, no society grew up that owed a debt to Atlantis, for the same rising of the world ocean that closed the land bridge between Yemen and Djibouti also broke the land bridge between America and the old world. The story of Naog did not touch there, and it seemed to Kemal absolutely clear what the cost of that was. Because they had no memory of Atlantis, it took the people of the Americas thousands of years longer to develop civilization—the city. Egypt was already ancient when the Olmecs first built amid the swampy land of the Bay of Campeche. And because they had no story of Naog, warning that the most powerful of gods rejected killing human beings, the old ethos of human sacrifice remained in full force, virtually unquestioned. The carnage of the Mexica—the Aztecs—took it to the extreme, but it was there already, throughout the Caribbean basin, a tradition of human blood being shed to feed the hunger of the gods.

Kemal could hardly say that the bloody warfare of the old world was much of an improvement over this. But it was different, and in his mind, at least, it was different specifically because of Naog. If he had not ridden out the flood to tell his story of the true God who forbade sacrifice, the old world would not have been the same. New civilizations might have risen more quickly, with no stories warning of the danger of city life. And those new civilizations might all have worshipped the same Dragon, or some other, as hungry for human flesh as the gods of the new world were hungry for human blood.

On the day that Kemal became sure that his Noah had actually changed the world, he was satisfied. He said little and wrote nothing about his conclusion. This surprised even him, for in all the months and years that he had searched hungrily for Atlantis, and then for Noah, and then for the meaning of Noah's saga, Kemal had assumed that, like Schliemann, he would publish everything, he would tell the world the great truth that he had found. But to his surprise he discovered that he must not have searched so far for the sake of science, or for fame, or for any other motive than simply to know, for himself, that one person's life amounted to something. Naog changed the world, but then so did Zawada, and so did Kormo, and so did the servant who skinned his elbows running down the hill, and so did Naog's father and mother, and . . . and in the end, so did they all. The great forces of history were real, after a fashion. But when you examined them closely, those great forces always came down to the dreams and hungers and judgments of individuals. The choices they made were real. They mattered.

Apparently that was all that Kemal had needed to know. The next day he could think of no reason to go to work. He resigned from his position at the head of the Atlantis project. Let others do the detail work. Kemal was well over thirty now, and he had found the answer to his great question, and it was time to get down to the business of living.

NOTES ON "ATLANTIS"

I was working on the concept that became my novel *Pastwatch: The Redemption of Christopher Columbus.* The technogimmick of the story was a machine that allowed you to *see* the past but not touch it or affect it. The scientific premise is absurd (as it always is with time travel): The flow of time would have to be tied to the rotations and revolutions of the Earth and the solar system and the galaxy, so that when you swam upstream through time there would somehow be a way of tracking causal events backward, not at this absolute site, but rather at this *relative* site.

Fortunately, science fiction readers long ago agreed to swallow such absurdities and just agree that we will allow silly time-travel stories to be taken seriously. And if you can accept stories where you travel back and forth in time, then why not stories where you only take a lookyloo?

Anyway, as I was working on Columbus—reading a decent biography and tying it in with all sorts of cultural things I was researching in Mesoamerica and Spain—I realized that I must also develop the culture of the people in the future who are using the timeview machinery to see into the past. Who are they? What do they look for? Why is anybody *paying* for this research?

I realized there were many obvious things that people would look for, and keep looking for as the resolution and range of the devices improved. There would be crimes to solve—I'm sure that finding who actually killed Jack the Ripper's victims would be a high priority, as would close examination of that grassy knoll in Dallas in 1963. And somebody would be bound to turn the time machine to look at Jesus' grave—if they could properly identify which of the victims of Roman crucifixion happened to be him.

Many things like that might be classed as "idle curiosity," but some would have genuine scientific value. And one of the biggest problems to resolve would be the widespread "great flood" story. Was there really such a flood? Or is it simply that cultures that have floods also have to invent a story of "the big one"?

There was an obvious time for a huge civilization–destroying flood to take place: after the most recent ice age, when melting glaciers sent torrential rivers flowing into shrunken seas.

At first, I thought of the Mediterranean Sea as an obvious place to look for such a flood. With worldwide sea levels down so far that Britain was a peninsula, surely the Mediterranean would be separated from the Atlantic, and then when the Atlantic refilled, there would be a flood that broke open the fountains of the great deep.

No dice. The Mediterranean, regardless of Ice Age or Warm Spell, would still have the Nile flowing into it. And as the glaciers melted, they would be pouring themselves into the Rhone, the Po, the Danube, the Dnieper. Even if the Atlantic refilled faster than the Mediterranean, there would never have been such a differential between them that the result would be truly cataclysmic.

What was true of the Mediterranean would be true of the Black Sea. Though the Bosphorus might have become dry land during the Ice Age, the melting glaciers would have been raising the Black Sea at least as fast as the Mediterranean. In fact, by my estimation I would think the Black Sea would fill *faster*.

Besides, why would there be enough of a civilization in the Black Sea for anyone to come away from it with tales that would spread throughout the world? Quick: Name the great civilization that arose on the shores of the Black Sea. You can't do it? Guess why.

Great civilizations grow up where certain conditions are met. Not only are there enough resources within reach to support a large population, there must be certain environmental challenges that greatly reward people who learn to work together in great public works projects. The cooperative ventures would then concentrate the population in a certain area where they might be wiped out by a single cataclysmic event.

In the Nile Valley, the annual floods made it easy to grow crops—but by creating granaries and guarding them together, much larger populations could sustain themselves through the dry season.

Whether the land is too wet and you have to have vast community cooperation to create drier farmland, as in Mesoamerica, or the land is dry and you have to irrigate from the existing rivers, as in Mesopotamia and the Indus, civilizations grow where cooperation is rewarded with surpluses that can sustain "high" cultures.

So where in Eurasia could there have been a place where it was likely for a civilization to grow, and yet a single flood that was specifically *not* a river flood but an *ocean* flood take place?

While I still had hopes for the Mediterranean or Black Sea—or maybe the Persian Gulf?—I talked to my friend Michael Lewis, a geographer at the University of North Carolina at Greensboro. I think it took him all of ten seconds to open the atlas and point to the Red Sea. "It's a rift valley," he said. "So almost no rivers flow into it. During the Ice Age, when it was cut off from the Indian Ocean, it would have dried up to a rump of what it is now—maybe even completely, like Lake Chad. And when the Ice Age ended and sea levels rose, it would have stayed low until the Indian Ocean broke through and flooded it in one amazing cataclysm. Anything and anyone in the Red Sea bed would have been swept away."

Looking at a map, it was obvious. The trouble was, the very lack of water that would leave it as a rump sea would also indicate that nobody could live there.

Except . . . there would have been a bit more water flowing out of the wadis that do feed the Red Sea. Water from the wadis of southwest Arabia and the Eritrean coast might well have created the kind of seasonal marshland that would reward public works projects. Around the mountains of the Dahlak Archipelago and in the valley of the Mits'iwa Channel, water might have collected into streams and swamps; dammed and channeled, the land might have become a protocivilization.

Anyway, it certainly looked more plausible than any of the other candidates for the job. In the Red Sea, there most definitely would have been a flood, and while it might have happened during a rainstorm, the bulk of the water would have been seawater from the Indian Ocean. There might have been advance warnings as the Indian Ocean rose and occasionally lapped over, sending tongues of water licking out across the sandy wastes of the isthmus joining Arabia and Africa. A gout of water might even have made it all the way over, sending a mini-flood down into the Red Sea basin, only to abate when the storm died.

Then came the big one, and this time, instead of just flicking out a tongue of water, the storm would keep enough surges flowing after the first one that a channel would wear through the sand, and as the flow increased, the channel would carve itself deeper and wider, until it would look like the bursting of a dam. With no early-warning system, people in the bottomlands would find the ocean pouring in on them, wave after wave, and many who sought the nearest high ground ("surely the flood won't go any higher than *this*") would also be swept away.

I knew I had my flood location. Then all I needed was my flood story.

Foolishly, I did not go back to reread the Gilgamesh epic before giving my Noah character a name echoing that alternate source of the flood story. Only after I had written and my friend Richard Gilliam had published "Atlantis" in the Atlanta World Fantasy Convention anthology (*Grails: Quests, Visitations and Other Occurrences*) did I make the head-slapping realization that Gilgamesh wasn't the flood guy, he went and *talked* to Utnapishtim, who was. Too late to fix it for that version; I'll change it when I write the novel *Pastwatch II: The Flood*. Meanwhile, the story "Atlantis" stands as I first wrote it.

GERIATRIC WARD

Sandy started babbling on Tuesday morning and Todd knew it was the end.

"They took Poogy and Gog away from me," Sandy said sadly, her hand trembling, spilling coffee on the toast.

"What?" Todd mumbled.

"And never brought them back. Just took them. I looked all over."

"Looked for what?"

"Poogy," Sandy said, thrusting out her lower lip. The skin of her cheeks was sagging down to form jowls. Her hair was thin and fine, now, though she kept it dyed dark brown. "And Gog."

"What the hell are Poogy and Gog?" Todd asked.

"You took them," Sandy said. She started to cry. She kicked the table leg. Todd got up from the table and went to work.

The university was empty. Sunday. Damn Sunday, never anyone there to help with the work on Sunday. Waste too much damn time looking up things that students should be sent to find out.

He went to the lab. Ryan was there. They looked over the computer readouts. "Blood," said Ryan, "just plain ain't worth the paper it's printed on."

"Not one thing," Todd said.

"Plenty of tests left to run."

"No tests left to run except the viral microscopy, and that's next week."

Ryan smiled. "Well, then, the problem must be viral."

"You know damn well the problem isn't viral."

Ryan looked at him sharply, his long grey hair tossing in the opposite direction. "What is it then? Sunspots? Aliens from outer space? God's punishment? The Jews? Yellow Peril?"

Todd didn't answer. Just settled down to doublechecking the figures. Outside he heard the Sunday parade. Pentecostal. Jesus Will Save You, Brother, When You Go Without Your Sins. How could he concentrate?

"What's wrong?" Ryan asked.

"Nothing's wrong," Todd answered. Nothing. Sweet Jesus, you old man, if I could live to thirty-three I'd let them hang my corpse from any cross they wanted. If I could live to thirty.

Twenty-four. Birthday June 28. They used to celebrate birthdays. Now everyone tried to keep it secret. Not Todd, though. Not well-adjusted Todd. Even had a few friends over, they drank to his health. His hands shook at night now, like palsy, like fear, and his teeth were rotting in his mouth. He looked down at the paper where his hands were following the lines. The numbers blurred. Have to have new glasses again, second time this year. The veins on his hands stuck out blue and evil-looking.

And Sandy was over the edge today.

She was only twenty-two; it hit the women first. He had met her just before college, they had married, had nine children in nine years—duty to the race. It must be child-bearing that made the women get it sooner. But the race had to go on.

Somehow. And now their older children were grown up, having children of their own. Miracles of modern medicine. We don't know why you get old so young, and we can't cure it, but in the meantime we can give you a little more adulthood—accelerated development, six-month gestation, puberty at nine, not a disease left you could catch except the one. But the one was enough. Not as large as a church door, but 'tis enough, 'twill serve.

His chin quivered and tears dropped down wrinkled cheeks onto the page.

"What is it?" Ryan asked, concerned. Todd shook his head. He didn't need comfort, not from a novice of eighteen, only two years out of college.

"What is it?" Ryan persisted.

"It's tears," Todd answered. "A salty fluid produced by a gland near the eye, used for lubrication. Also serves double-duty as a signal to other people that stress cannot be privately coped with."

"So don't cope privately. What is it?"

Todd got up and left the room. He went to his office and called the medical center.

"Psychiatric," he said to the moronic voice that answered.

Psychiatric was busy. He called again and got through. Dr. Lassiter was in.

"Todd," Lassiter said.

"Val," Todd answered. "Got a problem."

"Can it wait? Busy day."

"Can't wait. It's Sandy. She started babbling today."

"Ah," said Val. "I'm sorry. Is it bad?"

"She remembers her separation therapy. Like it was yesterday."

"That's it then, Todd," Val said. "I'm really sorry. Sandy's a wonderful woman, good researcher, but there's nothing we can do."

"Aren't we supposed to be able to see signs before she reaches this stage?"

"Usually," Val answered, "but not always. Think back, though. I'm sure you'll remember signs."

Todd swallowed. "Have you got a space, Val? You knew Sandy back in the old days, back when we were kids in the—"

"Is this pressure, Todd?" Val asked abruptly. "Appeal to friendship? Don't you know the law?"

"I know the law, dammit, I'm asking you, one medical researcher to another, is there room?"

"There's room, Todd," Val answered, "for the treatables. But if she's reverted to separation therapy, then what can I do? It's a matter of weeks. For your own safety you have to turn her over, never know what's going to happen during the final senility, you know. Hallucinations. Sometimes violence. There's still strength in the old bones."

"She's committed no crime."

"It's also the law," Val reminded him. "Good-bye."

Todd hung up the phone. Turn her over? He'd never thought it would come to Sandy so suddenly. He couldn't just turn her over, she'd

hate him, she had enough of herself left in herself to know what was going on. They'd been married thirteen years.

He went back to Ryan in the lab and told him to put the computers
on the viral microscopy tomorrow.

"That's unscientific, to rush it," said Ryan.

"Damned unscientific," Todd agreed. "Do it."

"OK," Ryan answered. "It's Sandy, isn't it?"

"It's handwriting," Todd said. "It's all over the walls."

Todd went home and found Sandy in the living room, cuddling a pillow and watching the tube. Someone was yelling at someone else. Sandy
didn't care. She was stroking the pillow, making love noises. Todd sat on
the chair and watched her for almost an hour. She never noticed him. She
did, however, change pillows.

"Gog," she said.

She listened for an answer, nodded, smiled, held the pillow to her
breasts. Todd chewed his fingernails. His heart was fluttering.

He went into the kitchen and fixed dinner. She ate, though she spilled
a great deal and threw her spoon on the floor.

He put her to bed. Then he showered, came back out, and crawled
into bed beside her.

"What the hell do you think you're doing," she challenged, her voice
husky and mature.

"Going to bed," Todd answered.

"Not in my bed, you bastard," she said, shoving at him.

"*My* bed, you mean," he said, even though he knew better.

She growled. Like a tiger, Todd thought. Then she clawed at his face.
Her nails were long. He lurched back, his face on fire with pain. The motion carried him off the bed. He landed heavily on the floor. His brittle
old bones ached at the impact. He felt for his eyes, to see if they were still
there. They were.

"If you ever come back," she said, "I'll have my husband eat you alive."

Todd didn't bother arguing. He went into the living room and curled
up on the couch. For the first time he wished that children still lived at
home nowadays. That even the two-year-old were there to talk to. He
touched the pillow, pulled it toward him, then stopped himself. Pillows.
One of the signs.

Not me, he thought.

He fell asleep surrounded by nightmares of childhood, attacked on all sides by sagging flesh and fragile bones and eyes and ears that had forgotten all they ever knew how to do.

He woke with the blood clotted stiffly on his face. His back was sore where he had struck the floor last night. He walked stiffly to the bathroom. When he washed the blood off his face the cuts opened again, and he spent a half hour stanching the bleeding.

When he left home, Sandy was sitting at the kitchen table, holding a tea party for herself and the pillows.

"Good-bye, Sandy," Todd said.

"More tea, Gog?" she answered.

He did not go to the lab. Instead he went to the library and used his top security clearance to gain access to the gerontology section. It was illegal to use security clearance for personal purposes, but who would know? Who would care, for that matter. He found a volume entitled *Psychology of Accelerated Aging* by V. N. Lassiter. He finished it at one o'clock.

Ryan looked irritated when Todd finally came in.

"We've been running the series without you," he said, "but holy hell, Todd, everybody's been on my back for doing it early. If you're going to give me a screwed-up order, at least be here to take the lumps."

"Sorry." Todd started looking over the early readouts.

"You won't find anything yet," Ryan said.

"I know," Todd answered. "But the meeting is on Friday."

Ryan slammed down a sheaf of papers on his desk.

"We'll make the report then," Todd went on.

"If we make a report then it will be worth exactly nothing," Ryan said angrily.

"If we make a report then—and we *will* make a report then—it will be as accurate as human understanding can make it. Do you think we'll miss anything now? There's nothing. Our blood is no different from the blood of our great-great-grandfathers who lived to be ninety-five. There are no microbes. And viruses are just corkscrews."

"If you do this," Ryan said, "I'll recommend that you be removed from your post and the viral microscopy series be run again."

Todd laughed. "Calm down," he said. "I'm twenty-four."

Ryan looked at the floor. "I'm sorry."

"Hey," Todd said, "don't worry about it. In a few months, you can run the whole thing over again if you want. And the guy after you, and the one after him, run it over and over and over again through eternity. I won't care. You'll have your time in the sun, Ryan. You'll have six years as head of the department and you'll write papers, conduct research, and then you'll roll over like the rest of us and wiggle your feet in the air for a while and then you'll die."

Ryan turned away. "I've got the point, Todd."

"Dr. Halking, boy," Todd said. "Dr. Halking to you until I'm dead." Todd walked to the window and opened it. Outside on the lawn was an afternoon rally of the Fatalists. "Hasten the day," they sang at the top of their decrepit lungs, white hair flashing in the breeze and the sunlight. "Take me away, death is the answer, don't make me stay."

"Shut the window," Ryan said. Todd opened it wider. Two students, graduate students about sixteen years old, took a few quick steps toward him.

"Relax," Todd said. "I'm not jumping."

Todd was still standing at the window when Val Lassiter came. "Ryan called me," Val said.

"I know," Todd answered. "I heard him call."

"Let's talk," Val answered. The students left the room. Val looked at Ryan, and he also left. "They're gone," Val said. "Let's talk."

Todd sat in a chair. "I know what you're thinking," Todd said. "I'm showing the signs."

"What signs?"

Todd sighed. "Don't give me any of that psychiatrist crap. I read your book. I've got it all: Tears, worries, inability to bear delay, impatience with friends, unwillingness to admit any possibility of hope, suicidal behavior— I'm so far gone that if Jesus whispered in my ear, 'You're saved,' I'd believe and be baptized and not be surprised at all."

"You shouldn't have read that book, Todd."

"I read the book but I'm not over the edge, Val. I will be, I know, but not yet. It's just Sandy—I was a fool, I let myself get too attached, you know? I can't handle it. Can't let go. Keep feeling there's got to be a way."

Val smiled and touched Todd's shoulder. "You've devoted your life to finding a way. So have I. So have all of us from the project. Geniuses all, even Sandy, what a damned shame she's the first to go. But the cure won't come overnight. Won't come by trying to reverse what's irreversible."

"Who says it's irreversible?" Todd demanded.

"Experience," Val said. "What, do you think you can go out of your discipline and outdo the experts in a sudden flash of inspiration? All you'll think of are ideas we've thought of and discarded long ago."

"How do you know it can't be reversed? We don't even know what causes the aging, Val. We don't even know if it *has* a cause—why is the cutoff point separation therapy? Why can't you help people once they revert to that?"

Val shrugged. "It's arbitrary. We can't do that much for others, either."

Todd shook his head, saying, "Val, you don't understand. Maybe what's going on in separation therapy is part of what *causes* the senility—"

Val stood impatiently. "I told you, Todd. You'll only think of things we already thought of. It can't be the cause because separation therapy began *after* the aging epidemic. It was tried as a *cure*. It was used so we would mature faster, so we would have more adult, productive years. Todd, you know that, you know it can't be the cause, what is this?"

Todd picked up a stack of readouts. "Forget it, Val. Tell everyone I'm over my breakdown. It's Sandy being over the edge. I just couldn't handle the grief awhile, OK?"

Val smiled. "OK. Have you turned her over yet?"

Todd stiffened. "No."

Val stopped smiling. "It's the law, Todd. Do it soon. Do it before I have to report it."

Todd looked up at Val with a sickening smile on his face. "And when will you have to report it, Val?"

Val looked at Todd for a moment, then turned and left. The others came back to the lab. They worked all afternoon and far into the night, pretending nothing had happened. At least Todd hadn't suicided. So many did these days, especially the brilliant ones; no one would have been surprised. But Todd they needed, at least for a while more, at least until the young ones had a chance to learn. Otherwise they'd be a few years deeper into the hole, there'd be a few more years' worth of learning lost, a little bit less that one man could hope to do in his short lifetime.

Todd called in sick the next morning. He was not sick. He took Sandy by the hand, led her to the car, and drove her to the childhouse. He flashed his security pass and rushed Sandy through the halls as quickly as possible, so no one would notice she was over the edge.

The rushing about left Todd's heart fluttering, his old hopeless heart, he thought, only a few more months, only a few more weeks of pumping away. They were met at the observation window by several young researchers; couldn't be out of college yet, maybe fifteen. Hair still young, eyes still bright, skin still smooth. Todd felt angry, looking at them.

They were impressed to be meeting *the* Todd Halking. "Gee, Dr. Halking," the heavyset young women enthused, "we never thought *our* work would have any application on the biological end of things."

"It probably doesn't," Todd said. "But we need to check every angle. This is my wife. She has a cold, so I'd advise you to keep your distance."

Sandy showed no sign of paying attention to the conversation around her. She only watched the large window in front of her. On the other side a child was playing with two stuffed animals. One was a bear, the other a lion.

"Poogy," Sandy whispered. "Gog."

A research supervisor walked into the observation room and began the testing. For a moment Todd tuned in to the heavyset woman's droning explanation: ". . . check to make sure the child's reliance is not pathological, in which case special treatment is necessary. In most cases separation therapy is judged to be safe, and so we proceed immediately. . . ."

The tests were simple—the supervisor knelt by the child and showed affection to each love object in turn, first by patting, then by kissing, then by taking the love object briefly and hugging it. Though the little girl showed some signs of anxiety when the researcher took the love object away for a moment to hug it, she was considered ready for therapy. "After all," the student explained to Todd, "for a five-year-old to show *no* anxiety would be as startling as extreme anxiety."

And so the separation therapy began. The attendant took both stuffed animals and left the room.

The little girl's anxiety was immediately more acute. She watched the door for a few moments, then stood up, went to the door, and tried to make it open. Of course the buttons didn't respond to her touch. She paced for a little while, then sat back down and waited, watching the door.

"You see," said the student, "you see how patient she is? That can be a sign of exceptional maturity."

Then the little girl ran out of patience. She began to call out. Her words were inaudible, but Todd could hear Sandy beside him, mumbling, "Poogy, Gog, Poogy, Gog," in time with the little girl's silent cries. She was reacting. Todd felt a shiver of fear run through him, upward, from his feet. She would react, but would it do any good?

The little girl was screaming now, her face red, her eyes bugging out. "She may, because she is an exceptionally affectionate and reliant child, continue this until she is unconscious," said the student. "We are monitoring her, however, in case she needs a sedative. If we can avoid the sedative, we do, because it does them good, like a purgative, to work it out of their system."

The little girl lay on the floor and kicked. She beat her head brutally against the floor. "Padded, of course," said the student. "Persistent little devil, isn't she?"

Todd noticed that tears were rolling down Sandy's cheeks. Profusively, making a latticework of tear tracks.

The little girl jumped up and ran as fast as she could against the wall, striking it with her head. The force of the impact was so great that she rebounded a full five feet and landed on her back. She jumped up again and screamed and screamed. Then she began running around the room in circles.

"Oh, well," said the student. "This could go on for hours, Dr. Halking. Would you like to see something else?"

"I'd like to continue watching a while longer," Todd said softly.

The little girl abruptly stopped moving and slowly removed all her clothing. Then she started tearing at her naked skin with her teeth and fingernails. Streaks of bloody wounds followed after her fingers.

"Uh-oh," said the student. "Self-destructive. Have to stop her, she might go for the eyes and cause permanent damage."

The last word was lost as the door slammed behind her. In a moment the observers saw the student researcher enter the therapy room. The little girl flew at her, screaming and clawing. The student, despite her weight, was well trained—she subdued the child quickly without sustaining or causing any wounds. Todd watched as the woman deftly forced a straitjacket on the child.

"Dr. Halking," one of the other students said, interrupting his observation. "I beg your pardon, but what is your wife doing?"

Sandy was removing her last stitch of clothing. Todd managed to catch her hands before she could rake her nails across her sagging bosom. The ancient hands were like claws where he held them—and madness poured strength into her arms. She broke free.

"Give me a hand here," Todd said, meaning to shout but only able to whisper because of the way his heart was beating.

When they finally forced her to the ground, shaking and exhausted, her own skin was streaked with blood, and some of the students had marks on them. Todd's face was bleeding, mostly where two-day-old wounds had reopened.

The matron of the childhouse came in almost immediately after they subdued Sandy. "What in heaven's name are you *doing* in here!" she demanded.

They told her. She narrowed her eyes and looked at Todd. "Dr. Halking, what do you mean bringing a woman who was over the edge into a childhouse? What did you mean letting her watch separation therapy? What in heaven's name were you *thinking* of? Are you trying to create catatonia? Are you trying to get some of my staff killed? You've certainly got some of them fired for letting this happen!"

Todd mumbled his apologies, urging her not to fire anyone. "It was all my fault, I lied to them, I—"

"Well, Dr. Halking, I'm calling the police at once. This woman is obviously ready to be turned over. Obviously. I can't understand a man of your stature playing these *games* with a woman's safety, and just plain *ignoring* the law—"

Todd apologized again, praised the fine work they were doing, told her he would make a favorable report on their behavior, and finally the matron calmed down. Todd managed to extricate himself. The matron did not call the police. Sandy took Todd's hand and followed him docilely out of the building.

When he got her home he let got of her hand. She stayed standing where he had let go of her. When he came back into the room a few minutes later, she was still standing there in exactly the same position.

He spoke to her, but she didn't answer. He took her hand and led her. She followed him to the bedroom. She stood by the bed when he let go. Gently he pushed her onto the bed. She lay on it, not moving. He raised her arm. She left it raised until he reached out and lowered it again.

He closed her eyes, because she wouldn't blink. Then he sat on the bed beside her and wept dry tears into his hands, his body shuddering with rapid, uncontrollable sobs, though not a sound came. Then he slept, feeling as sick as he had claimed to be that morning.

Sandy remained catatonic for the rest of the week. He hired a student from the university to come in and feed Sandy and clean up after her.

On Friday Todd and Ryan gathered their hastily prepared reports and flew to San Francisco for the meeting. Val Lassiter was on the same plane, but they all pretended not to know each other. The secrecy continued when they reached the city. The scientists were all put in separate hotels. They were brought to the meeting at different times, through different entrances. Some of the were instructed to wear casual clothes. Others wore business suits. One man wore a white uniform. Another wore a hard hat.

"Why all the secrecy?" Ryan asked Todd, laughing at a neurologist in a rather overdone fisherman's outfit.

"To prevent the public from getting too much hope if the papers report that this meeting is taking place," Todd answered.

"Why not? Why not a little hope?" Ryan asked.

"Why not a lot of heroin?"

Ryan looked coldly at Todd. "Dr. Halking, I find your despair disgusting."

Todd looked back and smiled. "And I find your insistence on hope touchingly naive."

The meeting went on. The reports varied between cautious negative statements and utter despair. Todd read Ryan's and his report toward the end of the first day. "Except for the viral microscopy reports, all were slowly and deliberately doublechecked. My assistant wants me to assure you that the viral microscopy reports were hurried through the second check. That is true, because the meeting couldn't wait and the computer *could* be made to work overtime."

There was some laughter.

"However, we never found any discrepancy between first and second runs on any other tests, and we did carefully check and found no discrepancies on the first run of the viral microscopy tests, either. Therefore, I can safely conclude that there is no significant difference between contemporary blood samples and the blood samples prior to the Premature Aging Phenomenon, except such differences as reflect our conquest of certain well-known diseases, and these antibodies were not stimulated until long after the PAP was first noted. Ergo—not significant."

There were some careful questions, easily answered, and they moved on. However jovial a presenter might be, the answer was always the same. No answers.

After the papers were presented, the data examined, the statistical results questioned and upheld, the heads of the projects gathered in one small room at the top of the old Hyatt Regency. Todd Halking and Val Lassiter arrived together. Only a couple of men were already there. On impulse, Todd walked to the chalkboard at one end of the room and wrote on it, "Abandon hope all ye who enter here."

"Not funny," Val said when Todd sat down next to him.

"Come on. They'll die laughing."

Val looked at Todd quizzically. "Get a grip, Todd," he said.

Todd smiled. "I have a grip. If not on myself, then on reality."

Everyone who came into the room saw the sign on the chalkboard. Some chuckled a little. Finally someone got up and erased the message.

The room was only half full. Todd got up and left the room, his aging bladder more demanding than it had been a few years—a few weeks!— before. He washed his hands afterward, and looked at himself in the mirror. He was haggard. His face cried out Death. He smiled at himself. The smile was ghastly. He went back to the room.

He was not yet seated when a military-looking man entered and said, "Ladies and gentlemen, the President of the United States." Everybody stood and applauded. The president walked in. No one could have recognized him from the publicity pictures. They all dated from his second campaign, and then he had not been bald.

"Well, you've done it," the president said. "And within my term of office. Thank you. The effort was magnificent. The results are remarkably thorough, I'm told by those who should know."

The president coughed into a handkerchief. He sounded like he had pleurisy.

"And if you're right," he said. "*If* you're right, the picture is pretty grim."

The president laughed. Todd wondered why. But a few of the scientists laughed, too. Including Anne Hallam, the geneticist. She spoke. "To the dinosaurs things once looked grim, too. A million mammals chewing on their eggs."

"The dinosaurs died out," the president said.

"No," Hallam answered. "Only the ones that hadn't become birds or mammals or some more viable type of reptile." She smiled at them all. Hope springs eternal, Todd thought. "It's small comfort," she went on, "but one thing this early aging has done: The species has shorter generations. We're better able to adapt genetically. Whatever happens, when mankind gets out of this we will not be the same as we were when we went in."

"Yes," Todd said cheerfully. "We'll all be dead."

Anne looked at him in irritation, and several people coughed. But the mood of joviality the president had set at first was gone now. Val wrote on his notebook and shoved it toward Todd as the president started talking again.

"You're speaking of aeons and species," the president said. "I must think of nations and societies. Ours is dying. If what you say is true, in a few years it will be dead. The nation. The way we live. Civilization, if I may use the romantic word."

Todd read Val's note. It said: "Shut your mouth, you bastard, it's bad enough already."

Todd smiled at Val. Val glared back.

People were telling the president: It's hardly that bleak, we weathered the worst already.

"Oh yes," the president agreed. "We lasted through the depression. We adapted to the collapse of world trade. We made the transition from the cities back to the farms, we have endured the death of huge industry and global interreactions. We have adapted to having our population cut in half, in less than half."

"What clever little adapters we are, Mr. President," Todd said, aware that he was breaking protocol to interrupt the president, and not particularly giving a damn. "But tell me, has anyone figured out an adaptation to death? Odd, isn't it, that in millions of years of evolution, nature has never managed to select for immortality."

Val stood, obviously angry. "Mr. President, I suggest that Dr. Halking be asked to contribute constructively or leave this meeting. There's no way we can accomplish anything with these constant interjections of pessimism."

There was a murmur, half of protest, half of agreement.

"Val," Todd said, "I'm only trying to be realistic."

"And what do you think *we* are, dreamers? Don't we know we're all old men and doomed to die?"

The president coughed, and Val sat down. "I believe," said the president, "that Dr. Halking will take this as a reminder that we are talking here as men of science, dispassionately. Impersonally, if you will. Now let's review. . . ."

They went over the findings again. "Is there any chance," the president asked again and again, "that you might be wrong?"

A chance, they all answered. Of course there's a chance. But we have done the best our instruments will let us do.

"What if you had more sophisticated instruments?" he asked.

Of course, they said. But we do not have them. You'll have to wait another generation, or two, or three, and by then the damage will be done. We'll never live to see it.

"Then," the president said, "we must get busy. Make sure your assistants and their assistants and their assistants as well know everything you know. Prepare them to continue your work. We can't give up."

Todd looked around the table as everyone nodded sagely, lips pursed in the identical expression of grim courage. The spirit of man: We shall overcome. Todd couldn't bear it anymore. Like his bladder, his emotions could be contained for progressively shorter periods of time.

"For Christ's sake, do you call this optimism?" he said, and was instantly embarrassed that tears came unbidden to his eyes. They would dismiss him as an emotional wreck, not listen to his ideas at all. Sound clinical, he warned himself. Try to sound clinical and careful and scientific and impartial and uninvolved and all those other impossible, virtuous things.

"I have the cure to the Premature Aging Phenomenon," Todd said. "Or at least I have the cure to the misery."

Eyes. All watching him intently. At last I have their attention, he thought.

"The cure to the misery is to go home and go to bed and stop trying. We've done all we can do. And if we can't cure the disease, we can live with it. We can adapt to it. We can try to be happy."

But the eyes were gone again, and two of the scientists came over to him and dabbed at his eyes with their handkerchiefs and helped him get up from the table. They took him to another room, where he sat (guarded by four men, just in case) and sobbed.

At last he was dry. He sat and looked at the window and wondered why he had said the things he had said. What good would it do? Men didn't have it in them to stop trying. We are not bred for despair.

And yet we learn it, for even in our efforts to repair the damage done by premature aging, we are as blind as lemmings, struggling to go down the same old road to a continent that a million years before had sunk under the sea—yet the road could not be changed. The age of forty had its tasks; therefore we must strive to live to forty, however far away it might be now.

The meeting ended. He heard voices in the hall. The words could not be deciphered, but through them all was the tone of boisterous good cheer, good luck my friend and I'll see you soon, here's to the future.

The door to Todd's private (except for the guards) room opened. Anne Hallam and Ryan came in, stepping quietly.

"I'm not asleep," Todd said. "Nor am I emotionally discommoded at the moment. So you needn't tiptoe."

Anne smiled then. "Todd, I'm sorry. About the embarrassment to you. It happens to all of us now and then."

Todd smiled back (thank God for a little warmth—how had she kept it?) and then shook his head. "Not then. Just now. Well, what did the meeting find out? Have the Chinese found a magic cure and only now are radioing the formula to Honolulu?"

Ryan laughed. "As if there *were* any Chinese anymore."

Anne said, "We decided two things. First, we haven't found the cure yet."

"Astute," Todd said, raising an imaginary glass to clink with hers.

"And second, we decided that there *is* a cure, and we will find it."

"And while you were at it," Todd asked, "did you decide that faster-than-light travel was possible, and declare that it would be discovered next week by two youngsters in France who by chance were walking in the field one day and plunged into hyperspace?"

"Not only that," Anne said, "but one of the children immediately will follow a rabbit down a hole and find herself in Wonderland."

"Blunderland," Todd added, and Anne and Todd laughed together with understanding and mutual compassion. Ryan looked at them, puzzlement in his eyes. Todd noticed it. The younger generation still knows only life: Ah, youthful Caesar, we who are about to die salute you, though we have no hope of actually communicating with you.

"But there is a cause," Anne insisted, "and therefore it can be found."

"Your faith is touching," Todd said.

"There's a cause for everything, we don't change overnight with no reason, or else nothing that any human being has ever called 'true' can be counted on at all. Will gravity fail?"

"Tomorrow afternoon at three," Todd said.

"Only if there's a cause. But sometimes—right now, with PAP—the cause eludes us, that's all. Why did the dinosaurs die out? Why did the apes drop from the trees and start talking and lighting fires? We can guess, perhaps, but we don't know; and yet there *was* a cause or there's no reason in the world."

"I rest my case," Todd said. "My basket case, to be precise."

Ryan's face twisted, and Todd laughed at him. "Ryan, the nearly dead are free to joke about death. It's only the living to whom death is tabu."

"Maybe," Anne Hallam said, leaning back in a chair (and the guards' eyes followed her, because they watched everybody, guarded everybody), "maybe there's some system, some balance, some ecosystem we haven't discovered until now, a system that demands that, when one species or group gets out of hand, that species changes, not for survival of the fittest, but for survival of the whole. Perhaps the dinosaurs were destroying the earth, and so they—stopped. Perhaps man was—no, we know man was destroying the earth. And we know we were stopped. Any talk of nuclear war now? Any chance of too much industry raping the earth utterly beyond of hope of survival?"

"And in a moment," Ryan said, his mouth curled with distaste, "you'll be mentioning the thought that God is punishing us for our sins. I, personally, find the idea ridiculous, and seeing two of our finest minds seriously discussing it is pathetic."

Ryan got up and left. Anne smiled again (warmly!) at Todd, patted his hand, and left. After a few minutes, Todd followed.

A plane ride east.

Midnight at the airport. Nevertheless, a crowd bustling through. At one end of the terminal, a ragged old man was shouting to an oblivious crowd.

Todd and the others tried to pass him without paying attention, but he called to them. "You! You with the briefcases, you in the suits!" Ryan stopped and turned, and so they all had to. Todd was irritated. He was tired. He wanted to get home to Sandy.

"You're scientists, aren't you!" the man shouted. They didn't answer. He took that for agreement. "It's your fault! The earth couldn't bear so many men, so many machines!"

"Let's get out of here," Todd said, and the others agreed. The old man kept calling after them. "Rape, that's all it was! Rape of a planet, rape of each other, rape of life, you bastards!" People stared at them all the way out of the terminal.

"There was a day," Ryan said, "when people expected science to work miracles, and cursed us when we failed. Now they curse us for the miracles we did give them."

Todd hunched his shoulders. Scientists hell. Who were scientists? People with blue security cards.

The old man's voice echoed even out in the parking lot: "The earth gets even! The violated virgins will have their revenge!"

Todd got in his car and drove home alone. Shaking.

When he got home he found all as he had left it. The student from the university had come in and fed Sandy—there were dishes in the sink that the boy apparently hadn't thought of cleaning up.

Sandy was where Todd had left her. Lying on the bed. Breathing. Her eyes were closed.

Todd lay on the bed beside her. He had carried despair with him to the meeting, and carried it as a burden multiplied many times over when he came back. With a gentle finger he traced the wrinkles that radiated from Sandy's eyes, followed the folds of skin down her neck, twisted the brown hair now showing grey roots, pressed his lips against her closed eyes. He could remember when the skin was smooth, not cracked and hard as parchment, not thin and vein-lined.

"I'm sorry," he said again and again, unsure who he was apologizing to or what for. "I'm so sorry."

And then he told his wife's unhearing ears about the conference. They had found nothing. And finding nothing, they could find no cure. You're going to die, he said softly into her ear. "You're going to die, I'd stop it if I could, but I can't, you're going to die."

He got up and sat at his desk. He wrote by hand on the blank envelope sitting there, because he felt too tired to type, too tired to reach up to the shelf above the desk and pick up the sheets of paper. The ink scrawled:

"Our senility is not just age. In the books it is possible to age gracefully. Let us age with grace and strength, please, not madly and with terror and in the darkness and clinging to our pillows and our blankets calling names of parents we never knew, names of soft friends who never answered us."

He stopped writing for as little reason as he had begun. He wondered who he had been writing to. He leaned back and touched the mattress. It was soft. He buried his hand in the blanket. It was soft.

On his knees by the bed, he clung to the blanket saying quietly, "Dappa," and then, "Coopie. Dappa, you're back."

Lying naked on the bed, curled up with a pillow tucked under his arm, he knew somewhere back in his mind that he was not quite what he should be, not quite thinking and acting as he ought. But it was too good to have Dappa and Coopie back.

He fell asleep with tears of comfort and relief spotting the sheets.

He woke with blood pumping upward out of his heart. His wife Sandy knelt on the bed, straddling him, the letter opener still in her hand, her face splotched red with his blood.

"Poogy," she said angrily, her face contorted. "You've got Poogy and I want him."

She stabbed him again, and Todd felt the letter opener in his chest. It fit as snugly and comfortably as a new organ that had long been missing from his body. It was, however, cold.

Sandy pulled out the letter opener and a new spout erupted and spattered. She stuck out her lower lip. "I'm taking Poogy now," she said. Then she reached down and pulled the bloody pillow from under his arm.

"Dappa," Todd said in feeble protest. But as the pillow moved away, cradled in his wife's arms, he saw clearly again, he recognized what was happening, and as his arms and legs got colder and the bloodspout weakened, he longed to cry out for help. But his voice did not work. There was no rescue.

Death and madness, he thought in the last moment left to him. They are the only rescuers. And where madness fails, death will do.

And it did.

NOTES ON "GERIATRIC WARD"

When I was just gearing up to begin my writing career, one of the writers who was teaching me was Harlan Ellison.

He didn't *know* he was teaching me. We hadn't met. I was just reading his anthologies—and, most importantly, the notes he included with the stories. His *Partners in Wonder, Dangerous Visions,* and *Again, Dangerous Visions* anthologies were a virtual writing course, especially since I had just finished reading all through the *Science Fiction Hall of Fame* and *Hugo Winners* volumes.

It was like having the entire history of science fiction laid out before me, and then when I got to the most recent generation of science fiction there was the added bonus of Ellison's essays and introductions. I got a sense of how he thought about stories, and how other writers thought about them—what they meant to do, the process they went through. I felt as if I'd been given a glimpse behind the curtain. I've tried to follow Ellison's example ever since—that's why there are notes accompanying all the stories in *Maps in a Mirror* and in this book as well.

My only regret was that I came on the scene too late to be part of

Ellison's *Dangerous Visions* project. I read about how *The Last Dangerous Visions* or *Final Dangerous Visions*—I heard both titles bandied about—was already closed, with multiple volumes' worth of stories just waiting for Ellison to write his introductions. Too late for me.

And then I got a phone call from Harlan—about something else, but in the process he invited me to submit a story. There was still room! I could make it in!

The trouble was, I'm not exactly a dangerous kind of guy. Oh, my fiction is revolutionary all right, but not in the traditional ways. Nobody has called me "edgy"—not lately—and even though I defy a lot of literary conventions, I don't do it in the recognizable ways so nobody notices it. When Harlan called me, I hadn't had enough published for anybody to detect just what I was doing that made me radically different (and quite a few bright lights in the field of sci-fi *still* don't have a clue), and so I thought I needed to come up with something that would be dazzling and dangerous in terms that would be recognizably so.

I thought and thought and thought . . .

And got nowhere.

Finally it occurred to me: If I write a story that is "dangerous" in exactly the way that the stories in the first two anthologies had been "dangerous," then I'm not being dangerous at all, am I? I'm actually being quite safe. A follower.

Instead of trying to live up to the *Dangerous Visions* tradition, I needed to simply find a story I cared about and believed in, write it as best I could, and send it off to Harlan Ellison to see if he thought I was worthy to be in the book.

The result was "Geriatric Ward," and Harlan took the story forthwith.

A year later. Two years. Five. *Locus* would report from time to time that Ellison was "working on" the book. That he would be "finished by . . ."

Then came a letter from Harlan—the same one he was sending all the other contributors. Sorry I'm so slow, I'll understand if you withdraw your story and publish it elsewhere, but let me know if you still want me to hold on to it.

By then I was making my living from novels, so the money wasn't an issue. I wanted to be in Harlan's book. So I told him to hang on to it.

Now it has been twenty years. Nobody's expecting to see *Final Dangerous Visions,* ever. And that's fine. Ellison already changed the world of sci-fi. He already helped teach me how to write.

So here is "Geriatric Ward," like a fossil suddenly brought to life. It represents the work I was doing in the first two years of my sci-fi writing career. I didn't keep it in my trunk, I kept it in Harlan's. To me it's as if it were written by a stranger. I don't even *know* that kid. And who does he think he is, writing about old age? What did *he* know?

HEAL THYSELF

There's a limit to how much you can shield your children from the harsh realities of life. But you can't blame parents who try. Especially when it's something you have to go out of your way to discuss.

My parents assure me that they would have talked about it someday, but it's not like the birds and the bees—there's not a certain age when you have to know. They were letting it slide. I was a curious kid. I had already asked questions that could have led there. They dodged. They waffled. I understand.

But then my childhood friend, Elizio, died of complications from his leukemia vaccination. I had been given mine on the same day, right after him, after jostling in line for twenty minutes with the rest of our class of ten-year-olds. Nobody else got sick. We didn't know anything was wrong with Elizio, either, not for months. And then the radiation and the chemotherapy, primitive holdovers from an era when medicine was almost indistinguishable from the tortures of the Inquisition. Nothing worked. Elizio died. He was eleven by then. A slow passage into the grave. And I demanded to know why.

They started to talk about God, but I told them I knew about heaven and I wasn't worried about Elizio's soul, I wanted to know why there wasn't some better way to prevent diseases than infecting us with semi-killed pseudo-viruses mixed with antigen stimulants. Was this the best the human race could do? Didn't God give us brains so we could solve these things? Oh, I was full of righteous wrath.

That was when they told me that it was time for me to take a trip to the North American Wild Animal Park. What did that have to do with my question? It will all become clear, they said. But I should see with my own eyes. Thus they turned from telling me nothing to telling me everything. Were they wise? I know this much: I was angry at the universe, a deep anger that was born of fear. My dear friend Elizio had been taken from me because our medicine was so primitive. Therefore anyone could die. My parents. My little sisters. My own children someday. Nothing was secure. And it pissed me off. The way I felt, the way I was acting, I think they felt that nothing but a complete answer, a visual experience, could restore my sense that this was, if not a perfect world, then at least the best one possible.

We left Saltillo that weekend, taking the high-speed train that connected Monterrey to Los Angeles. We got off in El Paso, the southern gateway to the Park. During the half-hour trip, I tried to make sense of the brochures about the Park, all the pictures, the guidebooks. But it was clear to me, even at the age of eleven, that something was being left out. That I was getting the child's version of what the Park contained. For all that the brochures described was a vast tract of savannahs, filled with wild animals living in their natural habitat, though it was an odd mixture of African, South American, European, and American fauna that they pictured. Of course, to protect the animals against the dangers of straying and the far greater menace of poaching, the Park was fenced about with an impenetrable barrier—*not* illustrated—of fences, ditches, wires, walls. The thing that made no sense at all, however, was the warning about absolute bio-security. All observations of the Park inside the boundaries were to take place from within completely bio-sealed buses, and anyone who tried to circumvent the bio-seal would be ejected from the Park and prosecuted. They did not say what would happen to anyone who succeeded in getting out into the open air.

Bio-sealed buses suggested a serious biohazard. And yet there was nothing in the brochures to suggest what that biohazard might be. It's not as if herds of bison could sneak onto the buses if you cracked the seal.

The answer to this mystery was no doubt the answer to my question about why Elizio died, and I impatiently demanded that my parents explain.

They urged me to be patient, and then took me right past the regular

buses and on to a nondescript door with the words—in small letters—
"Special Tours."

"What's so special?" I asked.

They ignored me. The clerk seemed to know without explanation
exactly what it was my parents wanted. Then I understood that my parents must have called ahead.

It was a private tour. And not on a bus. We were taken down an elevator into a deep basement, and then put aboard a train on which we rode
for more than an hour—longer than the trip from Saltillo to El Paso,
though I suspect we were going much slower. Underground, who can
tell?

We came up another elevator, and like the underground train, this one
had no trappings of tourism. This was a place where people worked;
gawking was only a secondary concern.

We were led by a slightly impatient-looking woman to a smallish
room with windows on four sides and dozens of sets of binoculars in a
couple of boxes. There were also chairs, some stacked, some scattered
about almost randomly. As if someone hadn't bothered to straighten up
after a meeting.

"Are they close?" asked Mother.

"We're here because the water is nearby," said the woman. "If they
aren't close now, they will be soon."

"Where's the water?" asked Father.

The woman pointed vaguely in a direction. It was clear she didn't
want us there. But Mother and Father had the gift of patience. They were
here for me, and bore the disdain of the scientist. If that's what she was.

The woman went away.

My parents picked up binoculars and searched. I also picked out a set
and tried to figure out how to focus it.

"It senses your vision automatically," Father explained. "Just look and
it will come into focus."

"Bacana," I said. I looked.

There was a lot of dry grassy land, interspersed with drier, sagebrushy
land. In one direction there were some trees. That must be where the water was.

"Spotted them yet?" Mother asked.

"To the left of the trees?" asked Father.

"There, too?"

"Where did you see them?"

"In the shade of that rock."

I searched and finally found what they were looking at.

Men and women. Long-haired. Filthy. Naked.

My strait-laced parents brought me here to see naked people?

Then I looked again, more closely. They weren't exactly people after all.

"Neanderthals," I said.

"Homo neanderthalensis," said Father.

"They've been extinct forever!"

"For about twenty thousand years, most conservative guess," said Father. "Maybe longer."

"But there they are," I said.

"There was a long debate," said Father. "About how the neanderthals died out."

"I thought that *Homo sapiens* wiped them out."

"It wasn't so simple. There was plain evidence of communities of *sapiens* and *neanderthalensis* living in close proximity for centuries. It wasn't just a case of kill-the-monsters. So there were several theories. One was that the two species interbred, but neanderthal traits were disprized to such a degree that they faded out. Like round eyes in China."

"How could they interbreed?" I asked. I was proud of my scientific erudition, as only eleven-year-olds can be. "Look at how different they are from humans."

"Not so different," said Mother. "They had rudimentary language. Not the complicated grammars we have now—basically just imperative verbs and labeling nouns. But they could call out to each other across a large expanse and give warning. They could greet each other by name."

"I was talking about how they look."

"But I was talking about brain function," said Mother. "Which is much more to the point, don't you think?"

"Another theory," said Father, "was that *Homo sapiens* evolved from the neanderthals. That one was discredited and then revived several times. It turns out it was the closest one to being right."

"You know, none of this explains why there are neanderthals out here in the North American Wild Animal Park."

"You surprise me, son," said my father. "I thought you would have leapt to at least some conclusion. Instead you seem to be passively awaiting our explanation."

I hated it when Father patronized me. He knew that, so he did it whenever he wanted to goad me into thinking. It always worked. I hated that, too.

"You brought me here because of the way I reacted to Elizio's death," I said. "And because you're famous scientists yourselves, you got to pull strings and get me a special tour. Not everybody sees this, right?"

"Actually, anybody can, but few want to," said Father.

"And the biohazard stuff, that suggests some kind of disease agent. What you said about the evolved-from-neanderthals scenario being close to correct suggests—there's some disease loose in the wild here that causes regular people to turn into cavemen?"

Father smiled wanly at Mother. "Smart boy," he said.

I looked at Mother. She was crying.

"Just tell me," I demanded. "No more guessing games."

Father sighed and put his arm around Mother and began to talk. It didn't take long to explain.

"The greatest breakthrough in the medical treatment of disease was the germ theory, but it took an astonishingly long time for doctors to realize that almost all human ailments were caused by infectious agents. A few were genetic—hemophilia, cystic fibrosis, sickle-cell anemia—but those all seemed to be recessive genes that conferred a benefit when you had one of them, and only killed you if you had two. All the others— heart disease, dementia, schizophrenia, strokes, nontraumatic cerebral palsy, multiple sclerosis, most cancers, even some *crimes*—all were actually diseases. What disguised them from researchers for so long was the fact that these diseases were passed along in the womb, across the placenta, mostly by disease agents composed of proteins smaller than DNA. Some were passed along in the ovum. So we had no way to compare a clean, healthy organism with an infected one until we finished mapping the human genetic code and realized that these diseases weren't there. When we finally tracked them down as loose proteins in the cells, we—"

"We?" I asked.

"I speak of our forebears, of course," said Father. "Our predecessors."

"You aren't in medical research."

"Our colleagues in science," said Father. "We've come a long way to have you quibble about my choice of pronouns. And anthropology is the science of which medicine is merely a subset."

I had a snappy retort about how nobody ever asks if there's an anthropologist in the house, but I kept it to myself, mostly because I didn't want to win points here, I wanted to hear the story.

"How do you inoculate an organism against in-utero infection?" asked Mother rhetorically. "How do you cleanse an ovum that has already been infected?"

"What we developed," Father began, then interrupted himself. "What *was* developed."

"What emerged from the development process," said Mother helpfully.

"Was," said Father, "an elegant little counter-infection. Learning from the way these protein bits worked, the researchers came up with a protein complex that hijacked the cell's DNA just the way these infectious agents did, only instead of slowly—or rapidly—destroying the host cell, our little counter-infection caused the human DNA to check aggressively inside the cell for proteins that didn't belong there. There are already mechanisms that do bits and parts of that, but this one worked damn near perfectly. Nothing was in that cell that didn't belong there. It even detected and threw out the wrong-handed proteins that caused spongiform encephalopathies."

"Now you're showing off, my love," said Mother.

"It was perfect," said Father. "And best of all, self-replicating yet nondestructive. Once you introduced it into a mother, it was in every egg in her body after a matter of days. Any child she bore would have this protection within it."

"It was perfect," said Mother. "The early tests showed that it not only prevented diseases, it cured all but the most advanced cases. It was the ultimate panacea."

"But they hadn't tested it for very long," said Father.

"There was enormous pressure," said Mother. "Not from outside, from *inside* the research community. When you have a cure for everything, how can you withhold it from the human race for ten years of longitudinal studies, while people die or have their lives wrecked by diseases that could be prevented with a simple inoculation."

"It had side effects," I said, guessing the end.

"Technically, no," said Father. "It did exactly what it was supposed to do. It eradicated diseases with smaller-than-bacteria agents. Period. Nothing else. The only reason that they didn't immediately spread the counter-infection throughout the world to save as many lives as possible was because of the one foreseeable hitch. Can you think of it? It's obvious, really."

I thought. I wish I could say I came up with it quickly, but my parents were nothing if not patient. And I did come up with it after a few false tries, which I can't remember now. The correct answer: "Aging is a disease. You get this counter-infection, you don't die."

"We were concerned about a population explosion," said Mother. "Even if people completely stopped having children, we weren't sure that the existing ecosphere could sustain a population in which all the existing children grew up to be adults while none of the adults died off to make room for them. Imagine all the children entering the workforce, while the older generation, newly vigorous and extremely unlikely to die, refused to retire. It was a nightmare. So, by the mercy of God, the counter-infection was restricted to a large longitudinal study centered on Manhattan, a smallish college town in Kansas."

"There was a quarantine, of sorts," said Father. "The participants accepted the rules—no physical contact with anyone outside the city during the two years of the study. In exchange, nobody dies of any kind of disease. They jumped at it."

"The counter-infection got loose!" I said.

"No. Everybody kept to the rules. This was science, not the movies," said Father. "But in the Manhattan Project, as we inevitably called it, for the first time the test included infants, newborns, children born after the study began, children *conceived* after the study began. We were so interested in the result with the aging population that it had never crossed our minds that . . . well, it *did* cure aging. The people who have it would never die of old age. The trouble was, the children were born—"

"As neanderthals," I said, making the obvious guess.

"And over time," said Father, "as cells were replaced, the adult bodies also tried to reshape themselves. It was fatal for them. You can't take an existing body and make it into something else like that. You had a few years of perfect health, and then your bones destroyed themselves in the frantic effort to grow into new shapes. The little ones, the ones who were changed in the womb, only they survived."

"And that's who I'm seeing out there," I said.

"It took fifteen years to find a way to sterilize them all without our counter-infection undoing the sterilization. By then there were so many of them that to keep them all in their natural habitat required a vast reserve. It really wasn't all that hard to get the citizens of this area to evacuate. Nobody wanted to be anywhere near Manhattan, Kansas. So once again, *Homo neanderthalensis* has a plot of ground here on Earth. *Homo neanderthalensis,* the most intelligent toolmaking species ever to evolve naturally."

"But how could the counter-agent cause us to revert to an earlier stage of evolution?" I asked.

"You weren't listening," said Father.

I thought for a moment. "*Homo neanderthalensis* isn't an earlier stage," I said. "There was no more evolution after that."

"Only a disease," said Father.

It seemed too incredible to me, as an eleven-year-old who prided himself on understanding the world. "Human intelligence is an *infection*?"

"Passed from mother to child through the ovum," said Mother. "By a disease agent that alters the DNA in order to replicate itself. We should have realized it from the fact that in-utero development recapitulates evolution, but there is no stage in which the fetus passes through a habiline form. We didn't evolve past it. The DNA is hijacked and we are born prematurely, grossly deformed by the disease. Neotonous, erect-standing, language-mad, lacking in sense of smell, too feeble to survive on our own even as adults, in need of clothing and shelter and community to a degree that the neanderthals never were. But . . . smart."

"So now," said Father, "do you understand why medical science has to rely on inoculation to fight off cancer, so that a small percentage—far smaller than ever before in human history, but not zero—a small percentage dies? Elizio died because the only alternative we've found is for this race of perfectly healthy, immortal, dimwitted beings to inherit the Earth."

I stood there for a long time in silence, watching the neanderthals, trying to see how their behavior was different from ours. In the years since then I have come to realize that there was no important difference. Being smarter hasn't made us *act* any differently from the neanderthals. We make better tools. We have a longer, more thorough collective memory in the form of libraries. We can talk much more fluently about the things we do. But we still do basically the same things. We *are* neanderthals, at heart.

But I did not understand this at the time. I was, after all, only eleven. I had a much more practical—and heartless—question.

"Why do we keep this park at all?" I asked. "I mean, they're going to live forever. And all the time they're alive, they pose a danger of this counter-infection getting loose outside the fence. Why haven't they all been killed and their bodies nuked or something so that the counter-agent is eliminated?"

Mother looked appalled at my ruthlessness, but Father only patted her arm and said, "Of course he thought of that, my love."

"But so young, to be so—"

"Practical?" prompted Father. "There was a long debate over exactly this issue, and it resurfaced from time to time, though not for decades now. The ones who argued for keeping the Park talked about the necessity of studying our ancestors, and some people talked about the rights of these citizens who, after all, can't help their medical condition and have committed no crime, but it was all a smokescreen. The real reason we didn't destroy them all, as you suggested, was because we didn't have the heart."

"They were our children," said Mother, crying again.

"At first," said Father. "And later, when they weren't children anymore, we still couldn't kill them. Because they had become our ancient parents."

Now, though, I have come to think that while they were both right, the answer is even deeper. We didn't kill them, and we continue not to kill them, despite the reality of all those dangers, because they are not "they" at all. There, but for the fact that we happen to be the tiniest bit ill, go we.

I had troubling dreams for months afterward. I had mood swings, alternating between aggression and despair. There were times when my parents wished they had just answered my questions about Elizio by taking me to the priest and getting me on the roster of altar boys.

But they were not wrong to take me there, any more than they had been wrong *not* to tell me up till then. I needed to know before my education was complete. Those who do not know, who continue through adulthood oblivious, in a sense remain children, forever naive. Within the fence of the North American Wild Animal Park is the Garden of Eden, and the people there eat freely of the Tree of Life. Here, outside, in this world of thorns, we dwell in the Valley of the Shadow of Death, madly eating of the fruit of the Tree of Knowledge, as much of it as we can get before we die.

You cannot straddle the boundary. If you bring children into the world on this side of the fence, you must take them to eat the fruit of the tree—not too young, not before they're able to bear it. But don't wait too long, either. Let them see, before you die, that death is truly the gift of a merciful God.

NOTES ON "HEAL THYSELF"

This is one of those stories that wanted to be a novel, but I couldn't get a handle on it. To make an idea into a novel, you have to have a character strong enough to carry the reader through the whole ride. A mere idea isn't enough for a whole book.

But it's enough for a story. It just hit me as I was reading up on the latest advances in the science of genetics: What if human intelligence, the vast jump from non-language-using animals to us talkers, came with a price?

There's a long tradition of great one-idea stories in science fiction. Think of Arthur C. Clarke's "The Nine Billion Names of God." It's just a weird thought—it's not as if Clarke actually believed in a religion where the purpose of the universe was for all of God's names to be uttered. But it was a *fun* idea, and what did it cost?

There were no characters in "Nine Billion Names," just as there are no characters in "Heal Thyself." Oh, yes, technically there are, but the whole point of the story isn't any individual person's choices, it's about the social order. The characters exist only in order to have somebody see and understand this situation for the first time.

I'm in good company here. There are no significant characters in Clarke's "The Star" or Asimov's "Nightfall" or Le Guin's "The Ones Who Walk Away from Omelas." Just an idea, which the author shows us in a short story.

Of course, readers are the ones who decide whether the idea is interesting or truthful or fun enough to be worth the read. All I know is that I couldn't let go of it until I wrote it down.

SPACE BOY

Todd memorized the solar system at the age of four. By seven, he knew the distance of every planet from the sun, including the perigee and apogee of Pluto's eccentric orbit, and its degree of declension from the ecliptic. By ten, he had all the constellations and the names of the major stars.

Mostly, though, he had the astronauts and cosmonauts, every one of them, the vehicles they rode in, the missions they accomplished, what years they flew and their ages at the time they went. He knew every kind of satellite in orbit and the distances and orbits that weren't classified and, using the telescope Dad and Mom had given him for his sixth birthday, he was pretty sure he knew twenty-two separate satellites that were probably some nation's little secret.

He kept a shrine to all the men and women who had died in the space programs, on the launching pad, on landing, or beyond the atmosphere. His noblest heroes were the three Chinese voyagers who had set foot on Mars, but never made it home. He envied them, death and all.

Todd was going into space. He was going to set foot on another planet.

The only problem was that by the time he turned thirteen he knew he was never going to be particularly good at math. Or even *average*. Nor was he the kind of athletic kid who looked like an astronaut. He wasn't skinny, he wasn't fat, he was just kind of soft-bodied with slackish arms no matter how much he exercised. He ran to school every day, his backpack bumping on his back. He got bruises on his butt, but he didn't get any faster.

When he ran competitively in PE he was always one of the last kids back to the coach, and he couldn't ever tell where the ball was coming when they threw to him, or, when it left his own hand, where it was likely to go. He wasn't the last kid chosen for teams—not while Sol and Vawn were in his PE class. But no one thought of him as much of a prize, either.

But he didn't give up. He spent an hour a day in the back yard throwing a baseball against the pitchback net. A lot of the time, the ball missed the frame altogether, and sometimes it didn't reach the thing at all, dribbling across the lawn.

"If I had been responsible for the evolution of the human race," he said to his father once, "all the rabbits would have been safe from my thrown stones and we would have starved. And the sabertooth tigers would have outrun whoever didn't starve."

Father only laughed and said, "Evolution needs every kind of body. No one kind is best."

Todd wouldn't be assuaged so easily. "If the human race was like *me,* then launching rockets and going into space would have to wait for the possums to do it."

"Well," said Father, "that would mean smaller spaceships and less fuel. But where in a spacesuit would they stow that tail?"

Really funny, Dad. Downright amusing. I actually thought about smiling.

He couldn't tell anybody how desperate and sad he was about the fact that he would probably have to become a high school drama teacher like his dad. Because if he *did* say how he felt, they'd make him go to a shrink again to deal with his "depression" or his "resentment of his father" the way they did after his mother disappeared when he was nine and Dad gave up on searching for her.

The shrink just wouldn't accept it when he screamed at him and said, "My mother's gone and we don't know where she went and everybody's stopped looking! I'm not depressed, you moron, I'm *sad.* I'm *pissed off!*"

To which the shrink replied with questions like, "Do you feel better when you get to call a grownup a 'moron' and say words like 'pissed'?" Or, worse yet, "I think we're beginning to make progress." Yeah, I didn't choke you for saying that, so I guess that's progress.

Nobody even remembered these days that sometimes people were just plain miserable because something really bad was going on in their lives and they didn't need a drug, they needed somebody to say "Let's go get your mother now, she's ready to come home," or "That was a great throw—look, after all these years, Todd's become a *terrific* pitcher and he's great at math so let's make him an astronaut!"

Ha ha, like that would ever happen.

Instead, he took a kitchen timer with him out to the back yard every afternoon, and when it went off he'd drop what he was doing and go inside and fix dinner. Jared kept trying to help, which was OK because Jared wasn't a complete idiot even though he was only seven and certifiably insane. Todd's arm was usually pretty sore from misthrowing the ball, so Jared would take his turn stirring things.

There was a lot of stirring, because when Todd cooked, he *cooked*. OK, he mostly opened soup cans or cans of beans or made mac and cheese, but he didn't nuke them, he made them on the stove. He told Dad that it was because he liked the taste better when it was cooked that way, but one day when Jared said, "Mom always cooked on the stove," Todd realized that's why he liked to do it that way. Because Mom knew what was right.

It wasn't *all* soup or beans or macaroni. He'd make spaghetti starting with dry noodles and plain tomato sauce and hamburger in a frying pan, and Dad said it was great. Todd even made the birthday cakes for all their birthdays, including his own, and for the last few years he made them from recipes, not from mixes. Ditto with his chocolate chip cookies.

Why was it he could calculate a half-recipe involving thirds of a cup, and couldn't find n in the equation $n = 5$?

He took a kind of weird pleasure from the way Dad's face got when he bit into one of Todd's cookies, because Todd had finally remembered or figured out all the things Mom used to do to make her cookies different from other people's. So when Dad got all melancholy and looked out the window or closed his eyes while he chewed, Todd knew he was thinking about her and missing her even though Dad *never* talked about her. I made you remember her, Todd said silently. I win.

Jared didn't talk about Mom, but that was for a different reason. For a year after Mom left, Jared talked about her all the time. He would tell everybody that the monster in his closet ate her. At first people looked at him with fond indulgence. Later, they recoiled and changed the subject.

He only stopped after Dad finally yelled at him. "There's no monster in your closet!" It sounded like somebody had torn the words from him like pulling off a finger.

Todd had been doing the dishes while Dad put Jared to bed, and by the time Todd got to the back of the house, Jared was in his room crying and Dad was sitting on the edge of his and Mom's bed and *he* was crying and then Todd, like a complete fool, said, "And you send *me* to a shrink?"

Dad looked up at Todd with his face so twisted with pain that Todd could hardly recognize him, and then he buried his face in his hands again, and so Todd went in to Jared and put his arm around him and said, "You've got to stop saying that, Jared."

"But it's true," Jared said. "I saw her go. I warned her but she did the very exact thing I told her *not* to do because it almost got my arm the time I did it, and—"

Todd hugged him closer. "Right, I know, Jared. I know. But stop saying it, OK? Because nobody's ever going to believe it."

"You believe me, don't you, Todd?"

Todd said, "Of course I do. Where else could she have gone?" Why not agree with the crazy kid? Todd was already seeing a shrink. He had nothing to lose. "But if we talk about it, they'll just think we're insane. And it made Dad cry."

"Well he made *me* cry, too!"

"So you're even. But don't do it anymore, Jared. It's a secret."

"Same thing with the monster's elf?"

"The monster itself? What do you mean?"

"The elf. Of the monster. I can't talk about the elf?"

Geeze louise, doesn't he let up? "Same thing with the monster's elf and his fairies and his dentist, too."

Jared looked at him like he was insane. "The monster doesn't have a dentist. And there's no such thing as fairies."

Oh, right, lecture *me* on what's real and what's not!

So it went on, days and weeks and months, Todd fixing dinner and Dad getting home from after-school play practices and they'd sit down and eat and Dad would tell funny things that happened that day, doing all the voices. Sometimes he *sang* the stories, even when he had to have thirty words on the same note till he came up with a rhyme. They'd all laugh and it was great, they had a great life . . .

Except Mom wasn't there to sing harmony. The way they *used* to do it was they'd take turns singing a line and the other one would rhyme to it. Mom could always make a great rhyme that was exactly in rhythm with the song. Dad was funny about it, but Mom was actually *good*.

Grief is like that. You live on, day to day, happy sometimes, but you can always think of something that makes you sad all over again.

Everybody had their secrets, even though everybody else knew them. Jared had his closet monster *and* its elf. Dad had his memory of Mom, which he never discussed with anyone. Todd had his secret dreams of going to other worlds.

Then on a cool Saturday morning in September, a few weeks after his thirteenth birthday, he was out in the side yard, screwing the spare hose onto the faucet so he could water Mom's roses, when he heard a hissing sound behind him and turned around in time to see a weird kind of shimmering appear in midair just a few feet out from the wall.

Then a bare child-size foot slid from nowhere into existence right in the middle of the shimmering.

If it had been a hairy claw or some slime-covered talon or the mandibles of some enormous insect, Todd might have been more alarmed. Instead, his fear at the strangeness of a midair arrival was trumped by his curiosity. All at once Jared's talk about Mother disappearing in the closet because she did the same thing *he* did when the monster "caught his arm" didn't sound quite as crazy.

The foot was followed, in the natural course of things, by a leg, with another foot snaking out beside it. The legs were bare and kept on being bare right up to the top, where Todd was vaguely disgusted to see that whoever was coming was *not* a child. It was a man as hairy as the most apelike of the guys in gym class, and as sweaty and naked as they were when they headed for the showers. Except that he was about half their size.

"Eew, get some pants on," said Todd, more by reflex than anything. Since the little man's head had not yet emerged, Todd didn't feel like he was being rude to a person—personhood really seemed to require a head, in Todd's opinion—but apparently the dwarf—no, the *elf,* it was pretty obvious that Jared must have been referring to something like this—must have heard him somehow because he stopped wriggling further out, and instead a hand snaked out of the opening and covered the naked crotch.

The elf must have been holding on to something on the other side of that opening, because all of a sudden, instead of wriggling further out, he simply dropped the rest of the way, hit the ground, and rolled. It reminded Todd of the way a pooping dog will strain and strain, making very little progress, and then all of a sudden the poop breaks off and drops. He knew it was a disgusting thought, which made him regret that there was no one there to say it to. Still, he couldn't help laughing, especially because this particular dropping was a stark-naked man about half Todd's size.

At the sound of Todd's laughter, the man rolled over and, now making no attempt at modesty, said, "Oh, it's you."

"Why, have we met?" asked Todd. "What are you doing naked in my backyard? I think that's illegal."

"In case you weren't watching," said the man, "I just squeezed through the worm, so it's not like any clothes I was wearing would have made it anyway. And what are you doing out here? You're never out here."

"I'm out here all the time," said Todd.

The elf pointed to the back yard, around the corner of the house. "You're always over there, throwing a ball at a fishnet. I admit I wondered why you haven't figured out that the net will *never* catch the ball."

"Who are you, and what are you doing here, and why did Jared know about you and the rest of us didn't, and where is my mother, what happened to her?"

"Do you mind if I get dressed first?"

"Yes, I do mind." If this was Todd's only chance to get his questions answered, he wasn't going to be put off. If the stories about elves and leprechauns were true—and now he had to figure they must have *some* basis in fact—they were tricky and dishonest and you couldn't take any of them at their word. Which meant that they would fit right into eighth grade. Todd was experienced at being suspicious.

"Too bad," said the elf.

The elf started walking toward the fence that separated the side yard from the front yard. Todd got in front of him to block his way.

The elf swatted him away. It *looked* like a swat, anyway—but it felt like the back of his hand sank two inches into Todd's shoulder and shoved him out of the way with all the force of a bulldozer. He smacked into the bricks of the side of the house, and slid sharply enough that his arm was scraped raw. His head also rang from the impact, and when he reached up his sore arm to touch his face, the right side of his forehead up near the hairline was bleeding.

"Hey!" Todd yelled at him. "You got no right to do that! That *hurt!*"

"Boo-hoo, poor baby," said the elf. He was kneeling now. It seemed he counted boards in the fence and then plunged his hand right down into the dirt in front of a certain board.

Todd had dug in this hard-clay soil. It was hard enough to dig when the soil was wet; when it was dry, it was like trying to dig a hole in the bottom of a dish using only a spoon. But the little man's hand plunged in as if the dirt were nothing but Jell-O and Todd began to realize that just because somebody was little didn't mean he wasn't strong.

The elf's hand came up with a metal strongbox. He punched buttons to do the combination of the lock, and then lifted it open. Inside were clothes in a plastic bag. Within a minute, the man had pants and a shirt on. They looked like they had been bought at Gap Kids—new enough but way too cute for a guy as hairy as this.

"Where did you get those shoes?" asked Todd. They were like clown shoes, much wider and longer than his feet. Almost like snowshoes.

"I had them specially made," the elf said irritably.

For the first time, Todd realized that despite the elf's fluency, he had an accent—English wasn't his native language. "Where are you from?" he asked.

"Oh, right, like you'd recognize the name," said the elf.

"I mean is it another country? Or . . ." Todd looked at the shimmering in the air, which was now *way* less visible and fading fast. "Like, another dimension?"

"Another planet," said the elf. "And your mouth can't make the sounds necessary to pronounce the real name. But your mother calls it 'Lilliput.'"

"My mother?" said Todd. All at once it felt like his heart was in his throat. "She's alive, like Jared said?"

"Of course she's alive, why wouldn't she be alive? I warned Jared about the worm and he warned your mother, but did she *believe* him? No, he was just a child, so now she's stuck there and she's starting to get annoyed about it."

"Starting? She's been gone four years."

"Time doesn't work the same way back home. Your mother's only been gone for about a week."

"Four years!" shouted Todd. "She's been gone four years and why hasn't she come home? If *you* can get here, why can't she?"

"Because she's too big to get where she needs to go," said the elf. "You think I'm small, but I'm a tall man in my world. Your mother—she's a giant. Only she's a big *weak* giant. A big weak naked giant because clothes don't do so well coming through the worm—"

"What worm? Where's the worm?"

The elf waved toward the shimmering in the air. "That's the worm's anus. The mouth is in the closet in Jared's bedroom."

"So there really is a monster there."

"Not a monster," said the elf. "A worm. It's not out to get anybody. It just sucks stuff in at one end of a connection between worlds. You'd be surprised how much energy is released where worlds connect, if you can bridge them, and worms can do it, so they attach the two worlds together and process things through. Like earthworms. Only worldworms don't move, they just sit there and suck."

"Suck *what*?" said Todd.

"I told you. Energy. They suck a star's worth of energy in a year."

"Out of Jared's *closet*?"

"No." The elf sounded scornful. "Out of the friction between universes. The differing timeflows—they rub up against each other because they aren't synchronized. Four years for you, a week for your mother—you think that timeflow difference doesn't *burn*?"

"Don't talk to me like I'm an idiot," said Todd. "How exactly was I supposed to know any of this? I didn't even know your universe existed."

"Your mother disappears and you don't *suspect* something?"

"Yeah, we suspected that somebody pointed a gun at her and made her go with them. Or she maybe ran away from us because she stopped loving Dad. Or she died in some freak accident and her body simply hasn't been found. But no, the idea of her disappearing into another universe with a different timeflow didn't come up much."

"I *heard* Jared tell your father."

"Jared told Dad about a monster in the closet! For pete's sake, if I hadn't seen you come out of midair myself I wouldn't believe it. What, are little kids taught all about the friction between timeflows in *your* world?"

The elf looked a little abashed. "Actually, no," he said. "In fact, I'm the scientist who finally figured out what's going on. I've been coming back and forth between worlds, riding the worm for years. Not just here, either, this is the fourth worm I've ridden."

"So you're like—what, the Einstein of the elves?"

"More like Galileo. Nobody believes me on my end of the worm, either. In fact, most of my science and math come from your world. Which is why I expected it to be obvious to *you*."

"Just because I'm from planet Earth I'm supposed to be a math genius? I guess that means that since you're an elf, you make great shoes. You probably made those stupid clown shoes yourself."

The elf glowered at him. "I'm not an elf. And I don't make shoes. I don't *wear* shoes back home. I wear them here because unless I wear shoes with wide soles to spread my weight, I sink too far into the ground, which slows me down and leaves tracks everywhere."

"They make you look stupid."

"I'd look a lot stupider up to my ankles in asphalt."

While they'd been talking, Todd had also been thinking. "You said Mom's been gone for only a week."

"The timeflow difference fluctuates, but that's about right."

"So she hasn't even begun to miss me yet. Us. Yet."

"She's a big baby about it. Cries all the time. Worse than your father."

Todd remembered hearing his father cry, how private that had been. "You spy on us?"

"The worm I'm riding comes out here, and to get home I have to go into your brother's bedroom. I'm not spying, I'm traveling. With my eyes and ears open." The elf sighed. "OK, so I stop and gather data. I'm a scientist. You're an interesting people. And you'll notice I called you *people,* not some insulting diminutive derogatory name like 'elves.'"

"Why doesn't Mom come home? If you can get through, why can't she?"

The elf—for lack of a better name—did a weird move with his fingers. He'd done it a couple of times before, and Todd finally realized that where he came from, it must be the equivalent of rolling his eyes. "Because like I said, in my world she's huge. And very . . . light. Insubstantial. She can't *do* anything. She can barely make her voice heard."

Todd tried to imagine what that might mean. "She's some kind of mist?"

The elf chuckled. "Yes, she has some foglike properties."

Todd took a threatening step toward him. "Don't laugh at my mother!"

"If you'd seen her during a windstorm, trying to hold on to trees, *anything* to keep from blowing away—"

"It's not funny!" Todd tried to shove him, but it was like hitting a brick wall. It hurt his hands, and the elf didn't even budge.

"You still don't get it," said the elf. "I'm very dense."

It took a moment for Todd to realize he meant *dense* like in physics instead of *dense* as in "kind of dumb."

"I want my mother back. And you're a lousy sack of crap to make fun of her when she's stuck in your world."

"Oh, and you didn't make fun of *me* at *all,* I take it," said the elf. "When I popped through naked, that wasn't funny to you?"

"It was disgusting. And if Mother could fit through the wormhole in the closet, she must have fit through the worm's . . . whatever, on *your* side. So she *can* fit."

"Anus," said the elf. "The worm's mouth is in your closet. Its anus, in my world, is on a lovely wooded hillside behind my house. And yes, it has a mouth and an anus on both worlds. It's a single organism, but its digestive systems are bidirectional. It eats both worlds at once."

"Eats *what?*" Now Jared's childhood fears of being eaten by the monster in the closet seemed too literally true.

"Eats time. Eats dark matter. Eats dust. I have no idea. Why does gravity suck? I'm just starting to try to figure out a whole branch of science that neither your world nor mine knows anything about."

Todd's mind jumped back to the real question. "My mother lives with you?"

"Your mother is living in the woods because there's more room for her there and she can avoid being seen. She can avoid having someone maliciously dissipate her."

"What?"

"Throw rocks at her, for instance, until she's so full of holes she can't stick together and the bits of her just drift away."

"What kind of sick people *are* you in that world!"

"She's a huge woman who looks as translucent as mist! The few who have met her don't think she's alive! *They* haven't been to this world. They're ignorant peasants, most of them. It's all very awkward." The elf leaned in close to Todd. "I'm doing everything I can to set things right. But please remember that I didn't take her to my world. She did that herself in spite of being warned. And I didn't put that stupid worm's mouth in your closet."

Then he got a strange look on his face. "Well, actually, I did, but not deliberately."

"You *put* it there?"

"The worm is apparently drawn to inhabited places. I don't know what it thinks we are, or if it thinks at all, but I've never seen a worm that wasn't close to the dwelling place of a sentient being. It may even be drawn to people who might want to use it to travel from world to world. It might have been aware of my passion for exploration, which is why the anus showed up in my front garden." Then, almost to himself: "Though it would have been much more convenient to have the *mouth* within easy reach."

"My mother didn't want to travel anywhere," said Todd. As he was saying it, he realized that maybe it wasn't Mother or even Jared who had drawn the worm to Jared's closet. There *was* someone in their family who had a passionate desire to travel to other planets.

"Your brother kept putting things through the worm," said the elf. "I'd find them in my garden. Wooden blocks. Socks. Underwear. A baseball cap. Little model cars. Plastic soldiers. A coat hanger. Money. And once a huge, misty, terrified cat."

Todd thought back to all the times things had disappeared. His favorite plastic soldiers. His baseball cap. His socks. His underwear. His Hot Wheels cars. Jared must have been stealing them to make them disappear down the wormhole. He had no idea where Jared got the cat, but it would have been just like him.

Of course, maybe Jared thought he was *feeding* the monster in the closet. Placating it, so it wouldn't come out of the closet and eat him. Was this how the worship of idols began? You put things in a certain place and they disappear into thin air—what could you imagine, except it was a hungry god?

And the kid was smart enough to figure out that if he needed to make stuff disappear, it might as well be something of Todd's. Amoral little dork.

"The first time I saw something appear in midair," said the elf, "it was broad daylight. I knew what it was—I'd been investigating worms for some time. It was a . . . hobby of mine. But I also knew that if people found out I had one in our neighborhood, I'd either be inundated with curiosity seekers, or plagued by pious people determined to sit around and see what the gods would give them, or I'd be arrested for witchcraft."

"Witchcraft? That's just superstition."

"Don't get superior with me. I've been studying your culture for years. On television you marry witches, but in real life you burn them. And if somebody in your world saw *me* plop out of the sky . . ."

"Which I just did."

". . . then what do you think would happen *here*?"

"Scientists would come and study the worm and—"

"You really are naive. No self-respecting scientist would come anywhere near something like this, because it would sound like pure tabloid journalism. They could lose their careers!"

"Is that what happened to you?" asked Todd. "Have you lost your career?"

"I don't have a career, exactly."

"You're not a scientist?"

"In our world, scientists are rare and they work alone."

Todd gave that the worst possible spin. "People think you're crazy and pay no attention to you."

"They'd think I was crazy and pay a *lot* of attention to me if I hadn't moved the anus."

It occurred to Todd that "moving the anus" could be rendered as "hauling ass," which he found amusing.

"Now look who's laughing," said the elf.

Todd got back to business. "You can *move* this thing."

"With enormous difficulty and great risk."

"So you could move it out of our closet. You didn't have to put it there!"

"I didn't put it in your closet. I moved it a hundred yards to a dense woods behind my house. I had no idea where it would go in *your* world. It moved a thousand miles. I couldn't plan its location here, and I'm not going to change it now. It happens to be well-hidden and convenient to a town with a decent library. It's perfect."

"Perfect for you. Really lousy for my mother and our whole family."

"I told you, that was not my fault." The elf sounded bored, which made Todd mad.

"Listen, you little runt, you get my mother back and then you get your worm out of our house and out of my yard!"

The elf was just as furious. "Listen yourself, you bug of a boy, don't give orders to a 'runt' who happens to be dense enough that I could reach into your chest with my bare hand and pull out your beating heart and stuff it into the worm's anus! You have 'suppository' written all over you."

There was a moment of silence while Todd realized that the elf was right. There was nothing Todd could do to threaten him; so it did no good to get angry or make demands. If he was going to get any help from the elf, he'd have to keep the conversation calm. So he said the first nonthreatening thing he could think of. "That's like what they did in *Temple of Doom*."

Exasperated, the elf said, "*What* is what *who* did? And where is the temple of doom?"

"It's a movie. An Indiana Jones movie. They pulled the beating heart out of their sacrificial victims."

"I don't have time to go to movies," said the elf. "I don't have time to talk to ignorant, pugnacious boys."

"What does pugnacious even mean?"

"It means that I apparently have become much more fluent in your ridiculously misspelled and underinflected language than you will ever be."

"Well, you're a scientist and I'm not." And then something else dawned on Todd. If the worm had been attracted to Todd, then it must also have been attracted to this guy and for maybe the same reason. "You're a space traveler."

"No I'm not."

"You travel between worlds."

"But not through space. My world doesn't exist in your space. No light from our sun can ever possibly reach this planet. You cannot board any kind of imaginable spacecraft and get from there to here no matter how long you flew. I am not a space traveler."

"You get from one planet to another. And you didn't have to build anything or get good grades in any subject or anything at all. It was just dumb luck, but you got to visit an alien world!"

"From your tone of voice, I suspect you're about to say, 'No fair!'"

"Well, why should *you* get to do it, and I can't!"

"Oh, you can—if you're stupid enough to reach into the throat of the worm and get sucked through and pooped out into a world where you're like a kind of atmospheric diarrhea."

"So what does that make you, interplanetary constipation or something?"

"It makes me sick of talking to you. I've got work to accomplish." The elf started walking away.

"Hey!" called Todd.

The elf didn't pause.

"What's your name!" Todd yelled.

The elf turned around. "You don't need my name!"

Why not? Did it give Todd some kind of magical power? Todd remembered a fairy tale about secret names that his mother used to read to them. "Then I'll call you Rumpelstiltskin!"

To his surprise, the elf came back, looking very angry. "What did you call me?"

"Rumpelstiltskin?" said Todd, remembering the heart-grabbing threat.

"Don't you ever call me that again."

Which almost made Todd call him that twenty times in a row. But no, he had to have this guy's cooperation if he was going to get his mother back. "Then tell me your name."

The elf stood there, irritably considering. "Eggo," he finally said.

Of all things. "Like the waffles?"

"Like *me*. My *name* is Eggo. And yes, your mother already explained about frozen toaster waffles. In my language it doesn't mean anything of the kind."

"What *does* it mean?"

"It means me, I told you! Just like Todd means you. It's a name, not a word."

The elf—Eggo—turned around and headed out across the back yard. Todd almost laughed, his gait was so ducklike as he swung those big shoes around each other so he didn't trip on his own feet. But it wasn't funny. Eggo was doing what he had to in order not to sink into the earth; what was Mother doing, to keep from dissolving into mist on the other side?

Todd went back into the house, determined to do something. He didn't know what, yet, but he had to act, stir things up, change things so that somehow Mom would come back and life would get back to normal. Or maybe it would get even worse, maybe people would die, but isn't that what they already believed happened to Mom? They'd already been through a death and now there was a chance to undo it.

And Todd knew that it was going to be him who did the undoing. Not because he was the smartest or strongest one in the family but because he had decided to. Because he was going to go through the worm and get Mom home. He was going to travel to another world. It's what he was born for.

He couldn't say that to anybody or they'd think he was crazy.

Not like seeing elves materialize in the back yard . . .

Dad was still asleep, as usual on a Saturday morning. Jared was up, but he hadn't left his room yet. Todd went in and sat beside the little sorted-out piles of Legos that Jared was drawing from to build his . . . what?

"It's like an amusement park ride," said Jared.

"It looks like a skyscraper."

"I put little Lego guys into this hole at the top and they bounce around inside and pop out here."

"That's not an amusement park, it's a machine for killing people."

"It's not for killing people," Jared said vehemently—but quietly, so Dad wouldn't wake up. "People are perfectly OK when they come through the other side. They are *alive*."

He's building the stupid worm, thought Todd. "You're right," said Todd. "They're perfectly all right when they come out the other end."

Jared looked up at him suspiciously.

"I met your elf," said Todd.

"There's no elf," said Jared.

"All my stuff you put through the mouth in the closet," said Todd. "By the way, thanks for stealing my Hot Wheels and all my other crap."

"I didn't steal anything."

"Mother's alive," said Todd. "I know it now."

But Jared didn't look relieved or happy or anything. In fact, he looked panicky. Only when Todd felt a strong hand on his shoulder did he realize that Dad must have come into the room and heard him.

Dad had never handled Todd roughly before, not like this. The grip on his shoulder was harsh—it hurt. And he dragged Todd so quickly out of the room that he could barely keep his feet under him. "Hey!" Todd yelled. "Hey, hey, what're you—"

But by then they were in Dad's room and the door slammed shut behind them. "What the *hell* do you think you're doing?" said Dad. He practically threw Todd onto the bed. Then he leaned over him, one hand on either side of him, his face angry and only about a foot away from Todd's. "Do you think it's funny to try to make your brother believe that all his childhood fantasies are true?"

"Dad," said Todd.

"It's all a joke to you, is that it?" Dad said, his voice a harsh whisper. "All that I've done, trying to make life normal again, you think it's really clever to undo it and make your brother think that your mother is still alive somewhere. Do you know what that would mean? That your mother *wants* to be away from us, that she *chose* to leave us like that. You think that's *better* than believing she's dead? Well you're wrong."

"It's not about believing anything," said Todd quietly, reasonably, trying to calm Father down.

And it worked, at least a little. Dad stopped looming over him and sat on the bed beside him. "What is it, then, Todd? Why are you telling your brother that he should believe his mother is alive?"

"Because she is, Dad," said Todd.

Dad turned away from him, slumped over, leaning on his knees. "It never ends."

"Dad," said Todd, "I didn't believe it, either. I thought she was dead until this very exact morning when I found out the truth. Something I saw with my own eyes. Dad, I'm not crazy and I'm not joking."

Dad was now leaning his forehead on his hands. "What do you think crazy people say, Todd?"

"They say there's a worm that passes between two worlds, and the mouth of it is in Jared's closet and it sucks things out of our world and drops them into another. And Mother's there, only she can't get back because the rules of physics are different in that place, and she's not as dense as we are here, so she can't hold on to things and she doesn't know how to find the mouth on the other side and the jerk who's studying the thing, the guy who moved the mouth of the worm into Jared's closet, he doesn't care about anything except his stupid science. And I can't go there myself and get Mom back if you don't help."

By the time Todd was through, Dad had sat up and was staring at him. "Yes, Todd," he finally said. "That's exactly what crazy people say."

"But I can prove it," said Todd.

Dad buried his face in his hands again. "God help us," he murmured.

"Dad, what if there's one chance in a million that I'm not crazy. Do you love me enough to give me that chance? Will you come and *look*?"

Dad nodded behind his hands. "Yeah, I'll look." He stood up. "Show me whatever you've got to show me, Todd."

Todd knew perfectly well that Dad still thought he was crazy. But he was at least willing to give him a chance. So Todd led the way back into Jared's room.

Jared was sitting on his bed, pressed into the corner of the room, holding a little Lego guy in one hand and gnawing on a finger. Not the nail, the whole finger in his mouth, chewing on it like it was gum.

"Get your hand out of your mouth, Jared, and come over here and help me," said Todd.

Jared didn't move.

"I've got to show Dad the worm's mouth," said Todd. "And you're the one who knows exactly where it is."

Jared didn't move.

"I can't believe you'd do this, Todd," said Dad. His voice was full of grief. "Jared's made so much progress, and now look."

"Listen to me, both of you! Mom's still alive on the other end of this thing! Stop trying to solve things, Dad, stop trying to make sense of it and just *watch*."

Todd picked up Jared's Lego thing, his representation of the worm, and took it to the closet and flung open the door.

He couldn't see anything at all like that slice of air out in the backyard. He walked back and forth in front of the closet, trying to get the right angle. Then he went to the drapes and opened them, letting sunlight flood in. It didn't help.

"Todd," said Dad.

"Jared," said Todd angrily, "if you don't help me, Dad's going to think we're both crazy and we'll *never* get Mom back. Now get off your butt and help me find it!"

Jared didn't move.

Todd took the Lego thing and stepped right into the closet and began waving his hand around, thrusting here and there, trying to accidentally find the hole in the air.

"Stop it," said Jared.

"What do you care whether I fall in or not?" said Todd. "Of course, if you guys aren't helping, I'll fall through just like Mom did, and I'll be just as helpless as she is on the other side, and then you'll lose us both, but at least Dad will know I'm not crazy!" Todd stopped and looked at his father. "Only now things will get really ugly, because the cops will want to know what happened to your son Todd, and they'll begin to get curious about how *two* people from the same family both disappeared under mysterious circumstances. I watch *Law & Order,* Dad. You'll be the prime suspect. And then they'll think *you're* crazy, unless *you* fall through the hole to prove it to them. And then Jared will be an orphan and there'll be some cops who are thrown out of the police force because they insist that they saw this man—this mass-murder suspect—disappear into thin air in his son's closet. Is that how you want this to go?"

Father was looking halfway between grief-stricken and terrified. But Jared had gotten off his bed and was padding across the floor, stepping over Lego piles. He took the Lego structure out of Todd's hands. Todd let him.

"Give me something," said Jared.

"Like what?"

"Your shoe."

"Why can't you use something of your own for once?" said Todd.

"I can't use my own stuff, because then it grabs hold of my hand and sucks me in."

"You mean it knows who *owns* things?"

"When I throw your crap in it doesn't grab my hand," said Jared.

"Then let *me* throw *your* crap in."

"Do you want Dad to see this or not?" demanded Jared.

Todd peeled his shoe off, but he didn't give it to Jared. "Shoes are expensive, in case you didn't know," he said. He rolled his dirty white sock off. "Socks are cheap."

"They also stink," said Jared. "You're such a pig, you never wash your clothes, you just wear them forever." But he took the sock and ducked into the closet—ducked *under* something—and then shoved Todd out. "Both of you watch," he said.

Then he held the sock out between his fingers and began swinging it back and forth like a floppy pendulum.

And then, on one of the outward swings, it stopped and didn't come back. It just hung there in the air, Jared holding on to the top of the sock, and something else holding on to the toe end.

"Now it's got it," said Jared. "Watch close because it's quick."

Jared let go. The sock disappeared.

But Todd had indeed been watching closely, and even though it happened fast, he saw that the sock was sucked into something by the toe.

Jared was pressed up against the closet doorframe. He was still scared of the thing. Smart kid.

"Get out of the closet, Jared," said Dad. His voice was soft. He was scared, too.

Jared sidled out.

Dad looked from Jared to Todd, back and forth. Then he settled on Todd. "Why didn't you tell me before?"

"Because up till this morning I thought the kid was wacked out."

"Thanks," said Jared.

"You mean you never saw him do this?" said Dad.

"Did it look like I knew where the thing was?" asked Todd.

"I've put things in that closet hundreds of times," said Dad.

"You have to come at it from the side," said Jared. "And kind of slow."

"And Mother did that?"

"She was trying to prove to me that there was nothing there. I told her how it worked, and so she was going to prove to me that it was just a nightmare. I begged her not to do it. I cried, I screamed at her, I threw things at her to get her to stop."

"Jared," said Dad, "that would just convince her that it was all the more important to prove it to you."

"It got her," said Jared. "I tried to pull her back but it got her whole arm and shoulder and her head so she couldn't even talk to me and then it just grabbed the rest of her, all at once, and ripped her leg right out of my hands." Jared was crying now. "I told you and told you but you didn't believe me and Todd finally said to stop talking about it because you'd think I was crazy."

Dad held Jared against him, patting his shoulder, letting him have his cry. He looked at Todd. "What happened this morning? What convinced you that it was real?"

So Todd told Dad all about Eggo the superdense scientist elf with duckfoot shoes, which sounded crazier the more he talked. He had to keep stopping and reminding Dad about the sock that disappeared, and half the time he was really reminding himself that this insane thing was real.

"I don't know what to make of all this," said Dad. "I don't know what to do. We can't tell this to the cops."

"We *could*," said Todd. "We could demonstrate it just like Jared did. I've got a lot of socks. But I don't think it would help. They'd just take over, they'd throw us out of the house and bring in a bunch of scientists but then *we'd* never get Mom back. Cause I don't care about studying this thing, I just want to go through it and get Mom."

"Not a chance," said Dad. "If anyone goes, I go."

"Dad," said Todd. "Think about it a minute. If *you* go, then there's no adult here in the house. Just me and Jared. Somebody's going to notice when you don't show up at work. They'll come here and find out you're gone."

"I'll come right back."

"Did *Mom* come right back?" said Todd. "No, because time flows differently there, it's only been a *week* for her, the guy said. So if you're gone even a few hours, that's days and weeks for us. So you're just as stuck as Mom is, and Jared and I are in foster homes somewhere far away from here while the cops try to figure out who murdered you and Mom because there's no chance they'll listen to two crazy kids, right?"

"So there's nothing we can do."

"I can go," said Todd.

"Not a chance," said Dad. "What can you do that I *can't* do?"

"You can cover up my absence," said Todd. "You can say I'm visiting Aunt Heather and Uncle Peace on their hippie commune which doesn't have a phone. You can say it's therapy because I'm still so messed up about Mom's death."

"That still doesn't get you *or* Mom back from . . . that other place."

"Right," said Todd. "But as long as you're *here,* at the house, you can help us. Because what is Mom's problem? She can't find the mouth on the other side so she can come through it. Eggo knows where it is, he comes through it all the time. So maybe it's in some place where she can't go. Maybe it's inside some building or in a public street where Eggo doesn't want her to be seen. Or maybe he *wants* to keep her captive so he just won't tell her."

"And you think *you* can find it?" asked Dad.

"No," said Todd. "I think you can move it and then show us where it's at."

"Move it?"

"Eggo moved the worm's anus on his side, and it moved the mouth of it into Jared's closet. So if you move the anus on *this* side, the mouth on *that* side should move, too."

"Then neither you nor Mom nor this Eggo person will know where it is," said Dad. "I can't believe I'm talking about moving some interstellar worm's ass."

"It's right out there by the garden hose," said Todd. "You give the thing an enema."

"What?" asked Dad.

"You stick the garden hose in and turn it on full blast."

"What makes you think that will work? It only digests in one direction."

"Eggo threatened to stuff my heart into the anus," said Todd. "You must be able to jam things through that way."

"Unless he was just making a stupid threat that wasn't actually possible."

"Then let's test it," said Todd.

A few minutes later, Dad was in his gym clothes instead of his pajamas and they stood in the back yard. Todd was afraid that he wouldn't be able to find the spot again, but by standing exactly where he had been when Eggo came through, he could see the very, very slight shimmering in the air. He made both Dad and Jared stand in that spot so they could find it. Then he went and got the garden hose and turned it on, just a trickle, and held the hose up so the water was running back down the green shaft of it.

He took it to the shimmering slice of air and tried to push it through. But it was just like waving it around in the air. It met no resistance, it found no aperture. He was just watering the lawn.

Then he remembered that Jared said you had to approach it from exactly the right angle. He tried to remember which direction Eggo's naked body had come through, and moved so he was standing at exactly the same angle from the hole. Then, very slowly, he extended the hose, holding it just behind the metal end where the water came out.

He felt just a little resistance, just *there,* but when he pushed harder, the hose slid aside and it was just air again.

Exact angle of approach. How much was Eggo's body tilted when it came through?

Todd brought his hand down and pushed the hose upward toward the spot where he had met resistance before. Now it felt solid. Real resistance. "I'm there," he said.

He tried to push the hose in. It went a little way, and to his surprise the water started squirting back at him, like when somebody covers the end of the hose with his thumb.

"Yow!" shouted Jared. "Cool!"

"You got it," said Dad.

"I can't push it through," said Todd. "I'm not strong enough."

"Or it only goes one way," said Jared.

"Help me!" Todd said to Dad.

A moment later, Dad was beside him, gripping Todd's hands over the hose. With his strength added on—or maybe entirely because of his strength, because Todd was certainly no strongman—the end of the hose suddenly moved and . . . disappeared.

So did the water. Nothing trickled back down the hose. The water was flowing somewhere else.

"Enema," said Jared. "Cool."

Dad let go.

"No!" said Todd. "We've got to move it."

"Where?" said Dad. "How?"

"We've got the hose jammed into it, don't we? Let's use it like a handle and shove it somewhere else."

"Where to?"

"I don't know," said Todd. "I don't think it matters. Eggo couldn't predict where it would move on *our* side, he could only move it where he wanted on *his* side. So let's move it where we want it and let the other side go wherever it goes."

"Maybe thousands of miles."

"What else can we do?" said Todd. "Wherever it is on that side, Dad, Mom hasn't been able to get to it. So we have to move it, and then when I get there, Mom and I have to find it."

"But how?" asked Dad. "If you and Mom are . . . misty or whatever . . ."

"Dad," said Todd. "It's probably going to be pretty easy to find. There's water coming out of it."

"Or fog," said Dad. "If things are mistier there."

"Water, fog—*something's* coming out of it right now. So let's move the thing, if we can."

It was only hard because the hose was so flexible. Twice when they tried to move the thing sideways, the hose slipped out, squirting them for a moment before it settled back to being just a trickle. Finally Dad had the idea of using the handle of the rake from the tool shed, and that worked.

He shoved it in beside the hose. It was rigid, and they were able to move the thing ten yards across the yard to the shed. The hose slid out as they went, spurting water for a moment when it did.

The shed door was still open, so they easily slid the worm's anus inside.

"Don't pull the rake out yet," said Dad. "Hold it in place."

He ran to the house and came back out with the digital camera. He took pictures of the hose from several angles. "I don't want to run the risk of not being able to get the hose back into it."

It was ten more minutes after that, but Dad got the printouts taped up on the inside walls of the shed. "OK," he said. "Pull out the rake."

It was a lot easier in that direction. *Out* was the direction that the anus wanted things to go.

Dad was all for putting the hose right back in, but Todd said no. "Think about it," said Todd. "I'm not even there yet. And time moves a lot slower there. If we start pumping water, somebody over there is going to notice it. Because it *better* be noticeable in a big way, or Mom and I will never find it."

"They've probably already noticed it," said Dad. "Even that trickle of water wasn't nothing. And what if somebody saw the rake handle?"

"It wasn't all that much water and it wasn't all that long," said Todd. "So give me time to get through and find Mom. Give me time to explain things to her. Eggo said it was hard to talk. Even if it only takes me ten minutes, how long is that *here,* where time goes so much quicker?"

"I see," said Dad. "Can we figure it out?"

"Eggo said maybe it fluctuates. I don't know. We don't want to wait too long, because what if a storm comes up and blows Mom and me to smithereens? So I think maybe . . . tomorrow? It's a Sunday."

"Too soon," said Jared. "Take your time. What if Mom isn't right there? What if it takes you a long time even to find her?"

"Then when?"

"Next week," said Dad. "A week from now. I can tell the school you're visiting your aunt and uncle, though we'll skip the hippie commune part. And next Saturday morning, we come out and give this thing a full-blast enema."

"Four years," said Jared. "Well, four years and four months. So that's two hundred and . . . twenty-five weeks. Two-twenty-five to one."

"You're doing all this math in your head?" said Todd. If *Todd* could've done that, he might've been able to become an astronaut.

"Sh," said Jared. "One week is 168 hours. Divide that by 225. That's about three-quarters of an hour. Forty-five minutes."

"I don't think it's that precise," said Todd.

"Even if I'm off by double," said Jared, "that gives you somewhere between twenty minutes and an hour and a half."

"You did that in your head?" asked Dad. "Why do your arithmetic grades suck so badly?"

Jared shrugged. "They make me do all these stupid problems and 'show my work.' What do I put down? 'Think think think'?"

"I don't know if that's enough time," said Todd. "I don't know how long it will take."

"It also means," said Dad, "if we run the water for 225 minutes, it will only be *one* minute on the other side."

"Yeah," said Todd, "but it'll mean that in one minute, 225 minutes' worth of water will come through."

"Man," said Jared. "That worm's gonna be doing some serious puking."

"What I'm saying," said Todd, "is that it'll be noticeable."

"And what I'm saying," said Dad, "is that if it takes you half an hour to get to the worm's mouth, we've got to be running that hose for nearly a week."

"Are you worried about the water bill?" said Todd.

"No," said Dad. "Just thinking that in a week, a lot of things might go wrong on our end."

"Dad," said Todd, "so many things can go wrong on both ends that it'll be a miracle if this works at all. But we can't leave Mom there without even trying, can we?"

A few minutes later, Todd was standing in Jared's closet. Stark naked. No point in having his clothes just disappear or whatever they did if you tried to go through the worm wearing them.

"Just make sure you have clothes waiting for Mom and me when we come through in the shed," said Todd.

"You're going to see Mom naked?" said Jared, like it was too weird to imagine.

"It's that or never see her again as long as any of us live," said Todd.

"Mom won't mind," said Dad. "She's in great shape, she kind of likes to show off." He laughed, but it was also kind of a sob.

"Here goes nothing," said Todd.

He reached out his hand.

"Higher," said Jared.

And then the mouth had him. It wasn't like something grabbing him. It was more like getting sucked up against the vacuum cleaner hose. Only instead of sticking to it, he got sucked right in.

He thought he'd come right out the other end, but he didn't. There was time. Like Jonah being stuck in the belly of the whale long enough to call on God to get him out. Only it wasn't a whale, was it, or a big fish, or whatever. It was a worm, like this one. Jonah gets tossed overboard right into the worm's mouth and then it takes him a while to find the mouth on the other side and then he comes through and he's on the beach. He's got to make sense of it somehow, right? So he tells people he was swallowed by a big fish and then God made the fish throw him up on the shore.

That thought took him only a minute. Or a second. Or an hour. And then Todd got distracted by what he was seeing. Stars. All of them distant, but shifting rapidly. As if he were moving through them at an incredible speed. Faster than light. No spaceship around him, no spacesuit, no way to breathe, only he realized that he didn't need to breathe, he could just look and see space all around him until a particular star up ahead didn't move off to the side, it came right at him, getting bigger and brighter, and then he dodged toward a planet and rushed toward the planet's surface, going way too fast, reentry was going to burn him up.

He didn't burn up. He didn't slow down, either. One moment he was plunging toward the planet's surface and the next moment, without any sensation of stopping, he was being squeezed headfirst out of a tight space with waves of peristaltic action. Like a bunch of crap. He could see the ground below him. He couldn't get his arms free. He was going to drop down and land on his face.

And with one last spasm of the worm's colon, that's exactly what happened.

It didn't hurt. He barely felt it. He barely felt anything.

He gathered his legs under him and got his hands in place, like a pushup, only the grassy ground felt like it was hardly there. Or maybe like his fingers weren't there. Then he realized that the bushes around him weren't bushes, they were trees. He was a giant here. A stark-naked, insubstantial giant.

He felt a breeze blowing. And on the breeze, a distant voice. Calling his name. "Todd," it was saying. And "no, no," it said.

He looked around, hoping it was Mother, hoping she was off in the distance somewhere. It *was* Mother, but she was not distant. She was entangled in the branches of some trees, not touching the ground at all.

"Hold on, Todd!" she called. It looked like she was shouting with all her strength, but the sound was barely audible. She couldn't be more than twenty feet away. Well, twenty feet compared to their body size—a lot farther compared to the size of the trees.

Hold on, she had said, and now he realized that the breeze was tugging at him, making him drift. He was still in kneeling position, but he was sliding across the ground.

Mother had the right idea, obviously. Get entangled in the branches. Get *caught* so the wind couldn't carry him like a stray balloon.

It took a while to get the knack of it. To move *through* the branches, heedless of how they poked into his skin. It didn't hurt, really. More like tickling sometimes, and sometimes a vague pressure. He figured the tickling was twigs and leaves, the pressure the heavier, more substantial, less-yielding branches.

Carefully, slowly, he made his way among the interlacing branches of the trees until he was close enough to Mother that neither of them had to shout, though their voices were still breathy and soft. "Don't eat anything," she warned him.

"How could I anyway?" he said.

"You can," she said. "And you can drink. But don't do it. It starts to change you. It makes you more solid."

"But isn't that good?"

"We could never go home," said Mother. "That's what *he* says, anyway. If I ever want to get home, I can't eat or drink."

"You haven't eaten or drunk anything in a week?" asked Todd.

"What are you doing here?" she said. "Why did you come through the hole in the closet?"

"Why did *you*?" he said. "Jared warned you."

"How could I believe him?" She started to cry. "Now we're both trapped here."

"Mom," said Todd. "Two things. First, we have a plan. Dad and Jared are going to help us find the worm's mouth."

"Worm's mouth?" she asked.

"And the second thing. It's been four years."

"No," she said. "A week. It's been a week."

"Four years," repeated Todd. "Look at me. I'm older. I'm bigger. Jared is, too. Four years we thought you were dead."

"A week," she murmured. "Oh, my poor children. My poor husband."

"Mom, you've got to be thirsty. You can't last a week without any water."

"I don't get as thirsty as I thought I would. But yes, I'm getting very weak now. I expected—I thought that pretty soon I'll just let go and blow away."

"Don't let go," said Todd. "Just hold on until they turn on the hose." Then he told her about the plan.

It was the longest week of Jared's life. He kept wanting to go out and check the worm's butt to make sure it was there in the shed. Or sit and stare at the mouth in the closet. But he knew if he did that, he'd start wanting to throw things in it. Or go through it himself so he could see Mom. It wasn't fair that Todd got to see her first, when Jared was the one who knew about it all along. But I saw her last, Jared told himself. That wasn't fair, either. And if I accidentally or on purpose go through the mouth, who'll help Dad? Who'll turn the hose on?

Who'll keep watch in case the elf comes back?

Because what Jared knew about the elf was this: He wasn't nice. He didn't want Mom to come back. Hadn't Jared begged him to bring her back, the first time he saw him after Mom went through? And the elf just shoved him away. It hurt so bad. The elf was so *strong*.

What if the elf came back and went through the mouth and saw Todd and Mom and realized what was happening and . . . and *killed* them? He might. He was selfish and cruel, Jared knew that about him. He didn't care about anybody. Oh, he asked questions, all the time, but he never answered any, he wouldn't tell anything. "You wouldn't understand anyway, you're just a child," he said. Well, children understand things, Jared wanted to scream at him. But he never did. Because if he got too demanding, if he got *mad,* the elf just left. And what if the elf shoved him again? He didn't want the elf to shove him. It hurt, deep inside, when he did that.

So Jared went through the days with Dad. Without Todd there, Jared and Dad had to do all kinds of jobs. He hadn't realized how hard Todd worked, all the things he did. Or how lonely it got without Todd there to gripe at and play with and yell at and fight over the television remote with.

He had thought all these years that it would be so nice if anyone would just believe him. But he hadn't thought through what that might mean. Believe him and then what? Well, then they would *do* something about it. But he thought it would be like the government would do it, the police, the fire department. Somebody official who already knew all about everything and they could just say, Oh, lost your mother in one of *those* things, of course, happens all the time, give us a minute . . . there! There's your mom!

But of course it couldn't work that way. Nobody knew anything about this. Nobody could just fix it. They had to do it themselves. So now the question was: Would Mom come back? Or had they just lost Todd, too? And if Todd couldn't come back, either, would the cops think Dad had killed him and Mom both and lock him up and put Jared in foster care? A part of him wished they had just left things alone. Losing Mom was bad. But losing everybody else, too, wouldn't exactly make anything better. If he had just kept it to himself. If he had just refused to put that sock into the monster's mouth when Todd told him to.

If . . .

Then it would be Jared's fault if Mom never came back. Even thinking like this, wasn't that the same is wishing Mom would never come home? I'm selfish and evil, Jared thought. I don't even deserve to have a mother.

And then, underneath all the wondering and worrying and blaming, there was this, like a constant drumbeat: hope. Mom was coming home. Todd would get her and Jared and Dad would show them where the mouth was on the other side by hosing the worm's butt, and they'd all be together again and it would be partly because Jared knew and showed them and helped make it happen.

He nearly flunked three different tests that week and the teachers were quite concerned at his sudden lapse in performance. It was hard to concentrate on anything. Hard to think that their stupid baby easy meaningless tests were worth taking. Hard even to listen to their sympathetic blabbing. "Is everything all right at home?" My brother just got swallowed up by the same monster that ate my mom, but we've got a plan, so, "Everything's fine." "Has anyone *done* anything to you?" Jared knew what they were asking, but apart from the worm in the closet eating his mom and his brother, Jared had to say that nobody had done anything to *him* at all.

And then it was Friday and he got to go home from school and fix himself some food and stay away from the closet because that would make him crazy, to sit and stare at the thing. Nothing was ever coming out of it, and nobody except the stupid elf was ever going into it again. There was nothing to see.

Except there he was when Dad got home, the closet door open and Jared sitting on the floor just looking at it, remembering Mom's look of panic as the thing caught hold of her and then how she looked, just her left shoulder and the rest of her body still in the closet, but not her head, not her right shoulder or arm, because they were going, and how Jared lunged and caught her but then she was torn right out of his arms. Like the thing had to get her in two swallows.

In two *bites*.

"Whatcha lookin' at?" Dad asked. Softly, which meant he didn't think anything was really funny.

"It didn't take Mom all at once," said Jared. "What if it bit her in half? What if she's dead and Todd can't ever bring her home?"

Dad took a slow breath. "Then Todd will tell us that when he gets back."

"And if he never comes back?"

"Then we'll move away from here."

"And leave somebody else to find it?"

"Jared, what can we do? Nuke the house? We didn't make this problem. Especially not you. It was done *to* us. And we're doing our best to undo it." He came and sat beside Jared. "Things can get a lot worse. Or they can get a lot better. But at least we're doing something, and we're doing the best thing we could think of, and what more can anybody do?"

Jared didn't answer. There wasn't an answer.

"Let's have dinner and watch a DVD tonight," said Dad. "What about a Harry Potter movie? What about all of them?"

"No magic," said Jared, shuddering in spite of himself. "No crap about people turning invisible or going back in time or three-headed dogs or vines that choke you or chessmen that try to kill you or teachers with a face on the back of their head."

"Charlotte's Web?"

"Dad, that's for kids."

So they watched *The Dirty Dozen* and when they threw those grenades down the shafts and the German officers in the bomb shelter were panicking and screaming, Jared felt a moment of breathless panic himself, but then he thought: At least the good guys were *doing* something, even though some of them were going to get killed in the process, even though some of them would never get home.

They were saving the world, maybe. Or helping to. We're just saving Mom.

But to Jared, that was better than saving the world. He didn't care about the world.

Saturday morning, Jared was up before the sun. He wanted to wake Dad, but he waited. And not long. Dad usually slept in on Saturday, but today he joined Jared at the breakfast table, pouring out Cheerios and stirring a couple of spoonfuls of brown sugar into the bowl and eating them, all without milk.

"That's so gross," said Jared.

"Better than watching the milk turn grey with sugar," said Dad.

"Do we have to wait till, like, noon or something?" asked Jared.

"There's a lot of oat bran in this stuff," said Dad. "I think I'll need to use the bathroom before I can go anywhere or do anything."

"Yeah, and you'll read a whole book in there."

"Reading, the best laxative." Dad said it in his Lee Marvin voice, which was a pretty good imitation.

"You might as well stick a plug in it," said Jared. "When you're reading, you never let fly."

"I can't believe you're speaking of the bodily functions of your father." This time Dad was doing Charles Bronson. It was nothing like Charles Bronson, actually, but somehow Jared knew that was who he was doing.

"We're giving an interstellar worm an enema today, Dad. I got rectums on my mind."

And Dad went into Groucho Marx. "I don't let anybody say my kid's got poop for brains."

"Poop?" said Jared.

"Got to get used to saying 'poop,' now that Mom's coming back."

"Is she, Dad?"

Dad's Groucho Marx grin didn't fade, but his voice came out like W. C. Fields. "I'll never lie to you, my boy. Now finish your breakfast, you bother me."

"That's all you got? Lee Marvin, a half-assed Charles Bronson, Groucho Marx, and W. C. Fields?"

"I did three others that you didn't catch," said Dad. "And besides, I had Cheerios in my mouth."

"Oh!" said Jared, doing the old family joke associated with Cheerios. "O-o-o-o-oh."

Which would have been the cue for Dad to launch into singing "We're off to see the wizard, the wonderful Wizard of Oh's," but instead he reached across the table and covered Jared's hand with his own. "I can't really eat much this morning, can you?"

"You see anything in my mouth?" said Jared.

Dad pushed back from the table. "I've gotta see a man about a hose."

Jared followed him out into the back yard. Dad unlocked the back shed and set down the clothes he had brought for Todd and Mom, while Jared unspooled the hose and dragged it across the lawn. Of course it got heavier the farther he pulled it, but it didn't slow him down. Quite the contrary—by the time he reached the shed, he was running.

"Careful," said Dad. "Let's do this methodically and get it right."

Jared watched as Dad found the gap in the air, following the pictures taped to the wall. Then he pushed it in, and kept pushing, and pushing. "Get me more slack, Jared."

Jared went back to the hose reel and pulled it until it was stretched tight. He could see Dad back in the shed, pushing more and more of it into the hole in the air, so it looked for all the world as if it were disappearing.

"It's pushing back," said Dad. "It wants to get it out."

"Wouldn't *you*?" asked Jared.

"Turn the water on. Full blast. Every bit of pressure the city can give us."

Jared turned the handle, turned and turned until it couldn't open any more. He could see Dad bracing his back against the shelves, pushing forward against the worm's efforts to expel the enema.

Jared walked closer to the shed, to ask whether any water was coming back or whether it was all getting through, when he saw the elf walking toward him across the back lawn.

Careful not to speed up, Jared continued toward the shed, but instead of talking or even letting himself look at what Dad was doing, he closed the door, loudly saying as he did so, "Hello, Eggo. Why didn't you tell me that was your name?" With any luck, Dad would realize that they didn't exactly want the elf to know what they were doing.

"You never asked," said Eggo. He headed toward the sideyard fence beyond where the worm's anus used to be and started stripping off his clothes in order to stow them back in the box. Only when he was down to his pants did he turn around and look at Jared, who was now leaning against the corner of the house, looking as nonchalant as he could.

"What are you watching?" he asked.

"All these years I see you, you never tell me anything. One time you talk to Todd, and suddenly you're full of information."

"You were a baby."

"I was, but I'm not now."

"So . . . what do you want to know?" Eggo returned to stripping off his pants. He was buck naked now, stuffing everything into a plastic bag before putting it into the box.

"When are you going to get Mom back to us?"

"I didn't take your mommy away from you," said Eggo. "It's none of my business."

"You're like half a worm," said Jared. "All asshole, no heart."

Eggo reburied the box and stood back up. By Jared's rough guess, it had been about five minutes since he started the water running. That was three hundred seconds. So in the other place, it wouldn't even have been running for two full seconds yet.

Eggo was looking at him. "What are you doing?"

"Math in my head," said Jared.

"I mean with the hose. The water's on, I can hear it, but you've got it flowing into the shed."

"Through the shed and out the back window," said Jared. "It's the only way to reach the very back of the yard without buying a longer hose."

But Eggo wasn't buying it. He was striding toward the shed now.

"It's none of your business!" cried Jared. "Haven't you done enough? Why don't you leave us alone!"

Eggo turned back to face Jared. "Everything's my business if I decide it is," he said. "What are you hiding in there?"

The elf glanced toward the place where there had once been a shimmering slit in the air. He walked toward it, searching. He waved his hand. "What have you done?" he said. He whirled and faced Jared. "You moved it, you little moron! Do you know what you've done? I'll never find it! It'll take months!"

"Good!" shouted Jared. "I hope it takes you *years,* because that'll be *centuries* here, and I won't ever have to see your ugly face and your ugly butt again!"

The elf's face was turning red as he strode toward Jared. His hand rose up as if to smack at him—to swat him into oblivion, as if he were a fly. But then the elf looked at the hose again and then at the shed and then he took off running straight toward it.

"Dad!" shouted Jared. "Don't try to fight him! He'll kill you!"

Eggo flung the door of the shed open—flung it so hard that it ripped from the hinges and sailed like a frisbee halfway across the lawn. Jared saw that Dad must have understood what was happening, because instead of holding on to the hose, he was gripping the chain saw and pulling the cord. It roared to life just as Eggo reached for the hose.

"Just how dense do you think you are!" shouted Dad.

Eggo backed off a little, but he was holding the hose now, pulling it out. "You moved it! You can't move it!"

"We already did," yelled Jared, "and you'll never get it back exactly where it was!"

"You're drowning my city!" shouted the elf.

"You kept my mother there when you could have brought her home!"

By now Dad had stepped out of the shed and was approaching Eggo. "Drop the hose!" he yelled. "I don't want to see how much damage this can do!"

Eggo roared and smacked at the chain saw with his left hand. It flew out of Dad's grasp, staggering him; but the elf came away from the encounter with his hand bleeding. No, spurting blood.

The deadman switch on the chain saw shut it down, now that nobody was gripping the handle. The sudden silence was deafening.

"What have you done to me!" wailed Eggo.

"You want me to call 911?" asked Jared.

"Drop the hose," said Dad.

"I'll bleed to death!"

"Drop the hose." Dad was picking up the chain saw again.

Eggo stamped his left foot repeatedly, spinning him in a circle as he howled and gripped his bleeding hand. It was as if he was screwing his right foot into the ground, and indeed it was already in the lawn up to the knee.

"You *are* Rumpelstiltskin, you little jerk," Jared said. "You told Todd that you weren't!"

"We're going to get them home, and you're not going to stop us," said Dad. The chain saw roared to life.

With a final howl, Eggo pulled his right foot out of the ground and ran into the house. Not through any of the doors—he leapt for the wall and his body hurtled through, leaving torn vinyl siding and broken studs and peeled-back drywall behind him. Jared ran to the gap in the wall in time to see Eggo dive through the worm's mouth.

He turned around to see Dad already back at the shed, pushing the hose back up into the worm's anus.

"What if he hurts them?" asked Jared. "He's gone back and he'll find them."

"We can only hope they're already on their way."

"The water only started a couple of seconds ago, in that world."

"Then I hope they aren't wasting any time," said Dad. "What else can we do?"

Once Mom understood what Todd was talking about, he began to ask her questions. She didn't know any answers. "If I try to go anywhere, either the wind starts lifting me or people see me and start throwing rocks or . . . screaming, or calling for other people to come and look and . . . I'm naked."

Todd knew perfectly well she was naked. But to his surprise, it didn't *feel* like she was naked. She was so misty that it was as if she were wearing the leaves behind her—he saw them better than he saw her.

"But you have to know where he comes from."

"He comes from the same hole in the air that we came through," said Mom.

"Then where does he *go*?"

"How can I tell, from here in the leaves?"

"I mean where does he *head*? Which way? Uphill? Downhill?"

"I'm sorry," she said. "Downhill. I just didn't—I can't think. It's like my mind is fading along with my body. I think bits of me have been blowing away. I'm being shredded. I'm leaving pieces of me in the tree. Todd, I don't even know if I *can* go home. Maybe if I get back there I'll die."

"You'll have a better chance there than here. Can you hold my hand?"

"I can't hold anything," she said.

But when he held out his hand to her, she took it. And he felt her hand in his. He could hold on to her. Better than he could hold on to the branches, because she wasn't so hard and unyielding; he didn't feel as if his body would tear itself apart if he held her too tightly. "Stay with me," he said. "We'll try to get closer to the mouth of the worm. If *he* goes this way, the mouth has got to be down here, too."

The faster they moved, the more control they had, or so it felt. Their feet touched the ground very lightly, but they didn't bounce up and into the air. With the wind coming from their right side, they had to keep correcting in order to move in the direction they intended. But soon enough they emerged from the trees and there was a town.

It looked vaguely oriental, mostly because of the shape of the roofs on the nearest houses. The colors of the walls had once been garish, but they were faded, the paint peeling. But there wasn't time to study the architecture. People were milling around in the streets, jabbering at each other. They didn't speak a language Todd had ever heard before. How could they? Only Eggo had had a chance to learn English. There'd be no talking with these people. No asking them for directions.

Then again, maybe it wouldn't be necessary. Because now he could see what they were all excited about. The street was covered with a drift of water. Not puddles, a drift—thicker than a mist or a fog, but not rushing anywhere, just hovering.

It was the trickle of water they had sent through the hose when they first tested it up the worm's anus. Only here, it was a lot of water.

Which meant that the original position of the worm's mouth wasn't far from here.

"Come on," he said to Mom, dragging her around the crowd.

"Wait," she said. "It's water from *our* world, isn't it? Todd, I'm so thirsty."

He couldn't force her to stay with him, though he thought it was a bad idea for her to head toward the people. He needn't have worried, though. They were apparently so freaked out by the water that it made them jumpy. When Mom started drifting through the crowd, they parted for her, and some of them screamed and ran away. She knelt in the pool of water and drank.

Todd could watch her gain solidity as she did. Apparently the lack of water had desiccated her, faded her. Now she was more solid, and more naked, but still it didn't bother him. It was like seeing a baby naked. There was a job to do, no time to worry about embarrassment.

He drifted toward her; but the moment he touched the water, it felt familiar and real—and cold and wet. He slogged through the water to where she knelt. "Let's go now, Mom, before they start figuring out just how solid we aren't."

She drank just a little more, then took his hand. They made better progress now that she could find a little better purchase for her feet, more strength in her legs. At the same time, being more solid made her more vulnerable to the wind.

They found the source of the water—a house. The people had broken down the door, apparently to find out what was causing the mini-flood, or perhaps to make sure no one was inside, drowning.

Todd also saw that the water trailed off in another direction. "When we moved it, the hose stayed with it for a few steps. I think the new location must be in that direction."

He pulled her along. She stopped and drank again. "I need that water," she said. "Don't leave it behind."

"There's plenty of water where we're going," he said.

"But you don't *know* where we're going. Just . . . this direction."

"Mom, we only took a few steps before the hose fell out, and here it's hundreds of yards. So the final location could be a mile farther on. We've got to keep moving."

A crowd of people, many of them children, were following them as they drifted out of the water and on up the streets. Todd tried to figure what a straight line would be, extending in the direction that the thick low fog had trailed off, but the streets weren't cooperating. He kept trying to double back to get in the line, but nothing led in the right direction.

Until finally they reached a street with a high fence enclosing a park, with green lawns and stately trees. He wasn't sure exactly where the line from the hosewater would have intersected with the park, but he knew it was bound to reach it somewhere. Quite possibly the real flood, when it came, would pour out in this park, which would make it much easier to see.

As if on command, there was a loud crashing sound not very far off, and when Todd looked in that direction, he saw a wall of water rushing toward them—toward the whole length of the fence.

There was no point in trying to face it head-on. They had to get around the flood, behind it. And for now, the only way to do that without having to slog through water was to get above it.

He led his mother up into one of the trees. But in this wide-open park, they couldn't climb hand over hand, tree to tree. There were wide gaps, and all they could do was leap, hoping they wouldn't get taken by the wind and drift away.

It was slow going, but they made steady progress, and Todd did a fair job of estimating how the breeze would influence their flight. It was kind of exhilarating, to leap out into the air and drift only slowly downward, over the rushing water.

And as they moved around the water, they found that it was flowing out of a huge house. The crashing sound had been the stone front wall of the house giving way, crumbling from the pressure of the thick fog. Which seemed absurd. Except that the water would be coming so hard and fast out of the hose on this end that it wasn't *water* pressure that knocked down the wall, it was the explosive force of air pressure.

He heard shouting behind him, which wasn't a surprise; but it was growing closer, which was. Most of the people had fled from the flood when they saw it coming at them through the wrought-iron fence. But now there was someone plunging ahead through the water. It was easier for him than it would have been for Todd or Mom—the water was only fog to him, though it was a very thick one.

It was Eggo. And he was aiming something at them.

A gun. He had a gun.

Eggo fired. The bullet passed through Todd. He felt it, but not as pain. More like a belch, a rumbling. But that didn't mean the damage wasn't real.

"Why are you doing this!" shouted Todd.

He could see that Eggo didn't hear him. "Keep going toward that house, Mother." He let go of her hand. "Go! Don't make all this a wasted effort!"

She went, looking at him once in anguish but plunging ahead.

Todd headed straight toward Eggo, who was reloading the thing. It was a muzzle-loader. He only had a musket. Thank heaven he hadn't figured out how to make an AK-47.

"Don't be stupid!" shouted Todd. "Stop it!"

Now the elf heard him. "No!" he shouted. "You wrecked everything!"

"The sooner we get back home, the sooner this flood will stop!"

"I don't care!" shouted Eggo. "That's the king's house, you fool! You destroyed the king's house!"

"And you can save it by driving us out of here! Let us go, and be the hero who ended the flood!"

Eggo's gun was loaded and he was pointing it right at Todd, who was close enough now that he thought this time it would probably hurt.

But Eggo didn't fire the thing. "All right!" he said. "Go! I'll shoot *past* you. Just get out of here. And act like you're afraid of me!"

"I won't be acting," murmured Todd.

But he couldn't change direction in midair, and he knew if he once got into that water, he'd never be able to take off again.

"Give me a push!" he shouted at Eggo.

Eggo ran at him and held up the barrel of his musket. Todd grabbed it, barely clung to it with his attenuated fingers, and then hung on for dear life as the elf swung him and threw him toward the palace, where Mom was just reaching the huge gap through which water was flowing.

Soon they were inside, grabbing sconces and chandeliers and furniture to keep them moving forward through the air over the flood. And finally they found it, the place where a huge, thick hose-end was spewing out an incredible volume of icy, jet-speed water. Todd made the mistake of being in the path of the blast and it felt like it had broken half his ribs. He dropped down into the water. Mom screamed and pulled herself down to help him, which saved *her* from getting blasted by another whip-like pass from the hose.

"We've got to get under it," he said. "Look for where the hose comes out of nothing. We have to climb the hose into the worm's mouth!"

Now it was Mom's turn to drag Todd, through the water, barely raising their heads above the surface to breathe. Finally they got behind the hose-end, and even though it was whipping around, the base of it, the place where it came out of nowhere, was fairly solidly in place.

The hose was exactly the right size for Todd to grip it. "You first!" he shouted to Mom. "Climb up the hose! When you get to the end, tell them to turn it off, but don't pull it out till I climb down after you!"

Mom gripped the house and when her hand inched up past the place where the hose disappeared, it also vanished. "Keep climbing," Todd urged her. "Don't stop no matter what you see. Don't let go!"

As Mom disappeared, he turned around to avoid watching her, and to take one last look around the room. There were soldiers in flamboyantly colored uniforms gathered in the doorways, aiming arrows at him. Oh, good, he thought. They don't have guns.

The chain saw lay discarded on the lawn. Jared stood near it, straddling the hose, watching as Dad wrestled with it like a python. He couldn't keep it from being thrust back at him, no matter how tightly he held it against the spot where it became invisible. Suddenly a loop of it would extrude and Dad would have to grasp it again, at the new end-point. Already several coils were on the floor. What if Mom and Todd weren't anywhere near the point where it emerged on the other side? What if all of this was for nothing?

And then, along with a coil of hose, a hand emerged out of nothingness in the shed.

Dad let go of the hose and took the hand, dragged at it.

Mother's head emerged from the wormhole. "Turn off the water!" she croaked. "Turn it off, but keep the hose—"

Jared was already rushing for the faucet. He turned it off, turned back to face her, and . . .

The hose lay completely on the ground, Mom tangled up in it. Nothing was poking into the worm's anus now. How would Todd get back?

Mom and Dad were hugging while at the same time Dad was trying to wrap a shirt around her, to cover her.

"What about Todd!" Jared shouted.

"He's coming," said Mom. "He's right behind me."

"The hose is out of the worm!"

Apparently they hadn't realized it until now. Father lunged for the hose-end, still dripping, and tried frantically to reinsert it. Mother, half-wearing the shirt now, tried to help him, but she was panting heavily and then she collapsed onto the hose.

Dad cried out and dropped the hose-end. "He's right behind me," Mom whispered.

Jared helped him get Mom up. She wasn't unconscious; once Dad was holding her, she could shuffle along. Dad led her toward the house.

Jared took up the hose again and started trying to feed it through. Finding the hole was hard; pushing the hose was harder.

Until he realized: It doesn't have to be the hose anymore. We aren't trying to pump water anymore.

He found the rake and fed the handle of it into the gap in the air. Rigid, the handle went in much more easily—which was to say, it took all of Jared's strength, but he could do it. He jammed the handle in all the way up to the metal of the rake and then held it there, gripping it tightly and bracing his feet against the lowest shelf on the wall of the shed.

The rake kept lunging toward him, pressing at him, shoving him backward, but he'd push it in again. It went on until he was too tired to hold it any longer and his belly and hips hurt where the rake had jabbed him, but still he held.

And then a hand came out of the hole along with a shove of the rake, and this time Jared shoved back only long enough to get out from behind the rake. It was practically shot out of the wormhole, and along with it came Todd.

Todd was bleeding all over from vicious-looking puncture wounds. "They shot me," he said, and then he fell into unconsciousness.

Mother spent two days in the hospital, rehydrating and recovering. They pumped her with questions about what had happened, where she was for four years and four months, but she told them over and over that she couldn't remember, that one minute she was putting Jared to bed, and the next minute she was lying out in the shed, gasping for breath, feeling as if someone had stretched her so thin that a gust of wind could blow her away.

They questioned Jared, too. And Dad. What did you see? How did you find them? Did you see who hurt your brother? And all they could say, either of them, was "Mom was just there in the shed. And after we helped her back into the house, we came out and Todd was there, too, bleeding, and we called 911."

Because Dad had told Mom and Jared, "No lies. Tell the truth. Up to Mom going and after Mom and Todd reappeared. No explanations. No guesses. Nothing. We don't know anything, we don't remember anything."

Jared didn't bother telling him that "I don't remember" was a huge lie. He knew enough to realize that telling the truth would convince everybody that they were liars, and only lies would convince anybody they were telling the truth.

Todd didn't recover consciousness after the surgery for three days, and then he was in and out as his body fought off a devastating fever and an infection that antibiotics didn't seem to help. So delirious that nothing he said made sense—to the cops and the doctors, anyway. Men with arrows. Elves. Eggo waffles. Worms with mouths and anuses. Flying through space. Floods and flying and . . . definitely delirium.

The cops found what looked like bloodstains on the chain saw, but since Todd's wounds were punctures and the stains turned out not to react properly to any of the tests for blood, the evidence led them nowhere. It might end up in somebody's X file, but what the whole event would not do was end up in court.

When Todd woke up for real, Dad and Jared were there by his bed. Dad only had time to say, "It's a shame if you don't remember anything at all," before the detective and the doctor were both all over him, asking how it happened, who did it, where the injuries were inflicted.

"On another planet," said Todd. "I flew through space to get there and I never let go of the hose but then it got sucked away from me and I was lost until I got jabbed in the shoulder with the rake and I held on and rode it home."

That was even better than amnesia, since the doctor assumed he was still delirious and they left Todd and Dad and Jared alone. Later, when Todd was clearly *not* delirious, he was ready with his own amnesia story, along with tales of weird dreams he had while in a coma.

The doctor's report finally said that Todd's injuries were consistent with old-fashioned arrows, the kind with barbs, only there were no removal injuries. It was as if the arrows had entered his body and dissolved somehow. And as to where Mom had been all those years, they hadn't a clue, and except for dehydration and some serious but generalized weight loss, she seemed to be in good health.

And when at last they were home together, they didn't talk about it much. One time through the story so everybody would know what happened to everybody else, but then it was done.

Mom couldn't get over how many years she had missed, how much bigger and older Todd and Jared had become. She started blaming herself for being gone that whole time, but Dad wouldn't let her. "We all did what made sense to us at the time," he said. "The best we could. And we're back together *now*. Todd has some interesting scars. You have to take calcium pills to recover from bone loss. There's only one thing left to take care of."

The mouth of the worm in the closet. The anus of the worm in the shed.

The solution wasn't elegant, but it worked. First they hooked the anus with the rake one last time, covered the top with a tarpaulin, and dragged it to the car. They drove to the lake and dragged the thing up to the edge of a steep cliff overlooking the water, then shoved it as far as they could over the edge, with Dad and Mom gripping Todd tightly so he wouldn't fall.

Let Eggo come back if he wanted. Given how tough he was, it probably wouldn't hurt him much, but it would be a very inconvenient location.

The mouth in the closet was harder, because they couldn't move it from their end. But a truckload of manure dumped on the front lawn allowed them to bring wheelbarrows full of it into the house and on into the bedroom, where they took turns shoveling it into the maw.

On the other side, they knew, it would be a fine mist of manure, spreading with the wind out across the town. Huge volumes of it, coming thick and fast.

And sure enough, by the time the manure pile was half gone, the mouth disappeared. Eggo must have moved it from his end. Which was all they wanted.

Of course, then they had to get the smell out of the house and spread a huge amount of leftover manure over the lawn and across the garden, and the neighbors were really annoyed with the stench in the neighborhood until a couple of rains had settled it down. But they had a great lawn the next spring.

Only one thing that Todd had to know. He asked Mom when they were alone one night, watching the last installment of the BBC miniseries of *Pride and Prejudice* after Dad and Jared had fallen asleep.

"What did you see?" he 'asked. "During the passage?" When she seemed baffled, he added, "Between worlds."

"See?" asked Mom. "What did *you* see?"

"It was like I was in space," said Todd, "only I could breathe. Faster than light I was going, stars everywhere, and then I zoomed down to the planet and . . . there I was."

She shook her head. "I guess we each saw what we wanted to see. Needed to see, maybe. No outer space for me. No stars. Just you and Jared and your dad, waiting for me. Beckoning to me. Telling me to come home."

"And the hose?"

"Never saw it," she said. "During the whole passage. I could *feel* it, hold tightly to it, but all I saw was . . . home."

Todd nodded. "OK," he said. "But it *was* another planet, just the same. Even if I didn't really see my passage through space. It was a real place, and I was there."

"You were there," said Mom.

"And you know what?" said Todd.

"I hope you're not telling me you ever want to go back."

"Are you kidding?" said Todd. "I've had my fill of space travel. I'm done."

"There's no place like home," said Mom, clicking her heels together.

NOTES ON "SPACE BOY"

The assignment from editors Gardner Dozois and Jack Dann was simple enough. Write an old-time adventure story that puts kids in space.

Hey, kids in space—isn't that what Card does?

I took on the assignment with the firm intention of fulfilling it literally. In fact, I was expecting that I'd write a story set in Battle School, so that it would not only be a kids-in-space adventure, it would be tied to the *Ender's Game* universe.

But then the deadline rolled around, and I hadn't thought of a single idea that worked well enough for me to be ready to write it. What I had was a weird story in which there *was* a monster in the closet, and it actually ate a kid's mom. But what does *that* have to do with kids in space? It's kids in the bedroom, for pete's sake!

Still . . . as I've told writing students for many years, the best stories often come from the juxtaposition of completely unrelated ideas. My own career is full of them. For instance:

My second novel, *Treason,* came from a map I doodled on which I started naming my imaginary countries with surnames from our present world; I combined it with a separate idea about people who could regenerate limbs at will, including limbs that weren't actually missing, so they'd come to parties with an extra arm or leg or other body part.

Hart's Hope came from an idea session with the very first writing class I taught, in which magical power came from blood, with the most power going to a woman who killed her own child; I combined it with an intriguing map I had drawn of a city in which, depending on what gate you enter through, you find a completely different place.

Even the original "Ender's Game" story came from one idea—a safe "battle room" in which soldiers trained for combat in space, but with walls to keep them from drifting away and getting lost; and then another idea, in which children are playing a complex space videogame but their commands get turned into orders followed by real pilots in a faraway space battle.

It's in the tension between these ideas, the struggle to make them fit, that creativity gets stimulated and you start to come up with stuff that's really cool—ideas that weren't going to come to you out of the blue.

So it was with this story. I had the monster-in-closet-eats-mom idea, and the need to have a kid travel from planet to planet. So . . . what if the monster in the closet is actually a living creature that, like an earthworm, survives on the energy differential between different universes? The same worm has both a mouth and an anus on both worlds, and objects that enter through one end are spewed out the other, intact—the creature "digests" only energy in a purer form. Solid objects and living creatures are just fiber.

I wrote to Gardner about this one, because it still didn't fit the parameters of the anthology. He told me to go ahead—perhaps because it was better than finding somebody else at such a late date—and I ended up with a story that I liked even more than I expected. After it first appeared in *Escape from Earth: New Adventures in Space,* "Space Boy" went on to become a Young Adult book on its own, from Subterranean Press, and I'm developing it into a film project. You never know what the desperation before a deadline can lead to.

ANGLES

3000

Hakira enjoyed coasting the streets of Manhattan. The old rusted-out building frames seemed like the skeleton of some ancient leviathan that beached and died, but he could hear the voices and horns and growling machinery of crowded streets and smell the exhaust and cooking oil, even if all that he saw beneath him were the tops of the trees that had grown up in the long-vanished streets. With a world as uncrowded as this one, there was no reason to dismantle the ruins, or clear the trees. It could remain as a monument, for the amusement of the occasional visitor.

There were plenty of places in the world that were still crowded. As always, most people enjoyed or at least needed human company, and even recluses usually wanted people close enough to reach from time to time. Satellites and landlines still linked the world together, and ports were busy with travel and commerce of the lighter sort, like bringing out-of-season fruits and vegetables to consumers who preferred not to travel to where the food was fresh. But as the year 3000 was about to pass away, there were places like this that made the planet Earth seem almost empty, as if humanity had moved on.

In fact, there were probably far more human beings alive than anyone had ever imagined might be possible. No human had ever left the solar system, and only a handful lived anywhere but Earth. One of the Earths, anyway—one of the angles of Earth. In the past five hundred years, millions had passed through benders to colonize versions of Earth where humanity had never evolved, and now a world seemed full with only a billion people or so.

Of the trillions of people that were known to exist, the one that Hakira was going to see lived in a two-hundred-year-old house perched on the southern coast of this island, where in ancient times artillery had been placed to command the harbor. Back when the Atlantic reached this far inland. Back when invaders had to come by ship.

Hakira set his flivver down in the meadow where the homing signal indicated, switched off the engine, and slipped out into the bracing air of a summer morning only a few miles from the face of the nearest glacier. He was expected—there was no challenge from the security system, and lights showed him the path to follow through the shadowy woods.

Because his host was something of a show-off, a pair of sabertooth tigers were soon padding along beside him. They might have been computer simulations, but knowing Moshe's reputation, they were probably genetic back-forms, very expensive and undoubtedly chipped up to keep them from behaving aggressively except, perhaps, on command. And Moshe had no reason to wish Hakira ill. They were, after all, kindred spirits.

The path suddenly opened up onto a meadow, and after only a few steps he realized that the meadow was the roof of a house, for here and there steep-pitched skylights rose above the grass and flowers. And now, with a turn, the path took him down a curving ramp along the face of the butte overlooking the Hudson plain. And now he stood before a door.

It opened.

A beaming Moshe stood before him, dressed in, of all things, a kimono. "Come in, Hakira! You certainly took your time!"

"We set our appointment by the calendar, not the clock."

"Whenever you arrive is a good time. I merely noted that my security system showed you taking the grand tour on the way."

"Manhattan. A sad place, like a sweet dream you can never return to."

"A poet's soul, that's what you have."

"I've never been accused of that, before."

"Only because you're Japanese," said Moshe.

They sat down before an open fire that seemed real, but gave off no smoke. Heat it had, however, so that Hakira felt a little scorched when he leaned forward. "There are Japanese poets."

"I know. But is that what anyone thinks of, when they think of the wandering Japanese?"

Hakira smiled. "But you *do* have money."

"Not from money-changing," said Moshe. "And what I don't have, which you also don't have, is a home."

Hakira looked around at the luxurious parlor. "I suppose that technically this *is* a cave."

"A homeland," said Moshe. "For nine and a half centuries, my friend, your people have been able to go almost anywhere in the world but one, an archipelago of islands once called Honshu, Hokkaido, Kyushu—"

Hakira, suddenly overcome by emotion, raised his hand to stop the cruel list. "I know that your people, too, have been driven from their homeland—"

"Repeatedly," said Moshe.

"I hope you will forgive me, sir, but it is impossible to imagine yearning for a desert beside a dead sea the way one yearns for the lush islands strangled for nearly a thousand years by the Chinese dragon."

"Dry or wet, flat or mountainous, the home to which you are forbidden to return is beautiful in dreams."

"Who has the soul of a poet now?"

"Your organization will fail, you know."

"I know nothing of the kind, sir."

"It will fail. China will never relent, because to do so would be to admit wrongdoing, and that they cannot do. To them you are the interlopers. The toothless Peace Council can issue as many edicts as it likes, but the Chinese will continue to bar those of known Japanese ancestry from even visiting the islands. And they will use as their excuse the perfectly valid argument that if you want so much to see Japan, you have only to bend yourself to a different slant. There is bound to be some angle where your tourist dollars will be welcome."

"No," said Hakira. "Those other angles are not *this* world."

"And yet they are."

"And yet they are not."

"Well, now, there is our dilemma. Either we will do business or we

will not, and it all hinges on that question. What is it about that archipelago that you want. Is it the land itself? You can already visit that very
land—and we are told that because of inanimate incoherency it *is* the
same land, no matter what angle *you* dwell in. Or is your desire really not
simply to go there, but to go there in defiance of the Chinese? Is it hate,
then, that drives you?"

"No, I reject both interpretations," said Hakira. "I care nothing for
the Chinese. And now that you put the question in these terms, I realize
that I myself have not thought clearly enough, for while I speak of the
beautiful land of the rising sun, in fact what I yearn for is the Japanese nation, on those islands, unmolested by any other, governing ourselves as we
have from the beginning of our existence as a people."

"Ah," said Moshe. "Now I see that we perhaps *can* do business. For it
may be possible to grant you your heart's desire."

"Me and all the people of the Kotoshi."

"Ah, the eternally optimistic Kotoshi. It means 'this year,' doesn't it?
As in, 'this year we return'?"

"As your people say, 'Next year in Jerusalem.' "

"A Japan where only the Japanese have ruled for all these past thousand years. In a world where the Japanese are not rootless wanderers, legendary toymakers-for-hire, but rather are a nation among the nations of
the world, and one of the greatest of them. Is *that* not the home you wish
to return to?"

"Yes," said Hakira.

"But that Japan does not exist in this world, not even now, when the
Chinese no longer need even half the land of the original Han China. So
you do not want the Japan of this world at all, do you? The Japan you
want is a fantasy, a dream."

"A hope."

"A wish."

"A *plan*."

"And it hasn't occurred to you that in all the angles of the world,
there might not be such a Japan?"

"It isn't like the huge library in that story, where it is believed that
among all the books containing all the combinations of all the letters that
could fit in all those pages, there is bound to be a book that tells the true

history of all the world. There are many angles, yes, but our ability to dif-
ferentiate them is not infinite, and in many of them life never evolved and
so the air is not breathable. It is an experiment not lightly undertaken."

"Oh, of course. To find a world so nearly like our own that a nation
called Japan—or, I suppose, Nippon—exists at all, where a language like
Japanese is even spoken—you do speak Japanese yourself, don't you?"

"My parents spoke nothing else at home until I was five and had to
enter school."

"Yes, well, to find such a world would be a miracle."

"And to search for it would be a fool's errand."

"And yet it *has* been searched for."

Hakira waited. Moshe did not go on.

"Has it been found?"

"What would it be worth to you, if it had?"

2024—*Angle* Θ

"You're a scientist," said Leonard. "This is beneath you."

"I have continuous video," said Bêto. "With a mechanical clock in it,
so you can see the flow of time. The chair moves."

"There is nothing you can do that hasn't been faked by somebody,
sometime."

"But why would I fake it? To publish this is the end of my career."

"Exactly my point, Bêto. You are a geologist, of all things. Geologists
don't have poltergeists."

"Stay with me, Leonard. Watch this."

"How long?"

"I don't know. Sometimes it's immediate. Sometimes it takes days."

"I don't have days."

"Play cards with me. As we used to in Faculdade. Look at the chair
first, though. Nothing attached to it. A normal chair in every way."

"You sound like a magician on the stage."

"But it *is* normal."

"So it seems."

"Seems? All right, don't trust me. *You* move it. Put it where you want."

"All right. Upside down?"

"It doesn't matter."

"On top of the door?"

"I don't care."

"And we play cards?"

"You deal."

2090

It is the problem of memory. We have mapped the entire brain. We can track the activity of every neuron, of every synapse. We have analyzed the chemical contents of the cells. We can find, in the living brain, without surgery, exactly where each muscle is controlled, where perceptions are rooted. We can even stimulate the brain to track and recall memory. But that is all. We cannot account for how memory is stored, and we cannot find where.

I know that in your textbooks in secondary school and perhaps in your early undergraduate classes you have read that memory was the first problem solved, but that was a misunderstanding. We discovered that after mapping a particular memory, if that exact portion of the brain was destroyed—and this was in the early days, with clumsy equipment that killed thousands of cells at a time, an incredibly wasteful procedure and potentially devastating to the subject—if that exact spot was destroyed, the memory was not lost. It could resurface somewhere else.

So for many years we believed that memory was stored holographically, small portions in many places, so that losing a bit of a memory here or there did not cause the entire sequence to be lost. This, however, was chimerical, for as our research became more and more precise, we discovered that the brain is not infinite, and such a wasteful system of memory storage would use up the entire brain before a child reached the age of three. Because, you see, *no memory is lost*. Some memories are hard to recover, and people often lose *track* of their memories, but it is not a problem of storage, it is a problem of retrieval.

Portions of the network break down, so tracks cannot be followed. Or the routing is such that you cannot link from memory A to memory X without passing through memories of such power that you are distracted from the attempt to retrieve. But, given time—or hyperstimulation of related memory tracks—all memories can be retrieved. All. Every moment of your life.

We cannot recover more than your perceptions and the sense you made of them at the time, but that does not change the fact that we *can* recover every moment of your childhood, every moment of this class. And we can recover every conscious thought, though not the unconscious streaming thought behind it. It is all stored . . . somewhere. The brain is merely the retrieval mechanism.

This has led some observers to conclude that there is, in fact, a mind, or even a soul—a nonphysical portion of the human being, existing outside of measurable space. But if that is so, it is beyond the reach of science. I, however, am a scientist, and with my colleagues—some of whom once sat in the very chairs where you are sitting—I have labored long and hard to find an explanation that is, in fact, physical. Some have criticized this effort because it shows that my faith in the nonexistence of the immaterial is so blind that I refuse to believe even the material evidence of immateriality. Don't laugh, it is a valid question. But my answer is that we cannot validly prove the immateriality of the mind by the sheer fact of our inability to detect the material of which it is made.

I am happy to tell you that we have received word that the journal *Mind*—and we would not have settled for anything less than the premier journal in the field—has accepted our article dealing with our findings. By no means does this constitute an answer. But it moves the field of inquiry and reopens the possibility, at least, of a material answer to the question of memory. For we have found that when neurons are accessed for memory, there are many kinds of activity in the cell. The biochemical, of course, has been very hard to decode, but other researchers have accounted for all the chemical reactions within the cell, and we have found nothing new in that area. Nor is memory electrochemical, for that is merely how raw commands of the coarsest sort are passed from neuron to neuron—rather like the difference between using a spray can as opposed to painting with a monofilament brush.

Our research, of course, began in the submolecular realm, trying to find out if in some way the brain cells were able to make changes in the atom, in the arrangement of protons and neutrons, or some information somehow encoded in the behavior of electrons. This proved, alas, to be a dead end as well.

But the invention of the muonoscope has changed everything for us. Because at last we had a nondestructive means of scanning the exact state of muons through infinitesimal passages of time, we were able to find some astonishing correlations between memory and the barely detectable muon states of slant and yaw. Yaw, as you know, is the constant—the yaw of a muon cannot change during the existence of the muon. Slant also seemed to be a constant, and in the materials which had previously been examined by physicists, that was indeed the case.

However, in our studies of brain activity during forced memory retrieval, we have found a consistent pattern of slant alteration within the nuclei of atoms in individual brain cells. Because the head must be held utterly still for the muonoscope to function, we could only work with terminally ill patients who volunteered for the study and were willing to die in the laboratory instead of with their families, spending the last moments of their lives with their heads opened up and their brains partially disassembled. It was painless but nevertheless emotionally disturbing to contemplate, and so I must salute the courage and sacrifice of our subjects, whose names are all listed in our article as co-authors of the study. And I believe that our study has now taken us as far as biology can go, given the present equipment. The next move is in the hands of physicists.

Ah, yes. What we found. You see? I became sidetracked by my thought of our brave collaborators, because I remembered their memories, which meant remembering who they were and what it cost them to . . . and I am being distracted again. What we found was: During the moment of memory retrieval, when the neuron was stimulated and went into the standard memory-retrieval state, there is a moment—a moment so brief that until fifteen years ago we had no computer that could have detected it, let alone measured its duration—when all the muons in all the protons of all the atoms in all the memory-specific RNA molecules in the nucleus of the one neuron—and no others!—change their slant.

More specifically, they seem, according to the muonoscope, to wink out of existence for that brief moment, and then return to existence with a new pattern of slants—yes, varying slants, impossible as we have been told that was—which exist for a period of time perhaps a thousand times longer than the temporary indetectability, though this is still a span of time briefer than a millionth of a picosecond, and during the brief existence of this anomalous slant state, which we call the "angle," the neuron goes through the spasm of activity that causes the entire brain to respond in all the ways that we have long recognized as the recovery of memory.

In short, it seems that the pertinent muons change their slant to a new angle, and in that angle they are encoded with a snapshot of the brain-state that will cause the subject to remember. They return to detectability in the process of rebounding to their original slant, but for the brief period before they have completed that rebound, the pattern of memory is reported, via biochemical and then electrochemical changes, to the brain as a whole.

There are those who will resent this discovery because it seems to turn the mind or soul into a mere physical phenomenon, but this is not so. In fact, if anything our discovery enhances our knowledge of the utterly unique majesty of life. For as far as we know, it is only in the living brain of organisms that the very slant of the muons within atoms can be changed. The brain thus opens tiny doorways into other universes, stores memories there, and retrieves them at will.

Yes, I mean other universes. The first thing that the muonoscope showed us was the utter emptiness of muons. There are even theorists who believe that there are no particles, only attributes of regions of space, and theoretically there is no reason why the same point in space cannot be occupied by an infinite number of muons, as long as they have different slants and, perhaps, yaws. For theoretical reasons that I do not have the mathematics to understand, I am told that while coterminous muons of the same yaw but different slants could impinge upon and influence each other, coterminous muons of different yaw could never have any causal relationship. And there could also be an infinite series of infinite series of universes whose muons are not coterminous with the muons of our universe, and they, too, are permanently undetectable and incapable of influencing our universe.

But if the theory is correct—and I believe our research proves that it is—it is possible to pass information from one slant of this physical universe to another. And since, by this same theory, all material reality is, in fact, merely information, it is even possible that we might be able to pass objects from one such universe to another. But now we are in the realm of fantasy, and I have spent as much time on this happy announcement as I dare. You are, after all, students, and my job is to pass certain information from my brain to yours, which does not, I'm afraid, involve mere millionths of a picosecond.

2024—Angle Φ

"I can't stand it, I can't. I won't live here another day, another hour."

"But it never harms us, and we can't afford to move."

"The chair is on top of the door, it could fall, it could hurt one of the children. Why is it doing this to us? What have we done to offend it?"

"We haven't done *anything,* it's just *malicious,* it's just *enjoying itself*!"

"No, don't make it angry!"

"I'm fed up! Stop this! Go away! Leave us alone!"

"What good is it to break the chair and smash the room!"

"No good. Nothing does any good. Go, get the children, take them out into the garden. I'll call a taxi. We'll go to your sister's house."

"They don't have room."

"For tonight they have room. Not another night in this evil place."

3000

Hakira examined the contract, and it seemed simple enough. Passage for the entire membership of Kotoshi, if they assembled at their own expense. Free return for up to ten days, but only at the end of the ten days, as a single group. There would be no refund for those who returned. But all that seemed fair enough, especially since the price was not exorbitant.

"Of course this contract isn't binding anyway," said Hakira. "How could it be enforced? This whole passage is illegal."

"Not in the target world, it isn't," said Moshe. "And that's where it would have to be enforced, nu?"

"It's not as if I can find a lawyer from that world to represent my interests now."

"It makes no sense for me to have dissatisfied customers."

"How do I know you won't just strand us there?" said Hakira. "It might not even be a world with a breathable atmosphere—a lot of angles are still mostly hydrocarbon gas, with no free oxygen at all."

"Didn't I tell you? I go with you. In fact, I have to—I'm the one who brings you through."

"Brings us? Don't you just put us in a bender and—"

"Bender!" Moshe laughed. "Those primitive machines? No wonder the near worlds are never found—benders can't make the fine distinctions that *we* make. No, I take you through. We go together."

"What, we all join hands and . . . you're serious. Why are you wasting my time with mumbo jumbo like this!"

"If it's mumbo jumbo, then we'll all hold hands and nothing will happen, and you'll get your money back. Right?" Moshe spread his hands. "What do you have to lose!"

"It feels like a scam."

"Then leave. You came to me, remember?"

"Because you got that group of Zionists through."

"Exactly my point," said Moshe. "I took them through. I came back, they didn't—because they were absolutely satisfied. They're in a world where Israel was never conquered by the surrounding Arab states so Jews still have their own Hebrew-speaking state. The same world, I might add, where Japan is still populated by self-governing Japanese."

"What's the catch?"

"No catch. Except that we use a different mechanism that is not approved by the government and so we have to do it under the table."

"But why does the *other* world allow it?" asked Hakira. "Why do they let you bring people in?"

"This is a rescue," said Moshe. "They bring you in as refugees from an unbearable reality. They bring you *home*. The government of Israel in that reality, as a matter of policy, declares that Jews have a right to return—even Jews from a different angle. And the government of Japan recently decided to offer the same privilege to you."

"It's still so hard to believe that anyone found a populated world that has Japanese at all."

"Well, isn't it obvious?" said Moshe. "Nobody *found* that world."

"What do you mean?"

"That world found *us*."

Hakira thought about it for a moment. "That's why they don't use benders, they have their own technology for reslanting from angle to angle."

"Exactly right, except for your use of the word 'they.'"

And now Hakira understood. "Not they. You. You're not from this world. You're one of them."

"When we discovered your tragic world, I was sent to bring Jews home to Israel. And when we realized that the Japanese suffered a similar tragic loss, the decision was made to extend the offer to you. Hakira, bring your people home."

2024—*Angle* Θ

"I told them I didn't want to see you."

"I know."

"I was sitting there playing cards and suddenly I'm almost killed!"

"It never happened that way before. The chair usually just . . . slid. Or sometimes floated."

"It was smashed to bits! I had a concussion, it's taken ten stitches, I'll have this scar on my face for the rest of my life!"

"But I didn't do it, I didn't know it would happen that way. How could I? There were no wires, you know that. You *saw*."

"Nossa. Yes. I saw. But it's not a ghost."

"I never said it was. I don't believe in ghosts."

"What, then?"

"I don't know. Everything else I think of sounds like fantasy. But then, telephones and satellite TV and movies and submarines once sounded like fantasy to anyone who thought of such ideas. And in this case, there've been stories of ghosts and hauntings and poltergeists since . . . since the beginning of time, I imagine. Only they're rare. So rare that they don't often happen to scientists."

"In the history of the world, real scientists are rarer than poltergeists."

"And if such things *did* happen to a scientist, how many of them might have done as you urged me to do—ignore it. Pretend it was a hallucination. Move to another place where such things don't happen. And the scientists who refuse to blind their eyes to the evidence before them—

what happens to them? I'll tell you what happens, because I've found seven of them in the past two hundred years—which isn't a lot, but these are the ones who published what happened to them. And in every case, they were immediately discredited as scientists. No one listened to them anymore. Their careers were over. The ones who taught lost tenure at their universities. Three of them were committed to mental institutions. And *not once* did anyone else seriously investigate their claims. Except, of course, the people who are already considered to be completely bobo, the paranormalists, the regular batch of fakers and hucksters."

"And the same thing will happen to you."

"No. Because I have you as a witness."

"What kind of witness am I? I was *hit in the head*. Do you understand? I was in the hospital, delirious, concussive, and I have the scar on my face to prove it. No one will believe me, either. Some will even wonder if you didn't beat me into agreeing to testify for you!"

"Ah, Leonard. God help me, but you're right."

"Call an exorcist."

"I'm a scientist! I don't want it to go away! I want to understand it!"

"So, Bêto, scientist, explain it to me. If it isn't a ghost to be exorcised, what is it?"

"A parallel world. No, listen, listen to me! Maybe in the empty spaces between atoms, or even the empty spaces within atoms, there are other atoms we can't detect most of the time. An infinite number of them, some very close to ours, some very far. And suppose that when you enclose a space, and somebody in one of those infinite parallel universes encloses the *same* space, it can cause just the slightest bit of material overlap."

"You mean there's something magic about boxes? Come on."

"You asked for possibilities! But if the landforms are similar, then the places where towns are built would be similar, too. The confluence of rivers. Harbors. Good farmland. People in many universes would be building towns in the same places. Houses. All it takes is one room that overlaps, and suddenly you get echoes between worlds. You get a single chair that exists in both worlds at once."

"What, somebody in our world goes and buys a chair and somebody in the other world happens to go and buy the same one on the same day?"

"No. I moved into the house, that chair was already there. Haunted houses are always old, aren't they? Old furniture. It's been there long enough, undisturbed, for the chair to have spilled a little and exist in both worlds. So . . . you take the chair and put it on top of the door, and the people in the other world come home and find the chair has been moved—maybe they even *saw* it move—and he's fed up, he's furious, he *smashes the chair.*"

"Ludicrous."

"Well, *something* happened, and you have the scar to prove it."

"And you have the chair fragments."

"Well, no."

"What! You threw them out?"

"My best guess is that *they* threw them out. Or else, I don't know, when the chair lost its structure, the echo faded. Anyway, the pieces are gone."

"No evidence. That clinches it. If you publish this I'll deny it, Bêto."

"No you won't."

"I will. I've already had my face damaged. I'm not going to let you shatter my career as well. Bêto, drop it!"

"I can't! This is too important! Science can't continue to refuse to look at this and find out what's really going on!"

"Yes it can! Scientists regularly refuse to look at all kinds of things because it would be bad for their careers to see them! You know it's true!"

"Yes. I know it's true. Scientists can be blind. But *not me*. And not you either, Leonard. When I publish this, I know you'll tell the truth."

"If you publish this, I'll know you're crazy. So when people ask me, I'll tell them the truth—that you're crazy. The chair is gone now anyway. Chances are this will never happen again. In five years you'll come to think of it as a weird hallucination."

"A weird hallucination that left you scarred for life."

"Go away, Bêto. Leave me alone."

2186

"I call it the Angler, and using it is called Angling."

"It looks expensive."

"It is."

"Too expensive to sell it as a toy."

"It's not for children anyway. Look, it's expensive because it's really high-tech, but that's a plus, and the more popular it becomes, the more the per-unit cost will drop. We've studied the price point and we think we're right on this."

"OK, fine, what does it do?"

"I'll show you. Put on this cap and—"

"I certainly will *not*! Not until you tell me what it does."

"Sure, I understand, no problem. What it does is, it puts you into someone else's head."

"Oh, it's just a Dreamer, those have been around for years, they had their vogue but—"

"No, not a Dreamer. True, we do use the old Dreamer technology as the playback system, because why reinvent the wheel? We were able to license it for a song, so why not? But the thing that makes this special is this—the recording system."

"Recording?"

"You know about slantspace, right?"

"That's all theoretical games."

"Not really just theoretical. I mean, it's well known that our brains store memory in slantspace, right?"

"Sure, yeah. I knew that."

"Well, see, here's the thing. There's an infinite number of different universes that have a lot of their matter coterminous with ours—"

"Here it comes, engineer talk, we can't sell engineering babble."

"There are people in these other worlds. Like ghosts. They wander around, and *their* memories are stored in *our* world."

"Where?"

"Just sitting there in the air. Just a collection of angles. Wherever their head is, in our world and a lot of other parallel worlds, they have their memories stored as a pattern of slants. Haven't you had the experience of walking into a room and then suddenly you can't remember why you came in?"

"I'm seventy years old, it happens all the time."

"It has nothing to do with being seventy. It happened when you were young, too. Only you're more susceptible now, because your own brain has so much memory stored that it's constantly accessing other slants. And sometimes, your head space passes through the head space of someone else in another world, and poof, your thoughts are confused—jammed, really—by theirs."

"My head just happens to pass through the space where the other guy's head just *happens* to be?"

"In an infinite series of universes, there are a lot of them where people about your height might be walking around. What makes it so rare is that most of them are using patterns of slants so different that they barely impinge on ours at all. And you have to be accessing memory right at that moment, too. Anyway, that's not what matters—that *is* coincidence. But you set up this recorder here at about the height of a human being and turn it on, and as long as you don't put it, say, on the thirtieth floor or the bottom of a lake or something, within a day you'll have this thing filled up."

"With what?"

"Up to twenty separate memory states. We could build it to hold a lot more, but it's so easy to erase and replace that we figured twenty was enough and if people want more, we can sell peripherals, right? Anyway, you get these transitory brain states. Memories. And it's the whole package, the complete mental state of another human being for one moment in time. Not a dream. Not *fictionalized,* you know? Those dreams, they were sketchy, haphazard, pretty meaningless. I mean, it's boring to hear other people *tell* their dreams, how cool is it to actually have to sit through them? But with the Angler, you catch the whole fish. You've got to put it on, though, to know why it's going to sell."

"And it's nothing permanent."

"Well, it's permanent in the sense that you"ll remember it, and it'll be a pretty strong memory. But you know, you'll *want* to remember it so that's a good thing. It doesn't damage anything, though, and that's all that matters. I can try it on one of your employees first, though, if you want. Or I'll put it on myself."

"No, I'll do it. I'll have to do it in the end before I'll make the decision, so I might as well do it from the start. Put on the cap. And no, it's not a toupee, if I were going to get a rug I'd choose a better one than this."

"All right, a snug fit, but that's why we made it elastic."

"How long does it take?"

"Objective time, only a fraction of a second. Subjectively, of course, well, you tell *us*. Ready?"

"Sure. Give me a one, two, three, all right?"

"I'll do one, two, three, and then flip it like four. OK?"

"Yeah yeah. Do it."

"One. Two. Three."

"Ah . . . aaah. Oh."

"Give it a few seconds. Just relax. It's pretty strong."

"You didn't . . . how could this . . . I . . ."

"It's all right to cry. Don't worry. First time, most people do."

"I was just . . . She's just . . . I was a *woman*."

"Fifty-fifty chance."

"I never knew how it felt to . . . This should be illegal."

"Technically, it falls under the same laws as the Dreamer, so, you know, not for children and all that."

"I don't know if I'd ever want to use it again. It's so strong."

"Give yourself a few days to sort it out, and you'll want it. You know you will."

"Yes. No, don't try to push any paperwork on me right now, I'm not an idiot. I'm not signing anything while my head's so . . . but . . . tomorrow. Come back tomorrow. Let me sleep on it."

"Of course. We couldn't ask for anything more than that."

"Have you shown this to anyone else?"

"You're the biggest and the best. We came to you first."

"We're talking exclusive, right?"

"Well, as exclusive as our patents allow."

"What do you mean?"

"We've patented every method we've thought of, but we think there are a lot of ways to record in slantspace. In fact, the real trouble is, the hardest thing is to design a record that doesn't bend space on the other side. I mean, people's heads won't go through the recording field if the recorder itself is visible in their space! What I'm saying is, we'll be exclusive until somebody finds another way to do it without infringing our patent. That'll take years, of course, but . . ."

"How many years?"

"No faster than three, and probably longer. And we can tie them up in court longer still."

"Look at me, I'm still shaking. Can you play me the same memory?"

"We could build a machine that would do that, but you won't want to. The first time with each one is the best. Doing the same person twice can leave you a little . . . confused."

"Bring me the paperwork tomorrow for an exclusive for five years. We'll launch with enough product to drop that price point from the start."

3001

It took a month for the members of Kotoshi to assemble. Only a few decided not to go, and they took a vow of silence to protect those who were leaving. They gathered at the southern tip of Manhattan, in the parlor of Moshe's house. They had no belongings with them.

"It's one of the unfortunate side effects of the technology we use," Moshe explained. "Nothing that is not organically connected to your bodies can make the transition to the new slant. As when you were born, you will be naked when you arrive. That's why wholesale colonization using this technology is impractical—no tools. Nor can you transfer any kind of wealth or art. You come empty-handed."

"Is it cold there?"

"The climate is different," said Moshe. "You'll arrive on the southern tip of Manhattan, and it will be winter, but there are no glaciers closer than Greenland. Anyway, you'll arrive indoors. I live in this house and use it for transition because there is a coterminous room in the other angle. Nothing to fret about."

Hakira looked for the technology that would transfer them. Moshe had spoken of this room. Perhaps it was much larger than bender technology, and had been embedded in the walls of the room.

Yet if they could not bring anything with them that wasn't part of their bodies, Moshe's people must have built their machinery here instead of importing it. Yet if they hadn't brought wealth, how had Moshe obtained the money to buy this house, let alone manufacture their slant-changing machinery? Interesting puzzles.

Of course, there were two obvious solutions. The first would be a disappointment, but it was the most predictable—that it was all fakery and Moshe would try to abscond with their money without having taken them anywhere at all. There was always the danger that part of the scam was killing those who were supposed to be transported so that there'd be no one left to complain. Foreseeing that, Hakira and the others were alert and prepared.

The other possibility, though, was the one that made Hakira's spine tingle. Theoretically, since slant-shifting had first been discovered as a natural function of the human brain, there was always the chance of nonmechanical transfer between angles. One of the main objections to this idea had always been that if it were possible, all the worlds should be getting constant visits from any that had learned how to transfer by mental power alone. The common answer to that was, How do you know they *aren't* constantly visiting? Some even speculated that sightings of ghosts might well be of people coming or going. But Moshe's warning about arriving nude would explain quite nicely why there hadn't been more visits. It's hard to be subtle about being nude in most human cultures.

"Do any of you," asked Moshe, "have any embedded metal or plastic in your bodies? This includes fillings in your teeth, but would also include metal plates or silicon joint replacements, heart pacemakers, nontissue breast implants, and, of course, eyeglasses. I can assure you that as quickly as possible, all these items will be replaced, except for pacemakers, of course, if you have a pacemaker you're simply not going."

"What happens if we *do* have some kind of implant?" asked one of the men.

"Nothing painful. No wound. It simply doesn't go with you. It remains here. The effect on you is as if it simply disappeared. And, of course, the objects would remain here, hanging in the air, and then fall to the ground—or the chair, since most of you will be sitting. But to tell the truth, that's the least of my problems—part of your fee goes to cleaning up this room, since the contents of your bowels also remain behind."

Several people grimaced.

"As I said, *you'll* never notice, except you might feel a bit lighter and more vigorous. It's like having the perfect enema. And, no matter how nervous you are, you won't need to urinate for some time. Well now, are we ready? Anyone want to step outside after all?"

No one left.

"Well, this couldn't be simpler. You must join hands, bare hands, skin to skin. Connect tightly, the whole circle, no one left out."

Hakira couldn't help but chuckle.

"Hakira is laughing," said Moshe, "because he mockingly suggested that maybe our method of transfer was some kind of mumbo jumbo involving all joining hands. Well, he was right. Only this happens to be mumbo jumbo that works."

We'll see, won't we? thought Hakira.

In moments, all their hands were joined.

"Hold your hands up, so I can see," said Moshe. "Good, good. All right. Absolute silence, please."

"A moment first," said Hakira. To the others, he said softly, "Nippon, this year."

With fierce smiles or no expression at all, the others murmured in reply, "Fujiyama kotoshi."

It was done. Hakira turned to Moshe and nodded.

They bowed their heads and made no sound, beyond the unavoidable sound of breathing. And an occasional sniffle—they *had* just come in from the cold.

One man coughed. Several people glared at him. Others simply closed their eyes, meditating their way to silence.

Hakira never took his eyes from Moshe, watching for some kind of signal to a hidden confederate, or perhaps for him to activate some machinery that might fill the room with poison gas. But . . . nothing.

Two minutes. Three. Four.

And then the room disappeared and a cold wind blew across forty naked bodies. They were in the open air inside a high fence, and around them in a circle stood men with swords.

Swords.

Everything was clear now.

"Well," said Moshe cheerfully, letting go and stepping back to join the armed men. One of them had a long coat for him, which he put on and wrapped around himself. "The transfer worked just as I told you it would—you're naked, there was no machinery involved, and don't you feel vigorous?"

Neither Hakira nor any of the people of Kotoshi said a thing.

"I did lie about a few things," said Moshe. "You see, we stumbled upon what you call 'slanting' at a much more primitive stage in our technological development than you. And wherever we went that wasn't downright fatal, and that wasn't already fully inhabited, there you were! Already overpopulating every world we could find! We had come upon the technique too late. So, we've come recruiting. If we're to have a chance at defeating you and your kind so we have a decent chance of finding worlds to expand into, we need to learn how to use your technology. How to use your weapons, how to disable your power system, how to make your ordinary citizens helpless. Since our technology is far behind yours, and we couldn't carry technology from world to world anyway, the way you can, this was our only choice."

Still no one answered him.

"You are taking this very calmly—good. The previous group was full of complainers, arguing with us and complaining about the weather even though it's *much* colder this time. That first group was very valuable— we've learned many medical breakthroughs from them, for instance, and many people are learning how to drive cars and how to use credit and even the theory behind computer programming. But you—well, I know it's a racial stereotype, but not only are you Japanese every bit as educated as the Jews from the previous group, you tend to be educated in mathematics and technology instead of medicine, law, and scripture. So from you we hope to learn many valuable things that will prepare us to take over one of your colonies and use it as a springboard to future conquest. Isn't it nice to know how valuable and important you are?"

One of the swordsmen let rip a string of sounds from another language. Moshe answered in the same language. "My friend comments that you seem to be taking this news extremely well."

"Only a few points of clarification are needed," said Hakira. "You are, in fact, planning to keep us as slaves?"

"Allies," said Moshe. "Helpers. Teachers."

"Not slaves. We are free to go, then? To return home if we wish?"

"No, I regret not."

"Are we free not to cooperate with you?"

"You will find your lives are much more comfortable if you cooperate."

"Will we be taught this mental method of transferring from angle to angle?"

Moshe laughed. "Please, you are too humorous."

"Is this a global policy on your world, or are you representing only one government or perhaps a small group not responsible to any government?"

"There is one government on this world, and we represent its policy," said Moshe. "It is only in the area of technology that we are not as advanced as you. We gave up tribes and nations thousands of years ago."

Hakira looked around at the others in his group. "Any other questions? Have we settled everything?"

Of course it was just a legal formality. He knew perfectly well that they were now free to act. This was, in fact, almost the worst-case scenario. No clothing, no weapons, cold weather, surrounded. But that was why they trained for the worst case. At least there were no guns, and they were outdoors.

"Moshe, I arrest you and all the armed persons present in this compound and charge you with wrongful imprisonment, slavery, fraud, and—"

Moshe shook his head and gave a brief command to the swordsmen. At once they raised their weapons and advanced on Hakira's group.

It took only moments for the nude Japanese to sidestep the swords, disarm the swordsmen, and leave them prostrate on the ground, their own swords now pointed at their throats. The Japanese who were not involved in that task quickly scoured the compound for more weapons and located the clumsy old-fashioned keys that would open the gate. Within moments they had run down and captured those guards who had been outside the gates. Not one got away. Only two had even attempted to fight. They were, as a result, dead.

To Moshe, Hakira said, "I now add the charge of assault and attempted murder."

"You'll never get back to your own world," said Moshe.

"We each have the complete knowledge necessary to make our own bender out of whatever materials we find here. We are also quite prepared to take on any military force you send against us, or to flee, if necessary. Even if we have to travel, we have *you*. The real question is whether we will learn the secret of mental reslanting from you before or after we build a bender for ourselves. I can promise you considerable lenience from the courts if you cooperate."

"Never."

"Oh, well. Someone else will."

"How did you know?" demanded Moshe.

"There is no world but ours with Japanese in it. Or Jews. None of the inhabited worlds have had cultures or languages or civilizations or histories that resembled each other in any way. We knew you were a con man, but we also knew the Zionists were gone without a trace. We also knew that someday we'd have to face people from another angle who had learned how to reslant themselves. We trained very carefully, and we followed you home."

"Like stray mongrels," said Moshe.

"Oh, and we do have to be told where the previous batch of slaves are being kept—the Zionists you kidnapped before."

"They'll all be killed," said Moshe nastily.

"That would be such a shame for you," said Hakira. He beckoned to one of his men, now armed with a sharp sword. In Japanese, he told his comrade that unfortunately, Moshe needed a demonstration of their relentless determination.

At once the sword flicked out and the tip of Moshe's nose dropped to the ground. The sword flicked again, and now Moshe lost the tip of the longest finger of the hand that he had been raising to touch his maimed nose.

Hakira bent over and scooped up the nose and the fingertip. "I'd say that if we get back to our world within about three hours, surgeons will be able to put these back on with only the tiniest scar and very little loss of function. Or shall we delay longer, and sever more protruding body parts?"

"This is inhuman!" said Moshe.

"On the contrary," said Hakira. "This is about as human as it gets."

"Are the people of your angle so determined to control every world you find?"

"Not at all," said Hakira. "We never interfered with any world that already had human life. You're the ones who decided on war. And I must say I'm relieved that the general level of your technology turns out to be so low. And that wherever you go, you arrive naked."

Moshe said nothing. His eyes glazed over.

Hakira murmured to his friend with the sword. The point of it quickly rested against the tender flesh just under Moshe's jaw.

Moshe's eyes grew quite alert.

"Don't even think of slanting away from us," said Hakira.

"I am the only one who speaks your language," said Moshe. "You have to sleep sometime. *I* have to sleep sometime. How will you know whether I'm really asleep, or merely meditating before I transfer?"

"Take a thumb," said Hakira. "And this time, let's make him swallow it."

Moshe gulped. "What sort of vengeance will you take against my people?"

"Apart from fair trials for the perpetrators of this conspiracy, we'll establish an irresistible presence here, watch you very carefully, and conduct such trade as we think appropriate. You yourself will be judged according to your cooperation now. Come on, Moshe, save some time. Take me back to my world. A bender is already being set up at your house—the troops moved in the moment we disappeared. You know that it's just a matter of time before they identify this angle and arrive in force no matter what you do."

"I could take you anywhere," said Moshe.

"And no doubt you're threatening to take me to some world with unbreathable air because you're willing to die for your cause. I understand that, I'm willing to die for mine. But if I'm not back here in ten minutes, my men will slaughter yours and begin the systematic destruction of your world. It's our only defense, if you don't cooperate. Believe me, the best way to save your world is by doing what I say."

"Maybe I hate you more than I love my people," said Moshe.

"What you love is our technology, Moshe, every bit of it. Come with me now and you'll be the hero who brings all those wonderful toys home."

"You'll put my finger and nose back on?"

"In my world the year is 3001," said Hakira. "We'll put them on you wherever you want them, and give you spares just in case."

"Let's go," said Moshe.

He took Hakira's hand and closed his eyes.

NOTES ON "ANGLES"

What can I say? This is a novel's worth of story that I was never able to tame into any useful shape. It's one of the best story ideas I've ever had, and what you just read (if you actually read it all) is the best I could do at putting it down in a coherent and, I hope, powerful way.

The original idea was: What if any enclosed space with right angles exerted a pressure on adjacent universes to have those angles matched? Sort of a feng shui thing—if someone was constructing a building, they would unconsciously align it with a building in the nearest "dimension" and there would be enormous pressure to make at least one room coincide *exactly*. If the builder didn't do this, it wouldn't feel right to people coming into the building, because though we aren't aware of it, we all sense the nearest dimensions.

But when the rooms exactly coincide, then a shimmering resonance begins, in which objects placed in the room exist in both dimensions at the same time.

This opened up the possibility that poltergeists—spirits that (supposedly) fling furniture around—were really people who were going crazy because *your* furniture was showing up in their house and they couldn't get rid of it! They'd move it out of the way, and you'd move it back! You were their poltergeist, and vice versa.

Besides the poltergeist thing, though, the idea of universes being very close together brought the possibility of space travel by the power of mind alone—that some people can go from universe to universe without knowing exactly where they're going. They just slide through somehow. Meanwhile, however, others can learn to do the same thing through technology, while others do it by linking people's minds together and bringing whole groups through.

That's all it remained, though—some ideas that I thought were really cool and couldn't let go of. I never found a way to fit the poltergeist thing into the time-traveler story. It finally came to life when I linked it with the situation of "homeless" nations on Earth—people like the Gypsies or (for many years) the Jews or the Kurds who, because of the vicissitudes of power, find themselves living in a land that somebody else insists belongs to *them*. Deprived of their homeland, they might use the possibility of travel into other universes as a way of getting, not just *a* homeland, but the very homeland that they had lost—only in a version of the universe in which that homeland was not occupied by humans. They wouldn't be displacing anybody.

That was the ragged idea on which I hung "Angles." I couldn't resist dropping in the poltergeist stuff, too. With only the dates at the head of each section to guide you, and some of the story threads leading, really, nowhere, I hope that the experience of reading this story wasn't *too* much like jumping from one universe to another without knowing quite how and why they were ever connected in the first place.

I think someday there might be a novel in this. When I think of yet another idea that will bind it all together.

II
FANTASY

VESSEL

Paulie hardly knew his cousins before that first family reunion in the mountains of North Carolina, and within about three hours he didn't want to know them any better. Because his mom was the youngest and she had married late, almost all the cousins were a lot older than Paulie and he didn't hit it off very well with the two that were his age, Celie and Deckie.

Celie, the girl cousin, only wanted to talk about her beautiful Arabians and how much fun she would have had if her mother had let her bring them up into the mountains, to which Paulie finally said, "It would have been a real hoot to watch you get knocked out of the saddle by a low branch," whereupon Celie gave him her best rich-girl freeze-out look and walked away. Paulie couldn't resist whinnying as she went.

This happened within about fifteen minutes of Paulie's arrival at the mountain cabin that Aunt Rosie had borrowed from a rich guy in the Virginia Democratic Party organization who owed her about a thousand big favors, as she liked to brag. "Let's just say that his road construction business depended on some words whispered into the right ears."

When she said that, Paulie was close enough to his parents to hear his father whisper to his mother, "I'll bet the left ears were lying on cheap motel pillows at the time." Mother jabbed him and Father grinned. Paulie didn't like the nastiness in Father's smile. It was the look that Grappaw always called "Mubbie's shit-eatin' smile." Grappaw was Father's father, and the only living soul who dared to call Father by that stupid baby nickname. In his mind, though, Paulie liked to think of Father that way. Mubbie Mubbie Mubbie.

Late in the afternoon Uncle Howie and Aunt Sissie showed up, driving a BMW and laughing about how much it would cost to get rid of the scratches from the underbrush that crowded the dirt road to the cabin. They always laughed when they talked about how much things cost; Mubbie said that was because laughing made people think they didn't care. "But they're always talking about it, you can bet." It was true. They hadn't been five minutes out of the car before they were talking about how expensive their trip to Bermuda had been ha-ha-ha and how much it was costing to put little Deckie into the finest prep school in Atlanta ha-ha-ha and how the boat salesmen insisted on calling thirty-footers "yachts" so they could triple the price but you just have to grit your teeth and pay their thieves' toll ha-ha-ha like the three billy goats gruff ha-ha-ha.

Then they went on about how their two older children were so busy at Harvard and some Wall Street firm that they just couldn't tear themselves away but they brought Deckie their little accident ha-ha-ha and they just bet that he and Paulie would be good friends.

Deckie was suntanned to the edge of skin cancer, so Paulie's first words to him were, "What, are you trying to be black?"

"I play tennis."

"Under a sunlamp?"

"I tan real dark." Deckie looked faintly bored, as though he had to answer these stupid questions all the time but he had been raised to be polite.

"Deckie? What's that short for? Or are you named after the floor on a yacht?" Paulie thought he was joking, like old friends joke with each other, but Deckie seemed to take umbrage.

"Deckie is short for Derek. My friends call me Deck."

"Are you sure they aren't calling you *duck*?" Paulie laughed and then wished he hadn't. Deckie's eyes glazed over and he began looking toward the house. Paulie didn't want him to walk off the way Celie had. Deckie was two years older than Paulie, and it was the important two years. Puberty had put about a foot of height on him and he was lean and athletic and his moves were languid and Paulie wanted more than anything to be just like Deckie instead of being a medium-height medium-strong medium-smart freckled twelve-year-old nothing.

So naturally he tried to cover up his stupid duck joke with an even lamer one. "Have you noticed how everybody in the family has a nickname that ends with *ie*?" Paulie said. "They might as well hyphenate that into the family name. You'd be Deck Ie-Bride, and Celie would be Ceel Ie-Caswell."

Deckie smiled faintly. "And you'd be Paul Ie-Asshole."

Paulie stood there blushing, flustered, until he finally realized that this was not a friendly joke, this was Deckie letting him know that he didn't exist. So Paulie turned and walked away from Deckie. Did Celie feel like this when she walked away from me? If she did then I'm a rotten shit to make somebody else feel like this. Why can't I just keep my mouth shut? Other people keep their mouths shut.

Later he saw Deckie and Celie hanging around together, laughing until tears ran down Celie's face. He knew they were talking about him. Or if they weren't they might as well be. That was the kind of laughter that never included Paulie, not at school, not at home, not here at this stupid family reunion in this stupid forty-room mansion that some stupid rich person called a "cabin." Whenever people laughed in real friendship, close to each other, bound by affection or mutual respect or whatever it was, Paulie felt it like a knife in his heart. Not because he was particularly lonely. He liked being alone and other people made him nervous so it's not like he suffered. It hurt him because it was exactly the way people were with Mubbie. Nobody liked him and he still kept joking with them as if they were friends, even Mother, she didn't like him either, any idiot could see that, they were probably staying together for the sake of "the child," which was Paulie of course. Or rather Mother was staying for Paulie's sake, and Mubbie was staying for Mother's money, which was always useful for tiding him over between sales jobs, which Mubbie always joked his way into losing after having piled up an impressive record of lost sales and mishandled contracts. I'm just like him, Paulie thought. I joke like him, I make enemies like him, people sneer at me behind my back the way they do with him, only I'm not even studly enough to get a rich babe like Mom to bail me through all the screwups that lie ahead of me in life.

If I could just learn to keep my mouth shut.

He even tried it for the next couple of hours, being absolutely silent, saying nothing to anybody. But of course the moment he wanted to shut up, that was when all the aunts and uncles and the older cousins had to come up and pretend to care about him. No doubt Mother had noticed that Paulie was by himself and told them to go include Paulie. People did what Mother said, even her older brothers and sisters. She just had a way of making suggestions that people started following before they even had a chance to think about whether they wanted to. So when Paulie tried to get by with nods and smiles, he kept hearing, "Cat got your tongue?" and "You can't be *that* shy" and even "You got something you shouldn't in your mouth, boy?" to which Paulie thought of about five funny answers, one of which wasn't even obscene, but at least he managed not to say them out loud and completely scandalize everybody and make himself the humiliated goat of the whole reunion, with Mother apologizing to everybody and saying, "I can assure you he wasn't raised that way," so that everybody understood that he got his ugly way of talking from Mubbie's side of the family. Of course, Mother would no doubt end up saying that *sometime* before the week was over, but maybe Paulie would get through the first day without having to hear it.

Dinner was bad. The dining room table was huge, but not big enough for everybody. Naturally, they had to have Nana, Mother's grandmother, at the table, even though she was so gaga that she had to be spoon-fed some poisonously bland gruel and never seemed to understand anything going on around her. Why didn't they send *her* to the second table with the little children of some of the older cousins, nasty little brats with no manners at all and a way of whining that made Paulie want to insert silverware really far down their throats? But no, that was Paulie's place.

Deckie and Celie were assigned to that table, too, but they ducked off into the kitchen to eat there, and bad as it was with the brats, Paulie knew it would be worse in the kitchen where he hadn't been invited. So he had to sit there and try to listen over the noise of the brats as Uncle Howie at the other table bragged about Deckie's tennis playing and how he could turn pro if he wanted, but of course he was going to Harvard and he'd simply use his tennis to terrorize his employees when he was running some company. "His employees won't have to try to lose in order to suck up to Deckie," Uncle Howie said. "They'll have to be such damn good tennis players that they can give him a good game. And that means his best executives will all be in top physical shape, which keeps the health costs down."

"Till one of them drops dead of a heart attack on the tennis court and the widow sues Deckie for making him play."

The whole table fell silent except for one person, who was laughing uproariously because after all, he made the joke. Mubbie, naturally. Paulie wanted to die.

After the dead silence, punctuated only by the laughter of one social corpse, Mother turned the conversation back to the achievements of the other children. It was a cruel thing for her to do, since naturally the others asked her about what Paulie was doing, and naturally she answered with offhand good humor, "Oh, you know, he gets along well enough. No psychiatrists' bills yet, and no bail money, so we're content." The others laughed at this, except Paulie. He wondered if maybe some of the older cousins had been to shrinks or had to be bailed out of jail, so that maybe Mom's little joke had a barb to it just like Father's did, only she knew how to do it subtly, so that even the victims had to laugh. But most likely nobody in this scrupulously correct family had ever been in a position where either a shrink or a bail bondsman was required.

Paulie ate as quickly as possible and excused himself and went to the room that had Deckie's stuff in it, too, piled on the other twin bed, but mercifully Deckie himself was off somewhere else being perfect and Paulie had some peace. His mother made him bring some books so when he was off by himself she could tell the others he was reading, and Paulie was smart enough to have packed books he already read at school so that when the adults asked him what he was reading he could tell them what the story was about, as if they cared. But the truth was that Paulie didn't like to read, it all seemed pretty thin to him, he could think up better stuff just lying around with his eyes closed.

They must have thought he was asleep, must have peered in the door and decided he was dead to the world, or they probably wouldn't have held their little confab out in the hall, Mother and her brothers and sister. The subject was Nana. "She's already got all her money in a trust that we administer," Mother was saying, "and she can afford a round-the-clock nurse, so what's the problem?"

But the others had all kinds of other arguments, which in Paulie's mind all boiled down to one: Nana was an embarrassment and as long as she remained in the Bride mansion in Richmond their family could never return to their rightful place among the finest families of Virginia. Paulie wanted to speak up and ask them why they didn't just put her in a bag, weight it down with rocks, and drop it into the James River, but he didn't. He just listened as every one of Nana's grandchildren except Mother made it plain that they had less filial affection than the average housecat. And even Mother, Paulie suspected, was opposing them because whoever ended up in that mansion would be established for all time as the leading branch of the family, and Mother couldn't stomach that, even though by marrying Mubbie she had removed herself from all possibility of occupying that position herself. At home she talked all the time about how her brothers and sisters put on airs as if they were all real Brides but the spunk was gone from the family after Mother and Father died when they went out sailing on the Chesapeake and got caught in the fringes of a spent hurricane. "Nana is the only remnant left of the old vigor," she would say.

"Drooling and grunting like a baboon," Father would always answer, then laugh as Mother ignored him.

"She still understands what's going on around her," Mother would say. "You can see it in her eyes. She can't talk or eat because Parkinson's has her, but it's not Alzheimer's, she's sharp as a tack and I have no doubt that if she could write or speak, she'd wipe my brothers and sisters right out of the will. And since she can't do that, she does the only thing she *can* do. She refrains from dying. I admire her for that."

"I refrain from dying every day," Mubbie would say, every time as if he hoped it would be funny if he just got to the right number of repetitions. "But you never admire *me* for that." At which Mother always changed the subject.

The conversation in the hall went the rounds until finally Aunt Rosie said, "Oh, never mind. Weedie's never going to bend"—Weedie was Mother, who preferred the nickname to Winifred—"and Nana can't live forever so we'll just go on."

They went away and Paulie wondered how Nana would feel if she could hear the way they talked about her. Didn't it ever occur to any of them that maybe she would be just as happy to be rid of them as they would be to be rid of her? Paulie tried to imagine what it would be like, to be trapped in a body that wouldn't do anything, to have to have somebody wipe your butt whenever you relieved yourself, to have to have somebody feed you every bite you ate, and know that they hated you for not being dead, or at least wished with some impatience that you'd just get *on* with it.

And then, drowning in self-pity, Paulie wondered whether it was really different from his own life. If Nana died, at least it would make a difference to somebody. They'd get a house. Somebody would move. People would have more money. But if I died, who'd notice? Hell, *I* probably wouldn't even notice. Not till it was time to eat and I couldn't pick up a fork.

It was dark by now but there was a full moon and anyway the parking lot around the so-called cabin was flooded with light, especially the tennis courts where the thwang, thunk, thwang, thunk, thwang of a ball being hit and bouncing off the court and getting hit again rang out in the night's stillness. Paulie got up from his bed where maybe he had fallen asleep for a while and maybe not. He walked through the upstairs hall and quietly down the stairs. Adults were gathered in the living room and the kitchen, talking and sometimes laughing, but nobody noticed him as he went outside.

He expected to see Deckie and Celie playing tennis, but it was Uncle Howie and Aunt Sissie, Deckie's parents, playing with intense grimaces on their faces as if this were the final battle in a lifelong war. They both dripped with sweat even though the night air here in the Great Smokies was fairly cool.

So where were Deckie and Celie? Not that it mattered. Not that they'd welcome Paulie's company if he found them. Not that he could even be sure they were together. He knew Deckie was out somewhere because his stuff was still piled on his bed. And the sounds of tennis had made Paulie assume he was playing with Celie. But for all he knew, Celie was in bed with the little girl cousins in the big attic dormitory. Still, he looked for them because at some level he knew they would be together, and for some perverse reason he always had to push and push until he forced people to tell him outright that they didn't want him around. The school counselor had told him this about himself, but hadn't told him how to stop doing it. In fact, Paulie was half-convinced that the counselor had only told him that as an oblique way of letting him know that he, too, didn't want Paulie around anymore.

There wasn't a sound coming from the pool, though the lights were on there, so Paulie didn't bother going in. He just walked the path around the chain-link fence that kept woodland animals from coming to drown in the chlorinated water. It wasn't till Celie giggled that Paulie realized they were in there after all, not swimming but sitting on the edge at the shallow end, their feet in the water, resting on the steps going into the water. Paulie stood and watched them, knowing that he was invisible to them, knowing he would be invisible even if he were standing right in front of them, even if he were walking on the damned water.

Then he realized that Celie was only wearing the bottom part of her two-piece swimming suit. Paulie's first thought was, How stupid, she's only eleven, she's got nothing to show anyway. Then he saw that Deckie had his hand inside the bottom of her swimsuit and he was kissing her shoulder or sucking on it or something, and that's why Celie was laughing and saying, "Stop it that tickles," and then Paulie understood that Deckie liked it that she didn't have any breasts yet and he knew just what Deckie was and in that moment relief swept over Paulie like a great cleansing wave because he knew now that despite Deckie's beautiful tan and beautiful body and charmed life, Deckie was the sick one and Paulie *didn't* want to be like him after all.

Only then did it occur to him that even though Celie was laughing, what Deckie was doing to her was wrong and for Paulie to stand there feeling *relieved* of all things was completely selfish and evil of him and he had to do something, he had to put a stop to it, then and there, if he was any kind of decent person at all, and if he didn't then he was just as bad as Deckie because he was standing there watching, wasn't he? And letting it happen.

"Stop it," he said. His voice was a croak and between the crickets and the breeze in the leaves and the thwang, thunk of the tennis match, they didn't hear him.

"Get your hands off her, you asshole!" Paulie yelled.

This time they heard him. Celie shrieked and pulled away from Deckie, looking frantically for the top of her swimsuit, which was floating about ten feet out. She splashed down the steps into the pool, reaching for it, as Deckie stood up, looking for Paulie in the darkness outside the chain-link fence. Their eyes met. Deckie walked around the pool toward him.

"I wasn't doing anything, you queer," said Deckie. "And what were you doing watching, anyway, you queer?"

The words struck home. Paulie answered not a word. They were face to face now, through the chain link.

"Nobody will believe you," said Deckie. "And Celie will never admit it happened. She wanted it, you know. She's the one that took off her top."

"Shut up," said Paulie.

"If you tell anybody, I'll just look disgusted and tell them that you and I quarreled and you warned me you'd do something to get me in trouble. They'll believe me. They know you're a weasel. A sneaking weasel queer."

"You can call me whatever you like," said Paulie. "But you and I both know what you are. And someday you'll mess with somebody's little girl and they won't just call the cops so your family lawyers can get you off, they'll come after you with a gun and blow the suntan right off your face."

Paulie said all that, but not until Deckie was on the other side of the pool, walking into the poolhouse. By then Celie had her top back on and was climbing out of the water. She didn't even turn to look at him. Paulie had saved her, but maybe she didn't want to be saved. And even if she did, he knew that she'd never speak to him again as long as he lived. He'd seen the wrong thing, he'd done the wrong thing, even when he was trying to do the right thing.

He didn't want to go to bed, not with Deckie lying there in the next bed. He thought of taking a swim himself, but the thought of getting in the water they had been using made him feel polluted. He walked away into the brush.

It got dark immediately under the trees, but not so dark he couldn't see the ground. And soon he found a path that led down to the stream, which made that curious rushing, plinking sound like some kind of random musical instrument that was both string and wind. The water was icy cold when he put his bare feet into it. Cold and pure and numbing and he kept walking upstream.

The trees broke open over the stream and moonlight poured down from almost straight overhead. The water had carved its way under some of the trees lining the banks. None had fallen, but many of them cantilevered perilously over the water, their roots reaching out like some ancient scaffolding, waiting for somebody to come in and finish building the riverbank. In the spring runoff or during a storm, all the gaps under the trees would be invisible, but it was the end of a dryish summer and there wasn't that much water, so the banks were exposed right down to the base. If I just lay down under one of these trees, when it rained again the water would rise and lift me up into the roots like a fish up to an octopus's mouth, and the roots would hold me like an octopus's arms and I could just lie there and sleep while it sucked the life out of me, sucked it right out and left me dry, and then I'd dissolve in the water and float down the river and end up in some reservoir and get filtered out of the drinking water and end up getting treated with a bunch of sewage or maybe in a toxic waste dump which pretty much describes my life right now so it wouldn't make much difference, would it?

The bank was higher on the left side now, and it was rocky, not clay. The stone was bone dry and shone ghostly white in the moonlight, except for one place, under a low outcropping, where the rock was glistening wet. When Paulie got closer he could see that there was water flowing thinly over the face of the rock. But how could that be, since all the rock above the overhang was dry? Only when he stooped down did he realize that there wasn't just shadow under that outcropping of stone, there was a cave, and the water flowed out of it. When the stream was high, the cave entrance must be completely under water; and the rest of the time it would be invisible unless you were right down under the overhang, looking up. Yet it was large enough for a person to slither in.

A person or an animal. A bear? Not hibernation season. A skunk? A porcupine? Maybe. So what? Paulie imagined coming home with spines in his face or smelling like a skunk and all he could think was: They'd have to take me away from here. To the doctor to get the spines out or back home to get the smell of me away from the others. They'd have to ride with him in the car all the way down the mountain, smelling him the whole way.

He ducked low, almost getting his face into the water, and soaking his shorts and the front of his T-shirt. He was right, you *could* get into the cave, and it was easier than it looked at first, the cave was bigger inside than it seemed from the size of the opening. The spring inside it had been eating away at the rock for a long time. And if there was an animal in here, it kept quiet. Didn't move, didn't smell. It was dark, and after a while when Paulie's eyes got used to the darkness it was *still* pitch black and he couldn't see his hand in front of his face, so he felt his way inward, inward. Maybe animals didn't use this cave because the entrance was underwater so much. Bats couldn't use it, that was for sure. And it would be a lousy place to hibernate since there was no getting out during the spring flood.

The water from the spring made a pool inside the cave, not a deep one, but pure and cold. The cleanest water Paulie would ever find in his life, he knew that. He dipped his hand into the water, lifted it to his mouth, drank. It tasted sweet and clear. It tasted like cold winter light. He crawled farther into the cave, looking for a place where he could lie down and dream and remember the taste of this water straight from the stone heart of the earth.

His hand brushed against something that wasn't rock, and it moved.

Paulie knelt there, hardly daring to breathe. No sound. No alarm. No movement of any kind. And he *could* see, just a little bit, just faint dark greys against the black of the background, and there wasn't any motion, none at all. He reached out and touched it again, and it moved again, and then tipped over and thudded softly and now when he handled it he realized it was a shoe, or not really a shoe but a moccasin, the leather dry and brittle, so it broke a little under his hand. Something clattered out of the moccasin when he lifted it up and when he cast around to find whatever it was, he realized it was a lot of things, small hard things, bones from somebody's feet. There was a dead body here. Someone had crawled into this cave and died.

And then suddenly in the darkness he could see, only he wasn't seeing anything that actually lay there. He was seeing an Indian, a youngish man, broad cheekbones, nearly naked, unarmed, fleeing from men on horseback, men on foot, running up the stream after him, calling and shouting and now and then discharging a musket. One of the musket balls took him, right in the back, right into a lung. Paulie almost felt it, piercing him, throwing him forward. After that he could hardly breathe, his lung was filling up, he was weak, he couldn't run anymore, but there was the cave here, and the water was low, and he had strength enough to climb up under the overhang, taking care not to brush against it and leave a stain of blood from his back. He would lie here and hide until the white men went on and he could come back out and go find his father, go find a medicine man who could do something about the blood in his lungs, only the white men didn't go away, they kept searching for him, he could hear them outside, and then he realized it didn't matter anyway because he was never going to leave this cave. If he coughed, he'd give himself away and they'd drag him out and torture him and kill him. If he didn't cough, he'd drown. He drowned.

Paulie felt the moment of death, not as pain, but as a flash of light that entered his body through his fingertips and filled him for a moment. Then it receded, fled into some dark place inside him and lurked there. A death hidden inside him, the death of a Cherokee who wasn't going to leave his home, wasn't going to go west to some unknown country just because Andrew Jackson said they had to go. He held inside him the death of a proud man who wasn't going to leave his mountains, ever. A man who had, in a way, won his battle.

He knelt there on all fours, gasping. How could he have seen all this? He had daydreamed for hours on end, and never had he dreamed of Indians; never had the experiences seemed so real and powerful. The dead Cherokee's life seemed more vivid, even in the moment of dying, than anything in Paulie's own experience. He was overwhelmed by it. The Cherokee owned more of his soul, for this moment, than Paulie did himself. And yet the Cherokee was dead. It wasn't a ghost here, just bones. And it hadn't possessed Paulie—he was still himself, still the bland nondescript nothing he had always been, except that he remembered dying, remembered drowning in his own blood rather than coughing and letting his enemies have the satisfaction of finding him. They would always think he got away. They would always think they had failed. It was a victory, and that was an unfamiliar taste in Paulie's mouth.

He stretched himself out beside the skeleton of the Indian, not seeing it, but knowing where the bones must be, the long bones of the arms, the ladder of the ribs, the vertebrae jumbled in a row, the cartilage that once connected them gone, dissolved and washed out into the stream many years ago.

And as Paulie lay there another image crept into his mind. Another person splashing through the stream, but it wasn't a sunny day this time, it was raining, it was bitterly cold. The leaves were off the trees, and behind him he could hear the baying of hounds. Could they follow his scent in the rain? Through the stream? How could they? Yet they came on, closer and closer, and he could hear the shouts of the men. "She went this way!"

She. Now Paulie became aware of the shape of the body he wore in this memory. A woman, young, her body sensitive to the chafing of the cloth across her small young breasts. And now he knew what she was fleeing from. The master wouldn't leave her alone. He came at her so often it hurt, and the overseer came after him as soon as he was gone, until finally she couldn't stand it, she ran away, and when they found her they'd whip her and if she didn't die from the lash then as soon as she was half-healed they'd come at her again, only this time she'd be kept chained and locked up and she wasn't going back, never, no matter what.

As she ran up the stream she saw the outcropping of rock and happened to stumble just then and splash on all fours into the icy river and then she looked up and saw that there was a cave and almost without thinking she climbed up into it and lay there shivering with the bitter cold, hardly daring to move, fearful that the chattering of her teeth would give her away. She slid farther up into the cave and then her hand found the half-decomposed leg of someone who had died in that cave and she shrieked in spite of herself and the men outside heard her but they didn't know where the shriek came from. They knew she was close but they couldn't find her and the dogs couldn't catch her scent so she lay there by the corpse of the dead Indian and shivered and prayed that the spirit of the dead would leave her alone, she didn't mean to bother him, she'd go away as soon as she could. In the meantime, she got more and more numb from the cold, and despite her terror at every shout she heard from the men outside, their voices got dimmer and dimmer until all she could hear was the rushing of the water and she got sleepy and closed her eyes and slept as the stream outside rose up and sealed the entrace of the cave and her breathing drew the last oxygen out of the air so that she was dead before the cold could kill her.

As before, the moment of her death came into Paulie's fingers like an infusion of light; as before, the light filled him, then receded to hide within him; as before, her last memories were more vivid in his mind than anything he had ever experienced himself.

I should never have drunk the water in this cave, thought Paulie. I've taken death inside me. It's a magic place, a terrible place, and now I'm filled with death. What am I supposed to do with this? How am I supposed to use the things I saw and felt and heard tonight? There's no lesson in this—this has nothing to do with my life, nothing to teach me. All that's different is that I know what it feels like to die. And I know that there are some people whose lives were worse than mine. Only maybe that's not even true, because at least they accomplished something by dying in this cave. They had some kind of small victory, and it's damn sure I've never had anything like that in *my* life. Since I'm the source of all my own problems, blundering and babbling my way through the world, who can I run away from in order to get free? This girl, this man who died here, they were lucky—they knew who their enemies were, and even if they died doing it, at least they got away.

He must have slept, because when he woke he was aware of aches and pains all over his body from lying on stone, from sleeping in the cool damp air of the cave. Fearless now of the dead, he felt around until he had traced the Cherokee's whole skeleton, and then, crawled farther in until he found the bones of the girl, the crumbling fabric of her cotton dress. He took a scrap of the dress with him, and a piece of the brittle leather of the Cherokee's moccasin. He put them in his pocket and crawled back to the entrance of the cave. Then he slid down, soaking his pants and shirt again.

The moon was low but it didn't matter, dawn was coming and there was enough light to find his way home, splashing through the stream until he came to the place where he had left his shoes. He wondered if his parents had even noticed he was gone. Probably not. It was damn sure Deckie wouldn't have told them he was missing. If Deckie even went to the room. Still, if they *did* notice he was gone, there might be some kind of uproar. He'd have to tell them where he was and what he was doing and why his feet and shirt and shorts were wet. He was still trying to think of some kind of lie when he came into the cabin, through the back door because there was a light on in the living room and maybe he could sneak into bed.

But no, there was someone in the kitchen, too, though the light was off. "Who's there?"

Reluctantly Paulie leaned into the kitchen door and saw, to his relief, that it was the nurse who looked after Nana. "I'm making her breakfast," the woman said, "but she's fretful. She moans when she's like that, unless somebody sits there with her, and I can't sit there with her and make her mush too, so would you mind since you're up anyway, would you mind just going in and sitting with her so she doesn't wake everybody up?"

The nurse was all right. The nurse wouldn't get him in trouble. He could hear Nana moaning from the main-floor bedroom that had been given over to her so nobody had to carry her frail old body up and down the stairs. The light was on in Nana's room and she was sitting up in her wheelchair, the strap around her ribs so she didn't fall over when the trembling became too strong. Paulie could see the cot where the nurse slept. It was silly, really—the nurse was a large, big-boned woman and the cot must barely hold her, not even room enough to roll over without falling out of bed. While tiny Nana had slept in a huge king-size bed. It would never have occurred to them, though, that Nana should get the cot. The nurse was of the serving class.

I am of the serving class, too, thought Paulie. Because I have more of my father's blood than my mother's. I don't belong among the rich people, except to wait on them. That's why I never feel like I'm one of them. Just like Father never belongs. We should be their chauffeurs and yard boys and butlers and whatever. We should wait on them and take their orders in restaurants. We should run their errands and file their correspondence. We all know it, even though we can't say it. Mother married down, and gave birth down, too. I should have been on a cot in someone's room, waiting for them to wake up so I could rush down and make their breakfast and carry it up to them. That's how the world is supposed to work. The nurse understands that. That's why she knew she could ask me to help her. Because this is who I really am.

Nana looked at him and moaned insistently. He walked to her, not knowing what she wanted or even if she wanted anything. Her eyes pierced him, sharp and unyielding. Oh, she wants something all right. What?

She looked up at him and started trying to raise her hands, but they trembled so much that she could hardly raise them. Still, it seemed clear enough that she was reaching out to him, staring into his eyes. So he held out his hands to her.

Her hands smacked against one of his. She could no more take hold of him than fly, so he took hold of her, one of her hands in both of his, and at once the trembling stopped, the effort stopped, and the unheld hand fell back into her lap on the wheelchair. "The nurse is fixing your breakfast," Paulie said lamely.

But she didn't answer. She just looked at him and smiled and then, suddenly, he felt that light that was hidden within him stir, he felt the pain in his back again from the musket ball, and now the death of the Cherokee swelled within him and filled him for a moment with light. And then, just as quickly, it flowed out of him, down through his fingertips just the way it had come. Flowed out of him and into her. Her face brightened, she dropped her head back, and as the last of the Cherokee's deathlight left him, she let out a final groan of air and died, her head flopped back and her mouth and eyes wide open.

Paulie knew at once what had happened. He had killed her. He had carried death out of the cave with him and it had flowed out of his hands and into her and she was dead and he did it. He sank to the floor in front of her and the weariness and pain of last night and this morning, the fear and horror of the two long-ago deaths that he had witnessed—no, experienced—and finally the enormity of what he had done to his great-grandmother, all of this overwhelmed him and when the nurse came into the room she found him crying silently on the floor. At once she took the old woman's pulse, then unstrapped her, lifted her out of the chair, and laid her on the bed, then covered her up to her neck. "You just stay there, son," she said to him, and he did, crying quietly while she went back to the kitchen and rinsed the dishes. It occurred to him to wonder that her response to death was not to waken everybody but rather to wash up after an uneaten breakfast. Then he realized: That's what the serving class is for, to clean up, wash up, hide everything ugly and unpleasant.

Hide everything ugly and unpleasant.

I didn't kill her, or if I did, I didn't mean to. And besides she wanted it. I think she saw the death in me and reached for it. I brought her what she couldn't get any other way, release from her family, from her body, from her memories of life unmatched by any power to live. Nobody will be sorry to see her dead, not really. Somebody can move into the Richmond mansion again and become the main bloodline of the Brides. The nurse will get another job and everything will be fine. So why can't I stop crying?

He hadn't stopped crying when the nurse went to waken Mother— even the nurse knew that it was Mother who had to be told first. And even though she held him and murmured to him, "Who could have guessed you'd be so tenderhearted," he couldn't stop crying, until finally he was shaking like the girl in the cave, shivering uncontrollably. I have another death in me, he thought. It's dangerous to come near me, there's another death in my fingers, the cold death of a slave girl waiting in some cave in my heart. Don't come near me.

Mother and Father left that morning, to take him home and make funeral arrangements in Richmond. Others would take care of arranging for the ambulance and the doctor and the death certificate. Others would dress the corpse. Mother and Father had to take their son, who, after all, had found the body. No one ever asked him what he was doing up at that hour, or where he had spent the night, and if anyone noticed that his shirt and pants were damp they never asked him about it. They just packed up his stuff while he sat, tearless now, on the sofa in the parlor, waiting to be taken away from this place, from the old lady who had drawn death out of his fingers, from the people who had jockeyed for position as they waited years for her to die, and from the children who played dark ugly games with each other by the swimming pool when no adult could see.

At last all the preparations were done, the car brought round, the bags loaded. Mother came and tenderly led him out onto the porch, down the steps, toward the car. "It was so awful for you to find her like that," she said to him, as if Nana had done something embarrassing instead of just dying.

"I don't know why I got so upset," said Paulie. "I'm sorry."

"We would have had to leave anyway," said Mubbie, holding the door open for him. "Even the Brides can't keep a family reunion going when somebody just died."

Mother glared at him over Paulie's head. He didn't even have to look up to see it. He knew it from the smirk on Mubbie's face.

"Paulie!" cried a voice. Paulie knew as he turned that it was Deckie, though it was unbelievable that the older boy would seek a confrontation right here, right now, in front of everybody.

"Paulie!" Deckie called again. He ran until he stopped right in front of Paulie, looking down at him, his face a mask of commiseration and kind regard. Paulie wanted to hit him, to knock the smile off his face; but of course if he tried to throw a punch Deckie would no doubt prove that he had taken five years of boxing or tae kwon do or something and humiliate Paulie yet again.

"Celie and I were worried about you," Deckie said. And then, in a whisper, he added, "We wondered if you stripped off the old lady's clothes so you could look at *her* naked, too."

The enormity of the accusation turned Paulie's seething anger into hot rage. And in that moment he felt the death stir within him, the light of it pour out into his body, filling him with dangerous light, right to the fingertips. He felt the terrible fury of the helpless slave girl, raped again and again, her determination to die rather than endure it anymore. He knew that all he had to do was reach out and touch Deckie and the slave girl's death would flow into him, so that in his last moments he would feel what a violated child felt like. It was the perfect death for him, true justice. There were a dozen adults gathered around, watching. They would all agree that Paulie hadn't done anything.

Deckie smiled nastily and whispered, "Bet you play with yourself for a year remembering me and Celie." Then he thrust out his hand and loudly said, "You're a good cousin and I'm glad Nana's last moments were with you, Paulie. Let's shake on it!"

What Deckie meant to do was to force Paulie to shake his hand, to humiliate himself and accept Deckie's dominance forever. What he couldn't know was that he was almost begging Paulie to kill him with a single touch. Death seeped out of Paulie, reaching for Deckie. If I just reach out . . .

"Shake his hand, for heaven's sake, Paulie," said Mother.

No, thought Paulie. Deckie is slime but if they killed every asshole in the world who'd be left to answer the phones? And with that thought he turned his back and got into the car.

"Paulie," said Mother. "I can't believe . . ."

"Let's go," said Father from the driver's seat.

Mother, realizing that Father was right and there shouldn't be a scene, slid into the front seat and closed the door. As they drove away she said, "Paulie, the trauma you've been through doesn't mean you can't be courteous to your own cousin. Maybe if you accepted other people's overtures of friendship you wouldn't be alone so much."

She went on like that for a while but Paulie didn't care. He was trying to think of why it was he didn't kill Deckie when he had the chance. Was he afraid to do it? Or was he afraid of something much worse, afraid that Deckie was right and Paulie had enjoyed watching, afraid that he might be just as evil in his own heart as Deckie was? Deckie should be dead, not Nana. Deckie should have been the one whose body shook so much he couldn't stand up or touch anybody. How long would Celie have sat still if Deckie had pawed at her with quivering hands the way that Nana reached out to me? God afflicts all the wrong people.

When they got home they treated Paulie with an exaggerated concern that was tinged with disdain. He could feel their contempt for his weakness in everything they said and did. They were ashamed that he was their son and not Deckie. If they only knew.

But maybe it wouldn't make any difference if they knew. Tanned athletic boys must sow their wild oats. They live by different rules, and if you have such a one as your own child, you forgive him everything, while if you have a child like Paulie, basic and ordinary and forgettable, you have to work all your life just to forgive him for that one thing, for being only himself and not something wonderful.

Mother and Mubbie didn't make him go to the funeral—he didn't even have to plead with them. And in later years, as the family reunion became an annual event, they didn't argue with him very hard before giving in and letting him stay home. Paulie at first suspected and then became quite sure that they were much happier leaving him at home because without him there, they could pretend that they were proud of him. They weren't forced to compare him quite so immediately with the ever taller, ever handsomer, ever more accomplished Deckie.

When they came home, Paulie would leave the room whenever they started going on about Sissie's and Howie's boy. He saw them cast knowing looks at each other, and Mother even said to him once, "Paulie, you shouldn't compare yourself to Deckie that way, there's no need for you to feel bad about his accomplishments. You'll have accomplishments of your own someday." It never occurred to her that by saying this, she swept away all the small triumphs of his life so far.

There were times in the years to come when Paulie doubted the reality of his memory of that family reunion. The light hiding within him stayed dark for weeks and months on end. The memory of the swimming pool faded; so did the memory of Nana's feebly grasping hands. So, even, did the memory of the death of the Cherokee and the runaway slave. But then one day he would move something in his drawer and see the envelope in which he kept the tattered fragment of a threadbare dress and the scrap of an ancient moccasin, and it would flood back to him, right down to the smell of the cave, the taste of the water, the feel of the bones under his hand.

At other times he would remember because someone would provoke him, would do something so awful that it filled him with fury and suddenly he felt the death rising in him. But he calmed himself at once, every time, calmed himself and walked away. I didn't kill Deckie that day. Why should I kill this asshole now? Then he would go off and forget, surprisingly soon, that he had the power to kill. Forget until the next time he saw the envelope, or the next time he was swept by rage.

He never saw Deckie again. Or Celie. Or any of his aunts and uncles or cousins. As far as he was concerned he had no family beyond Mother and Mubbie. It was not that he hated his relatives—except for Deckie he didn't think they were particularly evil. He learned soon enough that his family was, in a way, pretty ordinary. There was money, which complicated things, but Paulie knew that people without money still found reasons to hate their relatives and carry feuds with them from generation to generation. The money just meant you drove better cars through all the misery. No, Paulie's kinfolk weren't so awful, really. He just didn't need to see them. He'd already learned everything they had to teach him. One family reunion was enough for him.

NOTES ON "VESSEL"

This story began when I was invited to tour an area on the grounds of Guilford College in Greensboro, North Carolina, where I have lived for the past twenty-five years. I knew that it was a Quaker college, and that the Quakers had been a vital part of the Underground Railroad that brought runaway slaves to freedom during the Civil War, but until that tour I had never put it together that Guilford College itself might have been involved. (I grew up out West, where history is something that happened somewhere else.)

I was especially stirred by the stretch of a stream that had eroded its way under the broad roots of huge old trees. The runaway slaves would climb up under the roots and hide; the stream masked their scent from the dogs, and yet the runaways were dry, above the water level.

I was taken on the tour in hopes that I might be able to do something to publicize the historical importance of the site. It was slated to be in the path of a (useless) freeway that was planned to be built as a beltway around Greensboro, a city notorious for having roads that, like this beltway, don't actually go anywhere. Fortunately, without any help from me, the route was changed and the site was preserved.

Meanwhile, I had this place in my mind. Whom would I put there? Someone from our modern world. And what would happen to him because he was there?

This short story was the result. Acquiring the power to be a vessel of death was merely the first thought to come to mind that intrigued me enough to think about at length. It's a fantasy—I don't believe people can actually acquire such powers. Nor am I a believer in euthanasia—quite the contrary, I believe that allowing one person to "help" another die is a broad fast highway to murdering the old and crippled, a way to turn our society into something monstrous.

And yet there are people who are simply ready to die; what if there were someone who was ready to help them? Not only did I come up with this short story, I also had a whole novel planned out. But when it came time to write it, I simply didn't have it in me to write it. The prospect was too bleak. How could I find any hope in the story to make it worth reading? I ended up fulfilling the contract with *Treasure Box* instead—a bleak enough book!—and the novel version of "Vessel" died.

Meanwhile, the story had been held for a long time by a friend who wanted to publish it as part of a project that never got off the ground. So, years after I'd forgotten about the whole thing, I suddenly found myself with the rights back to a story that I thought was powerful and that had never been published. Just at that time I made my first visit to Spain, to attend a convention in Mataró. There it occurred to me that it would be cool to offer the Spanish sci-fi magazine *BEM* a story of mine that had never been published *anywhere* before, so that Spanish was the language of first publication. The editors liked the story, so it was published there first.

DUST

Through the Door in Oglethorpe's

Enoch Hunt wasn't the first kid who got lost in the toy department of Oglethorpe's. He wasn't even the first kid to get lost on purpose. But he *was* the first kid to hope that he wouldn't get found in time for Christmas.

Because on Christmas he wouldn't be in Dowagiac, Michigan. He'd be in Tucson, Arizona. No snow on the ground, no friends to show his stuff to, his grandparents a couple of thousand miles away. And with all of that, his mother probably wouldn't get better after all. Fifty-fifty chance, that's all the doctor gave her.

Enoch's dad treated him like a grown-up. "Son, you're twelve years old, I can tell you the truth, I don't have to pretend the way I do with the younger kids. Your mother isn't just a little sick. The disease she has is very rare, and they don't know a cure."

"How long does she have?" Enoch asked. This was a realistic question. Enoch always asked realistic questions when he could think of them. It fooled people into thinking he was very adult.

"They don't know," his father said. "I think I'm telling you this because I'm as scared as you are. They don't know if she's going to get better or not, they don't know *when* they'll know, they can't tell us anything except that some people who've had this have gotten better in Arizona. So we're going to Arizona."

"I don't want to go to Arizona," Enoch said. What he really meant was, "I don't want Mother to be sick," but he knew that wouldn't be realistic.

"If you were the sick one, Enoch, we'd go to Arizona for you, too." His father pulled out a little key ring, just like his, with one single key on it. "We've already rented an apartment there, Enoch. I got a key made up for you." It was a strange-looking key, with a hump right down the middle. They even had weird locks and keys in Arizona. "This key means we trust you," Father said. "This key means we care about Mother." Enoch took the key and hoped it would fall out of his pocket.

That was a few days ago. Today Enoch's dad took him to Oglethorpe's and let him look around in the toy department. Within a few minutes, Enoch decided to get lost, hoping that they wouldn't find him until his mom was better. Or maybe wouldn't ever find him at all. Because Enoch didn't want to live in a world where mothers got sick and fathers got scared. Mothers were supposed to live forever, and fathers aren't supposed to be afraid of anything. Didn't they *know* that?

Oglethorpe's was in a bunch of old houses strung together with brick walls so that it was like a maze, up and down stairs, in and out of doors and corridors, and the toy department was in the basements of the buildings, so it was even more confusing. All during the summer most of these rooms were kept locked up for storage—only during the Christmas seasons did they need it all for display space. Now Enoch was in the backmost room, where the toys were years out of date and covered with dust. It was there that he saw the crazy girl.

He was sure she must be crazy, because she looked so weird. Her hair was done up in four pigtails surrounding her face, sticking straight out like the rays of the sun in a kindergarten drawing. But the back of her hair was all done up like a beauty parlor. She was wearing a pink dress, but she had jeans sticking out of the bottom of the dress. And she had this weird-looking wart just under her left eye, a big old brown one that made her look like she was crying mud.

Enoch had never seen one human being look so ugly all at once. So he began kind of following her. He wasn't trying to *meet* her—she looked crazy enough to be dangerous, and Enoch didn't like to take chances. He just wanted to look at her a few more times to make sure she was real.

After a few minutes, though, he realized she was trying to get away from him. She moved away from him faster and faster, and began weaving in and out of the display racks, and backtracking when he wouldn't notice. It was like a game, and Enoch didn't mind playing along. Enoch named the game "Keep Exactly Fifteen Feet Away From the Weird-looking Girl."

He always named his games. He named everything. He was good at thinking up titles. He even kept a book in which he wrote down the important things that happened to him. Every page had a title. Like "The Day My Father Taught Me How to Throw a Football and Pulled His Shoulder," or "Why I Will Never Again Eat Radishes Straight from the Garden Without Washing Them."

His most recent entry was titled, "The Day My Father Told Me That My Mother Was Going to Die." But the title was all he could think of on that one. It just sat there in his book, a title and a blank page, because he couldn't think of anything else to say.

While he was thinking of that, the crazy girl got away. He had her trapped back in the corner of the oldest, dustiest room of all, and now she was gone. It made him angry. He didn't like failing at things.

He looked, but he couldn't find her anywhere. Had she given up and gone home? He didn't think so. She had been playing the game as much as he was—why would she suddenly quit?—so he went to the corner where she was when she disappeared.

Her footprints in the dust went right where he had seen her go—and then they just stopped, right in front of a pile of ancient Fort Apache sets. It was like she had got this far and then decided to fly the rest of the way. He wondered if maybe she was a witch. But that was impossible. There weren't any witches. But then—the crazy girl would look just right sitting on a broom.

If Enoch was going to be realistic, he had to stop thinking of things like ghosts or witches. Like his father always said, if something seems to be unexplainable, keep looking until you find the explanation.

He found it in the dust on the floor in front of the Fort Apache sets. One stack of boxes had been pulled out and then pushed back. The crazy girl was hiding behind the boxes.

Enoch had already pulled the boxes out before he realized he hadn't the faintest idea of what he'd say to her if he found her. "Gotcha"? "Olly olly oxen free"?

It didn't matter. She wasn't hiding behind the boxes. Instead there was a little door about four feet tall, with a sign on it that said "Employees Only." The sign was peeling away, and something was written on the door behind it in pencil. Enoch got close and read it. It said, "Abandon hope, all ye who enter here."

Enoch was not the sort of boy who went through doors that he wasn't supposed to go through. But if this was a place for those who had abandoned hope, then the door was made for him. And so he pushed it open, stepped through, and pulled the boxes back into place.

With the door still open, Enoch looked around. All he could see was a sort of janitor's closet, with rolls of toilet paper and packages of paper towels. But there were footprints and scuffs on the floor, leading to one of the piles. And sure enough there were footprints up a sort of stairway made of paper-towel packages, leading to a gap between the ceiling and the top of the wall.

Enoch inspected the door to make sure it wouldn't lock behind him. Then he closed it. There was a dim light seeping around the edges of the door. It was enough for Enoch to make his way to the top of the paper-towel stairway. But when he tried to look over the top of the wall, he could see nothing but darkness.

Enoch was not the sort of kid who went into dark places where he had never been before. But Enoch was here to get lost, and it would be a lot easier to get lost in a dark passageway than in the back rooms of the basement toy department. Besides, the crazy girl had come through here. It must be safe—she wasn't screaming, was she?

So he clambered over the wall, and hung his right leg down the other side, trying to find something to stand on. It occurred to him, while he was swinging his leg around, that the crazy girl might be standing below, watching him make an idiot of himself.

"Don't just stand there," he said. "Tell me how far down the ground is."

No answer. She wasn't there, of course.

He toyed with the idea of just dropping down. But what if the ground was farther away than he thought? What if he got stuck and couldn't get back? So he kept swinging his leg until his heel bashed into another wall.

Another wall. What he had almost dropped into wasn't a room, it was a space between walls. He really might have been stuck.

Carefully he straddled the space, which was only about two feet wide. The far wall was stone—part of the old foundation. And instead of a drop-off on the other side, there was a dirt floor in a kind of cave. Enoch knew it was a cave because he kept bumping his head in the darkness.

I am a complete idiot to be crawling around in a cave in the darkness, he decided. There could be side paths going off in any direction, and he'd never find his way back. But that was the idea, wasn't it? To get lost. And then he saw a light ahead of him.

Too bad. The cave didn't go on forever. It would let him out somewhere outside in Dowagiac, Michigan, and he would be recognized by somebody, and they would take him home, and he would have to go to Arizona.

Oh well. At least he could tell his friends about this cave. That was something. He didn't have to tell them he was following a crazy girl with four pigtails and a wart.

When he got out of the cave he spent a few minutes trying to figure out where he was. There weren't any buildings close by, which meant the cave was longer than he thought, going all the way from Oglethorpe's to the nearest woods.

But he couldn't see the end of this forest. Just trees and leaves and birds and grass and bushes and flowers and sunshine trickling down in little splashes—not a sign of a cornfield anywhere nearby. To be near Dowagiac and not see a cornfield *or* a building was almost incredible. That's why it took him so long to notice the *really* incredible thing.

In Dowagiac, Michigan, there were no leaves at all on the trees and a foot of snow on the ground. Here, wherever he was, it could be May 25th.

A small rock hit him in the head. He turned around, ready to yell at whoever threw it. But the crazy girl was standing there with a slingshot, and it was loaded, and it was aimed at his face.

"I found you," Enoch said.

"Did not," she said. "I found *you*."

"I was chasing you, wasn't I?"

"Around here, if I didn't want you to find me, you wouldn't have found me."

Enoch pointed at the slingshot. "What are you going to do, kill a giant?"

She shook her head. "He's already dead. Died last week. You should see the grave."

She was definitely crazy. Still, she had been here before, apparently—that was a brand-new-looking slingshot, all metal, and she hadn't been carrying it with her in the store. "Where is this place?" he asked.

"It's through the short door in Oglethorpe's," she said. "Didn't you watch how you got here?"

"Where is it on the *map*?"

"It isn't."

"It isn't what?"

"On the map. Look, what do you *think*? It's dead winter in Michigan."

"I know."

"The kind of places where it's spring in the middle of winter don't get *put* on maps."

"What about Australia? It's spring *there*."

"It's also on the other side of the world. Did you swim the Pacific Ocean or did you crawl a hundred feet through a cave under a second-rate toy store?"

"If you're not going to shoot me with that thing, would you mind pointing it somewhere else?"

She didn't point it somewhere else, which worried Enoch a little. "What did you follow me for, buddy?"

"Why not? It got me to this place, didn't it?"

"Don't give me that," she said. "You already knew the way."

"Did not."

"You got across the abyss in the dark, without knowing it was there?"

"The what?"

"The abyss. The space between the two walls."

"I kicked the far wall and straddled."

"Lucky for you. There are rats down there. If you live through the fall, and don't drown in the water, the rats will eat you alive."

"Don't try to scare me," Enoch said.

"Why not?" she asked.

"Because I scare real easy so it isn't even worth the bother. As a matter of fact, I'm scared right now. Would you mind pointing that somewhere else?"

She grinned. "I never met a boy who'd admit that he was scared of me."

"Who wouldn't be? You look like a freak."

She let go of the shank of the slingshot and touched her hair. "If my mother would let me have short hair, I wouldn't have to do this. I need it out of my face so I can aim."

"At me? You could be blind and hit me."

"At squirrels."

"You shoot at squirrels?"

"I get them, too. Dead as doorknobs."

If there was anything Enoch hated, it was kids who killed animals for fun. "That really makes me sick, you know that?"

"Sure," she said. "I bet you just love all the little animals."

"If it isn't hurting you, why should you kill it?"

"You're so sweet," she said. "I bet your mommy and daddy just love you to pieces."

The reference to his parents didn't make Enoch's mood any nicer. "Why don't you just take that slingshot and stuff it in your ear?" he asked.

"Why don't I stuff it in yours?" she answered. "Now there's an idea."

Just then a little bearded man about nine inches tall ran past through the grass, shouting, "Squirrel, squirrel!" That was when Enoch decided that this place was definitely not Dowagiac.

The Squirrels and the Little People

A squirrel came scampering along the ground after the nine-inch man.

"They're getting downright careless these days," the crazy girl said. She took aim with the slingshot.

Almost by reflex Enoch reached out and jostled her arm. The stone she was shooting struck the ground ten feet behind the squirrel. The squirrel ran away.

"You jerk!" she shouted at him.

"Squirrels! Squirrels!" shouted the little man.

"He got away, thanks to Bambi, here," the crazy girl said. The little man kept jumping up and down, pointing at the branches overhead, shouting. So Enoch looked up. Just in time to see two squirrels jumping down toward his face.

By reflex Enoch struck out at the animals before they hit him. But instead of falling to the ground and running away, the squirrels jumped right back onto his pants and began gnawing at his legs. He might have been more upset by this if a third squirrel weren't on his shoulder, biting savagely at his neck, probing for the jugular. These were no ordinary squirrels.

"Your eyes!" shouted the crazy girl. "Protect your eyes!"

"I'm working on saving my neck just now, thank you very much!" Enoch shouted back. He tore the one squirrel off his shoulder, but he lost a good deal of skin in the process. And now the squirrel was writhing in his hands, trying to bite off his fingers or scratch open his wrists, and Enoch hadn't the faintest idea how to kill it.

"Bash it into a tree!" the crazy girl shouted.

Enoch bashed it into a tree. It obligingly dropped like a stone to the ground and lay there. Soon he had done the same to the squirrels on his legs. Then he began prying extras off the crazy girl—she had nearly a dozen of them on her, and it took a good little while before they were all taken care of.

When the squirrels finally lay in neat little piles at the bases of nearby trees, Enoch stood and looked at the crazy girl.

"I definitely approve of squirrel-shooting," Enoch said.

"I figured you were probably on my side now."

"Excuse me," Enoch said, "but I think I hear someone clapping."

It was about a hundred of the little people. They were gathered around the squirrel bodies.

"Excellent work, O mighty one!" said a very short man in a Robin Hood cap.

"It was a trap," said the crazy girl.

"The nasty old squirrels can't fool *you*," said the little man. "Mind if we cart off the corpses?"

"Whatever you like," said the crazy girl.

"My neck hurts," Enoch said. "I don't mean to mention it, but those squirrels might have rabies."

The crazy girl looked at his neck. He could see that her face and neck were pretty scratched up, too. "Yeah, he was really going for you," she said.

"Excuse me, O Great Hunter," said the man in the Robin Hood cap. "This one isn't dead."

"Kill it yourself," the crazy girl snapped.

The little man shuddered and walked back to the pile of corpses. "We've got to do it ourselves," he said. "Our so-called friend won't help us."

Enoch was outraged. "Won't help you! We just stopped an *invasion*—"

"Never mind," said the crazy girl. She led him a few dozen yards into the woods, out of earshot. "Just forget them," she said. "They're ungrateful, and they aren't likely to change. Let me get something on your neck."

Something turned out to be a daub of mud that stung like hot mustard. "What are you trying to do, kill me?"

"I don't have any bandaids," she said. "This will have to do until we can get to the Healing Dust."

"Dust?"

"This place has its own system. No doctors, but the mud can make you feel a little better. And the Healing Dust can cure anything."

The mud *was* making him feel better. And the words "cure anything" gave Enoch a funny feeling. He didn't even recognize it, but the funny feeling was hope.

"How far is it to the Healing Dust?"

"I don't know. I'm not equipped with a speedometer or anything."

"How long does it take to get there?"

"That depends, doesn't it?"

"On what?"

"How many adventures we have along the way."

"I don't want any adventures. I just want the healing dust."

"Well, I've got bad news for you, buddy. The adventures are the way things work here. Nothing around here comes free. Only instead of paying with money, you pay with sweat and blood and courage. Got any of that?"

"Blood, anyway," Enoch said.

She grinned. "My name's Maureen, but if you call me that I'll kill you. I go by 'Mo.'"

Enoch wasn't a bit surprised. *Mo* was a perfect name for her. "I'm Enoch."

She giggled. This struck him as inappropriate, considering how silly *her* name was. "I'm sorry," she said. "It isn't your *name*. It's your *nick-name*."

"I don't have a nickname."

"Eeny," she said. "Short for Enoch. Eeny. And I'm Mo. Don't you get it?"

Enoch got it. "All we need is Meeny and Miny."

Mo held her slingshot up to the sky. "O noble slingshot, I christen thee 'Minotaur-slayer.'" She looped her belt over the slingshot. "I'll call it Miny for short. You can come up with Meeny."

"I don't have any weapons."

"You'll come up with something. You'll kill some evil knight and take his sword, or something."

Enoch doubted it. This place was more dangerous than he liked. But the pain from his neck and legs told him that the place was real enough, and there was a chance that there might really be something to this Healing Dust. If there was, it was worth some danger to get it. He fingered the key to the apartment in Arizona. The Healing Dust might save them from everything.

"OK," he said. "Take me to the Healing Dust."

"Why should I?" she asked.

"Because I helped you with the squirrels," he said.

"After you made me miss my first shot."

"All right, forget it. I don't need you to take me."

"Then how do you figure to get there?"

"I'll get one of those fairies to take me."

"Not a chance. Especially if you call them fairies. They *hate* that."

"In the stories the fairies always help you."

"The stories are all lies. This is real life. In real life, the little people are only out for themselves. They probably set up that little ambush, you know."

"I thought they were afraid of the squirrels."

"Oh, they *were*. Till I started killing the squirrels for them. Now it's been months since the squirrels have even come near the little people. So they aren't afraid anymore."

"But why would they set up an ambush, if you're the one keeping them safe?"

"They probably figured they could turn my skin into a five-year supply of leather."

"Are they so stupid they'd kill their protector for *leather*?"

"They're only nine inches tall, Eeny. How much brain do you think will fit into those teeny little heads?"

"Not very bright, is that it?"

"They're dumb as your thumb. And jerks, too. Rude and crude. Ungrateful. Disgusting little people."

"So why do you bother saving them from the squirrels?"

"Because it's the duty of a good knight to protect the weak and defenseless. Even the weak and defenseless who have no manners."

"You can't be a knight," Enoch said. "Knights are men."

And suddenly the discussion was over. Mo walked away from him into the woods. With her went his hope of finding the Healing Dust. "I'm sorry," he shouted, but she didn't turn back. He followed her, but in an amazingly short time she had managed to lose him. This wasn't a toy department in Oglethorpe's. This was a forest where Mo knew her way around and Enoch didn't. In a short time he discovered that he didn't even know the way back to the cave that led to Oglethorpe's. He was hopelessly lost.

When you are lost, his father always said, don't keep wandering around. Sit still in once place until you are found.

Well, fine, Dad, Enoch answered silently. But what if you're lost in an impossible forest where squirrels are killers and fairies actually exist, even if they *are* jerks. I could sit here until I starve to death before anybody finds me, except Mo, of course, and she isn't likely to be looking for me, since she's the one who lost me in the first place.

So Enoch began to wander around, searching for the Healing Dust or the cave entrance, whichever he found first. He kept a good lookout up in the branches overhead; he wasn't going to let a squirrel jump on his neck again. He was looking for squirrels, in fact, when Mo appeared out of nowhere and spoke to him.

"Not another step," she said.

"Hi," Enoch said. "Were you lost?"

"Very funny," she said. She walked over to him and pulled him back from the edge of a small clearing that was covered with last year's dead leaves. Then she bent and picked up a fallen branch and tossed it into the middle of the clearing. It did not bounce the way thrown branches usually do. Instead it splashed and almost immediately sank out of sight.

"Quicksand," said Mo.

"You can be a knight if you want to," Enoch said. "I can't think of a single reason why a girl shouldn't be a knight if she wants to be."

"You're welcome," she said.

"You saved my life."

"It's the duty of a knight to save the small and the stupid from destruction."

Enoch decided not to ask whether she considered him small. "I want to go to the Healing Dust," he said. "Will you take me there?"

"On two conditions."

"What are they?"

"First, Eeny, I am the knight and you are my squire. No, not even a squire. You're my *page,* and you must do everything that I command you. Otherwise, you'll mess everything up. I'm used to the way things work around here, and you'll have to get used to obeying me without asking *why* first. Like just now about the quicksand."

"Agreed."

"And the second condition is that if I take you to the Healing Dust, you'll go with me on my Quest."

"What's your quest?"

"I don't know."

"Then how am I supposed to go with you if you don't even know where we're going?"

"I know *where* it is. I just don't know *what* it is. There's a door I haven't been able to get through."

"I'm not that much smaller than you," Enoch said. "I'm not sure I could get through a space that *you* can't get through."

"It's trickier than that. I want you to help me figure out how to get through it. Two heads are better than one. Even if one of them is only yours."

"You're such a sweetheart, Mo."

"Coming or not?"

"I'll help you on your quest. But I don't know if I'll be much good to you."

"Neither do I. But you made it over the abyss, didn't you? You found your way through the cave, didn't you?"

"It wasn't hard to find my way. Just went straight and got to the end."

"*Straight!* Go straight and you end up somewhere in Nebraska! There are a dozen turns and I haven't marked them. You couldn't have gone straight."

"I didn't even have a light," Enoch said. "Of course I went straight."

She looked at him intensely, and apparently decided to believe him. "So you went straight. And found your way here. That means that either you're very lucky, or for some reason you're supposed to be here. Either way, you might be useful."

She turned her back on him and started off into the woods. Uncertain what she wanted him to do, Enoch just stood there for a moment. She stopped and looked back at him impatiently. "Are you coming or not?"

"Yes," he said, and he started toward her.

"Use your head next time," she said. "I shouldn't have to tell you *everything.*"

Enoch had never felt so stupid in his life. And yet he didn't mind at all. Mo was taking him to find the Healing Dust. And even the prospect of adventures along the way didn't bother him. This place was so unreal that he couldn't imagine really getting *hurt.*

"Everything comes out all right, doesn't it?" he asked.

"It always has so far," she said.

"I mean, we can't actually get killed or anything, can we?"

"Let me put it this way, Eeny. When I scrape my knee in this place, I still have a scab when I get back home."

"So what happens here—it really counts?"

"Sometimes," said Mo, "I think it counts double."

It should have frightened Enoch more than ever, but in fact it made him more eager to go on. What you got here could stay with you when you want back to the outside world. There was a chance, then, for his mother.

The Quest

There was no doubt about it—Mo knew her way around in this place. She half-trotted most of the time, even though there was scarcely a sign of a path to follow, and Enoch could hardly keep up with her. From time to time she would slow down and walk quietly, listening, watching. Enoch watched, too, until she said, "Look, Eeny, give me a break. Watch where you're going so you don't keep making so much noise. *I'll* watch for danger."

"What kind of danger?" he asked.

"The kind I'm watching for."

Just when Enoch was getting hungry, they came to an old apple orchard and had a meal.

"I thought it was supposed to be spring here," Enoch said.

"So?"

"So why are the apples ripe?"

"Aren't apples ripe in spring?"

"Where do you come from, Mo, the moon?"

"Farther. Chicago."

"You're kidding. A big city, and you know your way around the woods like this?"

"In the city you learn to walk soft, you learn to keep watching. It's the same thing." She threw a core at a tree trunk some thirty feet away. Right on target. "Besides, I've had a few months here to practice."

"Months? How long have you lived here in Dowagiac?"

"Moved in about the first of December."

"Then how could you have been in here for *months*? You haven't even lived in Dowagiac for three weeks."

Mo grinned. "A real mathematical wizard, aren't you. Look at your watch."

It was five o'clock.

"So what time did you come in here?"

"I don't know. We got to the store about four-thirty." Suddenly Enoch jumped to his feet. "Dad's looking all over the store for me."

"No he isn't. Besides, I thought you *wanted* to get lost."

"My dad *is* looking for me. What do *you* know about it?"

"He isn't looking for you because exactly one second has passed since you went into that door. Or maybe since you crossed the abyss. I've never bothered to time it out. It doesn't matter how many hours or days or weeks you stay in here. Come in at five, go out at five on the same day."

Enoch thought about that for a while. "You could live a whole life in here, and a whole other life out there."

"Right."

"If you like it so much here, Mo, how come you ever go back at all?"

"Escape."

Enoch laughed. "Escape is coming *in* here. That's escaping from reality." It was a realistic thing to say.

"When was the last time a squirrel jumped on your neck, genius? Where he bit you, how does that feel?"

"A little stiff."

"This is reality, pinbrain. After a few days of this, sometimes even a week, it gets so I can't stand it anymore, always having to watch out, always having to be quiet and careful. This is the real world here. This is life and death. Out there, that's escape. Out there I'm a child, and they protect me."

Enoch spat a seed out of his mouth.

"It's life and death out there, too."

Mo looked at him for a few moments. "Maybe it is, for some people. But that doesn't make this escape."

He nodded. She had got him thinking about things he'd rather forget. His own life in danger—that was easier these days, easier than other things.

"I said something wrong, didn't I?" Mo asked.

"Sure, why not?" Enoch smiled. "It's nice to know you can do something klutzy."

"Come here." She led him to a cottage, a storybook place with a thatched roof and shuttered windows instead of glass. She went boldly inside, without knocking. The house was neat and clean, though poor. No one was there.

"Do you know these people?"

"No," she said. "They're all dead."

"Oh."

"It was my second time in this place. I came to ask permission to eat the apples. A knight never steals, you see. They had been murdered, a man and wife. It wasn't nice. I buried them. My parents couldn't understand why I came home with bloodstains on my dress. They were scared half to death."

"Who did it?"

"The giants, I think. The little people say that they carry off children and raise them up to be slaves in their castles. I guess the parents objected to having their children carried off."

Enoch felt sick and angry, looking at the four small beds that the children must have slept in.

"I wanted to get revenge. But when I stood over their graves, trying to think up a good oath of vengeance, a redbird came and stood on the woman's grave. 'No,' she said. That's all. Just 'no.' And then a bluebird came and stood on the man's grave and said, 'Free the king from the Castle of Contempt.'" Mo reached under the smallest bed, and drew out a sword. It was small and light, as if it were made for her young arm. It glistened in the light from the door.

"That's how I learned my purpose here. I've come back every chance I could, learned all I could. I got this sword from the treasure of the dragon Drast. It wasn't such a big deal, though. It's easier to steal from a dragon than you think."

"What about the king?"

"I've found the castle, but I can't get in."

"Too well defended?"

"I've never seen a soul. I just can't get in the door. That's what I need you for, to help me get in."

"I'm not good at things like that."

"Like what?"

"Prying open doors."

"I already tried prying. Anything metal that I touch to the door turns into sand. Anything living that I touch to the door except my own skin turns to ashes. No fire, no heat. Just ashes. It's a problematical door."

"Magic?" To Enoch's surprise, he said something unrealistic and didn't even feel embarrassed about it.

"Of course," she said. "But what's the spell? I've said every magic word I could think of. I sat in front of the door eating apples for three days just talking and talking and talking, in hopes I'd accidently say the magic word."

"And *I'm* supposed to get you in?"

"That's the idea."

"You're going to be profoundly disappointed."

"Probably. But you're in here for a reason, Eeny. You don't get in here by accident. So why not figure maybe you're in here to help me in my Quest?"

"I hate it when you call me Eeny."

"Sorry."

He knew she'd keep on calling him that, though, until he had done something to earn her respect.

"You in high school?" Enoch asked.

"No. I'm only twelve." She sounded like she thought twelve was a disgusting age to be.

"Me, too," said Enoch.

She looked him over. "We are living proof of the fact that girls mature faster."

"How come I haven't seen you in seventh grade, then?"

"Because I haven't *been* yet."

Enoch understood then. She had been cutting school every day and coming here. "And you said this place wasn't escape," he said.

"I don't *go* to school," she said. "My father has an educational theory. He teaches me at home. He figures I'm going to grow up Christian if it kills me."

"It's obviously working," Enoch said.

She looked at him with fire in her eyes.

"I mean," Enoch explained, "you risk your life to do good. That's Christian, isn't it?"

"Not his way. Never mind. We've only got a few hours to go until dark. We need to get across Drast before nightfall."

From the orchard it was only a short way to a bare-rock mountain that rose sheer from a broad meadow. It was hard climbing at first, but Enoch soon got the knack of bracing himself against slight outcroppings and skinnying up furrows in the rock. The sun was bright and hot, and he was covered in sweat, but soon the slope began to level out, until gradually it became a flat, broad plain. It was only then, looking across the whole view, that he realized how regular this desert was, ridge after ridge like stone waves, with smooth plateaus in between, then another drop-off. "This Drast is a strange place," Enoch said.

"It isn't a place," Mo answered.

Only then did Enoch remember that Mo had mentioned the name Drast before. It was the name of a dragon.

"This is the *same* Drast?" he asked.

"Sure," she answered. "We're walking on his back."

"Kind of big, isn't he?"

"Sizes are all mixed up here," said Mo. "At least it keeps the giants away. They won't mess with a dragon."

"So why are *we* messing with him?"

"Us?" Mo laughed. "Do you ever notice the mosquito that bites you, until he's gone?" She drew her sword and thrust it under a lip of rock. No, not a lip of rock—one of the dragon's scales. Then she pried upward, and spat into the opening.

"Are you *crazy*?" Enoch demanded.

"It's what mosquitos do, except I don't eat anything. I like to think it gives him a little itch. To remember me by. You can see how I got away with the sword, though. I was so little he never even noticed me. The giants, now—he can see them. I like to think that when he flies out at night, he feels out of sorts because he's itching where I scratched him. I like to think he's so irritable that he kills a few extra giants, just to ease the itch."

They laughed about that for a while, then kept walking. The sun was getting low, and they didn't want to be on Drast's back when he took off for his evening flight.

They spent the night in a cave. Enoch wanted a fire to frighten off wild animals, but Mo forbade it. Instead they took turns sleeping. Enoch felt silly sitting there with a sword on his lap, but at least he didn't disgrace himself by falling asleep on duty.

The next day they came to the Castle of Contempt before noon. "That wasn't far," Enoch said.

"Things are quite conveniently located," Mo said.

Enoch laughed. "You sound like a realtor."

She only smiled slightly. "My father *is* a realtor."

"Oh," Enoch said. "Dowagiac isn't exactly a hot real estate market right now."

"I didn't say my father made any money at it, did I?"

Enoch looked at the castle. It wasn't much. The walls weren't particularly high; there was no moat; and there wasn't a single soldier to defend the place. "Where is everybody?" Enoch asked.

"I've never seen a soul here."

"Then how do you know this is the Castle of Contempt?"

"Isn't it obvious? No defenders, no moat, the walls are low—and still we can't get in. Whoever built this castle figured we were too stupid or weak to get inside. And so far he's been right. He has nothing but contempt for us."

"Our enemy?"

"The builder of the castle, anyway. Come on, look at it and see if you can figure a way in."

Mo led him to the obvious place first—the door. Enoch looked at it. Solid hardwood, snugly set into the wall.

"You can't even get a sword blade in the crack."

Enoch didn't hear her. He was too busy looking at the keyhole, a little odd-shaped keyhole on the right-hand side near the edge of the door.

Mo saw what he was looking at. "You can't pick the lock," she said. "Everything turns to sand or ashes."

But Enoch had the key out of his pocket, and he did not hesitate to touch it to the keyhole. He half-expected the key to dissolve into sand, even hoped that it would.

Instead, it fit snugly into the keyhole. He turned it in the lock. There was a clicking noise behind the door, and slowly, without either of them touching it, the door opened.

"Where'd you get that key!" Mo demanded.

"It's the key to our new apartment in Arizona."

"Well, fry my eggs," said Mo. "You really did it."

"And before lunchtime, too," Enoch said, feeling very pleased. The key was good for something after all.

The Battle to Free the King

Enoch was perfectly happy to let Mo pass through the door ahead of him. She was the one with the sword, after all. "What happens now?" he asked.

"How should *I* know?" she answered.

"Where's the king?"

"If you see a king, tell me and then we'll both know."

Enoch got the idea she wanted him to be quiet.

The doorway led into a large courtyard, which was cluttered with bright tents with slack banners. Every now and then a breeze came by, and the banners made a halfhearted effort to wave. Otherwise, there was not a motion or sound except the scuffing of their own feet on the dirt.

And then, suddenly, it began to rain. Not a cloud in the sky, not a clap of thunder, just a sudden downpour that drenched them immediately and turned the dirt to mud.

Instinctively Enoch dodged toward one of the tents. "Wait!" cried Mo. Enoch thought she wanted him to wait up for her, which was silly. She could just hurry. He was going to get into a tent before he drowned.

He was just opening a tent flap when she tackled him. Now he knew what the sportscasters meant when they said, "He took a good hit at the thirty-eight." A good hit was when your mouth filled up with mud and your bones got scattered in odd places throughout your body.

When he had cleared the mud out of his mouth, he asked the obvious question. "What did you do that for?"

"You are too dumb to live," she answered kindly.

"Maybe you don't know enough to come in out of the rain, but I do."

"What rain?" Mo asked.

It had stopped raining. But the ground was still wet. "So it stopped," Enoch said. "It *was* raining."

"Listen, Eeny. Around here, if it rains out of a clear blue sky, you *don't* walk into the nearest shelter. You stand in the rain and wait for your enemy to make his move."

"You mean the rain was magic?"

"The rain was water. It's the tents that I don't trust."

In answer to her suspicion, the tents all vanished at once, leaving the courtyard empty. Where the tents had been, however, the ground was dry.

"The tents were *real.*"

"Of course. Don't you understand by now, Eeny? *Everything* here is real. This isn't a TV magic show, where you know the magician is a clever fake. Around here, when he saws the lady in half, the guy doesn't put her in a box and she really ends up in two pieces."

"Now I'm getting worried," Enoch said.

"You're a real quick learner, Eeny."

The doors of the great hall stood open. Inside they could see a dim fire burning in the distance. Other than that they could see nothing. It was too dark inside and too bright outside.

"Maybe," Enoch said, "maybe the door is open because this is just where our enemy expects us to come in, and so we should go hunting for another door. Or maybe our enemy expects us to think that way, and so he opened this door so we'd be sure *not* to come in here."

"If we think like that, we'll end up crazy or dead within five minutes. Come on, Eeny."

"I don't have a weapon," Enoch pointed out. "I'd be useless to you in a battle."

"Just start explaining something to whoever attacks you, Eeny. They'll run away screaming, I promise you."

Mo led the way into the great hall. It took a few minutes for their eyes to become accustomed to the dark, but during that time there was no attack, not even a sound except the fire crackling in the cooking pit in the middle of the room. Most of the smoke rose to a hole in the roof; the rest filled the room, so that Enoch's eyes burned. Over the fire, a pig was roasting on a spit.

Around the outside walls of the great hall was a long, long table, and around the outside of the table was a long, long bench. On the bench were a couple of hundred men and women, dressed in brightly colored clothing, with food on the plates before them, with wine in their cups—and each and every person was dead. Killed by the person on one side of them, while they were in the process of murdering the person on the other side.

Enoch began to sing softly. "It's beginning to look a lot like Christmas."

"Can it," Mo said. She walked to a table and touched the food on a plate. "Still warm," she said.

Enoch couldn't think of anything to say to that. It was just as well, for the pig roasting over the fire took that opportunity to speak. "Hi. Would you like some ham? Help yourself."

It took a few moments to be sure who had spoken.

"That's right, it's me. Harvey Ham, here. Peter Porkchop. Billy Bacon. You'd have to go a long way before you got a hunk of meat as nice as me. The carving knife is right over there." The pig rolled its eyes toward a small table near the fire.

Enoch, always obedient, started for the carving knife.

"Hold still, pinhead," said Mo.

Enoch did as he was told.

"When a pig invites you to a ham dinner, I'd suggest you think twice before you RSVP."

"I'm just being generous," said the ham.

"Thanks kindly," Mo said. "We're vegetarians, at least for the moment."

Mo led the way to the head table. There was a large throne there, but it was empty, and there was no food on the plate. "The king wasn't in attendance," Mo pointed out.

"What would have happened if we had carved the ham?"

Mo shrugged.

"What if I had gone into the tent?"

"Listen, Enoch, that's why curious people make lousy knights. If you always have to find out what'll happen if you do some stupid thing, then your career will be brief. It's what you are willing to never find out that keeps you going in this business."

While Mo said this, she was busy looking around, poking at things on the table, studying the clothing of the nearest dead people.

"What are you looking for?" Enoch asked.

"I don't know. A clue or something. The king is in here somewhere, but I don't want to spend a year looking for him."

"You're just going to get hungrier," said the pig.

"You be quiet," Mo snapped at the animal.

"I hang here all day over a hot fire, nicely basted with garlic and butter, but do you think anyone ever eats? 'I'm sorry, but I already ate.' 'I'm sorry, but I'm a vegetarian.' And if they do eat, I get nothing but complaints. Needs more salt. Not hot enough. Do you think I ever get a word of thanks?"

"Thank you very much," Enoch said.

"Don't talk to him," Mo said. "It'll only encourage him." She turned over the king's empty plate to look on the bottom.

Something on the king's throne caught Enoch's eye. It was a small lizard about a half-inch long, poised at the back of the armrest. "Look at that," Enoch said.

The lizard was holding so still that Mo had a hard time seeing where he was.

"Is that the clue?" Enoch asked.

"I don't know."

"Does it talk? Hey, lizard, hi, how are you?"

"Eeny, don't talk to the lizard, you look like an idiot. Next thing you'll be talking to the chairs."

"Ever since a roast pig talked to me I've been open to conversing with anything," Enoch said.

"Well, leave the lizard alone. It looks dangerous."

The lizard moved slightly, bunching itself a little.

"Do lizards jump?" Enoch asked.

"Why?"

"If they do, this one's about to."

Without another word, Mo lunged with her sword and hacked down at the lizard, cutting it neatly in two. She was very quick.

"Good aim," Enoch said. "Remind me not to point it out if anybody I like is getting ready to jump."

"Listen, Eeny, didn't you learn anything from the squirrels? Anything that looks like it's going to jump on me, I make sure it doesn't."

Enoch remembered the wound on his neck and smiled at her. "If you were really nice, you would have only wounded it."

"You've got good eyes, Eeny. I didn't notice it had moved." They went around the head table and examined the body of the lizard. Mo picked up the front half. Something sparkled.

"Look," Enoch said. He took the back half of the body and showed her. Protruding slightly from the body was half of a clear, glowing green stone, cut like a Tiffany diamond. Mo mumbled something and took the matching half out of the front of the lizard.

"Let's put them together," Enoch said.

"Let's wait and do it later. Putting things together and taking them apart can have dire consequences here. It may cause us more problems than we want."

"It may solve all our problems."

Mo tossed her half-emerald to Enoch. "You're so smart, see what happens."

Enoch put the two halves together. Instantly there appeared before him in the air a three-dimensional model of the Castle of Contempt. When he rotated the stone, the outer walls were stripped away and room after room was revealed.

"A map," Mo said.

Enoch took the two halves of the stone apart. The map disappeared. "It doesn't show where the king is being kept."

"But it can show where the rooms are. We can save hours, and not miss anything."

The pig spoke up again from the fire. "That map isn't worth the thin air it's made out of. I advise you, don't pay the slightest attention to it."

"Let's get away from the pig. Bring out the map."

They easily found the secret passage behind the throne and ducked through it into a bedroom. And from there they explored every room of the castle and found nothing. No danger—and no king.

It was nearly dark.

"I'm getting hungry enough that the talking pig is beginning to sound like Canadian bacon to me," Enoch said.

"We're not eating the pig and that's final," said Mo. "Now let's get out of here for tonight. We can come back tomorrow and figure out something. But I have no intention of being here in the castle after dark."

It was a good idea, except that the door to the castle was closed and locked, and on this side there wasn't a keyhole.

So back they went to the great hall and sat down on the floor near the fire, where the light was brightest.

"If someone had told me when I went into Oglethorpe's that I'd end up spending a night in a room full of two hundred dead people," Enoch began.

"You would have come anyway," Mo said.

"Yeah, probably," said Enoch.

The pig sighed. "I don't suppose I could interest you in tripes," he said.

"No," Enoch answered sharply.

"Think of something," said Mo.

"I got us the map. I noticed the lizard. Now it's your turn."

"I'm always thinking. You're the one who needs to be reminded." So they lay in silence on the straw-covered stone floor, while the pig sizzled over the coals.

Enoch must have dozed off. He was wakened by something chewing on his arm. He opened his eyes and saw a red, fiery eye staring back at him.

"Excuse me, Mo," he said. "There seem to be rats in here."

Mo didn't answer. Enoch looked at where she had been lying. She was gone.

Enoch got to his feet. The fire was nothing but red coals now, and the rats were barely shadows. The one that was gnawing his arm was stubborn, but Enoch finally got him off. The others kept a reasonable distance, much to Enoch's relief. His arm hurt where the rat had been dining, but he had been living with the pain of the squirrels' attack for some time, and this new wound was almost unnoticeable.

Enoch walked nearer to the fire. The smell of roast ham was unbearable, and he was so hungry.

"Mm, mmm, good," mumbled the pig.

"Why didn't you wake me up when the rats came in?"

"I'm not allowed to bring up any subject except eating me."

"Where's Mo?"

"The skinny girl with the wart under her eye?"

"Yeah."

"I don't know."

"Did you see her leave?"

"Oh, of course. I'm very watchful. There isn't much else to do. There's firewood a few feet away behind you. If you like, you can brighten up this fire a bit. Just to cook me, mind you."

Enoch found the firewood, and soon had a few pieces going, just enough to let him see the edges of the room. All the people were gone. Their clothing, however, was neatly folded on the benches, and their weapons lay on the table. Enoch decided that nothing would ever surprise him again.

"Which way did she go?" Enoch asked.

"I can't say."

"Didn't you *see*?"

"Oh, yes, of course I *saw*."

"But you can't say."

"Would you like, for instance, roast pig's tongue?"

So the pig was under some sort of enchantment, and couldn't help him. Or maybe he could.

"What if I took you with me? Could you tell me if I were heading in the right direction?"

"That would depend on what our journey was *for*."

Enoch tried to find a way to outsmart the enchantment. "To find Mo so we can eat you."

"I can be of inestimable assistance."

Enoch got a thick robe from one of the piles of clothing and wrapped it around the pig. Then he lifted the animal, spit and all, and began to carry it away from the fire.

"Don't you need a torch?" asked the pig.

Enoch began to set down the pig while he went to fetch a torch from the wall.

The pig yelled. "Do you want your supper to be eaten by rats?"

"No," Enoch said. He carried the pig with him.

With the torch in his right hand and the pig under his left, Enoch headed for the secret door behind the throne.

"That isn't where your fellow diner is," said the pig. And the pig directed Enoch to another secret passage that could only be reached through a narrow slit by a window that looked like a shadow until the very moment that Enoch began to step into it. It turned into a stairway winding down.

"This isn't in the map," Enoch said.

"Do you believe everything you're told?" asked the pig.

As they went slowly down the stairway, Enoch kept up a one-sided conversation with the pig. "I noticed that even though all those dead people had warm food on their plates, not one of them was eating ham."

"They should have been. I taste unusually good."

"Which suggests that you weren't put on that spit until after they were all dead."

"If you refrigerate me, I make an excellent cold ham salad."

"What I'm wondering is whether you have anything to do with why the king wasn't at supper."

"He doesn't eat ham. Never does."

"What I'm wondering is what would happen if I pulled you off that spit."

"It would be so much harder to roast me then."

Enoch didn't try the experiment right then, however, because he had found Mo.

She was hanging by the wrists from manacles and chains. Her feet, also chained, were two feet off the floor. She looked tired and out of sorts.

"Took you long enough," she said nastily.

"If you at least had told me you were going," Enoch said.

"Then we'd both be chained up here."

Enoch looked around. It was a dungeon. He recognized some of the machinery as torture equipment. A rack. An iron maiden.

"What do you have with you?" asked Mo.

"The pig."

"Want a sandwich?" asked the pig.

"The pig! Of all the stupid—"

A roaring sound from the other side of the room interrupted Mo's remarks. It was a tiger, and it had an unkind expression on its face.

"Do you happen to have your sword with you, Mo?" Enoch asked.

"No," she answered. "I lost it in a battle with a gorilla. The gorilla was the one that put me up here. And then she dragged out the bodies of the eagle and the bear that had I already killed."

"Hey, this is a fun place," Enoch said. "Do you think this tiger only wants to chain me to the wall, too?"

The tiger roared.

"Not a chance," said Mo. "It wants you dead."

"If it's so set on killing me, why didn't *you* get killed?"

"I'm protected," said Mo.

The pig spoke up from under Enoch's arm. "She has a wart under her eye. Nothing in this place can kill her. But *you*—that's a different story."

Enoch was annoyed. "You might have mentioned this little difference between us before we set out on this quest, Mo."

Mo looked contrite. "I thought I could protect you."

Enoch looked away from her. "Listen, pig, if I'm going to be able to eat you for breakfast, I have to be alive in the morning. Any suggestions?"

"Get me off this spit," said the pig.

Enoch set down the pig and began pulling out the spit. A long metal rod, it was so greasy that he had a hard time holding on.

"That spit isn't going to do much good against that tiger," said Mo.

But almost as soon as he had the spit free of the pig, it began to shimmer. And it turned from a pointed metal rod into a dazzlingly bright silver thread.

"What do I do with *this*?" asked Enoch.

"It's perfect for slicing meat," said the pig. "In fact, the only thing it won't slice is you, so be careful."

Enoch got the idea, and swung the thread at the tiger. It missed, and then flipped around and cut the iron maiden neatly in half.

"It's sharp," Enoch said.

"Watch out for the tiger," Mo suggested.

The tiger was already leaping at Enoch. He had no time to do anything except hold the silver string in front of him like the string of a bow. It wasn't much of a shield. The tiger knocked him to the floor and landed on top of him. Enoch braced himself for the tiger's teeth, but they never bit him. The tiger had knocked him down, but on the way the silver thread had cut it in half to the shoulders.

"I suggest you keep holding on to the thread," said the pig. "If you aren't holding it, it will cut *you*."

Enoch was careful to keep hold of the thread as he got out from under the tiger.

By the time he was on his feet, there was a horse at the opposite side of the room. It was a beautiful animal, large and powerful, but Enoch figured he would probably never ride it, for its hoofs were fire, and fire dripped from its mouth in great drops. The horse reared up and whinnied, and fire spattered on the floor only a few feet from him.

Enoch did the only sensible thing. He turned his back on the horse and cut Mo's chains with a few swipes of the silver thread. He started to hand her the thread, but then it occurred to him that it would cut her hand off. And then he realized that if he set it down so she could take it, it would cut right through the floor and sink out of reach. It might even keep going until it reached the center of the earth.

Mo must have thought of the same thing, because she said, "It's your show, Eeny, baby."

So Enoch turned and faced the horse, wondering how he could learn to use his weapon in the next fifteen seconds.

"Think of it as a towel fight," Mo said.

After that it was easy. He just scrambled around and around the room, drawing the horse into corners or behind machines where it couldn't turn around. Then he snapped the string at the horse like a towel in the locker room at junior high, and it wasn't long before the horse was in just as bad condition as the tiger.

"And to think that during all those towel fights, I was really in training," Enoch said.

He cut the manacles off Mo's wrists and ankles as carefully as he could. As he was finishing, he noticed little flecks of cold on his hands. He looked closer, and in the torchlight he realized it was snowing.

"Snowing," said Mo. "It's always summer here."

"It's also indoors. Isn't indoor snow a little unusual here, too?"

"It's a bad sign," Mo said.

"On the contrary," said the pig. "It's a very good sign."

"It is?"

"It means that the king is getting some of his power back. You've been doing very well."

Something was wrong with this, though Enoch wasn't sure what. "Why would the king bring snow and cold, and his enemy brings summer all the time? Are we fighting for the wrong side?"

"Not at all," said the pig. "Winter is absolutely necessary for life to go on. Winter, then spring. Death, then life. If it were always summer, then it would always be the same. Nothing would *change*. Nothing would really be alive."

Enoch thought of his mother, thought of her dying, and he said, "No. It would be better if there were no death."

"Suit yourself," said the pig. "It's no skin off my snout. Or nose, rather."

Enoch glanced over at the pig, and it wasn't. A pig, that is. Instead it was a white-bearded man in a red gown with a white fur cape and a white fur belt. He was wearing huge boots, and on his head was the most extravagant of turbans. The costume was not exactly as Enoch had always seen it, but the man was recognizable.

"Santa Claus," Enoch said.

"Around here they usually call me the king," he answered. "The snow is mine."

"I thought you lived at the north pole," said Mo.

"Don't believe everything you hear. I live here, in the Castle of Care."

"Not the Castle of Contempt?"

"That's what my enemy named it. His specialty, you know. And yet it was a kind of warning. For instance, Mo, you didn't have contempt for that little lizard. If it had bitten you, it would have infected you the way it did all those other people, making you believe that the only way to get what you want is to get someone else out of the way."

"What happened to the pig?" asked Enoch.

"*I* am the pig. Or was. My enemy didn't have the power to finish me off, but he did catch me without friends one day and changed my shape and put me under a spell so that all I could say to people was suggest that they eat me."

"What if we *had* eaten you?"

"It would have killed me. And given you an excruciating headache, too. *You* were all for eating me, Eeny—don't think I didn't notice that. I'm glad Mo had more sense."

"Is it over now?" asked Enoch.

"Not really. Almost, though. Let's see—Mo found the secret room that my enemy built here, and you killed his tiger and his horse. I expect all we need to do now is call him here. My staff, please," said the king. "The silver string."

Enoch held out the string. "Won't it cut you?"

"Not *me*." The moment it touched the king's hand, the string turned into an ivory staff, taller by half than the old man, and as white as his beard.

"All right, Trickster," bellowed the king. "Front and center, right now!"

Immediately there appeared in the middle of the dungeon, surrounded by snow, a thin, woeful-looking little girl with tears running down her cheeks. "Mommy," said the child.

"None of that," said the king.

The child instantly turned into a man with a skull-like face. "You're such a sucker for children, I thought it was worth a try," he said.

"I must tell you, Trickster, I didn't like roasting."

"I thought you could take a joke."

"You've had your way long enough. Now I'll get rid of you without another word." The king held up his ivory staff and suddenly a foot of snow fell on the Trickster all at once, covering him completely. The Trickster did not move. He just sat there, buried in snow.

"It's only going to get colder down here," said the king. "Shall we go up and have some breakfast? It should be morning by now."

"I've been dying for a ham sandwich all night," Enoch said.

"We will *not* have ham," said the king.

Mo could not take her eyes off the pile of snow where the Trickster had been. "Is he dead?" she asked.

"For now," said the king. "But soon enough another liar will come along to try to tell us that death is the enemy of life and fool people into thinking that I'm just a jolly old elf who gives presents."

"Aren't you?" asked Enoch.

"Yes, but I have other jobs. Now, since you saved me, I'll give you your reward."

"All I want is the dust of healing," said Enoch.

"That's *your* affair," the king answered. "That isn't mine to give. All I can give you is a sip of water whenever you want it."

They were upstairs now, and out in the courtyard. It was not empty anymore. Now it was full of people and animals, and in the center of everything was a large fountain with two great spouts of water coming up.

"The fountain of wisdom and the fountain of love," said the king. "When they mix, they're just ordinary water. But when you drink from just one fount or the other, then you drink either the water of wisdom or the elixir of love. If you drink one, the other won't have any effect on you for at least a year. But after that, you can come back as often as you like. Don't bother coming to see *me*—I'll be much too busy. But feel free to have a drink from either fountain. Well, much to do, much to do. I have a few hundred years of work to catch up on. Roast pig indeed." The king disappeared inside the great hall.

Water of Wisdom

Because Mo and Enoch were young, the elixir of love did not tempt them. They drank instead from the fountain of wisdom. Immediately they were carried away in dreams. Here is the dream that Enoch saw:

His mother lay on a hospital bed, wasted and thin and cold-looking. A doctor touched her head, then felt gently for her pulse, then drew a sheet over her face. Enoch screamed and wept and vowed that he would not live another day with his mother gone.

But he lived another day. He saw himself with his father, going dully through the daily routines. Cooking, doing dishes, cleaning house, washing and folding clothes. Gradually they began to talk to each other. Soon they began to joke and smile. They watched TV together. They laughed. They had fun. And at the end of his dream, Enoch saw himself and his father talking about Mother and laughing about some of the crazy things that she used to do, and crying gently at the memory of her goodness. But not grieving.

Not grieving, for the grief had its end. That was the wisdom that the water taught him. That even after the end of the world, the world goes on. Even after the winter. Even after death.

He awoke from his dream and fingered the strange-shaped key in his pocket that had got him into the Castle of Care. He would use the key. He would no longer be afraid of anything.

As for Mo's dream, she awoke from it as quiet as Enoch did, and because she never asked him what he saw after drinking the water of wisdom, he never asked her either, and so he never knew.

Healing

On the way home they came to the edge of a vast desert. In the distance there were four or five tornadoes, but Enoch was not afraid of anything now. He went right to the desert's edge, and reached down into the deep dust, and filled his pockets. Only then did he hold some up to his mouth and breathe it in. He choked on it, but all the pain from all his wounds went away, and there was not so much as a scar. Mo did the same, and then she led him back to the cave that led to Oglethorpe's.

At the short door that said "Employees Only," Mo turned to him and shook his hand. "You turned out all right," she said. "Even if you'll never be a knight, you certainly graduated from page to squire in one trip."

"Thanks," said Enoch. And he felt vaguely sad as she strode boldly away, for he admired her so much, and she only liked him, and wouldn't miss him at all on her next adventure.

Enoch walked around and found his father, who hadn't even noticed that Enoch was missing. Enoch didn't come back to Oglethorpe's the next day, or the next, and after that he couldn't come for a whole year, because they moved to Tucson then.

In Tucson, Enoch was afraid to use the dust. He was afraid it wouldn't work so far away from the land that it came from. There were some days that he even doubted that his adventure with Mo was real. After all, it was such a crazy place. Killer squirrels, a talking roast pig, a fire-breathing horse, Santa Claus as the King of Care.

Then one day he saw how worried his father was, and he realized that living in Arizona was not helping. His mother was dying anyway.

So he went to his room, to the shoebox hidden away at the back of the closet, and opened it and touched the dust and held some of it in his hands, and he wondered if the dream of wisdom had been meant to prepare him for his mother's death. He decided it had not. It had only been meant to teach him that he mustn't try to put off death forever. This once he could use the dust and keep her from dying out of time. But when his parents were very old, he would not try to heal them again and again, and keep them alive forever. That was wisdom.

He baked half the dust into chocolate chip cookies, which his mother could not resist. The other half he served to her in applesauce at supper. She ate it to the bottom of the bowl.

And she got better. There was no mistaking it. She felt better at once, and gradually regained her strength, and before a year had gone by, she said at the dinner table one day, "Enoch. How would you like to have a white Christmas?"

He jumped up from the table and shouted for joy. "We're going to Dowagiac!" The dust had worked. His mother was completely cured.

The doctors all said it was because she had followed their advice and gone to Arizona. But that's how doctors stay in business, Enoch realized, by taking credit every time their patients happen not to die.

The Last Time Through the Door

All the time he was in Tucson, Enoch had thought that the moment he got back to Dowagiac he'd go through the short door again. But when he actually got to Oglethorpe's, he had second thoughts. And when he discovered that they hadn't yet opened the back basement rooms for the Christmas selling season, he was downright relieved.

He tried to tell himself that it was kid stuff anyway. That it was unrealistic. But the true reason he was glad not to go through the door was that he was scared. Last time he had Mo with him. And this time there was no crazy girl with her hair up in ugly pigtails hanging around in the basement. How would he handle the killer squirrels without her? What would he do if he ran into a giant? He had a vision of being trapped in a room with a fire-breathing horse, only this time without a silver thread. And so he went on home.

At school his friends were really glad to see him for the first two minutes of the first three class periods. Then they treated him perfectly normally, as if he had never been away. That was OK with Enoch. There were even a few new people, but Enoch talked to them as if he had known them as long as the others.

Not that everything was the same. A year at that age made a lot of difference. A lot of the other guys had grown four or five inches taller and had wispy mustaches. *All* of the girls were taller than Enoch, and looked about five years older. Enoch didn't mind. He had an appreciative eye.

He appreciated one girl in particular. She wore too much makeup, but that was a disease of the eighth grade; he could put up with that. She just fascinated him, even though she didn't talk much, even though she avoided his gaze. She even looked familiar. It wasn't until he heard someone call her Mo that he realized why.

"Mo?" he asked.

"Yeah, Eeny," she said. She looked miserable.

"It's really *you*?"

"Have you met?" asked a girl. "She didn't even come to school for the first time until after Christmas last year."

"We killed some squirrels together," said Enoch. It was OK to say that. Everyone took it as a joke, and so nobody asked any embarrassing questions. And in a few minutes they were alone by their lockers. Everybody else was in class, and they'd get in trouble, but Enoch figured what the heck. You don't have that many friends in the world who saved your life a couple of times.

"I thought your father didn't let you go to school."

"He thought I was getting too weird by myself all the time." She smiled, but it was unconvincing.

"Sorry I didn't recognize you. You're taller."

She looked even more miserable. "I know," she said.

"Hey, that's OK. You're not taller than the *other* girls or anything." No matter now hard he tried, he was just making it worse.

"I know," she said. "Eeny, have you tried to go through the short door yet?"

He shook his head.

"You're still shorter than I am. Maybe you still can."

Now he understood. She was too tall. "But can't you bend over?"

"Doesn't work," she said. "I tried. I tried scrunching down into my spine until my back ached. I kept trying until the clerks called my father and he saw me with my hair in those pigtails and he put me on restrictions for a month. Restrictions means watching channel forty-six all evening. I cried the whole time. Father thought I was repenting, and I wanted to die. Eeny, if you can get through that door again, I'll love you forever."

"What do you want me to do?" Of course she wanted him to do something for her.

She grinned. "That's true friendship, Eeny. You know I'm going to take advantage of you, and you don't mind."

"Actually, I do mind, but I owe you my life." Actually, he didn't mind—especially if she loved him forever, like she said. Somehow the idea of having her love him forever sounded pretty good. He looked at her face and finally realized the main reason he hadn't recognized her. "Where's the wart?"

Tears came to her eyes. "I didn't need it anymore, Eeny. So I let Mom get it removed."

She leaned on his shoulder for a moment and sobbed silently. Then she got hold of herself. "We better get to class or we'll be in detention your first day back to Dowagiac."

"I've been in worse places with you than detention."

She touched his hand. "Eeny, you're the only person who ever went with me through the short door. I've really missed you. I've done some incredible things since you left."

"So let's go to Oglethorpe's after school."

After school they talked all the way to Oglethorpe's. It wasn't hard to sneak through the labyrinth into the back rooms. And by the time they had the boxes out of the way of the short door, Enoch had a rough idea of all of her adventures.

"I buried the treasure chest at the base of an oak tree about ten yards west of the exact spot where you almost stepped into the quicksand. Do you think you can find it?"

"Yeah. What's in it?"

"Nothing special. Just enough gold and jewels to pay my way through college. With enough left over to let our whole class live in luxury for the rest of our lives."

"Is it heavy?"

"It doesn't take much gold these days to buy that many dollars. Eeny, am I being too greedy?"

"Not if I get a cut. Which side of the oak?"

"North. There's no shovel, but the soil isn't very hard to dig in. If you need my sword, it's hidden here." She pointed to a place on her rough map of the path through the cave. Last time he had been guided through somehow in the darkness. This time she gave him the pocket flashlight from her purse.

He fit through the door without bending, without scrunching down into his shoes. But he felt his hair brush the top of the doorframe, and he knew he'd not be making many trips after this.

When he got to the oak tree by the quicksand he knew that he was too late. The hole wasn't concealed, it was open. The treasure chest had been dug up. Probably by the little people. They were just rotten enough to steal from their benefactor.

He couldn't bear to go back empty-handed and disappoint her. Besides, with her sword in hand, back here in the place where he had helped to save the king, where he had got the healing dust that saved his mother, he couldn't just turn around and go back. It wasn't as if he'd keep Mo waiting—no matter how long he stayed, he would only seem to be gone a split second.

So he retraced the path they had taken before, through the apple orchard, over the back of the dragon Drast, and finally to the door of the Castle of Care. He needed no key now. The door stood open, and he had to stand in line for half an hour as the procession of sheep and cattle and wagons and jugglers and dancers and vendors and fine lords and ladies slowly passed through the door. The doorkeeper recognized his name and embraced him in the name of the king. "He doesn't have time to see you," said the doorkeeper.

"I know," said Enoch.

"But he wanted me to give you these." The doorkeeper handed him two ornate, jewel-encrusted flagons. "For you and the woman. So you can carry back the water of your choice."

"Hasn't Mo come back here herself?"

"Never. And it's been a good long time."

Enoch took the flagons and went to the fountain and filled them up. He slept the night in an inn outside the castle, free of charge because he was a friend of the king. And in the morning he got up and stood out on the road leading back to Oglethorpe's.

This was almost definitely his last trip. Surely there was some adventure for him before he went back. Hadn't Mo saved lives, slain monsters, befuddled witches, found hidden treasures? Surely he should do something like that, to be worthy of her.

No. He knew better. She was the brave one, the adventurer. He could do brave things now and then, if he had to. But he didn't know things that she knew without having to learn them. He hadn't the faintest idea how to handle the sword, to begin with. His only victory had come by snapping a silver cord like a towel. The best place for him was home, with memories.

So he walked home. Slowly, except when crossing the dragon's back; slowly, so that everything would stay imprinted in his mind. It was night before he got to the cave, but the little flashlight and Mo's map helped him through. He crossed the abyss and dropped down into the closet, pulled open the door and came out. Mo was standing where she had been when he left.

She was startled. "Why didn't you go?" she asked.

"I already went. I spent a couple of days in there."

"Oh. I've never stood outside and waited for somebody else."

"It wasn't there," he said. "Somebody already dug it up and took it."

She nodded, her eyes again filling with tears. "Well, it was silly of me to want it. How would I ever explain to people where it came from, anyway? My father would think I stole it." She grinned. "In fact, I did. But I stole it from a witch, and she stole it from a dragon, and I guess it's justice that somebody stole it from me." Her face darkened. "Probably those rotten little people. I hope the squirrels have a population explosion."

They laughed together, and then Enoch gave her the flagons. "Take your choice," he said. "Gifts to us from the King of Care."

"They're full."

"I filled them both with the water of wisdom," he said.

She looked gravely at the flagon. "I don't know. Should I drink it now?"

"No time like the present to get wise," he said.

She pulled out the stopper and lifted the flagon's mouth to her lips.

"Wait," Enoch said.

"Mm?"

"I lied," he said. "It isn't the water of wisdom."

"I know," she said. She reached over and pulled out the stopper of his flagon, too. "Drink, pinhead," she said.

"Cheers," said Enoch, and he drank the elixir of love to the last drop.

NOTES ON "DUST"

It was Kristine's and my first Christmas away from home together. We were in South Bend, Indiana, and we had lots of friends—but still, there was a lot of nostalgia for both of us. Ever since we started dating, we had combined the Christmas and New Year's traditions of both our families, so we would each be missing a double portion of what we had enjoyed during our years together in Utah.

But South Bend had wonders of its own. Though in those days it was a depressed factory town—American Motors was mostly gone, except for its garden tractor division—it still had the physical signs of the glory days of American cities with once-vibrant downtowns.

There was an old department store that was only one or two years from failure, it was plain. I remember carrying one of the kids with me— probably baby Emily—as I went down into the basement toy department. It was decorated for Christmas—employees were still trying to pretend the store had a reason to exist. And as I wandered around the shelf units, I came upon a back corner that had a door leading pretty much nowhere. Its position in the building suggested that if anything, it led out under the street.

More likely it was once the loading elevator leading up to the street, but I didn't think of that because hey, I'm a fantasy writer, and so I conjured up the image of a kid wandering away in the toy department at Christmastime and going into a passageway that led into . . .

Well, basically, into Narnia. Not Lewis's Narnia, but the same idea, a magical place with rules of its own that was no farther than a quick crawl through a door that should have been locked.

Because I had this idea in my head I decided that I'd write a Christmas story as our gift to friends and family. It would just be a lark, something I made up as I went along. I knew the starting place—that basement toy department in a dying store—and it would be easy enough to free-associate my way to a story.

The trouble is that free-associating leads you (a) straight into cliches, since your mind goes first to ideas you've seen before, and (b) into a really long story that nobody would have time to read at Christmas.

Still, I wrote it in a single sitting, we photocopied it, and then we sent it off to a list of a few select people.

My memory is that not a soul read it. Or if they did, nobody liked it enough to mention it. But that might be the slippage of memory—maybe one or two people actually mentioned it.

I knew it wasn't my best work, because I hadn't dropped sweat on the keyboard while typing it. But in another way it was a more personal story, less constructed than most of my work, more of a spew. So I continued to like it even as I decided not to bother offering it anywhere for publication.

I still liked it when we did a very small printing of it and offered it on our Website (http://www.hatrack.com) in a self-published mini-collection called *Doorways,* for whatever intrepid souls wanted to give it a try.

Again, the world didn't stop and people didn't beg me to print more copies so they could give them to all their friends. You'd think I could take a hint. But . . . I can't. To me it's still part of that first Christmas with just us.

HOMELESS IN HELL

If you don't get into heaven, you go to hell, right? That's what I'd always been taught. Heaven is Harvard, and hell a county technical college. If you finished high school, they've got to take you. Except that with hell, dying is the only diploma you're supposed to need.

I read those near-death-experience books, where they talked about how "the light" was full of warmth and love. Well, it *was* nice, but it sort of sets you up for disappointment, because when you're really dead and not just straying in there by accident, you get *past* that feel-good stage and suddenly you're *at* the light, and either it sucks you in or it shunts you away, like a magnet, and it all depends on how you're polarized.

I got pushed away.

Well, what did I expect, anyway? I used to go to church and all, but I wasn't much of a stickler on, like, telling the truth and helping my neighbor. And office supplies from work had a way of ending up at home. Not a lot, but I wasn't exactly perfect. Lots of looking upon women to lust after them. Just at the Victoria's Secret level. Quarreled with my wife a lot but I never hit her, though I did compare her to her mother way too often. Kind of the normal sins. I was sort of hoping they graded on the curve—I figured I was bound to make the top half. But no, it's straight percentage, you get one question wrong and you're out.

So what's the other choice? Hell, right? I start looking around, wondering if Dante was just making it all up and if not, which circle would I get into?

The answer is, Dante didn't know squat, there are no circles. You just find yourself on a street in hell and you go up to a door (and it's always the same door, no matter what the street is) and you see people going in and out, dressed to the nines, and you think, Cool, there are good clothes in hell, which stands to reason, really, and you go up to the door and you knock and the guy looks at you like you're a worm and he says, "Name?"

So I say my name and he makes this moue with his mouth like you sort of passed your expiration date about a month ago and he says, "Please, don't waste my time," and he starts to close the door in your face.

"Wait a minute," you say, "this is hell, right?"

"Hades," he says, and you can taste the contempt.

"Well I didn't make heaven, so you've got to let me in."

"No," he says, and then with a kind of faux patience he explains, "The place where, when you go there, they have to take you in, that's *home*. Not hell. We don't have to take just anybody. We're all about class here, nobody wants to look around and see *you*. There are real celebs inside. Stalin. Hitler. Caligula, for heaven's sake—oops, did I say that?"

"I'm not asking for the best seat in the house."

"There *is* no table insignificant enough for you."

I did a quick calculation—how many people ever lived on earth, how many would likely fail the entrance exam for heaven, and how many first-rank sinners would be ahead of me in line. "But . . . what do I do?"

"You bogey off and stop blocking the door."

"What do you think this is? Studio 54?"

He laughs. "Oh, no, it's much worse. It's like junior high. And you . . . ain't . . . cool."

And you get a big hand planted in your chest and when he pushes you don't fall, you *fly* across the street and smash into a building only it doesn't hurt—you're dead, remember?—and you're not injured and it begins to dawn on you, you're stuck in hell but you can't get in. You try a few other doors and the same guy is waiting behind every one of them to bounce you. And it's starting to rain. A thin cold drizzle, and even though you can't actually get injured, you *can* get cold and damp, or at least you *feel* like you've been left out in the cold, which in fact you have. You're not going to get sick, you're not going to starve, but you're also not going to get *in*.

Not that I was alone out there. There are a lot of streets in hell, and lots of homeless people wandering around. And they seem just about as crazy as the normal mix of homeless people. A few who look like they're waiting for a drug deal to go down, only I knew it was a fake, because what is there to buy or sell, and even if they're carrying—because you pretty much look the way you see yourself, so some people *are* armed— they aren't dangerous. If they had ever been truly dangerous, they'd be inside watching the strippers, or whatever they did inside Club Styx. These guys think if they look bad enough, if they say enough rude things to passersby, maybe someday they'll get by the bouncer. Ditto with the ones who look like hookers. They've got nothing to sell. But let's face it. Not everybody in hell is bright.

Then there are the crazies, shouting and preaching about Jesus and the end of the world, only it dawned on me pretty quickly that they aren't crazy—I mean, after you die there's no schizophrenia because there's no brain to malfunction. They're preaching because they're trying to tip the balance the other way, to show how righteous they are, denouncing sin, calling out the name of Jesus—or whoever, depending, but most of the shouters were, like, born again, only it apparently didn't take the way they thought.

I stood there watching them, and walked around watching them, and sat down and watched them, and no matter how hard I tried, I couldn't bring myself to care. It began to dawn on me just how *long* eternity was going to be, stuck on the streets of hell. I tried street after street, only nothing changed except the faces. The language didn't even change, because after you're dead all the languages become the same. They speak, and they think they're speaking Arabic or Tagalog, only what you hear is English, or at least you think it is. If you speak English. Anyway, you can understand everybody, and that's the worst, because you can't even go to a place where you don't understand the words people are saying so you can tune them out. You're always tuned in and it's so *boring.*

Daytime comes and goes, just like on earth, and gradually it began to dawn on me that this *was* earth. In fact, it was Washington DC, which is where I happened to buy the farm, hit by a car trying to cross Wisconsin in Georgetown on New Year's Eve 1999, which meant that whether the world ended that night the way everybody said it might, it definitely ended for me. I knew the streets. I could walk down the mall. Only everybody I saw was dead.

I thought for a while that the whole world must have died or some-thing, but then you'd think there'd be more newly dead people like me, you know, the whole government thing, if the world ended surely some significant percentage of them would go to hell, and surely they couldn't *all* qualify to get into Studio 666, so where were they? No, the world hadn't ended, just my little oxygen-consuming, carbon-dioxide-expelling bag of blood and bone.

And now that I was looking for it, I began to see the signs that life was going on. Things changed position. Garbage cans were in one place and then they were in another. Cars were parked somewhere and then they weren't. But you never actually saw them move. Nothing moved. It was like when they were in motion, they disappeared. And it occurred to me that it was like long-exposure photography. You set the exposure time really long, the aperture very small, and the only things you get are the things that don't move. Pedestrians, cars, anything that moves is gone.

It's like in hell time passes so slowly that living people are invisible to us. I had it figured out!

"You think you've got it figured out," said a fat man.

I looked at him, a little puzzled by why he was fat. I mean, surely when you die, you don't have to be fat anymore.

"It's how you see yourself," said the fat man. "You know how people said, 'Inside every fat person there's a thin person struggling to get out'? Not true. It's just another fat guy in there. In fact, usually a fatter guy."

"Can you lose weight?" I asked, because at least it was a conversation with somebody who wasn't trying to get wafted up into heaven or deeper into hell. And also it was kind of funny.

"You can look thinner," said the fat guy, "if you start to think of yourself as thin."

"So why can't you think of yourself as good, and get on up into heaven?"

He shook his head. "Those street preachers, they aren't thinking of themselves as good. They're thinking of themselves as righteous. Saved. Chosen."

"Better than everybody else."

"Bingo. Ditto with the bad dudes and the tough girls. They're needy, all of them, and needy doesn't get you off the street. Needy is what gets you *on* the street."

"If you've got it all figured out," says I, "what are you still doing here?"

"I'm conflicted," he said. "A common problem. Whenever I start going one direction, I do something to send me back the other." He grinned. "While *you,* you're talented."

Talented? "I'm not the one reading minds here. I mean, you've been answering stuff I didn't say."

"Yeah, I've got good hearing. I don't have to wait for you to speak. Because, you know, it's not like we actually have voices. We just sort of wish our thoughts to be heard, and then people close by can hear them. But your thoughts are actually just as loud, so to speak. So yeah, I can hear stuff. But you, you can see things."

I looked around. "No more than anybody else."

"Nope, nope, not so. I watched you. Crossing the street. You waited for the light."

"I did not. The lights don't change."

"And you dodged the pedestrians."

"There *are* no pedestrians."

"Nevertheless."

"I don't *see* them, so how can I dodge them?"

"Oh, you philosopher, you."

"What possible difference could it make to you?"

"I want to see how useful you are. What you can do."

"This is a job interview?"

"I've got an opening for an elf."

I looked him over, this time more carefully. No pipe clenched between his teeth, but his stomach was rather like a bowlful of jelly. "Am I supposed to laugh when I see you in spite of myself?"

"Clement Moore didn't actually see me," he said. "I'd long since stopped doing personal appearances by then. But you see, it doesn't make much difference. I've got this image in my face every Christmas—no, every Halloween and two months after—and it's all I can do to keep from wearing the red suit all year long. I used to be thin, when the Dutch were in charge of the image."

"What are you doing in hell? Aren't you supposed to be *Saint Nicholas?*"

"I'm not *in* hell. Any more than you are."

"Here's a clue, Nick. This ain't heaven."

"We're hovering, my friend. Or maybe we're volleying, like the shuttlecock in badminton, back and forth, almost one thing, almost another."

"Me, I'm just walking the streets."

"Dodging the pedestrians."

"I'm not a toymaker."

"Fine with me. That toymaking, that's just part of the myth. Hasn't anybody caught on that I'm *dead?* They don't issue us hammers and saws and set us to work making wooden toys. There's precious few of us can even see the living, and those that can move things in the material world, those are even more rare."

"So how do you come up with all those toys for good girls and boys?"

"When we need toys, which isn't as often as you think, we steal them."

"Ah," I said. "Now I'm beginning to get why you aren't in heaven. You aren't Santa Claus. You're Robin Hood."

"Mostly we break toys," said Santa. "Or hide them. It's not like we can move anything very far. And nowadays it's a cash economy. Come to think of it, it was back when I was alive, too. They used to draw pictures of me with bags of money, because that's what I did, my famous good deed, I paid a ransom in coin, saved some kids. Money's what we mostly use now, too. And because it's paper, it's even easier. Lighter. Even my less talented elves can move it."

I couldn't help it. He was so serious. I laughed. "Man, you had me going there. Santa Claus, stealing toys, breaking them, hiding them, dealing in cash. You got your elves out picking pockets?"

He didn't look amused. "Yes," he said. "I fail to see the humor."

"You're not putting me on?"

"I want to see if you can move things. In the material world."

"I told you, I can't even see the people, let alone pick their pockets, and even if I could, I've never been a thief." At once my conscience twinged. "At least, not deliberately. Not systematically."

"You got a better job offer?"

"I want a shot at heaven," I said. "As long as I'm not completely in hell, why not?"

"Me, too," said Santa. "Some years I've been *so* close."

"What about getting into the devil's workshop? Been close to that, too?"

He shrugged. "As a novelty act, they've invited me now and then. But not to stay. Strictly in the back door, you know."

"Why should I do this? I mean, you've been at this for what, fifteen hundred years? And you're still here."

"Got any better plans? It's not like you're running out of time."

"Santa, excuse me for saying this, but as far as I can tell, you're as looney as a one-legged duck."

He shook his head. "My friend, nobody's crazy here. We might be wrong about a lot of stuff, but we can't lie and we aren't crazy. Still, like I said, no hurry. Look me up if you decide Santa's gang of elves sounds more interesting than . . . whatever it is you're doing."

"How would I find you?"

He rolled his eyes. "Just ask. In case you didn't know it, I'm famous. People keep track of where I am."

"I was afraid I'd have to go to the north pole or something."

He shook his head, turned his back, and walked away.

He was right. I *could* see living people. And it wasn't a matter of slowing down or speeding up, either. It was more like you had to pay attention to something else, sort of look away and then be aware of what's going on at the edges of things. Only that's the strange thing—when you're dead, there are no edges. You have the habit, from all those years of binocular vision, of seeing only this window in front of you, with out-of-focus glimpses to the sides, and most dead people never get past that. But the fact is, when you're dead you don't have those limitations. You can see . . . well, you remember how people used to say that teachers seemed to have eyes in the back of their heads? Or it's like, you could feel someone's gaze on you, even though they were behind you? Well, that's how it is when you're dead, once you get the hang of it. You're aware in every direction. It's not really vision. It's just knowledge, but your mind kind of makes sense of it like vision. I wasn't consciously seeing those moving cars or pedestrians, so I didn't "know" they were there. But I was aware of them, aware of the people in the cars, aware of the people on the street, and some old reflex made me dodge them, weave among them without knowing it.

Thanks to the tip from Nick—I hate calling him Santa Claus because that name's too loaded down with cultural freight; I just have to laugh whenever I think of saying, "Hi, Santa!"—I got pretty good at seeing mortals. Got to be a habit, really, knowing where they were, knowing what they were doing. I found my range was pretty good, too, because this awareness thing, it isn't blocked by mere walls, I know who's coming around the corner before they actually come into my field of view. And I'm not a genius, either, I can imagine there's those that can see for miles, right through hills and cities and whatever else is in the way. Maybe see forever, if they've got the mind to sort through all the stuff you'd see in between.

And it wasn't just awareness. I could move stuff.

The thing is, touching the material world, changing it, that doesn't come the way awareness did—it isn't just automatically happening, so you only have to notice it. Ordinarily, when you're dead you simply don't affect the material world in any way. You don't sink through the earth or walk through walls, but only because you still have the respect for those surfaces you learned when you were alive. You *can* go through them, just as you can sink down into the earth, though that's extraordinarily boring, since nothing much is going on once you get past the earthworm and gopher level.

But you *can* affect things, not by touching or pushing or pulling, but by—oh, how else to say this?—by really, really wanting things to move. Yeah, OK, by *wishing.* But we're not talking about some wistful little desire. "Oh, I *wish* I could eat a candy bar again." No, it takes a desire so intense it consumes you, at least for the moment, the way a campfire consumes an empty marshmallow bag. You feel shrunken, thin, weak. But it's funny, because you also feel amazingly powerful. Like a superhero. Just because you got a chair to move.

Only how much can you really care about moving a chair? That's why poltergeists are so rare, and why they're usually so mean. They're angry all the time, and they move things around in order to cause fear in the living. That's the consuming desire—to make the living afraid of them. To have power. It's a pathetic thing, and it's definitely on the evil side of the ledger. Evil, but the bouncer doesn't let poltergeists into the nether-club, because they don't need somebody inside moving the furniture or spilling the drinks, I guess.

I'm no poltergeist. I'm not mad at anybody. OK, well, so, that's a lie. I'm pretty steamed about being stuck between heaven and hell, and I'm ticked off about getting killed before the prime of my life (at least I assume the prime was still ahead of me, seeing how nonprime the years I actually lived through seemed to be). So how was I going to move anything?

It was Nick who showed me how. Once I realized he'd been right about my seeing the living, I looked him up and he kind of took me under his wing, he and a few of his elves—who are *not* little and *not* cute, they're just dead people like me—and showed me the work they do.

It isn't just at Christmas, though Christmas is for them like tax time is for accountants. All through the year, Nick and his gang are watching out for children. They'll pick a kid—almost at random, or so it seems to me, though maybe there's some system in it, some signs they look for—and they just follow, watching. Most kids, their life is OK. Sure, they get yelled at, spanked, ignored, ridiculed, the normal stuff that makes life interesting, but most of them, somebody loves them, somebody's looking out for them, somebody thinks they're pretty good to have around. You can live through a lot of hard times, if you've got that.

There are other kids, though. Two kinds. Bullies and victims. And Nick's on the lookout for both. The victims, they break your heart. The ones that are getting tortured or beaten, there's not much we can do for them. The rage in the person hurting them, that's a powerful force, it matches any wish we can come up with, and then on top of that they've got bodies, which pretty much makes us helpless. What Nick's gang does in those cases is, they try their best to make it obvious to other living people what's going on. You know, cause a shirt to ride up so a bruise is visible, or get a neighbor to look in a window or hear a sound, something to make them suspicious. A lot of them call the cops or child welfare, if it's a country where the cops care, or where there *is* an agency whose job is to look out for kids. But a lot of them don't, and in the end, our hearts just break for those kids and we sort of just wait for them to join us. Because a lot of Nick's best recruits come from among those children. His scouts, so to speak. They've got a nose for it.

The neglected kids, though, Nick's gang can help a lot, there. We get food to them, sometimes. We open a door now and then—that's a lot harder and more complicated than you might think. And when they're alone, some of Nick's gang, they can't move things, but they can make sounds that the living can hear, so they sing to them or talk to them. Tell them stories. We get tagged as imaginary friends sometimes, but it's not like we're looking for credit. We just try to help the kids know they're not alone, that somebody cares what they're going through. And those singers, they do a sweet lullaby, I tell you. Songs that even the deaf can hear, cause they sing right into the mind. Sometimes I go with them, just to hear them sing. We can't save all their lives, but we can make what life they have a little better, and that's good. It's not like we think of death as all that big a deal, anyway. I mean, we *are* dead, and so death doesn't hold any fear for us. That's why we're generally not in the lifesaving business. When we can get a few crackers to a kid, sure, we'll do it, but . . . they'll just need more tomorrow, right? While a good song can live in their memory through a lot of dark nights of fear and loneliness.

But that's not the kind of work I do. I'm not a singer, and when I move things, I've got to be mad. It's my sense of injustice that has to get riled up. And so I'm on the bully patrol.

You know the kids I'm talking about. Some of them are physically violent, but most bullies do their damage with their mouths. They've got this instinct for the thing that makes a weaker kid hurt the most. Sometimes it's obvious—a kid with a big nose, you don't have to be a brain surgeon to figure out what to make fun of. But some of these bullies, it's like they can read minds. Their victim has a drunk mother, the bully goes straight to the mother jokes—how does he know? The girl who's lonely and scared she's not good enough for anybody, the bully girls taunt her clothes or play really mean jokes where they pretend to be her friend until she commits herself, says something that shows she really believes in their faux kindness, and then they can mock her. Some of the things they do are so elaborate, it takes so much thought and effort to do them, you can hardly believe someone would go to all that trouble just to make another person unhappy.

Well, that ticks me off. That gets me all intense, and I feel it building up, and I can move things.

The trouble is, what do I move? It's not like the bully deserves to die or anything, so I can't make the roof cave in on them. Death may not be a big deal to us, but murder still is, and one of the rules that seem to govern the universe is that while we can do a little messing around with the material world, we're not allowed to kill. Just can't do it. Wish all we want, but if the thing we try to move might kill somebody, it just won't budge.

So we've got to be resourceful. I mostly try for justice. A girl makes fun of another kid's big nose, I make sure the bully girl bumps into a door that wasn't quite where she thought it was. Big swollen nose, a shiner. Let her see how it feels to have other people stare at your face for a while. Or a bully boy who shoves little kids around—I can arrange for him to twist his ankle or trip and fall headlong right as he's going after a kid, make him look bad in front of everybody or distract him with a little pain. My favorite, though, is to make it so when the bully just touches his victim, I make the victim's nose bleed like a river, make him bruise up around his eye or jaw. Doesn't really hurt the victim when I do it, but it makes it look like the bully did a full-out assault, gets him in *so* much trouble. A few times the bully's been so frightened by the injury he "caused" that he gets control of his hostility and stops picking on kids.

But here's the problem. I'm working on justice, protecting kids from each other, trying to help change kids who've fallen in love with cruelty, help them start being a little more decent, learn a little compassion. But when you come right down to it, what am I actually doing? Causing pain. Hurting people. All in a good cause, right? But remember, the guy who judges you is the same one who said, "Turn the other cheek."

I tell myself, I'd turn my *own* cheek. But he never said I have to turn away and not notice when somebody else is getting slapped, right? I mean, he also said that it was better to tie a millstone around your neck and jump into the sea than to hurt one of the little ones.

But then I also have to be honest and tell myself that I'm hurting some of his little ones, too. The mean ones, the vicious ones, the ones that maybe he doesn't really think of as his. But if his capacity for forgiveness is infinite, the way some people say, then they're *all* his. Didn't he get ticked off at some moneychangers, though, and lash out with a scourge and knock over some tables? Surely he understands how we feel, those of us who are working on trying to stop the bullies.

You know the real problem? There are so few of us. Few who have the ability even to see the living—can't do much unless you can see what's going on!—and even fewer who, seeing, care. Because most of the dead, they just disconnect from the living. So mortals are mean to each other. Big deal. Get over it. Get on with your . . . well, your death. Whatever this is. You can't fix anything in the mortal world. You get no credit for it. You're already judged to be unworthy of heaven. So it's not like you've got a stake in what's going on.

Just a few of us who care about the kids and have the ability to do anything about it. So even if we're making a difference in the lives of some kids, there are thousands, millions of others that we never see. That's not a reason to stop, though. It's a reason to try harder. It's not like we sleep. That's something, anyway. We got twenty-four hours a day.

You do get tired, though. Not physically tired. Just tired in your soul. Seeing how many mean people there are. Seeing how eagerly the victims keep hoping that their parents will love them, that they'll find friends at school. And here we are, trying to help keep those hopes alive. It breaks your heart. It makes you want to despair sometimes, that despite all that hope, there's always a bully to dash it. Why do they hate happiness in other people so much? Especially the children—where do they learn to take such pleasure in someone else's misery?

Was I like that?

Oh, man, that's the thing that comes back again and again. Every rude thing I ever said to another kid. There was this guy in junior high and high school, we were friends, you know? In plays together, in band. He was smart and talented, and I liked him. But one day, I'm sitting there with a song going through my head, and for some reason I come up with a new lyric for it that makes fun of this friend. A song about Bruce, talking about how conceited he is. And, well, he *is,* not so much conceited as really excited about all the cool things he can do. I think back on it and I realize, he wasn't vain, he was just thrilled to keep discovering new things he could do, and he thought he could share his excitement with his friends. Well, I cured him of *that*. Cause it wasn't just the one song. I sang that to my friends and they all laughed and that was it for me, the first talent I ever had—a talent for musical meanness. I must have written twenty Brucie songs. Till Bruce stopped hanging around with us and it was no fun to sing it when he wasn't there. Made me look bad instead of clever.

I think back on that, I wonder where Nick was. Maybe Nick's gang saw me but figured, Bruce really *was* talented and smart, he really *didn't* need a loser like me for a friend. They didn't have to stop me, because I just wasn't important enough in Bruce's life for him to need rescue. I sure hope that's it. I hope I did no harm.

That's the kind of thing that goes through your mind when you're on bully patrol. Way too much self-examination, if you ask me, but you can't help it, you keep seeing yourself in the bullies as much as in the victims. They're all kids, after all. Even if they're rotten and mean, they're kids. They might still become something worthwhile.

Christmas, that's the tough time. I had a whole year of learning, mostly on American streets because I knew the culture well enough to recognize what was going on with the kids and to be able to think of ways to help them. And just when I'm getting pretty deft and clever at bully-stopping, Nick comes to me and says, "It's the Christmas rush. Bully patrol is over till after the big day."

It's obvious that it's Christmas. I mean, there's no missing it—because Nick's in a red suit. When the decorations go up, there's all these pictures of him looking like Norman Rockwell's Coke-drinking Santa, and he just can't hold on to his civilian image, the red suit just pops right out of him and that's how he looks. And it's a good thing I can't see myself in mirrors, because I've got to tell you, I wouldn't be at all surprised to find that I look really small and I'm wearing green. Sometimes you just want to yell at those advertising guys. Can't they leave us a little dignity?

Christmas and the elves. That's when the serious thievery begins.

Right, like you thought we actually made the toys! We're dead, and even if we were alive, most toys that kids actually want require serious machinery. Do you have any idea just how much equipment it takes to make one lousy little Lego? Let alone a whole *Toy Story* action figure. No, we don't make toys. We just redistribute them.

And not in the stores. Think about it—who goes to Toys R Us? People with no money? Hardly. So going to the parking lot and taking things out of one shopping cart and putting them in another, what good is that going to do? We can't move things far anyway—it just wipes us out even to jostle stuff. So none of this stuff about bags of toys going down chimneys. It's pretty rare for something to show up under the tree that Mom and Dad didn't know about in advance.

Besides, we have to be really intense in order to move things, right? So here's what we do on Christmas patrol.

We watch for people with more than they need to be out around poor people. Or for poor kids to be in a place where there's plenty of money changing hands. I'll be teamed up with one of the singing elves, and she'll distract the rich guy while he's handling his money, while I liberate a five-dollar bill or sometimes even a twenty and cause it to drift down to the floor. Then I stand watch over it, keeping it from being noticed by anyone until the singer is able to entice some poor kid to be close enough, and then I push the five or the twenty—or, heck, the buck or the quarter, cause sometimes that's all I can get—out into the open, where the kid can see it.

You know the amazing thing? The number of kids who immediately try to give it to the store owner, or take it straight to their parents. Well, once we give it to them, it's theirs to dispose of. The gift has been given. And when you think about it, maybe the best gift is for the kid with no money to give that twenty to the store owner, to prove that he doesn't really *need* that money, that it's more important to be a decent person than to have what money can buy. Or if he gives it to his parents, well, maybe that's food on the table. Sure, maybe it's booze, too, and that's why they're poor, but it's not the kid's fault, the kid did the right thing. He contributed to the family.

About half the kids, though, they hang on to the money, and that's fine, that's even better, because you know what? Almost every time, they use some of it to buy themselves a treat—ice cream or a candy bar, maybe a cooky—but then the rest of the money goes straight into buying a gift for somebody else. A little brother or sister. Mom or Dad. Sometimes a teacher who's been good to them. I even saw one kid who had four dollars and twenty-eight cents in his fist—change from the ice cream bar—and he sees a kid who looks even more poor than him, and he just walks up and gives it to him and says, "Merry Christmas." Right then I loved that kid so much. Because he got it. He understood. None of that stuff goes with you when you die. Only what you did for other people, or to them, and what they did for you, and to you. That's all you have with you when you're dead. That kid, when he dies, he's going to have so much cool stuff. Because he has a good heart. He won't be walking around the streets of hell, no place to stay. He'll fit right in with the light, he'll pass that entrance exam, they'll greet him with songs, you know? And I got him the fiver that he was able to mostly share. That's something.

That's Christmas. We just use the season to get gifts into the hands of children who don't have anything. It's about hope, just like what we do the rest of the year. That's what Nick does—he's in the hope business.

So it's the day after Christmas, and we're back on the regular schedule, but Nick, he comes to me—and the red suit hasn't faded yet, so he really looks like Santa Claus—he comes to me and says, "Want to take the long hike with me?"

I don't know what he's talking about, but I say, "Sure," because he wants me to and it's only thanks to him that I feel like I'm worth the space I take up, even on the streets of hell. Whatever the long hike is, it's not like I'll get tired or have to carry a pup tent on my back. So I say sure and off we go.

Straight up to the light.

And it's not a very long hike at all, not heading there. It's like, no matter where you are on earth, once you decide to find the light, there it is, just a little out of reach, up and over your shoulder. Nick, he goes like he knows the way, and I guess he does. Every year after Christmas, he goes back to the light and tries to get in. That's what I was along for. The other elves, I guess most of them have gone with him, some of them more than once. And I guess they were just as happy to have the new guy go along.

Because there goes Nick, straight into the light, and you think, "Man, this time he's going to make it. This time he's getting out of hell!"

He's in there so *long.* You have so much hope for him.

And then . . . pop. He's right back out. He looks at you. Shrugs his shoulders. "Better luck next time," he says.

Only I was new at this. And I'd been working on my sense of outrage all year, you know? And it's not like *I* was getting into heaven any time soon. I mean, if Nick can't pass the entrance exam, you think *I* stand a chance?

So I stand there and yell—not speaking loud, because it's not actually, sound, but I'm really intense, you know?—and I know I'm not supposed to get ticked off at the *light* for heaven's sake, but anyway, I yell, "Did you ever think that your stupid requirements might be too high? What've you got in there anyway, a bunch of pious martyrs? A bunch of goody-two-shoes never broke a rule in their lives? Well take a look at Nick here, he's on the front line, dead though he may be, he's trying to do something about it! I don't see *you* down there on the streets trying to make life better for kids! So what about *that,* huh? Ever think about how maybe some of the people in heaven aren't doing diddly-squat and maybe some of the people in hell are actually doing some good in the world?"

Finally I say enough that the intensity wears off and I remember who I'm talking to and I think, Man, it's going to take, like, ten thousand years to work off the sheer blasphemy of what I just said.

Only right then I hear something inside my mind, the way it must be when the singers do their lullabies for the suffering children. This voice, so soft, so kind, and all it says is, "Whatever you do for the least of my little ones, you've done it for me."

And it about knocks me over. He sees. He knows. What we're doing. What our work is. He knows, and he loves us for it, and yet . . .

And yet Nick still can't get in.

I look at him, and he shrugs again. "Yelling doesn't solve anything," he says.

And then he leads me on the long hike back. Yeah, that's the "long" part of the long hike. Getting to the light is quick. Getting back, that's hard and slow, because every step hurts, coming away from that beauty and going back to the plain old world with all the dead people preaching or being cool, and all the living people going about their business as if life were really long and they had all the time in the world. And you can't help but think, when you look at the living, you think: It's so easy for them, they can just *do* things, only they so rarely do anything that matters. So many children, all they need is a word and a smile, all they need is an act of kindness and generosity, something that any living person could give them, but so often they leave it up to the dead. But the ones who don't leave it up to us, the ones who are good to the kids, they're my friends, you know? They're my sisters and my brothers. I can't do anything to show them how I feel, but I'm glad they're alive. They're the only reason hell isn't more, well, hellish.

Finally we got back, down on the streets of hell. And Nick says, "Another year to go."

And I say, "Nick, thanks for letting me be part of it. Maybe it's not good enough for them, but it's good enough for me."

And he grins and even though he doesn't move, it feels like he just clapped me on the shoulder, and he says, "Then it's good enough for me, too." And off he goes.

Only there's something wrong with this picture. I'm seeing him but there's more to him than the red suit. There's a kind of jauntiness in his step, and even though that's probably my own mind creating the image that fits what I'm sensing about him, the fact is that it's still *true*. Nick just failed for the fifteen hundredth time to get into heaven, and he's almost dancing.

"Hey!" says I. "Hey, Santa!"

He turns around and there we are, face to face, and I say, "What are you so happy about?"

"It was a good Christmas," he says, all innocentlike, and I know he's not lying because you can't, but he's also not exactly answering me.

"How come you didn't make it this year?" I demanded.

"I don't think you get a list," he says.

"Bull," says I. "I came out of that light knowing every little sin I ever committed. You got the whole inventory, Nick. And I want to know what it is that keeps you out."

He turns around slowly, indicating the street around him. All the Christmas decorations are still up, of course, and there in every window, there's his face, Santa Claus, grinning and selling stuff. "It's all that," he says.

"What, the Christmas decorations?"

"The fact that it's my face and not his."

"*You* don't paint those pictures! *You* don't hang them up!"

"Yeah, but I like it that they're there. I like being famous. He never did."

"And that's it? That's all?"

"I don't even know if that's the reason," he says. "Because they don't give me a list of sins. But it's a story. Better than nothing, right?"

And off he goes, this time for real, and it's time to get back on the bully patrol, but a thought crosses my mind. Maybe the reason they don't give him a list of sins is because there isn't one. Not for him. Because there aren't any sins. He was in the light an awfully long time before he bounced out. What if he didn't get bounced at all? What if, every year, he chooses to come back even though he doesn't have to? Because he'd rather be here, homeless in hell, doing the work he does, than to be happy in heaven. In fact, maybe heaven would be hell to him, knowing that he *could* be leading us in helping kids, only there he is with a harp or whatever. So the only way for him to be in heaven is not to be in heaven. He's got work to do, and he's doing it, and *that's* heaven for him.

And then this really strange thought comes to me. What if that's all heaven is for anybody? What if everybody gets bounced down to the streets of hell, but if you find the right things to do, it becomes heaven for you? Look what I've got: A job to do that matters in the world. Good friends to work with. Nick leading me, a man I can look up to. Tell me what heaven's got that's any better than that.

Hey, it can't be true. I mean, if it *were* true, wouldn't Saint Francis and Saint Peter and all those guys be down here, working alongside us? No, heaven's heaven, and I'm in hell. Maybe Nick's an angel in disguise, and maybe he's just what he seems to be—another homeless dead guy desperate to figure out a way to get off the streets. What difference does it make?

I'm not in torment. In fact, I had a pretty merry Christmas. I saw a lot of sad things, but I saw some good things, and a few of those good things, I made them happen.

And then I thought, maybe I could make even more good things happen if I could just tell the living about how it is here, about how it works. I can't do it like an angel with a trumpet, so that everybody would have to believe. But I can tell it like a story. Making letters appear on a computer screen, that's a piece of cake compared to getting a five-dollar bill out of a wallet and onto the street. So I found a guy who leaves his computer on day and night, and I wrote all this down, and now you're reading it, and you can take it as fiction or you can take it as truth, it doesn't matter to me. I don't care what you believe. I just care what you do.

Well, I've taken just about as much time off as I can spare. Like the old joke says, "Back on your heads!" I'm up to my neck in it and there's only a few of us to shovel. Merry Christmas. God bless us every one. Suffer little children to come unto me. All that stuff.

NOTES ON "HOMELESS IN HELL"

Here's how it started. Somebody said, "Have a hell of a happy Christmas" and I was off and running.

See, we Mormons don't actually believe in the traditional Protestant or Catholic version of Hell. To us, that's as realistic as the Greek Hades or the River Styx. Just a myth, ripe to be used for entertainment. So when somebody said—or maybe I read it on a Christmas card—"Have a hell of a happy Christmas," I naturally thought it would be a cool joke to turn "hell" into a place where you really could have a merry Christmas.

I posted the story on Hatrack.com as a freebie for anybody who might get a kick out of it. Here's the irony. "Dust," which I actually took seriously, never raised much of a stir. But I heard back from a lot of people about "Homeless in Hell." Apparently there's a large contingent of people who are comfortable with the idea of Santa Claus as the devil, or vice versa, or something.

In the Dragon's House

In a fit of romantic excess, the builder of the house at 22 Adams gave this lovely street of grand Victorian mansions its one mark of distinction—a gothic cathedral of a house, complete with turrets, crenellated battlements, steep-pitched roofs, and even gargoyles at the downspouts.

One of the gargoyles—the one most easily visible to those who approached the front door—was a fierce dragon's head. In a thunderstorm the beast spewed great gouts of water, for it collected from the largest expanse of roofs. But this wet wyrm was no less to be avoided than its mythical fire-breathing forebears.

Inside the house, however, there was no attempt to be archaic or fey. Electricity was in the house from the beginning. In fact, it was the first house in Mayfield to be fully wired during construction, and the owner spared no expense. Knobs and wires were concealed behind the laths, and every room of any size had, not just one electric outlet, but four—one in each wall. A shameless extravagance. What would anyone ever need so many outlets *for*?

As the house was going up, passersby were known to tut-tut that the house was doomed to burn, having so much fire running up and down inside the walls. But the house did not burn, while others, less well-wired, sometimes did, as their owners overloaded circuits with multipliers and extension cords to make up for the electrical deficiency.

Between the gargoyle and the rumors of future fire, it was inevitable that the neighbors would call it "the dragon house." During the 1920s, the moniker changed a little, becoming "the Old Dragon's house," for during that time the owner was an old widower—the son of the original builder—who valued his privacy and had no concern for what the neighbors thought. He let the small garden surrounding the house go utterly to seed, so it was soon a jungle of tall weeds that offended the eye and endlessly seeded the neighbors' gardens.

When helpful or impatient neighbors from time to time came over and mowed the garden, the old man met them with hostility. As he grew older and more isolated, he threatened violence, first with a broom, then with a rake, and finally with a cane that might have been pathetic in the hands of such an old man. But he was so fiery in his wrath that even the boldest man quailed before him, and he soon became known among the neighbors as the Old Dragon. It was from him as much as the gargoyle that the house seemed to derive its name.

Finally, the neighbors went to court and got an injunction compelling the man to control the weeds on his property. The Old Dragon responded by hiring workmen to come and pave the entire garden, front and back, with bricks and cobblestones so that the only living things in the yard were the insects that wandered across it in search of likelier foraging grounds.

The old man lived out his days and when he died, the house went to a great niece who called it, not "the Old Dragon's House" but "the Albatross," and put it on the market the moment it was certified as hers.

That was when Michael's great-grandparents bought the place and turned it into the home he grew up in.

Normal Schwarzhelm had owned a chain of vaudeville theaters and had married his favorite headliner, Lolly Poppins. Just before vaudeville's collapse, Normal sold his theaters to a developer who was turning them all into movie houses, then invested the money and retired to Mayfield, the smallest and most charming of the towns on his little circuit.

Buying the Old Dragon's House was not Normal's idea, it was Lolly's. To her, it carried all the magic and romance of the legitimate stage, to which she had always aspired; her twenty years of doing slightly naughty comic songs followed by one tragic tear-jerking ballad had never been more than a stopgap until she got her "break."

Her break had turned out to be Normal, who adored her and

indulged her and had a wagonload of money. Of course he hadn't the power to get her into legitimate theatre now—he was out of the business, and she was too old and too well known for her shtick, which was looking surprised and confused at the double entendres in her own songs, followed by a whooping laugh when she finally got her own joke. Nobody in legitimate theatre would give her the roles she coveted.

But the Dragon's House had a copious cellar and, with a little excavation and remodeling and an additional dose of heavy-duty wiring for the lights, she fitted out a little underground theater where she could mount amateur productions to her heart's content. Which she did. She became the producer, the director, and a beloved character actress in a lively community theatre company that did everything from *Trojan Women* to *Macbeth,* from *The Importance of Being Earnest* to *The Women.* It should not be hard to guess which parts she played.

She also brought in old friends from vaudeville to take part in her shows, putting them up in her house and feeding them generously while they were there—a way to help out those in need without it looking like charity. "You're doing *me* a favor," she would insist. "These local amateurs need to see what a professional looks like!" To fit all her guests, she had workmen divide most of the bedrooms into small but cozy chambers, and as she did, she had the plumbing and wiring brought up to code, so that despite its age and ancient look, the Dragon's House had all the modern amenities.

While Lolly rehearsed and performed in the cellar, Normal climbed the stairs to the attic, where he, too, had a plethora of new wiring installed to support his passion—electric trains. The walls of the windowless room were lined with tables, and from the south wall a huge table projected into the middle, leaving only a narrow corridor. All the tables were covered with train tracks, trestles, bridges, hills, villages, and cities, with the walls expertly painted as mountains and farmland and, on one side, a river flowing into the sea.

Lolly invited all comers to the basement to watch her plays, but no one ever saw Normal's trains except the family, and then only a glimpse now and then, when calling him down to meals or to meet with his lawyer or broker. His hobby was not for display. It was a world where he alone could live. And over the years his fantasy life in the attic became quite an eccentricity, for now and then he would come downstairs and re-mark, "The dragon was lively today," or, "We had quite a thunderstorm in the attic," as if the train layout had its own weather and the occasional mythical beast to liven things up.

"Next thing you'll tell us," Lolly would say, "the little tiny people will start packing their little tiny clothes in little tiny suitcases and buy teensy-weensy tickets so they can ride the train."

He would look at her like she was crazy and say, "They're not *real*, Lolly." And she would roll her eyes heavenward as if to ask God to judge which of them was mad.

Lolly's first three children, fathered by her first three husbands, had been born during her vaudeville days and therefore loathed the theatre, absolutely refusing to take part in her plays. But her two children by Nor-mal, their son Herrick and their daughter Bernhardt—Herry and Harty—had no bad memories of backstage life, and so they happily threw themselves into every play. They were the princes murdered in the tower, they were Hansel and Gretel, they were young Ebenezer Scrooge and his beloved sister. When they weren't in rehearsal they were romping among the costumes and props and old set pieces stored on the north side of the cellar.

When Normal and Lolly died, no one minded that they left the house and all its contents to Herry and Harty. After all, they were Nor-mal's only children, and it was generous of him to leave a bit over a hun-dred thousand dollars to each of Lolly's other three children—a lot of money in those days. Most of the money, though, went to Herry and Harty, who kept up the tradition of theatricals in the basement until the city inspectors told them that the public safety laws had changed and there was no way to bring the cellar theater up to code without demolishing the building.

It was a sad day in the Old Dragon's House when the public perfor-mances ended, and while they still had guests over and put on shows from time to time, the regular community theater company moved to the local high school auditorium and Herry and Harty were no longer the heart and soul of it as they had been. They still contributed financially from time to time, but by the 1970s they had turned inward—not recluses, but focused on the life of their house.

With all those bedrooms, and no more retired vaudevillians to sleep in them and few plays to occupy their time, Herry and Harty cast about for something useful to do. The idea they hit upon was to take in strays.

Stray children, that is. Runaways. Beaten children. Orphans. They didn't take all—no, by no means, they were quite selective. For they knew that only a few children would respond to what they had to offer, and why waste time and effort with those they could not help? So they'd take a child in for a day or two, and if things weren't working, they'd pass him or her along—bathed, fed, with new clothes on their back—to the social workers who would find them the ordinary sort of foster care.

There were always a few children, however, whose eyes lighted up when they were given costumes to wear and lines to say, and now the occasional theatricals in the basement of the Old Dragon's House were performed mostly by children and teenagers playing all the parts, with local kids joining in, and an audience consisting of parents and friends. The lost children thrived in that company. Most of them did well in school; all of them went on to do well enough in life. For when you've been in good plays, you know how to work together with others and do your own part as well as you can and trust others to do theirs, and that's all you need to know in order to do well enough in a job or a marriage.

Harty had never married, but stayed on in the house with Herry and his wife, Cecilia. And when Cecilia died of breast cancer, Aunt Harty became surrogate mother to the four children and soon thought of them as her own. They were already teenagers before the transformation of the house to theatrical orphanage, but they loved what their home had become and didn't mind that when they came home for a visit there was rarely any room for them in the bedrooms. They might have slept in the big old bed in the front of the attic, but Harty didn't like to have people traipsing through her papa's train room to get to it, and so they'd end up sleeping on couches here and there—and, eventually, as their own families grew, in the nearby Holiday Inn.

But Michael was not one of the grandchildren—the grandchildren always had homes of their own in faraway cities and came to Mayfield only to visit. Michael did call Herry and Harty "Gramps" and "Granny," but it wasn't true. They were actually his great-uncle and great-aunt.

Michael's real grandmother was Portia Ringgold, Lolly's daughter by her third husband, a soldier who died of the flu after World War I. Portia was killed by alcohol in her fifties, though technically the cause of death was listed as "falling in front of a subway train." Michael's mother, Donna, was beaten to death by one of the "uncles" who came and went in her short, drug-addicted life.

Michael wasn't there for that sad day, however, for Herry and Harty had got wind of what was happening in their niece's life, and had offered to take care of Michael "for a while" so Donna could "recuperate." That was why Michael had no memory of calling anyone Mother. He knew only Gramps and Granny, and his only home was the little room at the back of the attic. They put him there because, as Gramps said, "The kids on the second floor come and go, but you're with us forever."

And that was why Michael Ringgold grew up in the Old Dragon's House.

At first, of course, he didn't know that was what the house was called. To him, it was simply "home." That's what Gramps and Granny called it. "I'm home!" "In our home we have certain rules." "We try to help these boys and girls feel at home." "This is a home, not a gymnasium!"

He wasn't aware yet that other people's homes didn't have theaters in the basement, or sad and angry children coming and going from time to time on the second floor, or locked doors in the attic from which strange sounds emerged at odd hours of the day or night, or a warm place on the backstairs where, when he sat very still, he could feel the throb, throb of a beating heart.

He did know, however, that Granny didn't like him to sit there in the warm place. Every time she saw him there, from earliest childhood, she would say, "What are you doing, boy? Why aren't you *playing*?" She would assign him some errand or, once he had learned to read, make him get a book and read something aloud to her—which was nice, he was proud of being a reader, he didn't mind that.

What he minded was the interruption. So when he heard someone coming down the narrow hall toward the back stairs that led to his attic room, he would scamper up to his bed and pretend to be sleeping. It never seemed to fool them. He tried pretending to be just waking up, but it was no good. "You were sitting there again, you dreamy dreamy boy," said Granny. Or, "He was in that *place* again," one of the visiting kids would call out.

Finally, when he was four, one of the visitors took pity on him and told him how they knew. "It's a wooden staircase, you moron," he said. "They can hear your feet when you run up to your room."

Oh.

Michael learned then to take his shoes off before he went to sit in the warm place. Then, when he heard someone coming, he walked up the stairs very slowly, stepping only at the outside edges of the steps so there were no creaks. It worked. Now the only time he was ever caught in the warm place was when he fell asleep there, and that hardly ever happened.

Because even though it was, as Granny assumed, a place for dreaming, it wasn't sleeping dreams he went for. And it wasn't because sleeping dreams were scarier—no, he had no nightmares as frightening as some of the dreams he had in the warm place. It was that the dreams in the warm place always seemed to make sense. They didn't just go from one thing to another in the silly way dreams did.

They felt like memories. Like he was thinking back on things he had done before. And whereas in sleeping dreams he always saw himself as if he were watching his own body from outside, in these memories he only *felt* himself. His own body. Stretching, taut, exhilarating dreams of having enormous strength and yet being amazingly light and being on fire inside, all the time. Dreams of flying. Dreams of falling down, hurtling toward the ground so fast that his vision went white and he came to himself gasping, as if he had just woken up, only he knew at the end of one of *those* dreams that he had never been asleep, for through it all he also remembered seeing the faded wallpaper and the part of the heavy-curtained window that his eyes were focused on even as he was moving through or over another world, in another body.

He knew it was another body because when he was walking around in the house, toddling on his little legs and falling down or bumping into things, it was definitely *not* the body he had in those dreams. In real life he was not strong and he could not fly and he never, never felt the fire inside.

Maybe in a weaker child that might have been an irresistible drug, to have those dreams in the warm place on the back stairs. But Michael Ringgold was strong without knowing it. Not strong of arm—he was as tough as any kid, but no tougher, and no one would mistake him for a blacksmith's apprentice. His throw could get to first base and he could chin himself up into a tree, and he didn't think to try for more. But there was another kind of strength which he had in good measure, without knowing it. Michael loved dreaming that he could fly with the heat throbbing inside him, but he also loved running around outside with the other kids, or lurking down in the theater watching a play rehearsal or helping paint the scenery. He loved trying to steal cookie dough in the kitchen when Granny's back was turned—he even loved getting rapped on the head with a spoon as he made it out the door with his mouth full, while Granny shouted after him, "You can get a disease from the eggs in that batter, you foolish boy!"

Michael had the strength to do what he chose to do, despite his own desires.

One night when he was seven he heard the sounds from behind the locked door. A humming sound, but with a bit of an edge to it. It sounded like Gramps's electric razor. Or a shower running somewhere in the house.

It wasn't quite dark yet, because it was a summer night on daylight savings time, and so even though there were shadows in the room and he had never before dared to get out of his bed when the sounds were there, tonight he decided he had to know, and so—because he was strong—he simply ignored his dread and got up. He only wore shoes for school and for church, but even though his feet had calluses from running across asphalt and climbing trees and scrambling through brambles, his soles felt extremely naked and vulnerable as he crossed the little space between his bed and the locked door that led deeper into the attic.

He turned the handle.

It turned freely, but he still couldn't open the door.

The sounds did not stop, either. It was as if his little effort to pull the door open were not worth noticing.

The keyhole was the old-fashioned kind, like the one on the door to the basement. But unlike the basement keyhole, this one seemed to have been plugged with something so he couldn't see through. Nor could he see anything under the door. Which might mean that it was dark in the locked room, or it might mean that it, too, had some kind of obstruction to keep light from passing.

So all his courage was wasted. He couldn't get through, and he couldn't see in.

Only he wanted to see, and this was the time.

What did he have in his dresser drawer? Whatever he had taken from his pockets all summer, stashed in the bottom drawer inside a cigar box. He chose two items: the tarnished baby spoon he had found by the creek behind the house, and the cheap little pocketknife he had got by trading four fine marbles to one of the boys who hadn't stayed long at the house because he kept making fun of the kids who were serious about rehearsing the play. It was Gramps's cut-down version of *Macbeth,* but the boy with the cheap knife never cared about it even when he was assigned to play Banquo, which meant he got to be a ghost in the dinner scene. And then he was gone, and Michael suspected he was the only person in the house who remembered him now at the end of summer, and that was only because he had this crummy little knife and somewhere in the past few weeks it had gradually dawned on him that he had been cheated.

Well, the knife wouldn't cut, and it wobbled in its handle, but maybe it could poke through whatever was blocking the keyhole.

And it did. One punch, straight through, and the blade broke and was stuck there in the keyhole.

Great. Now when Granny came up to clean, she'd see the blade sticking out and know that he had tried to break in. Only he hadn't, he just wanted to *see.*

Well, no, if he had been able to jimmy the lock, he would have opened the door. That was the truth and if he couldn't tell the truth to himself then he really *was* a liar like that one visiting girl said he was, when Michael told her that he said his prayers every night without Gramps or Granny watching over him to make him do it.

I want to see in there. And I don't want to get caught for having tried.

So he used the handle of the baby spoon. It wasn't the best tool—needlenose pliers were what he needed, and just imagine trying to explain to Gramps why he needed them. But the spoon handle did the job. By prying with it, he got the broken knifeblade to wiggle and finally come loose.

And now there *was* a hole, so tiny and narrow—thin as a blade, of course—that he couldn't actually see anything through it, except for one thing: There was light in that room. Bright light. Dazzling light. And all that buzzing, whirring, rushing. What was in there? Why would Gramps and Granny leave a light on in there?

There was a big attic window in the front of the house, and Michael had wondered for a long time whether the locked room ran the whole length of the house. But that wasn't the light of dusky evening coming through the keyhole, it was like a very bright naked bulb, a hundred-watter like the one in the basement storage room that you turned on by pulling on a chain that Michael could only reach by jumping. If there was always a light in the locked room, it would be visible through that front attic window, and if it were visible, there had been plenty of overcast and stormy days when Michael had been outside and would have seen that the attic was lit.

So the locked room didn't have any windows.

It's my brother in there, thought Michael. My secret brother, who already lived here before they brought me. The crazy one who actually killed my mother and they couldn't tell me about it because it was too terrible. He's chained in that room only they don't know he's broken the chain and he's just waiting for me to open the door so he can grab me and tear out my throat with his teeth like a wolf.

Or maybe it's my mother's body there, like Snow White when the dwarfs laid her out in a glass coffin to lie there looking beautiful till the prince came to kiss her awake, only the prince can't get there because the door is locked.

Or maybe the attic crawlspace would get him there.

There was a low door in the wall at the foot of his bed that Granny said led into the crawlspace. "We don't store anything there, it's just in case we get a dead rat or a bird's nest in there and we need to clean it out. Don't you go in there because the floor isn't finished and you'll put your foot right through the ceiling in the bedroom below and then we'll have to saw your leg off just to get you out." She said it with her I'm-pretending-it's-a-joke-but-take-heed look, and so of course he tried to get in there the second her back was turned, but even though he could turn the primitive wooden latch easily enough, when he tried to push the door open, it jammed against something immediately and he couldn't even see in.

Now, though, standing at the locked door, he looked over at his bed, whose foot was jammed in under the slope of the roof so he sometimes bumped the ceiling with his feet when he turned over too quickly in bed. And in that moment, perhaps because he actually wanted to know it, he understood exactly why the door hadn't opened. It was bumping into the continued downward slope of the ceiling. The door didn't open into the crawl space, it opened into the room.

Of course, that meant that to open it, Michael would have to move his bed. He had never tried to do that on purpose before—just accidentally before he learned just how angry Granny could get when she caught him lying on his back in the bed and shoving against the ceiling with his feet. "If I wanted footprints on the ceiling I would have moved to Australia where they walk around upside down all the time!" she said. And then she shoved the bed back into place with such vigor that the footboard of the bed made two indentations in the ceiling so the only real damage was what she had caused her own self. She hadn't liked it when Michael pointed this out to her, and so he learned a couple of lessons that day.

How quietly could he pull the bed out from the little door? And how far would he have to pull it before he could get through it?

The answers were: With only a couple of slight scraping sounds, and about a foot and a half.

He was sweating from the exertion of pulling the bed when he stuck his head through the opening and looked around.

It was very, very dark. But the longer he leaned there, his body half in, half out of the crawl space, the better he could see. There was light coming up from the outer edges of the room—faint light, because it really was full dusk outside and soon there'd be no light at all.

He could see the rafters like corduroy, row on row, with thick dust piled on them like snow on a fence rail. He thought of falling down through the ceiling. He thought of getting half there and realizing it was too dark to go on and then having it be so dark he couldn't find the door to get back into his room and then he'd feel a *hand* on his shoulder and a voice would say, "Hello, little brother . . ."

. . . and when he thought of *that* there was no way he was going in, not tonight. Tomorrow when it was light. And when the noises weren't coming from the locked room.

He pulled himself back into his little room. There was one horrible moment when the belt keeper on his jeans snagged against the doorframe and he thought he'd been grabbed. But then he was through the door and he slammed it shut—fortunately not making much noise because it was such a thin door and it didn't actually have a jamb to bump against. Then he scrambled to his feet, got round to the head of the bed, and shoved it hard against the wall.

Nothing could get through that door without moving the bed, and that would wake him up, so it was safe. Besides, he'd slept in this room all his life and nothing had ever come out of that little crawlspace door to get him anyway, had it? So why was he lying there under his covers, constantly lifting his head up to see if the door had moved. It had! No it hadn't. But maybe it had.

And then he woke up in the morning and didn't even remember about the crawlspace until he was in the front yard enjoying one of the last days of summer before second grade. He looked up at the front of the house and saw the attic balcony and window, and wondered, as he sometimes did, whether his brother ever looked out the window at him playing and hated him—and that was when he remembered the crawlspace last night. Only had it really happened? Wasn't it just a dream? Well, today he'd go in there when it was daylight and settle the question for once and all.

But he forgot about it again. He forgot it over and over except when he was too far away or too busy with something to bother running upstairs to do the experiment. He kept not doing it until he was away at school every day and then he really did forget. And then one of the visiting kids told him that all houses made weird noises at night. "It's just wind coming out of the toilet drainpipes," the girl said. "That and the house settling down to rest at night." And now that he thought about it, Michael realized that toilet drainpipes probably all made sounds like that from the wind whistling over them so it wasn't coming out of the locked room at all, it was from the pipes, and that was that. Mystery solved. Of course it wasn't his brother. He had no brother. That was just a nightmare.

One night, halfway through second grade, Gramps looked at him and said, "How tall are you anyway, boy?"

"Tall enough to pee standing up," said Michael, "but not tall enough to shave."

The visiting kids at the dinner table laughed and snorted.

"I hate it that you taught him to say that," said Granny.

"I didn't," said Gramps. "It's just the simple truth."

"It is so crude to use words like that."

"You heard your Granny, Michael. We have to call it 'chin depilation,' not 'shaving.' "

"I'm this tall," said Michael, standing up beside his chair again like he did during grace.

"That's what I thought," said Gramps. "Birds' nests are in grave danger from you now, young man. You're soon going to have to duck going under bridges."

"I'll just step over them," said Michael.

"You're not that tall," said one of the kids, a serious boy with round scars on his arms.

"It's a brag," said an older girl. "They always brag."

"It's a joke," said another girl.

"Nay," said Granny, " 'tis a jest, a jape."

Which was the cue for Gramps to do his gorilla act, saying, "I beat on my jest because I am one of the great japes." Only when he had finished and Granny spooned him on the butt and he fled back to his chair did he finally come to the point.

"We have an empty room on the second floor," said Gramps. "I think you're too tall for that little bed in the attic anymore."

"I like it fine, Gramps," said Michael.

"Yeah, he lives up there with his pet chicken," said one of the older boys. Another boy immediately made a choking sound.

Gramps glared at them both and they wilted a little, so Michael knew there was something bad or dirty about what they had said, though for the life of him he couldn't figure out what it was.

Gramps and Granny didn't do anything about it for a few weeks, but then one day when Michael came home from school, he found that all his stuff had been moved down into the little bedroom right at the foot of the back stairs, directly beneath his attic room.

It broke his heart, but he tried to hide it, and he must have done pretty well, because it wasn't till he was crying alone in his bed that he heard Granny's voice saying, "Good heavens, Michael, why are you crying?"

But he couldn't answer, he just clung to her for a long while until he wasn't crying anymore. "I'm OK," he said.

"But whatever were you crying about?"

"It's OK," he insisted.

"It's not OK, and if you don't answer me right now I'm going to go downstairs to *my* room and cry until *you* come down and ask me why *I'm* crying and I won't tell you, either."

"I just . . . I just guess I'm one of the visiting kids now, that's all," said Michael. "I don't mind, really."

"Why—that's absurd, you silly frumpus. Why would you think that?"

"'Cause Gramps said when I moved in, the kids on the second floor come and go."

"No, no—oh, you poor boy—you remember that? You weren't even three, how can you remember that? But don't you see? He was trying to reassure you because we thought that you might think that being up in the attic meant we didn't love you as much as the other kids, but the fact was that the bed up there is a child's bed and you're the only person who could sleep in it and it was the only space we had for you then. Gramps moved you down here because you're bigger, that's all. But you're not going to come and go, Michael. You're our very own. Our last little boy of our very own."

"I'm not your own," he said. "You're not even my Granny. You're my aunt."

"I'm your *great*-aunt, don't you forget. Only we shorten that to Graunt, and then Graunty, and then Grauny, only that sounds so theatrical and phony that we changed it to Granny. So you see? I'm your Granny *because* I'm your great aunt."

"And I suppose Gramps is short for great-uncle."

"Not at all. It's because he's grumpy. We called him Grumps when he was a boy, and it stuck, only somehow over the years it just changed to Gramps."

"So what is *my* name going to change to? Over the years?"

"I have no idea," said Granny. "Won't it be interesting to see? Over the years? Because you are going to be here for years and years. As long as you like. Until the day comes when *you* want to leave. To go off to college, or to get married to some nice girl."

"I'm not supposed to say 'pee' and *you* can talk about me marrying some girl?"

"Hardly seems fair, does it."

And he didn't feel like crying anymore and after a while he liked being on the same floor as the visiting kids and some of them even became friends, because they were almost his age.

Now and then he still went halfway up the back stairs to the warm place. But after the first few weeks, he didn't bother to go all the way up to his old room. It wasn't his room anymore, was it?

And down here, he never heard the sound of the wind rushing past the toilet drainpipes. He almost forgot about it. For years he almost forgot.

Seventh grade. The year that Granny and Gramps put on *Our Town, As You Like It,* and *Tom Sawyer.* The year that Michael Ringgold changed from clarinet to French horn because the junior high band had fourteen clarinets and no French horn player at all. The year that everybody was Indiana Jones for Halloween, so Michael and Gramps worked for a week to put together his costume so he could go trick-or-treating as the Lost Ark.

It was the year when they had such a blizzard the day after Christmas that the whole town of Mayfield shut down. The snow was no burden at the Old Dragon's House, of course, because with a troupe of boys and girls on hand, and plenty of snow shovels to go around, the front yard and sidewalk were soon clear right down to the cobbles and bricks. The kids were enthusiastic about the labor, too, because they carried the snow into the back yard in wheelbarrows and soon made such a mountain of snow that they could slide down it in all directions on sleds, inner tubes, and the seats of their pants.

It was great fun, and no one broke any bones this time, so the worst injury was probably the cut Michael got on his hand when his sled collided with another kid's snow shovel. He didn't mind—it was cold enough that his hands were too numb for the pain to be more than a dull throb—but the other kids began to complain that his blood was turning the snow all pink and it looked gross.

So he went inside and Granny almost fainted and in a few minutes she had Merthiolate poured over the wound and was stitching it up herself—a skill she had learned from her mother, who had done her share of backstage doctoring during vaudeville days. "Hold still so I can line up the edges of the wound so the skin matches up. Otherwise you'll look rumpled for the rest of your life."

"Will I have a scar?" asked Michael.

"Yes you will, so I hope you're not contemplating a life of crime, because it will make your palm print absolutely distinctive."

"I wish it was on my face," said Michael.

"I wish it *were* on my face," corrected Granny. "And whyever would you wish for such a foolish thing?"

"Scars are romantic."

"Romantic! Maybe once upon a time *dueling* scars were romantic. But sledding scars are definitely not. So I hope you're not going to go out and lie down on Mount Snowshovel and let the sleds run over you."

"I never would have thought of it if you hadn't suggested it."

She finished covering his palm with a bandage and winding it around with tape. "All packaged up so nicely we ought to put a stamp on it and mail it somewhere."

"Come on, this bandage is so thick I can't even pick my nose."

"Well if you expect me to do it for you, think again."

"So are you going to help me get some mittens on?"

"Apparently you are suffering from the delusion that you are going to go back outside and open up this wound after I went to all the trouble to stitch it closed."

"That *was* my plan, Gran."

"*My* plan is for you to stay here in the kitchen till you warm up. Whose plan do you think will prevail?"

"How about if I go lie down in my room?"

"That will certainly do, though I must warn you that if I look out back and see you on Mount Snowshovel again, you will have a nice set of scars on your squattenzone and I *will* stitch them all skewampus so that everyone who sees your backside will laugh at you."

"Who's ever going to see my backside?"

"Never you mind who, I can just promise you that you won't want them laughing."

"I won't go outside again," he said.

"Not even just to watch," said Granny.

"Not even just to watch." And Michael meant it, because now that he was warmer he really could feel the pain in his hand and it was nasty, a deep, hard throb that made it hard to think about anything else.

"Well, if you're really going up to bed, let me give you some cough medicine."

"I don't *have* a cough, Granny."

"This cough medicine has codeine in it," said Granny. "That's how it cures coughs—you fall asleep."

So he waited while she spooned the oversweet stuff into his mouth. He remembered that when he was little he liked it, but now it was way too sweet. It made him want to brush his teeth.

Up to his room he went, feeling just a little lightheaded by the time he got to the top of the stairs. And when he flopped down on his bed, the sudden move made his hand throb so hard that he almost fainted from the pain. He lay there wincing and panting for what seemed forever, refusing to cry. He finally worked up the gumption to get up and get a comic book to read, but the light coming into the room wasn't bright enough to read well, and he didn't want the overhead light on because it would be too bright, and in the end he fell asleep with the comic book on his chest.

When he woke up he was lying on the comic book and his hand hurt even worse, but differently, with the pain of deep healing rather than the pain of harsh injury. There was still light in the window, but it was the dim light of a winter evening and he could hear the sounds of dinner being eaten downstairs. He must have slept for hours and he was hungry.

Pain or no pain, he had missed lunch and he wasn't going to miss dinner, too. He swung his feet over the edge of the bed and stood up and then sat right back down, his head swimming. He had apparently lost a lot of blood outside in the snow. But after a few more minutes sitting on the edge of the bed, he was able to stand up and walk rather feebly toward the door, leaning on things as he went.

In the doorway, though, he heard gales of laughter from downstairs and suddenly he wasn't hungry after all, or at least not so hungry that he wanted to go walking into the bright crowded kitchen with all the kids gathered around the table. Granny would make a fuss over him but the other kids would mock him and tease him and it just made him tired. He wanted to be alone, like an injured animal that crawls off into the deepest thicket in the woods in order to either bleed to death or heal.

He might have turned back in to his own room, but that wasn't where he wanted to go. Without naming his goal, he walked along the narrow hall to the back of the house and then slowly climbed the stairs to the warm place.

He hadn't spent much time there this year. Perhaps none. Perhaps he hadn't sat in this place since sixth grade. Or fifth. He didn't remember. He only knew that this was the sheltered place where he needed to go when he felt like he felt right now.

He sat down on the step where he had always sat, but now he was bigger and his body didn't fit into the place as it used to. It really *had* been a long time, and he was going through a growth spurt, Granny said, and his legs were so long they stuck out of the bottoms of his pants like popsicle sticks.

He did not close his eyes because he never closed his eyes here.

Instead he let his gaze rest idly and unfocused on the wallpaper near the backstairs window and let the warmth of the place seep into him.

It came into him as it always did, in gentle increments with each throb of the heartbeat of the place. This time, though, the throbbing of the pain in his hand had its own rhythm that conflicted with the slower beat of the warm place, and it made him feel agitated at first, jumpy, restless. But then the warmth went to his hand and for a moment it actually burned, as if he had thrust his whole hand into a blazing fire, and he cried out with the sharpness of it.

And then he was caught up into a dream. Not of flying this time. No, he felt himself sliding and slithering through a dark passage through cold stone, downward mostly, but he couldn't really see anything except shadows against a dull red glow that seemed to increase with each of his breaths and quickly fade. He would brush against the sides or roof of the passage and feel the chill against his crusty skin, but the chill could never get very deep because he had so much warmth inside him.

Then the cold rock opened up and he was in a large open cavern with stalactites and stalagmites and a different sort of glow, a deeper red. The air was very hot here, as hot as the pain in Michael's palm, so there was a sort of balance, and it didn't bother him so much, it was just part of the place. He slipped among the stalagmites, feeling his body trail among them, bending easily around them, scraping on both sides but never injured. He had never realized how *long* his body was when he was in the dreams of this place, or how tightly and smoothly his arms could press up against his sides.

The underground chamber grew larger and brighter the farther in he went, and the stalagmites soon ceased. Instead the floor under his feet, under his belly, was as bumpy and yet smooth as the surface of boiling water, if you could harden boiling water into stone.

He came at last to a shore of an underground sea, only the sea was made of molten stone, seething and bubbling, smelling of sulphur. The blast of heat from the sea was worse than standing in front of Granny's oven when she had it really hotted up to broil something. And yet instead of making him want to back away, to retreat to some cool place, it seemed to waken a fire inside him and he wanted to be inside it the way he wanted to plunge into a swimming pool on a hot August day. Not that the sea of molten stone would be cool, but rather that the intense heat of it would bring this body the same kind of relief.

This body. What am I, when I dream like this. Not this boy, this weak walking boy clad in soft, easily sliced skin, not this cowering creature who slinks through the world creeping up backstairs and hiding from the laughter of his enemies.

Enemies? I have no enemies.

None who dare to show themselves, huddling little human.

Who are you?

I am the fire.

And with that thought, the body Michael wore in his dreams leapt up and spread its arms, its thin strong wings, and rose circling high above the sea of magma until he could sense, with senses he did not know he had, the roof of the great cavern, the crown of this bubble of air deep within the earth, and having reached the zenith of this dark sky, he plunged down, straight down into the hot red sea and his mind turned white inside and Michael sprawled unconscious upon the stair.

He became aware of himself again, stretched out across the steps, long and sinuous, his sleek feathery scales unperturbed by the wooden edges. His wings were folded up under him and his great jaws began to yawn.

No, that would be the other body, not this one. He stretched, and it was the arms of a boy that stretched. The hands of a boy that flexed, the eyes of a boy that opened.

It was dark, but it had been nearly dark when he had first crept to this place so that did not tell him how long he had been asleep. It couldn't have been long, because Granny would have checked on him when the other boys finished dinner and, not finding him in his room, would have looked first in this place.

He rose to his feet and was surprised at how small and light he was. An hour ago, he had thought himself rather tall and big—his man-height was coming on him these days, and he was taller than Granny, wasn't he, and almost as tall as Gramps?

He looked down at hands that were not wings, and again he flexed his fingers and realized that the bandaged hand did not hurt at all. Not so much as a twinge. The only discomfort was the awkwardness of the thick bandage.

He brought the bandage up to his mouth to bite at the tape, but then remembered that he had another hand, and used those fingers to prise up the end of the tape and peel it away. Granny's thorough packaging was unwrapped in only a few moments, and underneath it there was no wound at all, not even a scar. Only a few loops of black thread lying in his palm. He blew them away and there was then no way to tell which hand had been sliced.

Was this what happened when he plunged into the sea of fire? It made him whole?

You healed me?

But there was no answering thought as there had been in the dream. Just a faint buzzing, whirring, rushing sound.

Which, Michael now knew with absolute certainty, was not the sound of wind rushing past the drainpipes and playing them like an organ. It came from inside the locked windowless room where a bright light shone though no one ever entered to change the bulb. It sounded like razors, like can openers, and he had to know, he had to see.

He was up the stairs in a moment, his eye trying to peer through the keyhole. The tiny slit he had made years ago was still there, and as before, it showed only dazzling light.

In moments he had the bed back from the crawlspace door and was through it. It was dark, but he felt his way along the rafters, taking care to find the next one before taking his weight from the ones before. If there were spiderwebs or beetles he did not care; he was barely aware of the thick dust that rose from the rafters with each movement of a hand or foot. For one moment he thought he would sneeze, but he held it in by holding his breath, for he did not want to set the house on fire.

Fire? I make no fire when I sneeze.

Who are you, who healed me? Whose body is it that I dwell in, who was it took me diving into fire?

There was faint light up ahead. Far ahead, the length of the house. It was a couple of lines of dim light, and when at last he got there, he found that it was another crawlspace door, which was closed only by the same simple kind of latch as the door in his old attic room. He lifted the block of wood and the door opened easily at his push.

He was in the front room of the attic, the one that had the window and balcony overlooking the street. The only light in the room came from the streetlights' outside—that had been enough to make the faint glow around the edges of the crawlspace door.

But he could still hear the noise from the locked room, and there, opposite the window, was another door. This keyhole had not been blocked up—a bright glow shone plainly through it. And when Michael turned the handle and pulled, the door opened easily.

Four bright naked bulbs in ceiling fixtures made the dazzling light, and the razor sounds had come from five electric trains making their rounds along tracks that stretched completely around the room. The table surrounding the room even crossed in front of the doors, so the only way into the room was to duck down under the table and come up the other side, in the midst of a miniature world of villages, train stations, trestles and tunnels, hills and farms and rivers and a distant sea.

Who had built this? Why didn't anyone ever see it? Why did they leave the trains running, with no one here to play with them?

In one corner of the room, a mist seemed to gather. Michael watched it, fascinated. It was a cloud, he saw that now, emanating from the smoke-stacks of a tiny factory. No sooner had it formed than electricity began to spark from it. Michael felt his own hair standing up the way it did when you rubbed a balloon and held it near. The sparks crackled. A tiny bolt of lightning snapped from the cloud to a train track. There was a sharp cracking sound—miniature thunder. He could smell the ozone.

How was it done? He had never heard of a train layout with weather. A storm, of all things! No rain, but maybe that was coming.

The cloud kept jetting out of the smokestacks and now the whole ceiling was masked by it, so the light of the bulbs was dimmed. Lightning cracked here and there all around the room now, snapping down to the tracks. Each time, the trains hesitated for a moment but then went on.

Michael caught a whir of motion out of the corner of his eye. He spun to look. A train? But the only train in that part of the room was nowhere near the motion he had seen.

He looked intently at the painted, lichened landscape and again saw movement as a dragonfly suddenly leapt upward from the ground near the mouth of a tunnel. It flew rapidly around the room, so Michael could hardly get a look at it. There was something wrong, though. It did not move like a dragonfly, really. It had the long tail, but the wings were not a dragonfly's blur of translucence, they flapped like a bird's wings. Yet the skin of the tiny creature was as iridescent as a dragonfly's body, sparkling in the light, glimmering with each thread of lightning.

The creature did not shy away from the lightning, either. In fact it seemed drawn to it, darting toward each bolt as if it were drinking in the ozone that was left behind in the burnt air.

I know you, thought Michael.

"I know you," he whispered.

You don't know me, came the answer in his mind. You will never know me. You are incapable of knowing me, you poor worm.

You healed my hand. You took me flying with you and plunged me with you into the magma deep within the earth. "Thank you," Michael whispered.

In reply the tiny dragon lunged in the air just as a spark of lightning began to crackle downward and even though it happened in a mere instant, Michael thought he saw the dragon sparkle all over as if the lightning were inside it and it was the dragon that snapped downward to the electric track, leaving a trail of lightning behind it.

And it was gone.

The lights went out. The trains fell silent. Michael was in total darkness, surrounded by silence and the smell of ozone and another faint burnt smell.

You couldn't have died, thought Michael. After all these years that the trains have run in this room, and the lightning flashed, you couldn't have died on this very day when I first came here and saw you. It must be this way every time. You were reaching for the lightning. You must have reached for it, caught it like a surfer catching a wave, and ridden it down to earth. You must still be here . . . somewhere . . .

You are not really as small as the dragon I saw in this room. In all my dreams, the one thing I never felt was that you were small.

But there was no answering thought. Only the gradually increasing light as Michael's eyes became accustomed to seeing in the faint spill from the streetlights outside the window of the front attic room.

Who built this room? There had been something, some mention now that Michael thought about it, of Gramps's and Granny's father having electric trains—was it him, then? Yet how did he ever get a dragon to come here? He couldn't have made it. No man could make a living thing. The dragon was already alive, but it came here into the house and it has lived here all my life. I had the bedroom next to it. When I peered through the tiny slit in the keyhole, I was looking for the dragon.

When I sat in the warm place, I felt the beating of its huge, invisible heart. I felt its life come over me like a dream. I dwelt in its memories. It healed my hand.

What am I to this creature? A pet? A friend? A servant? A son? Its future prey?

Michael ducked under the table and left the train room, closing the door behind him. He made his way back through the crawl space and emerged again in the bedroom of his childhood.

He went downstairs into the room he had been sleeping in and took all the sheets and blankets off his bed and carried them up the backstairs to his old room. He knew he couldn't sleep on the child's bed there, so he spread them out on the floor. He went back down and gathered all his other things—not much, really, just clothing and his schoolbooks and a few toys and games and tools. It took only three trips, and he had moved upstairs again.

Only then did he hear the noises of the kids bounding up the stairs to the second floor, the water running in the bathrooms, lots of chatter and laughter and a few complaints and whines. Now he remembered—there had been a dress rehearsal of the New Year's play, *As You Like It*. They must have covered for him—he had a couple of smallish parts, being too young to compete for the leads in a grownup play. Granny must have thought he was sleeping and didn't let anyone wake him.

But now the rehearsal was over and everyone was going to bed and Granny would come looking for him, to see if he was hungry, to check on his hand.

He went to the head of the back stairs and started down just as Granny started up.

She looked down at the remnants of the bandage lying on the steps. "Why did you take it off?" she said. "That was foolish."

"It's all better," said Michael.

"Don't be absurd," said Granny. "It takes days for the wound to fully close, even with the stitches." She held out her hand. "Let me see the damage."

So went down a few more steps, and she came up a few, and he held out his hand to her.

"Don't be a goof, Michael," she said. "Show me the hand that you cut."

"This *is* the hand," he said, showing her the other as well.

She held both his hands, palm up, in hers and looked from one to the other, then up into Michael's eyes.

"What were you doing here?"

"I moved back into my old room," he said. "I want to live in my old room again."

"The bed's too small."

"I'll sleep on the floor."

"What happened to your hand, Michael?"

"I guess it wasn't as serious as you thought," he said.

"Don't be absurd, I should know how deep it was, and even if it was only a scratch it couldn't be healed like this. What did you do?"

"I came up to the warm place on the stairs," he said, "and I slept."

She looked in his eyes and perhaps she could see that he wasn't lying or perhaps she could see something else, something that forbade her to inquire more. Maybe she could see the dragon's eyes, just a glimpse of the dragon's eyes, looking out at her.

"I never came up here," she said softly. "After I was a little girl, and Mother sent me up to fetch Father for dinner, and I knocked on the door of his train room and he didn't hear me so I opened it."

"What did you see?" said Michael.

"What did *you* see?" she asked him in reply.

"Trains," he said.

"And?"

"Lightning."

She shuddered. "What did Papa do in there, Michael?"

"I don't know," he said. "He must have been very talented with . . . electric things."

"He was just an ordinary man. Rich, of course. Theatrical. He owned a lot of playhouses back in vaudeville days. But none of that should have let him create . . ."

"Weather," said Michael.

"You went inside," she said.

"It would be easier," said Michael, "if you gave me a key. I won't tell the other kids. I won't let anyone in. But now that I've seen it, you can't keep me out."

"It's dangerous," she said.

"So is crossing the street."

"That's an unbelievably inept analogy, Michael."

"I won't die in that room."

"Papa was only truly alive there," she said. "There were weeks when he hardly came out, and when he did, it was as though he was living in a dream. As though we weren't real. Only the train room was real."

"I know what's real," said Michael.

"I'll talk to Herry," she said. "To Gramps."

"I love you Granny," said Michael.

"Because you think I'll give you what you want?"

"Because you're good," he said.

"If I were really good," she said, "I would move out of this house and take you with me and never let you come here again. If I really loved you."

"I'd come back," he said. "I grew up in the dragon's heart."

Tears came to her eyes. "Papa talked about dragons. It was part of his . . ."

"He wasn't crazy," said Michael. "They live in the fire. The fires under the earth are like home to them. And they fly the lightning. They soar into the storm and they search for the lightning and when they catch it just right they ride it down to earth."

"Don't tell me any more," she said. "You can't have inherited his madness. None of Papa's blood is in your veins."

"It's not madness."

"The house does it. Letting you sleep in the attic, I never should have done that."

"He came to the house because he loves the lightning, and there's so much electricity here. In the theater lights in the basement. And up here, in the tracks, the trains. That's all. It's not madness, it's real. He came up out of the earth because all the electricity called to him."

"How do you know this?"

"Because I've felt how he hungers for it. I felt it, too. That's what called me into the train room. That's what drew me, I know it now. He's all through this house. It didn't matter where you had me sleep. Once I felt his heartbeat here on the back stairs, I knew him, Granny."

"And when was that?" she asked softly.

"The first day I came here," he said. "When you and Gramps took me up these stairs and told me I would live here forever. I felt his heartbeat as we climbed the stairs. That's how I knew that I was truly home. Because it was warm there. And I'd never been warm like that before."

"Why didn't you tell me what was happening to you?"

"I didn't know it myself until today. Until I said it out loud to you just now." He bent down—for he was standing two steps above her—and kissed her forehead. "I love you, Granny. I'll be safe here. I'll be careful. Don't be afraid for me. Look."

He held his hands out to her.

"He healed my hand. It really happened. He's looking out for me."

But even as he said it, he knew it was not true. Dragons don't look out for human beings. Dragons don't care.

She pressed his hands against her cheeks. "God help us, Michael."

To which he had no answer. If God helps us, he thought, he does it through other people. It was you and Gramps who took me in when I needed a home—but maybe it was God who made you my great-aunt and great-uncle. It was the dragon who healed my hand—but maybe it was God who brought me to the house where the dragon lives.

Or maybe not.

"I'm hungry," said Michael. "Is there any dinner left?"

"Yes," she said, coming to herself again. "Yes, of course. I kept some of it warm in the oven for you. Shepherd's pie."

"Nasty stuff," said Michael, sliding past her, putting his arm around her, walking with her down the stairs. "I don't know why you work so hard to poison us with stuff like that."

"I saved you half a pie because I know how you love it," she said.

"Only half? When I didn't have lunch? What were you thinking?"

"Don't get smart with me."

"You want me to get stupid? I can do that."

"No you can't," she said. "It takes *real* brains to do that."

It was an old joke between them, but it felt far more meaningful now. Almost portentous. But then, anything they said would sound that way, now that they knew each other's secrets. Some of them, anyway.

The dragon gargoyle on the house at 22 Adams pours water out of its mouth whenever it rains, and it splashes on the cobbles of the garden and in a bad storm it can soak the shoes of whoever is standing at the

door. The house is so unusual—gothic amid Victorians, the garden cob-
bled and bricked, and the torrent of boys and girls running in and out of
the house at all hours—that people drive from all over town sometimes
just to see the Old Dragon's House.

None of them guess that every night in the back room of the attic,
the old dragon watches over the sleeping boy whose body is growing into
one that someday he can use, someday he can wear, allowing him to
emerge from the wiring of the house and bear a living body up into the
sky, soaring once again on gossamer wings, his wyrmtail curling under
him, seeking lightning in the storm so he can ride back down to earth.
One ride per body, alas, for it burns up on the ride and shatters against the
earth as the dragon within it plunges down into the earth.

But then, one ride on a single bolt of lightning is enough to keep a
dragon going for a thousand years.

And the boy would love that moment, when it came.

They always did.

NOTES ON "IN THE DRAGON'S HOUSE"

This story was almost the novel I did instead of *Magic Street*.

The idea began with the dragon. I had signed on with Marvin Kaye
to submit something to an anthology of longish dragon stories he was editing, and I wanted to come up with something other than the ordinary
dragon.

What I thought of was the idea that lightning striking the ground
might be dragons. Or, rather, dragons might *ride* the lightning and derive
their energy from it. What if dragons lived on electricity? Creatures that
only rose up with thunderstorms and then rode the weather front for a
thousand miles until the electricity dissipated.

And then it occurred to me: Through all of history, lightning would
have been pretty much the only thing that dragons could thrive on. But
now we have all these houses that are virtual caves of electricity, room after room surrounded with wires.

What if dragons became visible only when they went out to ride the
lightning? Only nowadays they don't have to do it at all, because they can
live like drug addicts, sucking electricity out of houses and buildings.

OK, I had my dragon. I had a house for him to live in. But who were the people sharing the house with him, and what would the dragon mean to them?

The story grew in my head until I had almost too much material to work with. I pared down the history as much as I could—but still couldn't resist a very slow beginning to the story as I gave a history of the house where the dragon dwelt.

Once I got into the story, I liked the characters so well that there was no way I could get the story all the way to the ending I intended—a sacrificial riding of the lightning, a dragon with a boy on its back, forcing it to destroy itself and set the house, and the treasure in it, free.

After all, it was going to be a book called *The Dragon Quintet,* not "Novel by Orson Scott Card, with four additional stories by these other writers." I had to get "In the Dragon's House" well ended at a respectable length.

The result is that the story ends—and it does end—just when things were starting to get interesting. I put a novel's opening on a novelette.

But I didn't worry, because I was going to write the novel, wasn't I? I had a good contract with Del Rey to write another contemporary fantasy like *Enchantment*. And even though the idea for *Magic Street* had been stewing for many years longer, I was terrified of writing *that* book because every important character in it was African-American, and I knew I was going to blow it, even with the help of friends who had grown up in the upper-middle-class black community in Los Angeles.

So I was getting started, ready to beat the deadline and turn in the novel version of *The Dragon's House,* when my wife called to my attention the fact that the short story hadn't come out yet, the anthology wasn't finished, and my novel for Del Rey had a good chance of coming out *before* the anthology. If I used "Dragon's House" for the novel, I would violate the exclusivity clause in my contract for the anthology.

That is not a nice thing to do.

So I turned around *again* and forced myself to swallow my fears and write *Magic Street* after all.

Someday, though, I'll have at this tale again and see if I can make it into the book I think it's supposed to be.

INVENTING LOVERS ON THE PHONE

You want to know what Deeny's life was like? It can be summed up in the sentence her father said when she got a cellphone.

"Who the hell's gonna call *you*?"

Deeny said what she always said when her father, otherwise known as "Treadmarks," put her down. She said nothing at all. Just left the room. Which was what ol' Treadmarks wanted. But it was what Deeny also wanted. In fact, on that one point they agreed with each other completely, and since their relationship consisted almost entirely of Deeny getting out of whatever room her father was in, one could almost say that they lived in perfect harmony.

In the kitchen, her mother was thawing fish sticks and slicing cucumbers. Deeny stood there for a moment, trying to figure out what possible dinner would need those two ingredients, and no others.

"You've got a zit, dear," said her mother helpfully.

"I always have a zit, Mother," said Deeny. "I'm seventeen and I have the complexion of dog doo."

"If you washed . . ."

"If I didn't eat chocolate, if I didn't eat fatty foods, if I used Oxy-500, if I didn't have the heredity you and Treadmarks gave me . . ."

"I wish you wouldn't call your father that. It doesn't even make sense."

Come on, Mom, you *wash* his underwear. "It's because everyone rolls right over him at work. I feel kind of sorry for the old guy."

Mother made a show of speaking silently, mouthing the words, "He can hear you."

"Come on, Mom, you know what a nothing he is on the job. He's nearly forty and so far the only thing he ever accomplished was getting you pregnant. And he only did *that* the one time."

As usual, Deeny had gone too far. Mother turned, her face reddening. "You get out of this kitchen, young lady. Not that you *deserve* to be called a lady of any kind. The mouth you have!"

Deeny's hand was already in her pocket. She pressed the button on her phone. It immediately rang.

"Excuse me, Mother," she said. "Somebody actually *wants* to talk to me."

Her mother just stood there looking at her, a fish stick in her hand.

Deeny made a show of looking at the phone. "Oh, not Bill again." She pressed the END button.

"Who's Bill?"

"A guy who calls sometimes," said Deeny.

"You've only had that cellphone for a couple of hours," said Mother. "How would he get your number if you don't want him to call?"

"He probably bribed somebody. He's such an asshole."

"Deeny, that language just makes you sound cheap."

"Well, I'm not cheap. I'm priceless. You said so yourself."

"When you were four and used to sing that little song."

"That little song you made me rehearse for hours and hours so you could show me off to your friends."

"You were darling. They loved it. And so did you. I never saw you turn your back on an audience."

"Oh really?" said Deeny. Holding the cell phone above her head like castanets, she sashayed out of the kitchen, heading for her room.

When she got there she flopped back on her bed, feeling sick and lost. It would be different if her parents weren't right about everything. But they were. She was exactly the loser her father thought she was. And she wasn't a lady, or darling, and she probably *would* be cheap, if she could get a guy to look at her at all. But when there are no buyers, what does it matter whether your price is high or low?

Even though she tried to tune out everything Treadmarks said, he made sure she never forgot for a single day how tragically disappointing she was as a human being. It's like he couldn't stand for her to feel good about herself for a single second. An *A* in a class? "Study hard, kid, it's a sure thing you're never gonna have a husband to support you." A new top? "Why didn't you leave it in the store where it might get bought by somebody who can wear that kind of thing?" At the office on the days she helped out after school, she tried to do everything right but it was never good enough. And if she tried to talk to him, ever, about anything, he'd get this impatient, bored look and about two sentences in he'd say, "Some of us have things to do, Deeny, will you get to the point?"

It would have been different if she didn't agree with him. She really did screw up everything she touched. She really was a leper at school. She never got calls from boys. She never even got *looks* from boys.

It wasn't that she had no friends. She had plenty of friends. Well, two. Both losers like her, when she looked at it rationally. When they were together, though, they fed on each other's insanity and fancied themselves the superior of everyone else at school.

Rivka, alias Becky, always sneered at the popular girls' sheeplike insistence on dressing alike and wearing their hair alike and even having the exact same half-inch of absolutely smooth, no-pudge abdomen showing between their thin little tops and their tightass jeans. Deeny kept it to herself that it was all she could do, when she saw those perfect waistlines, not to pinch her own little three-quarter-inch flab slab just to remind herself that skimpy little tops were only the stuff of dreams for her.

Lex, on the other hand—who had tried to get them to call her Luthor in fifth grade and Alexis in ninth, to which they had responded by calling her Blecch for an entire month—always mocked them for how airheaded they were. Even the smart ones. Especially the smart ones. Maybe Deeny would enjoy Lex's wit more if she were actually smarter than the girls whose lack of brains she made fun of, but half the time it was Lex who was wrong, and it just made all three of them look like idiots.

Yeah, Deeny had friends, all right. The way some people got impetigo.

Not that she didn't like them. She liked them fine. She just knew that, socially speaking, she'd be better off alone than hanging out with these two aggressively hostile Jewesses—the term they both insisted on.

All the way to school on the bus next morning (another mark of Cain on her brow), Deeny rehearsed how she'd get into school another way and absolutely avoid them all day, except when she had classes with them, which was every period except A Cappella, because neither of them could carry a tune in a gas can.

Yet when she got to school, her mind had wandered onto another subject—her cellphone, as a matter of fact—and it wasn't till she heard Becky's greeting—that endlessly cheery "Hey, tush flambee!"—that she remembered that she was supposed to be doing evasive maneuvers.

What the hell. Her social standing was past saving. And she didn't care anyway. And besides, she had the phone. Not that she'd ever have the courage to use it.

So on their way up to the front door, threading their way among the other kids, Becky and Lex talked loudly on purpose so everybody could hear them being crude.

"Is there something about being Jewish that makes us have huge boobs?" said Lex. "Or is it because our ancestors lived in eastern Europe for so many centuries and all that borscht and potatoes made them cows?"

"I don't have huge boobs," said Deeny quietly. "I hardly have any boobs at all."

"Which makes me wonder if you aren't secretly a shiksa," said Lex. "I mean, why do you even bother to wear bras?"

"Because I have nipples," said Deeny grimly, "and if I don't wear a bra, they chafe."

"You've never heard of undershirts?" said Lex.

"You two make me sick," said Becky. "These things aren't accidents. God gives big boobs to the women he wants to send babies to. The boobs bring the boys, the boys bring the babies, God is happy, and we get fat."

"Is that a new midrash?" asked Lex.

"So I'm meant to be a nun?" said Deeny. "Why didn't he go all the way and make me Catholic?"

"You'll get them," said Becky. "You're a late bloomer, that's all."

If there was anything Deeny hated worse than when Becky and Lex flaunted their udders, it was when they tried to make her feel better about her unnoticeables. Because she didn't actually feel bad about them. She looked at what the two of them carried around with them and it looked to her like it was about as convenient has having two more big textbooks to carry to every single class all day.

So, as they talked about the curse of bigness—while sticking their chests out so far they could barely open their lockers—Deeny fidgeted. Her hand was in her purse. She was turning the cellphone over and over in her fingers. And somewhere along the line, without quite deciding, she pushed the button and the cellphone rang.

She ignored it for the first ring.

"These morons who bring cellphones to school," said Becky. "And most of them aren't even drug dealers, so what's the point? What kind of emergency is it where someone says, 'Quick! Call a teenager! Thank God they're all carrying cellphones now!'"

Perfect moment, thought Deeny. Because she was actually blushing for real, just imagining the embarrassment of pulling out a cellphone in front of Becky at this exact moment. So . . . she pulled out the cellphone and pushed the TALK button.

Of course, all that happened was that the "test ring" shut off and the last number called got dialed—but since that number was her home phone, and nobody was there during the day, and her last-century parents didn't bother with an answering machine, what could go wrong?

She held the phone to her ear and turned away from the others. As she did, she saw both Becky and Lex do their oh-my-god takes.

"Not now," Deeny hissed into the phone.

"Sellout," murmured Becky.

Deeny knew she was joking.

"No," said Deeny. "I told you no."

"She's dealing," said Lex. "I knew it."

"It must take every penny she earns at her dad's office to pay for a cell," said Becky. "How needy can you get?"

"Maybe her parents are paying."

"Shakespeare based Shylock on her mother and Simon Legree on her father. I don't think so."

"Oh, right, from Shakespeare's famous play *Uncle Hamlet's Cabin*."

As they nattered on, Deeny retreated farther from them and said, very softly—so softly that everyone around her was bound to be listening and hear her—"I told you I can't talk at school and no, I wasn't faking." Then she punched the END button, turned the phone off, and jammed it back into her purse.

Becky and Lex were looking at her skeptically. "Oh, right," said Lex. "Like . . . faking what? An orgasm?"

They weren't buying it.

But she said nothing. Stuck with the charade. Let her face turn red with embarrassment. Walked to her own locker and opened it—no combination to spin, she had deliberately broken the lock the first day of school and made it a point never to keep anything in the locker that she cared about keeping. "So the homework elf didn't come back," she said.

"Oh, now she's pretending that she doesn't want to talk about it," said Becky. "Like she isn't dying to feed us some line of bull doo about some imaginary boyfriend."

"There's no boyfriend," said Deeny.

"Give me that," said Lex. And before Deeny could register what Lex was doing, she had snatched the purse right off Deeny's shoulder and in an instant was brandishing the cellphone.

"Hey, give that back," said Deeny. Immediately, those words made her flash on all the times in grade school when one of the Nazi children—i.e., the popular kids—grabbed something away from her—a sandwich, her homework—and how futile and pathetic Deeny had always sounded, whining, "Hey, give that back, give that back, don't throw it in there, please, please." Sickened at the memory, she shut her mouth and folded her arms and leaned against her locker to tough it out. Which might have made her look cool if her locker hadn't been open so that leaning made her fall right in.

Becky smirked at her as she awkwardly pushed herself back out of the locker. "You know, if you had boobs you couldn't fall into your locker. At least not sideways."

"Thanks for the reminder."

"Redial last number," said Lex as she pushed SEND. She was looking at the little LCD display. So she'd recognize the phone number at once, having called it a thousand times since they met in fourth grade.

Only Lex didn't say a thing about the number. And when she held it to her ear, her eyes widened.

"Sorry," she said. "Wrong number." She pushed END and handed the phone back to Deeny, blushing as she did.

Deeny hadn't known that Lex could blush.

"Well?" demanded Becky.

"Ask Dinah," said Lex. "Apparently she's been seeing somebody without telling us."

Deeny was stunned. Lex was playing along. Unbelievable.

"*Seeing* somebody?" said Becky. "Adults who are having affairs 'see' somebody. High school girls *date*. And not somebody, guys."

"Sounded more like seeing somebody to me," said Lex. "If you don't believe me, push redial."

"Not a chance," said Deeny, as Becky reached for the phone. "*Real* friends don't spy. Or assume that I'm lying." She meant it—but she had to put a smile on it, because after all, if Lex was playing along, Deeny didn't want to antagonize her *too* much. Still, she had to act pissed off because she *would* be pissed off at Lex taking her phone—and she knew she *would* be pissed off because she *was* pissed off.

"He's probably twenty-five," said Lex. "Either a garage mechanic or an investment banker—"

"Oh, like *those* two professions sound the same," said Becky.

"Same kind of I-know-everything-and-you're-as-ignorant-as-fish attitude," said Lex.

"Well what did he say?"

"Try, 'Hello, Deeny.' Like he had caller ID."

"Cellphone numbers don't show up on caller ID," said Becky.

"So maybe he has a special cellphone whose number he gave only to Deeny," said Lex.

"Maybe he got Deeny *her* phone and his is the only one on speed dial," said Becky, really getting into it now. "So she isn't paying for it at all."

"But she's a kept woman now," said Lex, "and so he thinks he owns her, he can call her whenever and wherever he wants, only she longs for her independence, and so she's going to dump him, but he won't accept it and starts to stalk her and take pictures of her with spycams and then he puts them out on the internet only with other women's bodies so they're really pornographic."

"Oh, like mine wouldn't be sexy enough to be pornographic," said Deeny.

"Oh, it would," said Lex, "except it would only appeal to men who go for boys without weenies."

"Oh, who *is* he?" demanded Becky. "Forget all the other stuff, who got you this phone?"

Deeny noticed how Lex's joke had now become the "true" story—she'd been given the phone by a boyfriend. And it felt bad to have them actually believe the lie, even if it *was* exactly the lie she had bought the phone for.

"I pay for it myself," said Deeny. "Out of my savings. I can only afford the first three payments and then they'll cancel my account. I got it so I could fake having a boyfriend but I was never going to try to fool *you* guys."

"Ha, ha," said Lex.

"So you're really not going to tell us?" said Becky.

"There's nobody, honest," said Deeny. "I only faked it that time because it pisses me off when you try to console me about wearing size A-minus. Tell her, Lex. You don't have to play along any longer."

She had expected Lex to break into a grin and say, "All right, Deeny-bopper."

Instead, Lex's face got cold and hard. "Play it that way, stud," said Lex. "I guess you'll be talking about it with your *real* friends." And she stalked off.

Becky rolled her eyes. "I don't mind if you want to keep it a secret. And Lex won't stay mad. She never does."

I've only known her three years longer than you have, so duh, yes, I know that. "Thanks, Becky," said Deeny. "I'm not going to keep carrying it. It was a dumb idea, anyway." Especially if you two won't believe me when I tell you the absolute truth.

Together they headed off to Calculus, which was a hell of a way to start the day, especially because she had no intention of ever using a logarithm in her entire life after high school. She was only taking it because the district had passed a new ruling just before her sophomore year that all phrosh and sophs had to take four years of math, and since she had already taken honors Algae Trichinosis her freshman year, it was too late to start out with remedial so her fourth year could be geometry.

The nice thing about Calculus was that since she had already passed her first semester, now all she needed was a D in the second semester because the college of her choice would already have admitted her before her final grades came in. So she didn't actually have to pay attention in class. Her mind could wander. And it did.

How far is Lex going to take this? She had to recognize Deeny's home phone number. She had to know she was hearing the blat-rest-blat of a ringing telephone, and not a voice. So why was she doing this whole injured-friend routine?

There was no figuring Lex out when she got some gag going. Like the time Becky had said "Oh, you talk too much" to her, and for five whole days Lex hadn't said another word, not one, nada, not even when teachers called on her. It was like she had gone on strike, and by the end Becky was begging her to say something, anything. "Tell me to go eff myself, just say *something*." That Lex, what a kidder. In an overdone assholical way.

Didn't use the phone all the rest of that day. Didn't even bring it to school the next day because she forgot and left it on the charging stand. Then she brought it on Friday because what the hell, she was paying for it, wasn't she?

Pep rally after school. Attendance required. "Enforced pep," said Becky. "What a Nazi concept. Sieg Tigers."

Lex was still being a butt, making snide remarks about how Deeny had a whole secret life that only her *real* friends got to know about. And all those perky cheerleaders making brilliant impromptu speeches about how, like, our team does so much better if we, like, really have spirit, they were really irritating, too, especially because so many of the other kids were getting into it and yelling and chanting and cheering, the whole mob-mentality thing. And it didn't help to have Becky mumbling *her* snide remarks. "You want them to have spirit, try wearing that cute little skirt without panties, that'll make those boys play hard." Oh, that was funny, Becky, why not laugh so hard you fall off the back of the bleachers.

So what was there to do, really, except push the button and then rush over to the edge of the bleachers and turn away from everybody and pretend to be having a phone call.

There was so much noise that she didn't actually have to make up anything to say. Just mumble mumble mumble, and then laugh, and then smile, and then imagine him saying something kind of dirty, and smirking at what he said, and then he says something *really* dirty, and so she makes a face but it's plain she really likes hearing it even though she pretends to be mad.

Twenty-five-year-old mechanic. Covered with grease but arms so strong he just lifts the car up onto the jack. Or investment banker. Who never wears anything under his suit except his shirt, "In case you only got a little time for me, baby," he says, "I don't want to waste any of it."

Yeah, right.

But don't let the "yeah, right" show on your face, moron. A laugh. A smile. A little offended. Then delighted. Then . . . yeah, they're looking, not just Lex and Becky, but other kids, too, looking at Deeny, can you imagine that, watching her have a love life, even if it's only with the beep beep beep of the ring tone at home.

Only now that she thought about it, there wasn't a beep beep beep.

Had one of her parents picked up the phone? Come home early from work maybe, and the phone rang, and they picked it up, only she didn't hear them saying, "Hello? Hello? Who's there?" because there was so much noise here at the pep rally.

She pressed END, stuffed the phone in her purse, and then just sat there, looking out over the basketball court with all the stupid streamers that somebody was going to have to climb up and cut down before the game anyway, so why go to all that trouble in the first place, and I wonder what my parents heard on the phone when they picked it up, was I actually saying stuff *out loud* about what the investment banker does or doesn't wear? Even if I was, they couldn't possibly have heard me. Except that my mouth was right by the mike and they didn't have a pep rally going on there at home so they probably *could* hear and she hoped it was her father—let *him* hear her talking about how maybe somebody wanted sex with his loser daughter, sit on *that* and spin—

But if it was Mom . . .

Please don't let it be Mom. Please don't let her go to the drugstore and buy me condoms or make an appointment for me to go to the doctor and get a prescription for the Pill or the Patch or whatever remedy she decides is right for her little flat-chested princess who has about as much use for birth control as fish have for deodorant.

Lex was sitting beside her. Close, leaning in, so she could whisper and still be heard. "Who *is* he?"

Deeny turned to her, then leaned away, because Lex was right there in her face. Nobody was near enough to hear.

"You of all people should know," said Deeny.

"Why, is it someone I know?"

"It's *nobody*." It's my wishful thinking. It's my pathetic loser attempt to make people think I have a love life, somebody who cares enough to call. And I don't even *care* what people think, except I bought the phone and I put on this little show so I do care, don't I, which makes me just as needy as any other loser. People smell the need like dogs, like wolves, and if they're like Daddy they torment you because they know they can get away with it because losers have no claws.

Lex was angry. Sat up straight, looking forward, down toward the stupid pep rally where they were either acting out the kama sutra in cheerleader outfits or trying to spell something with their bodies. But then she must have decided that being mad wasn't going to get what she wanted, because her face softened and she turned back to Deeny, rested her chin in one hand, and contemplated her.

"I know from his voice that he's not a kid," she said. "I was thinking college student, but the way you're acting now, I'm thinking—married guy."

"How can you know anything from his voice?" said Deeny, disgusted now with this whole game.

"I know he exists," said Lex. "I know he's a guy. I know he doesn't sound like any of these little boys. He doesn't talk like high school."

And it finally dawned on Deeny that Lex wasn't lying. She actually heard something. There *was* a voice when she took the phone and called.

Which meant that someone at home must have picked up. "It must have been my father," said Deeny. "The only number I had ever called was my home phone. My father must have been home this morning."

Lex rolled her eyes. "A, I *know* your father's voice, give me some credit. And B, I *saw* the number on the screen and it wasn't your home phone."

"Well then I don't know who it was because I've never dialed any other number," said Deeny. "It really was a wrong number."

"Oh, a wrong number that says, 'I can't stop thinking about you either, Deeny'?"

Now Deeny understood. "Oh, how sick can you get. So I was playing around with the phone and yes, it was a dumb thing to do, but let it go now, OK? You're as bad as the Nazis, making fun of me. Just let it go."

Lex's astonishment looked genuine. "I'm not making fun of you, I think you're in trouble somehow, I think maybe you're doing something really dumb or really cool and I just want to know, I want to be your *friend,* but if you want to keep it all to yourself that's fine with me, that's *no skin off my ass!*"

She was shouting by the end because Deeny was going down the bleachers as fast as she could, getting away, getting off by herself. Lex believed it. Lex wasn't making fun of her. Lex really talked to somebody. Somebody who said things like "I can't stop thinking of you either, Deeny."

Only there wasn't anybody that Deeny couldn't stop thinking about. There was just a phone she got so she could make fun of all the girls with cellphones talking to their stupid boyfriends who were only sixty yards away talking on *their* cellphones at *their* lockers. And maybe she *did* want people to think she really might have a boyfriend, some older guy who wasn't in high school, so she could seem mysterious and mature so people would think the reason she never connected with anybody at high school except Becky and Lex was because she had a life outside, a life far more exciting and dangerous than any of the Nazis had here at school.

Somebody answered the phone when Lex pressed TALK.

Outside the gym, over in the grove where the smokers and lovers gathered to light up and pet, Deeny took out her phone and pressed TALK and looked at the number.

It was a number she'd never seen before. With an area code in front of it that she'd never heard of. Long distance. Oh, that was great, all she needed was long-distance charges, she'd lose the phone the first month at that rate.

She was about to press END but then there was a voice.

"I dreamed of you last night, Deeny."

Tinny as it was, coming out of the tiny little speaker eighteen inches away, Deeny could still tell that it was a man's voice. Deep. With a bit of humor in it. And he knew her name.

She brought the phone up to her ear. "Who is this?" she asked.

"You gotta stay out of my dreams, Deeny. I wake up and I can't get back to sleep, thinking about you."

"How did you get my number?"

He laughed. "Deeny, you called *me,* remember?"

"Lex called you. My friend Lex. She pushed the button. And how do you know my name, anyway? Do you work for the cellphone company?"

"I know your name because you whispered it to me in my dream," he said. "I know your name because I whispered it myself as I slid your shirt up your body and kissed you all the way down your—"

Deeny mashed the END button and cast the phone down onto the pine needles.

One of the nearby smokers laughed. "Oooh, lovers' quarrel," he said.

"None of your effin' business," said Deeny.

"If my business was effin', you'd be the first one I'd eff," said the smoker, and his buddies laughed.

Deeny picked up the phone. "I don't have time for little boys."

But as she walked away, she was thinking, This is the first time any boy at this school ever made a rude sexual comment about *me.* And he did it because of the phone.

The damn thing works.

Too well, that's how it works. This was supposed to be a game of let's pretend. So who was the guy on the other end?

She pushed TALK.

The display showed her home phone number. It rang. Beep. Beep. Beep. No answer. No man's voice.

She turned to the couple who were kissing and touching and pressing up against each other next to the big oak tree at the center of the grove.

"Lovers are so fickle," she said. "One minute taking your shirt off, the next minute not even answering the phone."

They broke their kiss long enough to turn and look at her, gap-lipped, for a long moment.

"As you were," she said.

They returned to their kiss, his hands moving along the bare skin between her jeans and her top, her hands playing with his pockets, with his butt. Deeny wanted to scream, it made her so jealous, it made her so angry. It made her want so much to press TALK and have somebody really be there. Somebody who wanted her so much he couldn't keep his hands off her. And with any luck, maybe it would be somebody who didn't say things like "If my business was effin', you'd be the first one I'd eff."

She remembered the voice on the phone, the impossible voice, the unknown phone number. The thought of him made her shiver. And as she walked toward the buses, she wondered whether shivering was one of the early warning signs of love.

She did not use the phone over the weekend.

On Saturday Mother went to temple and Treadmarks went outside and squatted by the lawn mower, pretending to have some understanding of mechanical things, but actually half-mooning the neighborhood with his butt crack. Thus he offended the God of Israel two ways, by working on the Sabbath and by making it so embarrassing to believe that man had been made in his image.

Deeny showed her faith by not working, and her freethinking by not going to temple. Basically she sat around and tried to read three different books and a magazine and couldn't keep her mind on any one of them because she kept thinking of what it might be like for a man—not a boy, a man—to slide his hands under her shirt and lift it upward and then kiss her naked flesh. Since her naked flesh would include her flabby belly, it kind of interfered with the fantasy, and she kept switching between imagining that he preferred bodies with a little loose flesh and imagining that her flesh was somehow magically tightened over the smooth hard muscles of a girl who uses the ab roller fifty reps every day.

She told herself that there was no point in picking up the phone because who would see her do it?

And on Sunday, Deeny managed not to pull the cellphone out of her purse all morning. She didn't touch it till Mother offered to take her to the mall, and even then it was only because her father called out to her as they were heading out the door.

"Aren't you taking your phone? In case loverboy calls?"

Deeny wondered for one panicked moment how Treadmarks could possibly know about the guy on the phone. Until Mother answered him. "Dear, I think 'Bill' was just made up."

"Oh, yes, Bill," said Father. "Aren't you afraid he might call?"

Deeny thought back to Thursday and remembered that she had said she was trying to avoid Bill's calls. "I don't want to talk to him even if he does," she said.

"Then leave the phone with me," said Father. "If he calls, I'll get rid of him for you."

Deeny reached into her purse, lifted up the phone, and dropped it back inside. "No thanks," she said.

"So you *want* him to call."

Mother sighed. "He doesn't exist, dear."

"That is my fondest wish, Mother," said Deeny, "but alas it has not yet come true." And they were out the door.

It was such a weird confrontation. Treadmarks mocking her by pretending that he believed some guy was trying to call her. Mother defending Deeny by calling her a liar. Which she was, of course, except that even though Bill was a lie, there really *was* a guy on the phone. Or at least there had been. And now she was afraid to push the TALK button, for fear he would be there, and for fear that he would not.

When Monday came around, the phone weighed heavy in her purse, and she toyed with the idea of simply leaving it home. She even decided to do that, for a few minutes, but after breakfast she went back to her room for no other reason than to take it out of her drawer and put it in her purse. She told herself it was so that Treadmarks wouldn't find it and do something sickening like getting her cellphone number and calling it and leaving fake messages on her voicemail. Which he was not above doing. Though it did sound like more work than he was wont to attempt on his own.

So there she was on the bus again, phone in her purse, and just like Thursday and Friday, she switched it on and set it to test the current ringing sound when she pressed the OK button. All the time telling herself she wasn't actually going to push it. She was just going to forget she even had a phone in her purse.

Unless it just . . . rang. Unless somebody called her.

Nobody called.

But something else was going on.

Word had spread, apparently. She was getting looked at by kids who usually glanced past her as if she had no more existence than gum on the sidewalk—to be stepped around, lest she stick to their shoe, but otherwise ignored. Today, though, they fell silent in their conversations and glanced at her, some of them covertly, but others quite openly, as if she had forgotten to wear pants. And one time she overheard the words "older guy" and she realized that either Becky or Lex had been indiscreet.

Wasn't that what she wanted, though? She could hardly be mad at them for making her, if not famous, then notorious. And maybe it wasn't them at all, maybe it was one of the other kids at the pep rally. It's not as if they had had any privacy there in the bleachers in the gym.

They were talking about her. Holding her in awe. Or maybe not, maybe they disapproved—that's what it looked like in that group where she heard the words "older guy," no doubt the very next words from somebody else were those little "tsk-tsk" clicks or even the more direct "what a whore." Well, disapproval from shmucks like that was like an Oscar and the Nobel Prize combined, minus the statue and the cash, of course.

And by lunchtime, Lex and Becky had far more to report. After she had assured them that he had *not* called again and no, she had never slept with him, they were full of news about what everybody was saying. "They are so sure he's from the college and he's some big brain from the physics department."

"Big brain, I like that," said Deeny.

"So he isn't?" asked Becky.

"College is in his past, not his present, and definitely not his future," said Deeny. As if she knew. But he sounded like a college kind of guy. Clear-sounding, confident, and he didn't have to hunt for words, they were just there, whatever words he needed. Not that he had said that many of them.

"And what *I* heard," said Lex, "is that he's a married man older than your dad and it's like some kind of electric complex—"

"Electra," said Deeny, "as in *Mourning Becomes.*"

Lex rolled her eyes. "Puh-leeeeeze, like I wasn't the first one to discover the psych book and tell you both about all the weird sex crap back in sixth grade."

"You just take so much pride in being smarter than everybody, Deeny," said Becky. "It's your worst feature."

"But at least I've got no tits, so you still look real sexy when you stand next to me."

Lex did her build-a-wall pantomime between them, saying, as she always did, "Please don't fight, girls, it will worry the children."

"So everybody's talking," said Deeny. "What can I do about that?" Except enjoy it.

"Amazingly enough," said Lex, "none of the stories reflect any credit on *you.*"

"Like we expected anything else?" said Deeny. "But at least they notice me."

"So . . . what'll you do if the school counselor calls you in?" said Lex.

"Why would a counselor want to see me?"

What a stupid question. She hadn't even finished lunch when Ms. Reymondo walked by and said, "Come see me, would you, Deeny?"

"When?"

"Anytime," she said.

"Cool," said Deeny. "How about July?"

"How about now?" said Ms. Reymondo, with her sweet-as-nails smile.

"I'm still digesting," said Deeny.

"She farts a lot when she's doing that," said Lex.

"And people have been known to puke when she farts, especially after cole slaw," said Becky. "Do you have a big solid wastebasket in your office, Ms. Reymondo? The kind with holes don't do much good when you're puking."

Ms. Reymondo faked a chilly little laugh. "You girls are so clever, I just can't keep up with you. I always envied the smart girls when I was in high school."

That was enough to get Deeny out of her chair, because she knew it would only be moments before Lex did something really offensive, like fake-puking on her lunch tray or blowing milk out her nose, which she could do at will. "I'll come now, Ms. Reymondo."

And sure enough, it was about the rumors. "Deeny, I hope you know that if you are in some kind of . . . inappropriate relationship, you can always speak to me in strictest confidence."

"So you don't obey the law?" said Deeny.

"What?"

"The law that says that if there is some kind of child abuse, you have to report it to the appropriate authorities."

"So there *is* abuse?" She looked so eager.

"No, there's no abuse. I'm doing just fine. Nobody's boffing me or even feeling me up, which is more than half the girls in this school can say."

"I don't see why you're being so hostile."

"Oh, no, that's all wrong, Ms. Reymondo. You sound defensive. You're supposed to say, 'And how does it make you feel, to talk about other girls having sex and getting felt up?' "

"I know how it makes you feel," said Ms. Reymondo. "It makes you feel like you've somehow struck a blow against authority and aren't you cool. Only I'm not any kind of authority, God knows, and what you're doing now is blowing smoke up the ass of a person who is only trying to help you."

"Help me what?"

"Help you get out of a situation that might be getting out of control."

"The only thing out of my control," said Deeny, "is getting called in to your office and losing half my lunch period just so I can hear you discuss your ass and whether you're getting any smoke blown up it."

"You're free to go," said Ms. Reymondo. "But I hope you remember how you treated a person who only wanted to be your friend."

Deeny paused at the door. "*Friends* aren't paid by the state or the county or whatever, and *friends* don't have the power to order me to their office."

"When you're in trouble, friends are the people who can help you, whether they're getting paid for it or being treated like shit by bratty little girls who think they're so smart they can handle relationships with older men."

For a moment, Deeny wanted to say she was sorry. After all, if she really were dating some older man and it started getting weird or something, maybe she would need to turn to somebody and maybe it would be . . .

No, it would never be Ms. Reymondo, whose answer to everything was that the Anglo patriarchy took what they wanted and therefore equality for women and people of color was nothing but a joke. It irritated Deeny that Ms. Reymondo always included Jews in her "people of color" classification, an idea whose wrongness could be verified by the naked eye. Not to mention Ms. Reymondo herself, who looked like she had just stepped off the boat from northern Spain and had about as much color as your average Frenchman.

So Deeny didn't apologize, she just fled, telling herself that no doubt Ms. Reymondo had been treated more rudely by other students. And then thinking, maybe not. Maybe I'm the worst kid she's ever faced. And why would I talk that way? Why am I suddenly so defiant? I've spent my whole time in high school mousing around and only talking big when I'm alone and safe with my friends. And now I'm talking to school counselors like I was some kind of hardened hoodlum. Stuff I used to think to myself and tell Lex and Beck about later, I said out loud, and I didn't get killed.

And on a whim, she reached into her purse, and there in the counselors' hallway, she made her cellphone ring.

He wouldn't be on it. There'd be nobody there. But she could *pretend* to be taking a call from an imaginary lover and see what Ms. Reymondo made of *that*.

Ms. Reymondo came out of her office and saw her just as she pulled the phone out of her purse. Deliberately Deeny turned her back and spoke softly into the phone. "Oh, right, like you call me *now*," she said. "I'm taking so much crap because of you."

The phone wasn't beeping.

"Nothing to say?" she said.

"I thought you wanted it this way," said the man.

The same man, sounding manlier than ever. And while his words might be the kind of whiny and apologetic thing you'd get from the kind of guy Ms. Reymondo would probably date, his tone was teasing so she knew he wasn't really asking for validation or something.

"I was waiting for you to call," said Deeny.

"You're the one with the buttons to push," said the man. And then, when Deeny didn't answer, he said what she was waiting for him to say. "I wish I were there to push them," he said, laughing at himself just a little. "Touch them, anyway. With my fingers, maybe. Or maybe not."

Deeny blushed and giggled, wondering what buttons he meant, knowing perfectly well, or hoping she knew, or . . . something. This was what love felt like, this confusion, wasn't it? Especially knowing that if Ms. Reymondo could hear the other side of this conversation she'd spot her knickers.

"Legal age is sixteen," she whispered, "and I'm seventeen, so what's stopping you?"

"There's a limit to what I can do over the phone," he said.

"My point exactly."

"It's a limit we have to live with," he said.

"So you're all talk, is that it?"

"Yes," he said. "That's it." And then the line went silent.

Deeny couldn't believe it. Here she was, practically begging him to show up at her door naked, and he just blows her off and *hangs up*?

Ms. Reymondo was standing across the corridor from her when Deeny put the phone back in her purse.

"Legal age is eighteen," she said.

"I'm not talking about drinking," said Deeny.

"Drinking age is twenty-one," said Ms. Reymondo. "The legal age of consent is eighteen in this state."

"My father's a lawyer," said Deeny. "And you don't know squat."

"It's my job to know squat," said Ms. Reymondo. "So if this guy is trying to get in your pants, it's really not up to you to say yes to him. And, by the way, I happen to know your father is definitely *not* a lawyer. Don't lie to a counselor who has studied your file."

"I guess that means you know everything about me. All the yearnings of a teenage heart. You really 'get' the youth of today, Ms. Reymondo. We have no secrets from *you,* because as our *friend,* you've got our files."

Ms. Reymondo glared at her and walked away, maybe—just maybe—swinging her butt a little bit more than usual. We're getting a bit *huffy,* Ms. Reymondo. I don't think that's very *professional,* Ms. Reymondo.

I am such a bitch. This phone is doing bad things to me. All these years, the only thing keeping me from complete bitchery has been my shyness. With cellphone in hand, the real me comes out and shows that I suck worse than the Nazis have ever thought.

He doesn't want to be with me. He only wants to talk to me on the phone.

All that week, there was buzz about her at school. And then the next week, there wasn't. She'd been moved from one slot to another—from dweebish Jewgirl to whore-of-older-men—but now that she was safely slotted again, she could be ignored. Even Ms. Reymondo seemed to be taking screw you for an answer. It was just . . . . over.

The phone had done all it was supposed to do, and the change in her life amounted to nada. Unless you counted the monthly phone bill.

I'll cancel and give the phone back.

But she didn't do it. Couldn't. Because even though she hadn't pressed TALK since Monday, she didn't want to cut herself off from the possibility of talking to him again.

All week she'd had so many ups and downs it scared her a little. She actually had to look up bipolar disorder in order to make sure she didn't fit their list of symptoms. One minute she's thinking, He'll change his mind, he'll come to me, or he'll tell me where he is and I'll go to *him.* The next minute, He won't come here because he's seen me and he could never pretend to be aroused by my body *in person.* It's like those phone-sex fakes, where it's some fat fifty-year-old woman in her kitchen cooing in her little sixteen-year-old vixen voice to fifty-year-old men who are paying through the nose to a 900 number to live out their fantasy of having sex with women so young it was almost illegal. Wouldn't they just gag if they could see who was talking to them.

He's just a phone-sex line.

Why would I want a guy like that touching me anyway? His hands creeping around on my body like big fat spiders. His lips slobbering on me and he calls it "kissing" like I wouldn't just puke on his bald spot.

He's not like that. He loves me, and he's not *old,* he's just older than me.

Older than me, and doesn't want to *be* with me.

Now everybody thinks I'm a whore, and I don't even get laid.

On Saturday she was so angry and hurt and confused and ashamed that she actually got up and went to temple with Mother. Treadmarks didn't even say anything snide as they went—probably because he knew that Mother was feeling triumphant and he didn't want the fight that would happen if he said something disparaging about religion. But all that happened was, Deeny felt like the worst kind of hypocrite because the reason she was depressed was because she couldn't commit adultery, and she was busy coveting her neighbor, but couldn't get him to come over and live up to his promises of sin. What kind of blasphemy was it for her to even be there?

All the time she was there, and all the way home, she kept looking at every guy and thinking, is it him? Are you the one? And the more ludicrous they were, the better. She almost wanted to go up to a couple of them—the ones who glanced at her a little bit more than the others—and say, "Have you been calling me?" But of course she didn't, not with her mother there, not with a little shred of sanity still hanging around somewhere in her head, saying, "Oh, right," to all her wackier notions.

On Monday, she left the cellphone in her drawer. A whole week without it. And Lex and Becky didn't even notice, or if they did they said nothing about it. It was all over. Just like that.

Only not really. Because she *was* in that different slot.

It was on the bus. Jake Wu, a guy who rode it sometimes and sometimes didn't. Half Chinese and kind of cute, thin and looked great in clothes, but hey, he was on the bus, so he couldn't actually be cool, right? And he always hung out with a different crowd, the chess-club types, the math-club types, sort of the stereotypical oriental-American, intellectual and college-bound and probably going to be an electrical engineer or a physicist.

And he sat down beside her.

"I hear you been dating an older guy," he said.

Like that, no preamble, no hi, not even a decent interval like he had to work up the courage.

"It's over," she said. And when she said it, she realized it was true and it made her sad but it also relieved her because it meant she had made the decision and she knew it was the right one.

"Are you still broken up about it? So I should act, like, sad? Because I'd be faking it."

Faking it, which would mean he wasn't sad it was over with her older guy. Too cool. "You don't have to fake anything," she said.

"Cool," he said. "So you want to go out with a really mature high school senior?"

"Why, do you know any?" she asked.

She could see it right then in his eyes that she'd stung him with that. And it occurred to her that maybe she wasn't the only person on the planet who felt rejected and was scared all the time whenever she had to face somebody of the opposite sex. And unlike her, *he* had the guts to do something in spite of being scared.

Though come to think of it, she *had* done something, hadn't she. Even if it *was* over.

"I was kidding," she said. "I'd like to go out with a mature high school senior, if you mean you."

"I meant me," he said.

"My schedule's not real crowded right now," said Deeny. "So if you kind of pick a day, I'll choose a different day to wash my hair and walk the dog."

He grinned. "Heck, I was hoping that's what we could do on our date."

"Which? Hair or dog?"

"You got a dog?" he asked.

"No."

"Me neither," he said. "My mother has fish but she frowns on me washing them. So . . . your hair or mine?"

She made a show of examining his hair. "Yours is thick and straight and probably looks like this no matter what you do. Whereas mine is a challenge, real problem hair, a complete bitch to deal with. So we'll wash yours."

"I see you like to do things the easy way."

"If that's an assumption," she said, "my knee knows where your balls are."

"I assume nothing," he said. "Whereas you assume I've *got* balls."

"I know you do," she said.

"Jeans that tight?"

"It took balls to sit here," she said. "What with me being a leper."

"Leper hell," he said. "Everybody just figured you were out of reach."

"I didn't notice anybody reaching."

"Cause guys don't like to fail, so if they thought they'd fail with you, they wouldn't try."

"And you're different?"

"Yeah," he said. "I asked."

And here's the funny thing. He really did pick her up, take her over to his house, where his mother and father looked on as if they had only just discovered that their teenage son was strange, while Deeny washed his hair, then ratted it into a fright wig, and then washed it and combed it out again, with all the snarls and screaming that such an operation entailed.

"What do you want to know, I'll tell you everything, only stop the torture!" he cried.

"I can leave your hair like this."

"I'm going to shave it all off if you do," he said.

But she didn't leave it like that, and he didn't shave it off, and while she was quite sure that his parents still did not have any place for a Jewess in their plans for their number-one son, she could also tell that they kind of liked it that he had actually had fun.

It was, in fact, great. Not great for a first date. Just flat-out great.

Best thing was, next morning Lex and Becky were actually happy for her instead of criticizing him and picking him apart the way the three of them had always picked apart every guy that any other girl was dating. Who knew that they'd be so sensitive when it was one of *them* who was dating the guy? None of them had ever put it to the test before.

The only teasing was when Becky said, "Wouldn't you know, the one without boobs gets the first date."

"With a Chinese guy," said Lex. "Chinese women don't have boobs, either, so he probably thinks women who got 'em are, like, alien." That was as close to disparaging as either of them ever got.

She'd gone on a couple more dates with Jake Wu and her life was actually looking livable when there was another pep rally and she ducked out of it after making sure she'd been seen by the attendance people and instead of going out to the grove, she went around by the buses. It was way early for that, the drivers were still over in a group chatting and smoking and whatever else it was drivers did. But when she got on the bus it didn't actually register with her that she was alone.

Not until a couple of Nazis got on and it was obvious that it wasn't an accident, they had gotten on this particular bus at this particular time because they knew she was there and they knew she was alone.

"Hey, Deeny," said Truman Hunter. With a name like that he should have been manly, but instead he had kind of a receding chin but everybody knew his folks had a *lot* of money and it made him cool by default.

"Hey," said Deeny. And made an instant decision. She stood up. "I guess Becky and Lex are running late so I'm going to . . ."

Truman got right in her face, his body up against hers. Either she had to let him press against her, or sit back down.

She sat.

"She changed her mind," said Ryan Wacker. The kind of guy who scared offensive linemen on opposing football teams. Ryan knelt on the seat in front of hers as Truman sat down beside her, pressing her against the wall of the bus.

"Leave me alone, asshole," she said fiercely.

"We were just curious about what it was some old guy found so fascinating. We just wanted a look, you know? The magical mystery tour."

And while he was talking, like they had planned it out—or done it before—Ryan Wacker's hands flashed out and caught her wrists and pinned them against the back of her seat, while Truman got his hands under her sweater and pushed it up, snagging her bra on the way and pushing it up, too, so her chest was bare in front of them and Truman said, "Well, it can't have been the boobs, unless she's got another pair stashed somewhere, cause these are for shit," and Ryan laughed, and Deeny didn't even think of screaming because she didn't want anybody to see her like this, to know she had been so humiliated, that it had been so *easy* to humiliate her. She just wanted them to finish whatever they were going to do and go away.

Truman got her pants unzipped and unbuttoned, but she braced her legs against the seat in front and squirmed as best she could to keep him from getting her pants down.

"Look, she's getting into it," said Truman.

But Ryan, who had the job of trying to control her, wasn't amused. His fingers pressed into her wrists until she thought he was going to snap her bones it hurt so bad and he whispered "Hold still sweetheart" like he was her lover. And then it was only seconds till her pants and underpants were down around her ankles and Truman had his hand between her legs and she was crying helplessly and then the bus rocked just a little bit as the driver got on.

"I don't know what the hell you kids are doing but not on my bus, got it?"

He hadn't finished the sentence before Truman had her sweater pulled back down and all of a sudden he and Ryan were both standing up, blocking the driver's view of her while she pulled up her pants and rezipped them and then reached under her sweater and pulled her bra back down into place.

"Friend of ours was crying," said Truman, "and we were trying to make her feel better."

"I know exactly what you were doing, asshole," said the driver. "And I also know your big asshole buddy is a football player but here's a clue, boys. You're just high school tough, and that's pure pussy to me. I was in the Gulf War killing badass Iraqis with my bare hands when you were still holding Mommy's hand to go wee-wee in the girls' bathroom, so please, please try something."

"You got us wrong," said Ryan.

Deeny felt Truman's breath on her face. "Say anything and I'll f—— you with a file," he whispered.

She turned her face away from him.

"Call me anytime," he said, loud enough this time for the driver to hear. "I'm always willing to listen."

"Get away from her, asshole," said the driver. "Now."

Truman waited just a moment longer, to show how free he was. Then he sauntered down the aisle. It was small satisfaction to Deeny that when they passed him and started down the steps, he planted his foot on Truman's ass and shoved them both out onto the parking lot.

Truman bounded up, limping but too mad to let the pain stop him. "You just f——ed yourself, big man, you just lost your job!" Ryan was trying to get him to shut up.

The driver leaned out the door. "You think that girl is scared of you, but if you try to get me fired, you just see what she says to the board of inquiry. Think she'll stand by you?"

Truman looked at her. Ryan looked at her. She thought of Truman with a file in his hands, while Ryan held her against the ground. She thought of how it felt to have him touch her. Look at her naked. Mock her to her face.

She held up both hands, displaying one finger on each. One for each of them.

They went away.

The bus driver came back to her. "You OK?" he asked. "You OK?"

And she just kept nodding until she could finally control her voice enough to say, "Really, please, I'm fine."

"They get away with shit like that because they're in school and Daddy's got money, but someday they're going to go after somebody with a gun and the gun won't care how much money the family has or how good their lawyers are, because lawyers can't bring assholes back from the dead, much as they'd like to try."

"You," said Deeny, "are a poet."

He grinned. She managed a half-assed smile back.

And then sat there while other kids piled onto the bus and then emptied back out, stop by stop, until there were only six kids left and it was her stop.

She went into the house. Nobody was home, of course. Nobody to talk to, but she wasn't going to talk to them anyway. Not to them, not to Lex or Becky, not yet anyway, and not to Jake Wu, not ever to him. Not to anybody.

Except there she was in her room, naked and wet from the fifteen minutes in the shower, three times soaping herself and rinsing it off and she still felt dirty, there she was naked and it wasn't her underwear she was getting out of her drawer, it was this, this cellphone, whose batteries were probably run down, yeah just one little bar, not ten seconds worth of battery, but she pressed PHONE OPTIONS, RINGER OPTIONS, RING TONES, TEST, and then OK.

It rang. She held it up to her ear.

And he answered. "Deeny, I'm so sorry, I'm so sorry."

All she could do was cry. He knew. She didn't even have to tell him. He knew.

After a while she could talk, and even though he knew she told him. How it felt. How ugly and dirty.

"Because it was by force," he said. "It was meant to degrade you. It wouldn't feel that way with a man you loved. It wouldn't be that way."

"You're only saying that because you wanted to do the same thing, all along, that's what you wanted."

"No," he said. "No, Deeny. I only wanted you to have whatever it was you wanted. A lover on the phone, that's what you wanted, and I could do that, so I did."

"Who *are* you? Why do I get you on the phone when I call *nothing*?"

"I'm nothing," he said. "I'm ashes. I'm dust. I'm an exhaled breath."

"What's your *name*!" she demanded.

"My name is Listener," he said. "My name is The One Who Always Cares."

"Bullshit!" she screamed into the phone, and then repeated it about six times, louder each time until she felt like she was ripping her own throat out from the inside.

"My name," he whispered, "is Carson. Vaughn Carson. I lived all of twenty-five years and I died when I put my car into a tree and it killed the girl who was with me because all I could think about was showing off to her so maybe I could get laid that night and she said, Please slow down, you can't control the car at this speed, so I went faster and I can't . . . leave here. I don't want to. I can't go on because if I do I'll have to face . . . what I did."

"You just faced it," said Deeny. "Telling me."

"No," he said. "You don't know. All I did was *tell* you. I can't—I'm a coward. That's what we are, the ones who linger here. Cowards. We just can't go on. We're too ashamed."

"So you haunt cellphones?" She couldn't keep the derision out of her voice. Did he expect her to believe this? Of course, she *did* believe it, because it made more sense than any other possibility that had occurred to her. So the dead live on. And some of them can't bear to take the next step, so here they are.

"We never haunt *things*," he said. "Not houses, not any *thing*. It's people. We have to find some way to make ourselves . . . noticeable. To people. Somebody who knows how to look at other people and really see them. Somebody who's willing to accept that a person might be where a person couldn't be. Or a voice might be coming out of something that shouldn't have a voice."

"Why me?" she said. "And besides, Lex heard you, too."

"Lex heard what she expected *you* to hear. Not the same voice, but the *idea* of the same voice. The voice you were hungry for."

"I wasn't 'hungry' for a man," she said.

"You were hungry to have people think of you differently at school. But what you chose, what you *pretended,* was a man. A lover on the phone. And I could do that. I remember it . . . not how it felt because I don't even have the memory of my senses, but I remember that I once felt it, whatever it was, and I liked it, and so I talked about what I did that I knew made girls . . . shiver. And ask for more. And let me do more. I remembered that. It's what you wanted. I couldn't miss it—you were screaming it."

"No I wasn't," she said. "I never said it to anybody."

"I told you, I can't *hear.* I can only *know.* You were like a siren, moving through the streets. You were so lonely and angry and hurt. And I—"

You pitied me. She didn't say it into the phone, because the battery was already dead, and anyway, he could hear her whether she spoke aloud or not.

"No," he said. "Not really. No, I was attracted to you. I thought, here's what she needs, I could do that."

"Why bother?" she said.

"I've got anything else to do?" he asked.

"Granting wishes for sex-starved ugly teenage girls?"

"See, that's the thing," he said. "You're not ugly."

"I thought you couldn't see."

"I can't. But I know what *you* see, and you're completely wrong, the very things that you hate about yourself are the things that seem most sweet to me. So young, fragile, so real, so kind."

Oh, right, Miss Bitch herself, let's check this with Ms. Reymondo and see what *she* thinks.

"Stop listening to Treadmarks," said the voice. The man. Carson. Vaughn.

"You really *are* raiding my brain," she said.

"You know what? Your father is really just doing the best he can to deal with the fact that he lusts for you. You haunt his dreams."

"Oh, make me puke," she said. "That's such a lie."

"He never actually thought it through, but by treating you so badly, he guarantees that you'll hate him and so he'll never be able to get near you and try the things he keeps dreaming of doing. He hates himself every time he sees you. It's very complicated and it doesn't make him a good father, but at least he's not as bad a father as he could have been."

"What, were you a shrink?"

"Come on, I've been dead for seventeen years, I've had time to figure out what makes people tick. Never had a clue while I was alive, no one ever does."

"So how many other girls have you talked dirty to."

"You're the first."

"Come on."

"The first who ever heard me."

"Lex was first."

"She heard me because you wanted her to."

Deeny began to cry again. "I didn't really. I didn't know what I wanted."

"Nobody ever does. So we try for what we *think* we want and hope it works out. Like me and Dawn. I thought I wanted to impress her so she'd sleep with me. All I did was scare her and then kill her. That wasn't what I wanted. What I really wanted was . . . to marry her and make babies with her and be a father and watch my kids grow up and if I'd married her, if I hadn't killed us, then maybe our first child would have been a girl and maybe she would have looked like you and when she was so lost and angry and hungry and sad, then maybe I could have put my arms around her, not like your poor father wants to, but like a *real* father, my arms like a safe place for you to hide in, my words to you nothing but the truth, but the truth put in such a way that it could heal you. Show you yourself with different eyes, so you could see who you really are. The dreamer, the poet, the singer, the wit. The beauty—yes, don't laugh at me, you don't know how men see women. There are boys who only see whether you look like the right magazine covers, but men look for the whole woman, they really do, *I* did, and you *are* beautiful, exactly as you are, your body and mind and your kindness and loyalty and that sharp edge you have, and the light of life inside you, it's so beautiful, if only you could see what I *know* you are."

"The only guy who sees it is a dead guy on the phone," she said.

He chuckled. "So far, maybe you're right," he said. "Because you're still in high school, and the only males you know are just boys. Except a few. This Wu kid, he's not bad. He saw you."

"Only after I got a reputation as a whore."

"No, I know better than that. I really *know.* He saw you *before.* Before me. He just took a while to work up the courage."

"Because his friends would make fun of him if he—"

"The courage to face a woman in all her beauty and ask if she'd give a part of it to him, just for a few hours, and then a few hours more. You don't know how hard that is. It's why the assholes get all the best women—because they don't understand either the women or themselves well enough to know how utterly undeserving they are. But look at the guys who did that to you today. Look what they confessed about themselves. They already knew that the only way they could get any part of your beauty and your pride was to take it by force, because a woman like you would never give it to trivial little animals like them. All they could do was tear at you, rip it up a little. But they could never *have* it, because a woman of true beauty would never even think of sharing it with *them.*"

To her surprise, the words he said flowed into her like truth and even though they didn't take away what had happened that afternoon on the bus, it took away some of the sting. It didn't hurt so bad. She could breathe without gasping at the pain and shame of it.

"Now I know what I wanted," she said.

"What?"

"On the phone," Deeny said. "What I wanted on the phone."

"Not a lover?"

"No," she said.

And in her mind, she did not say the word aloud, but she thought it all the same, knowing he would hear.

What I needed was a father.

"Can I call you again?" she said. "Please?"

"Whenever you want, Deeny," he said.

"Until you decide you can go on," she said. "It's OK with me if you go, whenever you want, that's OK. But while you're still here, I can call?"

"Just pick up the phone. You don't even have to press the buttons. It doesn't even have to have any juice. Just pick up the phone and I'll be there."

And he was.

Six years later. Deeny was married. Not to Jake Wu, though they came close, until it became clear that his family really did expect that his career would swallow her up and she realized she couldn't live that way, and couldn't bear their disappointment if she didn't. But the guy she married was just like Jake. Not in any obvious superficial way, but just like him all the same, in the way he treated her, in the things he wanted from her. Only he didn't want her to become a support for his life. The man she married wanted them to support each other. And now she had his baby, their firstborn child, a girl, and she could see that he loved the baby, that he was going to be a great father.

And that was why she came to the cemetery. She had finally found Vaughn Carson, even though he had never told her where his body was. Maybe he didn't know, or maybe he didn't care, or maybe he simply didn't notice how much she wondered. But she found him, anyway, in a cemetery two states away. How he got from where he lived and died to where she was as a teenager—maybe she really had been calling out like a siren. Or maybe it was one hunger calling to another.

However he had found her, now she'd found him back, and here she was, standing at his grave, a single red rose in one hand, a cellphone in the other.

"You're so silly," he said when she opened the phone. "It's just dust now. Dust in a box."

"I just wanted to tell you," she said. "That my husband is a wonderful father."

"I know," he said. "I told you he would be when I gave you my permission to marry him."

"No, you're not hearing me. It isn't that he's a wonderful father, it's that I *know* he's a wonderful father. How do you think I know what a wonderful father even is?"

She didn't have to say, Because I had you. She knew he heard what was in her heart.

"So what I'm saying," she said, "is that you've had that daughter. Not the way you wanted. Not with Dawn. But you found a fatherless girl and you led her out of despair and instead of marrying somebody like my own father because I thought that's what I deserved, I married somebody . . . good."

"Good," he said. His voice was only a whisper.

"And so," she said, "it's done. You can go on."

"Go on," he said.

"You can face whatever it is you have to face, because you've done the thing you hungered most to do. You've done it, and you can go on."

"Go on," he whispered.

"And I will love you forever, Vaughn Carson, even when you aren't on the phone anymore. Because you *were* on the phone when I needed you."

"Needed you," he echoed.

She laid the rose on the engraved plate that was set in concrete at the head of the grave. It softened the stainless steel of death a little. Even though the rose, too, was dying now. It was still, for this brief moment, vivid and red as blood.

She took the phone from her ear and kissed it. "Good-bye, Daddy," she said. "I'll miss you. But I'm glad I had you for as long as I did."

"Long as I did," he echoed. And then one last sigh. "Good-bye." And she thought she heard something else as if he had laid it gently inside her heart instead of speaking it aloud. "My daughter."

NOTES ON "INVENTING LOVERS ON THE PHONE"

It turns out that Janis Ian and I had been fans of each other's work for a long time without suspecting the other felt the same way. I, of course, memorized all the words to "At Seventeen" and played her first album over and over. But being a consumer of pop music, not a connoisseur, I had no idea of what had happened to her after that wonderful early work, or what course her life had taken.

But we made contact—both AOL users, it turned out—and emailed each other until we had a chance to meet at a concert she gave in Raleigh, North Carolina. I brought my daughter Emily with me and we loved the concert. Her new songs were better than ever, and Janis is a stunning performer on the stage, a born actress.

She took time to visit with us after the show and the friendship was cemented. A while later, when we held the first (and only) EnderCon—a convention for fans of *Ender's Game*—Janis not only came, she performed and offered a master class. Talk about generous!

I wasn't her only friend in the world of sci-fi, though; with Mike Resnick she was editing an anthology of science fiction and fantasy stories based on her songs (*Stars: Original Stories Based on the Songs of Janis Ian*). When she invited me, of course I accepted.

It was a pleasure to listen to everything and find the story I wanted to write.

Oddly enough, though, I kept coming back to a single phrase in "At Seventeen" about invented lovers on the phone. That lyric had haunted me as a teenager, too, the idea of being so lonely that you *pretend* to be talking to someone just to hear yourself in a conversation. And the "vague obscenities" part—well, that song came out just as I was busy inventing sexual desire (every teenager thinks that he invented it) and I understood that, too. This was long before I ever heard any public mention of the idea of "phone sex," but Janis Ian, natural-born sci-fi writer that she is, had not only thought of it, she had taken it a step further.

When Janis wrote that lyric we all used telephones that were tied to the wall. Now it's cellphones—but cellphones make the sad little girl of her song all the more believable. Now she has her phone there at school, and she can walk around where others might hear her and pretend she has a boyfriend who is too cool or too old to attend this crappy high school. I liked this girl, the sad defiance of her attitude.

Of course, it was an anthology of sci-fi and fantasy stories. Janis said they didn't have to be speculative fiction, but the literary story I first intended to write would have belonged in a different kind of publication. So I found the daemon in the cellphone and wrote this tale.

By the way, at the time I wrote this, individual cellphone numbers did *not* show up on caller ID, the way they do now.

WATERBABY

First off you got to know about Tamika, how it was with her and water. First time she got into a pool, she was only two, we had those tube things around her arms to hold her up and me and Sondra, we were both there in the water, she was our baby and no way she was going to be out of our sight for a second, so we were both there kind of holding her up and making sure those air things really kept her from sinking. So Sondra was kind of holding her on one side and me on the other and Tamika just laughed and shrieked and we could feel how she was kicking and wiggling her arms and it sort of came to me how maybe by holding on to her I was holding her back, and so I let go, figuring Sondra had her on the other side anyway, so she'd be safe. Only later on Sondra tells me she had the same thought at the same moment and *she* let go and right away, Tamika starts moving forward through the water, kicking her legs, pulling with her arms, smiling and keeping her head above water and there was no mistake about it, she was swimming. By the end of that day we had those tubes off her arms and never looked back. She was born for the water, she was born to swim.

It's been like that ever since. We just couldn't keep her away from swimming pools. We called her our waterbaby, she'd catch sight of a pool and one way or another, in five seconds she'd be in the water. We took to dressing her all summer in a swimsuit instead of underwear cause if we didn't, she'd go in fully dressed or stark naked, but she was going in, right now. Anybody with a pool, they were Tamika's best friends whether Sondra and I liked them or not. At three years old she'd head on out the front door to go over to a house with a pool. We had to put locks high up on the door to keep her in. Sometimes it was scary, she loved the water so much, but we were proud, too, because that girl could swim, Your Honor. You had to see her. She'd go underwater quick as a fish, move like a blur, pop up so far from where she went under you'd be sure there had to be a second kid, nobody could move that fast. When she dove off the board— she was never afraid of heights as long as there was water under her—she was like a bird, but even so, when she slipped into the water it's like there wasn't even a splash, the water opened up to take her in. I can hardly think of her except soaking wet, drops glistening on her brown skin like jewels in the sunlight, smiling all the time, she was so beautiful, she was so happy.

Tamika said it all the time. "Oh, Daddy, oh Mama, I wish I didn't ever have to come out of the water. I wish I was a fish and I could *live* in the water." And Sondra would always say, "You're no fish, Tamika, you're just our own little waterbaby, we found you in a rain puddle and fished you out and took you home and dried you off and your daddy wanted to name you Tunafish but I said, No, she's Tamika." Said that all the time when Tamika was three and four. By the time Tamika was six, she'd say, "Oh, Mama, not that again," but she still loved to hear it.

Sondra and me, our dream was to make enough money to get a house with a pool so she didn't always have to go somewhere else to swim. But you know how it is, that wasn't going to happen. We used to joke that the closest thing to a swimming pool we'd ever have was the waterbed me and Sondra slept on. My parents thought we were crazy when we bought that bed. "Black people don't sleep on waterbeds," my daddy told me. "Black people have more sense with their dollars." I wish to Jesus I'd listened to my daddy.

It was a hot summer night, you know how it gets here in LA late in August, you got the ceiling fan going full blast and no covers on top of you but you still got sweat dripping all along your body like rain and your pajamas are soaked and you toss and turn all night and you're half the time dreaming and half the time thinking about work and problems and worries and you can't even tell where one leaves off and the other begins. And so that's why I thought it was a dream at first. I was there on the waterbed only something was moving under me. The bed was rocking a little and I thought that meant Sondra had gotten up or just lain back down or something, only it kept rocking and I could hear her breathing and she was asleep, and then I felt something bump into me. From below.

Like a fish in the water, a big fish, it bumped me hard. I was awake right away, only I wasn't sure I was awake, you know? How you're thinking that you're dreaming that you're awake, only maybe you are awake, only you know that it's still part of the dream? I felt something start pummeling me from below. Like fists punching straight up at me, pounding on my back from inside the waterbed. Hard enough to almost hurt. Little fists. And I got this picture in my mind of a mermaid trapped inside the waterbed, pounding on me to get me to get *off* and that's when I woke up, or anyway that's when I rolled over and got off the bed, and I was thinking, This dream's too much for me. I got up and went to the bathroom and took a piss and got a drink and I was kind of shaking from the dream, it was so real, and then I thought, I gotta look in on the kids, and I knew it was dumb but whenever I felt afraid from a dream or a noise in the night, even if I knew it was nothing, I still had to look at the kids and make sure they were all right.

The boys were fine, the four-year-old, the two-year-old, breathing steady and soft in their beds. And from the door of Tamika's room she looked fine, too, in a jumble of covers, only then I thought, how can she stand to have so much blanket on her in this heat? So I went over to see if she was maybe sweating too much and I ought to pull off the covers and she wasn't there. Just her pillow and the covers all wadded up where she must have kicked them in the night and a damp area on the sheets where she'd been sweating and dreaming just like the rest of us.

She must have gotten up to go to the bathroom, I thought.

Only I knew it wasn't that at all. I knew right then that I hadn't been dreaming. All the times Tamika had wished she was a fish in the water, tonight somehow she'd dreamed her way or wished her way into the only pool of water in the house that was big enough to hold her and she had somehow realized where she was and knew it was me sleeping right above her and she'd pounded on me to wake up and save her and what was I doing still standing here in her room feeling the sheet when she was drowning?

I knew I was crazy—that's why I started calling her name, just shouting it, even though I knew it would wake up the boys and wake up Sondra, because I was still hoping I was wrong, that she'd hear me and she'd call out to me from the bathroom or from the kitchen, "I'm in here, Daddy, what's wrong?" only she didn't make a sound but I keep on yelling her name so maybe there in the water she can hear me and she'll know I'm coming. I run into the kitchen and open the high cupboard where we keep the sharp knives and I get the big heavy meat-chopping knife cause I know I can get that one through the rubber of the waterbed and then I'm heading back to my bedroom and Sondra sees me coming with this big knife shouting Tamika's name and I don't know what she's thinking but she grabs me and tries to stop me and I just flung her away, that's why she had that cut on her head, I didn't hit her, I was only thinking, Don't slow me down, my baby's in that water and I've got to get her out.

So the boys are crying and Sondra's crying but all I know is, Tamika's been under there too long, the whole time I was peeing and getting a drink and looking at the boys and checking her bed and getting this knife, she's been under there alone in the dark scared to death and trying to hold her breath. She could hold her breath a long time, but who knows how much air she had in her when she found herself under there? It's not like diving in when you can take a deep breath.

That was all going through my mind while I'm pulling off the sheet and the pad and I raise up the knife and I think, I can't just jab down into this waterbed, I don't know where Tamika is, I don't want this knife to go right on through into my baby. So I press down on the corner and make sure she's not under there and then I jab with the knife, and that mattress skin is tough, it just shies away under the knife, it's not till the third time that I get that knife through and the water starts gushing out and I'm pulling the blade through the mattress, ripping through and now it cuts real smooth and Sondra isn't crying anymore, she's saying, "Where's Tamika? Where's Tamika?" Well I cut about a five-foot slice along my side of the waterbed and there's water sloshing around, a real stink from the algae and the chemicals, it's like the filthiest industrial pond and I'm thinking, My baby's in that muck, I've got to get her out. So I plunge in my arms up to my neck, some of that stuff sloshes right into my mouth and I spit it out but I can't feel her under there and my first thought is, Thank the Lord, it was just a dream.

But I know it's not a dream. I yell to Sondra, "Push her over here," and Sondra knows what I'm talking about by now, she knows Tamika didn't answer me when I called, so she doesn't ask me what I'm talking about, she just gets on her side of the bed and pushes straight down onto the mattress and she cries out cause she felt Tamika under the water and Sondra says "I pushed her!" and right then I feel her bump up against my hands there in the dark water, and I grab on to her ankle and I start pulling and then with my left hand I find her arm and I pull now with both arms and she just comes sloshing right out, water all over everything, but I got my baby out of there.

No, I'm not thinking about how she got in there, all I'm thinking is, How long was she under? Is she breathing? And no, she wasn't breathing. And I start yelling to Sondra, "Call 911!" And she grabs the phone and I hear her calling while I'm pressing on Tamika's chest and water whooshes out of her mouth and then I go back and forth between pressing on her and blowing air into her little mouth and I'm still doing that when the paramedics come and pull me out of the way and they take over and get her on oxygen and you already heard them testify about how they saved her life.

Or partly saved her, anyway. There was brain damage from being without air so long, and so she doesn't walk right and she has a hard time talking and she's forgotten how to read but that's still our little Tamika in there, we know she's there, our little waterbaby, she's just got to learn how to do all those things again.

As for what that social worker said, I didn't confess to anything, but I did say what she said I said. Because she was explaining to us how our little girl wasn't coming home till they could find out what really happened that night, and I knew she didn't believe us because who would? Who could believe this story? How does a little girl who's having dreams on a hot night suddenly get inside a waterbed mattress? She's dreaming, she's wishing she was in the water, and suddenly her wish comes true? If I hadn't cut into that waterbed myself, if I hadn't felt her fists pounding me from inside it, I would never have believed it. But Sondra saw that there wasn't no cut in that mattress till the cut she saw me make, and she pushed our baby over to me, she felt it, she knows what's true, and we were the only ones there, and if I was making up some lie to tell you, don't you think I'd make up a better one than this?

My lawyer, he as much as told me to make up something better. He says to me, You got to realize that it isn't what's true that matters, it's what a jury can actually believe, and nobody's going to believe what you're telling me. And he starts telling me all these maybes, like Maybe you dropped a ring into the waterbed so you cut into it to try to get it out and maybe your daughter thought she could help you find it and when your back was turned she went into the water to look for the ring and you didn't realize she was trapped under there until too late.

But I said to him, When I put my hand on God's word and promise the Lord God that I'll tell the truth, that's what I'll do, even if it means I lose my baby, even if it means I go to jail, because my family needs the Lord now more than ever, more than they need me, so I'm not going to spit in the eye of Jesus. I will tell it the way it happened. And as for that so-called confession, all I ever said was, "Lay it all on me. I'll move out of the house so you'll know Tamika will be safe, but you let her go home to her mama and her brothers." I didn't confess to nothing, but I took all their suspicions on myself so that when I left the house they'd let her go back home. And I kept my word, I haven't come near the house this whole time, Sondra and I talk on the phone and I've talked to Tamika on the phone cause even though she doesn't talk so good she can still hear me and I can tell her how much I love her. And no matter how this trial comes out, I know that my baby said to me, one time on the phone she said, "Thank you Daddy," and I knew she was thanking me for waking up when she pounded on me and for getting her out of the water.

If I hadn't believed in the impossible then I would never have cut into that waterbed. I would have stripped off the sheet and seen there was no break in the mattress and I would've known there's no way she could be in there, and we would have searched the whole house and yard for Tamika and called the cops and woke the neighbors and after a while somebody would have realized there was some big lump inside the waterbed and if we'd got one of the cops to cut into the mattress or a paramedic or even a neighbor, with a bunch of witnesses, then I wouldn't be on trial, it'd just be some story in *Weekly World News* and I wouldn't be trying to make some jury believe the impossible.

But my baby would be dead.

So I'm glad I'm here and I'm glad I'm on trial, because I'd rather go to jail and never see my baby again, as long as I know she's alive and she's with her mama and her brothers and she's got a chance to be herself again. But I'd rather be with her. My boys need me, and she needs me. I'm a good father to my family, I never raised a hand against them, I work hard and I make a fair living. Put me in jail and that's all gone, Sondra has to go to work or live off welfare or what her family and my family can spare. But whatever we go through, that's fine, we thank Jesus all the same, because our baby's alive.

And maybe I do deserve to go to jail. Cause I'm not the one who put her in the water, but I am the one who pulled her out too late.

NOTES ON "WATERBABY"

This story was born in the process of inventing *Magic Street*. The premise of the novel is that magic erupts into the world in the middle of Baldwin Hills, an upper-middle-class black neighborhood in Los Angeles. But what form would such an eruption take? How would people know that something terrible was loose among them?

Wishes, I thought. Their wishes come true, but in horrible ways that distort the lives of everyone they love.

Having slept on a waterbed for many years, I was aware of the way that early waterbeds could get a wave action going. When you're lying on the surface of something that ripples and undulates like water, you're bound to imagine a whole aquarium of aquatic life underneath you. What if you felt something bump into you? Something large under the water, in a place where it couldn't possibly be? That idea had been in my mind for years; now, thinking of wishes gone awry, I was able to put that old nasty thought to good use. What if the large swimmer in your waterbed was your own child, the one who loves to swim, whose secret wish is to swim like a fish inside . . . the nearest body of water large enough to hold you?

Horrible enough, but then the aftermath: No one would believe you.

After I wrote this first-person account, I had no idea how to use it in the novel. Would I interrupt the book with first-person stories like this? For a couple of years I had myself persuaded that I'd go that route. But another part of me recognized this immediately as a retreat from the novel I *should* write. For every time the narrative flow was interrupted by these first-person tales, the action of the novel would stop cold. The readers would quickly realize that these first-person stories wouldn't go anywhere. They were there just to show how cool and arty the author is.

So instead, when I wrote *Magic Street* I referred to the incidents in this story and used these people as characters, but I did not use the actual story—I didn't stop the forward movement of the third-person narrative of *Magic Street*.

It's easy for an author to subvert his own work by showing off his own dazzling licks as a writer. But when you're writing fiction, there's some serious work going on—and it's not just the writer doing it. When I write the words of my narrative, each reader is using them as a guide to create, in his own mind, the sights and sounds, the causes and effects, the characters and their feelings and pasts. I'm guiding the reader into a small village of characters with more or less relationship with the world the reader already knows, and if I'm doing a good job, the reader is able to collaborate with me easily in creating this sequence of memories.

So why should I interrupt the reader in this good work, which both of us are enjoying, and require the reader to drop that thread and pick up a completely new one, in a different voice and point of view, when I could accomplish the same task without all the distraction? When I make the reader turn away from the story and characters and notice *me* and the tricks *I'm* doing, then what am I? I'm like a movie director who is constantly distracting the audience with odd camera angles or weird color effects, just to prove what an artiste I am. I'm like a playwright who jumps up on the stage after a particularly funny or moving scene and shouts, "Don't look at those actors, look at *me*. I'm the one who wrote that scene you liked so well! Clap for *meeeeeeeee*!"

In other words, it's a pitiful kind of neediness that leads a writer to be more interested in impressing his readers than in allowing them to fully involve themselves in the construction of the vicarious memories I promised to give them. It's easy and cheap to dazzle the reader; it's hard work to stay invisible and guide the reader seamlessly through the experience of the tale.

Which is not to say that I never succumb to the temptation. Particularly in short stories, where the time invested in the tale is so much less, I'm as likely as anyone to play a few games and have some fun.

But most of the time, I'm quite serious about what I write, and so, like a good playwright or director, I stay off the stage, I stay out of the shot, I let the readers go about the business of living the vicarious lives I've created for them.

That's why this story still existed as a separate entity. When *Galaxy Online* asked for a story, this is one that was available, because its words would never appear in the pages of *Magic Street*. I thought this was a very good story—but it didn't belong in what I wanted to be an even better book.

KEEPER OF LOST DREAMS

Mack Street was not born. He was, in the words of the immortal bard, "from the womb untimely ripped."

Unfortunately, there was no evil Macbeth that needed slaying by someone who was not "of woman born." Still, Mack Street always knew that his life had a purpose—perhaps a great one, perhaps a small one, but a purpose all the same. How else could he explain the fact that he was alive at all?

He did not know why his mother decided to abort him, or why she waited so long. Was the abortion a spiteful vengeance when his father left her only a few months before their baby's due date? Was she merely indecisive, and it took her seven months to make up her mind to get rid of the kid?

And why, when she realized the appalling fact that he was breathing, perhaps even crying those weak mews of a premature baby, did she take him all the way to Baldwin Park, far from the nearest path, and cover him with leaves so that it would take a miracle for someone to find him and keep him alive?

Still, he *was* found, by a couple of boys in search of a safe place to smoke their first joints. Just before they would have discovered that they had been cheated, and the "weed" was, in fact, merely a weed, a common and slightly nauseating one at that, the smaller boy saw the pile of leaves move, and he pulled them away to reveal a naked baby that looked too small to be real.

The bigger boy insisted that it *wasn't* real, or at least wasn't human. "Everybody knows that baby coyotes look human," he said.

"You telling me this one gone grow up to be a niggah coyote?" said the smaller boy.

"Come on," said the bigger boy. "Do the smoke first, then we tell somebody about the baby."

"If it do us like it do my big brother, we ain't gone tell nobody nothing for about half a day. This a tiny baby, he gonna die."

"Little dick like that, he ain't no niggah," said the bigger boy, but already he was putting the supposed weed back in the Ziploc bag. "You want to take him somewhere, you do it without old Raymo, I don't want nobody asking me questions when I got a bag of weed on me."

"Bag of weed your mama's black ass," said the smaller boy. "I bet they rolled up broccoli or something anyway, they ain't gone give *us* nothing."

"Don't you go talking about my mama's ass, Ceese."

Which might have led to an argument, seeing how they were both on edge and a little pissed off at each other, but Ceese picked up the baby and it wiggled and mewed and he thought, Just like a baby kitten, and then he remembered how Raymo once took a baby kitten and stepped on its head just to see it squish. Ceese decided not to stick around, even though the thing with the kitten was a couple of years ago and Raymo had puked his guts out and threw the brain-covered shoe away and got a licking for "losing" it. You just never knew what Raymo was going to do. As his mama often told him at the top of her voice, he wasn't the kind of guy who ever seemed to "learn his lesson."

So Ceese took off with the aborted baby and ran all the way home and when he showed it to *his* mama she screamed and ran next door and woke up Miz Smitcher, who was a night shift nurse, and Miz Smitcher called the emergency room to alert them, and then put Ceese, still holding the baby, in the back seat of her Civic, belted him in, and drove like a crazy woman all the way to the hospital, cussing the whole time about how people ought to have a license to own a uterus.

"People so crazy they won't let them buy a gun can go right out and make a baby without asking anybody's permission, and when they *get* a baby they just throw it away."

Then Miz Smitcher had a sudden ugly thought and leaned over the seat to glare at Ceese. "That ain't *your* baby, is it, boy?"

"Watch the road, dammit!" yelled Ceese, seeing how the big truck in front of them had come to a stop and Miz Smitcher hadn't.

Miz Smitcher slammed on the brake so fast that Ceese got flung forward till his chin smacked against the seat, and of course the baby had already flown out of his hands, bounced off the back of the front seat, and dropped like a rock onto the floor.

"It's dead!" screamed Ceese.

"Pick it up, you coprocephalic!" shouted Miz Smitcher.

Ceese leaned over and picked up the baby.

"Is it all right?" said Miz Smitcher.

"Ain't you gone ask if *I'm* all right?" demanded Ceese.

"I *know* you all right, cause you giving me sass and acting stupid! Now what about that baby!"

"He's breathing," said Ceese. "You got so many McDonald's wrappers on the floor, I guess he didn't hit all that hard."

"That baby plain determined not to die," said Miz Smitcher. She flipped off the people behind her, who were honking their brains out. Then she turned on her blinkers like she thought that would make her car an ambulance, caught up with the truck, whipped around it, and kept on going at top speed till she lurched to a stop in the turnaround at the emergency entrance.

Which is how Mack Street happened not to die under a pile of leaves in Baldwin Park, and instead got fostered out to Ceese's neighborhood.

Well, technically, he was fostered to Miz Smitcher, who took to calling him her little miracle, though more likely she felt guilty about jamming the brakes and throwing him onto the floor and she wanted to make sure if there was some brain damage or something, she'd be able to make it up to him.

But Miz Smitcher worked nights and slept days, and baby Mack slept nights and yelled his lungs out while she was trying to sleep, so it turned out he was sort of fostered to whatever mother was home and willing to take him. Not a one of them took him to heart the way Miz Smitcher did, so mostly he just lay around until somebody remembered to feed him or wipe his butt, except when somebody's kid decided he'd be a great baby doll or a cool squirmy football and incorporated him into a game.

Some folks said that that was why Miz Smitcher gave him the last name Street—because he was raised by most every family on the block. Wasn't a soul asked, and so not a soul was told, that Street was Miz Smitcher's last name before she got married and divorced, and Mack was the nickname of her favorite uncle. Mack didn't find it out till after she died and he went through her things. She just wasn't much of a talker or a self-explainer. If she loved you, you'd have to guess it from her cooking and buying clothes for you, cause you'd never know it from a word or a touch.

Still, despite the lack of affection in Mack's life, he certainly didn't lack for stimulation. Being fed mud pies or flying through the air as a forward pass is bound to keep a baby somewhat alert. By the time he started school he was pretty much fearless. He'd take any dare, seeing as how there was nothing he could be asked to eat or do that he hadn't already eaten or done worse. "There's an angel watching over that boy," said Miz Smitcher, when somebody told her of another of the crazy things Mack did.

Dare-taking was what he did to win a place, however strange it was, among the kids at school. It wasn't where he lived.

For Mack, the real excitement in his life came in dreams. It wasn't till he was seven years old that he first found out that other people only dreamed when they were asleep. For Mack, dreams had a way of popping up day or night. It was the reason the other kids sometimes saw him slow down in the middle of a game and go sort of slack-jawed, staring off into space. When that happened, kids would just say, "Mack's gone," and go off and continue their game without him.

Most dreams he could shrug off and pay no heed to—they weren't worth missing out on recess time or getting barked at by grumpy teachers in school, the kind who actually expected their lessons to be listened to.

But some dreams captivated him, even though he didn't understand them.

There was one in particular, it started when Mack was ten. He was in a vehicle—he wasn't sure it was a car, because a car shouldn't be able to drive on roads like this. It started out on a dirt road, with ragged-looked trees around, kind of a dry California kind of woods. The road began to sink down while the ground stayed level on both sides, till they were dirt walls or steep hills, and sometimes buttes. And the road began to get rocky, only the rocks were all the size of cobblestones, rounded like river rocks, and they hurtled along—Mack and whoever else was in the vehicle—as if the rocks were pavement.

The rocks glistened black in the sunlight, like they'd been wet recently. The cobbly road started to go up again, steeper and steeper, and then it narrowed suddenly and they were almost jammed in between high cliffs with a thin trickly waterfall coming from the crease where the cliffs joined together.

So they backed out—and here was where Mack knew it wasn't him driving, because he didn't know how to back a car. If it was a car.

Backed out and headed down until the canyon was wide enough that they could turn around, and then they rushed along until they found the place where they had gone wrong. When the road reached the lowest point, there was a narrow passage off to the left leading farther down, and now Mack realized that this wasn't no road, this was a river that just happened to be dry. And the second he thought of that, he heard distant thunder and he knew it was raining up in the high hills and that little trickle of a waterfall was about to become a torrent, and there'd be water coming down the other branch of the river, too, and here they were trapped in this narrow canyon barely wide enough for their vehicle, it was going to fill up with water and throw them down the canyon, bashing against the cliffs, rounding them off just like one of the river rocks.

Sure enough here comes the water, and it's just as bad as he thought, spinning head over heels, getting slammed this way and that, and out the windows all he can see is roiling water and stones and then the dead bodies of the other people in the vehicle as they got washed out and crushed and broken against the canyon walls and suddenly . . .

The vehicle shoots out into open space, and there's no cliffs anymore, just air on every side and a lake below him and the vehicle plunges into the lake and sinks lower and lower and Mack thinks, I got to get out of here, but he can't find a way to open it, not a door, not a window. Deeper and deeper until the vehicle comes to rest on the bottom of the lake with fish swimming up and bumping into the windows and then a naked woman comes up, not sexy or anything, just naked because she never heard of clothes, she swims up and looks at him and smiles and when she touches the window, it breaks and the water slowly oozes in and surrounds him and he swims out and she kisses his cheek and says, Welcome home, I missed you so much.

Mack didn't have to take a psychology class to guess what this dream was about. It was about getting born way too soon. It was about getting to the lowest point, completely alone, and then he'd find his mother, she'd come to him and open the door and let him come back into her life.

He believed his dream so much that he was sure he knew now what his mother looked like, skin so black it was almost blue, but with a thinnish nose, like those men and women of Sudan in the *African Peoples* book at school. Maybe I *am* African, he thought. Not African-American, like the other black kids in his class, but truly African without a drop of white in him.

But then why would his mother have thrown him away?

Maybe it wasn't his mother. Maybe she was drugged and the baby was taken out of her and carried off and hidden and she doesn't even know he was ever alive, but Mack knew he would find her someday, because the dream was so real it had to be true.

Later he told the dream to a therapist—the one they sent him to about his "seizures," as they called those trances when he stopped to watch a dream. The therapist listened and nodded wisely and then explained to him, "Mack, dreams come from deep inside you, some chain of meaning so deep it has no words or pictures, so your brain dresses it up in pictures that it already knows. So from deep inside there's this idea of going down a passage that's both a river and a road, so your brain makes it into a canyon and when it starts to push you and push you, your brain puts water in the dream, forcing you out, and when the deep inner story says that you plunge out into air, then you see it as a plunge out of a canyon, and then who comes and saves you? Your mother."

"So you're saying this is the way my brain makes sense of my memory of being born," said Mack.

"That's one possible interpretation."

"There's another?"

"I haven't thought of it yet, but there might be."

"But it's my mother, anyway, like I always thought."

"I believe that in dreams, if it looks like your mother and you think it's your mother, it's your mother."

"Cool," said Mack. All he cared about was that he knew what his mother looked like. Mack was as black as they come, but his mother was even blacker, and that was cool. But if she was under water, then that wasn't so cool. He hoped that his dream didn't mean that she was drowned. Maybe it just meant she swam a lot.

Or maybe it didn't mean a damn thing.

That was the only one of his strong dreams in which he felt like himself, though, and the therapist didn't have any explanation for that. "What do you mean, you don't feel like yourself?"

"I mean that in the dreams, I'm not me. Except that one about the road that turns out to be a river."

"Well, who are you then?"

"Somebody different every time."

"Tell me about those dreams," the therapist said.

"I can't," said Mack. "That wouldn't be right."

"What do you mean? You can tell me anything."

"I can tell you *my* dreams," said Mack. "But these ones ain't mine."

The therapist thought that was totally crazy reasoning. "They're in your head, Mack. That makes them yours!"

And Mack couldn't explain why he knew that the therapist was wrong, and they weren't his own.

He just knew that when he dreamed about finding himself as a baby, about his hands reaching down and picking up this infant, it wasn't his dream, it was Ceese's. Ceese still lived in the neighborhood, but he didn't have much to do with Mack—it was Raymo who told the story all the time about how he and Ceese found Mack. The way Raymo told it, Ceese wanted to leave the baby and smoke weed, but Raymo insisted that they take the baby back and save its life, making out how he was the hero. But in the dream that came into Mack's mind, he saw the real story, how Ceese was the one who did the saving, and Raymo wanted to leave the baby there in the leaves.

But Mack didn't talk to anybody about his dream of the true story, because they'd think he was crazy. Not that they didn't already, but Mack knew that if they got to thinking he was *really* crazy, they'd lock him away somewhere. And the worst part of *that* idea was, what kind of dreams would they stick in his head there in the crazy house?

Cause Mack knew it was other people putting these dreams into his mind. Most of the time he didn't know whose dream he was having, though some of them, he knew they had to come from a teacher, and others, he had a pretty good guess who in the neighborhood was having this dream.

The thing was, he didn't know if they actually had the same dream, at least not exactly the way he saw it. Because the dreams he saw, they were always so sad, that if other people really knew they had such dreams inside them, how could they get through a single day without crying?

Mack didn't cry for them, though. Because it wasn't his dream.

Like the Johnsons, the ones whose daughter got brain-damaged when she half-drowned in their waterbed, Mack didn't know if the dream he caught from their house was Mr. Johnson's or Mrs. Johnson's or maybe it was Tamika's, a dream left over from back when she was a pretty girl who lived for swimming. In the dream she was diving and swimming in a pool of water in the jungle, with a waterfall, like in a movie. She kept diving deeper and deeper and then one time when she came up, there was a thick plastic barrier on the top of the water and she was scared for just a second, but then she saw that her daddy and mommy were lying on top of the plastic and she poked them and they woke right up and saw her and smiled at her and pulled open the plastic and lifted her out.

If Mack hadn't known something about Tamika's story—or at least the story Mr. Johnson told about how it happened, before they took him off to jail—he might have thought this was just another version of his own dream of being born. Maybe he would have thought, This is how birth dreams come to folks who weren't aborted and left to die in the park under a bunch of leaves.

But instead he saw it as maybe Mr. Johnson's dream of how he wished it had happened, instead of having Tamika trapped under the water all that time till cells in her brain started dying before he realized where she was and cut into the mattress and pulled her out. If only he'd found her right away, the first time she bumped into him from inside the waterbed.

Or maybe it was Mrs. Johnson's dream, since she never felt her daughter inside the mattress at all. Maybe it's how *she* wished it had happened, both of them feeling her poking them so they believed it right away and got her out in time.

Or maybe it was Tamika's dream. Maybe this was how she remembered it, in the confusion of her damaged brain. Diving and swimming, deeper and deeper, until she came up inside her parents' waterbed and they did indeed pull her out and hug her and fuss over her and kiss her like in the dream. The hug and kiss of CPR, but to Tamika, maybe that's what love felt like now.

The thing is, it was a good dream. Maybe when he woke up from it, Mr. Johnson cried—if he was the one who dreamed it. But it made Mack feel good. The diving and swimming were wonderful. And so was the opening of the plastic barrier and the mother and father waiting to hug the swimming girl.

After Mack talked to the therapist, even though he never told this dream, he tried to think of it the way the therapist did. This dream has a mother in it, and a father, so maybe it's really my own dream about a mother and father, only I think it *isn't* my dream because my real mother and father rejected me. So I had this deep dream about opening up a barrier and finding myself surrounded with loves and kisses, only on top of that dream, my brain supplied some of the details from the real story of how Tamika got half drowned in the waterbed. Maybe it's all me, and I'm just sort of twisted up about who's who inside my own head.

Around and around Mack went, thinking about how his brain worked—or didn't work—and why he had these dreams, and how he might be getting dreams sent to him from other people.

Until the day when Yo Yo moved in to Baldwin Hills.

She wasn't down in the flat, where Mack lived, and all his friends. She bought a house up in the hills, near the top of the winding road that led to the very place in the park where Mack had been found. She had doctors and lawyers and big-shot accountants and a movie agent and a semi-famous director living on her street. There was a lot of money there, and expensive cars, and fine tailored suits and evening gowns, and people with responsibilities.

But Yo Yo—or Yolanda White, as she was listed in the phone book—she wasn't like them. She wasn't trying to look respectable like those other folks, who, as Raymo said, were trying to "get everything white folks had in the hopes that white folks won't be able to tell the difference, which wasn't *never* gone happen." Yo Yo rode a motorcycle—a big old hog of a cycle, which made noise like a train as she spiraled up the winding roads at any hour of the day or night. Yo Yo didn't wear those fine fashions, she was in jeans so tight around a body so sleek and lush it made teenage boys like Mack fantasize about the day the threads just gave way and those jeans just peeled open like a split banana skin and she'd wheel that bike on over and get off it all naked with the jeans spilling on down and she'd say, "Teenage boy with concupiscent eyes, I wonder if you'd like to take a ride with me."

That wasn't no *dream,* Mack knew, that was just him wishing. Yo Yo had that effect on a boy, and Mack wasn't so strange he could get confused about the difference between his wishes and Yo Yo's dream.

He knew Yo Yo's dream when it came to him. In fact, he'd pretty much been waiting for it, since he was pretty familiar with all the regular dreams in his neighborhood, and the ones that turned up only at school. All the deep dreams that kept coming back the same. He noticed easy enough when the new dream came on a night when that motorcycle echoed through the neighborhood and somebody shouted out a string of ugly words that probably woke more babies than the motorcycle he was cussing about.

The new dream was a hero dream, and in it he was a girl—which was always a sure sign to him that it was *not* his own dream. He definitely wasn't one of those girls-trapped-in-a-boy's-body. But in the dream, this girl had on tight jeans and Mack sure liked how they felt on him. He liked how the horse felt between his legs when he rode—even though when he came out of the dream he knew that in the real world it was a motorcycle and not a horse.

In the dream, Yo Yo—because that's who it had to be—rode a powerful horse through a prairie, with herds of cattle grazing in the shade of scattered trees, or drinking from shallow streams. But the sky wasn't the shining blue of cowboy country, it was sick yellow and brown, like the worst day of smog all wrapped up in a dust storm.

And up in that smog, there was something flying, something ugly and awful, and Yo Yo knew that she had to fight that thing and kill it, or it was going to snatch up all the cattle, one by one or ten by ten, and carry them away and eat them and spit out the bones. In the dream Mack saw that mountain of bones, and perched on top of it a creature like a banana slug, it was so filthy and slimy and thick, only after creeping and sliming around on top of the pile of bones it unfolded a huge pair of wings like a moth and took off up into the smoky sky in search of more because it was always hungry.

The thing is, through that whole dream, Yo Yo wasn't alone. It drove Mack crazy because try as he might, he couldn't bend the dream, couldn't make the girl turn her head and see who it was riding with her. Sometimes Mack thought the other person was on the horse behind her, and sometimes he thought the other person was flying alongside, like a bird, or running like a dog. Whoever or whatever it was, however, it was always just out of sight.

And Mack couldn't help but think: Maybe it's me.

Maybe she needs me and that's why I'm seeing this dream.

Because in the dream, when the girl rides up to the mountain of old bones, and the huge slug spreads its wings and flies, and it's time to kill it or give up and let it devour the whole herd, the girl suddenly realizes that she doesn't have a gun or a spear or even so much as a rock to throw. Somehow she lost her weapon—though in the dream Mack never notices her having a weapon in the first place. She's unarmed, and the flying slug is spiraling down at her, and then suddenly the bird or dog or man who is with her, he—or it—leaps at the monster. Always it's visible only out of the corner of her eye, so Mack can't see who it is or whether the monster just kills it or whether it sinks its teeth or a beak or a knife into the beast. Because just at the moment when Yo Yo is turning to look, the dream stops.

Not like regular dreams, which fade into wakefulness. Nor was it like Mack's other waking dreams, which he gradually felt slipping away until they were gone. No, this dream, when it ended, ended quick, as if he had suddenly been shoved out of a door into the real world. He'd blink his eyes, still turning his head to see . . . nothing. Except maybe some of his friends laughing and saying, "Mack's back!"

For both these reasons—Mack's fantasies of Yolanda on the motorcycle, Mack's hope that somehow it might be him accompanying Yolanda on horseback to face the slug with her—he keyed in on her as the meaning of his life. All this time, he wasn't an abortion-gone-wrong, an accidental survivor. He was born to be here in the flat of Baldwin Hills as Yo Yo's bike roared up the street and into the mountain. He was born to love her. He was born to serve her. He was born to die for her in the jaws of the giant slug, if that's what she needed from him.

So Mack didn't miss a single whisper as the adults began to work themselves up about the "problem" in the neighborhood. Somebody complained to the police about the noise, but then word got around that Yolanda's bike had passed the noise test, which only got them angrier.

"If that machine isn't loud enough to get confiscated, then why do we have noise pollution laws in the first place?" demanded Miz Smitcher.

"If we can't get rid of the bike," said Ceese's mom, "then we have to get rid of the girl."

"There's no way she *owns* that house," said old lady James. "Tart like that, how could she pay for it? Some man's keeping her."

"That's the old Parson house," said Miz Smitcher. "Mr. Parson was blind and deaf when they carted him off to the old folks' home, and Mrs. Parson was out of there like a shot. You think *she's* keeping that Yo Yo?"

The suggestions came thick and fast then. Maybe she's squatting there, and the Parsons—or the new owners, if there are any—don't even know she's living in their house.

Maybe she really *is* a tart, but she makes so much money at it she actually bought the house cash. "And paid for it in quarters," cackled old lady James, "like a true two-bit whore!"

Maybe she's a niece of Mr. Parsons and they just weren't able to say no to her.

Maybe she's the girlfriend of a drug lord who bought the house to keep her in it. ("Drug lords can afford better-looking women than that!" sniped Ceese's mom.)

But after all the speculation, the answer was simple enough. Hershey LeBlanc, a lawyer who lived four doors down from her and swore the koi in his pond went insane from the noise of her motorcycle, looked up the deed and found that the house did indeed belong to Yolanda White, who paid for the house with one big fat check. "But the house has a covenant," LeBlanc announced triumphantly.

"A covenant?" asked Miz Smitcher.

"A restriction," said LeBlanc. "Left over from years and years ago, when this was a white neighborhood."

"Oh my lord," said Ceese's mom. "The deed says the house can never be sold to a black person, is that it?"

"Well, to be precise, it specified a 'colored person,'" said LeBlanc.

"Those things don't hold up in court anymore," said Miz Smitcher. "Not for years."

"Besides," said old lady James. "Half the houses up there must have covenants like that, or used to."

"And how hypocritical would we have to be to try to throw her out of her house on the basis of on account of she's *colored*," hooted Ceese's mom. "I mean, this whole neighborhood is as black as God's armpit, for crying out loud."

"As black as God's armpit!" cackled old lady James. "That is the most racist thing I ever heard."

"If that's the most racist thing you ever heard," said Ceese's mom, "then you went deaf a lot younger than I thought."

"We won't kick her out because she's black," said LeBlanc. "We'll nullify the sale because the deed still had that covenant and she didn't challenge it. We'll sue her because she left the racist covenant in her deed, which is an offense to the whole neighborhood."

"So she'll just change the deed and strike out the covenant," said Ceese's mom.

"But by then she'll know we want her out of here," said LeBlanc. "Maybe she'll just sell it."

"To a white family, I'll bet!" said Miz Smitcher. "After all, her deed forbids her to sell to a 'colored family.'"

They all had a good, nasty laugh over that. But when he left, Hershey LeBlanc vowed that he'd find one legal pretext or another to get her out of the neighborhood—or at least stop the loud motorcycle noise at all hours.

That's how it was that Mack found himself walking up the long winding avenue that spiraled into the mountain. He didn't go up there much, once he had satisfied his curiosity about the spot where he had been found—not that he was sure where that spot was, since Raymo and Ceese couldn't agree with each other about where it was, nor did either of them pick the same place twice. And ever since he had become so fascinated with Yo Yo, he had made it a point *not* to go look at her house, because the last thing he wanted to be when he grew up was a stalker.

Today's visit wouldn't be stalking, though. He had heard her bike roar in at four a.m., so he imagined that about noon on a summer Wednesday should be just about right for a sixteen-year-old dream-ridden crazy boy from the flat of Baldwin Hills to go knocking on Yolanda White's door.

Except there was a locked gate in the fence.

Ordinarily that sort of thing was no barrier to Mack. He and his friends weren't even slowed down, let alone stopped, by little things like fences as they roamed the neighborhood. He could be over this simple white-painted wrought-iron fence in five seconds—less, if he had a running start.

But it wouldn't be such a good start to the conversation if she came to the door and demanded to know how he got into her yard.

So Mack walked right on past the house—eyeing it surreptitiously, but seeing not a sign of life—and kept on up the avenue till he reached the edge of the park. He stood there looking down into the basin where rainwater collected. When it rained heavily, all the runoff from this high valley would pour down into the basin, and there was a tall standing drainpipe which, when the basin got deep enough, would carry away the water through a big pipe that ran under the street. That's what kept the whole street from becoming a river in every rainstorm.

And that pipe was the place that Mack thought of as his birthplace. Not that he really believed that his mother had been lying there when some abortionist pulled him out of her. But whenever he saw that pipe, he felt something powerful flowing out of it, like the blood rushing through his body, and he knew that whatever it was that made him Mack Street was still connected to this basin, to that pipe. It was because of whatever flowed from that pipe that he hadn't died up there, buried in leaves. That's what he believed, because it made more sense than believing that his whole life was just a dumb accident.

He was contemplating that pipe, that basin, the underbrush and the leaves that collected there, when he heard the unmistakable sound of a motorcycle engine revving up.

He had waited too long.

He whirled around and raced down the road—even though he had
clear memories of running down a hill when he was three and falling
and skinning his knees and hands so bad that Miz Smitcher actually
cried when she saw the injury. He threw himself onto the mercy of
gravity, forcing his legs to stay ahead of his body so he didn't fall over
and skid sixty yards. The automatic gate in the driveway was opening
when he reached it and hurled himself against it like a bug on a wind-
shield.

Yo Yo was just easing the bike down the driveway when Mack suddenly appeared clinging to her gate. She stopped and looked at him and
he must have seemed pretty pathetic or something, because she busted out
laughing and killed the motor.

The silence was louder than the engine had been.

"Well?" said Yo Yo. "Did you want to say something, or are you just
hoping they make bashing-your-face-into-a-moving-gate an Olympic
event?"

"I wanted to talk to you," said Mack. "I got to warn you."

"What, somebody sent their crazy teenage boy to tell me to stop riding my bike?"

Mack was astonished. "How did you know I was crazy?"

She just broke up laughing. Practically fell off the bike. "Peel yourself
off my gate and come in here," she said. "I been looking for a crazy boy,
and I guess I just found him."

Two minutes later, there he was inside her house, sitting on her floor
because there really wasn't a stick of furniture in the living room apart
from the thronelike chair on which she sat and the lamp beside it—not
even a TV or boombox or anything, just a chair, a lamp, and a stack of
books.

He blurted out everything he'd heard them saying about her, except-
ing only the remark about the quarters. How the covenant excluded
black people so she couldn't live there, or maybe she couldn't live there
because she didn't change the deed, but anyway it was all about the bike
and they were really mad and she'd better do something or they'd cause
her a lot of trouble.

"Why you telling me this, boy?"

Well, now, that had him stumped. Not that he didn't know the reason, but he couldn't say, Because I love you. It would hurt too much when she laughed at him for loving a grown woman like her.

"I like your bike," he said.

She laughed anyway. "Want to ride it?"

"Don't got a license."

"Yeah, but that would only matter if I cared." She got up and left the room and came back with two helmets. "Either one of these fit onto that huge head of yours?"

Mack didn't even mind her saying that, since it was true—he always had to set the plastic tab on the back of a baseball cap to the last notch, and even then it would perch on his head like an egg.

But one of the helmets fit him, or at least he could force it on past his ears, and in no time he was sitting on the bike as she showed him the controls, how to clutch and shift gears, how to speed up, how to brake. "Miz White," he said, "I can't make my hands and feet do four different things at the same time."

"In the first place," she said, "Miz White is my mama, I'm Yolanda. Yo Yo if I feel like letting you call me that to my face. In the second place, look how stupid most motorcycle riders look. I can promise you, they really are that dumb, and if *they* can ride, so can you. So let's go through it again and you show me that you know what your hands and feet are good for."

Five minutes later, after a few pathetic false starts, Mack found himself riding Yo Yo's motorcycle down the driveway and out the gate, with Yo Yo herself sitting behind him with her arms around his waist and her breasts pressing into his back and the bike vibrating so much he couldn't hardly see. He drove slow, and when he came out of the driveway he turned right, uphill, toward the basin.

He drove fast enough that the bike kept its balance, but not a bit faster. And when he got to the top, he slowed down and stopped.

Yolanda reached around him and turned the key and the engine shut off.

"Now *that* was about the saddest excuse for a bike ride I've ever had," she said. "A man gets on a bike, he's supposed to feel the power of it, he's supposed to pour on the speed."

Ashamed, all he could say was "Sorry."

"Don't tell me you didn't *want* to go fast."

"Course I did," said Mack.

"I've heard about you, crazy boy. I've heard you take any dare anybody ever gives you and you're not afraid of a damn thing."

Mack nodded, wondering how his school reputation ever reached a grownup, especially this one that all the other grownups hated. It occurred to him that he might not be the first kid to be on her bike when her body pressed up close, and that made him angry and sad and foolish-feeling.

"So how come you were scared to go fast on this bike? It's made for speed, Sneed!"

" 'Cause if I crashed the bike," said Mack, "*you* might get hurt."

She just sat there for a second, then got off the bike and came around the front of it and stood there leaning on the handle and looking in his eyes. "Is that some line you use or something?"

Mack didn't know what she meant by that.

"Because if it isn't, it should be. It's the first line I've heard from a man in a long time that didn't make me want to puke. In fact, it made me want to kiss you."

And being Yo Yo, she reached right out and peeled the helmet off his head, which wasn't easy, and for a second or two he thought he might lose an ear in the process, but the helmet came off eventually, and his ears stayed where they belonged, and she reached out and took his head between her hands to kiss him right on the lips and then . . .

She stopped.

The expression on her face changed.

The hands holding his head slackened and then pulled away.

"Lord Jesus be my Savior," she whispered. "It can't be you."

Mack didn't know what she meant by that, but for one brilliant, wonderful, terrible second he thought: She's my mother. She must have been about thirteen when she had me aborted, that's something I never thought about, that maybe she was just a child. But she never knew I was alive till she put her hands on my head and then she somehow knew, maybe she felt the dream inside me, she *knew* I was her baby.

But right along with that thought came another one: I got all hot and hard for my own *mama* and that makes me about the sickest bastard in Baldwin Hills.

And he tried to get off the cycle to get away from her, but then realized that if he was standing up instead of sitting down she'd *see* just what had been on his mind when he thought she was going to kiss him, so he sat back down, and then she said, "No, baby, no. I'm not your mama. Whoever that poor woman was, she ain't me."

Was she reading his mind?

"No, I don't read minds," she said. "I just know *men* so well I can read their faces."

"No," he said. "Don't lie to me."

"OK," she said. "I read minds sometimes. Or more like I read souls. And when I put my hands on your head, I saw something inside your mind."

"What did you see?" asked Mack.

"I saw that you're filled with love."

With love or *something,* thought Mack.

"I saw that this spot is holy ground to you," she said.

And he trembled that she could have seen such a thing, just by touching him. Or did she have the story from Ceese or Raymo?

"And I saw that you're the one who found my lost dream."

"What do you mean?" he asked.

"My dream," she said. "When I was a little girl, when it was still horses I wanted to ride, back when I didn't know black girls didn't grow up to ride horses. I dreamed a dream of riding, but then I got older and I stopped having that dream. It was so long lost that I'd forgotten I even had it, though now I can see that my riding this bike must have been like a distant echo of it. Only when I put my hands on your head, after I heard the love crying out from your heart, and after I felt the holiness of this place inside you, then I saw a dream, and it was my dream, and you been dreaming it for me, keeping it for me all these years."

"No, ma'am," said Mack. "I only started dreaming it once you moved here."

"Well, now, that's sweet," she said. "I guess it was inside me all along, only lost. But either way, it's you that found it, and you that brought it back to me, and that makes you my friend for life, Mack Avenue."

"Mack Street," said Mack.

"I always give my friends a new name," she said.

"I'd rather you gave me that kiss."

She laughed, and she kissed him right on the mouth, and it wasn't no auntie kiss, and it wasn't quick. But even so, it also wasn't the kiss she would have given him before she found her dream inside his head, and he knew it, and he was just a little disappointed.

"I'm a minister, you know," she said.

"I didn't know that."

"Well, nobody else does, either," she said. "Because I haven't found the God I want to preach about. But I'm wondering right here if maybe I ain't some kind of John the Baptist, looking around for Jesus. Because you, Mack Avenue, you're the Keeper of Lost Dreams, and that's a God that's been needed in this world for a long time."

"But it's a bad dream," said Mack.

"No it's not," she said. "It's the best dream of my whole life. It's the dream I love best."

"But there's that monster. That slug with wings."

"And I've got to kill it," she said, "and I don't have any weapons. I know all that. It's my dream, you know."

"But doesn't that scare you?"

"No sir," said Yo Yo. "Why do you have to ask? In my dream, have you ever felt me be afraid?"

He realized, when she asked, that he'd never felt a speck of fear in her.

A car screeched to a halt. Slowly Mack brought himself out of his gazing into Yo Yo's eyes and turned to see Miz Smitcher slamming the door of the car and stalking toward Yo Yo with murder in her eyes.

"Who do you think you are, getting my boy up on that monster and letting him drive it! He got no driver's license, you crazy bitch!"

"Watch who you calling a crazy bitch," said Yolanda mildly. "If I really *was* a crazy bitch, you wouldn't have the balls to call me that."

Miz Smitcher turned to Mack. "You get off that bike, Mack Street, and get in that car."

Mack turned to Yolanda. What should I do, he wanted to ask her.

She grinned at him. "I'll see you later, Mack Avenue."

"No you won't!" screeched Miz Smitcher. "You come within twenty yards of him and I'll have you in jail for corrupting a minor! You hear me? There's laws protecting young boys from predatory women like you!"

"Mama bird," said Yolanda, "I got no plans to steal away your little chick."

"I'll have you out of this neighborhood, you and that bike! Now I see you using that thing to lure young boys into your den of depredation!"

Yolanda laughed out loud. "A woman with tits like mine, why would I ever need a bike to lure boys!"

That was so outrageous that even Miz Smitcher couldn't think of a thing to say, and Miz Smitcher *never* couldn't think of something to say. Instead she grabbed Mack by the wrist as he was getting off the bike and nearly made him lose his balance as she dragged him to the car and shoved him in through the driver's side with a push so hard he smacked the top of his head on the glass on the other side. And in no time she had that car turned around and headed down the hill, but Mack could still hear Yo Yo's laughter behind him.

"She's a minister," he said.

"You shut up," said Miz Smitcher. "You ain't thinking straight and you *won't* be thinking straight for about two hours after having that woman's arms around you and her *kissing* you."

Mack was outraged. "You mean somebody *called* you?"

"Well I didn't have no psychic vision if *that's* what you're thinking!"

"She's a minister, Miz Smitcher, it was a . . . a Christian kiss."

"Well, there's a billion Christians in this world, and most of them got started with a kiss like that. So you're not to go near her again, you hear me? I'll get her out of this neighborhood if I have to buy a gun and shoot that bike."

"All right," said Mack.

"You agreeing with me, just like that?"

"Yes ma'am."

"Well, now I know you're lying. A boy your age doesn't just say yes ma'am about staying away from a woman like that."

Mack was thinking like crazy, trying to find a way to get Miz Smitcher out of this rage she was in. And then he got it. "Miz Smitcher, I just thought maybe she was my mama. Maybe she come back here to look and see what become of her baby."

That was it. That was the answer. Because all of a sudden Miz Smitcher's eyes got all teary and she pulled the car over in front of the neighbor's house and just hugged him to her and said, "Oh, you poor baby, of course you'd think she was your mama, her looking like she does. Exactly the kind of woman who'd have an abortion and leave the baby in the weeds."

That wasn't exactly what Mack had meant, but it would do.

"So you didn't have the hots for her, you thought she was your *mama!*" Miz Smitcher began to laugh. She put the car back in gear and drove the thirty yards to the curb in front of her house and by the time she got the car parked she was laughing so hard tears were coming down her face.

Two things stuck with Mack from that car ride with Miz Smitcher. First one was, that was the first time he could ever remember her hugging him. Second thing was, You tell somebody something they want to hear, and they'll believe it even if it's the biggest old lie you ever made up.

He promised her everything she asked him to promise—that he'd never ride that bike again, that he'd never go to That Woman's house again, that he'd never talk to her again, that he'd never even *think* of her again. The only true thing he said to her was when she made him say, "I know she could not possibly be my mama."

That night he halfway hoped he'd dream Yolanda's dream, but he didn't. He picked up half a dozen other dreams, including one that he thought might be Miz Smitcher's, and which he never watched all the way through. Yolanda's dream never came, but in the morning he realized, Well of course I didn't dream her dream and I never will again, because I gave it back to her and now it's for *her* again.

But I still got my own dream, he thought. Nothing yesterday was really much like that dream of roads and rocks and cliffs and floods, except I was running down the street like hurtling along the canyon, and at the end of it, a woman reached out and held my head and kissed me and she tasted sweet as love.

NOTES ON "KEEPER OF LOST DREAMS"

Like "Waterbaby," "Keeper of Lost Dreams" was conceived as part of *Magic Street*. Indeed, in a way it was this story where *Magic Street* finally came to life. I had known, ever since talking with Queen Latifah, that I wanted to have a motorcycle-riding woman of power in the book, and I knew magic was going to erupt into Baldwin Hills, and I knew that I was going to build the story around a black man as the hero, because that's what my friend Roland Brown had asked me to do. But I didn't know who that man was going to be, or how any of the pieces of the story were going to fit together. I had a fleeting image in my mind of a bunch of people rising into the air in a great circle, but beyond that . . . nothing.

During the time when I thought I was going to have lots of short tales like "Waterbaby" in the book, I began to think: The hero needs to be someone who becomes aware of all their wishes. Somebody who knows all the people in the neighborhood and will understand the connection between their deep wishes and the terrible things that happen in the real world.

It was in that idea that the character of Mack Street was born. The actual dream in this story is the result of free association and the geography of dreams, the way that places flow into each other in unexpected ways that are often truer than the way they fit together in the real world. I free-associated the dream the way I did the things that Ender finds in the Fantasy Game after he passes the Giant's Drink. It's just whatever cool stuff came into my head while I was writing, and then I made sense of it as best I could after the fact.

In effect, then, this story was my exploratory first draft of *Magic Street,* the way that "A Plague of Butterflies" was a first draft of *Wyrms.* After writing this and then waiting for a while, I was able to start drawing together the elements that became the story as a whole. Without "Keeper of Lost Dreams," there would be no *Magic Street,* which is, I believe, one of the best things I've ever written.

I assumed the story would never be published, but, as with "Waterbaby," I received a request for a story from an editor, in this case Al Sarrantonio, who was putting together an anthology of stories called *Flights: Visions of Extreme Fantasy.* The concept was to do a *Dangerous Visions* in the fantasy genre. I wasn't sure how extreme "Keeper of Lost Dreams" might be, but I had the story, it hadn't been published, and so I sent it to him and he decided that it fit the concept of the anthology well enough.

I don't really think of my work in terms of whether it's "extreme" or not—at least not until after I've written it. I remember, early in my career, how shocked I was when people reacted to *A Planet Called Treason* as if I had written something offensively violent. I was just telling what my character went through—and I didn't write the violence graphically, either. There's no gore in my work. Still, the book was published by the SF Book Club with a warning that some might find it offensive. I guess that made me an "edgy" writer. I had no clue. I just did what I still do: Tell the story that feels important and true to me as clearly as I can.

The same thing happened when my story "America" (part of *Folk of the Fringe*) was published. A reviewer commented that it was hard to believe that what might be the "sexiest" story so far that year had been written by, of all people, Orson Scott Card. I didn't know what to make of the comment. Should I be offended or proud that the reviewer was so surprised that a sexy story could come from me? But as I was writing it, I didn't think of it as a sexy story. I thought of it as the way this character would experience these events.

So it may be that readers who encountered my story in Sarrantonio's anthology found mine the tamest and least "extreme" of the stories; or maybe this tale fit right in. I have no idea. I guess that's what editors are for. Of course, at this stage of my career, I have no idea whether they're buying a story because they actually like the story, or because it's worth wasting a little space on it in order to be able to put my name on the cover. That's the danger of being an established name in the field—my name carries a certain weight because of other things I've already written, so that it can be one of the reasons a potential buyer might pick up a book, irrespective of whether it's one of my better stories.

It's one of the dangers of being an established writer with a long track record—you can get careless and lazy and people will still publish your work. The trouble is, I don't ever *feel* careless or lazy; would I even notice it if I did become that way? I have to watch the reactions of people around me very closely. I know how to write a story that feels professional, so I can fool even the people closest to me into thinking that a work is "done" long before it's really ready. So I look for a spark of enthusiasm and surprise in them before I'm sure I'm on to something with a new story.

Of course, that can backfire. I mean, at some point aren't the people who love me best *not* supposed to show surprise when I actually write something good?

MISSED

Tim Bushey was no athlete, and if at thirty-one middle age wasn't there yet, it was coming, he could feel its fingers on his spine. So when he did his hour of exercise a day, he didn't push himself, didn't pound his way through the miles, didn't stress his knees. Often he relaxed into a brisk walk so he could look around and see the neighborhoods he was passing through.

In winter he walked in midafternoon, the warmest time of the day. In summer he was up before dawn, walking before the air got as hot and wet as a crock pot. In winter he saw the school buses deliver children to the street corners. In summer, he saw the papers getting delivered.

So it was five-thirty on a hot summer morning when he saw the paperboy on a bicycle, pedaling over the railroad tracks and up Yanceyville Road toward Glenside. Most of the people delivering papers worked out of cars, pitching the papers out the far window. But there were a few kids on bikes here and there. So what was so odd about him that Tim couldn't keep his eyes off the kid?

He noticed a couple of things as the kid chugged up the hill. First, he wasn't on a mountain bike or a street racer. It wasn't even one of those banana-seat bikes that were still popular when Tim was a kid. He was riding one of those stodgy old one-speed bikes that were the cycling equivalent of a '55 Buick, rounded and lumpy and heavy as a burden of sin. Yet the bike looked brand-new.

And the boy himself was strange, wearing blue jeans with the cuffs rolled up and a short-sleeved shirt in a print that looked like . . . no, it absolutely was. The kid was wearing clothes straight out of *Leave It to Beaver.* And his hair had that tapered buzzcut that left just one little wave to be combed up off the forehead in front. It was like watching one of those out-of-date educational films in grade school. This kid was clearly caught in a time warp.

Still, it wouldn't have turned Tim out of his planned route—the circuit of Elm, Pisgah Church, Yanceyville, and Cone—if it hadn't been for the bag of papers saddled over the rack on the back of the bike. Printed on the canvas it said, "The Greensboro Daily News."

Now, if there was one thing Tim was sure of, it was the fact that Greensboro was a one-newspaper town, unless you counted the weekly *Rhinoceros Times,* and, sure, maybe somebody had clung to an old canvas paper delivery bag with the *Daily News* logo—but that bag looked new.

It's not as if Tim had any schedule to keep, any urgent appointments. So he turned around and jogged after the kid, and when the brand-new ancient bicycle turned right on Glenside, Tim was not all that far behind him. He lost sight of him after Glenside made its sweeping left turn to the north, but Tim was still close enough to hear, in the still morning air, the faint sound of a rolled-up newspaper hitting the gravel of a country driveway.

He found the driveway on the inside of a leftward curve. The streetlight showed the paper lying there, but Tim couldn't see the masthead or even the headline without jogging onto the gravel, his shoes making such a racket that he half-expected to see lights go on inside the house.

He bent over and looked. The rubber band had broken and the paper had unrolled itself, so now it lay flat in the driveway. Dominating the front page was a familiar picture. The headline under it said:

BABE RUTH, BASEBALL'S
HOME RUN KING, DIES
CANCER OF THROAT CLAIMS LIFE
OF NOTED MAJOR LEAGUE STAR

I thought he died years ago, Tim thought.

Then he noticed another headline:

INFLATION CURB SIGNED BY TRUMAN
PRESIDENT SAYS BILL INADEQUATE

Truman? Tim looked at the masthead. It wasn't the *News and Record,* it was the *Greensboro Daily News.* And under the masthead it said:

TUESDAY MORNING, AUGUST 17, 1948 . . . PRICE: FIVE CENTS.

What kind of joke was this, and who was it being played on? Not Tim—nobody could have known he'd come down Yanceyville Road today, or that he'd follow the paperboy to this driveway.

A footstep on gravel. Tim looked up. An old woman stood at the head of the driveway, gazing at him. Tim stood, blushing, caught. She said nothing.

"Sorry," said Tim. "I didn't open it, the rubber band must have broken when it hit the gravel, I—"

He looked down, meant to reach down, pick up the paper, carry it to her. But there was no paper there. Nothing. Right at his feet, where he had just seen the face of George Herman "Babe" Ruth, there was only gravel and moist dirt and dewy grass.

He looked at the woman again. Still she said nothing.

"I . . ." Tim couldn't think of a thing to say. Good morning, ma'am. I've been hallucinating on your driveway. Have a nice day. "Look, I'm sorry."

She smiled faintly. "That's OK. I never get it into the house anymore these days."

Then she walked back onto the porch and into the house, leaving him alone on the driveway.

It was stupid, but Tim couldn't help looking around for a moment just to see where the paper might have gone. It had seemed so real. But real things don't just disappear.

He couldn't linger in the driveway any longer. An elderly woman might easily get frightened at having a stranger on her property in the wee hours and call the police. Tim walked back to the road and headed back the way he had come. Only he couldn't walk, he had to break into a jog and then into a run, until it was a headlong gallop down the hill and around the curve toward Yanceyville Road.

Why was he so afraid? The only explanation was that he had hallucinated it, and it wasn't as if you could run away from hallucinations. You carried those around in your own head. And they were nothing new to him. He'd been living on the edge of madness ever since the accident. That's why he didn't go to work, didn't even have a job anymore—the compassionate leave had long since expired, replaced by a vague promise of "come back anytime, you know there's always a job here for you."

But he couldn't go back to work, could only leave the house to go jogging or to the grocery store or an occasional visit to Atticus to get something to read, and even then in the back of his mind he didn't really care about his errand, he was only leaving because when he came back, he'd see things.

One of Diana's toys would be in a different place. Not just inches from where it had been, but in a different room. As if she'd picked up her stuffed Elmo in the family room and carried it into the kitchen and dropped it right there on the floor because Selena had picked her up and put her in the high chair for lunch and yes, there were the child-size spoon, the Tupperware glass, the Sesame Street plate, freshly rinsed and set beside the sink and still wet.

Only it wasn't really a hallucination, was it? Because the toy was real enough, and the dishes. He would pick up the toy and put it away. He would slip the dishes into the dishwasher, put in the soap, close the door. He would be very, very certain that he had not set the delay timer on the dishwasher. All he did was close the door, that's *all*.

And then later in the day he'd go to the bathroom or walk out to get the mail and when he came back in the kitchen the dishwasher would be running. He could open the door and the dishes would be clean, the steam would fog his glasses, the heat would wash over him, and he knew *that* couldn't be a hallucination. Could it?

Somehow when he loaded the dishwasher he must have turned on the timer even though he thought he was careful not to. Somehow before his walk or his errand he must have picked up Diana's Elmo and dropped it in the kitchen and taken out the toddler dishes and rinsed them and set them by the sink. Only he hallucinated not doing any such thing.

Tim was no psychologist, but he didn't need to pay a shrink to tell him what was happening. It was his grief at losing both his wife and daughter on the same terrible day, that ordinary drive to the store that put them in the path of the high school kids racing each other in the Weaver

500, two cars jockeying for position, swerving out of their lanes, one of them losing control, Selena trying to dodge, spinning, both of them hitting her, tearing the car apart between them, ripping the life out of mother and daughter in a few terrible seconds. Tim at the office, not even knowing, thinking they'd be there when he came home from work, not guessing his life was over.

And yet he went on living, tricking himself into seeing evidence that they still lived with him. Selena and Baby Di, the Queen Dee, the little D-beast, depending on what mood the two-year-old was in. They'd just stepped out of the room. They were upstairs, they were in the back yard, if he took just a few steps he'd see them.

When he thought about it, of course, he knew it wasn't true, they were dead, gone, their life together was over before it was half begun. But for that moment when he first walked into the room and saw the evidence with his own eyes, he had that deep contentment of knowing that he had missed them by only a moment.

Now the madness had finally lurched outside of the house, outside of his lost and broken family, and shown him a newspaper from before he was born, delivered by a boy from another time, on the driveway of a stranger's house. It wasn't just grief anymore. He was bonkers.

He went home and stood outside the front door for maybe five minutes, afraid to go in. What was he going to see? Now that he could conjure newspapers and paperboys out of nothing, what would his grief-broken mind show him when he opened the door?

And a worse question was: What if it showed him what he most wanted to see? Selena standing in the kitchen, talking on the phone, smiling to him over the mouthpiece as she cut the crusts off the bread so that Queen Dee would eat her sandwiches. Diana coming to him, reaching up, grabbing his fingers, saying, "Hand, hand!" and dragging him to play with her in the family room.

If madness was so perfect and beautiful as that, could he ever bear to leave it behind and return to the endless ache of sanity? If he opened the door, would he leave the world of the living behind, and dwell forever in the land of the beloved dead?

When at last he went inside there was no one in the house and nothing had moved. He was still a little bit sane and he was still alone, trapped in the world he and Selena had so carefully designed: Insurance enough to pay off the mortgage. Insurance enough that if either parent died, the other could afford to stay home with Diana until she was old enough for school, so she didn't have to be raised by strangers in daycare. Insurance that provided for every possibility except one: that Diana would die right along with one of her parents, leaving the other parent with a mortgage-free house, money enough to live for years and years without a job. Without a life.

Twice he had gone through the house, picking up all of Diana's toys and boxing them, taking Selena's clothes out of the closet to give away to Goodwill. Twice the boxes had sat there, the piles of clothes, for days and days. As one by one the toys reappeared in their places in the family room or Diana's bedroom. As Selena's dresser drawers filled up again, her hangers once again held dresses, blouses, pants, and the closet floor again was covered with a jumble of shoes. He didn't remember putting them back, though he knew he must have done it. He didn't even remember deciding not to take the boxes and piles out of the house. He just never got around to it.

He stood in the entryway of his empty house and wanted to die.

And then he remembered what the old woman had said.

"That's OK. I never get it into the house anymore these days."

He had never said the word "newspaper," had he? So if he hallucinated it and she saw nothing there in the driveway, what was it that she never got into the house?

He was back out the door in a moment, car keys in hand. It was barely dawn as he pulled back into that gravel driveway and walked to the front door and knocked.

She came to the door at once, as if she had been waiting for him.

"I'm sorry," he said. "It's so early."

"I was up," she said. "I thought you might come back."

"You just have to tell me one thing."

She laughed faintly. "Yes. I saw it, too. I always see it. I used to pick it up from the driveway, carry it into the house, lay it out on the table for him. Only it's fading now. After all these years. I never quite get to touch it anymore. That's all right." She laughed again. "I'm fading, too."

She stepped back, beckoned him inside.

"I'm Tim Bushey," he said.

"Orange juice?" she said. "V8? I don't keep coffee in the house, because I love it but it takes away what little sleep I have left. Being old is a pain in the neck, I'll tell you that, Mr. Bushey."

"Tim."

"Oh my manners. If you're Tim, then I'm Wanda. Wanda Silva."

"Orange juice sounds fine, Wanda."

They sat at her kitchen table. Whatever time warp the newspaper came from, it didn't affect Wanda's house. The kitchen was new, or at least newer than the 1940s. The little Hitachi TV on the counter and the microwave on a rolling cart were proof enough of that.

She noticed what he was looking at. "My boys take care of me," she said. "Good jobs, all three of them, and even though not a one still lives in North Carolina, they all visit, they call, they write. I get along great with their wives. The grandkids are brilliant and cute and healthy. I couldn't be happier, really." She laughed. "So why does Tonio Silva haunt my house?"

He made a guess. "Your late husband?"

"It's more complicated than that. Tonio was my first husband. Met him in a war materials factory in Huntsville and married him and after the war we came home to Greensboro because I didn't want to leave my roots and he didn't have any back in Philly, or so he said. But Tonio and I didn't have any children. He couldn't. Died of testicular cancer in June of '49. I married again about three years later. Barry Lear. A sweet, dull man. Father of my three boys. Account executive who traveled all the time and even when he was home he was barely here."

She sighed. "Oh, why am I telling you this?"

"Because I saw the newspaper."

"Because when you saw the newspaper, you were embarrassed but you were *not* surprised, not shocked when it disappeared. You've been seeing things yourself lately, haven't you?"

So he told her what he'd told no other person, about Selena and Baby Di, about how he kept just missing them. By the end she was nodding.

"Oh, I knew it," she said. "That's why you could see the paper. Because the wall between worlds is as thin for you as it is for me."

"I'm not crazy?" he asked, laughing nervously.

"How should I know?" she said. "But we both saw that paper. And it's not just us. My kids, too. See, the—what do we call it? haunting? evidences?—it didn't start till they were grown up and gone. Barry Lear was busy having his stroke and getting downright eager to shed his old body, and I was taking care of him best I could, and all of a sudden I start hearing the radio playing music that my first husband and I used to dance to, big band sounds. And those newspapers, that paperboy, just like it was 1948, the year we were happiest, the summer when I got pregnant, before the baby miscarried and our hearts broke and just before Christmas he found out about the cancer. As if he could feel Barry getting set to leave my life, and Tonio was coming back."

"And your kids know?"

"You have to understand, Barry provided for us, he never hit anybody or yelled. But he was a completely absent father, even when he was home. The kids were so hungry for a dad, even grown up and moved away they still wanted one, so when they came home for their father's funeral, all three of them saw the same things I was seeing. And when I told them it was happening before Barry died, that it was Tonio, the man who wasn't their father but wanted so badly to be, the man who would have been there for them no matter what, if God hadn't taken him so young—well, they adopted him. They call him their ghost."

She smiled but tears ran down her cheeks. "That's what he came home for, Tonio, I mean. For my boys. He couldn't do it while Barry was here, but as Barry faded, he could come. And now the boys return, they see his coffee cup in the dish drain, they smell his hair oil in the bathroom, they see the newspapers, hear the radio. And they sit there in the living room and they talk. To me, yes, of course, but also to him, telling him about their lives, believing—knowing—that he's listening to them. That he really cares, he *loves* them, and the only reason they can't see him is because he just stepped out, they only *just* missed him, he's bound to be in the next room, he can hear every word they say."

Tim nodded. Yes, that's how it was. Just how it was.

"But he's fading now." She nodded. "They don't need him so much. The hole in their lives is filled now." She nodded again. "And in mine. The love of my life. We had unfinished business, you see. Things not done."

"So why did I see it? The paperboy, the newspaper—I never knew Tonio, I'm not one of your sons."

"Because you live like I do, on the edge of the other side, seeing in. Because you have unfinished business, too."

"But I can never finish it now," he said.

"Can't you?" she answered. "I married Barry. I had my boys. Then Tonio came back and gave them the last thing they needed. You, now. You could marry, you know. Have more children. Fill that house with life and love again. Your wife and baby, they'll step back, like Tonio did. But they won't be gone. Someday maybe you'll be alone again. Big empty house. And they'll come back. Don't you think? Selena—such a lovely name— and your baby Diana. Just in the next room. Around you all the time. Reminding you when you were young. Only by then Diana might not need to be a baby anymore. It won't be toys she leaves around, it'll be schoolbooks. Hairbrushes. And the long hairs you find on your pillow won't be Selena's color anymore. It'll be grey. Or white."

He hadn't told her about still finding Selena's hair. She simply knew.

"You can go on with your life without letting go," said Wanda. "Because you don't really lose them. They're just out of reach. I look around Greensboro and I wonder, how many other houses are like mine? Haunted by love, by unfinished love. And sometimes I think, Tonio isn't haunting us, we're the ones who are haunting *him*. Calling him back. And because he loves us, he comes. Until we don't really need him anymore."

They talked a little more, and Tim went home, and everything was different, and everything was gloriously the same. It wasn't madness anymore. They really *were* just out of reach, he really *had* just missed them. They were still in the house with him, still in his life.

And, knowing that, believing it now, he could go on. He visited Wanda a couple of times a week. Got to know each of her sons on their visits. Became friends with them. When Wanda passed away, he sat with the family at the funeral.

Tim went back to work, not at the company where he and Selena had met, but in a new place, with new people. Eventually he married, they had children, and just as Wanda had said, Selena and Diana faded, but never completely. There would be a book left open somewhere, one that nobody in the house was reading. There would be a whiff of a strange perfume, the sound of someone humming a tune that hadn't been current for years.

Right along with his new family, he knew that Diana was growing up, in a house full of siblings who knew about her, loved the stories of her childhood that he told, and who came to him, one by one, as the years passed, to tell him privately that once or twice in their childhood, they had seen her, the older sister who came to them during a nightmare and comforted them, who whispered love to them when friends at school had broken their hearts, whose gentle hand on their shoulder had calmed them and given them courage.

And the smiling mother who wasn't their mother but there she was in the doorway, just once, just a fleeting glimpse. Selena, looking at the children she had never given birth to but who were still hers, partly hers, because they were his, and he would always be a part of her even though he loved another woman now and shared his life with her.

Sometime, somewhere down the road, his life would draw to a close and he would see them again, face to face, his family, his first family, waiting for him as Tonio had waited for Wanda all those years. He could wait. There was no hurry. They were only moments out of reach.

NOTES ON "MISSED"

I can't remember now if the local paper asked me for a Halloween story—I think they did, but it might be that I'm conflating this story with a multi-author serial that the same newspaper put together a few years later. It might be that I came up with the idea, called them, and asked if they would consider running a piece of scary fiction and, if so, how long it ought to be.

Whether they initiated it or I did, the result was this story, set in a specific neighborhood. In fact, the house where Tim finds the newspaper is the home of our friends the Jensens. If you can't tip your hat to friends or family now and then, what's the fun of being a fiction writer?

I began this story frivolously enough. It was a lark; write a newspaper horror story for Halloween.

But it turned serious almost at once. I had only just started running. After our last child, Erin Louisa, died on the day she was born, I had suddenly come face to face with mortality. People I loved could die. I could die—and at the weight I was carrying at the time, I probably would, sooner rather than later. I got serious about getting my body under control and started exercising. I never became the kind of runner Tim was—but I knew something about what it felt like, to run.

And so I suppose it wasn't just coincidence that I made this a story about the worst thing in the world—to have a family and lose it. It was what I was going through at the time, in a very small way. And things like that, things from real life, are going to show up even in the "frivolous" fictions of a writer who's just doing something for the fun of it.

III
LITERARY

50 WPM

Y ou know a lot of these guys?"

"No. We didn't fight the same war."

"I thought you went to Vietnam."

"Oh, sure, yeah. But I never fired a rifle at anybody, and nobody ever fired one at me. I never even left Saigon."

"But I always thought . . ."

"What?"

"You know."

"What?'

"Your hand. Your fingers. The missing ones. I thought that happened in Vietnam."

"It did. . . . There he is."

"Who?"

"My guardian angel."

"Man, if I got a guardian angel I hope mine ain't *dead*."

"Yeah, well, he was joking, too, I think. Got in country, he saw I was kind of green. You know. I was young, I'd never been out of Hickory, I didn't know a thing, so he says to me, I'm your guardian angel, I'll not only keep you alive in this hellhole, I'll even keep you sane."

"Well, one out of two ain't bad."

"I know you don't mean anything by it, son, and there's nothing wrong with joking, but I got my fingers resting on the name of a friend who died saving my life."

"Sorry, Dad. You know I didn't mean . . ."

"Funny thing is, your grandpa had it all figured out so my life wouldn't *need* saving. See these hands? All seven fingers? Would you believe I used to be a typist?"

"That before or after you were front man for the Beatles? No, sorry, I want to hear. Dad, I do. Really."

Your grandpa was a grunt in World War II. Volunteered the day after Pearl Harbor, and when they saw how that country boy could shoot, he was infantry all the way. He wasn't stupid, he didn't volunteer for anything, didn't get himself into Airborne or the Marines, turned down sergeant's stripes three times. He just knew how to shoot, so they had him on the front lines in North Africa, Sicily, and in slow motion all the way up the boot of Italy.

He told me it got so he didn't even bother learning the name of a new guy till he'd been there for a week, so many guys got blown away just cause they were new and didn't know enough to keep their heads down. Dad and the other guys'd tell 'em, but they just didn't have survivor instinct, that's what Dad called it. The sense to know just how far you had to bend over to keep from giving them a target.

Helmets don't stop bullets, son. You got a helmet so you don't get killed when a bullet knocks a chip out of a stone wall and the chip comes and hits you in the head. But somebody aims right at you, that helmet just adds a little more metal to get slammed into your skull.

Anyway, Pop comes to me when I'm thirteen years old, summer before eighth grade, and he says, "No, I'm not going to teach you how to shoot. Knowin' how to shoot got me three and a half years on the front lines killin' guys and having guys get killed all around me. What you're going to do this summer, boy, you're going to learn how to *type*."

Now, I didn't even hardly know what typing was. Something girls took in high school, something you saw secretaries doing when my mom took me with her to pay, like, the water bill or something. Pop had to drag me there, I ain't kidding, kid, had to drag me up to the high school and sign me up for summer school typing. Bought me a typewriter, too, and he didn't have a lot of money, that was a big deal, we had to be the only people we knew had a typewriter on their kitchen table, it sat there during meals and everything. At least an hour a day, he set the kitchen timer on me and it was worth half the skin on my butt to fiddle with it and cheat. So I sat there and typed, and a lot of the time he was watching me. Stuff like "Don't look at the keys!" and "Spell it like it's written, you moron!"

No, he actually called me shit-for-brains, but your mother doesn't like me talking to you the way my pop talked to me. And yes, this is about how Daniel I. Keizer saved my life. Look, forget it, let's go find your mother and your sisters.

It's not like I tell this story a lot, son. So I don't know which parts to take out so it's entertaining.

It's about my father trying to save my life. That's why he made me take typing class. He says to me, "Bobby, there's gonna be a war. There's always gonna be a war. First thing they do, they find out what you can do. Me, I could shoot the shit off a squirrel's ass so clean he'd think he wiped himself, so they put me in the dust and the mud and had people tryin' to kill me, and all I got in exchange was the GI Bill, but I never got me a single one of my buddies back, they stayed just as dead as they were when I left 'em behind in Italy. Well, that ain't gonna happen to you, Bobby. You go into that recruiting office and where they say skills, you put down, 'typing, fifty words per minute.' That's the magic number, boy. You type fifty words a minute—and that's fifty words without a single mistake, every minute, page after page—and they never put you near a rifle. After Basic, you just sit at a desk and type and type and type, and when the war's over you go home and you ain't dead and nobody you knew in the army is dead because they were all typing, too, or giving orders from some nice safe place ten or twenty miles back or five thousand miles even. That's where I want you in the war."

So I says to him, Pop, what if I *want* to fight, and he says, "Bobby, you volunteer for infantry, I'll kill you myself so I don't have to worry about you getting killed by somebody else. Better me than a stranger. Your mother and I, we'll cry over your grave, but we sure as hell never gonna sit there waiting for some letter or some telegram from the government to find out whether you made it through another day of people shooting at you. You get me?"

Didn't matter whether I got it or not, I was going to learn to type. And that first summer, I kept telling him to go ahead and kill me, because hell couldn't be worse than breaking my fingers on that damn machine.

But by the end of that summer, I was typing thirty words a minute, and that's *after* you take off ten words a minute for each typo.

All through eighth grade he makes me type all my homework—and that was before computers, hardly anybody typed their stuff, not in Hickory anyway—and I had to practice an hour a day and then every Saturday morning first thing, he'd time me and correct my paper and if I ever did worse than the week before—lower speed or more typos—then I couldn't go anywhere with my friends that whole weekend.

By the end of eighth grade I was typing fifty words a minute, just like he wanted. He let me off then, no more hour-a-day practices, but those weekly tests kept right on, and any week I didn't stay over fifty words per minute, I was back to the practicing.

So I graduate high school and Johnson's escalating the war in Vietnam and everybody who went to college got to sit it out and I could've, too, you can bet I got accepted at college—I mean, hell, kid, I could *spell,* I could *type,* that made me an intellectual in the hills of western Carolina. But, see, I figured I'd get drafted, put in my two years, and then come out with the government paying all my college bills cause I'd be a veteran. I wasn't worried about no war, kid, cause Pop took care of that, I could *type.*

No, it worked just like Pop said. I come in there looking and talking like a hillbilly and I put down on my form that I can type 50 wpm and the recruiter looks at me and says, "It's a federal offense to lie on this form," and I says to him, I ain't lyin', man, and so he sets me down at his own desk and opens a book and puts a paper in the machine and looks at his watch and says, "Go."

Well I made that thing sound faster than a machine gun. A minute later he says to stop and what I got on that page isn't fifty words, it's ninety words, all spelled right and pretty as you please. And then he says, "Do it again," and this time he doesn't say stop after a minute, he just has me keep typing and typing. I blew through three sheets of paper and the other recruiters are standing around laughing and he looks over my typing and I didn't make a single damn mistake and even including changing sheets, I was over ninety words per minute.

I don't know what he wrote in my file, but even in Basic I kept getting called out of my company to go type stuff for the base commander and when I got to Vietnam I think I'd fired a rifle exactly once. My pop, he knew what he was talking about. I was going to live through that war.

Course it wasn't really as easy as all that. Cause I kept thinking about how other guys were going to go out into the jungle and lay down their lives, and the worst that was going to happen to me was getting my fingers smudgy when I changed ribbons. But when I wrote that to my mom in a letter, my pop read it, too, and he wrote back to me cussing a blue streak right there on the paper and he says, "It's just as much part of the war to type up orders and reports. Somebody's gonna sit in that chair in that nice clean office and usually it's some lily-assed faggot son of a congressman but this damn war it's gonna be a hillbilly from Hickory N.C." In those days you could still say faggot, son, it was a different world. Wasn't better, just different.

So I get to Nam, my orders put me right in the typing pool in an office building in downtown Saigon, and that's where Danny Keizer spotted me.

Danny wasn't in the typing pool. He was the guy in charge of all the guys who typed up orders every day. You know, sending this regiment to that place and telling where supplies had to go. And it was pretty high level, I mean, the stuff he typed got sent to other offices where other guys had to type up fifty more orders just to carry out the orders Danny's office sent them. And Danny comes into the typing pool and there I am, showing off, typing as fast as I can, and he says, "What're you typin' there, ass-face, 'Now is the time for all good men' or 'When in the course of human events'?" And he comes over and looks at my paper and he gives this low whistle and twenty minutes later some guy comes over and lays a paper on top my machine and it says I'm assigned to the office of sit-and-dick-around-with-Danny effective immediately.

No, that wasn't the real name, but that was the job description whenever we weren't actually working. I mean, Danny kept that office humming, he did his job and made sure we did ours, but as soon as we were done for the day, all he wanted to do was have fun, and he'd take along whoever wanted to go.

Which wasn't me.

I had fun, it just wasn't the same fun. Come on, you know your gran, she's Baptist through and through and that means I never even *danced* when I was growin' up and I sure as hell never smoked or drank, and as for women, well, there wasn't no double standard in my parents' house, they said a boy should be just as virgin as a girl till he was married, and my pop let it be known that if I wanted to keep my dick it was going to stay inside my pants and not go gettin' anybody pregnant. And I wasn't one of those kids, the second he's away from home, he goes wild. I may not be as die-hard Baptist as my folks were, but I was then, and no way was I going to go out whoring and drinking with Danny I. Keizer and his cronies.

So Danny sees I'm not going, of course, and he asks why and I tell him, not judgmental or nothing but still, you know, how it was against my Christian upbringing. The other guys just groan and I figure I'm gonna get a hard time, but Danny, he just puts a hand on my shoulder and says, "Good for you, got more brains than all the rest of us put together." They still go out, mind you, and I stay in, but he didn't let 'em give me any crap about it, they just went and I just didn't and after a while they kind of liked it that way, it meant they had somebody sober when they got back to, you know, help get the booze and the vomit off 'em and get 'em to bed. And believe me, there was nothing I saw about their condition when they came back that made me want to take up drinkin' or whorin' or smokin' dope.

But one day Danny says to me—and it wasn't that long after I got there, either—he says, "Let's go to a place I know and have lunch." So we go to this canteen about three blocks away, they served pretty good food and there were reporters there too so you knew it was a place where you wouldn't puke or get the runs from eating the food. Always crowded. And Danny sat me down and I said, I can't afford to eat in no restaurants, and he says, "I can afford to buy this restaurant because my father is a car dealer in Minnesota and he makes so damn much money he can give thousands of dollars to politicians which is why I'm here."

And I says, Your pop got his politician friends to send you to Nam?

And for a second he didn't know I was joking but then he did and he says, "Very funny, Deacon."

I hated it when they called me that, and I says to him, My pop *is* a deacon and I'm not.

And he says, "I'm sorry, man. I guess I just keep saying the wrong thing, is that it?" And then he tells me about how he had his college deferment, but he was such a screwup he ended up getting kicked out of college and about fourteen seconds later he was drafted, because his dad was a Democrat but the local draft board was mostly Republican and they hated him big time. His dad didn't even try to get him out, he just pulled some strings—and Danny said it was Hubert Humphrey who pulled 'em, and maybe his dad even said it was, but I mean, come on, Hubert Humphrey was Vice-President of the United States, who the hell would listen to *him*? Anyway, Danny only typed, like, negative twenty words a minute because he made so many typos, but they assigned him to the typing pool anyway, and the way he tells it—the way he told it—the guys in charge of the typing pool kept trying to get him kicked out and the orders kept coming back that Danny was a *permanent* member of the typing pool, so finally the only way they could keep things going smooth was to put him in charge of the typing pool himself. Or anyway that's how he told it. But I also think it had something to do with him being just, you know, a likable guy. The officers around him, they liked working with him, so they promoted him. That simple.

I liked him, too. Couldn't help it and I didn't try not to. Even though I knew he was a hard drinker, and I figure half those half-American Vietnamese kids they talk about must look like Danny, he never talked about that kind of thing with me. Never even swore—hell, I swore more than he did, my pop used to say he came from a long line of Swearin' Baptists, and he didn't care if I swore, too, as long as I never did it in front of my mother, which I never did. Though they said a lot worse things than just swearing, which I never could bring myself to say. Anyway, he never talked rough around me at all, never even swore. Just talked about . . . everything else. Everything except the war.

He asked about my family, how I grew up, and finally I says to him, Am I, like, a sociology project or something? And he says to me, "What I hope is that you're a friend," and then he made a face so I'd know that he meant it but he wasn't queer or anything, but after that he told me everything about his own life and his family and everything. Every lunch, or almost every lunch. Every lunch that some officer didn't take him along to lunch with *him,* Danny would take me down to lunch with him, and he always paid, even though I tried to pay my share, he just laughed and said, "Somebody stateside bought a Chevy from my dad today for five hundred bucks more than he should've paid, so lunch is on him."

And all the time we were talking, he kept giving me advice. On the streets of Saigon, he'd say, "Don't ever go in there, you get VD just from window-shopping," and he'd say, "Look out for little kids with their shirts buttoned up, cause the VC like to strap grenades to them and send them over to GIs to blow them up." He told me the parts of town never to go into, and he especially told me all kinds of stuff about what it was like in combat. What the booby traps looked like, how walking point is the safest place because the VC always wait till you're past their ambush so they can kill the main bunch of guys in the middle, how if you hate your lieutenant all you got to do is salute him and he's a dead man, some VC sniper'll get him. And all the time I'm thinkin', How the hell do *you* know about combat, Mr. Danny I. Son-of-a-Guy-Who-Owns-Politicians?

And I guess he knew I was skeptical because he says to me, "Bobby, this isn't like other wars. Desk jobs aren't safe here. Just cause you don't take a rifle to work doesn't mean the other guy isn't trying to kill you. They love nothing better than killing GIs walking around Saigon, thinking they're safe. You're never safe. We're all combat troops, and the guys who don't realize it are the ones who're gonna die. That's why I ask every guy I know who's been in combat, I ask 'em how to stay alive and they tell me because anything can happen. One day they're gonna come into our office and hand out weapons and say, Congratulations, boys, you're all infantry now, and they'll take us out and get us killed *unless* we got some idea what we're doing."

That's when he told me he was my guardian angel. "You're going to amount to something, Bobby," he says to me. "You need to stay alive."

And I just laughed cause what does it matter what happens to a boy from Hickory, except to my mother and daddy, but he says, "No sir, it's the way you type. Maybe at first your pop made you learn, maybe you hated it then"—cause, see, I already told him about that—"but the way you type now, that's ambition. You got to be the best. That's in you, to be the best. So that means you're worth keeping alive. So I'm your guardian angel. My job is to teach you what you got to know to stay alive in this war."

I says to him, My daddy already saw to it I know what I need to know, but he says, "Every soldier needs a guardian angel, it's the only way you get through the war, I promise you." And I says, Who's your guardian angel, Hubert Horatio Humphrey? And he says to me, "I got no guardian angel, God doesn't waste time on screwups like me," and I says, If you believe in Jesus he'll forgive all your sins, and he says, "I like Jesus too much to ever repent of my sins, cause as long as I don't repent, he doesn't have to pay for them," and that was pretty much the end of our discussion of religion.

He never took advice from me, though. Like when he typed, he was fast, but he wasn't very accurate. Typos on every order he ever sent out. I tried to tell him to slow down so he wouldn't make mistakes, and he just said, "Faster I type, faster they're out of here." And when I told him I thought that stunk cause a mistake on those orders could get somebody killed, he just looks at me like I'm crazy and he says, "Bobby, even when the orders are exactly right they get somebody killed." Afterward I thought of all kinds of things to say to that, like how maybe if the orders were right the guys who died might accomplish something first, but I never said it to him cause I knew with him it was all the same. He didn't want my advice cause he didn't want anybody's advice cause he didn't care enough to want to get better at anything. Except staying alive.

So he'd come back to that guardian angel thing now and then. "Don't do that," he'd say. "This is your guardian angel speaking." And then I'd laugh and sometimes I'd do it anyway and sometimes I wouldn't—you know, just stuff like going out in a jeep with a guy when we had a pass, or going up to a kid and giving him a candy bar. "Listen to me, Bobby, and someday I'll save your life."

So we were sitting in that very restaurant, the first one he ever took me to, and there's the usual crowd, all kinds of soldiers and reporters and Vietnamese businessmen and officers and whatever, and I see this kid come in, little beggar kid, they come in, you know, to beg, cause the doors are open with ceiling fans, the place wasn't air-conditioned, I mean this was Vietnam, we didn't even have air-conditioning in Hickory in those days. So I see this little beggar kid, and I've seen a hundred just like him, five hundred, only there's something wrong. He's going from table to table just like they did, only I keep watching him, not even thinking about why, I'm listening to Danny, only I can't take my eyes off the kid.

And Danny says, "What're you looking at?" and he turns and sees the kid and he waves the kid over to our table and he pulls out a candy bar to give him and all of a sudden I know.

"His shirt's buttoned up," I says to Danny, and without even thinking about it, I'm standing up, I stood up so fast I knocked my chair over and I remember somebody cussing cause my chair fell against him, and I says, "Danny, no, his *shirt's buttoned up.*" But it's like Danny doesn't even hear me, he's holding out the candy bar to the kid and the kid's right there in front of him and I'm around the table, reaching for him, grabbing to pull him away, and at the exact moment that Danny is between me and the kid, the kid blows up.

Wasn't even grenades, they said, it was high-tech explosives. It was a big enough deal it made the papers back in the States. Mostly I think because reporters got killed. Hell, everybody in the place got killed or so blown up they were in the hospital for months, they strapped enough explosives on the kid that people were killed on the street outside, that's how bad it was.

Except me. They told me it was a miracle that all that happened to me was getting three fingers blown off.

Only it wasn't a miracle, it was Danny. He was right between me and the kid. He took the whole blast that was meant for me. I mean, I got knocked back fifteen feet and I blacked out, it's not like *nothing* hit me, my head hit the floor so hard I had a concussion and it took a month for my ears to heal, but I was no more than six feet from the kid, I should have been dead, blown to bits like those other guys, but there I was lying on the floor and when I came to—and I was only out for, like, a couple of minutes—when I came to, everything was silent, cause of my ears, you know, and when I tried to get up my head hurt, but I had to see if Danny was OK, you know? I had to see about Danny. And I sit up and I got stuff smeared all over my eyes but I wipe them off and I look and the whole place looks like a tornado hit a meat locker, it's all bloody and pieces of people are everywhere and I'm thinking, This is combat. Danny was right, the war is everywhere and this is combat.

Only the one thing I don't see is Danny. And I start to get up to see if maybe he got thrown over me, you know, right over my head so he's behind me, only as I get up my clothes move wrong and I think, my legs are cut off inside my pants, I mean that's what it looked like, I was getting up only my clothes didn't move right, and then I realize, those aren't my clothes. I pull at them and I've got another whole uniform spread out on my body like somebody had held it up against me to see if it fit. Only it was torn open in front, it was really only just the back half of a uniform, and then I recognize the shirt, the stripes on the sleeve, the way they were rolled up. It was Danny's uniform. It got blown clean off him. Or he got blown clean out of it. And the stuff I wiped off my face, that was probably . . . that was.

Oh God. Oh God. This is why I don't tell the story. He saved my life, see? I had got around behind him to pull him away from the kid, and it just happened that he was exactly, he was so perfectly between me and the kid that he took it all for me. Everything. Except where I was reaching my right hand around to grab him. What happened to my hand, that's what would have happened to my whole body except for Danny. He was my guardian angel.

No, not just because he took it all for me. Think about it. Lord knows I had plenty of time to think about it. A month in the hospital, and then coming home with my damn Purple Heart and Pop calling it my million-dollar wound till I got so sick of it I moved out and went to college just to get away from home, and the whole time I was thinking about Danny, and he really *was* my guardian angel, because if he hadn't told me to watch out for kids with their shirts buttoned up, if he hadn't pounded it into me that when you see something like that you just get out, you don't talk about it, you just *go*—I mean, I would've still been sitting at that table. Maybe getting something out of my pockets to give the kid. The only reason I was exactly behind Danny was because I was on my feet getting the hell out of there the second I realized that kid had his shirt buttoned up.

Only it wasn't just that, either. Cause if Danny had listened to me, if he'd headed for the door like me, we'd both be dead. Everybody in that place was dead, or had pieces blown off them a lot worse than fingers, you know. I'm the only guy walked out of that place. And if Danny hadn't bent over to give that kid a candy bar, if he'd run for it like I was running for it, you wouldn't be here and neither would I. It was just like he fell on a grenade to save his buddy in a foxhole. And sometimes I even think that he *knew* he was doing it. I mean, he's the one who taught *me* to look for a kid like that, he taught *me* to get out of there, only when the time comes he doesn't even see it? Come on. I think he knew. I think he chose between me and him, or anyway he knew that the only way I'd live is if I had protection, and he decided my life mattered.

And when I get to thinking that way, for a long time I thought, Wrong, Danny I. Keizer. Wrong. My life wasn't worth saving. I haven't done one thing important enough to be worth you or anybody else dying for. That's why I never came to the Wall before. I couldn't face him.

And then they blow up the World Trade Center and you come home and you start talking about volunteering so you can fight the way Pop did in World War II and the way I did in Vietnam and I realized for the first time. I looked at you and I thought, No way are those bastards going to take you away from me, but then I looked at your sisters and your mother and I thought, What if they blew up the school where one of my girls was? Or the grocery store when your mom was shopping? And I knew you had to go, 'cause you thought it was right, and if you went, I knew you might die because that happens, guys die, there's a wall full of guys here who died.

No, hell no, I didn't bring you here so you'd change your mind. I brought you here because I finally knew I could face Danny. Because I *had* done something with my life. I really *was* worth saving.

You. You're the thing I did. You and your sisters. Your mom and I had you all, and I worked all my life paying the bills and I also tried to raise you decent, we both did, and whether it was because of us or in spite of us, you're a great kid, you're a good *man,* and your sisters, they're terrific, too, and I knew I could face Danny cause I had you here with me.

See, I taught you how to type, but I also taught you how to shoot, because it isn't my choice. It's your choice. But right here at this wall, here's my guardian angel. I wanted him to meet you. I don't know where you'll go or what you'll do, but I'd like to think you got somebody with you like I did, watching over you. Because I know you'll do right, but when it's all over, I don't want your name on a wall somewhere. I want you to come home to me, just as bad as Pop ever wanted me to come home. You do whatever you think is right, but let Danny watch over you, and if he sometime whispers in your ear, then by God you listen, you hear me?

NOTES ON "50 WPM"

When "50 WPM" first appeared in an anthology of stories about the
Vietnam War and its aftermath (*In the Shadow of the Wall: An Anthology of
Vietnam Stories That Might Have Been,* ed. Byron R. Tetrick), this "author
note" was included with it. Even now, I really have nothing more to add:

I didn't serve in Vietnam. Born in 1951, I wasn't eligible for the draft
until the lottery came along, and my number was above the cutoff. By
then—1969—the war had already been declared pointless by a government that was now sending soldiers to Vietnam to die just to save face for
America, the sort of cause I have never thought worth the expenditure of
more than six bucks and a hangnail.

So I spent those years of my life either as a theatre student at Brigham
Young University or as a missionary in São Paulo, Brazil, reading everything about the war but experiencing nothing. Yet I am a lifelong student
of matters military and was not an opponent of the war as originally sold
to the American people; I cared and care about what happened in Vietnam, and have shed my share of tears at the Wall. How could I write
about Vietnam and the Wall, when I had no personal experience there and
did not pay any price myself, though I was of that generation?

I struggled with that issue for months, wanting to contribute a story,
but not knowing what sort of story I had a right to tell. And then I
realized—I should write, not about the kind of war that most of the guys
whose names are on that wall were fighting, but the kind of war that I
would inevitably have fought, had I been drafted. Physically soft and not
particularly skilled at anything the infantry needs, and highly unlikely to
be tagged as having the leadership that makes one an officer, the only
thing that stood out was my typing. I was fast. No, let me get technical
here, I was *damn* fast, and accurate, too. There's not a chance that I would
have seen action. Even if I went to Vietnam, I would have been in an office somewhere. This story, then, is about the kind of war I might have
fought, though none of the characters in it are in any way like me.

FEED THE BABY OF LOVE

When Rainie Pinyon split this time she didn't go south, even though it was October and she didn't like the winter cold. Maybe she thought that this winter she didn't deserve to be warm, or maybe she wanted to find some unfamiliar territory—whatever. She got on the bus in Bremerton and got off it again in Boise. She hitched to Salt Lake City and took a bus to Omaha. She got herself a waitressing job, using the name Ida Johnson, as usual. She quit after a week, got another job in Kansas City, quit after three days, and so on and so on until she came to a tired-looking café in Harmony, Illinois, a small town up on the bluffs above the Mississippi. She liked Harmony right off, because it was pretty and sad—half the storefronts brightly painted and cheerful, the other half streaked and stained, the windows boarded up. The kind of town that would be perfectly willing to pick up and move into a shopping mall only nobody wanted to build one here and so they'd just have to make do. The help-wanted sign in the café window was so old that several generations of spiders had lived and died on webs between the sign and the glass.

"We're a five-calendar café," said the pinched-up overpainted old lady at the cash register.

Rainie looked around and sure enough, there were five calendars on the walls.

"Not just because of that *Blue Highways* book, either, I'll have you know. We already had these calendars up before he wrote his book. He never stopped here but he could have."

"Aren't they a little out of date?" asked Rainie.

The old lady looked at her like she was crazy.

"If you already had the calendars up when he wrote the book, I mean."

"Well, not *these* calendars," said the old lady. "Here's the thing, dar-lin'. A lot of diners and whatnot put up calendars after that *Blue Highways* book said that was how you could tell a good restaurant. But those were all fakes. They didn't *understand*. The calendars have all got to be *local* cal-endars. You know, like the insurance guy gives you a calendar and the car dealer and the real estate guy and the funeral home. They give you one every year, and you put them all up because they're your friends and your customers and you hope they do good business."

"You got a car dealer in Harmony?"

"Went out of business thirty years ago. Used to deal in Studebakers, but he hung on with Buicks until the big dealers up in the tri-cities un-derpriced him to death. No, I don't get his calendar anymore, but we got two funeral homes so maybe that makes up for it."

Rainie almost made a remark about this being the kind of town where nobody goes anywhere, they just stay home and die, but then she decided that maybe she liked this old lady and maybe she'd stay here for a couple of days, so she held her tongue.

The old lady smiled a twisted old smile. "You didn't say it, but I know you thought it."

"What?" asked Rainie, feeling guilty.

"Some joke about how people don't need cars here, cause they aren't going anywhere until they die."

"I want the job," said Rainie.

"I like your style," said the old lady. "I'm Minnie Wilcox, and I can hardly believe that anybody in this day and age named their little girl Ida, but I had a good friend named Ida when I was a girl and I hope you don't mind if I forget sometimes and call you Idie like I always did her."

"Don't mind a bit," said Rainie. "And nobody in this day and age *does* name their daughter Ida. I wasn't *named* in this day and age."

"Oh, right, you're probably just pushing forty and starting to feel old. Well, I hope I never hear a single word about it from you because I'm right on the seventy line, which to my mind is about the same as driving on empty, the engine's still running but you know it'll sputter soon so what the hell, let's get a few more miles on the old girl before we junk her. I need you on the morning shift, Idie, I hope that's all the same with you."

"How early?"

"Six a.m. I'm sad to say, but before you whine about it in your heart, you remember that *I'm* up baking biscuits at four-thirty. My Jack and I used to do that together. In fact he got his heart attack rolling out the dough, so if you ever come in early and see me spilling a few tears into the powdermilk, I'm not having a bad day, I'm just remembering a good man, and that's my privilege. We got to open at six on account of the hotel across the street. It's sort of the opposite of a bed-and-breakfast. They only serve dinner, an all-you-can-eat family-style home-cooking restaurant that brings 'em in from fifty miles around. The hotel sends them over here for breakfast and on top of that we get a lot of folks in town, for breakfast *and* for lunch, too. We do good business. I'm not poor and I'm not rich. I'll pay you decent and you'll make fair tips, for this part of the country. You still see the nickels by the coffee cups, but you just give those old coots a wink and a smile, cause the younger boys make up for them and it's not like it costs that much for a room around here. Meals free during your shift but not after, I'm sorry to say."

"Fine with me," said Rainie.

"Don't go quittin' on me after a week, darlin'."

"Don't plan on it," said Rainie, and to her surprise it was true. It made her wonder—was Harmony, Illinois, what she'd been looking for when she checked out in Bremerton? It wasn't what usually happened. Usually she was looking for the street—the down-and-out half-hopeless life of people who lived in the shadow of the city. She'd found the street once in New Orleans, and once in San Francisco, and another time in Paris, and she found places where the street used to be, like Beale Street in Memphis, and the Village in New York City, and Venice in LA. But the street was such a fragile place, and it kept disappearing on you even while you were living right in it.

But there was no way that Harmony, Illinois, was the street, so what in the world was she looking for if she had found it here?

Funeral homes, she thought. I'm looking for a place where funeral homes outnumber car dealerships, because my songs are dead and I need a decent place to bury them.

It wasn't bad working for Minnie Wilcox. She talked a lot but there were plenty of town people who came by for coffee in the morning and a sandwich at lunch, so Rainie didn't have to pay attention to most of the talking unless she wanted to. Minnie found out that Rainie was a fair hand at making sandwiches, too, and she could fry an egg, so the workload kind of evened out—whichever of them was getting behind, the other one helped. It was busy, but it was decent work—nobody yelled at anybody else, and even when the people who came in were boring, which was always, they were still decent and even the one old man who leered at her kept his hands and his comments to himself. There were days when Rainie even forgot to slip outside in back of the café and have a smoke in the wide-open gravel alleyway next to the dumpster.

"How'd you used to manage before I came along?" she asked early on. "I mean, judging from that sign, you've been looking for help for a long time."

"Oh, I got by, Idie, darlin', I got by."

Pretty soon, though, Rainie picked up the truth from comments the customers made when they thought she was far enough away not to hear. Old people always thought that because *they* could barely hear, everybody else was half-deaf, too. "Oh, she's a live one." "Knows how to work, this one does." "Not one of those young girls who only care about *one thing*." "How long you think she'll last, Minnie?"

She lasted one week. She lasted two weeks. It was on into November and getting cold, with all the leaves brown or fallen, and she was still there. This wasn't like any of the other times she'd dropped out of sight, and it scared her a little, how easily she'd been caught here. It made no sense at all. This town just wasn't Rainie Pinyon, and yet it must *be,* because here she was.

After a while even getting up at six a.m. wasn't hard because there was no life in this town at night so she might as well go to bed as soon as it turned dark and then dawn was a logical time to get up. There was no TV in the room Rainie took over the garage of a short-tempered man who told her "No visitors" in a tone of voice that made it clear he assumed that she was a whore by nature and only by sheer force of will could he keep her respectable. Well, she was used to letting the voice of authority make proclamations about what she could and couldn't do. Almost made her feel at home. And, of course, she'd do whatever she wanted. This was 1990 and she was forty-two years old and there was freedom in *Russia* now so her landlord, whatever his name was, could take his no-visitors rule and apply it to his own self. She saw how he sized up her body and decided she was nice-looking. A man who sees a nice-looking woman and assumes that she's wicked to the core is confessing his own desires.

After work Rainie didn't have anywhere much to go. She ate enough for breakfast and lunch at the café that dinner didn't play much of a part in her plans. Besides, the hotel restaurant was too crowded and noisy and full of people's children running around dripping thick globs of gravy off their plates. The chatter of people and clatter of silverware, with Montovani and Kostelanetz playing in the background—it was not a sound Rainie could enjoy for long. And when she passed the piano in the hotel lobby the one time she went there, she felt no attraction toward it at all, so she knew she wasn't ready to surface yet.

One afternoon, chilly as it was, she took off her apron after work and put on her jacket and walked in the waning light down to the river. There was a park there, a long skinny one that consisted mostly of parking places, plus a couple of picnic tables, and then a muddy bank and a river that seemed to be as wide as the San Francisco Bay. Dirty and cold, that was the Mississippi. It didn't call out for you to swim in it, but it did keep moving leftward, flowing south, flowing downhill to New Orleans. I know where this river goes, thought Rainie. I've been where it ends up, and it ends up pretty low. She remembered Nicky Villiers sprawled on the levee, his vomit forming one of the Mississippi's less distinguished tributaries as it trickled on down and disappeared in the mud. Nicky shot up on heroin one day when she was out and then forgot he'd done it already and shot up again, or maybe he didn't forget, but anyway Rainie found him dead in the nasty little apartment they shared, back in the winter of—what, '68? Twenty-two years ago. Before her first album. Before anybody ever heard of her. Back when she thought she knew who she was and what she wanted. If I'd had his baby like he asked me, he'd still be dead and I'd have a fatherless child old enough to go out drinking without fake ID.

The sky had clouded up faster than she had thought possible—sunny but cold when she left the café, dark and cloudy and the temperature dropping about a degree a minute by the time she stood on the riverbank. Her jacket had been warm enough every other day, but not today. A blast of wind came into her face from the river, and there was ice in it. Snowflakes like needles in it. Oh yes, she thought. This is why I always go south in winter. But this year I'm not even as smart as a migratory bird, I've gone and got myself a nest in blizzard country.

She turned around to head back up the bluff to town. For a moment the wind caught her from behind, catching at her jacket and making it cling to her back. When she got back to the two-lane highway and turned north, the wind tried to tear her jacket off her, and even when she zipped it closed, it cut through. The snow was coming down for real now, falling steadily and sticking on the grass and on the gravel at the edges of the road. Her feet were getting wet and cold right through her shoes as she walked along in the weeds, so she had to move out onto the asphalt. She walked on the left side of the road so she could see any oncoming cars, and that made her feel like she was a kid in school again, listening to the safety instructions. Wear light clothing at night and always walk on the left side of the road, facing traffic. Why? So they can see your white, white face and your bright terrified eyes just before they run you down.

She reached the intersection where the road to town slanted up from the Great River Road. There was a car coming, so she waited for it to pass before crossing the street. She was looking forward to heading southeast for a while, so the wind wouldn't be right in her face. It'd be just her luck to catch a cold and get laryngitis. Couldn't afford laryngitis. Once she got that it could linger for months. Cost her half a million dollars once, back in '73, five months of laryngitis and a canceled tour. Promoter was going to sue her, too, since *he* figured he'd lost ten times that much. His lawyer talked sense to him, though, and the lawsuit and the promoter both went away. Those were the days, when the whole world trembled if I caught a cold. Now it'd just be Minnie Wilcox in Jack & Minnie's Harmony Café, and it wouldn't exactly take *her* by surprise. The sign was still in the window.

The car didn't pass. Instead it slowed down and stopped. The driver rolled down his window and leaned his head out. "Ride?"

She shook her head.

"Don't be crazy, Ms. Johnson," he said. So he knew her. A customer from the café. He pulled his head back in and leaned over and opened the door on the other side.

She walked over, just to be polite, to close the door for him as she turned him down. "You're very nice," she began, "but—"

"No buts," he said. "Mrs. Wilcox'll kill me if you get a cold and I could have given you a ride."

Now she knew him. The man who did Minnie's accounting. Lately he came in for lunch every day, even though he only went over the café books once a week. Rainie wasn't a fool. He was a nice man, quiet and he never even joked with her, but he was coming in for her, and she didn't want to encourage him.

"If you're worried about your personal safety, I got my two older kids as chaperones."

The kids leaned forward from the back seat to get a look at her. A boy, maybe twelve years old. A girl, looking about the same age, which meant she was probably younger. "Get in, lady, you're letting all the heat out of the car," said the girl.

She got in. "This is nice of you, but you didn't need to," she said.

"I can tell you're not from around here," said the boy in the back seat. "Radio says this is a *bad* storm coming and you don't walk around in a blizzard after dark. Sometimes they don't find your body till spring."

"Dougie," said the man.

That was the man's name, too, she remembered. Douglas. And his last name . . . Spaulding. Like the ball manufacturer.

"This is nice of you, Mr. Spaulding," she said.

"We're just coming back down from the Tri-Cities Mall," he said. "They can't wear last year's leather shoes cause they're too small, and their mother would have a fit if I suggested they keep wearing their sneakers right on through the winter, so we just had the privilege of dropping fifty bucks at the shoe store."

"Who are you?" asked the girl.

"I'm Ida Johnson," she said. "I'm a waitress at the café."

"Oh, yeah," said the girl.

"Dad said Mrs. Wilcox had a new girl," said Dougie. "But you're not a girl, you're *old.*"

"Dougie," said Mr. Spaulding.

"I mean you're older than, like, a teenager, right? I don't mean like you're about to get Alzheimer's or anything, for Pete's sake, but you're not *young,* either."

"She's *my* age," said Mr. Spaulding, "so I'd appreciate it if you'd get off this subject."

"How old are *you,* then, Daddy?" asked the girl.

"Bet he doesn't remember," said Dougie. He explained to Rainie. "Dad forgets his age all the time."

"Do not," said Mr. Spaulding.

"Do so," said Dougie. It was obviously a game they had played before.

"Do not, and I'll prove it. I was born in 1948, which was three years after World War II ended, and five years before Eisenhower became president, and *he* died at Gettysburg, Pennsylvania, which was the site of a battle that was fought in 1863, which was 127 years ago last July, and here it is November which is four months after July, and November is the eleventh month and so I'm four times eleven, forty-four."

"No!" the kids both shouted, laughing. "You turned *forty-two* in May."

"Why, that's good news," he said. "I feel two years younger, and I'll bet Ms. Johnson does, too."

She couldn't help but smile.

"Here we are," he said.

It took her a moment to realize that without any directions, he had taken her right to the garage with the outside stair that led to her apartment. "How did you know where to take me?"

"It's a small town," said Mr. Spaulding. "Everybody knows everything about everybody, except for the things which nobody knows."

"Like Father's middle name," said the girl.

"Get on upstairs and turn your heat on, Ms. Johnson," said Mr. Spaulding. "This is going to be a bad one tonight."

"Thanks for the ride," said Rainie.

"Nice to meet you," said Dougie.

"Nice to meet you," echoed the girl.

Rainie stood in the door and leaned in. "I never caught *your* name," she said to the girl.

"I'm Rose. *Never* Rosie. Grandpa Spaulding picked the name, after *his* aunt who never married. I personally think the name sucks pond scum, but it's better than Ida, don't you agree?"

"Definitely," said Rainie.

"Rosie," said Mr. Spaulding, in his warning voice.

"Good night, Mr. Spaulding," said Rainie. "And thanks for the ride."

He gave a snappy little salute in the air, as if he were touching the brim of a nonexistent hat. "Any time," he said. She closed the door of the car and watched them drive away. Up in her room she turned the heater on.

During the night the snow piled up a foot and a half deep and the temperature got to ten below zero, but she was warm all night. In the morning she wondered if she should go to work. She knew Minnie would be there and Rainie wasn't about to have Minnie decide that her "new girl" was soft. She almost left the apartment with only her jacket for warmth, but then she thought better and put on a sweater under it. She still froze, what with the wind blowing ground snow in her face.

At the café the talk was that four people died between Chicago and St. Louis that night, the storm was so bad. But the café was open and the coffee was hot, and standing there looking out the window at the occasional car passing by on the freshly plowed road, Rainie realized that in Louisiana and California she had *never* felt as warm as this, to be in a café with coffee steaming and eggs sizzling on the grill and deadly winter outside, trying but failing to get at her.

When Mr. Spaulding came into the café for his lunch just after one o'clock, Rainie thanked him again.

"For what?"

"For saving my life yesterday."

He still looked baffled.

"Giving me a ride up from the river."

Now he remembered. "Oh, I was just doing Minnie a favor. She never thought you'd stay a week, and here you've stayed for more than a month already. She would have reamed me out royal if we had to dig your corpse out of a snowdrift."

"Well, anyway, thanks." But she wasn't saying thanks for the ride, she realized. It was something else. Maybe it was the kids in the back seat. Maybe it was the way he'd talked to them. The way he'd *kept on* talking with them even though there was an adult in the car. Rainie wasn't used to that. She wasn't used to being with kids at all, actually. And when she did find herself in the presence of other people's children, the parents were always shushing the kids so they could talk to *her.* "I liked your kids," said Rainie.

"They're OK," he said. But his eyes said a lot more than that. They said, You must be good people if you think well of my kids.

She tried to imagine what it would have been like, if her own parents had ever been with her the way Mr. Spaulding was with *his* children. Maybe my whole life would have been different, she thought. Then she re-membered where she was—Harmony, Illinois, otherwise known as the last place on Earth. No matter whether her parents were nice or not, she prob-ably would have hated every minute of her childhood in a one-horse town like this. "Must be hard for them, though," she said. "Growing up miles from anywhere like this."

All at once his face closed off. He didn't argue or get mad or any-thing, he just closed up shop and the conversation was over. "I suppose so," he said. "I'll just have a club sandwich today, and a diet something."

"Coming right up," she said.

It really annoyed her that he'd shut her down like that. Didn't he *know* how small this town was? He'd been to college, hadn't he? Which meant he must have lived away from this town *sometime* in his life. Have some perspective, Spaulding, she said to him silently. If your kids aren't dying to get out of here now, just give them a couple of years and they will be, and what'll you do *then*?

As he sat there eating, looking through some papers from his brief-case, it began to grate on her that he was so pointedly ignoring her. What right did he have to judge her?

"What put a bug up *your* behind?" asked Minnie.

"What do you mean?" said Rainie.

"You're stalking and bustling around here like you're getting set to smack somebody."

"Sorry," said Rainie.

"One of my customers insult you?"

She shook her head. Because now that she thought about it, the reverse was true. She had insulted *him,* or at least had insulted the town he lived in. What was griping at her wasn't him being rude to her, because he hadn't been. He simply didn't like to hear people badmouthing his town. Douglas Spaulding wasn't in Harmony because he never had an idea that there was a larger world out there. He was a smart man, much smarter than the job of smalltown accountant required. He was here by choice, and she had talked as if it was a bad choice for his children, and this was a man who loved his children, and it really bothered her that he had closed her off like that.

It bothered her so much that she went over and pulled up a chair at his table. He looked up from his papers, raised an eyebrow. "This a new service at Jack & Minnie's Café?"

"I'm willing to learn," said Rainie. "I'm not a bigot against small towns. I just sort of took it for granted that small towns would feel oppressive to kids because the small town I grew up in felt oppressive to *me.* If that's a crime, shoot me."

He looked at her in wonder. "I don't have an idea on God's Earth what you're talking about."

"A minute ago when you shut me down," she said, really annoyed now. "You can't tell me that shutting people down is so unimportant that you don't even remember doing it."

"I ordered my lunch is all I did," said Spaulding.

"So you *do* remember," she said triumphantly.

"I just wasn't interested in continuing that conversation."

"Then don't shut a person down, Mr. Spaulding. Tell them that you don't appreciate what they said, but don't just cut me off."

"It honestly didn't occur to me that you'd even notice," he said. "I figured you were just making small talk, and the talk just got too small."

"I wasn't making small talk," said Rainie. "I was really impressed with your kids. It's a sure thing *I* was never that way with *my* father."

"They're good kids." He took another bite and looked down at his paper.

She laid her hand on the paper, fingers spread out to cover the whole sheet and make it unreadable.

He sat up, leaned back in his chair, and regarded her. "The place isn't crowded, the lunch rush is over, so it can't be that you need my table."

"No sir," said Rainie. "I need your attention. I need just a couple of minutes of your attention, Mr. Spaulding, because in your car yesterday I caught a whiff of something I've heard about but I always thought it was a legend, a *lie,* like Santa Claus and the tooth fairy and the Easter bunny."

He got a little half-smile on his face, but there was still fire in his eyes. "Since when is Santa Claus a lie?"

"Since I was six years old and got up to pee and saw Dad putting together the bike on the living room floor."

"It strikes me that what you saw was proof that Santa Claus was real. Flesh and blood. Putting together a bike. Making cookies for you in the kitchen."

"That wasn't Santa Claus, that was Dad and Mom, except that my mom didn't make cookies for *me,* she made them for *her,* all neat and round and lined up exactly perfect on the cooky tray, Lord help me if I actually *touched* one, and Dad couldn't get the bike together right, he had to wait till the stores opened the day after Christmas so he could get the guy in the bike shop to put it together."

"So far you haven't proved that Santa Claus was fake, you just proved that he wasn't good enough for you. If Santa Claus couldn't be perfect, you didn't want any Santa Claus at all."

"Why are you getting so mad at me?"

"Did I invite you to sit at this table, Ms. Johnson?"

"Dammit, Mr. Spaulding, would you call me Ida like everybody else?"

"Dammit, Ms. Johnson, why are you the only person in town who doesn't call me Douglas?"

"Begging your pardon, *Douglas.*"

"Begging yours, *Ida.*"

"All I was trying to say, *Douglas,* when I brought up Santa Claus, *Douglas,* was that in your car I saw a father being easy with his children, and the children being easy with their dad, right in front of a stranger, and I never thought that happened in the real world."

"We get along OK," said Douglas. He shrugged it off, but she could see that he was pleased.

"So for a minute in your car I felt like I was part of that and I guess it just hurt my feelings a little when you shut me down back then. It didn't seem fair. I didn't think my offense was so terrible."

"Like I said. I wasn't punishing you."

"All right then. More coffee?"

"No thanks."

"Pie? Ice cream?"

"No thanks."

"Well then why do you keep calling me over to your table?"

He smiled. Laughed almost. So it was all right. She felt better, and she could leave him alone then.

After he left, after all the lunch customers had gone and she was washing down the tables and wiping off the saltshakers and emptying the ashtrays, Minnie came over to her and looked her in the eye, hard and angry.

"I saw you sitting down and talking with Douglas," she said.

"We weren't busy," said Rainie.

"Douglas is a decent man with a happy family."

Now Rainie understood. In her own way, Minnie was just like the guy who rented her the room over the garage. Always assuming that because she was a good-looking woman, she was on the make. Well, she *wasn't* on the make, but if she was, it wouldn't be any of Minnie's business or anybody else's except her own. What *was* it about this place? Why did everybody always assume that sex was the foremost thing in a single forty-two-year-old woman's mind?

"I'm glad for him," Rainie said.

"Don't you make no trouble for that good man and his good wife," said Minnie.

"I said something that I thought maybe offended him and I wanted to make sure everything was all right, that's all. I was trying to make sure I hadn't alienated a customer." Even as she explained, Rainie resented having to make an explanation.

"Do you think I'm a fool? Do you think I'm such a fool as to think *you're* a fool? Since he first laid eyes on you he's been in here every day. And now you're going over sitting at his table arguing with him and then making him laugh. I've got half a mind to fire you right now and send you on your way, except I like you and I'd like to keep you around. But I don't like you so much I'm willing to have you making things ugly for people around here. You can make a mess here and then just walk away, but me and my customers, we'll have to keep living with whatever it is you do, so don't do it. Am I clear?"

Rainie didn't answer, just furiously wiped at the table. She hadn't been reamed out like that since . . . her *mother* was the last one to ream her out like this, and Rainie had left *home* over it, and it made her so *mad* to have to listen to it all over again, she was forty-two years old and she *still* had some old lady telling her what she could and couldn't do, laying down rules, making conditions and regulations, and claiming that she *liked* her while she was doing it.

Minnie waited for a minute till it was clear Rainie wasn't going to answer. "All right then," said Minnie. "I've got enough in the register to give you your pay. Take off the apron, you can go."

I don't need your money or your job, you poor old fool, I'm Rainie Pinyon, I sing and write songs and play the piano and cut albums, I've got a million-dollar ranch in the Horse Heaven Hills of eastern Washington and an agent in LA who calls me sweetheart and sends me checks a couple of times a year, checks large enough even during the bad years that I could buy your two-bit café and move it to Tokyo and never even miss the money.

Rainie thought all that, but she didn't say it. Instead she said, "I'm sorry. I'm not going to mess around with anybody's life, and I'll be careful with Mr. Spaulding."

"Take off the apron, Ida."

Rainie whirled on her. "I *said* I'd do what you wanted."

"I don't think so," said Minnie. "I think you got the same tone of voice I heard in my daughter when she had no intention of doing what I said, but promised to do it just to get me off her back."

"Well I'm not your daughter. I *thought* I was your friend."

Minnie looked at her, steady and cold, then shook her head. "Ida

Johnson, I can't figure you out. I never thought you'd last a week, and I *sure* never figured you for the type who'd try to hold on to a lousy job like this one after the tongue-lashing I just gave you."

"To tell you the truth, Mrs. Wilcox, I never figured myself that way, either. But I don't want to leave."

"Is it Douglas Spaulding? Are you in love?"

"I used up love a dozen years ago, Mrs. Wilcox, and I haven't looked to recharge the batteries since then."

"You mean to tell me *you* been without a man for twelve years?"

"I thought we were talking about whether I was in love."

"No such thing." Minnie looked her up and down. "I'll bet you didn't wear a bra during the bra-burning days, did you?"

"What?"

"Your chest has dropped so low you could almost tuck 'em into your belt. I don't know what a man would find attractive about you anyway."

It was such an insulting, outrageous thing to say that Rainie was speechless.

"You can stay, as long as you don't call me Mrs. Wilcox, that just drives me crazy, call me Minnie."

Things went right back to normal, mostly because Douglas Spaulding didn't come in again for more than a week, and when he did come back, he wasn't alone. He was part of a group of men—most of them in suits, but not all—who came into the café walking on the balls of their feet like dancers, like running backs. "You're all full of sass," said Minnie to one of the men.

"Time to feed the baby!" he answered.

Minnie rolled her eyes. "I know. Jaynanne Spaulding's gone out of town again."

"Dougie's Christmas present to her—a week with her folks up in Racine."

"Present to him*self*," said Minnie.

"Taking care of the kids for a solid week, you think that's a picnic?"

"Those kids take care of themselves," said Minnie. "Douglas Spaulding's just a big old kid himself. And so are you, Tom Reuther, if you want my opinion."

"Minnie, honey, nobody ever has *time* to want your opinion. You give it to us before we even have a chance to wish for it."

Minnie held up a ladle of her Cincinnati chili. "You planning to eat your lunch or wear it, Tom?"

One of the other men—a mechanic, from the black stains on his overalls—piped up from the two tables they had pushed together in the middle of the room. "He's already wearing every bit of food you ever served him. Can't you see it hanging over his belt?"

"Under my belt or over it, Minnie, I wear your food with pride," said Tom. Then he blew her a kiss and joined the others.

Douglas was already sitting at the table, laughing at nothing and everything, just like the others. He really *did* seem to be just a big old kid right then—there was nothing of the father about him now. Just noise and laughing and moving around in his chair, as if it might just kill him if he ever sat still for more than ten seconds at a time. Rainie half expected to look down and see him wearing too-short or too-long jeans with holes in the knees, showing one knee skinned up and scabbed over, and maybe raggedy sneakers on his feet. She was almost disappointed to see those shiny sensible oxfords and suitpants with the hems just right. He didn't *not* look at her, but he didn't particularly look at her, either. He was just generally cheerful, being with his friends, and he had plenty of good cheer to share with anybody who happened to come along.

"You going to order separate checks and make my life miserable?" asked Rainie of the group at large.

"Just give the bill to Doug," said Tom.

"You can make one total and we'll divvy it up ourselves," said Douglas. "It'll be easy, because we're all having exactly the same thing."

"Is that right?"

"Beans!" cried Tom.

"Beans! Beans! Beans!" chanted several of the others.

"We gots to have our daily beans, ma'am," Tom explained, "cause we gots to feed the baby of love!"

"I got a double batch of chili with extra cinnamon!" called Minnie from behind the counter. "This time somebody had the *brains* to call ahead and warn me!"

Tom immediately pointed an accusing finger at Douglas. "What is this, Spaulding! A sudden attack of maturity and consideration for others? Malicious *foresight*? For shame!"

Douglas shrugged. "Last time she ran out."

"Chili for everybody," said Rainie. "Is that all? Nothing to drink?"

"What is the drink of the day?" asked one of the men.

"Whose turn is it anyway?" asked another.

"Tom's turn," said Douglas.

They turned toward him expectantly. He spread his hands out on the table, and looked them in the eye, as if he was about to deliver the state of the union address. Or a funeral prayer. "Seven-Up," said Tom. "A large Seven-Up for everybody."

"Are you serious?" asked Douglas. "And what's for dessert, toothpaste?"

"The rule is no alcohol at lunch," said Tom, "and beyond that we're free to be as creative as we like."

"You're giving creativity a bad name," said Douglas.

"Trust me," said Tom.

"If all we get today is Seven-Up," said the mechanic, "you are going to spend the entire evening as primordial slime."

"No, he's going to spend the night in *hell,*" said another.

At the soda machine, spurting the Seven-Up into the glasses, Rainie had to ask. "What in the world are they *talking* about?"

"It's a game they play," said Minnie. "It's notorious all over town. More satanic than Dungeons and Dragons. If these boys weren't so nice they'd probably be burnt at the stake or something."

"Satanic?"

"Or secular humanist or whatever. I get those two things mixed up. It's all about feeding beans to the baby and when you win you turn into God. Pagan religion and evolution. I asked Reverend Blakely about it and he just shook his head. No wonder Jaynanne leaves town whenever they play."

"Aren't you going to serve up the chili?"

"Not till they're through with whatever nonsense they do about the drinks."

Rainie loaded the drinks onto the tray and headed back to what she was now thinking of as the Boys' Table. Whatever it was that Douglas

Spaulding and his friends had turned into, it was suddenly a lot more interesting to her, now that she knew that at least some groups in the town disapproved of it. Evolution and paganism? It sounded like it was right up her alley.

She started to load off the glasses at each place, but Tom beckoned to her frantically. "No, no, all here in front of me!" With one arm he swept away the salt and pepper shakers, the napkin dispenser, the sugar canister, and the red plastic ketchup bottle. "Right here, Miss Ida, if you don't mind."

She leaned over Tom's left shoulder and set down the whole tray without spilling a drop from any of the glasses. Before she stood up, she glanced at Douglas, who was right across from Tom, and caught him looking down the neck of her dress. Almost immediately he looked away; she didn't know whether he knew she saw him looking or not.

My boobs may have sagged a little, Minnie, but I still got enough architecture to make the tourists take a second glance.

There were other customers, but while she was dropping off their orders she kept an eye on the Boys' Table. Tom *had* been creative, after all—he had packets of Kool-Aid in his suitcoat pocket, and he made quite a ritual of opening them and putting a little of every flavor in each glass. They foamed a lot when he stirred them, and they all ended up a sickly brownish color.

She heard the mechanic say, "Why didn't you just puke in the glasses to start with and avoid the middleman?"

"Drink, my beloved newts and emus, drink!" cried Tom.

They passed out the glasses and prepared to drink.

"A toast!" cried Douglas, and he rose to his feet. Everybody in the café was watching, of course—how often does somebody propose a toast at noon in a smalltown café?—but Rainie kept right on working, laying down plates in front of people.

"To the human species!" said Douglas. "And to all the people in it, a toast!"

"Hear hear!"

"And to all the people who only wish they were in it, I promise that when I am supreme god, you will *all* be human at last!"

"In a pig's eye!" shouted the mechanic joyously.

"I'll drink to that!" cried Tom, and with that they all drank.

The mechanic did a spit take, putting a thin brown Kool-Aid and Seven-Up fog into the air. Tom must have had some inner need to top that; as he finished noisily chug-a-lugging his drink, Rainie could see that he intended to throw the glass to the floor.

Apparently Minnie saw the same glint in his eye. Before he could hardly move his arm she screeched at him, "Not on your life, Tom Reuther!"

"I paid for it last time," said Tom.

"You didn't pay for all the lunch customers who never came back. Now you boys sit down and be quiet and let folks have their lunch in peace!"

"Wait a minute!" cried Douglas. "We haven't had the song yet."

"All right, do the song and then shut up," said Minnie. She turned back to the chili and resumed dipping it out into the bowls, muttering all the while, ". . . drive away my customers, spitting all over, breaking glasses on the floor . . ."

"Whose turn to start?" somebody asked.

The mechanic rose to his feet. "I choose the tune."

"Not opera again!"

"Better than opera," said the mechanic. "I choose that pinnacle of indigenous American musical accomplishment, the love theme from Oscar Mayer."

The boys all whooped and laughed. The man next to him rose to his feet and sang what must have been the first words that came into his mind, to the tune of the Oscar Mayer wiener jingle from—what, twenty years ago? Rainie had to laugh ironically inside herself. After all my songs, and all the songs of all the musicians who've suffered and sweated and taken serious drugs for their art, what sticks in the memory of my generation is a song about a kid who wishes he could be a hot dog so he'd have friends.

"I wish I had a friend in my nostril."

The next man got up and without hesitation sang the next line. "In fact I know that's where he'd want to be."

And the next guy: "Cause if I had a friend in my nostril."

"Cheat, cheat, too close to the first line!" cried Tom.

"Bad rhyme—same word!" said the mechanic.

"Well what else am I supposed to do?" said the guy who sang the line. "There's no rhyme for 'nostril' in the English language."

"Or any other," said Douglas.

"Like you're an expert on Tadzhiki dialects or something," said Tom.

"Wastrel!" shouted the mechanic.

"That doesn't rhyme," said Douglas.

"Leave it with nostril," said Tom. "We'll simply heap scorn upon poor Raymond until he rues the day."

"You are so gracious," said Raymond.

"Dougie's turn," said the mechanic.

"I forgot where we were," said Douglas, rising to his feet.

The mechanic immediately jumped up and sang the three lines they had so far:

> *I wish I had a friend in my nostril,*
> *I know that's where he'd really want to be,*
> *Cause if I had a friend in my nostril . . .*

Rainie happened to be passing near the Boys' Table at that moment, and she blurted out the song lyric that popped into her mind before Douglas could even open his mouth:

> *He could eat the boogers I don't see!*

Immediately the men at the table leaped to their feet and gave her a standing ovation, all except Tom, who fell off his chair and rolled on the floor. The only people who didn't seem to enjoy her lyric were Minnie, who was glaring at her, and Douglas, who stared straight ahead for a moment and then sat down—laughing along with the others, but only as much as conviviality required.

I'm sorry I stole your thunder, Rainie said silently. Whenever I think of the perfect clincher at the end of a verse, I always blurt it out like that, I'm sorry.

She went back to the counter and got the chili, which Minnie had already laid out on a tray. "Are you trying to make my customers get indigestion right here in the diner?" Minnie hissed. "Boogers! *Eating* them. My land!"

"I'm sorry," said Rainie. "It just came out."

"You got a barnyard mouth, Ida, and it's nothing to be proud of," said Minnie. She turned away, looking huffy.

When Rainie got back to the table with the chili, the men were talking about her. "She got the last line, and it was a beaut, and so she's first," said Tom. "That's the law."

"It may be the law," said Douglas, "but Ida Johnson isn't going to want to feed the baby."

"Maybe I do and maybe I don't," said Rainie.

Douglas closed his eyes.

"Dougie's just sore because he could *never* think of a line to top Ida's," said Raymond.

"Retarded parrots could think of better lines than *yours,* Raymond," said the mechanic.

"Retarded parrot *embryos,*" said another man.

"What baby do you feed, and what do you feed it?" asked Rainie.

"It's a game," said Tom. "We kind of made it up. Dougie and I."

"All of us," said Douglas.

"Dougie and me first, and then everybody together. It's called Feed the Baby of Love Many Beans or Perish in the Flames of Hell."

"Greg had the idea in the first place," said Douglas.

"Yeah, well, Greg moved to *California* and so we spit upon his memory," said Tom.

At once everybody made a show of spitting—all to their left, all at once. But instead of actually spitting, they all said, in perfect unison, "Ptui."

"Come on, Ida," said Tom. "It's at Douglas's house. The game's all about karma and reincarnation and trying to progress from primordial slime to newt to emu to human until finally you get to be supreme god."

"Or not," said the mechanic.

"In which case your karma decides your eternal fate."

"In heaven with the Baby of Love!"

"Or in hell with the Baby of Sorrows!"

"I don't think so," said Rainie. She was noticing how Douglas didn't seem too eager to have her come. "I mean, if Douglas's wife leaves town whenever you play, then it must be one of those male-bonding things and I've never been good at male bonding."

"Oh, great," said Tom, "now she thinks we're gay."

"Not at all," said Rainie. "If I thought you were gay I'd be there with bells on. The refreshments are always great at gay parties. It's you pickup-basketball-game types who think beer and limp pretzels are a righteous spread."

Raymond rose to his feet. "Behold our nuncheon feast, Your Majesty," he said. "Do we look like the beer and pretzels type?"

"No, you actually look like the boys who always made disgusting messes out of the table scraps on their school-lunch trays."

"That's it!" cried Tom. "She understands us! *And* she put a brilliant last line on the song. Tonight at seven, Idie baby, I'll pick you up."

From the look on Douglas's face, Rainie knew that she should say no. But she could feel the loneliness of these past few weeks in this town—and, truth to tell, of the months, the *years,* before—like a sharp pain within her. Being on the fringes of this group of glad friends made her feel like . . . what? Like her best days living on the street. That's what it was. She had found the street after all. Grown up a little, most of them wearing suits, but here in this godforsaken town she had found some people who had the street in their souls, and she couldn't bear to say no. Not unless Douglas *made* her say it.

And he didn't make her say it. On the contrary. She looked him in the eye and he half smiled and gave her a little shrug. Suit yourself, that's what he was saying. So she did.

"OK, so I'll be there," she said.

"But you should be aware," said Tom, "we probably aren't as fun as your gay friends' parties."

"Naw," she said, "they stopped being fun in the eighties, when they started spending all their time talking about who had AIDS and who didn't."

"What a *downer,*" said Raymond.

"Bad karma!" said the mechanic.

"No problem," said Tom. "That just means she'll end up in hell a lot."

"Do I need to bring anything?" asked Rainie.

"Junk food," said Tom. "Nothing healthy."

"That's Tom's rule," said Douglas. "You can bring anything you want. I'll be putting out a vegetable dip."

"Yeah, right," said Raymond. "Mr. Health."

"Mr. Quiche," said another man.

"Tell her what we *dip* in your vegetable dip, Dougie."

"Frankfurters show up a lot," said Douglas. "And Tootsie Rolls. Once Tommy stuck his nose into the dip, and then the Health Department came and closed us down."

"Ida!" Minnie's voice was sharp.

"I'm about to get fired," said Rainie.

"Minnie can't fire you," said Tom. "Nothing bad can ever happen to Those Who Feed the Baby!"

But the expression on Minnie's face spoke eloquently about the bad things that could happen to her waitress Ida Johnson. As soon as Rainie got behind the counter with her, she whispered in Minnie's ear, "I can't help it that it's at Douglas's house. Count the chaperones and give me credit for a little judgment."

Minnie sniffed, but she stopped looking like she was about to put a skewer through Rainie's heart.

The Boys' Table lasted a whole hour, and then Douglas looked at his watch and said, "Ding."

"The one-o'clock bell," cried Tom.

Raymond whistled between his teeth.

"The one-o'clock whistle!"

And in only a few moments they had their coats on and hustled on out the door. They might act like boys for an hour at noon, but they were still grown-ups. They still had to get back to work, and right on time, too. Rainie couldn't decide if that was sad or wonderful. Maybe both.

By the time Rainie's shift was over, Minnie was her cheerful self again. Whether that meant that Minnie trusted her or she had simply forgotten that Rainie was going to feed the baby with the boys tonight, Rainie was glad not to have to argue with her. She didn't want anything to take away the strange jittery happiness that had been growing inside her all afternoon. She had no idea what the game was about, but she knew she liked these men, and she was beginning to suspect that maybe this game, maybe these boys were the reason she had stopped her wandering at this café in Harmony, Illinois. If there'd been a place in town that sold any clothes worth buying, Rainie would have bought a new outfit. As it was, she spent a ridiculous amount of time fretting over what to wear. It had to be that the sheer foolish immaturity of these boys had infected her. She was like a virgin girl getting ready for her first date. She laughed at herself—and then took off all her clothes and started over again.

She spent so much time choosing what to wear that she put off buying any refreshments until it was almost too late. As it was, all she had time to do was rush to the corner grocery and buy the first thing that she saw that looked suitable—a giant bag of peanut M&Ms.

"I hear you're going to feed the baby," said the zit-faced fat thirty-year-old checkout girl, who'd never given her the time of day before.

"How do these stories get started?" said Rainie. "I don't even *have* a baby."

She got back to her apartment just as Tom pulled up in a brand-new but thoroughly mud-spattered pickup truck. "Hop in before you let all the heat out!" he shouted. He was rolling before she had the door shut.

Douglas Spaulding's house was just what she expected, right down to the white picket fence and the veranda wrapped around the white clapboard walls. Simple, clean lines, the walls and trim freshly painted, with dark blue shutters at the windows and lights shining between the pulled-back curtains. A house that said Good plain folks live here, and the doors aren't locked, and if you're hungry we've got a bite to eat, and if you're lonely we've got a few minutes to chat, anytime you feel like dropping by. It was an island of light in the dark night. When she opened the door of Tom's pickup truck, she could hear laughter from the parlor, and as she picked her way through the paths in the snow to get to the front porch, she could look up and see people moving around inside the house, eating and drinking and talking, all so at ease with each other that it woke the sweetest flavors in her memory and made her hungry to get inside.

They were laying the game out on the dining room table—a large homemade board, meadow green with tiny flowers and a path of white squares drawn around the outside of it. Most squares had either a red heart or a black teardrop, with a number. In the middle of the board was a dark area shaped like a giant kidney bean with black dotted lines radiating out from it toward the squares. And in the middle of the "bean" were a half-dozen little pigs that Rainie recognized as being from the old Pig Out game, plus a larger pig from some child's set of plastic barnyard animals.

"That's the pigpen," said the mechanic, who was counting beans into piles of ten. Only he wasn't dressed like a mechanic anymore—he was wearing a white shirt and white pants with fire-engine-red suspenders. He was also wearing a visor, like the brim of a baseball cap. Rainie remembered seeing people wear visors like that on TV. In old Westerns or something. Who wore them? Bank tellers? Bookies? She couldn't remember.

"What's your name?" asked Rainie. "I've been thinking of you as the guy in overalls cause I never caught your name."

"If I'd'a knowed you was a-thinkin' of me, Miss Ida, I'd'a wore my overalls again tonight, just to please you." He grinned at her.

"Three *Ida*s in the same sentence," said Rainie. "Not bad."

"It's a good thing she didn't think of you as 'that butt-ugly guy,' " said Tom. "You're a lot better-looking when you keep *that* particular feature covered up."

"Look what Miss Ida brung us," said the mechanic. "*M*'s."

Immediately all the men in the vicinity of the table hummed in unison. "Mmmmm. Mmmmm."

"Not just *M*'s, but *peanut M*'s."

Again, only twice as loud: "MMMMMM! MMMMMM!"

Either M&Ms were part of the ritual, or they were making fun of her. Suddenly Rainie felt unsure of herself. She held up the bag. "Isn't this OK?"

"Sure," said Douglas. "And I get the brown ones." He had a large bowl in his hand; he took the bag of M&Ms from her, pulled it open, and poured it into the bowl.

"Dougie has a thing for brown M&Ms," said the mechanic.

"I eat them as a public service," said Douglas. "They're the ugly ones, so when I eat them all the bowl is full of nothing but bright colors for everyone else."

"He eats the brown ones because they make up forty percent of the package," said Tom.

"Tom spends most of his weekends opening bags of M&Ms and counting them, just to get the percentages," said an old man that hadn't been at the café.

"Hi, Dad," said Douglas. He turned and offered the old man the bowl of M&Ms.

The old man took a green one and popped it in his mouth. Then he stuck out his right hand to Rainie. "Hi," he said. "I'm Douglas Spaulding. Since he and his son are also Douglas Spaulding, everybody calls me Grandpa. I'm old but I still have all my own teeth."

"Yeah, in an old baby-food jar on his dresser," said Tom.

"In fact, he has several of *my* teeth, too," said the mechanic.

Rainie shook Grandpa's hand. "Pleased to meet you. I'm . . ." Rainie paused. For one crazy moment she had been about to say, I'm Rainie Pinyon. "I'm Ida Johnson."

"You sure about that?" asked Grandpa. He didn't let go of her hand.

"Yes, I am," she said. Rather sharply.

Grandpa raised his eyebrows and released her hand. "Welcome to the madhouse."

Suddenly there was a thunderous pounding on the stairs and Rose and Dougie burst into the room. "Release the pigs!" they both shouted. "Pig attack! Pig attack!"

Douglas just stood there laughing as his kids ran around the table, grunting and snorting like hogs as they reached into every bowl for chips and M&Ms and anything else that looked vaguely edible, stuffing it all into their mouths. The men all laughed as the kids ran back out of the room. Except Grandpa, who never cracked a smile. "What is the younger generation coming to?" he murmured. Then he winked at Rainie.

"Where should I sit?" she asked.

"Anyplace," said Tom.

She took the chair at the corner. It seemed the best place—the spot where she'd have to sit back away from the table because the table leg was in the way. It felt just a little safer to her, to be able to sit a little bit outside of the circle of the players.

The mechanic leaned over to her and said, "Cecil."

"What?" Rainie asked.

"My name," he said. "Don't tell anybody else."

Tom, who was sitting next to her, said in a loud whisper, "We all pretend that we think his name is 'Buck.' It makes him feel more manly."

"What do I *call* you?" asked Rainie. "If I'm supposed to keep Cecil a secret."

"Now you've gone and told," said Cecil.

"Call him Buck," said Tom.

"Does anybody else really call him that?" asked Rainie.

"I will if you will," said Tom.

"Time for a review of the rules!" said Douglas, as he took the last place at the table, which happened to be in the middle of the table on the side across from Rainie, so she'd be looking at him throughout the game.

"I hate to make you have to spend time going over everything for me," said Rainie.

"They repeat the rules every time anyway," said Grandpa.

"Cause Grandpa's getting senile and forgets them every time," said Tom.

"They repeat them because they're so proud of having thought them up themselves," said Grandpa.

The game was pretty complicated. They used plastic children's toys—little robots or dinosaurs—as their playing pieces. The idea of the game was to roll three dice and get around the board. Each time they passed Start they were reborn as the next-higher life-form, from slime to newt to emu to human; the winner was the first human to reach Start and therefore become supreme god.

"Then the supreme god turns over his karma cards. If he's got more good than bad karma, then whoever has the most good karma comes in second. But if the supreme god has more bad karma than good, then whoever has the most *bad* karma comes in second," said Douglas.

"So bad karma can be good?" asked Rainie.

"Never," said Tom. "What kind of person are you? No, if the supreme god turns out to have bad karma, it's a terrible disaster for the known universe. We all sing a very sad song and cry on the way home."

"The last time bad karma triumphed, Meryl Streep and Roseanne Barr released that movie *She-Devil,*" said Douglas.

"So you see, the consequences can be dire," said Tom.

"She didn't even get to do an accent," said Cecil, his tone mournful and hushed.

"And . . . and *Ed Begley Junior* had to play Roseanne Barr's husband," said Raymond.

"Only John Goodman is man enough to do that and live," said Cecil.

"So you see," said Tom, "our game isn't just a *game*. It has consequences in the real world."

Douglas continued with the rules. Every time you landed on a teardrop or a heart, you had a chance to pray to either the Baby of Sorrows or the Baby of Love, depending. In order to pray, you had to make an offering of as many beans as the number shown on the square. "So beans are like money," said Rainie.

"Ugly money," said Raymond.

"Nasty money," said Tom.

"Filthy lucre," said Grandpa.

"We hate beans," said Cecil. "Nobody wants beans. Only *greedy, nasty, selfish people* try to get a lot of beans."

"Of course, you have no chance of winning unless you have a lot of beans," said Douglas. "But if it ever looks like you are too interested in getting beans, then we hold a bean council and punish you."

"I never did like beans," said Rainie.

"Good thing," said Cecil. "But watch out, because Tom is a miserable bean thief and he'll steal your beans when you're not looking."

"*If* I actually cared for beans," said Tom, "I'd be an excellent bean thief."

"If your prayer is granted," Douglas said, going on with the rules, "then you get a power card. There are evil powers and good powers, depending on which baby you pray to. When you use an evil power you get a bad karma card, and when you use a good power you get a good karma card. Good power cards are always played on other people—they never benefit the person who plays them. Evil power cards are always vicious and selfish and vindictive."

"That's not in the rules," said Cecil.

"But it's the truth," said Douglas. "Good people never use evil power cards."

"Dougie's just sore because of the time we ganged up on him and killed him every time he stuck his nose out of hell," explained Tom.

"I tried to reason with them."

"He whined all night. It only goaded us to new depths of cruelty."

"They had no pity."

"We were nature red in tooth and claw," said Tom. "You were unfit to survive."

They went on with the rules but at the end Rainie could hardly remember half of them. "You just tell me what to do and I'll get the hang of it."

She started the game with five power cards. All of them were handwritten, the good powers in red ink, the evil powers in black. She had three evil cards and two good ones. One of the good ones said:

"BUTT-INSKI"
Allows you to
cause 2 other
players to swap
all power cards

Two of the evil power cards said:

"UP THE PIGGAGE"
ADD 2 PIGS TO THE PEN

and

"YOUR KARMA IS
MY KARMA"
ALLOWS YOU TO SWAP
KARMA CARDS WITH
ANOTHER PLAYER

The last two cards, one good, one evil, made Rainie laugh out loud. The evil one said:

RELEASE
THE
PIGS!!

The good one, on the other hand, said:

RELEASE
THE
PIGS!!
For the good of the
whole.

"What's funny?" asked Tom.

"Is there any difference between releasing the pigs on somebody from a good power card as opposed to an evil power card?" she asked.

"All the difference in the world!" cried Raymond.

"When you release the pigs for the good of the whole," said Cecil, "it's a noble act, a kind and generous sacrifice for the benefit of the entire community, without a single thought of personal benefit."

"Whereas," said Tom, "releasing the pigs from an evil power card is the act of a soulless, cruel, despicable human being."

"But I mean, is the actual pig attack any different?"

"Not a whit," said Douglas.

"Absolutely identical," said Tom.

"I'm betting that Ida has her a couple of Release-the-Pigs cards," said Raymond.

"How many beans are you betting?" asked Tom.

"Five beans says she does."

"Oh, yeah?" said Tom. "Well, *ten* beans says she *does*."

"That's what *I* said," said Raymond.

"No, you said *five* beans," said Tom.

"Roll the dice, Ida," said Grandpa, "or we'll never get started."

"The fate of the world hangs in the balance," said the quiet guy at the other end of the table—Rainie couldn't remember his name. He looked very sad, even when he laughed.

"Because you are first," said Douglas, "and because you have never played before, you may use the lobster dice to begin."

The lobster dice were just like the other dice—there were about a dozen scattered around the table—except that they had a red lobster printed on the face that should have had the one-spot.

"The lobster dice have special significance," said Douglas. "And if you should be so fortunate as to have a lobster turn up on your roll, it changes your move. For instance, if you roll the three dice and get two fives and a lobster, the total isn't eleven, it's ten-lobster."

"How many do I move for the lobster?"

"One," said Douglas.

"Per lobster," added Tom.

"So that's eleven," said Rainie.

Douglas and Tom both made a show of looking stricken. "An unbeliever," said Douglas. "I never would have thought it of you."

Tom addressed the others. "If she can't tell the difference between eleven and ten-lobster, then what if she rolls, like, *four-lobster-lobster?*"

They all shook their heads and made mournful noises.

"I worry about you, Ida," said Douglas. "You seem to have an unhealthy grip on reality."

"Nay," said Cecil, "reality hath an unhealthy grip on *her.*"

"Maybe I'm not worthy to use the lobster dice," said Rainie.

"Ah," said Douglas. "That's all right then."

"What is?"

"As long as you think you might be unworthy, then you *are* worthy."

"Thinking I'm unworthy makes me worthy?"

"Here are the sacred lobster dice," said Douglas. "You found the perfect last line for the song. You served us our beans and brought us our drinks. No one is worthier than you."

He spoke with such simplicity and sincerity that, even though she knew he was joking, she couldn't help but be touched. "I'm honored," she said, and meant it. She took the dice and rolled.

Two of the dice showed lobsters. The other die showed an ace. Some of the men gasped.

"One-lobster-lobster," murmured Cecil.

"The first roll of the game."

"Surely good karma will triumph tonight."

"Tell me," said Cecil, "are you perchance a visitor from another realm, temporarily dwelling among us mortals in disguise?"

"No," she said, laughing.

"Have you not been sent by the Baby of Love," Cecil insisted, "to bring the blessing of healing to a world of woe?"

Rainie reached out her hand toward Cecil. "Flesh and blood, see?"

He touched her hand, cradled it gently in his, as if it were a porcelain rose. "Ah," he said, "she is real. I know it, for I have touched her."

"She's not a real person," said Grandpa. "She's a ghost. Can't you tell? We're being haunted here tonight. Ida Johnson is just a figment of her own imagination."

The others chuckled, and Rainie laughed. But as she took her hand back from Cecil, she felt strangely shy. And when she looked at Grandpa, she found him gazing at her very steadily.

"I'm not a ghost," she said softly.

"Yes she is," said Grandpa to the others. "She can fool you boys, but not these old eyes. I know the difference."

"One-lobster-lobster," said Douglas. "Let's get this game moving!"

The game got moving. It took only a few minutes for Rainie to get into the spirit of it. The game was about life and death, but what happened with the dice was almost trivial compared to what they all did to each other with the power cards. The game had hardly begun when the blond guy at the other end of the table—Jack?—played a card on her that said:

"THE GRASS IS ALWAYS GREENER . . ."
Allows you to swap power
cards with another player

and in one moment she found herself with a handful of completely different cards. It wasn't Jack's turn, or hers—he just felt like playing it.

In a moment, though, she saw why. Douglas had landed on a square whose pigpath—the line connecting it to the pigpen—had only three dots on it. Jack played one of her former Release-the-Pigs cards, and they all whooped and hollered and lined up the baby pigs at the head of the pigpath, with Momma Pig last in line.

"This is pointless," said Douglas. "I'm still primordial ooze. I can't regress any farther than that."

"I want you in hell," said Jack.

"But I won't go to hell. I don't have any karma at all yet."

"You personally released the pigs on me twice last time. Tonight you're *never* going to be reincarnated."

"Grudge-holding is beneath you, Jack."

Jack burst into a country-music song.

> *If I can't hold me a woman,*
> *Then a grudge will have to do.*
> *The woman I'd hold against myself,*
> *But the grudge I'll hold against you.*

Rainie had never heard the song before, so she figured he had made it up. The tune was actually pretty good.

The pigs were about to start charging down the pigpath when Jack played her former card adding two pigs to the pen. Now there were even more pigs on the path, and since they leapfrogged instead of taking turns, the pigs were bound to reach Douglas. Each pig that got to him would cost him two life-pennies, except for Momma, who would cost him four. Since everybody started with only ten life-pennies, he was doomed.

"I need the lobster dice," said Douglas.

"You need an angel from heaven," said Jack.

Tom handed Jack the two bad karma cards he got for playing evil power cards.

"Oh, these are bad," sad Jack.

"Only what you deserve," said Douglas.

"Well, before we sic the pigs on you, Dougie, let's try *this*." Where-upon Jack laid down another of Rainie's old cards, the one that allowed him to swap karma with Douglas. Since Douglas had none and Jack had two bad karma cards, it meant that when Douglas died his karmic balance would be negative and he'd go to hell.

"You are one seriously evil dude tonight, Jack," said Raymond. "I like your style. Let's see what happens with this one." He laid down an evil power card that said:

"ANGRY OINKERS"
DOUBLES THE DAMAGE OF
ALL PIGS ON A GIVEN PIG
ATTACK

"Hey, how dead can I get?" asked Douglas.

"We won't find out on this turn," said Grandpa. He laid down a good power card that said:

"FAIR IS FAIR"
Causes the person
who released the
pigs to take the
damage from a
pig attack (only
when pigs are
released on
someone else)

"Son of a *gun*!" shouted Jack. "You can't do this to me!"

"Can so."

"I'm not even on a pigpath!" It was true. Jack's playing piece—the plastic triceratops—was on a square with no path connecting it to the pigpen.

"Doesn't matter," said Tom. "You're taking the damage from the attack on Douglas, so the pigs will still follow *his* pigpath."

"And since you just played that evil power on Douglas switching your karma, you get a new evil power card of your very own," said Grandpa. "So if you die, you'll go to hell."

The pigs started down the path. As each baby pig advanced to a new dot on the path, Jack got to roll one die. If he got a one or a two, the pig was "popped" and returned to the pen. He wasn't lucky—he only popped two pigs, so five reached him and he was dead before Momma could even start her run down the path.

Just before the last pig reached him, though, he played the other Release-the-Pigs card that he had got from Rainie, and since this one was "for the good of the whole" he got a good karma card for it. "Ha!" he said. "It's a ten and my bad karma card was only a four. I'll go to heaven, and Douglas *still* has to face the pigs!"

So once again the pigs were lined up and started down the path. Rainie looked again at the cards she had gotten from Jack. One of them said:

<u>"PERHAPS I CAN HELP"</u>
Allows you to heal
another player of
all damage.
(Will not work after
they have been
killed)

She waited until Douglas was down to his last two life-pennies, and played the card.

"You are my hero," he said.

"You're just too young to die," said Rainie.

"There's still some more pigs," Jack pointed out.

"Not enough to kill me," said Douglas.

"But," said Tom, "what if *Momma rides again*!" He slapped down an evil power card that said:

"MOMMA RIDES AGAIN"
CAUSES THE MOMMA PIG TO COME
DOWN THE PATH TWICE.

"This has gone too far!" cried Cecil. "I say Momma is drunk as a skunk." He laid down a good power card called <u>"SOUSED SOW"</u> that was supposed to keep Momma home.

"I hate do-gooders," said Raymond. He laid down an evil power card that said:

"I HATE
DO-GOODERS"
Allows you to
cancel a Good
power before it
takes effect

"So Momma rides twice," said Tom. "That'll be eight life-pennies if she makes it both times, and that plus the two babies and you *could* die, Douglas."

"Good to know," said Douglas. "Is this how you talk to your patients?"

"I'm a dermatologist," said Tom. "My patients don't die, they just put bags over their heads."

"Let's make sure of this," said Raymond, laying down another card.

"PIGS CAN FLY"
PIGS MOVE 2 SQUARES
EACH STEP INSTEAD OF 1

"I'm dead," said Douglas. And it was true. The pigs came down the path, Momma twice, and all his life-pennies were gone.

"Dead and in hell," said Jack cheerfully.

"Boy am I nice," said Grandpa, laying down a card.

"Not 'Boy Am I Nice'!" wailed Jack.

But it *was* the Boy-Am-I-Nice card. Grandpa took on himself all of the bad karma Douglas had gotten from Jack, leaving Douglas with no karma at all. "And that counts as good karma," said Douglas, "and so I go to heaven."

"No, no, no," moaned Jack.

"I'm in heaven while you're in *hell,* Jack," said Douglas. "Which is the natural order of the universe."

"Do people get to stay in heaven if they gloat?" asked Rainie.

"Absolutely. It's about the only fun thing that people in heaven are allowed to do," said Grandpa.

"And you should know, Grandpa," said Jack.

"All my old friends have gone to heaven," said Grandpa, "and not one of them is having any fun at all."

"They talk to you?" asked Rainie.

"No. They send me postcards that say 'Having a wonderful time. Wish you were here.' They're all gloating."

The game went on, the power cards flying thick and fast, with everybody praying like crazy to get more power cards. When someone didn't have enough beans to pray, somebody would invariably lend him a few. And Rainie noticed that there actually was a remarkable amount of bean-stealing when people weren't looking. In the meantime, Douglas had eaten every single brown peanut M&M in the bowl. "It really does look more festive when you do that," said Rainie.

"Do what?"

"Take the brown ones out. It looks so much brighter."

"Sometimes he leaves only the red and green ones," said Raymond. "At Christmastime, especially."

Douglas got out of heaven after three turns there, and before long he had caught up with the others—or rather, the others had been sent back or killed or whatever so often that he was about even with them. Jack, however, was never even able to get past the slime stage and up to the level of newt. "The game knows," said Douglas. "Slime thou art, and slime thou shalt remain."

"Makes me want to go *wash*," said Jack.

"That's a question," said Douglas. "If slime washed, what would it wash off? I mean, what seems dirty to slime?"

The game ebbed and flowed, people ganging up on each other and then, at odd moments, pitching in and helping somebody out with a good power card. Rainie began to realize that crazy as it was, this game really *was* like life. Even though people could only do to each other whatever was permitted by the power cards they randomly drew, it took on the rhythms of life. Things would be going great, and then something bad would happen and everything would look hopeless, and then you'd come back from the dead and the dice would be with you again and you'd be OK. They didn't take it easy on Rainie, and she played with the same gusto as everyone else, but the dice were with her, so that she seemed to make up her losses quite easily, and seemed to have exactly the power card she needed time after time.

Then Rainie prayed successfully to the Baby of Sorrow and the evil card she drew was an event, not a power.

"TAKE A BREAK"
EVERYONE RELAX, EAT SOME
FOOD (AT HOST'S EXPENSE),
CALL YOUR SPOUSES OR
WHATEVER. AFTER ALL,
WHAT'S LIFE FOR?

"About time!" said Tom. "I'm hungry."

"You've had your hands in the potato chips all night," said Douglas.

"That just means my hands are greasy."

"Nobody can eat just one," added Raymond.

They were already up from the table and moving toward the kitchen. "Should I draw another power card to replace this?" asked Rainie.

"Naw," said Jack. "When the card says take a break, we take a break. You can finish your turn when we get back."

In the kitchen, Douglas was nuking some lasagna.

"It doesn't have that revolting cottage cheese this time, does it?" Raymond was asking when Rainie came in.

"It's ricotta cheese," said Douglas.

"Oh, excuse me, ricotta cheese."

"And I made the second pan without it, just for you."

"Oh, I have to wait for the second pan, eh?"

"Wait for it or wear it," said Douglas.

Rainie pitched in and helped, but she noticed that none of them seemed to expect her to do the dishes. They cleaned up after themselves right along, so that the kitchen never got disgusting. They weren't really little boys after all.

The lasagna was pretty good, though of course the microwave heated it unevenly so that half of it was burning hot and the other half was cold. She carried her plate into the family room, where most of them were eating.

"They'll call them 'the oughts,'" Grandpa was saying.

"They'll call what 'the oughts'?" asked Rainie.

"The first ten years of the next century. You know, 'ought-one,' 'ought-two.' When I was a kid people still remembered the oughts, and people always talked about them that way. 'Back in ought-five.' Like that."

"Yeah, but back then they still used the word *ought* for zero, too," said Douglas. "Nobody'd even know what it meant today."

"People won't use *ought* even if they *ought* to," said Tom. Several of the men near him dipped a finger into whatever they were drinking and flicked a little of the liquid onto Tom, who bowed his head graciously.

"What about *zero*?" said Raymond. "Just call the first two decades 'the zeroes' and 'the teens.' "

"People aren't going to say 'zero-five,' " said Douglas. "Besides, zero has such a negative connotation. 'Last year was a real zero.' "

"Aren't there any other words for zero?" asked Rainie.

"I've got it!" said Tom. "The zips! Zip-one, zip-two, zip-three."

"That's it!" cried Raymond.

Douglas tried it out. " 'Back in zip-nine, when Junior got his Ph.D.' That works pretty well. It has style."

" 'I know what's happening, you young whippersnapper,' " said Cecil, putting on an old man's voice. " 'I remember the nineties! I didn't grow up in the zips, like you.' "

"This is great!" said Tom. "Let's write to our congressman and get it made into a law. The next decade will be called 'the zips'!"

"Don't make it a law, or they'll find a way to tax it," said Raymond.

"Fine with me," said Tom, "if I get a percentage for having thought of it."

Rainie noticed when Grandpa got up, set his plate down, and stepped outside. Probably going for a smoke, thought Rainie. And now that she thought of smoking, she wanted to. And now that she wanted to, she found herself getting up without a second thought. It was cold outside, she knew, and her coat wasn't *that* warm, but she needed to get out there.

And not just for the cigarette. In fact, when she got outside and looked into her purse, she realized that she didn't have any cigarettes. When had she stopped carrying them? How long had she not even noticed that she didn't have any?

"Nasty habit," said Grandpa.

She turned. He was sitting on the porch swing. Not smoking.

"I thought you came out here to smoke," said Rainie.

"Naw," he said. "I just got to thinking about the people I knew who remembered the oughts, and I liked thinking about them, and so I came out here so I could hold the thought without getting distracted."

"Well, I didn't mean to disturb you."

"No problem," said Grandpa. "I'm old enough that my thoughts aren't very complicated anymore. I get hold of one, it just goes around and around until it bumps into a dead brain cell and then I just stand there and wonder what I was thinking about."

"You're not so old," said Rainie. "You hold your own with those young men in there."

"I am *so* old. And *they* aren't all that young anymore, either."

He was right. This was definitely a party of middle-aged men. Rainie thought back to the beginning of her career and remembered that in those days, people in their forties seemed so powerful. They *were* the Establishment, the ones to be rebelled against. But now that she was in her forties herself she understood that if anything middle-aged people were *less* powerful than the young. They had less chance of changing anything. They seemed to fit into the world, not because they had made the world the way it was or because they even particularly liked it, but because they had to fit in so they could keep their jobs and feed their families. That's what I never understood when I was young, thought Rainie. I knew it with my head, but not with my heart—that pressure of feeding a family.

Or maybe I *did* know it, and hated what it did to people. To my parents. Maybe that's why my marriages didn't last and I never had any babies. Because I never wanted to be forty.

Surprise. I'm past forty anyway, and lonely to boot.

"I've got a question I want you to answer," she said to Grandpa. "Straight, no jokes."

"I knew you'd get around to asking."

"Oh, really?" she said. "Since you're so knowledgeable, do you happen to know what the question is?"

"Maybe." Grandpa got up and walked near her and leaned against the porch railing, whistling. The breath came out of his mouth in a continuous little puff of vapor.

He looked unbearably smug, and Rainie longed to take him down just a notch. "OK, what did I want to know?"

"You want to know why I called you a ghost."

That was exactly what she wanted to ask, but she couldn't stand to admit that he was right. "That *wasn't* my question, but as long as you bring it up, why *did* you say that? If it was a joke I didn't get it. You hurt my feelings."

"I said it because it's true. You're just haunting us. We can *see* you, but we can't touch you in any way."

"I have been touched in a hundred places since I came here."

"You got nothing at risk here, Ida Johnson," said Grandpa. "You don't care."

Rainie thought of Minnie. Of Douglas and his kids. "You're wrong, Grandpa Spaulding. I care very much."

"You care with your heart, maybe, but not with your soul. You care with those feelings that come and go like breezes, nothing that's going to last. You're playing with house money here. No matter how it comes out, you can't lose. You're going to come away from Harmony, Illinois, with more than you brought here."

"Maybe so," said Rainie. "Is that a crime?"

"No ma'am. Just a discovery. Something I noticed about you and I didn't think you'd noticed about yourself."

"Well ain't you clever, Grandpa." She smiled when she said it, so he'd know she was teasing him, not really being snide. But it hurt her feelings all over again, mostly because she could see now that he was right. How could anything she did here be *real,* after all, when nobody even knew her right name? In a way Ida Johnson *was* her right name—it was her *mother's* name, anyway, and didn't Douglas Spaulding have the same name as *his* father? Didn't he give the same name to his son? Why couldn't she use her mother's name? How was that a lie, really, when you looked at it the right way? "Ain't you clever. You found out my secret. Grandpa Spaulding, Grey Detective. Sees a strange woman in his parlor one November evening and all at once he knows everything there is to know about her."

Grandpa waited a moment before answering. And his answer wasn't really an answer. More like he just let slip whatever her words made him think of. "My brother Tom and I did that one summer. Kept a list of Discoveries and Revelations. Like noticing that you were a ghost."

Every time he said it, it stung her deeper. Still, she tried to keep her protest playful-sounding. "When you prick me, do I not bleed?"

He ignored her. "We made another list, too. Rites and Ceremonies. All the things we always did every year, we wrote them down, too, when we did them that summer. First stinkbug we stepped on. First harvest of dandelions."

"They got chemicals to kill the dandelions now," said Rainie.

"Stinkbugs, too, for that matter," said Grandpa. "Very convenient."

Rainie looked through the window. "They're settling back down to play the game in there."

"Go on back in then, if you want. Haunt whoever you want. Us mortals can't determine your itinerary."

She was tired of his sniping at her. But it didn't make her angry. It just made her sad. As if she had lost something and she couldn't even remember what it was. "Don't be mean to me," she said softly.

"Why shouldn't I?" he answered. "I see you setting up to do some harm to my family, Ida Johnson or whoever you are."

It couldn't be that Rainie was doing something to tip everybody off how much she was attracted to Douglas Spaulding, to the idea of him. It had to be that people around here were just naturally suspicious. "Do you say that to every stranger in town, or just the women?"

"You're one hungry woman, Ida Johnson," said Grandpa, cheerfully enough.

"Maybe I haven't been getting my vitamins."

"You can get pretty malnourished on a diet of stolen food."

That was it. The last straw. She didn't have to put up with any more accusations. "I'm done talking with you, old man." She meant to make a dramatic exit from the porch, but the door to the parlor wouldn't open.

"That door's painted shut," he said helpfully. "You want the other one." He pointed around to the far side of the bay window, where the door she had come out of was open a crack. The noises of the men at the table surged and faded like waves on the shore.

She took two steps toward that door, stalking, angry, and then realized that Grandpa was laughing. For a moment she wanted to slap him, to stop him from thinking he was so irresistibly wise, judging her the way adults always did. But she didn't slap him. Instead she plunked back down on the swing beside him and laughed right along.

Finally they both stopped laughing; even the silent gusts of laughter settled down; even the lingering smiles faded. It was cold, just sitting there, not talking, not even swinging.

"What was your question, anyway?" he asked out of nowhere.

For a moment she couldn't think what he was talking about. Then she remembered that she had denied that he was right when he guessed her question. "Oh, nothing," she said.

"It was important enough for you to come out here into the cold, wasn't it? Might as well ask me, cause here I am, and next week you can't be sure, I'm seventy-four going on seventy-five."

She still couldn't bring herself to admit that he had been right. Or rather, she couldn't admit that she had lied about it. "It was a silly question."

He said nothing. Just waited.

And as he waited, a question did come to her. "Your grandson, Dougie, he said that there were some things that nobody in town knew, and one of them was his father's middle name."

Grandpa Spaulding sighed.

"You can tell *me*," said Rainie. "After all, I'm a ghost."

"Douglas has never forgiven me for naming him the way I did. And sometimes I'm sorry I did it to him. How was I supposed to know that the name would turn trendy—as a girl's name? To me it was a boy's name, still is, a name full of sweat and sneakers and flies buzzing and jumping into the lake off a swing and almost drowning. A name that means open windows and hot fast crickets chirping in the sultry night."

"Summer," she said. A murmur. A whisper. A sweet memory on a cold night like this.

"That's right," he said. "I named him Douglas Summer Spaulding."

She nodded, thinking that Summer was the kind of name a sentimental, narcissistic fourteen-year-old girl would choose for herself. "You're lucky he didn't sue you when he came of age."

"I explained it to him. The way I explained it to my wife. I wanted to name him for something perfect, a dream to hold on to, or at least to wish for, to *try* for."

"You don't have to try for summer," said Rainie. "You just have to have the guy come and service the air conditioner."

"You don't believe that," he said, looking appalled.

"Oh, aren't ghosts allowed to tease old eccentrics?"

"I didn't name him for just any old summer, you know. I named him for one summer in particular. The summer of 1928, to be exact, the perfect summer. Twelve years old. Living in Grandpa's and Grandma's boardinghouse with my brother Tom. I knew it was perfect even at the time, not just thinking back on it. That summer was the place where God lived, the place where he filled my heart with love, the moment, the long exquisite twelve-week moment when I discovered that I was alive and that I liked it. The next summer Grandpa was dead, and the next year the Depression was under way and I had to work all summer to help put food on the table. I wasn't a kid anymore after summer 1928."

"But you were still alive," Rainie said.

"Not really," said Grandpa. "I *remembered* being alive, but I was coasting. Summer of '28 was like I had me a bike at the top of Culligan Hill and from up there I could see so far—I could see *past* the edge of every horizon. All so beautiful, spread out in front of me like Grandma's supper table, strange-looking and sweet-smelling and bound to be delicious. And so I got on the bike and I pushed off and never had to touch the pedals at all, I just coasted and coasted and coasted."

"Still coasting?" asked Rainie. "Never got to the supper table?"

"When you get down there and see things close, it isn't a supper table anymore, Rainie. It turns out to be the kitchen, and you aren't there to eat, you're there to fix the meal for other people. Grandma's kitchen was the strangest place. Nothing was anywhere that made sense. Sugar in every place except the canister marked sugar. Onions out on the counter and the knives never put away and the spices wherever Grandma last set them down. Chaos. But oh, Rainie, that old lady could cook. She had miracles in her fingers."

"What about you? Could you cook?"

He looked at her blankly.

"When you stopped coasting and found out that life was a kitchen."

"Oh." He remembered the stream of the conversation. "No," he said, chuckling. "No ma'am, I was no chef. But I didn't have to do it alone.

Didn't get married till I got back from the war, twenty-nine years old in 1945, I still got the mud of Italy under my fingernails and believe me, I've scrubbed them plenty, but there was my Marjory, and she gave me three children and the second one was a boy and I named him Douglas after myself and then I named him for the most perfect thing I ever knew, I named him for a dream . . ."

"For a ghost," said Rainie.

He looked at her so sadly. "For the opposite of a ghost, you poor child."

Douglas opened the parlor door and leaned out into the night. "Aren't you two smart enough to come in out of the cold?"

"One of us is," said Grandpa, but he didn't move.

"We're starting up," said Douglas, "and it's still your turn, Ida."

"Coming," said Rainie, getting up.

Douglas slipped back inside.

She helped Grandpa Spaulding out of the swing. "Don't get me wrong," he said, patting her back as she led the way to the door. "I like you. You're really something."

"Mmm," said Rainie.

"And if I can feel that way about you when you're pretending to be something you're not, think how much I'd like you if you actually told the truth about something."

She came through the door blushing, with anger and with embarrassment and with that thrill of fear—was she found out? Did Grandpa Spaulding somehow know who she really was?

Maybe he did. Without knowing the name Rainie Pinyon, maybe he knew exactly who she was anyway.

"Whose turn is it?" asked Tommy.

"Ida's," somebody said.

"What is she, an emu?"

"No, human. Look, she's a human."

"How did she get so far without us noticing?"

"Not to worry!" cried Douglas Summer Spaulding. He raised a red-lettered card over his head. "For the good of the whole—Release the Pigs!"

The others gave a rousing cheer.

"Give me my good karma," said Douglas. Then he grinned sheep-ishly in Rainie's face. "You have only five life-pennies and there are seven piglets and the pigpath is only three dots long, so I sincerely hope with all my heart that your karmic balance is of a sort to send you to heaven, because, dear lady, the porkers from purgatory are going to eat your shorts."

"Heaven?" said Rainie. "Not likely."

But she popped every one of the pigs before they got to her. It was like she couldn't roll anything but ones and twos.

"Grandpa's right," said Tommy. "She really *is* a ghost! The pigs went right through her!"

Then she rolled eighteen, three sixes, and it was enough to win.

"Supreme god!" Tommy cried. "She has effed the ineffable!"

"What's her karmic balance?"

She flipped over the karma cards. Three evils and one good, but the good was a ten and the evils were all low numbers and they balanced ex-actly.

"Zero counts as good," said Douglas. "How could anyone have sup-posed otherwise? So I bet I come in second with a balance of nine on the good side."

They all tallied and Grandpa finished last, his karmic balance a nega-tive fifty.

"That's the most evil I ever saw in all the years we've been feeding the baby," said Tommy. He switched to a Midwestern white man's version of black dialect. "Grandpa, you bad."

Grandpa caught Rainie's eye and winked. "It's the truth."

They all stayed around and helped finish off the refreshments and clean up from dinner, talking and laughing. Tom was the first to go. "If you're coming with me, Ida, the time is now."

"Already?" She shouldn't have said that, but she really did hate to go. It was the best night she'd had in months. Years.

"Sorry," he said. "But I've got to scrape some moles off people's faces first thing tomorrow, and I have to be bright-eyed and bushy-tailed or I accidentally take off noses and ears and people get so *testy* with me when I do that."

"That's fine, I really don't mind going."

"No, you go on ahead, Tom," said Douglas. "Somebody else can take her home."

"I can," said Raymond.

"Me too," said Jack. "Right on my way."

They all knew where she was living, of course. It made her smile. Whether I knew them or not, they cared enough about me to notice where I lived. Smalltown nosiness could be ugly if you looked at it one way, but kind of sweet and comforting if you looked at it another way entirely.

After a while she drifted away from the conversation in the kitchen and began wandering a little in the house. It was a bad habit of hers—her mother used to yell at her about it when she was a little kid. *Don't* go wandering around in strangers' houses. But curiosity always got the better of her. She drifted into the living room. No TV, lots of books. Fiction, biography, history, science—so that's what accountants read. I never would have guessed.

And then up the stairs, just to see what was there. Not meaning to pry. Just wanting to *know.*

Standing in the upstairs hall, in the near darkness, she could hear the children breathing. Which room is which, she wondered. The bathroom had the nightlight in it; she could see that the first two rooms belonged to the kids, one on the right, one on the left. The other two rooms had to be the one Douglas shared with his absent wife, and Grandpa's. A houseful. The extended family. Three generations present under one roof. This is the American home that everyone dreams of and nobody has. Dad goes off to work, Mom stays home, Grandpa lives right with you, there's a white picket fence and probably a dog in a nice little doghouse in the back yard. Nobody lives like this, except those who really work at it, those who know what life is supposed to be like and are determined to live that way.

Lord knows Mom and Dad weren't like this. Fighting all the time, clawing at each other to get their own way. And who's to say that Douglas and Jaynanne aren't like that, too? I haven't seen them together, I don't know what they're like.

But she did know. From the way the kids were with their father. That doesn't come out of a home torn apart with power struggles, with mutual fear and loathing.

She walked down the hall—just to see—and opened the last two doors. The one on the right had to be Grandpa's room, and she closed the door immediately. The one on the left had the big bed. Douglas's room.

She would have closed the door and gone downstairs at once, except that in the faint light from the bathroom nightlight she caught a glimpse of bright reflection from an old familiar shape, and suddenly she was filled with a longing that was so familiar, so right, that she couldn't resist it, not even for a moment. She snapped on the light and yes, it was what she had thought, a guitar, leaning against the wall beside the dresser that was obviously his—cluttered on top, no knickknacks.

Pulling the door almost closed behind her, she walked to the guitar and picked it up. Not a particularly good make, but not a bad one. And the strings were steel, not that wimpy nylon, and when she strummed them softly they were perfectly in tune. He has played this guitar today, she thought. And now my hands are holding something that his hands have held. I don't share the having of children with him, I don't share this sweet impossible house with him, but he plays this instrument and I can do that, too.

She didn't mean to play, but she couldn't help herself. It had been so long since she had even wanted to touch a musical instrument that, now that the hunger had returned to her, she had no will to resist it. Why should she? It was music that defined who she was in this world. It was music that gave her fame and fortune. It was music that was her only comfort when people let her down, which was always, always.

She played those old mournful melodies, the plucked-out ones, not the strumming tunes, not the dancey, frolicking ones. She played softly, gently, and hummed along, no words, no words . . . words would come later, after the music, after the mood. She remembered the hot African wind coming across the Mediterranean and drying her after a late-night swim on a beach in Mallorca. She remembered the lover she had had then, the one who yelled at her when he was drunk but who made love in the morning like no man had ever made love to her before, gluttonously, gorgeously, filling her like the sun coming up over the sea. Where was he now? Old. He'd be in his sixties now. He might be dead now. I didn't have his baby, either, but he didn't want one. He was a sunrise man, he was always gone by noon.

Tossing and turning, that's what sleep was like in Mallorca. Sticky and sweaty and never more than a couple of hours at a time. In the darkness you get up and stand on the veranda and let the sea breeze dry the sweat off you until you could go back inside and lie down again. And there he'd be, asleep, yes, but even though you were facing away from him you knew he'd reach out to you in his sleep, he'd hold you and press against you and his sweat would be clammy on your cold body, and his arm would arch over you and his hand would reach around you and cup your breast, and he'd start moving against you, and through it all he'd never even wake up. It was second nature to him. He could do it in his sleep.

What did Mallorca have to do with Harmony, Illinois? Why were tunes of hot Spanish nights coming out of this guitar here in the cold of December, with Christmas coming on and the little dying firs and pines standing up in the tree lots? It was the dream of love, that's what it was, the dream but not the memory of love because in the long run it never turned out to be real. In the long run she always woke up from love and felt it slip away the way dreams slip away in the morning, retreating all the faster the harder you try to remember them. It was always a mirage, but when she got thirsty for it the way she was now, it would come back, that dream, and make her warm again, make her sweat with the sweetness of it.

Maybe there was a noise. Maybe just the movement at the door. She looked up, and there were young Dougie and Rose, both of them awake, their faces sleepy but their eyes bright.

"I'm sorry," said Rainie, immediately setting the guitar aside.

"That's Dad's guitar," said Rose.

"You're good," said Dougie. "I wish I could play like that."

"I wish *Dad* could play like that," said Rose, giggling.

"I shouldn't be in here."

"What was that song?" asked Dougie. "I think I've heard it before."

"I don't think so," said Rainie. "I was making it up as I went along."

"It sounded like one of Dad's records."

"Well, I guess I'm not very original-sounding," said Rainie. She felt unbelievably awkward. She didn't belong in this room. It wasn't her room. But there they were in the doorway, not seeming to be angry at all.

"Can't you play some more?" said Dougie.

"You need your sleep," said Rainie. "I shouldn't have wakened you."

"But we're already awake," said Rose. "And we don't have school to-morrow, it's Saturday."

"No, no," said Rainie. "I have to get home." She brushed apologetically past them and hurried down the stairs.

Everybody was gone. The house was quiet. How long had she played?

Douglas was in the kitchen, making a honey sandwich. "It's my secret vice," he said. "It's making me fat. Want one?"

"Sure," she said. She couldn't remember ever having a honey sandwich in her life. She watched him pull the honey out of the jar, white and creamy, and spread it thickly on a slice of bread.

"Lid or no lid?" he asked.

"No lid," she said. She picked it up and bit into it and it was wonderful. He bit into his. A thin strand of honey stretched between his mouth and the bread, then broke, leaving a thread of honey down his chin.

"It's messy, but I don't care," he said.

"Where do you buy bread like this?"

"Jaynanne makes it," he said.

Of course. Of course she makes bread.

"Where is everybody?" she asked.

"Went home," said Doug. "Don't worry about a ride. They all had wives waiting for them, and I don't, so I said I'd take you home."

"No, I don't want you to have to go out on a night like this."

"I figured we'd leave a note on Minnie's door telling her you'd be late tomorrow."

"No," said Rainie. "I'll be there on time."

"It's after midnight."

"I've slept less and done more the next day. But I hate to have you have to drive me."

"So what would you do, walk?"

I'd sleep in your bed, Rainie said silently. I'd get up in the morning and we'd make breakfast together, and we'd eat it together, and then when the kids got up we'd fix another breakfast for them, and they'd laugh with us and be glad to see us. And we'd smile at each other and remember the sweetness in the dark, the secret that the children would never understand until twenty, thirty years from now. The secret that I'm only beginning to understand tonight.

"Thanks, I'll ride," said Rainie.

"Dad's out seeing to the dog. He worries that the dog gets too cold on nights like this."

"What, does he heat the doghouse?"

"Yes, he does," said Douglas. "He keeps bricks just inside the fireplace and then when he puts the fire out at night he wraps the hot bricks in a cloth and carries them outside and puts them in the doghouse."

"Does the dog appreciate it?"

"He sleeps inside with the bricks. He wags his tail. I guess he does." Douglas's bread was gone. She reached up and wiped the honey off his chin with her finger, then licked her finger clean.

"Thanks," he said.

But she could hear more in his voice than he meant to say. She could hear that faint tremble in his voice, the hesitation, the uncertainty. He could have interpreted her gesture as motherly. He could have taken it as a sisterly act. But he did not. Instead he was taking it the way she meant it, and yet he wasn't sure that she really meant it that way.

"Better go," he said. "Morning comes awful early."

They bundled up and went outside. They met Grandpa coming around the front of the house. "Night," Grandpa said.

"Night," said Rainie. "It was good talking to you."

"My pleasure entirely," he said. He sounded perfectly cheerful, which surprised her. Why should it surprise her?

Because I'm planning to do what he warned me not to do, thought Rainie. I'm planning to sleep with Douglas Spaulding tonight. He's mine if I want him, and I want him. Not forever, but tonight, this sweet lonely night when my music came back to me in his house, sitting on his bed, playing his guitar. Jaynanne can spare me this one night, out of all her happiness. There'll be no pain for anyone, and joy for him and me, and there's nothing wrong with that, I don't care what anyone says.

She got in his car and sat beside him, watching the fog of his breath in the cold air as he started the engine. She never took her eyes off him, seeing how the light changed when the headlights came on inside the garage, how it changed again as he leaned over the backseat, guiding the car in reverse down the driveway. He pressed a button and the garage door closed after them.

No one else was on the road. No one else seemed even to exist—all the houses were dark and still, and the tires crunching on snow were the only noise besides the engine, besides their breathing.

He tried to cover what was happening with chat. "Good game tonight, wasn't it?"

"Mm-hm," she said.

"Fun," he said. "Crazy bunch of guys. We act like children, I know it."

"I like children," she said.

"In fact, my kids are more mature than I am when I'm with those guys."

She remembered speaking to them tonight, their faces so sleepy. "I woke them, I'm afraid. I was playing your guitar. That's a bad habit of mine, intruding in people's houses. Sort of an invited burglar or something."

"I heard you playing," he said.

"Clear downstairs? I thought I was quieter than that."

"Steel strings," he said. "And the vents are all open in the winter. Sound carries. It was beautiful."

"Thanks."

"It was—beautiful," he said again, as if he had searched for another word and couldn't think of one. "It was the kind of music I've always longed for in my home, but I've never been good enough on the guitar to play like that myself."

"You keep it in tune."

"If I don't the dog barks."

She laughed, and he smiled in return. She couldn't stop looking at him. The heater was on now, so his breath didn't make a fog. The streetlights brightened his face; then it fell dark again. He's not that handsome. I'd never have looked at him twice if I'd met him in LA or New York. He would have been just another accountant there. So many bright lights in the city, how can someone like this ever shine there? But here, in the snow, in this small town, I can see the truth. That this is the true light, the one that all those neon lights and strobes and spots and halogens are trying to imitate but never can.

They pulled up in front of her apartment. He switched off his lights. The dark turned bright again almost immediately, as the snow reflected streetlights and moonlight.

I can't sleep with this man, thought Rainie. I don't deserve him. I made my choice many years ago, and a man like him is forever out of reach. Sleeping with him would be another self-deception, like so many I've indulged in before. He'd still be Jaynanne's husband and Dougie's and Rose's father and I'd still be a stranger, an intruder. If I sleep with him tonight I'd have to leave town tomorrow, not because I care what anybody thinks, not because anybody'd even know, but because I couldn't stand it, to have come so close and still not belong here. This is forbidden fruit. If I ate of it, I'd know too much, I'd see how naked I am in my own life, my old life.

He opened his car door.

"No," she said. "You don't need to help me out."

But he was already walking around the car, opening her door. He gave her a hand getting out. The snow squeaked under their feet.

"Thanks for the ride," she said. "I can get up the stairs OK."

"I know," he said. "I just don't like dropping people off without seeing them safe inside."

"You'd walk *Tom* to the door?"

"So I'm a sexist reactionary," he said. "I can't help it, I was raised that way. Always see the woman safely to the door."

"There aren't many rapists out on a night like this," said Rainie.

Ignoring her arguments, he followed her up the stairs and waited while she got the key out and unlocked the deadbolt and the knob. She knew that he'd ask to come inside. Knew that he'd try to kiss her. Well, she'd tell him no. Not because Minnie and Grandpa told her to, but because she had her own kind of integrity. Sleeping with him would be a lie she was telling to herself, and she wouldn't do it.

But he didn't try to kiss her. He stepped back as she pushed open the door and gave a little half-wave with his gloved hand and said, "Thanks."

"For what?" she asked.

"For bringing your music into my house tonight."

"Thanks," she said. It touched her that it seemed to mean so much to him. "Sorry I woke your kids."

He shook his head. "I never would have asked you to play. But I hoped. Isn't that stupid? I tuned my guitar for you, and then I hid it upstairs, and you found it anyway. Karma, right?"

It took a moment for her to realize what it meant, him saying that. In this town she had never touched a musical instrument or even told anybody that she played guitar. So why did he know to tune it for her?

"I'm such a fool," she whispered. "I thought my disguise was so perfect."

"I love your music," he said. "Since I heard the first note of it. Your songs have been at the heart of all the best moments of my life."

"How did you know?"

"You've done it before," he said. "Dropped out. Lived under an assumed name. Right? It took a while for me to realize why you looked so familiar. I kept coming back in to the café until finally I was sure. When you talked to me that day, you know, when you chewed me out, your voice—I had just listened to your live album that morning. I was pretty sure then. And tonight when you played, then I really knew. I wasn't going to say anything, but I had to thank you . . . for the music. Not just tonight, all of it. I'm sorry. I won't bother you again."

She was barely hearing him, though; her mind had snagged on the phrase he said before: Her songs had been at the heart of all the best moments of his life. It made her weak in the knees, those words. Because it meant that she *was* part of this, after all. Through her music. Her songs had all her longings in them, everything she'd ever known or felt or wished for, and he had brought those songs into his life, had brought *her* into his home. Of course Dougie thought she sounded like his dad's records—they had grown up hearing her songs. She did belong there in that house. He had probably known her music before he even knew his wife.

And now he was going to turn away and go on down the stairs and out to his car and *leave her here alone* and she couldn't let him go, not now, not now. She reached out and caught his arm; he stopped on the next-to-top step and that put them at the same level, and she kissed him. Kissed him and clung to him, kissed him and tasted the honey in his mouth. His arms closed around her. It was maddening to have their thick winter coats between them. She reached down, still kissing him, and fumbled to unbutton her coat, then his; she stepped inside his coat as if it were his bedroom. She pressed herself against him and felt his desire, the heat of his body.

At last the endless kiss ended, but only because she was ready to take him inside her room, to share with him what she knew he needed from her. She stepped up into her doorway and turned to lead him in.

He was rebuttoning his coat.

"No," she said. "You can't go now."

He shook his head and kept fastening the buttons. He was slow and clumsy, with his gloves on.

"You want me, Douglas Spaulding, and I need you more than you know."

He smiled, a shy, embarrassed smile. "Some fantasies can't come true," he said.

"I'm not fantasizing you, Douglas Spaulding."

"I'm fantasizing *you*," he answered.

"I'm real," she said. "You want me."

"I do," he said. "I want you very much."

"Then have me, and let me have you. For one night. Like the music. You've had my music with you all these years. I want the memory of your love with *me*. Who could begrudge us that?"

"Nobody would begrudge us anything."

"Then stay with me."

"It's not me you love," said Douglas, "and it's not my love you want."

"No?"

"It's my life you love, and my life you want."

"Yes," she said. "I want your life inside me."

"I know," he said. "I understand. I wanted this life, too. The difference between us is that I wanted it so much I did the things you have to do to get it. I set aside my career ambitions. I moved away from the city, from the center of things. I turned inward, toward my children, toward my wife. That's how you get the life I have."

Against her will, there were tears in her eyes. Feeling him slip away she wanted him all the more. "So you have it, and you won't share, is that it?"

"No, you don't understand," he said. "I can't give it to you."

"Because you're afraid of losing it yourself. Afraid of what all these small-minded people in this two-bit town will think."

"No, Rainie Pinyon, I'm not afraid of what they'll think of me, I'm afraid of what I'll know about myself. Right now, standing here, I'm the kind of man who keeps his promises. An hour from now, leaving here, I'd never be that kind of man again. It's the man who keeps his promises who gets the kind of life I have. Even if nothing else changed, I'd know that I was not that man anymore, and so everything would be changed. It would all be dust and ashes in my heart."

"You are a selfish bastard and I hate you," said Rainie. At the moment she said it, she meant it with all her heart. He was forbidding her. He was refusing her. She had offered him real love, her best love, her whole heart. She had allowed herself to *need him* and he was letting some idiotic notion of honor or something get in the way even though she knew that he wanted her too.

"Yeah," he said. He turned and walked down the stairs. She closed the door and stood there with her hand on the knob as she heard him start the car and drive away. It was hot in her apartment, with the heater on, with her coat on. She pulled it off and threw it against the door. She pulled off her sweater, her shoes, all her clothes and threw them against the walls and crawled into bed and cried, the way she used to cry when her mother didn't let her do what she *needed* to do. Cried herself to sleep.

She woke up with the sun shining into her window. She had overslept. She was late for work. She jumped out of bed and got dressed, hurrying. Minnie will be furious. I let her down.

But by the time she had her clothes on, she knew the truth. She had overslept because in her heart she knew she was done with this place. She had no reason to get up early because working for Minnie Wilcox wasn't her job anymore. She had found all that she was looking for when she first dropped out and went searching. Her music was back. She had something to sing about again. She could go home.

She didn't even pack. Just took her purse with all her credit cards and walked to the post office, which was where the buses stopped. She didn't care which one—St. Louis, Chicago, Des Moines, Cairo, Indianapolis, any bus that got her to an airport city would do. It turned out to be St. Louis.

By the time she saw the Gateway Arch she had written a song about feeding the baby of love. It turned out well enough that it got her some decent radio airplay for the first time in years, her first top-forty single since '75.

> *Tried to walk that lonely highway*
> *Men and women, two by two*
> *Promising, promising they will be true*
> *You went your way, I'll go my way*
> *Feeling old and talking new*
> *Whatever happened to you?*
> *I wonder what happened to you?*

> *Spoke to someone in the air*
> *Heard but didn't heed my prayer*
> *Couldn't feed it anyway*
> *Didn't have the price to pay*
> *You got to feed the baby*
> *Hungry, hungry, hungry baby*
> *Got to feed the baby of love*

She had her music back again, the only lover that had ever been faithful to her. Even when it tried to leave her, it always came home to her in the end.

NOTES ON "FEED THE BABY OF LOVE"

This story was born during the months just before I got married, when I was already living in the apartment Kristine and I were going to share after the wedding. One of my favorite singer-songwriters of all time is Joni Mitchell—her music is still locked into my heart, and her lyrics pop up all the time. During those lonely months before the wedding, I was at a magazine store in downtown Salt Lake City and found a story about Joni Mitchell and read it in the store (yes, in my poverty I was that kind of "customer").

In the story I learned that at one point she had dropped out and disappeared; the idea that came into my mind (or was it in the article?) was that she must have needed to get back on the street again, as one of her song lyrics says.

That night, playing her albums (a stack of about five records on a turntable/record changer—we're talking the Stone Age here), I jotted the notes for a story about a rock singer who goes, not to the "street," but to a small town in Utah, where she brings her rock 'n' roll expectations to a place where people don't share them. She falls in love with a young Mormon husband who loves her music and her, but at the last minute he can't be false to his wife, can't throw away the values that have shaped him into the kind of man this rock singer fell in love with. The idea is that you can't have it both ways—you can't be *this* person and have *that* experience.

I knew perfectly well that this was a seriously old-fashioned story, but it was also a true one. I was about to make some pretty serious covenants with my wife-to-be, which I intended to keep. But . . . I was also going to be pursuing a career (such was my overweening confidence) in which I might meet famous people and encounter the temptations that come to the rich and famous. I was keenly aware of all the Hollywood and New York artistic types who thought that their talent gave them a free ticket to break their word and hurt anyone they wanted to, because, after all, they were "geniuses." So in a way, this story idea was a reminder to myself that genius excuses nothing. So what if you're a really talented writer or actor or singer or athlete? If you're false to your wife, if you can't keep your word, then you still suck as a human being.

In other words, I was forewarning and, perhaps, forearming myself. Though none of that was consciously in my mind at the time, I can assure you! I simply thought of it as a cool story idea.

The trouble is, it was a cool story idea that I wasn't ready to write. Because I wrote it. It's a miserable little fragment called "Spider Eyes." I'm tempted to include it here just so that you can nod your heads and say, Yep, Card's right, that story is a real toilet-stuffer.

The problem, I see now, is that I couldn't write the story because I had never actually been married. I was looking at marriage from the wrong direction. Starry-eyed and naive, I had no idea how hard and how powerful this thing could be. I also had no idea, really, of what the life of a professional artist of any kind could be like, how frightening it was to get up every morning knowing that if you didn't perform *today* at least as well as you did yesterday, your career could simply disappear. So the story

I wrote then was shallow, empty, nothing, because I was too ignorant about the real world to write it.

But there it sat, in the back of my mind, waiting.

Skip a decade. *Ender's Game* has been published. I get an invitation from LucasFilm Games to come out to "the ranch" in Marin County and consult with them on some games. They're paying for the ticket—do you think I'm going to pass this up?

I had a great time, meeting some marvelously creative game designers and seeing how they think and plan in order to create great electronic games. But one of the best experiences wasn't at "the ranch"—it was at the home of one of the designers, where they trotted out a game designed by Greg Johnson, who didn't even work for LucasFilm Games.

The game was Feed the Baby of Love Many Beans or Perish in the Flames of Hell, and every scrap of gameplay in the story you just read comes from Greg's wonderfully irreverent game. (He later made me a game board of my own so I could own it and play it, and from time to time I trot it out and we play a round of it.) The real fun of the game, however, was that beyond the gameplay itself, Greg and the other guys had surrounded it with all kinds of unrelated rituals that bound them together as a community, so that the game itself, the *outcome* of the game, was both more and less than it seemed. More, because the game had become a symbol of their camaraderie and they pretended it had magical resonance in the real world; and less, because the game itself didn't actually matter, and nobody minded much who won and who lost.

One more element was needed before I could put things together and write a story. I was invited to take part in an anthology of stories in honor of Ray Bradbury (*The Bradbury Chronicles,* ed. William F. Nolan and Martin H. Greenberg). For this occasion, Bradbury had generously allowed a group of writers to set stories in the worlds he had created.

I knew immediately that, much as I loved his Martian and October Country stories, it was *Dandelion Wine* that I was going to visit. I loved that book. I didn't read it as a little kid, required by teachers to put on Doug Spaulding's sneakers—I read it in my late teens, as a sophisticated college student, and it melted me back into my childhood and made me see it through gold-colored glasses. Unlike the disillusionists of this world, who insist that the darkest of all possible views must be the "real" one, I knew in reading *Dandelion Wine* that the truth ran the other way. Living through childhood can be difficult and painful, but in fact, with relatively rare exceptions, it is also a glorious time that we're simply too short and too shortsighted to see. It is childhood that shapes our lives; it is the hopeful child inside us that gives us the faith that allows us to try things and achieve things in adulthood.

So, even though I was a sci-fi writer, I knew I was going to write an absolutely realistic but, I hoped, poetic story that echoed the optimism in the midst of struggle that marked *Dandelion Wine* as Bradbury's finest writing.

And I knew, without even having to think about it, that the story I was going to write was "Spider Eyes"—only this time, Rainie Pinyon would find Douglas Spaulding as a grownup, a husband and father, vulnerable to her, drawn to her—but still determined to be the man he was supposed to be.

The trouble was that *Dandelion Wine* was set in the 1930s, and the rock 'n' roll culture simply took place too late. It would not work.

That's when the character of the grandfather was born. *He* was the Douglas Spaulding of *Dandelion Wine,* but the town and the world were not changed, and he wanted his grandson to hold that world together for his own children.

I knew exactly the town where I wanted the story set, too. It was Nauvoo, the onetime Mormon capital on the banks of the Mississippi, just across from the southern tip of Iowa. Not because of any Mormon connection—this time around, the hero was not going to be Mormon—but because I had visited Nauvoo and fallen in love with the slightly shabby but still living downtown, the old houses, the river just down from the bluff. I thought: This is just the kind of place where Rainie Pinyon might get off the bus and go to the café (where I had recently dined) and order their slightly crusty fried eggs and decide, I think I'll work here for a while.

The elements were all together, and I knew it was going to be one of the best things, if not *the* best thing, I had ever written. Which scared me so much that I put off writing it for about as long as I could. The deadline for the Bradbury anthology was looming. And finally, while visiting in the home of friends in Sterling, Virginia, I sat down at their dining room table and wrote the thing in one sitting.

It was exactly what I wanted it to be.

The trouble was, it was just a short story. It appeared in the anthology and whoever read it, read it, but then it was gone. I thought of expanding it into a novel, but I was afraid the weight of it would be too much. I tried developing it as a screenplay, writing one version of it myself and then getting my friend and partner Aaron Johnston to write what turned out to be a very good draft. Someday, using ideas Aaron and I came up with for the screenplay, I may write that novel version yet.

But here's one of the barriers. Where would I publish it?

I'm a genre writer. I'm known as a writer of kids-in-space stories. Even though I take those stories very seriously as literature—indeed, more seriously than I think most "literary" writers take their productions—it means I'm on the wrong side of the apartheid fence in the literary world. We who actually write for the joy of our readers instead of to impress them are considered tainted. I could easily get a small press to publish the book, but I would have zero chance of getting a novel version of "Feed the Baby of Love" published in a serious way by a major publisher. They have too much contempt for a genre they do not understand and for a kind of writing they and their literary community forsook long ago.

It would be so easy to add a little magic to the story and make it a contemporary fantasy. Then I could sell it without a problem.

Not a chance. Sometimes a story has to be what it is. This is one of those times.

Of course, I might be delusional here. This story might be so personal that I'm the only reader who thinks it's as wonderful as I think it is. In which case, it's a mercy that it *hasn't* been available to the general public for all these years, because I've been allowed to maintain my illusions. I still have them, though, and intend to keep them. This story, more than any other I've written, tells the truth about what life is for.

IV

HATRACK RIVER

GRINNING MAN

The first time Alvin Maker run across the grinning man was in the steep woody hills of eastern Kentuck. Alvin was walking along with his ward, the boy Arthur Stuart, talking either deep philosophy or the best way for travelers to cook beans, I can't bring to mind now which, when they come upon a clearing where a man was squatting on his haunches looking up into a tree. Apart from the unnatural grin upon his face, there wasn't all that much remarkable about him, for that time and place. Dressed in buckskin, a cap made of coonhide on his head, a musket lying in the grass ready to hand—plenty of men of such youth and roughness walked the game trails of the unsettled forest in those days.

Though come to think of it, eastern Kentuck wasn't all that unsettled by then, and most men gave up buckskin for cotton during summer, less they was too poor to get them none. So maybe it *was* partly his appearance that made Alvin stop up short and look at the fellow. Arthur Stuart, of course, he did what he saw Alvin do, till he had some good reason to do otherwise, so he stopped at the meadow's edge, too, and fell silent too, and watched.

The grinning man had his gaze locked on the middle branches of a scruffy old pine that was getting somewhat choked out by slower-growing flat-leaf trees. But it wasn't no tree he was grinning at. No sir, it was the bear.

There's bears and there's bears, as everyone knows. Some little old brown bears are about as dangerous as a dog—which means if you beat it with a stick you deserve what you get, but otherwise it'll leave you alone.

But some black bears and some grizzlies, they have a kind of bristle to the hair on their backs, a kind of spikiness like a porcupine that tells you they're just spoiling for a fight, hoping you'll say a cross word so's they can take a swipe at your head and suck your lunch back up through your neck. Like a likkered-up river man.

This was that kind of bear. A little old, maybe, but as spiky as they come, and it wasn't up that tree cause it was afraid, it was up there for honey, which it had plenty of, along with bees that were now so tired of trying to sting through that matted fur that they were mostly dead, all stung out. There was no shortage of buzzing, though, like a choir of folks as don't know the words to the hymn so they just hum, only the bees was none too certain of the tune, neither.

But there sat that man, grinning at the bear. And there sat the bear, looking down at him with its teeth showing.

Alvin and Arthur stood watching for many a minute while nothing in the tableau changed. The man squatted on the ground, grinning up; the bear squatted on a branch, grinning down. Neither one showed the slightest sign that he knew Alvin and Arthur was even there.

So it was Alvin broke the silence. "I don't know who started the ugly contest, but I know who's going to win."

Without breaking his grin, through clenched teeth the man said, "Excuse me for not shaking your hands but I'm a-busy grinning this bear."

Alvin nodded wisely—it certainly seemed to be a truthful statement. "And from the look of it," says Alvin, "that bear thinks he's grinning you, too."

"Let him think what he thinks," said the grinning man. "He's coming down from that tree."

Arthur Stuart, being young, was impressed. "You can do that just by grinning?"

"Just hope I never turn my grin on *you*," said the man. "I'd hate to have to pay your master the purchase price of such a clever blackamoor as you."

It was a common mistake, to take Arthur Stuart for a slave. He was half Black, wasn't he? And south of the Hio was all slave country then, where a Black man either was, or used to be, or sure as shooting was bound to become somebody's property. In those parts, for safety's sake,

Alvin didn't bother correcting the assumption. Let folks think Arthur Stuart already had an owner, so folks didn't get their hearts set on volunteering for the task.

"That must be a pretty strong grin," said Alvin Maker. "My name's Alvin. I'm a journeyman blacksmith."

"Ain't much call for a smith in these parts. Plenty of better land farther west, more settlers, you ought to try it." The fellow was still talking through his grin.

"I might," said Alvin. "What's your name?"

"Hold still now," says the grinning man. "Stay right where you are. He's a-coming down."

The bear yawned, then clambered down the trunk and rested on all fours, his head swinging back and forth, keeping time to whatever music it is that bears hear. The fur around his mouth was shiny with honey and dotted with dead bees. Whatever the bear was thinking, after a while he was done, whereupon he stood on his hind legs like a man, his paws high, his mouth open like a baby showing its mama it swallowed its food.

The grinning man rose up on *his* hind legs, then, and spread *his* arms, just like the bear, and opened his mouth to show a fine set of teeth for a human, but it wasn't no great shakes compared to bear's teeth. Still, the bear seemed convinced. It bent back down to the ground and ambled away without complaint into the brush.

"That's my tree now," said the grinning man.

"Ain't much of a tree," said Alvin.

"Honey's about all et up," added Arthur Stuart.

"My tree and all the land round about," said the grinning man.

"And what you plan to do with it? You don't look to be a farmer."

"I plan to sleep here," said the grinning man. "And my intention was to sleep without no bear coming along to disturb my slumber. So I had to tell him who was boss."

"And that's all you do with that knack of yours?" asked Arthur Stuart. "Make bears get out of the way?"

"I sleep under bearskin in winter," said the grinning man. "So when I grin a bear, it stays grinned till I done what I'm doing."

"Don't it worry you that someday you'll meet your match?" asked Alvin mildly.

"I got no match, friend. My grin is the prince of grins. The king of grins."

"The emperor of grins," said Arthur Stuart. "The Napoleon of grins!"

The irony in Arthur's voice was apparently not subtle enough to escape the grinning man. "Your boy got him a mouth."

"Helps me pass the time," said Alvin. "Well, now you done us the favor of running off that bear, I reckon this is a good place for us to stop and build us a canoe."

Arthur Stuart looked at him like he was crazy. "What do we need a canoe for?"

"Being a lazy man," said Alvin, "I mean to use it to go downstream."

"Don't matter to me," said the grinning man. "Float it, sink it, wear it on your head or swallow it for supper, you ain't building nothing right here." The grin was still on his face.

"Look at that, Arthur," said Alvin. "This fellow hasn't even told us his name, and he's a-grinning *us*."

"Ain't going to work," said Arthur Stuart. "We been grinned at by politicians, preachers, witchers, and lawyers, and you ain't got teeth enough to scare us."

With that, the grinning man brought his musket to bear right on Alvin's heart. "I reckon I'll stop grinning then," he said.

"I think this ain't canoe-building country," said Alvin. "Let's move along, Arthur."

"Not so fast," said the grinning man. "I think maybe I'd be doing all my neighbors a favor if I kept you from ever moving away from this spot."

"First off," said Alvin, "you got no neighbors."

"All mankind is my neighbor," said the grinning man. "Jesus said so."

"I recall he specified Samaritans," said Alvin, "and Samaritans got no call to fret about me."

"What I see is a man carrying a poke that he hides from my view."

That was true, for in that sack was Alvin's golden plow, and he always tried to keep it halfway hid behind him so folks wouldn't get troubled if they happened to see it move by itself, which it was prone to do from time to time. Now, though, to answer the challenge, Alvin moved the sack around in front of him.

"I got nothing to hide from a man with a gun," said Alvin.

"A man with a poke," said the grinning man, "who *says* he's a black-smith but his only companion is a boy too scrawny and stubby to be learning his trade. But the boy is just the right size to skinny his way through an attic window or the eaves of a loose-made house. So I says to myself, this here's a second-story man, who lifts his boy up with those big strong arms so he can sneak into houses from above and open the door to the thief. So shooting you down right now would be a favor to the world."

Arthur Stuart snorted. "Burglars don't get much trade in the woods."

"I never said you-all looked smart," said the grinning man.

"Best point your gun at somebody else now," said Arthur Stuart quietly. "Iffen you want to keep the use of it."

The grinning man's answer was to pull the trigger. A spurt of flame shot out as the barrel of the gun exploded, splaying into iron strips like the end of a worn-out broom. The musket ball rolled slowly down the barrel and plopped out into the grass.

"Look what you done to my gun," said the grinning man.

"Wasn't me as pulled the trigger," said Alvin. "And you was warned."

"How come you still grinning?" asked Arthur Stuart.

"I'm just a cheerful sort of fellow," said the grinning man, drawing his big old knife.

"Do you like that knife?" asked Arthur Stuart.

"Got it from my friend Jim Bowie," said the grinning man. "It's took the hide off six bears and I can't count how many beavers."

"Take a look at the barrel of your musket," said Arthur Stuart, "and then look at the blade of that knife you like so proud, and think real hard."

The grinning man looked at the gun barrel and then at the blade. "Well?" asked the man.

"Keep thinking," said Arthur Stuart. "It'll come to you."

"You let him talk to White men like that?"

"A man as fires a musket at me," said Alvin, "I reckon Arthur Stuart here can talk to him any old how he wants."

The grinning man thought that over for a minute, and then, though no one would have thought it possible, he grinned even wider, put away his knife, and stuck out his hand. "You got some knack," he said to Alvin.

Alvin reached out and shook the man's hand. Arthur Stuart knew what was going to happen next, because he'd seen it before. Even though Alvin was announced as a blacksmith and any man with eyes could see the strength of his arms and hands, this grinning man just had to brace foot to foot against him and try to pull him down.

Not that Alvin minded a little sport. He let the grinning man work himself up into quite a temper of pulling and tugging and twisting and wrenching. It would have looked like quite a contest, except that Alvin could've been fixing to nap, he looked so relaxed.

Finally Alvin got interested. He squished down hard and the grinning man yelped and dropped to his knees and began to beg Alvin to give him back his hand. "Not that I'll ever have the use of it again," said the grinning man, "but I'd at least like to have it so I got a place to store my second glove."

"I got no plan to keep your hand," said Alvin.

"I know, but it crossed my mind you might be planning to leave it here in the meadow and send me somewheres else," said the grinning man.

"Don't you ever stop grinning?" asked Alvin.

"Don't dare try," said the grinning man. "Bad stuff happens to me when I don't smile."

"You'd be doing a whole lot better if you'd've frowned at me but kept your musket pointed at the ground and your hands in your pockets," said Alvin.

"You got my fingers squished down to one, and my thumb's about to pop off," said the grinning man. "I'm willing to say uncle."

"Willing is one thing. Doing's another."

"Uncle," said the grinning man.

"Nope, that won't do," said Alvin. "I need two things from you."

"I got no money and if you take my traps I'm a dead man."

"What I want is your name, and permission to build a canoe here," said Alvin.

"My name, if it don't become 'One-handed Davy,' is Crockett, in memory of my daddy," said the grinning man. "And I reckon I was wrong about this tree. It's your tree. Me and that bear, we're both far from home and got a ways to travel before nightfall."

"You're welcome to stay," said Alvin. "Room for all here."

"Not for me," said Davy Crockett. "My hand, should I get it back, is going to be mighty swoll up, and I don't think there's room enough for it in this clearing."

"I'll be sorry to see you go," said Alvin. "A new friend is a precious commodity in these parts." He let go. Tears came to Davy's eyes as he gingerly felt the sore palm and fingers, testing to see if any of them was about to drop off.

"Pleased to meet you, Mr. Journeyman Smith," said Davy. "You too, boy." He nodded cheerfully, grinning like an innkeeper. "I reckon you couldn't possibly be no burglar. Nor could you possibly be the famous Prentice Smith what stole a golden plow from his master and run off with the plow in a poke."

"I never stole nothing in my life," said Alvin. "But now you ain't got a gun, what's in my poke ain't none of your business."

"I'm pleased to grant you full title to this land," said Davy, "and all the rights to minerals under the ground, and all the rights to rain and sunlight on top of it, plus the lumber and all hides and skins."

"You a lawyer?" asked Arthur Stuart suspiciously.

Instead of answering, Davy turned tail and slunk out of the clearing just like that bear done, and in the same direction. He kept on slinking, too, though he probably wanted to run; but running would have made his hand bounce and that would hurt too much.

"I think we'll never see *him* again," said Arthur Stuart.

"I think we will," said Alvin.

"Why's that?"

"Cause I changed him deep inside, to be a little more like the bear. And I changed that bear to be a little bit more like Davy."

"You shouldn't go messing with people's insides like that," said Arthur Stuart.

"The Devil makes me do it," said Alvin.

"You don't believe in the Devil."

"Do so," said Alvin. "I just don't think he looks the way folks say he does."

"Oh? What does he look like then?" demanded the boy.

"Me," said Alvin. "Only smarter."

Alvin and Arthur set to work making them a dugout canoe. They cut down a tree just the right size—two inches wider than Alvin's hips—and set to burning one surface of it, then chipping out the ash and burning it deeper. It was slow, hot work, and the more they did of it, the more puzzled Arthur Stuart got.

"I reckon you know your business," he says to Alvin, "but we don't need no canoe."

"*Any* canoe," says Alvin. "Miss Larner'd be right peeved to hear you talking like that."

"First place," says Arthur Stuart, "you learned from Tenskwa-Tawa how to run like a Red man through the forest, faster than any canoe can float, and with a lot less work than this."

"Don't feel like running," said Alvin.

"Second place," Arthur Stuart continued, "water works against you every chance it gets. The way Miss Larner tells it, water near killed you sixteen times before you was ten."

"It wasn't the water, it was the Unmaker, and these days he's about give up on using water against me. He mostly tries to kill me now by making me listen to fools with questions."

"Third," says Arthur Stuart, "in case you're keeping count, we're supposed to be meeting up with Mike Fink and Verily Cooper, and making this canoe ain't going to help us get there on time."

"Those are two boys as need to learn patience," says Alvin calmly.

"Fourth," says Arthur Stuart, who was getting more and more peevish with every answer Alvin gave, "*fourth* and final reason, you're a *maker,* dagnabbit, you could just think this tree hollow and float it over to the water light as a feather, so even if you had a reason to make this canoe, which you don't, and a safe place to float it, which you don't, you sure don't have to put me through this work to make it by hand!"

"You working too hard?" asked Alvin.

"Harder than is needed is always too hard," said Arthur.

"Needed by whom and for what?" asked Alvin. "You're right that

I'm not making this canoe because we need to float down the river, and I'm not making it because it'll hurry up our travel."

"Then why? Or have you give up altogether on doing things for reasons?"

"I'm not making a canoe at all," says Alvin.

There knelt Arthur Stuart, up to his elbows in a hollowed-out log, scraping ash. "This sure ain't a house!"

"Oh, *you're* making a canoe," said Alvin. "And we'll float in that canoe down that river over there. But *I'm* not making a canoe."

Arthur Stuart kept working while he thought this over. After a few minutes he said, "I know what you're making."

"Do you?"

"You're making *me* do what you want."

"Close."

"You're making me make this tree into something, but you're also using this tree to make me into something."

"And what would I be trying to make *you* into?"

"Well, I think *you* think you're making me into a maker," said Arthur Stuart. "But all you're making me into is a *canoe*-maker, which ain't the same thing as being an all-around all-purpose maker like yourself."

"Got to start somewhere."

"You didn't," says Arthur. "You was born knowing how to make stuff."

"I was born with a knack," says Alvin. "But I wasn't born knowing how to use it, or when, or why. I learned to love making for its own sake. I learned to love the feel of the wood and the stone under my hands, and from that I learned to see inside it, to feel how it felt, to know how it worked, what held it together, and how to help it come apart in just the right way."

"But I'm not learning any of that," says Arthur.

"Yet."

"No sir," says Arthur Stuart. "I'm not seeing inside nothing, I'm not feeling inside nothing except how my back aches and my whole body's pouring off sweat and I'm getting more and more annoyed at being made to labor on a job you could do with a wink of your eye."

"Well, that's something," says Alvin. "At least you're learning to see inside yourself."

Arthur Stuart fumed a little more, chipping away burnt wood as he did. "Someday I'm going to get fed up with your smugness," he says to Alvin, "and I won't follow you anymore."

Alvin shook his head. "Arthur Stuart, I tried to get you not to follow me this time, if you'll recall."

"Is *that* what this is about? You're punishing me for following you when you told me not to?"

"You said you wanted to learn everything about being a maker," says Alvin. "And when I try to teach you, all I get is pissing and moaning."

"You also get work from me," says Arthur. "I never stopped working the whole time we talked."

"That's true," says Alvin.

"And here's something you didn't consider," says Arthur Stuart. "All the time we're making a canoe, we're also *un*making a tree."

Alvin nodded. "That's how it's done. You never make something out of nothing. You always make it out of something else. When it becomes the new thing, it ceases to be what it was before."

"So every time you do a making, you do an unmaking, too," says Arthur Stuart.

"Which is why the Unmaker always knows where I am and what I'm doing," says Alvin. "Because along with doing my work, I'm also doing a little bit of his."

That didn't sound right or true to Arthur Stuart, but he couldn't figure out an argument to answer it, and while he was trying to think one up, they kept on a-burning and a-chipping and lo and behold, they had them a canoe. They dragged it to the stream and put it in and got inside it and it tipped them right over. Spilled them into the water three times, till Alvin finally gave up and used his knack to feel the balance of the thing and then reshape it just enough that it had a good balance to it.

Arthur Stuart had to laugh at him then. "What lesson am I supposed to learn from *this*? How to make a *bad* canoe?"

"Shut up and row," said Alvin.

"We're going downstream," said Arthur Stuart, "and I don't have to row. Besides which all I've got is this stick, which is no kind of paddle."

"Then use it to keep us from running into the bank," said Alvin, "which we're about to do thanks to your babbling."

Arthur Stuart fended the canoe away from the bank of the stream, and they kept on floating down until they joined a larger stream, and a larger, and then a river. All the time, Arthur kept coming back to the things Alvin said to him, and what he was trying to teach, and as usual Arthur Stuart despaired of learning it. And yet he couldn't help but think he had learned *something,* even if he had no idea at present what the thing he learned might be.

Because folks build towns on rivers, when you float down a river you're likely as not to come upon a town, which they did one morning with mist still on the river and sleep still in their eyes. It wasn't much of a town, but then it wasn't much of a river, and they weren't in much of a boat. They put in to shore and dragged the canoe onto the bank, and Alvin shouldered his poke with the plow inside and they trudged on into town just as folks was getting up and about their day.

First thing they looked for was a roadhouse, but the town was too small and too new. Only a dozen houses, and the road so little traveled that grass was growing from one front door to the next. But that didn't mean there was no hope of breakfast. If there's light in the sky, somebody's up, getting a start on the day's work. Passing one house with a barn out back, they heard the ping-ping-ping of a cow getting milked into a tin pail. At another house, a woman was coming in with the night's eggs from a chicken coop. That looked promising.

"Got anything for a traveler?" asked Alvin.

The woman looked them up and down. Without a word she walked on into her house.

"If you wasn't so ugly," said Arthur Stuart, "she would have asked us in."

"Whereas looking at you is like seeing an angel," said Alvin.

They heard the front door of the house opening.

"Maybe she was just hurrying in to cook them eggs for us," said Arthur Stuart.

But it wasn't the woman who came out. It was a man, looking like he hadn't had much time to fasten his clothing. In fact, his trousers were kind of droopy, and they might have started laying bets on how quick they'd drop to the porch if he hadn't been aiming a pretty capable-looking blunderbuss at them.

"Move along," the man said.

"We're moving," said Alvin. He hoisted his poke to his back and started walking across in front of the house. The barrel of the shotgun followed them. Sure enough, just as they were about even with the front door, the trousers dropped. The man looked embarrassed and angry. The barrel of the blunderbuss dipped. The loose birdshot rolled out of the barrel, dozens of tiny lead balls hitting the porch like rain. The man looked confused now.

"Got to be careful loading up a big-barrel gun like that," Alvin said. "I always wrap the shot in paper so it don't do that."

The man glared at him. "I did."

"Why, I know you did," said Alvin.

But there sat the shot on the porch, a silent refutation. Nevertheless, Alvin was telling the simple truth. The paper was still in the barrel, as a matter of fact, but Alvin had persuaded it to break open at the front, freeing the shot.

"Your pants is down," said Arthur Stuart.

"Move along," said the man. His face was turning red. His wife was watching from the doorway behind him.

"Well, you know, we was already planning to," said Alvin, "but as long as you can't quite kill us, for the moment at least, can I ask you a couple of questions?"

"No," said the man. He set down the gun and pulled up his trousers.

"First off, I'd like to know the name of this town. I reckon it must be called 'Friendly' or 'Welcome.' "

"It ain't."

"Well, that's two down," said Alvin. "We got to keep guessing, or you think you can just tell us like one fellow to another?"

"How about 'Pantsdown Landing'?" murmured Arthur Stuart.

"This here is Westville, Kentuck," said the man. "Now move along."

"My second question is, seeing as how you folks don't have enough to share with a stranger, is there somebody who's prospering a bit more and might have something to spare for travelers as have a bit of silver to pay for it?"

"Nobody here got a meal for the likes of you," said the man.

"I can see why this road got grass growing on it," said Alvin. "But your graveyard must be full of strangers as died of hunger hoping for breakfast here."

On his knees picking up loose shot, the man didn't answer, but his wife stuck her head out the door and proved she had a voice after all. "We're as hospitable as anybody else, except to known burglars and thieving prentices."

Arthur Stuart let out a low whistle. "What you want to bet Davy Crockett came this way?" he said softly.

"I never stole a thing in my life," said Alvin.

"What you got in that poke, then?" demanded the woman.

"I wish I could say it was the head of the last man who pointed a gun at me, but unfortunately I left it attached to his neck, so he could come here and tell lies about me."

"So you're ashamed to show the golden plow you stole?"

"I'm a blacksmith, ma'am," said Alvin, "and I got my tools here. You're welcome to look, if you want."

He turned to address the other folks who were gathering, out on their porches or into the street, a couple of them armed.

"I don't know what you folks heard tell," said Alvin, setting down his poke, "but you're welcome to look at my tools." He drew open the mouth of the poke and let the sides drop so his hammer, tongs, bellows, and nails lay exposed in the street. Not a sign of a plow.

Everyone looked closely, as if taking inventory.

"Well, maybe you ain't the one we heared tell of," said the woman.

"No, ma'am, I'm the exact one, if it was a certain trapper in a coonskin cap named Davy Crockett who was telling the tale."

"So you confess to being that Prentice Smith who stole the plow? And a burglar?"

"No, ma'am, I just confess to being a fellow as got himself on the wrong side of a trapper who talks a man harm behind his back." He gathered up his bag over the tools and drew the mouth closed. "Now, if you-all want to turn me away, go ahead, but don't go thinking you turned away a thief, because it ain't so. You pointed a gun at me and turned me away without a bite to eat for me or this hungry boy, without so much as a trial or a scrap of evidence, just on the word of a traveler who was as much a stranger here as me."

The accusation made them all sheepish. One old woman, though, wasn't having any of it. "We know Davy, I reckon," she said. "It's you we never set eyes on."

"And never will again, I promise you," said Alvin. "You can bet I'll tell this tale wherever I travel—Westville, Kenituck, where a stranger can't get a bite to eat, and a man is guilty before he even hears the accusation."

"If there's no truth to it," said the old woman, "how did you know it was Davy Crockett a-telling the tale?"

The others nodded and murmured as if this were a telling point.

"Cause Davy Crockett accused me of it to my face," said Alvin, "and he's the only one who ever looked at me and my boy and thought of burglaring. I'll tell you what I told him. If we're burglars, why ain't we in a big city with plenty of fine houses to rob? A burglar could starve to death, trying to find something to steal in a town as poor as this one."

"We ain't poor," said the man on the porch.

"You got no food to spare," said Alvin. "And there ain't a house here with a door that even locks."

"See?" cried the old woman. "He's already checked our doors to see how easy they'll be to break into!"

Alvin shook his head. "Some folks see sin in sparrows and wickedness in willow trees." He took Arthur Stuart by the shoulder and turned to head back out of town the way they came.

"Hold, stranger!" cried a man behind them. They turned to see a large man on horseback approaching slowly along the road. The people parted to make way for him.

"Quick, Arthur," Alvin murmured. "Who do you reckon this is?"

"The miller," said Arthur Stuart.

"Good morning to you, Mr. Miller!" cried Alvin in greeting.

"How did you know my trade?" asked the miller.

"The boy here guessed," said Alvin.

The miller rode nearer, and turned his gaze to Arthur Stuart. "And how did you guess such a thing?"

"You spoke with authority," said Arthur Stuart, "and you're riding a horse, and people made way for you. In a town this size, that makes you the miller."

"And in a bigger town?" asked the miller.

"You'd be a lawyer or a politician," said Arthur Stuart.

"The boy's a clever one," said the miller.

"No, he just runs on at the mouth," said Alvin. "I used to beat him but I plumb gave out the last time. Only thing I've found that shuts him up is a mouthful of food, preferably pancakes, but we'd settle for eggs, boiled, scrambled, poached, or fried."

The miller laughed. "Come along to my house, not three rods beyond the commons and down the road toward the river."

"You know," said Alvin, "my father's a miller."

The miller cocked his head. "Then how does it happen you don't follow his trade?"

"I'm well down the list of eight boys," said Alvin. "Can't all be millers, so I got put out to a smith. I've got a ready hand with mill equipment, though, in case you'll let me help you to earn our breakfast."

"Come along and we'll see how much you know," said the miller. "As for these folks, never mind them. If some wanderer came through and told them the sun was made of butter, you'd see them all trying to spread it on their bread." His mirth at this remark was not widely appreciated among the others, but that didn't faze him. "I've got a shoeing shed, too, so if you ain't above a little farrier work, I reckon there's horses to be shod."

Alvin nodded his agreement.

"Well, go on up to the house and wait for me," said the miller. "I won't be long. I come to pick up my laundry." He looked at the woman that Alvin had first spoken to. Immediately she ducked back inside the house to fetch the clothes the miller had come for.

On the road to the mill, once they were out of sight of the villagers, Alvin began to chuckle.

"What's so funny?" asked Arthur Stuart.

"That fellow with his pants around his ankles and birdshot dribbling out of his blunderbuss."

"I don't like that miller," said Arthur Stuart.

"Well, he's giving us breakfast, so I reckon he can't be all bad."

"He's just showing up the town folks," said Arthur Stuart.

"Well, excuse me, but I don't think that'll change the flavor of the pancakes."

"I don't like his voice."

Well, that made Alvin perk up and pay attention. Voices were part of Arthur Stuart's knack. "Something wrong with the way he talks?"

"There's a meanness in him," said Arthur Stuart.

"May well be," said Alvin. "But his meanness is better than hunting for nuts and berries again, or taking another squirrel out of the trees."

"Or another fish." Arthur made a face.

"Millers get a name for meanness sometimes," he said. "People need their grain milled, all right, but they always think the miller takes too much. So millers are used to having folks accuse them. Maybe that's what you heard in his voice."

"Maybe," said Arthur Stuart. Then he changed the subject. "How'd you hide the plow when you opened your poke?"

"I kind of opened up a hole in the ground under the poke," said Alvin, "and the plow sank down out of sight."

"You going to teach me how to do things like *that*?"

"I'll do my best to teach," said Alvin, "if you do your best to learn."

"What about making shot spill out of a gun that's pointed at you?"

"My knack opened the paper, but his own trousers, that's what made the barrel dip and spill out the shot."

"And you didn't make his trousers fall?"

"If he'd pulled up his suspenders, his pants would've stayed up just fine," said Alvin.

"It's all unmaking though, isn't it?" said Arthur Stuart. "Spilling shot, dropping trousers, making them folks feel guilty for not taking you in."

"So I should've let them drive us away without breakfast?"

"I've skipped breakfasts before."

"Well, aren't you the prissy one," said Alvin. "Why are you suddenly so critical of the way I do things?"

"You're the one made me dig out a canoe with my own hands," said

Arthur Stuart. "To teach me making. So I keep looking to see how much making *you* do. And all I see is how you unmake things."

Alvin took that a little hard. Didn't get mad, but he was kind of thoughtful and didn't speak much the rest of the way to the miller's house.

So nearly a week later, there's Alvin working in a mill for the first time since he left his father's place in Vigor Church and set out to be a prentice smith in Hatrack River. At first he was happy, running his hands over the machinery, analyzing how the gears all meshed. Arthur Stuart, watching him, could see how each bit of machinery he touched ran a little smoother—a little less friction, a little tighter fit—so more and more of the power from the water flowing over the wheel made it to the rolling millstone. It ground faster and smoother, less inclined to bind and jerk. Rack Miller, for that was his name, also noticed, but since he hadn't been watching Alvin work, he assumed that he'd done something with tools and lubricants. "A good can of oil and a keen eye do wonders for machinery," said Rack, and Alvin had to agree.

But after those first few days, Alvin's happiness faded, for he began to see what Arthur Stuart had noticed from the beginning: Rack was one of the reasons why millers had a bad name. It was pretty subtle. Folks would bring in a sack of corn to be ground into meal, and Rack would cast it in handfuls onto the millstone, then brush the corn flour into a tray and back into the same sack they brought it in. That's how all millers did it. No one bothered with weighing before and after, because everyone knew there was always some corn flour lost on the millstone.

What made Rack's practice a little different was the geese he kept. They had free rein in the millhouse, the yard, the millrace, and—some folks said—Rack's own house at night. Rack called them his daughters, though this was a perverse kind of thing to say, seeing as how only a few laying geese and a gander or two ever lasted out the winter. What Arthur Stuart saw at once, and Alvin finally noticed when he got over his love scene with the machinery, was how those geese were fed. It was expected that a few kernels of corn would drop; couldn't be helped. But Rack always took the sack and held it, not by the top, but by the shank of the sack, so kernels of corn dribbled out the whole way to the millstone. The geese were on that corn like—well, like geese on corn. And then he'd take big sloppy handfuls of corn to throw onto the millstone. A powerful lot of kernels hit the side of the stone instead of the top, and of course they dropped and ended up in the straw on the floor, where the geese would have them up in a second.

"Sometimes as much as a quarter of the corn," Alvin told Arthur Stuart.

"You counted the kernels? Or are you weighing corn in your head now?" asked Arthur.

"I can tell. Never less than a tenth."

"I reckon he figures he ain't stealing, it's the geese doing it," said Arthur Stuart.

"Miller's supposed to keep his tithe of the ground corn, not double or triple it or more in gooseflesh."

"I don't reckon it'll do much good for me to point out to you that this ain't none of our business," said Arthur Stuart.

"I'm the adult here, not you," said Alvin.

"You keep saying that, but the things you do, I keep wondering," said Arthur Stuart. "I'm not the one gallivanting all over creation while my pregnant wife is resting up to have the baby back in Hatrack River. I'm not the one keeps getting himself throwed in jail or guns pointed at him."

"You're telling me that when I see a thief I got to keep my mouth shut?"

"You think these folks are going to thank you?"

"They might."

"Put their miller in jail? Where they going to get their corn ground then?"

"They don't put the *mill* in jail."

"Oh, you going to stay here, then? You going to run this mill for them, till you taught the whole works to a prentice? How about me? You can bet they'll love paying their miller's tithe to a free half-Black prentice. What are you *thinking*?"

Well, that was always the question, wasn't it? Nobody ever knew, really, what Alvin was thinking. When he talked, he pretty much told the truth, he wasn't much of a one for fooling folks. But he also knew how to keep his mouth shut so you didn't know what was in his head. Arthur Stuart knew, though. He might've been just a boy, though more like a near-man these days, height coming on him kind of quick, his hands and feet getting big even faster than his legs and arms was getting long, but Arthur Stuart was an expert, he was a bona fide certified scholar on one subject, and that was Alvin, journeyman blacksmith, itinerant all-purpose dowser and doodlebug, and secret maker of golden plows and reshaper of the universe. He knew Alvin had him a plan for putting a stop to this thievery without putting anybody in jail.

Alvin picked his time. It was a morning getting on toward harvest time, when folks was clearing out a lot of last year's corn to make room for the new. So a lot of folks, from town and the nearby farms, was queued up to have their grain ground. And Rack Miller, he was downright exuberant in sharing that corn with the geese. But as he was handing the sack of corn flour to the customer, less about a quarter of its weight in goosefodder, Alvin scoops up a fine fat gosling and hands it to the customer right along with the grain.

The customer and Rack just looks at him like he's crazy, but Alvin pretends not to notice Rack's consternation at all. It's the customer he talks to. "Why, Rack Miller told me it was bothering him how much corn these geese've been getting, so this year he was giving out his goslings, one to each regular customer, as long as they last, to make up for it. I think that shows Rack to be a man of real honor, don't you?"

Well, it showed *something,* but what could Rack say after that? He just grinned through clenched teeth and watched as Alvin gave away gosling after gosling, making the same explanation, so everybody, wide-eyed and happy as clams, gave profuse thanks to the provider of their Christmas feast about four months off. Them geese would be monsters by then, they were already so big and fat.

Of course, Arthur Stuart noticed how, as soon as Rack saw how things was going, suddenly he started holding the sacks by the top, and taking smaller handfuls, so most of the time not a kernel fell to the ground. Why, that fellow had just learned himself a marvelous species of efficiency, returning corn to the customer diminished by nought but the true miller's tithe. It was plain enough that Rack Miller wasn't about to feed no corn to geese that somebody else was going to be feasting on that winter!

And when the day's work ended, with every last gosling gone, and only two ganders and five layers left, Rack faced Alvin square on and said, "I won't have no liar working for me."

"Liar?" asked Alvin.

"Telling them fools I meant to give them goslings!"

"Well, when I first said it, it wasn't true *yet,* but the minute you didn't raise your voice to argue with me, it became true, didn't it?" Alvin grinned, looking for all the world like Davy Crockett grinning him a bear.

"Don't chop no logic with me," said Rack. "You know what you was doing."

"I sure do," said Alvin. "I was making your customers happy with you for the first time since you come here, and making an honest man out of you in the meantime."

"I already *was* an honest man," said Rack. "I never took but what I was entitled to, living in a godforsaken place like this."

"Begging your pardon, my friend, but God ain't forsaken this place, though now and then a soul around here might have forsaken *Him.*"

"I'm done with your help," said Rack icily. "I think it's time for you to move on."

"But I haven't even looked at the machinery you use for weighing the corn wagons," said Alvin. Rack hadn't been in a hurry for Alvin to check them over—the heavy scales out front was only used at harvest time, when farmers brought in whatever corn they meant to sell. They'd roll the wagons onto the scales, and through a series of levers the scale would be balanced with much lighter weights. Then the wagon would be rolled back on empty and weighed, and the difference between the two weights was the weight of the corn. Later on the buyers would come, roll on their empty wagons and weigh them, then load them up and weigh them again. It was a clever bit of machinery, a scale like that, and it was only natural that Alvin wanted to get his hands on it.

But Rack wasn't having none of it. "My scales is my business, stranger," he says to Alvin.

"I've et at your table and slept in your house," says Alvin. "How am I a stranger?"

"Man who gives away my geese, he's a stranger here forever."

"Well, then, I'll be gone from here." Still smiling, Alvin turned to his young ward. "Let's be on our way, Arthur Stuart."

"No sir," says Rack Miller. "You owe me for thirty-six meals these last six days. I didn't notice this Black boy eating one whit less than you. So you owe me in service."

"I gave you due service," says Alvin. "You said yourself that your machinery was working smooth."

"You didn't do nought but what I could have done myself with an oilcan."

"But the fact is I did it, and you didn't, and that was worth our keep. The boy's worked, too, sweeping and fixing and cleaning and hefting."

"I want six days' labor out of your boy. Harvest is upon us, and I need an extra pair of hands and a sturdy back. I've seen he's a good worker and he'll do."

"Then take three days' service from me *and* the boy. I won't give away any more geese."

"I don't have any more geese to give, except the layers. Anyway I don't want no miller's son, I just want the boy's labor."

"Then we'll pay you in silver money."

"What good is silver money here? Ain't nothing to spend it on. Nearest city of any size is Carthage, across the Hio, and hardly anybody goes there."

"I don't use Arthur Stuart to discharge my debts. He's not my—"

Well, long before those words got to Alvin's lips, Arthur Stuart knew what he was about to do—he was going to declare that Arthur wasn't his slave. And that would be about as foolish a thing as Alvin could do. So Arthur Stuart spoke right up before the words could get away. "I'm happy to work off the debt," he says. "Except I don't think it's possible. In six days I'll eat eighteen more meals and then I'll owe another three days, and in those three days I'll eat nine meals and I'll owe a day and a half, and at that rate I reckon I'll never pay off that debt."

"Ah yes," says Alvin. "Zeno's paradox."

"And you told me there was never any practical use for that 'bit of philosophical balderdash,' as I recall you saying," says Arthur Stuart. It was an argument from the days they both studied with Miss Larner, before she became Mrs. Alvin Smith.

"What the Sam Hill you boys talking about?" asked Rack Miller.

Alvin tried to explain. "Each day that Arthur Stuart works for you, he'll build up half again the debt that he pays off by his labor. So he only covers half the distance toward freedom. Half and half and half again, only he never quite gets to the goal."

"I don't get it," says Rack. "What's the joke?"

By this point, though, Arthur Stuart had another idea in mind. Mad as Rack Miller was about the goslings, if he truly needed help at harvest time he'd keep Alvin on for it, unless there was some other reason for getting rid of him. There was something Rack Miller planned to do that he didn't want Alvin to see. What he didn't reckon on was that this half-Black "servant" boy was every bit smart enough to figure it out himself. "I'd like to stay and see how we solve the paradox," says Arthur Stuart.

Alvin looks at him real close. "Arthur, I got to go see a man about a bear."

Well, that tore Arthur Stuart's resolve a bit. If Alvin was looking for Davy Crockett, to settle things, there might be scenes that Arthur wanted to see. At the same time, there was a mystery here at the millhouse, too, and with Alvin gone Arthur Stuart had a good chance at solving it all by himself. The one temptation was greater than the other. "Good luck," said Arthur Stuart. "I'll miss you."

Alvin sighed. "I don't plan to leave you here at the tender mercy of a man with a peculiar fondness for geese."

"What does *that* mean?" Rack said, growing more and more certain that they were making fun of him underneath all their talk.

"Why, you call them your daughters and then cook them and eat them," says Alvin. "What woman would ever marry you? She wouldn't dare leave you alone with the children!"

"Get out of my millhouse!" Rack bellowed.

"Come on, Arthur Stuart," said Alvin.

"I *want* to stay," Arthur Stuart insisted. "It can't be no worse than the time you left me with that schoolmaster." (Which is another story, not to be told right here.)

Alvin looked at Arthur Stuart real steady. He was no Torch, like his wife. He couldn't look into Arthur's heartfire and see a blame thing. But somehow he saw something that let him make up his mind the way

Arthur Stuart wanted him to. "I'll go for now. I'll be back, though, in six days, and I'll have an accounting with you. You don't raise a hand or a stick against this boy, and you feed him and treat him proper."

"What do you think I am?" asked Rack.

"A man who gets what he wants," said Alvin.

"I'm glad you recognize that about me," said Rack.

"Everybody knows that about you," said Alvin. "It's just that you aren't too good at picking what you ought to be wanting." With another grin, Alvin tipped his hat and left Arthur Stuart.

Well, Rack was as good as his word. He worked Arthur Stuart hard, getting ready for the harvest. A late summer rain delayed the corn in the field, but they put the time to good account, and Arthur was given plenty to eat and a good night's rest, though it was the millhouse loft he slept in now, and not the house; he had only been allowed inside as Alvin's personal servant, and with Alvin gone, there was no excuse for a half-Black boy sleeping in the house.

What Arthur noticed was that all the customers were in good cheer when they came to the millhouse for whatever business they had, especially during the rain when there wasn't no field work to be done. The story of the goslings had spread far and wide, and folks pretty much believed that it really had been Rack's idea, and not Alvin's doing at all. So instead of being polite but distant, the way folks usually was with a miller, they gave him hail-fellow-well-met and he heard the kind of jokes and gossip that folks shared with their friends. It was a new experience for Rack, and Arthur Stuart could see that this change was one Rack Miller didn't mind.

Then, the last day before Alvin was due to return, the harvest started up, and farmers from miles around began to bring in their corn wagons. They'd line up in the morning, and the first would pull his wagon onto the scale. The farmer would unhitch the horses and Rack would weigh the whole wagon. Then they'd hitch up the horses, pull the wagon to the dock, the waiting farmers would help unload the corn sacks—of course they helped, it meant they'd be home all the sooner themselves—and then back the wagon onto the scale and weigh it again, empty. Rack would figure the difference between the two weighings, and that difference was how many pounds of corn the farmer got credit for.

Arthur Stuart went over the figures in his head, and Rack wasn't cheating them with his arithmetic. He looked carefully to see if Rack was doing something like standing on the scale when the empty wagon was being weighed, but no such thing.

Then, in the dark of that night, he remembered something one of the farmers grumbled as they were backing an empty wagon onto the scale. "Why didn't he build this scale right at the loading dock, so we could un-load the wagon and reweigh it without having to move the durn thing?" Arthur Stuart didn't know the mechanism of it, but he thought back over the day and remembered that another time a farmer had asked if he could get his full wagon weighed while the previous farmer's wagon was being unloaded. Rack glared at the man. "You want to do things your way, go build your own mill."

Yes sir, the only thing Rack cared about was that every wagon get two weighings, right in a row. And the same system would work just as well in reverse when the buyers came with their empty wagons to haul corn east for the big cities. Weigh the empty, load it, and weigh it again. When Alvin got back, Arthur Stuart would be ready with the mystery mostly solved.

Meanwhile, Alvin was off in the woods, looking for Davy Crockett, that grinning man who was singlehandedly responsible for getting two separate guns pointed at Alvin's heart. But it wasn't vengeance that was on Alvin's mind. It was rescue.

For he knew what he'd done to Davy and the bear, and kept track of their heartfires. He couldn't see into heartfires the way Margaret could, but he could see the heartfires themselves, and keep track of who was who. In fact, knowing that no gun could shoot him and no jail could hold him, Alvin had deliberately come to the town of Westville because he knew Davy Crockett had come through that town, the bear not far behind him, though Davy wouldn't know that, not at the time.

He knew it now, though. What Alvin saw back in Rack's millhouse was that Davy and the bear had met again, and this time it might come out a little different. For Alvin had found the place deep in the particles of the body where knacks were given, and he had taken the bear's best knack and given the same to Davy, and Davy's best knack and gave as much to the bear. They were evenly matched now, and Alvin figured he had some responsibility to see to it that nobody got hurt. After all, it was partly Alvin's fault that Davy didn't have a gun to defend himself. Mostly it was Davy's fault for pointing it at him, but Alvin didn't have to wreck the gun the way he did, making the barrel blow apart.

Running lightly through the woods, leaping a stream or two, and stopping to eat from a fine patch of wild strawberries on a riverbank, Alvin got to the place well before nightfall, so he had plenty of time to reconnoiter. There they were in the clearing, just as Alvin expected, Davy and the bear, not five feet apart, both of them a-grinning, staring each other down, neither one budging. That bear was all spiky, but he couldn't get past Davy's grin; and Davy matched the bear's single-minded tenacity, oblivious to pain, so even though his butt was already sore and he was about out of his mind with sleepiness, he didn't break his grin.

Just as the sun set, Alvin stepped out into the clearing behind the bear. "Met your match, Davy?" he asked.

Davy didn't have an ounce of attention to spare for chat. He just kept grinning.

"I think this bear don't mean to be your winter coat this year," said Alvin.

Davy just grinned.

"In fact," said Alvin, "I reckon the first one of you to fall asleep, that's who the loser is. And bears store up so much sleep in the winter, they just flat-out don't need as much come summertime."

Grin.

"So there you are barely keeping your eyelids up, and there's the bear just happy as can be, grinning at you out of sincere love and devotion."

Grin. With maybe a little more desperation around the eyes.

"But here's the thing, Davy," said Alvin. "Bears is better than people, mostly. You got your bad bears, sometimes, and your good people, but on average, I'd trust a bear to do what he thinks is right before I'd trust a human. So now what you got to wonder is, what does that bear think will be the right thing to do with you, once he's grinned you down?"

Grin grin grin.

"Bears don't need no coats of human skin. They do need to pile on the fat for winter, but they don't generally eat meat for that. Lots of fish, but you ain't a swimmer and the bear knows that. Besides, that bear don't think of you as meat, or he wouldn't be grinning you. He thinks of you as a rival. He thinks of you as his equal. What *will* he do? Don't you kind of wonder? Don't you have some speck of curiosity that just wants to know the answer to that question?"

The light was dimming now, so it was hard to see much more of either Davy or the bear than their white, white teeth. And their eyes.

"You've already stayed up one whole night," said Alvin. "Can you do it again? I don't think so. I think pretty soon you're going to understand the mercy of bears."

Only now, in his last desperate moments before succumbing to sleep, did Davy dare to speak. "Help me," he said.

"And how would I do that?" asked Alvin.

"Kill that bear."

Alvin walked up quietly behind the bear and gently rested his hand on the bear's shoulder. "Why would I do that? This bear never pointed no gun at me."

"I'm a dead man," Davy whispered. The grin faded from his face. He bowed his head, then toppled forward, curled up on the ground, and waited to be killed.

But it didn't happen. The bear came up, nosed him, snuffled him all over, rolled him back and forth a little, all the time ignoring the little whimpering sounds Davy was making. Then the bear lay down beside the man, flung one arm over him, and dozed right off to sleep.

Unbelieving, Davy lay there, terrified yet hopeful again. If he could just stay awake a little longer.

Either the bear was a light sleeper in the summertime, or Davy made his move too soon, but no sooner did his hand slide toward the knife at his waist than the bear was wide awake, slapping more or less playfully at Davy's hand.

"Time for sleep," said Alvin. "You've earned it, the bear's earned it, and come morning you'll find things look a lot better."

"What's going to happen to me?" asked Davy.

"Don't you think that's kind of up to the bear?"

"You're controlling him somehow," said Davy. "This is all your doing."

"He's controlling himself," said Alvin, careful not to deny the second charge, seeing how it was true. "And he's controlling you. Because that's what grinning is all about—deciding who is master. Well, that bear is master here, and I reckon tomorrow we'll find out what bears do with domesticated humans."

Davy started to murmur a prayer.

The bear laid a heavy paw on Davy's mouth.

"Prayers are done," intoned Alvin. "Gone the sun. Shadows creep. Go to sleep."

That's how it came about that when Alvin returned to Westville, he did it with two friends along—Davy Crockett and a big old grizzly bear. Oh, folks was alarmed when that bear come into town, and ran for their guns, but the bear just grinned at them and they didn't shoot. And when the bear gave Davy a little poke, why, he'd step forward and say a few words. "My friend here doesn't have much command of the American language," said Davy, "but he'd just as soon you put that gun away and didn't go pointing it at him. Also, he'd be glad of a bowl of corn mush or a plate of corn bread, if you've got any to spare."

Why, that bear plumb ate his way through Westville, setting down to banquets without raising a paw except to poke at Davy Crockett, and folks didn't even mind it, it was such a sight to see a man serve gruel and corn bread to a bear. And that wasn't all, either. Davy Crockett spent a good little while picking burrs out of the bear's fur, especially in the rumpal area, and singing to the bear whenever it crooned in a high-pitched tone. Davy sang pert near every song that he ever heard, even if he only heard it once, or didn't hear the whole thing, for there's nothing to bring back the memory of tunes and lyrics like having an eleven-foot bear poking you and whining to get you to sing, and when he flat-out couldn't remember, why, he made something up, and since the bear wasn't altogether particular, the song was almost always good enough.

As for Alvin, he'd every now and then pipe up and ask Davy to mention whether it was true that Alvin was a burglar and a plow-stealing prentice, and each time Davy said no, it wasn't true, that was just a made-up lie because Davy was mad at Alvin and wanted to get even. And whenever Davy told the truth like that, the bear rumbled its approval and stroked Davy's back with his big old paw, which Davy was just barely brave enough to endure without wetting himself much.

Only when they'd gone all through the town and some of the outlying houses did this parade come to the millhouse, where the horses naturally complained a little at the presence of a bear. But Alvin spoke to each of them and put them at ease, while the bear curled up and took him a nap, his belly being full of corn in various forms. Davy didn't go far, though, for the bear kept sniffing, even in his sleep, to make sure Davy was close by.

Davy was putting the best face on things, though. He had his pride.

"A man does things for a friend, and this here bear's my friend," said Davy. "I'm done with trapping, as you can guess, so I'm looking for a line of work that can help my friend get ready for the winter. What I mean is, I got to earn some corn, and I hope some of you have jobs for me to do. The bear just watches, I promise, he's no danger to your livestock."

Well, they heard him out, of course, because one tends to listen for a while at least to a man who's somehow got himself hooked up as a servant to a grizzly bear. But there wasn't a chance in hell that they were going to let no bear anywhere near their pigsties, nor their chicken coops, especially not when the bear clearly showed no disposition to earn its food honestly. If it would beg, they figured, it would steal, and they'd have none of it.

Meanwhile, as the bear napped and Davy talked to the farmers, Alvin and Arthur had their reunion, with Arthur Stuart telling him what he'd figured out. "Some mechanism in the scale makes it weigh light when the wagon's full, and heavy when it's empty, so the farmers get short weight. But then, without changing a thing, it'll weight light on the buyers' empty wagons, and heavy when they're full, so Rack gets extra weight when he's selling the same corn."

Alvin nodded. "You find out if this theory is actually true?"

"The only time he ain't watching me is in the dark, and in the dark I can't sneak down and see a thing. I'm not crazy enough to risk getting myself caught sneaking around the machinery in the dark, anyway."

"Glad to know you got a brain."

"Says the man who keeps getting himself put in jail."

Alvin made a face at him, but in the meantime he was sending out his doodlebug to probe the machinery of the scale underground. Sure enough, there was a ratchet that engaged on one weighing, causing the levering to shift a little, making short weight; and on the next weighing, the ratchet would disengage and the levers would move back, giving long weight. No wonder Rack didn't want Alvin looking over the machinery of the scale.

The solution, as Alvin saw it, was simple enough. He told Arthur Stuart to stand near the scale but not to step on it. Rack wrote down the weight of the empty wagon, and while it was being pulled off the scale, he stood there calculating the difference. The moment the wagon was clear of the scale, Alvin rounded on Arthur Stuart, speaking loud enough for all to hear.

"Fool boy! What were you doing! Didn't you see you was standing on that scale?"

"I wasn't!" Arthur Stuart cried.

"I don't think he was," said a farmer. "I worried about that, he was so close, so I looked."

"And I say I saw him stand on it," said Alvin. "This farmer shouldn't be out the cost of a boy's weight in corn, I think!"

"I'm sure the boy didn't stand on the scale," Rack said, looking up from his calculation.

"Well, there's a simple enough test," said Alvin. "Let's get that empty wagon back onto the scale."

Now Rack grew alarmed. "Tell you what," he said to the farmer, "I'll just *give* you credit for the boy's weight."

"Is this scale sensitive enough to weigh the boy?" asked Alvin.

"Well, I don't know," said Rack. "Let's just estimate."

"No!" cried Alvin. "This farmer doesn't want any more than his fair credit, and it's not right for him to receive any less. Haul the wagon back on and let's weigh it again."

Rack was about to protest again, when Alvin said, "Unless there's something wrong with the scale. There wouldn't be something wrong with the scale, now, would there?"

Rack got a sick look on his face. He couldn't very well confess. "Nothing wrong with the scale," he said gruffly.

"Then let's weigh this wagon and see if my boy's weight made any difference."

Well, you guessed it. As soon as the wagon was back on the scale, it showed near a hundred pounds lighter than it did the first time. The other witnesses were flummoxed. "Could have sworn the boy never stepped on that scale," said one. And another said, "I don't know as I would have guessed that boy to weigh a hundred pounds."

"Heavy bones," says Alvin.

"No sir, it's my brain that weighs heavy," said Arthur Stuart, winning a round of laughter.

And Rack, trying to put a good face on it, pipes up, "No, it's the food he's been eating at my table—that's fifteen pounds of it right there!"

In the meantime, though, the farmer's credit was being adjusted by a hundred pounds.

And the next wagon to come on the scale was a full one, while the scale was set to read heavy. In vain did Rack try to beg off early—Alvin simply offered to keep on weighing for him, with the farmers as witnesses so he wrote down everything square. "You don't want any of these men to have to wait an extra day to sell you their market grain, do you?" Alvin said. "Let's weigh it all!"

And weigh it all they did, thirty wagons before the day was done, and the farmers was all remarking to each other about what a good corn year it was, the kernels heavier than usual. Arthur Stuart did hear one man start to grumble that his wagon seemed to be lighter this year than in any previous year, but Arthur immediately spoke up loud enough for all to hear. "It don't matter if the scale is weighing light or heavy—it's the difference between the full weight and the empty weight that matters, and as long as it's the same scale, it's going to be correct." The farmers thought that over and it sounded right to them, while Rack couldn't very well explain.

Arthur Stuart figured it all out in his head and he realized that Alvin hadn't exactly set things to rights. On the contrary, this year Rack was getting cheated royally, recording credits for these farmers that were considerably more than the amount of corn they actually brought in. He could bear such losses for one day; and by tomorrow, Alvin and Arthur both knew, Rack meant to have the scale back in its regular pattern—light for the full wagons, heavy for the empty ones.

Still, Alvin and Arthur cheerfully bade Rack farewell, not even commenting on the eagerness he showed to be rid of them.

That night, Rack Miller's lantern bobbed across the yard between his house and the mill. He closed the mill door behind him and headed for the trap door leading down to the scale mechanism. But to his surprise, there was something lying on top of that trap door. A bear. And nestled in to sleep with the bear wrapped around him was Davy Crockett.

"I hope you don't mind," said Davy, "but this here bear took it into his head to sleep right here, and I'm not inclined to argue with him."

"Well, he can't, so that's that," said the miller.

"You tell him," said Davy. "He just don't pay no heed to my advice."

The miller argued and shouted, but the bear paid no mind. Rack got him a long stick and poked at the bear, but the bear just opened one eye, slapped the stick out of Rack's hand, then took it in his mouth and crunched it up like a cracker. Rack Miller proposed to bring a gun out, but Davy drew his knife then. "You'll have to kill me along with the bear," he said, "cause if you harm him, I'll carve you up like a Christmas goose."

"I'll be glad to oblige you," said Rack.

"But then you'll have to explain how I came to be dead. If you manage to kill the bear with one shot, that is. Sometimes these bears can take a half-dozen balls into their bodies and still swipe a man's head clean off and then go fishing for the afternoon. Lots of fat, lots of muscle. And how's your aim, anyway?"

So it was that next morning, the scale still weighed opposite to Rack's intent, and so it went day after day until the harvest was over. Every day the bear and his servant ate their corn mush and corn bread and drank their corn likker and lay around in the shade, with onlookers gathering and lingering to see the marvel. The result was that witnesses were around all day and not far off at night. And it went on just the same when the buyers started showing up to haul away the corn.

Stories about the bear who had tamed a man brought more than just onlookers, too. More farmers than usual came to Rack Miller to sell their corn, so they could see the sight; and more buyers went out of their way to come to buy, so there was maybe half again as much business as usual.

At the end of the whole harvest season, there was Rack Miller with a ledger book showing a huge loss. He wouldn't be paid enough by the buyers to come close to making good on what he owed the farmers. He was ruined.

He went through a few jugs of corn likker and took some long walks, but by late October he'd given up all hope. One time his despair led him to point a pistol at his head and fire, but the powder for some reason wouldn't ignite, and when Rack tried to hang himself he couldn't tie a knot that didn't slip. Since he couldn't even succeed at killing himself, he finally gave up even that project and took off in the dead of night, abandoning mill and ledger and all. Well, he didn't mean to abandon it—he meant to burn it. But the fires he started kept blowing out, so that was yet another project he failed at. In the end, he left with the clothes on his back and two geese tucked under his arms, and they honked so much he turned them loose before he was out of town.

When it was clear Rack wasn't just off on a holiday, the town's citizens and some of the more prominent farmers from round about met in Rack Miller's abandoned house and went over his ledger. What they learned there told them clear enough that Rack Miller was unlikely to return. They divided up the losses evenly among the farmers, and it turned out that nobody lost a thing. Oh, the farmers got paid less than Rack Miller's ledger showed, but they'd get a good deal more than they had in previous years, so it was still a good year for them. And when they got to inspecting the property and found the ratchet mechanism in the scale, then the picture was crystal clear.

All in all, they decided, they were well rid of Rack Miller, and a few folks had suspicions that it was that Alvin Smith and his half-Black boy who'd turned the tables on this cheating miller. They even tried to find out where Alvin might be, to offer him the mill in gratitude. Someone had heard tell he came from Vigor Church up in Wobbish, and a letter there did bring results—a letter in reply, from Alvin's father. "My boy thought you might make such an offer, and he asked me to give you a better suggestion. He says that since a man done such a bad job as miller, maybe you'd be better off with a bear, especially if the bear has him a manservant who can keep the books."

At first they laughed off the suggestion, but after a while they began to like it, and when they proposed it to Davy and the bear, they cottoned to it, too. The bear got him all the corn he wanted without ever lifting a finger, except to perform a little for folks at harvest time, and in the winter he could sleep in a warm dry place. The years he mated, the place was a little crowded with bearflesh, but the cubs were no trouble and the mama bears, though a little suspicious, were mostly tolerant, especially because Davy was still a match for any of *them,* and could grin them into docility when the need arose.

As for Davy, he kept true books, and fixed the scale so it didn't ratchet anymore, giving honest weight every time. As time went on, he was so well-liked that folks talked about running him for mayor of Westville. He refused, of course, since he wasn't his own man. But he allowed as how, if they elected the bear, he'd be glad to serve as the bear's secretary and interpreter, and that's what they did. After a year or two of having a bear as mayor, they up and changed the name to Bearsville, and the town prospered. Years later, when Kenituck joined the United States of America, it's not hard to guess who got elected to Congress from that part of the state, which is how it happened that for seven terms of Congress a bear put its hand on the Bible right along with the other Congressmen, and then proceeded to sleep through every session it attended, while its clerk, one Davy Crockett, cast all its votes for it and gave all its speeches, every one of which ended with the sentence "Or at least that's how it looks to one old grizzly bear."

NOTES ON "GRINNING MAN"

Robert Silverberg contacted me with an invitation. He had an idea for an anthology that would actually make money. What if leading writers of fantasy and science fiction wrote new stories set in their most popular imaginary universes? Presumably, all the fans of all the writers would desperately need to own the book, so everybody would get royalties based on each other's audience size.

Excellent idea—as long as one of the authors was Stephen King. Or so we discovered eventually.

At that point, however, Silverberg was only inviting me to take part in the sci-fi book, *Far Horizons*. For that I would revisit the *Ender's Game* universe and write a new story. I had kept in the back of my mind the vague idea that someday I might go back and write something more about Ender Wiggin, but I was busy filling other contracts and never gave it much thought. Now I had a reason to do it—the advance was amazingly high for a novelet in an anthology—and what I came up with was "Investment Counselor," one of the stories collected in my little Ender anthology *First Meetings*.

What tantalized me, though, was Silverberg's fantasy anthology, *Legends*. I wheedled. "I write fantasy, too." Silverberg hadn't known that. "I have a series about an American frontier wizard named Alvin Maker." How interesting. "Too bad you couldn't squeeze me into the fantasy book." Hmmm.

Nobody can be more graciously noncommittal than Robert Silverberg when he doesn't intend to say yes.

A while later—weeks? months?—Bob contacted me again, with the news that one of the *real* fantasy authors had dropped out, so . . . could I get him a story?

Don't ever let anybody tell you that whining never pays.

Ever since I was a little kid and could sing the whole Davy Crockett theme song and knew the story of how he *grinned* a bear down out of a tree I'd harbored a secret love for the idea of a man and a bear becoming, in a way, friends. Now, with my Alvin Maker universe, I had a perfect setting. Using characters I already knew well—Alvin and his ward and pupil, Arthur Stuart—I could have them run into Davy Crockett and see what they could make of him.

All I had in mind when I started writing was the meeting in the woods, and even that wasn't planned. I just let it flow. Once Davy left the scene, though, I had no idea where to go from there. Until it dawned on me that my best character wasn't really Davy, it was the bear. Once I realized that the bear was the protagonist of the tale, the rest became pure fun to write. I think this just may be the most *fun* of all the stories I've ever written, and I wish with all my heart I could someday see it made into a film. I just want to see that bear in Congress.

THE *YAZOO QUEEN*

Alvin watched as Captain Howard welcomed aboard another group of passengers, a prosperous family with five children and three slaves.

"It's the Nile River of America," said the captain. "But Cleopatra herself never sailed in such splendor as you folks is going to experience on the *Yazoo Queen*."

Splendor for the family, thought Alvin. Not likely to be much splendor for the slaves—though, being house servants, they'd fare better than the two dozen runaways chained together in the blazing sun at dockside all afternoon.

Alvin had been keeping an eye on them since he and Arthur Stuart got here to the Carthage City riverport at eleven. Arthur Stuart was all for exploring, and Alvin let him go. The city that billed itself as the Phoenicia of the West had plenty of sights for a boy Arthur's age, even a half-black boy. Since it was on the north shore of the Hio, there'd be suspicious eyes on him for a runaway. But there was plenty of free Blacks in Carthage City, and Arthur Stuart was no fool. He'd keep an eye out.

There was plenty of slaves in Carthage, too. That was the law, that a black slave from the South remained a slave even in a free state. And the greatest shame of all was those chained-up runaways who got themselves all the way across the Hio to freedom, only to be picked up by Finders and dragged back in chains to the whips and other horrors of bondage. Angry owners who'd make an example of them. No wonder there was so many who killed theirselves, or tried to.

Alvin saw wounds on more than a few in this chained-up group of twenty-five, though many of the wounds could have been made by the slave's own hand. Finders weren't much for injuring the property they was getting paid to bring on home. No, those wounds on wrists and bellies were likely a vote for freedom before life itself.

What Alvin was watching for was to know whether the runaways were going to be loaded on this boat or another. Most often runaways were ferried across the river and made to walk home over land—there was too many stories of slaves jumping overboard and sinking to the bottom with their chains on to make Finders keen on river transportation.

But now and then Alvin had caught a whiff of talking from the slaves—not much, since it could get them a bit of lash, and not loud enough for him to make out the words, but the music of the language didn't sound like English, not northern English, not southern English, not slave English. It wasn't likely to be any African language. With the British waging full-out war on the slave trade, there weren't many new slaves making it across the Atlantic these days.

So it might be Spanish they were talking, or French. Either way, they'd most likely be bound for Nueva Barcelona, or New Orleans, as the French still called it.

Which raised some questions in Alvin's mind. Mostly this one: How could a bunch of Barcelona runaways get themselves to the state of Hio? That would have been a long trek on foot, especially if they didn't speak English. Alvin's wife, Peggy, grew up in an Abolitionist home, with her papa, Horace Guester, smuggling runaways across river. Alvin knew something about how good the Underground Railway was. It had fingers reaching all the way down into the new duchies of Mizzippy and Alabam, but Alvin never heard of any Spanish- or French-speaking slaves taking that long dark road to freedom.

"I'm hungry again," said Arthur Stuart.

Alvin turned to see the boy—no, the young man, he was getting so tall and his voice so low—standing behind him, hands in his pockets, looking at the *Yazoo Queen*.

"I'm a-thinking," said Alvin, "as how instead of just looking at this boat, we ought to get on it and ride a spell."

"How far?" asked Arthur Stuart.

"You asking cause you're hoping it's a long way or a short one?"

"This one goes clear to Barcy."

"It does if the fog on the Mizzippy lets it," said Alvin.

Arthur Stuart made a goofy face at him. "Oh, that's right, cause around you that fog's just bound to close right in."

"It might," said Alvin. "Me and water never did get along."

"When you was a little baby, maybe," said Arthur Stuart. "Fog does what you tell it to do these days."

"You think," said Alvin.

"You showed me your own self."

"I showed you with smoke from a candle," said Alvin, "and just because I *can* do it don't mean that every fog or smoke you see is doing what I say."

"Don't mean it ain't, either," said Arthur Stuart, grinning.

"I'm just waiting to see if this boat's a slave ship or not," said Alvin.

Arthur Stuart looked over where Alvin was looking, at the runaways. "Why don't you just turn them loose?" he asked.

"And where would they go?" said Alvin. "They're being watched."

"Not all that careful," said Arthur Stuart. "Them so-called guards has got jugs that ain't close to full by now."

"The Finders still got their sachets. It wouldn't take long to round them up again, and they'd be in even more trouble."

"So you ain't going to do a thing about it?"

"Arthur Stuart, I can't just pry the manacles off every slave in the South."

"I seen you melt iron like it was butter," said Arthur Stuart.

"So a bunch of slaves run away and leave behind puddles of iron that was once their chains," said Alvin. "What do the authorities think? There was a blacksmith snuck in with a teeny tiny bellows and a ton of coal and lit him a fire that het them chains up? And then he run off after, taking all his coal with him in his pockets?"

Arthur Stuart looked at him defiantly. "So it's all about keeping you safe."

"I reckon so," said Alvin. "You know what a coward I am."

Last year, Arthur Stuart would have blinked and said he was sorry, but now that his voice had changed the word "sorry" didn't come so easy to his lips. "You can't heal everybody, neither," he said, "but that don't stop you from healing *some*."

"No point in freeing them as can't stay free," said Alvin. "And how many of them would run, do you think, and how many drown themselves in the river?"

"Why would they do that?"

"Because they know as well as I do, there ain't no freedom here in Carthage City for a runaway slave. This town may be the biggest on the Hio, but it's more southern than northern, when it comes to slavery. There's even buying and selling of slaves here, they say, flesh markets hidden in cellars, and the authorities know about it and don't do a thing because there's so much money in it."

"So there's nothing you can do."

"I healed their wrists and ankles where the manacles bite so deep. I cooled them in the sun and cleaned the water they been given to drink so it don't make them sick."

Now, finally, Arthur Stuart looked a bit embarrassed—though still defiant. "I never said you wasn't *nice*," he said.

"Nice is all I can be," said Alvin. "In this time and place. That and I don't plan to give my money to this captain iffen the slaves are going southbound on his boat. I won't help pay for no slave ship."

"He won't even notice the price of our passage."

"Oh, he'll notice, all right," said Alvin. "This Captain Howard is a fellow what can tell how much money you got in your pocket by the smell of it."

"*You* can't even do that," said Arthur Stuart.

"Money's his knack," said Alvin. "That's my guess. He's got him a pilot to steer the ship, and an engineer to keep that steam engine going, and a carpenter to tend the paddlewheel and such damage as the boat takes passing close to the left bank all the way down the Mizzippy. So why is he captain? It's about the money. He knows who's got it, and he knows how to talk it out of them."

"So how much money's he going to think *you* got?"

"Enough money to own a big young slave, but not enough money to afford one what doesn't have such a mouth on him."

Arthur Stuart glared. "You don't own me."

"I told you, Arthur Stuart, I didn't want you on this trip and I still don't. I hate taking you south because I have to pretend you're my property, and I don't know which is worse, you pretending to be a slave, or me pretending to be the kind of man as would own one."

"I'm going and that's that."

"So you keep on saying," said Alvin.

"And you must not mind because you could force me to stay here iffen you wanted."

"Don't say 'iffen,' it drives Peggy crazy when you do."

"She ain't here and you say it your own self."

"The idea is for the younger generation to be an improvement over the older."

"Well, then, you're a mizzable failure, you got to admit, since I been studying makering with you for lo these many years and I can barely make a candle flicker or a stone crack."

"I think you're doing fine, and you're better than that, anyway, if you just put your mind to it."

"I put my mind to it till my head feels like a cannonball."

"I suppose I should have said, Put your heart in it. It's not about *making* the candle or the stone—or the iron chains, for that matter—it's not about *making* them do what you want, it's about *getting* them to do what you want."

"I don't see you setting down and *talking* no iron into bending or dead wood into sprouting twigs, but they do it."

"You may not see me or hear me do it, but I'm doing it all the same, only they don't understand words, they understand the plan in my heart."

"Sounds like making wishes to me."

"Only because you haven't learned yourself how to do it yet."

"Which means you ain't much of a teacher."

"Neither is Peggy, what with you still saying 'ain't.'"

"Difference is, I know how *not* to say 'ain't' when she's around to hear it," said Arthur Stuart, "only I can't poke out a dent in a tin cup whether you're there or not."

"Could if you cared enough," said Alvin.

"I want to ride on this boat."

"Even if it's a slave ship?" said Alvin.

"Us staying off ain't going to make it any less a slave ship," said Arthur Stuart.

"Ain't you the idealist."

"You ride this *Yazoo Queen,* Master of mine, and you can keep those slaves comfy all the way back to hell."

The mockery in his tone was annoying, but not misplaced, Alvin decided.

"I could do that," said Alvin. "Small blessings can feel big enough, when they're all you got."

"So buy the ticket, cause this boat's supposed to sail first thing in the morning, and we want to be aboard already, don't we?"

Alvin didn't like the mixture of casualness and eagerness in Arthur Stuart's words. "You don't happen to have some plan to set these poor souls free during the voyage, do you? Because you know they'd jump overboard and there ain't a one of them knows how to swim, you can bet on that, so it'd be plain murder to free them."

"I got no such plan."

"I need your promise you won't free them."

"I won't lift a finger to help them," said Arthur Stuart. "I can make my heart as hard as yours whenever I want."

"I hope you don't think that kind of talk makes me glad to have your company," said Alvin. "Specially because I think you know I don't deserve it."

"You telling me you *don't* make your heart hard, to see such sights and do nothing?"

"If I could make my heart hard," said Alvin, "I'd be a worse man, but a happier one."

Then he went off to the booth where the *Yazoo Queen*'s purser was selling passages. Bought him a cheap ticket all the way to Nueva Barcelona, and a servant's passage for his boy. Made him angry just to have to say the words, but he lied with his face and the tone of his voice and the purser didn't seem to notice anything amiss. Or maybe all slave owners were just a little angry with themselves, so Alvin didn't seem much different from any other.

Plain truth of it was, Alvin was about as excited to make this voyage as a man could get. He loved machinery, all the hinges, pistons, elbows of metal, the fire hot as a smithy, the steam pent up in the boilers. He loved the great paddlewheel, turning like the one he grew up with at his father's mill, except here it was the wheel pushing the water, stead of the water pushing the wheel. He loved feeling the strain on the steel—the torque, the compression, the levering, the flexing and cooling. He sent out his doodlebug and wandered around inside the machines, so he'd know it all like he knew his own body.

The engineer was a good man who cared well for his machine, but there was things he couldn't know. Small cracks in the metal, places where the stress was too much, places where the grease wasn't enough and the friction was a-building up. Soon as he understood how it ought to be, Alvin began to teach the metal how to heal itself, how to seal the tiny fractures, how to smooth itself so the friction was less. That boat wasn't more than two hours out of Carthage before he had the machinery about as perfect as a steam engine could get, and then it was just a matter of riding with it. His body, like everybody else's, riding on the gently shifting deck, and his doodlebug skittering through the machinery to feel it pushing and pulling.

But soon enough it didn't need his attention anymore, and so the machinery moved to the back of his mind while he began to take an interest in the goings-on among the passengers.

There was people with money in the first-class cabins, with their servants' quarters close at hand. And then people like Alvin, with only a little coin, but enough for the second-class cabins, where there was four passengers to the room. All *their* servants, them as had any, was forced to sleep belowdecks like the crew, only even more cramped, not because there wasn't room to do better, but because the crew was bound to get surly iffen their bed was as bad as a blackamoor's.

And finally there was the steerage passengers, who didn't even have no beds, but just benches. Them as was going only a short way, a day's journey or so, it made plain good sense to go steerage. But a good many was just poor folks bound for some far-off destination, like Thebes or Corinth or Barcy itself, and if their butts got sore on the benches, well, it wouldn't be the first pain they suffered in their life, nor would it be their last.

Still, Alvin felt like it was kind of his duty, being as how it took him so little effort, to sort of shape the benches to the butts that sat on them. And it took no great trouble to get the lice and bedbugs to move on up to the first-class cabins. Alvin thought of it as kind of an educational project, to help the bugs get a taste of the high life. Blood so fine must be like fancy likker to a louse, and they ought to get some knowledge of it before their short lives was over.

All this took Alvin's concentration for a good little while. Not that he ever gave it his whole attention—that would be too dangerous, in their world where he had enemies out to kill him, and strangers as would wonder what was in his bag that he kept it always so close at hand. So he kept an eye out for all the heartfires on the boat, and if any seemed coming a-purpose toward him, he'd know it, right enough.

Except it didn't work that way. He didn't sense a soul anywheres near him, and then there was a hand right there on his shoulder, and he like to jumped clean overboard with the shock of it.

"What the devil are you—Arthur Stuart, don't sneak up on a body like that."

"It's hard not to sneak with the steam engine making such a racket," said Arthur, but he was a-grinnin' like old Davy Crockett, he was so proud of himself.

"Why is it the one skill you take the trouble to master is the one that causes me the most grief?" asked Alvin.

"I think it's good to know how to hide my . . . heartfire." He said the last word real soft, on account of it didn't do to talk about makery where others might hear and get too curious.

Alvin taught the skill freely to all who took it serious, but he didn't put on a show of it to inquisitive strangers, especially because there was no shortage of them as would remember hearing tales of the runaway smith's apprentice who stole a magic golden plowshare. Didn't matter that the tale was three-fourths fantasy and nine-tenths lie. It could get Alvin kilt or knocked upside the head and robbed all the same, and the one part that was true was that living plow inside his poke, which he didn't want to lose, specially not now after carrying it up and down America for half his life now.

"Ain't nobody on this boat can see your heartfire ceptin' me," said Alvin. "So the only reason for you to learn to hide is to hide from the one person you shouldn't hide from anyhow."

"That's plain dumb," said Arthur Stuart. "If there's one person a slave has to hide from, it's his master."

Alvin glared at him. Arthur grinned back.

A voice boomed out from across the deck. "I like to see a man who's easy with his servants!"

Alvin turned to see a smallish man with a big smile and a face that suggested he had a happy opinion of himself.

"My name's Austin," said the fellow. "Stephen Austin, attorney-at-law, born, bred, and schooled in the Crown Colonies, and now looking for people as need legal work out here on the edge of civilization."

"The folks on either hand of the Hio like to think of theirselves as mostwise civilized," said Alvin, "but then, they haven't been to Camelot to see the King."

"Was I imagining that I heard you speak to your boy there as 'Arthur Stuart'?"

"It was someone else's joke at the naming of the lad," said Alvin, "but I reckon by now the name suits him." All the time Alvin was thinking, what does this man want, that he'd trouble to speak to a sun-browned, strong-armed, thickheaded-looking wight like me?

He could feel a breath for speech coming up in Arthur Stuart, but the last thing Alvin wanted was to deal with whatever fool thing the boy might take it into his head to say. So he gripped him noticeably on the shoulder and it just kind of squeezed the air right out of him without more than a sigh.

"I noticed you've got shoulders on you," said Austin.

"Most folks do," said Alvin. "Two of 'em, nicely matched, one to an arm."

"I almost thought you might be a smith, except smiths always have one huge shoulder, and the other more like a normal man's."

"Except such smiths as use their left hand exactly as often as their right, just so they keep their balance."

Austin chuckled. "Well, then, that solves the mystery. You *are* a smith."

"When I got me a bellows, and charcoal, and iron, and a good pot."

"I don't reckon you carry that around with you in your poke."

"Sir," said Alvin, "I been to Camelot once, and I don't recollect as how it was good manners there to talk about a man's poke or his shoulders neither, upon such short acquaintance."

"Well, of course, it's bad manners all around the world, I'd say, and I apologize. I meant no disrespect. Only I'm recruiting, you see, them as has skills we need, and yet who don't have a firm place in life. Wandering men, you might say."

"Lots of men a-wanderin'," said Alvin, "and not all of them are what they claim."

"But that's why I've accosted you like this, my friend," said Austin. "Because you weren't claiming a blessed thing. And on the river, to meet a man with no brag is a pretty good recommendation."

"Then you're new to the river," said Alvin, "because many a man with no brag is afraid of gettin' recognized."

"Recognized," said Austin. "Not 'reckonize.' So you've had you some schooling."

"Not as much as it would take to turn a smith into a gentleman."

"I'm recruiting," said Austin. "For an expedition."

"Smiths in particular need?"

"Strong men good with tools of all kinds," said Austin.

"Got work already, though," said Alvin. "And an errand in Barcy."

"So you wouldn't be interested in trekking out into new lands, which are now in the hands of bloody savages, awaiting the arrival of Christian men to cleanse the land of their awful sacrifices?"

Alvin instantly felt a flush of anger mixed with fear, and as he did whenever so strong a feeling came over him, he smiled brighter than ever and kept hisself as calm as could be. "I reckon you'd have to brave the fog and cross to the west bank of the river for that," said Alvin. "And I hear the Reds on that side of the river has some pretty powerful eyes and ears, just watching for Whites as think they can take war into peaceable places."

"Oh, you misunderstood me, my friend," said Austin. "I'm not talking about the prairies where one time trappers used to wander and now the Reds won't let no white man pass."

"So what savages did you have in mind?"

"South, my friend, south and west. The evil Mexica tribes, that vile race that tears the heart out of a living man upon the tops of their ziggurats."

"That's a long trek indeed," said Alvin. "And a foolish one. What the might of Spain couldn't rule, you think a few Englishmen with a lawyer at their head can conquer?"

By now Austin was leaning on the rail beside Alvin, looking out over the water. "The Mexica have become rotten. Hated by the other Reds they rule, dependent on trade with Spain for second-rate weaponry—I tell you it's ripe for conquest. Besides, how big an army can they put in the field, after killing so many men on their altars for all these centuries?"

"It's a fool as goes looking for a war that no one brought to him."

"Aye, a fool, a whole passel of fools. The kind of fools as wants to be as rich as Pizarro, who conquered the great Inca with a handful of men."

"Or as dead as Cortez?"

"They're all dead now," said Austin. "Or did you think to live forever?"

Alvin was torn between telling the fellow to go pester someone else and leading him on so he could find out more about what he was planning. But in the long run, it wouldn't do to become too familiar with this fellow, Alvin decided. "I reckon I've wasted your time up to now, Mr. Austin. There's others are bound to be more interested than I am, since I got no interest at all."

Austin smiled all the more broadly, but Alvin saw how his pulse leapt up and his heartfire blazed. A man who didn't like being told no, but hid it behind a smile.

"Well, it's good to make a friend all the same," said Austin, sticking out his hand.

"No hard feelings," said Alvin, "and thanks for thinking of me as a man you might want at your side."

"No hard feelings indeed," said Austin, "and though I won't ask you again, if you change your mind I'll greet you with a ready heart and hand."

They shook on it, clapped shoulders, and Austin went on his way without a backward glance.

"Well, well," said Arthur Stuart. "What do you want to bet it isn't no invasion or war, but just a raiding party bent on getting some of that Mexica gold?"

"Hard to guess," said Alvin. "But he talks free enough, for a man proposing to do something forbidden by King and by Congress. Neither the

Crown Colonies nor the United States would have much patience with him if he was caught."

"Oh, I don't know," said Arthur Stuart. "The law's one thing, but what if King Arthur got it in his head that he needed more land and more slaves and didn't want a war with the U.S.A. to get it?"

"Now there's a thought," said Alvin.

"A pretty smart thought, I think," said Arthur Stuart.

"It's doing you good, traveling with me," said Alvin. "Finally getting some sense into your head."

"I thought of it first," said Arthur Stuart.

In answer, Alvin took a letter out of his pocket and showed it to the boy.

"It's from Miz Peggy," said Arthur. He read for a moment. "Oh, now, don't tell me you knew this fellow was going to be on the boat."

"I most certainly did not have any idea," said Alvin. "I figured my inquiries would begin in Nueva Barcelona. But now I've got a good idea *whom* to watch when we get there."

"She talks about a man named Burr," said Arthur Stuart.

"But he'd have men under him," said Alvin. "Men to go out recruiting for him, iffen he hopes to raise an army."

"And he just happened to walk right up to you."

"He just happened to listen to you sassing me," said Alvin, "and figured I wasn't much of a master, so maybe I'd be a natural follower."

Arthur Stuart folded up the letter and handed it back to Alvin. "So if the King *is* putting together an invasion of Mexico, what of it?"

"Iffen he's fighting the Mexica," said Alvin, "he can't be fighting the free states, now, can he?"

"So maybe the slave states won't be so eager to pick a fight," said Arthur Stuart.

"But someday the war with Mexico will end," said Alvin. "Iffen there is a war, that is. And when it ends, either the King lost, in which case he'll be mad and ashamed and spoilin' for trouble, or he won, in which case he'll have a treasury full of Mexica gold, able to buy him a whole navy iffen he wants."

"Miz Peggy wouldn't be too happy to hear you sayin' 'iffen' so much."

"War's a bad thing, when you take after them as haven't done you no harm, and don't mean to."

"But wouldn't it be good to stop all that human sacrifice?"

"I think the Reds as are prayin' for relief from the Mexica don't exactly have slavers in mind as their new masters."

"But slavery's better than death, ain't it?"

"Your mother didn't think so," said Alvin. "And now let's have done with such talk. It just makes me sad."

"To think of human sacrifice? Or slavery?"

"No. To hear you talk as if one was better than the other." And with that dark mood on him, Alvin walked to the room that so far he had all to himself, set the golden plow upon the bunk, and curled up around it to think and doze and dream a little and see if he could understand what it all meant, to have this Austin fellow acting so bold about his project, and to have Arthur Stuart be so blind, when so many people had sacrificed so much to keep him free.

It wasn't till they got to Thebes that another passenger was assigned to Alvin's cabin. He'd gone ashore to see the town—which was being touted as the greatest city on the American Nile—and when he came back, there was a man asleep on the very bunk where Alvin had been sleeping.

Which was irksome, but understandable. It was the best bed, being the lower bunk on the side that got sunshine in the cool of the morning instead of the heat of the afternoon. And it's not as if Alvin had left any possessions in the cabin to mark the bed as his own. He carried his poke with him when he left the boat, and all his worldly goods was in it. Lessen you counted the baby that his wife carried inside her—which, come to think of it, she carried around with her about as constantly as Alvin carried that golden plow.

So Alvin didn't wake the fellow up. He just turned and left, looking for Arthur Stuart or a quiet place to eat the supper he'd brought on board. Arthur had insisted he wanted to stay aboard, and that was fine with Alvin, but he was blamed if he was going to hunt him down before eating. It wasn't no secret that the whistle had blowed the signal for everyone to come aboard. So Arthur Stuart should have been watching for Alvin, and he wasn't.

Not that Alvin doubted where he was. He could key right in on Arthur's heartfire most of the time, and he doubted the boy could hide from him if Alvin was actually seeking him out. Right now he knew that the boy was down below in the slave quarters, a place where no one would ask him his business or wonder where his master was. What he was about was another matter.

Almost as soon as Alvin opened up his poke to take out the cornbread and cheese and cider he'd brought in from town, he could see Arthur start moving up the ladderway to the deck. Not for the first time, Alvin wondered just how much the boy really understood of makering.

Arthur Stuart wasn't a liar by nature, but he could keep a secret, more or less, and wasn't it just possible that he hadn't quite got around to telling Alvin all that he'd learned how to do? Was there a chance the boy picked that moment to come up because he *knew* Alvin was back from town, and *knew* he was setting hisself down to eat?

Sure enough, Alvin hadn't got but one bite into his first slice of bread and cheese when Arthur Stuart plunked himself down beside him on the bench. Alvin could've eaten in the dining room, but there it would have given offense for him to let his "servant" set beside him. Out on the deck, it was nobody's business. Might make him look low class, in the eyes of some slaveowners, but Alvin didn't much mind what slaveowners thought of him.

"What was it like?" asked Arthur Stuart.

"Bread tastes like bread."

"I didn't mean the bread, for pity's sake!"

"Cheese is pretty good, despite being made from milk that come from the most measly, mangy, scrawny, fly-bit, sway-backed, half-blind, bony-hipped, ill-tempered, cud-pukin', sawdust-fed bunch of cattle as ever teetered on the edge of the grave."

"So they don't specialize in fine dairy, is what you're saying."

"I'm saying that if Thebes is spose to be the greatest city on the American Nile, they might oughta start by draining the swamp. I mean, the reason the Hio and the Mizzippy come together here is because it's low ground, and being low ground it gets flooded a lot. It didn't take no scholar to figure that out."

"Never heard of a scholar who knowed low ground from high, any-how."

"Now, Arthur Stuart, it's not a requirement that scholars be dumb as mud about . . . well, mud."

"Oh, I know. Somewhere there's bound to be a scholar who's got book-learnin' *and* common sense, both. He just hasn't come to America."

"Which I spose is proof of the common sense part, bein' as this is the sort of country where they build a great city in the middle of a bog."

They chuckled together and then filled up their mouths too much for talking.

When the food was gone—and Arthur had et more than half of it, and looked like he was wishing for more—Alvin asked him, pretending to be all casual about it, "So what was so interesting down with the servants in the hold?"

"The slaves, you mean?"

"I'm trying to talk like the kind of person as would own one," said Alvin very softly. "And you ought to try to talk like the kind of person as was owned. Or don't come along on trips south."

"I was trying to find out what language those score-and-a-quarter chained-up runaways was talking."

"And?"

"Ain't French, cause there's a cajun what says not. Ain't Spanish, cause there's a fellow grew up in Cuba what says not. Nary a soul knew their talk."

"Well, at least we know what they're not."

"I know more than that," said Arthur Stuart.

"I'm listening."

"The Cuba fellow, he takes me aside and he says, Tell you what, boy, I think I hear me their kind talk afore, and I says, What's their language, and he says, I think they be no kind runaway."

"Why's he think that?" said Alvin. But inside, he's noticing the way Arthur Stuart picks up exactly the words the fellow said, and the accent, and he remembers how it used to be when Arthur Stuart could do any voice he heard, a perfect mimic. And not just human voices, neither, but birdcalls and animal cries, and a baby crying, and the wind in the trees or the scrape of a shoe on dirt. But that was before Alvin changed him, deep inside, changed the very smell of him so that the Finders couldn't match him up to his sachet no more. He had to change him in the smallest, most hidden parts of him. Cost him part of his knack, it did, and that was a harsh thing to do to a child. But it also saved his freedom. Alvin couldn't regret doing it. But he could regret the cost.

"He says, I hear me their kind talk aforeday, long day ago, when I belong a massuh go Mexico."

Alvin nodded wisely, though he had no idea what this might mean.

"And I says to him, How come black folk be learning Mexica talk? And he says, They be black folk all over Mexico, from aforeday."

"That would make sense," said Alvin. "The Mexica only threw the Spanish out fifty years ago. I reckon they was inspired by Tom Jefferson getting Cherriky free from the King. Spanish must've brought plenty of slaves to Mexico up to then."

"Well, sure," said Arthur Stuart. "So I was wondering, if the Mexica kill so many sacrifices, why didn't they use up these African slaves first? And he says, Black man dirty, Mexica no can cook him up for Mexica god. And then he just laughed and laughed."

"I guess there's advantages to having folks think you're impure by nature."

"Heard a lot of preachers in America say that God thinks *all* men is filthy at heart."

"Arthur Stuart, I know that's a falsehood, because in your life you never been to hear a *lot* of preachers say a blame thing."

"Well, I heard *of* preachers saying such things. Which explains why our God don't hold with human sacrifice. Ain't none of us worthy, white or black."

"Except I don't think that's the opinion God has of his children," said Alvin, "and neither do you."

"I think what I think," said Arthur Stuart. "Ain't always the same thing as you."

"I'm just happy you've taken up thinkin' at all," said Alvin.

"As a hobby," said Arthur Stuart. "I ain't thinkin' of takin' it up as a trade or nothin'."

Alvin gave a chuckle, and Arthur Stuart settled back to enjoy it.

Alvin got to thinking out loud. "So. We got us twenty-five slaves who used to belong to the Mexica. Only now they're going down the ·Mizzippy on the very same boat as a man recruiting soldiers for an expedition *against* Mexico. That's a downright miraculous coincidence."

"Guides?" said Arthur Stuart.

"I reckon that's likely. Maybe they're wearing chains for the same reason you're pretending to be a slave. So people will think they're one thing, when actually they're another."

"Or maybe somebody's so dumb he thinks that chained-up slaves will be good guides through uncharted land."

"So you're saying maybe they won't be reliable."

"I'm saying maybe they think starving to death all lost in the desert ain't a bad way to die, if they can take some white slaveowners with them."

Alvin nodded. The boy did understand that slaves might prefer death, after all. "Well, I don't speak Mexica, and neither do you."

"Yet," said Arthur Stuart.

"Don't see how you'll learn it," said Alvin. "They don't let nobody near 'em."

"Yet," said Arthur Stuart.

"I hope you ain't got some damn fool plan going on in your head that you're not going to tell me about."

"Don't mind telling you. I already got me a turn feeding them and picking up their slop bucket. The predawn turn, which nobody belowdecks is hankering to do."

"They're guarded day and night. How you going to start talking to them anyway?"

"Come on now, Alvin, you know there must be at least one of them speaks English, or how would they be able to guide anybody anywhere?"

"Or one of them speaks Spanish, and one of the slaveowners speaks it too, you ever think of that?"

"That's why I got the Cuba fellow to teach me Spanish."

That was brag. "I was only gone into town for six hours, Arthur Stuart."

"Well, he didn't teach me *all* of it."

That set Alvin to wondering once again if Arthur Stuart had more of his knack left than he ever let on. Learn a language in six hours? Of course, there was no guarantee that the Cuban slave knew all that much Spanish, any more than he knew all that much English. But what if Arthur Stuart had him a knack for languages? What if he'd never been a mimic at all, but instead a natural speaker-of-all-tongues? There was tales of such—of men and women who could hear a language and speak it like a native right from the start.

Did Arthur Stuart have such a knack? Now that the boy was becoming a man, was he getting a real grasp of it? For a moment Alvin caught himself being envious. And then he had to laugh at himself—imagine a fellow with *his* knack, envying somebody else. I can make rock flow like water, I can make water as strong as steel and as clear as glass, I can turn iron into living gold, and I'm jealous because I can't also learn languages the way a cat learns to land on its feet? The sin of ingratitude, just one of many that's going to get me sent to hell.

"What're you laughing at?" asked Arthur Stuart.

"Just appreciating that you're not a mere boy anymore. I trust that if you need any help from me—like somebody catches you talking to them Mexica slaves and starts whipping you—you'll contrive some way to let me know that you need some help?"

"Sure. And if that knife-wielding killer who's sleeping in your bed gets troublesome, I expect you'll find some way to let me know what you want written on your tombstone?" Arthur Stuart grinned at him.

"Knife-wielding killer?" Alvin asked.

"That's the talk belowdecks. But I reckon you'll just ask him yourself, and he'll tell you all about it. That's how you usually do things, isn't it?"

Alvin nodded. "I spose I do start out asking pretty direct what I want to know."

"And so far you mostly haven't got yourself killed," said Arthur Stuart.

"My average is pretty good so far," said Alvin modestly.

"Haven't always found out what you wanted to know, though," said Arthur Stuart.

"But I always find out something useful," said Alvin. "Like, how easy it is to get some folks riled."

"If I didn't know you had another, I'd say that *was* your knack."

"Rilin' folks."

"They do get mad at you pretty much when you say hello, some-times," said Arthur Stuart.

"Whereas nobody ever gets mad at you."

"I'm a likable fellow," said Arthur Stuart.

"Not always," said Alvin. "You got a bit of brag in you that can be annoying sometimes."

"Not to my friends," said Arthur, grinning.

"No," Alvin conceded. "But it drives your family insane."

By the time Alvin got to his room, the "knife-wielding killer" had woke up from his nap and was somewhere else. Alvin toyed with sleeping in the very same bed, which had been his first, after all. But that was likely to start a fight, and Alvin just plain didn't care all that much. He was glad to have a bed at all, come to think of it, and with four bunks in the room to share between two men, there was no call to be provoking anybody over who got to which one first.

Drifting off to sleep, Alvin reached out as he always did, seeking Peggy, making sure from her heartfire that she was all right. And then the baby, growing fine inside her, had a heartbeat now. Not going to end like the first pregnancy, with a baby born too soon so it couldn't get its breath. Not going to watch it gasp its little life away in a couple of desperate minutes, turning blue and dying in his arms while he frantically searched inside it for some way to fix it so's it could live. What good is it to be a seventh son of a seventh son if the one person you can't heal is your own firstborn baby?

Alvin and Peggy clung together for the first days after that, but then over the weeks to follow she began to grow apart from him, to avoid him, until he finally realized that she was keeping him from being with her to make another baby. He talked with her then, about how you couldn't hide from it, lots of folks lost babies, and half-growed children, too, the thing to do was try again, have another, and another, to comfort you when you thought about the little body in the grave.

"I grew up with two graves before my eyes," she said, "and knowing how my parents looked at me and saw my dead sisters with the same name as me."

"Well you was a torch, so you knew more than children ought to know about what goes on inside folks. Our baby most likely won't be a torch. All she'll know is how much we love her and how much we wanted her."

He wasn't sure he so much persuaded her to want another baby as she decided to try again just to make him happy. And during this pregnancy, just like last time, she kept gallivanting up and down the country, working for abolition even as she tried to find some way to bring about freedom short of war. While Alvin stayed in Vigor Church or Hatrack River, teaching them as wanted to learn the rudiments of makery.

Until she had an errand for him, like now. Sending him downriver on a steamboat to Nueva Barcelona, when in his secret heart he just wished she'd stay home with him and let him take care of her.

Course, being a torch she knew perfectly well that was what he wished for, it was no secret at all. So she must need to be apart from him more than he needed to be with her, and he could live with that.

Couldn't stop him from looking for her on the skirts of sleep, and dozing off with her heartfire and the baby's, so bright in his mind.

He woke in the dark, knowing something was wrong. It was a heartfire right up close to him; then he heard the soft breath of a stealthy man. With his doodlebug he got inside the man and felt what he was doing—reaching across Alvin toward the poke that was tucked in the crook of his arm.

Robbery? On board a riverboat was a blame foolish time for it, if that was what the man had in mind. Unless he was a good enough swimmer to get to shore carrying a heavy golden plowshare.

The man carried a knife in a sheath at his belt, but his hand wasn't on it, so he wasn't looking for trouble.

So Alvin spoke up soft as could be. "If you're looking for food, the door's on the other side of the room."

Oh, the man's heart gave a jolt at that! And his first instinct was for his hand to fly to that knife—he was quick at it, too, Alvin could see that it didn't much matter whether his hand was on the knife or not, he was always ready with that blade.

But in a moment the fellow got a hold of hisself, and Alvin could pretty much guess at his reasoning. It was a dark night, and as far as this fellow knew, Alvin couldn't see any better than him.

"You was snoring," said the man. "I was looking to jostle you to get you to roll over."

Alvin knew that was a flat lie. When Peggy had mentioned a snoring problem to him years ago, he studied out what made people snore and fixed his palate so it didn't make that noise anymore. He had a rule about not using his knack to benefit himself, but he figured curing his snore was a gift to other people. *He* always slept through it.

Still, he'd let the lie ride. "Why, thank you," said Alvin. "I sleep pretty light, though, so all it takes is you sayin' 'roll over' and I'll do it. Or so my wife tells me."

And then, bold as brass, the fellow as much as confesses what he was doing. "You know, stranger, whatever you got in that sack, you hug it so close to you that somebody might get curious about what's so valuable."

"I've learned that folks get just as curious when I *don't* hug it close, and they feel a mite freer about groping in the dark to get a closer look."

The man chuckled. "So I reckon you ain't planning to tell me much about it."

"I always answer a well-mannered question," said Alvin.

"But since it ain't good manners to ask about what's in your sack," said the man, "I reckon you don't answer such questions at all."

"I'm glad to meet a man who knows good manners."

"Good manners and a knife that don't break off at the stem, that's what keeps me at peace with the world."

"Good manners has always been enough for me," said Alvin. "Though I admit I would have liked that knife better back when it was still a file."

With a bound the man was at the door, his knife drawn. "Who are you, and what do you know about me?"

"I don't know nothing about you, sir," said Alvin. "But I'm a blacksmith, and I know a file that's been made over into a knife. More like a sword, if you ask me."

"I haven't drawn my knife aboard this boat."

"I'm glad to hear it. But when I walked in on *you* asleep, it was still daylight enough to see the size and shape of the sheath you keep it in.

Nobody makes a knife that thick at the haft, but it was right proportioned for a file."

"You can't tell something like that just from looking," said the man. "You heard something. Somebody's been talking."

"People are always talking, but not about you," said Alvin. "I know my trade, as I reckon you know yours. My name's Alvin."

"Alvin Smith, eh?"

"I count myself lucky to have a name. I'd lay good odds that you've got one, too."

The man chuckled and put his knife away. "Jim Bowie."

"Don't sound like a trade name to me."

"It's a Scotch word. Means light-haired."

"Your hair is dark."

"But I reckon the first Bowie was a blond Viking who liked what he saw while he was busy raping and pillaging in Scotland, and so he stayed."

"One of his children must have got that Viking spirit again and found his way across another sea."

"I'm a Viking through and through," said Bowie. "You guessed right about this knife. I was witness at a duel at a smithy just outside Natchez a few years ago. Things got out of hand when they both missed—I reckon folks came to see blood and didn't want to be disappointed. One fellow managed to put a bullet through my leg, so I thought I was well out of it, until I saw Major Norris Wright setting on a boy half his size and half his age, and that riled me up. Riled me so bad that I clean forgot I was wounded and bleeding like a slaughtered pig. I went berserk and snatched up a blacksmith's file and stuck it clean through his heart."

"You got to be a strong man to do that."

"Oh, it's more than that. I didn't slip it between no ribs. I jammed it right *through* a rib. We Vikings get the strength of giants when we go berserk."

"Am I right to guess that the knife you carry is that very same file?"

"A cutler in Philadelphia reshaped it for me."

"Did it by grinding, not forging," said Alvin.

"That's right."

"Your lucky knife."

"I ain't dead yet."

"Reckon that takes a lot of luck, if you got the habit of reaching over sleeping men to get at their poke."

The smile died on Bowie's face. "Can't help it if I'm curious."

"Oh, I know, I got me the same fault."

"So now it's your turn," said Bowie.

"My turn for what?"

"To tell your story."

"Me? Oh, all I got's a common skinning knife, but I've done my share of wandering in wild lands and it's come in handy."

"You know that's not what I'm asking."

"That's what I'm telling, though."

"I told you about my knife, so you tell me about your sack."

"You tell everybody about your knife," said Alvin, "which makes it so you don't have to use it so much. But I don't tell nobody about my sack."

"That just makes folks more curious," said Bowie. "And some folks might even get suspicious."

"From time to time that happens," said Alvin. He sat up and swung his legs over the side of his bunk and stood. He had already sized up this Bowie fellow and knew that he'd be at least four inches taller, with longer arms and the massive shoulders of a blacksmith. "But I smile so nice their suspicions just go away."

Bowie laughed out loud at that. "You're a big fellow, all right! And you ain't afeared of nobody."

"I'm afraid of lots of folks," said Alvin. "Especially a man can shove a file through a man's rib and ream out his heart."

Bowie nodded at that. "Well, now, ain't that peculiar. Lots of folks been afraid of me in my time. But the more scared they was, the less likely they was to admit it. You're the first one actually said he was afraid of me. So does that make you the *most* scared? Or the least?"

"Tell you what," said Alvin. "You keep your hands off my poke, and we'll never have to find out."

Bowie laughed again—but his grin looked more like a wildcat snarling at its prey than like an actual smile. "I like you, Alvin Smith."

"I'm glad to hear it," said Alvin.

"I know a man who's looking for fellows like you."

So this Bowie was part of Austin's company. "If you're talking about

Mr. Austin, he and I already agreed that he'll go his way and I'll go mine."

"Ah," said Bowie.

"Did you just join up with him in Thebes?"

"I'll tell you about my knife," said Bowie, "but I won't tell you about my business."

"I'll tell you mine," said Alvin. "My business right now is to get back to sleep and see if I can find the dream I was in before you decided to stop me snoring."

"Well, that's a good idea," said Bowie. "And since I haven't been to sleep at all yet tonight, on account of your snoring, I reckon I'll give it a go before the sun comes up."

Alvin lay back down and curled himself around his poke. His back was to Bowie, but of course he kept his doodlebug in him and knew every move he made. The man stood there watching Alvin for a long time, and from the way his heart was beating and the blood rushed around in him, Alvin could tell he was upset. Angry? Afraid? Hard to tell when you couldn't look at a man's face, and not so easy even then. But his heartfire blazed and Alvin figured the fellow was making some kind of decision about him.

Won't get to sleep very soon if he keeps himself all agitated like that, thought Alvin. So he reached inside the fellow and gradually calmed him down, got his heart beating slower, steadied his breathing. Most folks thought that their emotions caused their bodies to get all agitated, but it was the other way around, Alvin knew. The body leads, and the emotions follow.

In a couple of minutes Bowie was relaxed enough to yawn. And soon after, he was fast asleep. With his knife still strapped on, and his hand never far from it.

This Austin fellow had him some interesting friends.

Arthur Stuart was feeling way too cocky. But if you *know* you feel too cocky, and you compensate for it by being extra careful, then being cocky does you no harm, right? Except maybe it's your cockiness makes you feel like you're safer than you really are.

That's what Miz Peggy called "circular reasoning" and it wouldn't get him nowhere. Anywhere. One of them words. Whatever the rule was.

Thinking about Miz Peggy always got him listening to the way he talked and finding fault with himself. Only what good would it do him to talk right? All he'd be is a half-Black man who somehow learned to talk like a gentleman—a kind of trained monkey, that's how they'd see him. A dog walking on its hind legs. Not an *actual* gentleman.

Which was why he got so cocky, probably. Always wanting to prove something. Not to Alvin, really.

No, *expecially* to Alvin. Cause it was Alvin still treated him like a boy when he was a man now. Treated him like a son, but he was no man's son.

All this thinking was, of course, doing him no good at all, when his job was to pick up the foul-smelling slop bucket and make a slow and lazy job of it so's he'd have time to find out which of them spoke English or Spanish.

"Quién me comprénde?" he whispered. "Who understands me?"

"Todos te compréndemos, pero calle la boca," whispered the third man. We all understand you, but shut your mouth. "Los blancos piensan que hay solo uno que hable un poco de inglés."

Boy howdy, he talked fast, with nothing like the accent the Cuban had. But still, when Arthur got the feel of a language in his mind, it wasn't that hard to sort it out. They all spoke Spanish, but they were pretending that only one of them spoke a bit of English.

"Quieren fugir de ser esclavos?" Do you want to escape from slavery?

"La única puerta es la muerta." The only door is death.

"Al otro lado del rio," said Arthur, "hay rojos que son amigos nuestros." On the other side of the river there are Reds who are friends of ours.

"Sus amigos no son nuestros," answered the man. Your friends aren't ours.

Another man near enough to hear nodded in agreement. "Y ya no puedo nadar." And I can't swim anyway.

"Los Blancos, que van a hacer?" What are the Whites going to do?

"Piensan en ser conquistadores." Clearly these men didn't think much of their masters' plans. "Los Mexicos van comer sus corazones." The Mexica will eat their hearts.

Another man chimed in. "Tú hablas como cubano." You talk like a Cuban.

"Soy americano," said Arthur Stuart. "Soy libre. Soy . . ." He hadn't learned the Spanish for "citizen." "Soy igual." I'm equal. But not really, he thought. Still, I'm more equal than you.

Several of the Mexica Blacks sniffed at that. "Ya hay visto, tu dueño." All Arthur understood was "dueño," owner.

"Es amigo, no dueño." He's my friend, not my master.

Oh, they thought that was hilarious. But of course their laughter was silent, and a few of them glanced at the guard, who was dozing as he leaned against the wall.

"Me de promesa." Promise me. "Cuando el ferro quiebra, no se maten. No salguen sin ayuda." When the iron breaks, don't kill your-selves. Or maybe it meant don't get killed. Anyway, don't leave without help. Or that's what Arthur thought he was saying. They looked at him with total incomprehension.

"Voy quebrar el ferro," Arthur repeated.

One of them mockingly held out his hands. The chains made a noise. Several looked again at the guard.

"No con la mano," said Arthur. "Con la cabeza."

They looked at each other with obvious disappointment. Arthur knew what they were thinking: This boy is crazy. Thinks he can break iron with his head. But he didn't know how to explain it any better.

"Mañana," he said.

They nodded wisely. Not a one of them believed him.

So much for the hours he'd spent learning Spanish. Though maybe the problem was that they just didn't know about makery and couldn't think of a man breaking iron with his mind.

Arthur Stuart knew he could do it. It was one of Alvin's earliest les-sons, but it was only on this trip that Arthur had finally understood what Alvin meant. About getting inside the metal. All this time, Arthur had thought it was something he could do by straining real hard with his mind. But it wasn't like that at all. It was easy. Just a sort of turn of his mind. Kind of the way language worked for him. Getting the taste of the language on his tongue, and then trusting how it felt. Like knowing somehow that even though *mano* ended in *o*, it still needed *la* in front of it instead of *el*. He just knew how it ought to be.

Back in Carthage City, he gave two bits to a man selling sweet bread, and the man was trying to get away with not giving him change. Instead of yelling at him—what good would that do, there on the levee, a half-Black boy yelling at a White man?—Arthur just thought about the coin he'd been holding in his hand all morning, how *warm* it was, how right it felt in his own hand. It was like he understood the metal of it, the way he understood the music of language. And thinking of it warm like that, he could see in his mind that it was getting warmer.

He encouraged it, thought of it getting warmer and warmer, and all of a sudden the man cried out and started slapping at the pocket into which he'd dropped the quarter.

It was burning him.

He tried to get it out of his pocket, but it burned his fingers and finally he flung off his coat, flipped down his suspenders, and dropped his trousers, right in front of everybody. Tipped the coin out of his pocket onto the sidewalk, where it sizzled and made the wood start smoking.

Then all the man could think about was the sore place on his leg where the coin had burned him. Arthur Stuart walked up to him, all the time thinking the coin cool again. He reached down and picked it up off the sidewalk. "Reckon you oughta give me my change," he said.

"You get away from me, you Black devil," said the man. "You're a wizard, that's what you are. Cursing a man's coin, that's the same as thievin'!"

"That's awful funny, coming from a man who charged me two bits for a five-cent hunk of bread."

Several passersby chimed in.

"Trying to keep the boy's quarter, was you?"

"There's laws against that, even if the boy is Black."

"Stealin' from them as can't fight back."

"Pull up your trousers, fool."

A little later, Arthur Stuart got change for his quarter and tried to give the man his nickel, but he wouldn't let Arthur get near him.

Well, I tried, thought Arthur. I'm not a thief.

What I am is, I'm a maker.

No great shakes at it like Alvin, but dadgummit, I thought a quarter hot and it dang near burned its way out of the man's pocket.

If I can do that, then I can learn to do it all, that's what he thought, and that's why he was feeling cocky tonight. Because he'd been practicing every day on anything metal he could get his hands on. Wouldn't do no good to turn the iron hot enough to melt, of course—these slaves wouldn't thank him if he burned their wrists and ankles up in the process of getting their chains off.

No, his project was to make the metal soft without getting it hot. That was a lot harder than hetting it up. Lots of times he'd caught himself straining again, trying to *push* softness onto the metal. But when he relaxed into it again and got the feel of the metal into his head like a song, he gradually began to get the knack of it again. Turned his own belt buckle so soft he could bend it into any shape he wanted. Though after a few minutes he realized the shape he wanted it in was like a belt buckle, since he still needed it to hold his pants up.

Brass was easier than iron, since it was softer in the first place. And it's not like Arthur Stuart was fast. He'd seen Alvin turn a gun barrel soft while a man was in the process of shooting it at him, that's how quick *he* was. But Arthur Stuart had to ponder on it first. Twenty-five slaves, each with an iron band at his ankle and another at his wrist. He had to make sure they all waited till the last one was free. If any of them bolted early, they'd all be caught.

Course, he could ask Alvin to help him. But he already had Alvin's answer. Leave 'em slaves, that's what Alvin had decided. But Arthur wouldn't do it. These men were in his hands. He was a maker now, after his own fashion, and it was up to him to decide for himself when it was right to act and right to let be. He couldn't do what Alvin did, healing folks and getting animals to do his bidding and turning water into glass. But he could soften iron, by damn, and so he'd set these men free.

Tomorrow night.

Next morning they passed from the Hio into the Mizzippy, and for the first time in years Alvin got a look at Tenskwa-Tawa's fog on the river.

It was like moving into a wall. Sunny sky, not a cloud, and when you looked ahead it really didn't look like much, just a little mist on the river. But all of a sudden you couldn't see more than a hundred yards ahead of you—and that was only if you were headed up or down the river. If you kept going straight across to the right bank, it was like you went blind, you couldn't even see the front of your own boat.

It was the fence that Tenskwa-Tawa had built to protect the Reds who moved west after the failure of Ta-Kumsaw's war. All the Reds who didn't want to live under White man's law, all the Reds who were done with war, they crossed over the water into the west, and then Tenskwa-Tawa . . . closed the door behind them.

Alvin had heard tales of the west from trappers who used to go there. They talked of mountains so sharp with stone, so rugged and high that they had snow on them clear into June. Places where the ground itself spat hot water fifty feet into the sky, or higher. Herds of buffalo so big they could pass by you all day and night, and next morning it still looked like there was just as many as yesterday. Grassland and desert, pine forest and lakes like jewels nestled among mountains so high that if you climbed to the top you ran out of air.

And all that was now Red land, where Whites would never go again. That's what this fog was all about.

Except for Alvin. He knew that if he wanted to, he could dispel that fog and cross over. Not only that, but he wouldn't be killed, neither. Tenskwa-Tawa had said so, and there'd be no Red man who'd go against the Prophet's law.

A part of him wanted to put to shore, wait for the riverboat to move on, and then get him a canoe and paddle across the river and look for his old friend and teacher. It would be good to talk to him about all that was going on in the world. About the rumors of war coming, between the United States and the Crown Colonies—or maybe between the free states and slave states within the U.S.A. About rumors of war with Spain to get control of the mouth of the Mizzippy, or war between the Crown Colonies and England.

And now this rumor of war with the Mexica. What would Tenskwa-Tawa make of that? Maybe he had troubles of his own—maybe he was working even now to make an alliance of Reds to head south and defend their lands against men who dragged their captives to the tops of their ziggurats and tore their hearts out to satisfy their god.

Anyway, that's the kind of thing going through Alvin's mind as he leaned on the rail on the right side of the boat—the stabberd side, that was, though why boatmen should have different words for right and left made no sense to him. He was just standing there looking out into the fog and seeing no more than any other man, when he noticed something, not with his eyes, but with that inward vision that saw heartfires.

There was a couple of men out on the water, right out in the middle where they wouldn't be able to tell up from down. Spinning round and round, they were, and scared. It took only a moment to get the sense of it. Two men on a raft, only they didn't have drags under the raft and had it loaded front-heavy. Not boatmen, then. Had to be a homemade raft, and when their tiller broke they didn't know how to get the raft to keep its head straight downriver. At the mercy of the current, that's what, and no way of knowing what was happening five feet away.

Though it wasn't as if the *Yazoo Queen* was quiet. Still, fog had a way of damping down sounds. And even if they heard the riverboat, would they know what the sound was? To terrified men, it might sound like some kind of monster moving along the river.

Well, what could Alvin do about it? How could he claim to see what no one else could make out? And the flow of the river was too strong and complicated for him to get control of it, to steer the raft closer.

Time for some lying. Alvin turned around and shouted. "Did you hear that? Did you see them? Raft out of control on the river! Men on a raft, they were calling for help, spinning around out there!"

In no time the pilot and captain both were leaning over the rail of the pilot's deck. "I don't see a thing!" shouted the pilot.

"Not *now*," said Alvin. "But I saw 'em plain just a second ago, they're not far."

Captain Howard could see the drift of things and he didn't like it. "I'm not taking the *Yazoo Queen* any deeper into this fog than she already is! No sir! They'll fetch up on the bank farther downriver, it's no business of ours!"

"Law of the river!" shouted Alvin. "Men in distress!"

That gave the pilot pause. It *was* the law. You had to give aid.

"I don't see no men in distress!" shouted Captain Howard.

"So don't turn the big boat," said Alvin. "Let me take that little row-boat and I'll go fetch 'em."

Captain didn't like that, either, but the pilot was a decent man and pretty soon Alvin was in the water with his hands on the oars.

But before he could fair get away, there was Arthur Stuart, leaping over the gap and sprawling into the little boat. "That was about as clumsy a move as I ever saw," said Alvin.

"I ain't gonna miss this," said Arthur Stuart.

There was another man at the rail, hailing him. "Don't be in such a hurry, Mr. Smith!" shouted Jim Bowie. "Two strong men is better than one on a job like this!" And then he, too, was leaping—a fair job of it, too, considering he must be at least ten years older than Alvin and a good twenty years older than Arthur Stuart. But when he landed, there was no sprawl about it, and Alvin wondered what this man's knack was. He had supposed it was killing, but maybe the killing was just a sideline. The man fair to flew.

So there they were, each of them at a set of oars while Arthur Stuart sat in the stern and kept his eye peeled.

"How far are they?" he kept asking.

"The current might've took them farther out," said Alvin. "But they're there."

And when Arthur started looking downright skeptical, Alvin fixed him with such a glare that Arthur Stuart finally got it. "I think I see 'em," he said, giving Alvin's lie a boost.

"You ain't trying to cross this whole river and get us kilt by Reds," said Jim Bowie.

"No sir," said Alvin. "Got no such plan. I saw those boys, plain as day, and I don't want their death on my conscience."

"Well where are they now?"

Of course Alvin knew, and he was rowing toward them as best he could. Trouble was that Jim Bowie didn't know where they were, and he was rowing too, only not quite in the same direction as Alvin. And seeing as how both of them had their backs to where the raft was, Alvin couldn't even pretend to see them. He could only try to row stronger than Bowie in the direction he wanted to go.

Until Arthur Stuart rolled his eyes and said, "Would you two just stop pretending that anybody believes anybody, and row in the right direction?"

Bowie laughed. Alvin sighed.

"You didn't see nothin'," said Bowie. "Cause I was watching you looking out into the fog."

"Which is why you came along."

"Had to find out what you wanted to do with this boat."

"I want to rescue two lads on a flatboat that's spinning out of control on the current."

"You mean that's *true*?"

Alvin nodded, and Bowie laughed again. "Well I'm jiggered."

"That's between you and your jig," said Alvin. "More downstream, please."

"So what's your knack, man?" said Bowie. "Seeing through fog?"

"Looks like, don't it?"

"I think not," said Bowie. "I think there's a lot more to you than meets the eye."

Arthur Stuart looked Alvin's massive blacksmith's body up and down. "Is that *possible*?"

"And you're no slave," said Bowie.

There was no laugh when he said *that*. That was dangerous for any man to know.

"Am so," said Arthur Stuart.

"No slave would answer back like that, you poor fool," said Bowie. "You got such a mouth on you, there's no way you ever had a taste of the lash."

"Oh, it's a *good* idea for you to come with me on this trip," said Alvin.

"Don't worry," said Bowie. "I got secrets of my own. I can keep yours."

Can—but will you? "Not much of a secret," said Alvin. "I'll just have to take him back north and come down later on another steamboat."

"Your arms and shoulders tell me you really are a smith," said Bowie. "But. Ain't no smith alive can look at a knife in its sheath and say it used to be a file."

"I'm good at what I do," said Alvin.

"Alvin Smith. You really ought to start traveling under another name."

"Why?"

"You're the smith what killed a couple of Finders a few years back."

"Finders who murdered my wife's mother."

"Oh, no jury would convict you," said Bowie. "No more than I got convicted for *my* killing. Looks to me like we got a lot in common."

"Less than you might think."

"Same Alvin Smith who absconded from his master with a particular item."

"A lie," said Alvin. "And he knows it."

"Oh, I'm sure it is. But so the story goes."

"You can't believe these tales."

"Oh, I know," said Bowie. "You aren't slacking off on your rowing, are you?"

"I'm not sure I want to overtake that raft while we're still having this conversation."

"I was just telling you, in my own quiet way, that I think I know what you got in that sack of yours. Some powerful knack you got, if the rumors are true."

"What do they say, that I can fly?"

"You can turn iron to gold, they say."

"Wouldn't that be nice," said Alvin.

"But you didn't deny it, did you?"

"I can't make iron into anything but horseshoes and hinges."

"You did it once, though, didn't you?"

"No sir," said Alvin. "I told you those stories were lies."

"I don't believe you."

"Then you're calling me a liar, sir," said Alvin.

"Oh, you're not going to take offense, are you? Because I have a way of winning all my duels."

Alvin didn't answer, and Bowie looked long and hard at Arthur Stuart. "Ah," said Bowie. "That's the way of it."

"What?" said Arthur Stuart.

"You ain't askeered of me," said Bowie, exaggerating his accent.

"Am so," said Arthur Stuart.

"You're scared of what I know, but you ain't a-scared of me taking down your 'master' in a duel."

"Terrified," said Arthur Stuart.

It was only a split second, but there were Bowie's oars a-dangling, and his knife out of its sheath and his body twisted around with his knife right at Alvin's throat.

Except that it wasn't a knife anymore. Just a handle.

The smile left Bowie's face pretty slow when he realized that his precious knife-made-from-a-file no longer had any iron in it.

"What did you do?" he asked.

"That's a pretty funny question," said Alvin, "coming from a man who meant to kill me."

"Meant to scare you is all," said Bowie. "You didn't have to do that to my knife."

"I got no knack for knowing a man's intentions," said Alvin. "Now turn around and row."

Bowie turned around and took hold of the oars again. "That knife was my luck."

"Then I reckon you just run out of it," said Alvin.

Arthur Stuart shook his head. "You oughta take more care about who you draw against, Mr. Bowie."

"You're the man we want," said Bowie. "That's all I wanted to say. Didn't have to wreck my knife."

"Next time you look to get a man on your team," said Alvin, "don't draw a knife on him."

"And don't threaten to tell his secrets," said Arthur Stuart.

And now, for the first time, Bowie looked more worried than peeved. "Now, I never said I *knew* your secrets. I just had some guesses, that's all."

"Well, Arthur Stuart, Mr. Bowie just noticed he's out here in the middle of the river, in the fog, on a dangerous rescue mission, with a couple of people whose secrets he threatened to tell."

"It's a position to give a man pause," said Arthur Stuart.

"I won't go out of this boat without a struggle," said Bowie.

"I don't plan to hurt you," said Alvin. "Because we're not alike, you and me. I killed a man once, in grief and rage, and I've regretted it ever since."

"Me too," said Bowie.

"It's the proudest moment of your life. You saved the weapon and called it your luck. We're not alike at all."

"I reckon not."

"And if I want you dead," said Alvin, "I don't have to throw you out of no boat."

Bowie nodded. And then took his hands off the oar. His hands began to flutter around his cheeks, around his mouth.

"Can't breathe, can you?" said Alvin. "Nobody's blocking you. Just do it, man. Breathe in, breathe out. You been doing it all your life."

It wasn't like Bowie was choking. He just couldn't get his body to do his will.

Alvin didn't keep it going till the man turned blue or nothing. Just long enough for Bowie to feel real helpless. And then he remembered how to breathe, just like that, and sucked in the air.

"So now that we've settled the fact that you're in no danger from me here on this boat," said Alvin, "let's rescue a couple of fellows got themselves on a homemade raft that got no drag."

And at that moment, the whiteness of the fog before them turned into a flatboat not five feet away. Another pull on the oars and they bumped it. Which was the first time the men on the raft had any idea that anybody was coming after them.

Arthur Stuart was already clambering to the bow of the boat, holding onto the stern rope and leaping onto the raft to make it fast.

"Lord be praised," said the smaller of the two men.

"You come at a right handy time," said the tall one, helping Arthur make the line fast. "Got us an unreliable raft here, and in this fog we wasn't even seeing that much of the countryside. A second-rate voyage by any reckoning."

Alvin laughed at that. "Glad to see you've kept your spirits up."

"Oh, we was both praying and singing hymns," said the lanky man.

"How tall *are* you?" said Arthur Stuart as the man loomed over him.

"About a head higher than my shoulders," said the man, "but not quite long enough for my suspenders."

The fellow had a way about him, right enough. You just couldn't help but like him.

Which made Alvin suspicious right off. If that was the man's knack, then he couldn't be trusted. And yet the most cussed thing about it was, even while you wasn't trusting him, you still had to like him.

"What are you, a lawyer?" asked Alvin.

By now they had maneuvered the boat to the front of the raft, ready to tug it along behind them as they rejoined the riverboat.

The man stood to his full height and then bowed, as awkward-looking a maneuver as Alvin had ever seen. He was all knees and elbows, angles everywhere, even his face, nothing soft about him, as bony a fellow as could be. No doubt about it, he was ugly. Eyebrows like an ape's, they protruded so far out over his eyes. And yet . . . he wasn't bad to look at. Made you feel warm and welcome, when he smiled.

"Abraham Lincoln of Springfield, at your service, gentlemen," he said.

"And I'm Cuz Johnston of Springfield," said the other man.

"Cuz for 'Cousin,'" said Abraham. "Everybody calls him that."

"They do *now*," said Cuz.

"*Whose* cousin?" asked Arthur Stuart.

"Not mine," said Abraham. "But he looks like a cousin, don't he? He's the epitome of cousinhood, the quintessence of cousiniferosity. So when I started calling him Cuz, it was just stating the obvious."

"Actually, I'm his father's second wife's son by her first husband," said Cuz.

"Which makes us step-strangers," said Abraham. "In-law."

"I'm particularly grateful to you boys for pickin' us up," said Cuz, "on account of now old Abe here won't have to finish the most obnoxious tall tale I ever heard."

"It wasn't no tall tale," said old Abe. "I heard it from a man named Taleswapper. He had it in his book, and he didn't never put anything in it lessen it was true."

Old Abe—who couldn't have been more than thirty—was quick of eye. He saw the glance that passed between Alvin and Arthur Stuart.

"So you know him?" asked Abe.

"A truthful man, he is indeed," said Alvin. "What tale did he tell you?"

"Of a child born many years ago," said Abe. "A tragic tale of a brother who got kilt by a treetrunk carried downstream by a flood, which hit him while he was a-saving his mother, who was in a wagon in the middle of the stream, giving birth. But doomed as he was, he stayed alive long enough on that river that when the baby was born, it was the seventh son of a seventh son, and all the sons alive."

"A noble tale," said Alvin. "I've seen that one in his book my own self."

"And you believe it?"

"I do," said Alvin.

"I never said it wasn't true," said Cuz. "I just said it wasn't the tale a man wants to hear when he's spinning downstream on a flapdoodle flatboat in the midst of the Mizzippy mist."

Abe Lincoln ignored the near-poetic language of his companion. "So I was telling Cuz here that the river hadn't treated us half bad, compared to what a much smaller stream done to the folks in that story. And now here *you* are, saving us—so the river's been downright kind to a couple of second-rate raftmakers."

"Made this one yourself, eh?" said Alvin.

"Tiller broke," said Abe.

"Didn't have no spare?" said Alvin.

"Didn't know I'd need one. But if we ever once fetched up on shore, I could have made another."

"Good with your hands?"

"Not really," said Abe. "But I'm willing to do it over till it's right."

Alvin laughed. "Well, time to do this raft over."

"I'd welcome it if you'd show me what we done wrong. I can't see a blame thing here that isn't good raftmaking."

"It's what's under the raft that's missing. Or rather, what ought to be there but ain't. You need a drag at the stern, to keep the back in back. And on top of that you've got it heavy-loaded in front, so it's bound to turn around any old way."

"Well I'm blamed," said Abe. "No doubt about it, I'm not cut out to be a boatman."

"Most folks aren't," said Alvin. "Except my friend Mr. Bowie here. He's just can't keep away from a boat, when he gets a chance to row."

Bowie gave a tight little smile and a nod to Abe and his companion. By now the raft was slogging along behind them in the water, and it was all Alvin and Bowie could do, to move it forward.

"Maybe," said Arthur Stuart, "the two of you could stand at the *back* of the raft so it didn't dig so deep in front and make it such a hard pull."

Embarrassed, Abe and Cuz did so at once. And in the thick fog of midstream, it made them mostly invisible and damped down any 'sound they made so that conversation was nigh impossible.

It took a good while to overtake the steamboat, but the pilot, being a good man, had taken it slow, despite Captain Howard's ire over time lost, and all of a sudden the fog thinned and the noise of the paddlewheels was right beside them as the *Yazoo Queen* loomed out of the fog.

"I'll be plucked and roasted," shouted Abe. "That's a right fine steamboat you got here."

"Tain't our'n," said Alvin.

Arthur Stuart noticed how little time it took Bowie to get himself up on deck and away from the boat, shrugging off all the hands clapping at his shoulder like he was a hero. Well, Arthur couldn't blame him. But it was a sure thing that however Alvin might have scared him out on the water, Bowie was still a danger to them both.

Once the dinghy was tied to the *Yazoo Queen,* and the raft lashed alongside as well, there was all kinds of chatter from passengers wanting to know obvious things like how they ever managed to find each other in the famous Mizzippy fog.

"It's like I said," Alvin told them. "They was right close, and even then, we still had to search."

Abe Lincoln heard it with a grin, and didn't say a word to contradict him, but he was no fool, Arthur Stuart could see that. He knew that the raft had been nowheres near the riverboat. He also knew that Alvin had steered straight for the *Yazoo Queen* as if he could see it.

But what was that to him? In no time he was telling all who cared to listen about what a blame fool job he'd done a-making the raft, and how dizzy they got spinning round and round in the fog. "It twisted me up into such a knot that it took the two of us half a day to figure out how to untie my arms from my legs and get my head back out from my armpit." It wasn't all that funny, really, but the way he told it, he got such a laugh. Even though the story wasn't likely to end up in Taleswapper's book.

Well, that night they put to shore at a built-up rivertown and there was so much coming and going on the *Yazoo Queen* that Arthur

Stuart gave up on his plan to set the twenty-five Mexica slaves free that night.

Instead, he and Alvin went to a lecture being held that night in the dining room of the riverboat. The speaker was none other than Cassius Marcellus Clay, the noted anti-slavery orator, who persisted in his mad course of lecturing against slavery right in the midst of slave country. But listening to him, Arthur Stuart could see how the man got away with it. He didn't call names or declare slavery to be a terrible sin. Instead he talked about how much harm slavery did to the owners and their families.

"What does it do to a man, to raise up his children to believe that their own hands never have to be set to labor? What will happen when he's old, and these children who never learned to work freely spend his money without heed for the morrow?

"And when these same children have seen their fellow human, however dusky of hue his skin might be, treated with disdain, their labor dispraised and their freedom treated as nought—will they hesitate to treat their aging father as a thing of no value, to be discarded when he is no longer useful? For when one human being is treated as a commodity, why should children not learn to think of all humans as either useful or useless, and discard all those in the latter category?"

Arthur Stuart had heard plenty of abolitionists speak over the years, but this one took the cake. Because instead of stirring up a mob of slave-owners wanting to tar and feather him, or worse, he got them looking all thoughtful and glancing at each other uneasily, probably thinking on their own children and what a useless set of grubs they no doubt were.

In the end, though, it wasn't likely Clay was doing all that much good. What were they going to do, set their slaves free and move north? That would be like the story in the Bible, where Jesus told the rich young man, Sell all you got and give it unto the poor and come follow me. The wealth of these men was measured in slaves. To give them up was to become poor, or at least to join the middling sort of men who have to pay for what labor they hire. Renting a man's back, so to speak, instead of owning it. None of them had the courage to do it, at least not that Arthur Stuart saw.

But he noticed that Abe Lincoln seemed to be listening real close to everything Clay said, eyes shining. Especially when Clay talked about them as wanted to send Black folks back to Africa. "How many of you would be glad to hear of a plan to send *you* back to England or Scotland or Germany or whatever place your ancestors came from? Rich or poor, bond or free, we're Americans now, and slaves whose grandparents were born on this soil can't be sent *back* to Africa, for it's no more their home than China is, or India."

Abe nodded at that, and Arthur Stuart got the impression that up to now, the lanky fellow probably thought that the way to solve the Black problem was exactly that, to ship 'em back to Africa.

"And what of the mulatto? The light-skinned Black man who partakes of the blood of Europe and Africa in equal parts? Shall such folk be split in two like a rail, and the pieces divvied up between the lands of their ancestry? No, like it or not we're all bound together in this land, yoked together. When you enslave a black man, you enslave yourself as well, for now you are bound to him as surely as he is bound to you, and your character is shaped by his bondage as surely as his own is. Make the Black man servile, and in the same process you make yourself tyrannical. Make the Black man quiver in fear before you, and you make yourself a monster of terror. Do you think your children will not see you in that state, and fear you, too? You cannot wear one face to the slave and another face to your family, and expect either face to be believed."

When the talk was over, and before Arthur and Alvin separated to their sleeping places, they had a moment together at the rail overlooking the flatboat. "How can anybody hear that talk," said Arthur Stuart, "and go home to their slaves, and not set them free?"

"Well, for one thing," said Alvin, "I'm not setting *you* free."

"Because you're only pretending I'm a slave," whispered Arthur.

"Then I *could* pretend to set you free, and be a good example for the others."

"No you can't," said Arthur Stuart, "because then what would you do with me?"

Alvin just smiled a little and nodded, and Arthur Stuart got his point. "I didn't say it would be easy. But if everybody would do it—"

"But everybody won't do it," said Alvin. "So them as free their slaves, they're suddenly poor, while them as don't free them, they stay rich. So now who has all the power in slavery country? Them as keep their slaves."

"So there's no hope."

"It has to be all at once, by law, not bit by bit. As long as it's permitted to keep slaves anywhere, then bad men will own them and get advantage from it. You have to ban it outright. That's what I can't get Peggy to understand. All her persuasion in the end will come to nothing, because the moment somebody stops being a slaveowner, he loses all his influence among those who have kept their slaves."

"Congress can't ban slavery in the Crown Colonies, and the King can't ban it in the States. So no matter what you do, you're gonna have one place that's got slaves and the other that doesn't."

"It's going to be war," said Alvin. "Sooner or later, as the free states get sick of slavery and the slave states get more dependent on it, there'll be a revolution on one side of the line or the other. I think there won't be freedom until the King falls and his Crown Colonies become states in the union."

"That'll never happen."

"I think it will," said Alvin. "But the bloodshed will be terrible. Because people fight most fiercely when they dare not admit even to themselves that their cause is unjust." He spat into the water. "Go to bed, Arthur Stuart."

But Arthur couldn't sleep. Having Cassius Clay speaking on the riverboat had got the belowdecks folk into a state, and some of them were quite angry at Clay for making White folks feel guilty. "Mark my words," said a fellow from Kenituck. "When they get feelin' guilty, then the only way to feel better is to talk theirself into believing we *deserve* to be slaves, and if we deserve to be slaves, we must be very bad and need to be punished all the time."

It sounded pretty convoluted to Arthur Stuart, but then he was only a baby when his mother carried him to freedom, so it's not like he knew what he was talking about in an argument about what slavery was really like.

Even when things finally quieted down, though, Arthur couldn't sleep, until finally he got up and crept up the ladderway to the deck.

It was a moonlit night, here on the east bank, where the fog was only a low mist and you could look up and see stars.

The twenty-five Mexica slaves were asleep on the stern deck, some of them mumbling softly in their sleep. The guard was asleep, too.

I meant to free you tonight, thought Arthur. But it would take too long now. I'd never be done by morning.

And then it occurred to him that maybe it wasn't so. Maybe he could do it faster than he thought.

So he sat down in a shadow and after a couple of false starts, he got the nearest slave's ankle iron into his mind and began to sense the metal the way he had that coin. Began to soften it as he had softened his belt buckle.

Trouble was, the iron ring was thicker and had more metal in it than either the coin or the buckle had had. By the time he got one part softened up, another part was hard again, and so it went. It began to feel like the story Peggy read them about Sisyphus, whose time in Hades was spent pushing a stone up a mountain, but for every step up, he slid two steps back, so after working all day he was farther from the top than he was when he began.

And then he almost cussed out loud at how stupid he had been.

He didn't have to soften the whole ring. What were they going to do, slide it off like a sleeve? All he had to do was soften it at the hinge, where the metal was thinnest and weakest.

He gave it a try and it was getting all nice and soft when he realized something.

The hinges weren't connected. The one side wasn't joined to the other. The pin was gone.

He took one fetter after another into his mind and discovered they were all the same. Every single hinge pin was missing. Every single slave was already free.

He got up from the shadows and walked out to stand among the slaves.

They weren't asleep. They made tiny hand gestures to tell Arthur to go away, to get out of sight.

So he went back into the shadows.

As if at a signal, they all opened their fetters and set the chains gently on the deck. It made a bit of racket, of course, but the guard didn't stir. Nor did anyone else in the silent boat.

Then the Black men arose and swung themselves over the side away from shore.

They're going to drown. Nobody taught slaves to swim, or let them learn it on their own. They were choosing death.

Except that, come to think of it, Arthur didn't hear a single splash.

He stood up when all the slaves were gone from the deck and walked to another part of the rail. Sure enough, they were overboard all right— all gathered on the raft. And now they were carefully loading Abe Lincoln's cargo into the dinghy. It wasn't much of a dinghy, but it wasn't much of a cargo, either, and it didn't take long.

What difference did it make, not to steal Abe's stuff? They were all thieves, anyway, since they were stealing themselves by running away. Or that was the theory, anyway. As if a man, by being free, thereby stole something from someone else.

They laid themselves down on the raft, all twenty-five, making a veritable pile of humanity, and with those at the edges using their hands as paddles, they began to pull away out into the current. Heading out into the fog, toward the Red man's shore.

Someone laid a hand on his shoulder and he near jumped out of his skin.

It was Alvin, of course.

"Let's not be seen here," Alvin said softly. "Let's go below."

So Arthur Stuart led the way down into the slave quarters, and soon they were in whispered conversation in the kitchen, which was dark but for a single lantern that Alvin kept trimmed low.

"I figured you'd have some blame fool plan like that," said Alvin.

"And I thought you was going to let them go on as slaves like you didn't care, but I should've knowed better," said Arthur Stuart.

"I thought so, too," said Alvin. "But I don't know if it was having Jim Bowie guess too much, or him trying to kill me with that knife—and no, Arthur Stuart, he did *not* stop in time, if there'd been a blade in that knife it would have cut right through my throat. Could have been the fear of death made me think that I didn't want to face God knowing I could have freed twenty-five men, but chose to leave them slaves. Then again, it might have been Mr. Clay's sermon tonight. Converted me as neat as you please."

"Converted Mr. Lincoln," said Arthur Stuart.

"Might be," said Alvin. "Though he doesn't look like the sort who ever sought to own another man."

"I know why you had to do it," said Arthur Stuart.

"Why is that?"

"Because you knew that if you didn't, I would."

Alvin shrugged. "Well, I knew you'd made up your mind to try."

"I could have done it."

"Very slowly."

"It was working, once I realized I only had to go after the hinge."

"I reckon so," said Alvin. "But the real reason I chose tonight was that the raft was here. A gift to us, don't you think? Would have been a shame not to use it."

"So what happens when they get to the Red man's shore?"

"Tenskwa-Tawa will see to them. I gave them a token to show to the first Red they meet. When they see it, they'll get escorted straight to the Prophet, wherever he might be. And when *he* sees it, he'll give them safe passage. Or maybe let them dwell there."

"Or maybe he'll need them, to help him fight the Mexica. If they're moving north."

"Maybe."

"What was the token?" asked Arthur Stuart.

"A couple of these," said Alvin. He held up a tiny shimmering cube that looked like the clearest ice that had ever been, or maybe glass, but no glass had ever shimmered.

Arthur Stuart took it in his hand and realized what it was. "This is water. A box of water."

"More like a *block* of water. I decided to make it today out on the river, when I came so close to having my blood spill into the water. That's partly how they're made. A bit of my own self has to go into the water to make it strong as steel. You know the law. 'The maker is the one . . .'"

"The maker is the one who is part of what he makes," said Arthur Stuart.

"Get to sleep," said Alvin. "We can't let nobody know we was up tonight. I can't keep them all asleep forever."

"Can I keep this?" said Arthur Stuart. "I think I see something in it."

"You can see everything in it, if you look long enough," said Alvin. "But no, you can't keep it. If you think what I got in my poke is valuable, think what folks would do to have a solid block of water that showed them true visions of things far and near, past and present."

Arthur reached out and offered the cube to Alvin.

But instead of taking it, Alvin only smiled, and the cube went liquid all at once and dribbled through Arthur Stuart's fingers. Arthur looked at the puddle on the table, feeling as forlorn as he ever had.

"It's just water," said Alvin.

"And a little bit of blood."

"Naw," said Alvin. "I took that back."

"Good night," said Arthur Stuart. "And . . . thank you for setting them free."

"Once you set your heart on it, Arthur, what else could I do? I looked at them and thought, somebody loved them once as much as your mama loved you. She died to set you free. I didn't have to do that. Just inconvenience myself a little. Put myself at risk, but not by much."

"But you saw what I did, didn't you? I made it soft without getting it hot."

"You done good, Arthur Stuart. There's no denying it. You're a maker now."

"Not much of one."

"Whenever you got two makers, one's going to be more of a maker than the other. But lessen that one starts gettin' uppity, it's good to re-member that there's always a third one who's better than both of them."

"Who's better than you?" asked Arthur Stuart.

"You," said Alvin. "Because I'll take an ounce of compassion over a pound of tricks any day. Now go to sleep."

Only then did Arthur let himself feel how very, very tired he was. Whatever had kept him awake before, it was gone now. He barely made it to his cot before he fell asleep.

Oh, there was a hullabaloo in the morning. Suspicions flew every which way. Some folks thought it was the boys from the raft, because why else would the slaves have left their cargo behind? Until some-body pointed out that with the cargo still on the raft, there wouldn't have been room for all the runaways.

Then suspicion fell on the guard who had slept, but most folks knew that was wrong, because if he had done it then why didn't he run off, instead of lying there asleep on the deck till a crewman noticed the slaves was gone and raised the alarm.

Only now, when they were gone, did the ownership of the slaves become clear. Alvin had figured Mr. Austin to have a hand in it, but the man most livid at their loss was Captain Howard hisself. That was a surprise. But it explained why the men bound for Mexico had chosen this boat to make their journey downriver.

To Alvin's surprise, though, Austin and Howard both kept glancing at him and young Arthur Stuart as if they suspected the truth. Well, he shouldn't have been surprised, he realized. If Bowie told them what had happened to his knife out on the water, they'd naturally wonder if a man with such power over iron might have been the one to slip the hinge pins out of all the fetters.

Slowly the crowd dispersed. But not Captain Howard, not Austin. And when Alvin and Arthur made as if to go, Howard headed straight for them. "I want to talk to you," he said, and he didn't sound friendly.

"What about?" said Alvin.

"That boy of yours," said Howard. "I saw how he was doing their slops on the morning watch. I saw him talking to them. That made me suspicious, all right, since not one of them spoke English."

"Pero todos hablaban español," said Arthur Stuart.

Austin apparently understood him, and looked chagrined. "They *all* of them spoke Spanish? Lying skunks."

Oh, right, as if slaves owed you some kind of honesty.

"That's as good as a confession," said Captain Howard. "He just admitted he speaks their language and learned things from them that even their master didn't know."

Arthur was going to protest, but Alvin put a hand on his shoulder. He did *not,* however, stop his mouth. "My boy here," said Alvin, "only just learned to speak Spanish, so naturally he seized on an opportunity to practice. Unless you got some evidence that those fetters was opened by use of a slop bucket, then I think you can safely leave this boy out of it."

"No, I expect he *wasn't* the one who popped them hingepins," said Captain Howard. "I expect he was somebody's spy to tell them Blacks about the plan."

"I didn't tell nobody no plan," said Arthur Stuart hotly.

Alvin clamped his grip tighter. No slave would talk to a white man like that, least of all a boat captain.

Then from behind Austin and Howard came another voice. "It's all right, boy," said Bowie. "You can tell them. No need to keep it secret anymore."

And with a sinking feeling, Alvin wondered what kind of pyrotechnics he'd have to go through to distract everybody long enough for him and Arthur Stuart to get away.

But Bowie didn't say at all what Alvin expected. "I got the boy to tell me what he learned from them. They were cooking up some evil Mexica ritual. Something about tearing out somebody's heart one night when they were pretending to be our guides. A treacherous bunch, and so I decided we'd be better of without them."

"*You* decided!" Captain Howard growled. "What right did *you* have to decide."

"Safety," said Bowie. "You put me in charge of the scouts, and that's what these were supposed to be. But it was a blame fool idea from the start. Why do you think them Mexica left those boys alive instead of taking their beating heart out of their chests? It was a trap. All along, it was a trap. Well, we didn't fall into it."

"Do you know how much they cost?" demanded Captain Howard.

"They didn't cost *you* anything," said Austin.

That reminder took a bit of the dudgeon out of Captain Howard. "It's the principle of the thing. Just setting them free."

"But I didn't," said Bowie. "I sent them across river. What do you think will happen to them there—*if* they make it through the fog?"

There was a bit more grumbling, but some laughter, too, and the matter was closed.

Back in his room, Alvin waited for Bowie to return.

"Why?" he demanded.

"I told you I could keep a secret," said Bowie. "I watched you and the boy do it, and I have to say, it was worth it to see how you broke their irons without ever laying a hand on them. To think I'd ever see a knack like that. Oh, you're a maker all right."

"Then come with me," said Alvin. "Leave these men behind. Don't you know the doom that lies over their heads? The Mexica aren't fools. These are dead men you're traveling with."

"Might be so," said Bowie, "but they need what I can do, and you don't."

"I do so," said Alvin. "Because I don't know many men in this world can hide their heartfire from me. It's your knack, isn't it? To disappear from all men's sight, when you want to. Because I never saw you watching us."

"And yet I woke you up just reaching for your poke the other night," said Bowie with a grin.

"Reaching for it?" said Alvin. "Or putting it back?"

Bowie shrugged.

"I thank you for protecting us and taking the blame on yourself."

Bowie chuckled. "Not much blame there. Truth is, Austin was getting sick of all the trouble of taking care of them Blacks. It was only Howard who was so dead set on having them, and he ain't even going with us, once he drops us off on the Mexica coast."

"I could teach you. The way Arthur Stuart's been learning."

"I don't think so," said Bowie. "It's like you said. We're different kind of men."

"Not so different but what you can't change iffen you've a mind to."

Bowie only shook his head.

"Well, then, I'll thank you the only way that's useful to you," said Alvin.

Bowie waited. "Well?"

"I just did it," said Alvin. "I just put it back."

Bowie reached down to the sheath at his waist. It wasn't empty. He drew out the knife. There was the blade, plain as day, not a whit changed.

You'd've thought Bowie was handling his long-lost baby.

"How'd you get the blade back on it?" he asked. "You never touched it."

"It was there all along," said Alvin. "I just kind of spread it out a little."

"So I couldn't see it?"

"And so it wouldn't cut nothing."

"But now it will?"

"I think you're bound to die, when you take on them Mexica, Mr. Bowie. But I want you to take some human sacrificers with you on the way."

"I'll do that," said Bowie. "Except for the part about me dying."

"I hope I'm wrong and you're right, Mr. Bowie," said Alvin.

"And I hope you live forever, Alvin Maker," said the knife-wielding killer.

That morning Alvin and Arthur Stuart left the boat, as did Abe Lincoln and Cuz, and they made their journey down to Nueva Barcelona together, all four of them, swapping impossible stories all the way. But that's another tale, not this one.

NOTES ON "THE *YAZOO QUEEN*"

Just as I was about to start writing *The Crystal City,* the penultimate book in the Alvin Maker series, Bob Silverberg told me that he had the go-ahead for a second anthology in the *Legends* series. *Crystal City* was going to take place in Nueva Barcelona—New Orleans; I had just read a book about Lincoln that told about his trips down the Mississippi, once with a cousin of his. Since I had to get Alvin and Arthur down the river to New Orleans anyway, I might as well have them meet Lincoln on the way.

As I always do with the Tales of Alvin Maker, I cast about to see who else might have been on the river at that time, and found Jim Bowie, among others. With a cast of characters like that, I knew I couldn't lose.

But I found a way to really mess myself up. Because *"Yazoo Queen"* became so productive that I couldn't bear to tear myself away. "Grinning Man" had stood completely alone—if you never read it, the novels would make perfect sense anyway. But after what happened in *"Yazoo Queen,"* I couldn't just *drop* these characters. I realized that *Crystal City* needed to continue the story right where it left off.

Which made *"Yazoo Queen,"* in effect, Chapter Zero of *The Crystal City.* Only it was under an exclusivity contract with *Legends* and so it couldn't appear in the book. Nor could I make it available online.

What I was doing was, in effect, making *Crystal City* the direct sequel of a story that those who owned all the Alvin Maker books nevertheless did not have. It would inevitably refer back to events on the river that they could not read about unless they bought Silverberg's anthology—which, if I remember correctly, would not come out until considerably after *The Crystal City* was published.

I did my best to play fair with the readers. In the opening chapter of *Crystal City,* I made sure that the key information was clearly presented so that the readers would not be completely lost. However, these clues were also tantalizing hints that there was a good story there that the readers were not being told. Which was the truth.

The better solution would have been to make *"Yazoo Queen"* Chapter One of *The Crystal City* after all, and write something else about Alvin Maker for *Legends.* But the *Legends* deadline would not wait; nor would the *Crystal City* deadline. I had no other Alvin story that was ready to write.

Thus is literature shaped by the calendar.

So for those readers of *Crystal City* who were annoyed by the way the book opened, I agree with you completely. It was wrong of me. I apologize. But now you've got the missing story, along with a lot of others, so stop kvetching. I won't do it again. I hope.

V

MORMON STORIES

When I call these "Mormon stories" I don't mean to imply that they are religious. Quite the contrary, they are most definitely not. I don't write religious stories—I think real religion is far too serious to be put in the hands of fiction writers. If a religion has truth in it, that truth will not be helped by surrounding it with lies.

I do, however, write stories that deal with characters who have religious faith. My Women of Genesis series (*Sarah, Rebekah, Rachel and Leah*) and *Stone Tables* are about important figures from the first two books of the Bible. I take very seriously the responsibility to present them fairly, with the motives and beliefs the scripture assigns to them. My task in those books was to flesh them out, to make their lives seem more complete and real to the modern reader. But at no point did I try to deal with points of doctrine, or attempt to persuade people to believe as I believe, or give readers a "spiritual experience."

Indeed, I have contempt for artists who attempt, through their art, to convey spirituality. I believe they could undertake such an enterprise only because they have no idea what spirituality is; they have mistaken it for emotionalism. But emotionalism is a cheap effect. Any actor knows how to make an audience cry; to make them cry using those tricks and then label it a "spiritual experience" is, in my opinion, fraud.

I'm a believer—I believe that God lives and touches our lives. I even believe that we have a responsibility to help each other find our way to faith and obedience to the things God teaches. But I think that should be done openly, the way I did it when I served as a missionary in Brazil in my early twenties, or the way I have conversed candidly about my faith with any individual who sincerely asked. But such conversations are private, and they have no place in my fictional writings.

No, these stories are "Mormon" because they were written by a

Mormon, about Mormon culture, for Mormon readers. They are *culturally* Mormon.

Because the Mormon religion requires all adult members of the Church to be ministers to each other in one "calling" or another, it consumes an enormous amount of our time. We go to ordinary schools in the nations where we live; we hold ordinary jobs; we vote (or don't vote) like ordinary citizens, and are obliged to obey the same laws as everyone else. But in our private lives, we are thrust together in small communities called "wards" (parishes, more or less), consisting of about sixty to a hundred households, and there we spend a lot of our time, fulfilling our callings by teaching each other and helping each other live as better Latter-day Saints.

The result is that almost every Latter-day Saint—every Mormon—lives in a tiny village. That village might be right in the middle of a huge city or spread out over a wide stretch of countryside, but we all belong to a community about the size of a nomadic tribe or a decent-size medieval village. We are familiar with every face; we know which children belong to which parents; many of us know every single person's name.

Not only that, but because the organization of the Church is the same in every ward, we can move into a new ward and immediately know people—at least by their job description. The top man is the bishop; the top woman, the Relief Society president. Name the calling, and we know what role that person serves in this particular small town. It's like moving from town to town and knowing that every single one of them will have exactly one butcher, one baker, and one candlestick maker; all you have to do is find out which face goes with which job and you know *something* about them. You know what you can expect of them; and as soon as you are given a calling, they know what to expect of you.

Of course, the callings change. The bishop this year might be teaching children in Primary the next; no calling in the ward is permanent. So there is a hidden social system, too, one that you don't begin to learn until you've lived in a ward for some time. Regardless of calling, there are certain people who can be counted on to help and take part in everything, and others who are of only shaky reliability. There are those who are deeply knowledgeable about the gospel, and those whose understanding is superficial. There may also be poisonous gossips or ambitious climbers. Gradually, over time, you come to know the true order of the town.

Then one day the people even higher up will decide that the ward has grown too big and divide it into two separate congregations, so the whole thing starts over again as two new villages take shape and discover who they are together.

This way of organizing our lives is so foreign to the experience of most Americans that it doesn't even occur to them how different Mormons' lives are. We don't dress like the Amish or Chassidim (though we do try to dress modestly), so it's not plainly visible, but we experience church life in a radically different way from any other group of Christians. It is safe to say that for most of us—for those of us who are actively engaged in the life of the ward—we *live* in Mormonism and only *visit* American culture.

Mormon life thus has a religious intensity that most others don't have, simply because of the amount of time and attention we put into our church activities. I have lived in Greensboro, North Carolina, for nearly a quarter of a century—almost half my life—but in truth, it is only since I started writing a column for a local weekly ("Uncle Orson Reviews Everything" in *The Rhinoceros Times*) that I felt like I actually became a part of Greensboro. Before that, I was driving around Greensboro and shopping in Greensboro and sending my kids to school in Greensboro but I *lived* in the Guilford Ward for seven years and then the Summit Ward ever since.

Mormons reading this will know exactly what I'm talking about. Non-Mormons may just shake their heads and mutter, "Weird."

But you have to understand this in order to understand what's going on with these four stories—and why they even exist.

Because within Mormon culture there are subcultures. For instance, Mormon life in the "Mormon Corridor"—Eastern Idaho, Utah, and parts of Arizona, where many a town is half Mormon or more—is very different from Mormon life in, say, California, where Mormons are common but not predominant, or in the East and South, where Mormons are relatively rare and we are awash in a sea of Baptists or Methodists or Presbyterians or Catholics.

There are many Mormons who refer to Utah as "Zion," and really believe that it's only there, in valleys sheltered by the Rocky Mountains, and surrounded by communities consisting almost entirely of fellow Latter-day Saints, that the Mormon religion reaches its true fruition.

Then there are others, like me, who believe that Mormonism is at its best where we are not in the majority, where the differences between our lives and the lives of unbelievers are clearly drawn, where it's not "good business" to be seen in church meetings and hold prominent callings, and where the kids dealing drugs in the high school are not the same teenage boys blessing the sacrament on Sunday.

Here in North Carolina, our teenagers need each other in order to help sustain each other's identity as Latter-day Saints; adults depend on each other and are tolerant of variations. If you show up and do your calling, then we don't care what political party you belong to, you're one of us. Also, wards are spread out over large stretches of cities and country-side, so that people of every walk of life and every income level gather together to worship.

In the Mormon Corridor, by contrast, members are expendable—there are so many Mormons you can afford to ostracize those who don't believe *exactly* the way you do. And wards are so bunched together that zoning laws shape the church to a dysfunctional degree—everybody in the ward makes pretty much the same amount of money and lives in pretty much the same-size house, and never has to deal with anyone markedly poorer or different from themselves. When wards are smaller than Zip Codes, it's easy to forget that it's faith and obedience that bind us together, not the superficial similarities of income and career.

In other words, in "Zion," Mormons are far more likely to get con-fused about where worldly values leave off and religious values begin. Whereas in places where Mormons are a small minority, the lines are clear and everyone can see them. Of course there are good and bad Mormons in all different situations, and there are sick and healthy wards both in and out of "Zion." Maybe it's just a matter of preference.

As a fiction writer, my stories serve as social commentary, whether I mean them to or not (and usually I don't). I faithfully report the kinds of things that real people do, and explain as best I can the reasons why they do them. That's what fiction is for.

But when I'm writing for the general audience, I can't address issues that exist only in Mormon culture. So, from time to time—and you can see that it is comparatively rarely—I find it useful to write a fiction that is set within Mormon culture, or within the Mormon belief system. Knowing that non-Mormons probably will never read it, I don't bother to explain cultural elements that Mormons all recognize immediately. In these cases I am writing fiction that is "inside."

Usually, in such cases, my purpose is satire. In the classic sense: I am humorously and ironically calling attention to flaws in society with the idea that these flaws should be corrected. My book *Saintspeak: The Mormon Dictionary* has precisely that purpose—by defining terms that Mormons use in ways peculiar to ourselves, I can also comment on Mormon life and suggest ways that, as a people, we might do better.

So if you are not a Mormon, and you read these stories, you may find them boring, because the issues at stake mean little to you; or you may find them strange and vaguely exotic, like reading Alexander McCall Smith's Botswana novels. Or you may recognize the similarities as well as the differences and find some value for your own understanding of the place of people within their culture.

"Christmas at Helaman's House" was written many years ago and was intended to be the first chapter of a novel; it still may become that. Mormons have—or had, and in my opinion *should* have—a deep suspicion of capitalism and the markers of wealth. Too often in Mormon communities wealth is taken as a sign of God's favor. But I've learned through many conversations and much correspondence that I am far from being the only one in the Church who thinks we've gone too far and need to recover Joseph Smith's insistence that there should be—and is—a better way. So no matter how many Mormons you hear talking like free-market capitalists, remember that there are also a lot of Mormons whose loathing for the competitive economy is a tradition older than Marxism.

"Neighbors" was created as a retelling of the story of Christ, as if he had been born to a couple from a Mormon ward. On one level it's an anti-gossip satire, but on another level it's a take on the way we all safely interpret dangerous things in ways that don't require us to change our lives.

"God Plays Fair Once Too Often" is probably too much of a parable to really work as fiction. I had intended it for publication in a Mormon journal, but realized that it would probably be too offensively jocular for many Latter-day Saints. The problem is that I don't take the book of Job seriously as doctrine or scripture. The account of God making a bet with the devil is not just ludicrous but offensive to me—it's not how the universe works. And I find none of the explanations of why bad things happen to good people even remotely useful. So for me it's fair game for satire, but many other Mormons are bound to think I'm making light of sacred things. As a result, the only publication this received was in the program book for a Dutch science-fiction convention in Rotterdam many years ago. What they made of it I don't know, but they wanted to publish something that hadn't been published before, this was all I had, and they accepted it.

"Worthy to Be One of Us" was created for an anthology of LDS fiction edited jointly by me and my friend David Dollahite (*Turning Hearts: Short Stories on Family Life*). Dave is a scientist working in family studies, particularly fatherhood studies, and we wanted to create an anthology of useful fiction that would show family life from a Mormon perspective. What I was dealing with in my story was the issue of status in the Mormon Church. The leaders of the Church fill important roles, and those I have known personally are usually very good men who can be trusted to fill those roles wisely and well. But surrounding them is too often a penumbra of social class derived from rank. In the Church Office Building they are surrounded, as often as not, by toadies and sycophants who are nauseating in a Uriah Heep kind of way; it makes me wonder how the Church leaders can bear it. I can only assume they are mostly unaware of how they are exploited, fawned over, misrepresented, and lied to by so many of their underlings.

A few generations ago, however, the social aspects of the situation were even worse. Salt Lake City high society was absolutely dominated by those who were called to be General Authorities of the Church, with social rank completely determined by the station and seniority of your family's MRGA—Most Recent General Authority.

Early in Kristine's and my marriage we ran into one of the surviving examples of this pernicious attitude. My great-grandfather (my father's mother's father) was George F. Richards, who for a while was the President of the Quorum of the Twelve, making him the senior Apostle and the designated successor to the President of the Church. He died too soon and never succeeded to the presidency, but his ranking was very high.

Kristine and I were living in Salt Lake when the time for the annual George F. Richards Family Reunion rolled around. George F. and his wife had had fifteen children, twelve of whom lived to have children of their own, so the gathering would be huge. The reunion was to be held at Sugarhouse Park, and my grandmother asked Kristine and me, since we were living close by, to take charge of providing the name tags.

We thought of the bright idea of color-coding the name tags to identify which of George F.'s dozen children each person was descended from. As people approached the reunion, we would ask their names, write them on the right color tag, and then everybody would know something about them. It was very genealogical, very Mormon, and rather fun, Kristine and I thought.

Until we ran into the LeGrand Richards problem. Uncle LeGrand was the only child of George F. who also became an Apostle, and since he was still alive at the time of this reunion, he was the only Living General Authority at the gathering. I had met him several times, and in fact he had performed Kristine's and my wedding ceremony (though we did not expect him to remember). When he came near our table, we called out (as we had to everyone), "Come and get your name tags!" He waved us off, and, rather snappishly, remarked, "I don't need a name tag." Well, of course he didn't. Everyone knew who he was. So Kristine and I laughed it off, though it would have been *nice* if his own descendants could have been visibly linked to him by the color-coded tags.

That's what we thought—until we met some of those descendants. We called out to them, and they were the only people in the whole gathering to act rather huffish and snooty toward us when we explained what we were doing. "Which of George F.'s children are you descended from?" I asked.

The woman looked at me as if I were an idiot. "LeGrand, of course," she said. The tone was absolutely clear: How could I have been so hopelessly ignorant as not to know they were of the sacred family of the Most Recent General Authority?

Kristine and I laughed over it (we still do) but I was also deeply ashamed of them. They were my cousins, after all, but they were also

crushing snobs, and their status derived entirely, not from any achievements of their own, but from what one of their ancestors did—as if it
made them a different kind or class of people from the rest of us. Except
that *every single person* at that gathering was descended from a President of
the Quorum of the Twelve—a higher status than LeGrand had ever
achieved—and so it was ludicrous to pull social rank.

Even though they accepted the name tags we wrote for them, they
didn't wear them—we saw the tags lying atop the nearest garbage can
only a few moments later. So at that family reunion, the way you could
tell LeGrand and at least one branch of his family was by their lack of a
name tag. They were just too cool for the rest of us.

Uncle LeGrand was a beloved Apostle—by me as much as anyone.
And I still loved hearing him speak in Conference until he died some
years later. But from then on, there was a little sad memory in my heart
whenever I saw and thought of him. For all his many contributions to the
Church (for instance, his missionary book *A Marvelous Work and a Wonder*), he had failed to raise at least some of his family with the humility expected of Christians. The lesson taught by the Savior when he pointed to
his disciples and said, "These are my mother and my brothers," was apparently lost on them.

I single them out only because I'm in that family and had occasion to
see their behavior firsthand. But snobbery based on Church rank and
prominence is a pernicious disease in the Mormon Church. Even though
the doctrine is clear—children of General Authorities can go to hell just
as fast and just as far as anyone else, if they so choose—snobbery is more
the rule than the exception. I've heard it as recently as the priesthood session of the most recent General Conference (April 2007), when one of
the speakers, in order to prove the "success" of a particular group of
young men, listed how many had become mission presidents and temple
presidents and General Authorities of the Church.

When the speaker said that, I turned to the man beside me and said,
"I'm just a priests' quorum instructor and a cultural arts director. I guess
my youth leaders failed with me. I might as well give up and go have a
beer." He laughed, but he knew what I was saying and had also felt the
sting. When Church ranking is used as a measure of "success" in raising
faithful Latter-day Saints, it brands all the ordinary, hardworking, faithful

fathers and mothers in the Church who have *not* reached those rare prominent offices as failures. It's actually a rather shocking thing to do—but such snobbish insults happen all the time, without anyone batting an eye.

"Worthy to Be One of Us," then, is a story of a particular family; but it's also a story of what should actually matter in a family and in an organization that purports to be, and tries to be, the Kingdom of God on earth.

And if you're not a Mormon, I can't imagine why this would matter to you one bit. What do *you* care whether one Mormon is unkind to another because of who his or her family is or isn't?

But then, the tendency toward snobbery *is* a human universal. So even if you're outside the culture in which this story takes place, perhaps it will have some resonance for you. And for that reason, these four Mormon stories are included in a collection that is otherwise definitely *not* geared toward a religious audience.

Christmas at Helaman's House

There were times when he wanted to give up and live in a tent rather than fight with the contractors one more time, but in the end Helaman Willkie got the new house built and the family moved in before Christmas. Three days before Christmas, in fact, which meant that, exhausted as they all were from the move, they *still* had to search madly through the piles of boxes in the new basement to find all the Christmas decorations and get them in place before Santa showed up to inaugurate their new heat-trapping triple-flue chimney.

So they were all tired, weary to the bone, and yet they walked around the house with these silly smiles on their faces, saying and doing the strangest things. Like Joni, Helaman's sixteen-year-old daughter, who every now and then would burst into whatever room Helaman was in, do a pirouette, and say, "Daddy, Daddy, I have my own room!" To which he would reply, "So I heard." To which she would say, hugging him in a way calculated to muss his hair, "You really do love me, now I *know* it."

Helaman's old joke was that none of his children had ever been impossible, but they had all been improbable more than once. Twelve-year-old Ryan had already been caught twice trying to ride his skateboard down the front staircase. Why couldn't he slide down the banister like any normal boy? Then at least he'd be polishing it with his backside, instead of putting dings in the solid oak treads of the stair. Fourteen-year-old Steven had spent every waking moment in the game room, hooking the computers together and then trying out all the software, as if to make sure that it would still work in the new house. Helaman had no evidence that Steven had yet seen the inside of his own bedroom.

And then there was Lucille, Helaman's sensible, organized, dependable, previously sane wife, kissing all the appliances in the kitchen. But the truth was that Lucille's delight at the kitchen came as a great relief to Helaman. Till then he had been worried that she was still having doubts about the house. When the movers left, she had stood there in the main-floor family room, staring at the queen-size hide-a-bed looking so forlorn and small on the vast carpet. Helaman reassured her that in no time they'd have plenty of furniture to fill up the room, but she refused to be reassured. "We're going to buy a truckload of furniture? When our mortgage is bigger than the one on our first store back in 1970?"

He started to explain to her that those were 1970 dollars, but she just gave him that how-stupid-do-you-think-I-am look and said, "I took economics in college, Helaman. I was talking about how I *felt*."

So Helaman said nothing. He had long since learned that when Lucille was talking about how she *felt,* none of the things he could think of to say would be very helpful. He couldn't even begin to put into words what *he* felt—how proud he had been of this house he had caused to exist for her, how much he needed to know that it made her happy. After all their years of struggling and worrying to try to keep the business afloat, and then struggling and worrying about the huge debts involved in starting up the branch stores, he knew that Lucille deserved to have a fine house, the *finest* house, and that he deserved to be the man who could give it to her. Now all she could think about was the huge amount of money the house had cost, and Helaman felt as though someone had taken the very breath out of him.

Until she came into the kitchen and squealed in delight. It was exactly the sound his daughters made—an ear-piercing yelp that gave him headaches whenever Trudy and Joni got excited for more than a minute at a time. He had almost forgotten that it was hereditary, that they got that glass-shattering high note from Lucille. She hadn't been surprised and happy enough to make that sound in years. But she made it now, and said, "Oh, Helaman, it's beautiful, it's perfect, it's the perfect kitchen!" It made up for her reaction to the family room. If it hadn't, he would have despaired—because he had worked hard to make sure that the kitchen was irresistible. He had kept careful track of everything she had ever admired in magazines or home shows; he had bought all new appliances, from the can opener and toaster to the microwave and the breadmaker; he had brought those all into the house himself and had his best crew install everything and test it so it ran perfectly. He had inventoried every utensil in her old kitchen and bought a brand-new replacement; they had chosen new silverware and pans and dishes for daily use, and he had arranged it as close to the way she had her old kitchen arranged as possible, even when the arrangement made no sense whatever. And he had kept her out of the kitchen—with tape across the door—all the time he was doing it, and all during the move itself, until that moment when he told her she could tear away the ribbon and walk through the door. And she squealed and kissed all the appliances and opened all the drawers and said, "Just where I would have put it!" and "I can't believe there's room for everything and there's *still* counter space!" and "How did you get them all out of the old kitchen without my seeing you do it?"

"I didn't," Helaman told her. "I bought all new ones."

"Oh, you're such a tease," she said. "I mean, here's the old garlic press. I've never even used it."

"Now you have two of them."

And when she realized that he meant it, that he had really duplicated all her utensils and put them away exactly as she had always had them, she started to cry, which was a sign of happiness even more certain than the squealing.

So yes, they loved the house, all of them. Wasn't that what he built it for? For them to feel exactly this way about it? But what he hadn't expected was his own feeling of disappointment. He couldn't match their enthusiasm; on the contrary, he felt sad and uncertain as he walked through the house. As if after all his struggling to cause this house to exist, to be perfect, now that it was done he had no reason to be here. No, that wasn't quite the feeling. It was as if he had no *right* to be here. He strode through the house with all the rights of ownership, and yet he felt like an interloper, as if he had evicted the rightful occupants and stolen the place.

Am I so used to struggling for money all my life that when I finally have visible proof that the struggle is over, I can't believe it? No, he thought. *What I can't believe is* me. *I don't belong in a place like this. In my heart, I think of myself in that miserable three-bedroom tract house in*

Orem with the four makeshift bedrooms Dad built in the basement so all his six kids could have rooms of our own. Well, I'm not a wage man like Dad, and my kids will not be ashamed of where they live, and my wife will be able to invite any woman in the ward into her home without that look of apology that Mother always had when she had to bring chairs from the dining room just so there'd be enough places for her visitors to sit.

Yet even when he had told himself all these things, reminded himself of the fire that had burned inside him all during the building of the house, he still felt empty and disappointed and vaguely ashamed, and he just didn't understand it. It wasn't fair that he should feel like this. He had *earned* this house.

Well, what did he expect, anyway? It was like Christmas itself: The gifts were never as good as the preparations—the shopping and hiding and wrapping. He felt as he did because he was tired, that's all. Tired and ready for it to be the day after Christmas when he could get back to running his little empire of five Willkie's stores, which sprawled on their parking lots in choice locations up and down the Wasatch Front, beaming their cheery fluorescent lights to welcome people in to the wonderful world of dis-count housewares. This had been a record Christmas, and maybe getting the accountants' year-end reports would make him feel better.

Then again maybe it wouldn't. Maybe this is what it is, he thought, that makes all those lonely women come to see the bishop and complain about how they're so depressed. Maybe I'm just having the equivalent of postpartum blues. I have given birth to a house with the finest view in the Darlington Heights Ward, I'm sitting here looking out of a window larger than any of the bathrooms, the twinkling lights of Salt Lake Valley on Christmas Eve spread out before me, with Christmas carols from the CD player being pumped through twenty-two speakers in nine rooms, and I can't enjoy it because I keep getting the postpartum blues.

"They're *hee*-eere!" sang out Trudy. So the new love of her life (the second in December alone) must be at the door. At eighteen she was their eldest child and therefore the one nearest to achieving full human status. Unlike Joni, Trudy still spelled her name with a *y*, and it had been more than a year since she stopped drawing the little eyes over the *u* to make it look like a smile in the middle of her signature. At church yesterday she had fallen in love with the newly returned missionary who bore his testimony in a distinctly Spanish accent. "Can I invite him to come over for the hanging of the stockings?" she pleaded. In vain did Helaman tell her that it would be no use—his *own* family would want to have him all night, it was his first Christmas with them since the 1980s, for heaven's sake! But she said, "I can at least ask, can't I?," and Lucille nodded and so Helaman agreed, and to his surprise the young elder had said yes. Helaman took a mental note: Never underestimate the ability of your own daughters to attract boys, no matter how weird you think your girls have grown up to be.

And now the young elder was here, no doubt with so many hormones flowing through him that he could cause items of furniture to mate with each other just by touching them. Helaman had to get up out of the couch and would play father and host for a couple of hours, all the time watching to make sure the young man kept his hands to himself.

It wasn't till he got to the door and saw *two* young men standing there that he realized that Trudy had said *they're* here. He recognized the elder, of course, looking missionary-like and vaguely lost, but the other was apparently from another planet. He was dressed normally, but one side of his head was mostly shaved, and the other side was partly permed and partly straight. Joni immediately attached herself to him, which at least told Helaman what had brought him to their door on Christmas Eve— another case of raging hormones. As to *who* he was, Helaman deduced that he was either a high school hoodlum she had invited over to horrify them or one of the bodacious new boys from the Darlington Heights Ward that she had been babbling about all day. In fact, if Helaman tried very hard he could almost remember the boy as he looked yesterday at church, in a lounge-lizard jacket and loosened tie, kneeling at the sacrament table, gripping the microphone as if he were about to do a rap version of the sacrament prayer. Helaman had shuddered at the time, but apparently Joni was capable of looking at such a sight and thinking, "Wow, I'd like to bring that home."

By default Helaman turned to Trudy's newly-returned missionary and stuck out his hand. "Feliz Navidad," said Helaman.

"Feliz Navidad," said the missionary. "Thanks for inviting me over."

"I didn't," said Helaman.

"*I* did, silly," said Trudy. "And you're supposed to notice that Father said Merry Christmas in Spanish."

"Oh, sorry," said the missionary. "I've only been home a week and everybody was saying Feliz Navidad all the time. Your accent must be good enough that I didn't think twice."

"What mission were you in?"

"Colombia Medellín."

"Do I just call you Elder or what?" asked Helaman.

"I've been released," said the missionary. "So I guess my name is Tom Boke again."

Joni, of course, could hardly bear the fact that Trudy's beau had received more than a full minute of everyone's attention. "And this is *my* first visitor to the new house," said Joni.

Helaman offered his hand to Joni's boy and said, "I know a good lawyer if you want to sue your barber."

Joni glared at him but since the boy showed no sign of understanding Helaman's little jest, she quickly stopped glaring.

"I'm Spencer Raymond Varley," said the boy, "but you can call me Var."

"And you can call me Brother Willkie," said Helaman. "Come on in to family room A and we'll tell you which cookies Joni baked so you can avoid them and live."

"Daddy, *stop* it," said Joni in her cute-whiny voice. She used this voice whenever she wanted to pretend to be pretending to be mad. In this case it meant that she really *was* mad and wanted Helaman to stop goading young Var.

Helaman was too tired to banter with her now, so he pried her off his arm, where she had been clinging, and promised that he'd be good from now on. "I was only teasing the spunky young lad out of habit."

"His father is *the* Spence Varley," Joni whispered. "He drives a Jag."

Well, *your* father is *the* Helaman Willkie, he answered silently. And I'll be able to get you great prices on crock pots for the rest of your natural life.

The family gathered. They munched for a while on the vegetables and the vegetable dip, the fruits and the fruit dip, and the chips and the chip dip. Helaman felt like a cow chewing its cud as he listened to the conversation drone on around him. Lucille was carrying the conversation, but Helaman knew she loved being hostess and besides, she was even worse than the girls, waiting to pounce on Helaman and hush him up if he started to say anything that might embarrass a daughter in front of her male companion for the evening. Usually Helaman enjoyed the sport of baiting them, but tonight he didn't even care.

I don't like having these strangers in our home on Christmas Eve, he thought. But then, I'm as much a stranger in *this* house as they are.

By the time Helaman connected back to the conversation, Joni was regaling her fashion-victim boyfriend with the story of the marble floor in the entryway. "Father *told* the contractor to lower the floor in the entryway or the marble would stand an inch above the living room carpet and people would be falling down or stubbing their toes forever. And the contractor said he wouldn't do it unless Father accepted the fact that this would make them three days late and add a thousand dollars to the cost of the house. And so Father gets up in the middle of the night—"

"You've got to know that I warned them while they were putting *in* the entryway floor that they needed to drop it an inch lower to hold the marble, and they completely ignored me," said Helaman. "And now it had the staircase sitting on it and it really would have been a lot easier to just install a parquet floor instead, but I had promised Lucille a marble entryway and the contractor had promised *me* a marble entryway and—"

"Father," said Joni, "I was going to tell the *short* version."

"And now he said he wouldn't do it," said Helaman, and then fell silent.

"*So,*" said Joni, "as *somebody* was saying, Father got up in the middle of the night—"

"Six in the morning," said Helaman.

"*Let* her tell the story, Helaman," said Lucille.

"And he got the chainsaw out of the garage," said Joni, "and he cut this big gaping hole in the middle of the entry floor and you know what? They realized that Daddy *really meant it.*"

They laughed, and then laughed all the harder when Helaman said, "Remember the chainsaw if you're ever thinking of keeping my daughter out after her curfew."

Even as he laughed, though, Helaman felt a sour taste in his mouth from the chainsaw story. It really *had* cost the contractor money and slowed down the house, and when Helaman had stood there, chainsaw in hand, looking in the first light of morning down into the hole he had just made, he had felt stupid and ashamed, when he had *meant* to feel vindicated and clever and powerful. It took a few minutes for him to realize that his bad feelings were really just because he was worried about somebody walking in without looking where they were going and falling down into the basement, so he wrestled a big sheet of plywood over and laid it *mostly* over the hole, leaving just enough of a corner that the contractor couldn't help but know that the hole was there. And then it turned out that *that* wasn't the reason he felt stupid and ashamed after all, because when he'd finished he *still* had to come home and take a shower just to feel clean.

Of course, while he was thinking of this, they had gone on with the second marble story, only now it was Trudy telling it. "So this lady from across the street comes over and Mom thinks she's going to welcome us into the neighborhood, and so she holds the door open and invites the woman inside, and the first thing she says is 'I hear you're going to have marble in the foyer of your new house,' and Mom says yes, and then the woman—"

"Sister Braincase, I'll bet," said Var.

"Who?" asked Lucille.

"Sister Barnacuse," said Var. "We call her Braincase because she's going bonkers."

"How compassionate of you," murmured Lucille.

"*Any*way," said Trudy, "whoever she was—Mrs. Barnacuse—said, 'Well, I hope it isn't that miserable *fox* marble.' And Mother just stands there and she's trying to think of what fox marble might mean. Was it a sort of russet shade of brown or something? She'd never heard of a color called *fox*. And then all of a sudden it dawns on her that the woman means *faux* marble, and even though the marble in the entry *is* real, Mother says to her, 'No, the marble *we* have is *faux*.' As if it was something to be proud of. And the woman says, 'Oh, well that's different,' and she goes away."

Var laughed uproariously, but Tom Boke only sat there with a polite missionary grin, which Helaman supposed he probably perfected back before he really knew the language, when he had to sit and listen to whole conversations he didn't understand. Finally the young man shared with them the reason for his failure to laugh. "What's foe marble?" he asked.

"Faux," said Lucille. "French for false."

"It means fake," Ryan said, in one of the brief moments when his mouth wasn't full of chips. "But ours is real. And our toilets flush silently."

"Ryan," said Lucille in her I'm-still-acting-sweet-but-you'd-better-do-this voice, "why don't you go down and pry your brother away from the computer and ask him to come up and meet our guests?"

Ryan went.

"Old Braincase is such a snob," said Var, "but the truth is all the marble in *her* house really *is* faux, but we think the contractor sort of misled her about it and she's the only one who doesn't know that there's not an ounce of real marble in her whole house." Var cackled uproariously.

"How sweet of you not to break her heart by telling her," said Lucille. "We'll keep the secret, too."

"Guided tour time!" cried Joni. "Please, before we hang the stockings or anything? I want Var to see my room."

"This is the best time to do it," Helaman said to Var. "It'll be the last time her floor is visible till she goes away to college."

Var smiled feebly at Helaman's joke, but Tom Boke actually managed to laugh out loud. I'll count that as my first Christmas present, Helaman said silently. In fact, if you do that again I'll ask you to marry my daughter, just so I can have somebody to laugh at my jokes around this house.

This house this house this house. He was tired of saying it, tired of thinking it. Six thousand square feet not counting the garage or the basement, and he had to take yet another tour group to see every single square foot of it. The living room, the parlor, the dining room, the kitchen, the pantry so large you could lose children in it, the breakfast room, the library, and back to the main-floor family room—giving the tour was almost aerobic.

Then downstairs to family room B, the big storage room, and the game room with the new pool table and two elaborate computer setups so the boys wouldn't fight over who got to play videogames. Not to mention the complete guest apartment with a separate entrance, a kitchenette, two bedrooms, and a bathroom, just in case one of their parents came to live with them someday in the future.

Then all the way up two flights of stairs to see the bedrooms—eight of them, even though they only used five right now. "Who knows how many more we'll need?" said Helaman, joking. "We're still young, we'll have more to fill 'em up."

But Lucille looked just the tiniest bit hurt and Helaman regretted saying it immediately, it was just a dumb joke and for *that* he had caused her to think about the fact that she'd blown out a fallopian tube in an ectopic pregnancy two years after Ryan was born and even though the doctors said there shouldn't be a problem they hadn't conceived a child since. Not that their present crop of children gave them any particular incentive to keep trying.

No, thought Helaman, I must never come to believe my own jokes about my family. Most of the time they're great kids, I've just got the blues tonight and so everything they do or say or *think* is going to irritate me.

"*Will* you have more children?" asked Tom.

It was an appalling question, even from a recently returned missionary who had gone so native that he was barely speaking English. "I think that's for the Lord to decide," said Lucille.

They were all standing in the master bathroom now, with Ryan dribbling an imaginary basketball and then slam-dunking it in the toilet. Tom Boke stood there after Lucille's words as if he were still trying to understand them. And then, abruptly, he turned to Trudy. "I'm sorry," he said, "but I've got to go."

"Where?" asked Trudy. "We haven't even done the stockings yet."

"I didn't know it would take so long to see the house," said Tom. "I'm sorry."

"*See,* Dad?" said Trudy. "If you'd just learn how to give shorter tours, I might actually someday get to . . ."

But before she could finish affixing blame on Helaman, even though it was Lucille who had insisted on the tour for her daughters' gentlemen callers, Tom Boke had already left the master bathroom and was heading out the master bedroom door.

"Get him, Father," said Trudy. "Don't let him go!"

"If *you* can't keep him," said Helaman, "what makes you think he'll stay for *me*?" But he followed Tom all the same, because the young man had looked quite strange when he left, as if he were sick or upset, and Helaman didn't feel right about just letting him go back out into the cold.

He caught up with him at the front door—Helaman assumed that the only thing that slowed Tom down was the fact that it was so easy to get lost when you came down the back stairs. "Tom," said Helaman. "What's wrong?"

"Nothing, sir."

But the expression on Tom's face declared his "nothing" to be a lie. "Are you going to be sick? Do you need to lie down?"

Tom shook his head. "I'm sorry," he said. "It's just . . . I just . . ."

"Just what?"

"I just don't belong here."

"You're welcome under our roof, I hope you know that."

"I meant America. I don't know if I can live in America anymore."

To Helaman's surprise the young man's eyes had filled with tears. "I don't know what you're talking about," Helaman said.

"Everybody here has so *much*." Tom's gaze took in the entryway with its marble floor, opening onto the living room, the dining room, the library. "And you keep it all for yourselves." The tears spilled out of his eyes.

Helaman felt it like a slap in the face. "Oh, and people don't keep things for themselves down in Colombia?"

"The poor people scratch for food while the drug lords keep everything they can get their hands on. Only the mafia have houses as large . . ."

The comparison was so insulting and unfair that Helaman was filled with rage. He had never hit anyone in anger in his life, not even as a child, but at this moment he wanted to lash out at this boy and make him take it back.

But he didn't, because Tom took it back before he even finished saying it.

"I'm sorry," Tom said. "I didn't mean to compare . . ."

"I earned every penny of the price of this house," said Helaman. "I built my business up from nothing."

"It's not your fault," said Tom. "Why should you think twice about living in a house like this? I grew up in this ward, I never saw anything wrong with it until I went to Colombia."

"I *didn't* grow up in this ward," said Helaman. "I *earned* my way here."

"The Book of Moses says that in Zion they had no poor among them. Well, Darlington Heights has achieved *that* part of building Zion, because no poor people will ever show their faces *here*."

"Why aren't you home telling your own parents this, instead of troubling *my* house?"

"I didn't mean to trouble you," said Tom. "I wanted to meet your daughter."

"So why don't you just stay and meet her, instead of judging me?"

"I told you," said Tom. "It's *me,* not you. I just don't belong here. Enjoy your new house, really, it's beautiful. It's not your fault that I taught so many people whose whole house was smaller than your bathroom. But the Spirit dwelt there in their little houses, some of them, and they were filled with love. I guess I just miss them." The tears were flowing down his cheeks now, and he looked really embarrassed about it. "Merry Christmas," he said, and he ducked out the door.

Helaman had no sooner closed the door behind him than Trudy was down the stairs railing at him. "I always knew that you'd drive one of my boyfriends away with all your teasing and the horrible things you say, Daddy, but I never thought you'd send one away in *tears.*"

"What did you *say* to him, Helaman?" asked Lucille.

"It wasn't anything I said," Helaman answered. "It was our bathroom."

"He *cried* because of your *bathroom*?" asked Trudy. "Well thank heaven you didn't show him your cedar closet, he might have killed himself!"

Helaman thought of explaining, but then he looked at Trudy and didn't want to talk to her. He couldn't think of anything to say to that face, anyway. She had never whined and demanded and blamed like this when she was little. Only since the money. Only since the money started happening.

What am I turning my daughter into? What will she become in this house?

Helaman wasn't feeling the blues anymore. No, it was much worse. He was suffocating. It was desolation.

Helaman's hand was still on the doorlatch. He looked at Lucille. "Do the stockings without me," he said.

"No, please, Helaman," said Lucille.

"Oh, good job, Trudy," said Joni. "Now everybody's going to be mad at each other on our first Christmas in the new house."

"I think I'd better go home now," said Var.

"*I* can't help it if my father and my sister both went insane tonight," said Joni. "Don't go, Var!"

Everyone's attention had shifted to Joni's pleading with Var; Helaman used the break to slip out the front door, Lucille's remonstrance trailing him out into the cold night air until at last he heard her close the door and Helaman could walk along the sidewalk in the silence.

The houses rose up like shining palaces on either side of him. Mrs. Braincase's pillared mansion across the street. The huge oversized bi-level two doors down. All the houses inflated as if somebody had been pumping air into them up and down the street. Christmas lights in ever-so-tasteful color-coordinated displays on the trees and along the rooflines. Every house saying, I have succeeded. I have arrived. I am somebody, because I have money.

He imagined that it wasn't him walking along this sidewalk tonight, but a Colombian family. Maybe a father and mother and their two daughters and two sons. Big as these houses were, would any of them have room for them tonight?

Not one. These houses were all too small for that sort of thing. Oh, somebody might slip them a twenty, if anybody wasn't too terrified of robbers to open the door in the first place. But there'd be no room for them to sleep. After all, they might have fleas or lice. They might steal.

Helaman stopped and turned around, looking back at his house from a distance. I can't live here, he thought. That's why I've been so depressed. Like the day I cut out the entry floor and forced them to redo it—I was powerful and strong, wasn't I! And yet all I had the power to do was get my own way by bullying people. I built this house to prove that I had what it takes to get a house in Darlington Heights. And now I'll never see this house without imagining that poor Colombian family, standing outside in the cold, praying for somebody to open the door and let them come inside where it was warm.

What am I doing here, living in one of these houses? I hated these people when I was a kid. I hated the way they looked down on my family. The way they could never quite imagine Dad or Mom in a leadership calling, even though they were always there helping, at every ward activity, every service project, bringing food, making repairs, giving rides.

Mom in the nursery, Dad as permanent assistant to four scoutmasters, and all the time Helaman knew that it was because they weren't educated, they talked like farm people because that's where *they* grew up, they didn't have money and their car was ugly and their house was small, while people with nowhere near the kindness and love and goodness and testimony got called to all the visible, prominent callings.

Helaman remembered one time when he was thirteen, sitting there in the office of his bishop, who told him how he needed to set goals in his life. "You can't separate the Church from your career," he said. "When Sterling W. Sill had the top insurance agency in the state of Utah, he got called to the First Council of the Seventy. My goal is to have the top agency by the time I'm forty, and then serve wherever the Lord calls me from then on." The unspoken message was, I'm already bishop and I'm already rich—see how far I've come.

Helaman had come out of that interview seething with rage. I don't believe you, he had insisted silently. The Lord doesn't work that way. The Lord doesn't value people by how much money they make, the two things have nothing to do with each other. And then Helaman had gone home and for the first time in his life, at age thirteen he saw his father the way that bishop must have seen him—as a failure, a man with no money and no ambition, a man with no *goals*. A man you couldn't possibly respect. Helaman's prayers that night had been filled with rage. He stayed up finding scriptures: It's as hard for a camel to pass through the eye of a needle as for a rich man to get into heaven; let him who would be the greatest among you first be the servant of all; he who would find his life must lose it; sell all you have and give it to the poor and come follow me; they were not rich and poor, bond and free, but all were partakers of the heavenly gift. All those ideas still glowed in Helaman's memory as they had that night, and when he finally slept it was with the sure knowledge that it was his father, the quiet servant without ambition for himself, who was more honorable in the sight of God than any number of rich and educated men in the Church. It was the beginning of his testimony, that peaceful certainty that came that night.

What Helaman had never realized until right now, on this cold Christmas Eve, standing on this street of mansions, was that he had also believed the other story as well, the one the bishop told him. Maybe it was because he still had to see that bishop there on the stand, week after week, and then watch him become stake president and then go off as a mission president; maybe it was because Helaman was naturally ambitious, and so his heart had seized on the bishop's words. Whatever the reason, Helaman had not modeled his life on his father's life, despite that testimony he had received that night when he was thirteen. Instead he had followed the path of the people who had looked down on his father. He had built a house in their neighborhood. He had brought his children to dwell among them. He had proved to them that he was exactly as good as they were.

And that was why he felt so empty, there in his new house, even though his whole family loved the place, even though he had worked so hard to build it. Because the fact that he lived there meant that he was exactly as good as those people who had despised his father, and he knew that it was his father who was good, not them.

Not me.

Lucille even tried to stop me, he thought. She knew. That was why she kept saying, We don't need such a big house. We don't need all those rooms. I don't have to have a separate sewing room—I *like* sewing in the family room with everybody around me.

Helaman had been deaf to all she said; he had taken it for granted that she was only saying these things because she always worried about money and because she was too unselfish to ever ask for anything for herself; he knew that secretly she really wanted all these fine things, these big rooms, these well-earned luxuries.

Only once had she put her foot down. The architect had specced out gold fixtures everywhere, and Lucille had rejected it immediately. "I'd feel like I had to wash my hands before I could touch the faucet to turn it on," she said. Helaman was all set to go ahead anyway, on the assumption that she really wanted them after all, until she looked him in the eye and said, "I will never use a bathroom with gold fixtures, Helaman, so if you put them in, you'd better build me an outhouse in the back yard."

Even then, what had finally convinced him was when she said that chrome fixtures went better with all the towels because they didn't have a color of their own to clash with.

I wasn't listening, thought Helaman. She was telling me exactly what the Spirit told me that night in my childhood, showing me in the scriptures what my goals should be and what I should think about money. And I knew she was right, yet I still went ahead and built this house and now I can't bear to live in it because every room, every bit of wainscoting, every polished oak molding, every oversized room is a slap in the face of my father. I was so angry at those snobs that I had to get even with them by becoming just like them. I don't belong here, I don't want to live among people who would build and live in houses like these, and yet here I am.

Tom Boke stood in my house and wept because I had so much, and I kept it all for myself. I am the opposite of my father. I had the money to do good in the world, and I used it to build a monument to Helaman Willkie, to win the respect of people whose respect isn't worth having.

He was trembling with the cold. He had to go inside, and yet he couldn't bring himself to take another step toward that house.

It's a beautiful house, said a voice inside him. You earned it.

No, he answered silently. I earned the right to live in a house big enough for my family, to meet our needs, to keep us warm and dry. There is no work in the world that a person can do that can earn him the right to live in a house like *this,* when so many others are in want. I sinned in building it, and I will sin every time I put a key in the lock on that door as if it were my right to take this much of the bounty of God's Earth and keep it for just my family to use.

The door to the house opened and light spilled out onto the porch, onto the bare trampled ground that didn't yet have a lawn. It was Lucille, coming outside to find him. Lucille, wearing a coat and carrying another, looking for her husband to keep him warm. Lucille, who had understood the truth about this house all along, and then loved him enough to let him build it anyway. Would she love him enough to let him abandon it now?

He could not walk back to the house, but he could always walk to his wife, and so he called out to her and strode on trembling, uncertain legs toward where she waited for him.

"Here's a coat," she said. "If you don't have the brains to stay indoors, at least wear the coat. I don't want to have to bury you in the back yard, not till the landscapers come in the spring, anyway."

He took her teasing with good cheer, as he always did, but all he could really think about was the impossibility of telling her what he needed to tell her. It was so hard to think of the words. So hard to know how to begin.

"So can I stay out here and talk to you?" said Lucille.

He nodded.

"The house is too big, isn't it," she said. "That missionary has told you about poverty and you took the news as if you'd never heard of it before and now you feel guilty about living here."

As so often before, she had guessed enough about what was in his heart that he could say the rest himself. "It wasn't the boy, what he said. I was already unhappy here, I just didn't know it."

"So what do we do, Helaman? Sell it?"

"Everybody will think we built a house bigger than we could afford and *had* to sell it."

"Do you care?"

"There'll be rumors that Willkie Housewares is in financial trouble."

"It's not a corporation. The stock won't drop in value because of a rumor."

"The kids will never forgive me."

"*That* is possible."

"And I don't know if I could ever look myself in the eye, if I gave you a kitchen like that and then took it away because of some crazy idea that living here means I'm ashamed of my father."

"Your father loves this house, Helaman, he's been over here a dozen times during the building of it, and if he hadn't promised your sister Alma that he'd spend Christmas with *her* family in Dallas he'd be here with us tonight."

"What about you?"

"Moving is a pain and I won't like doing it twice," she said. "But you already know that I never wanted a house this big."

"But I wanted you to have it. I wanted you never to be like my mother, living in a ward where all the other women looked down on her, raising a family with no money in a tiny house."

"*Our* old house wasn't tiny, it was just small."

"You love the new kitchen. I don't want you to give up the new kitchen."

"You sweet, foolish man, I love the kitchen because you took so much care to make it perfect for me."

"I'll give it all up," said Helaman. "Because I can't live with myself if

I stay in a place like this. But how can I take it away from you and the kids? Even if you didn't really want it, even if you never asked for it, I gave it to you anyway and I can't take it back."

"So, will you rent an apartment near the main store and come visit us on weekends? Helaman, I couldn't bear it if this house came between us. Why do you think I didn't try to stop you from building it? Because I knew you wanted it so much, you were so hungry for it—not for yourself, but to give it to us. You needed so much to give this to us. Well, you *have* given it to us, and the kids and I love it. You meant to build it for the best motives, and as soon you realized that maybe it wasn't such a good idea, you were filled with remorse. The Lord doesn't expect you to sell it and live in a tent."

"Sell all you have and give it to the poor and come follow me," Helaman quoted.

"That was what he said to a rich *young* man. You're middle-aged."

"And you're just saying whatever you think will get me back into the house where it's warm."

"Well, what *are* you going to do, then? Never come back inside again?"

To Helaman's surprise, he found tears running down his cheeks, his face twisting into a grimace of weeping. "I can't," he said. "If I go back inside then it means I'm just like *them*."

"So don't *be* just like them," said Lucille, putting her arms around him. "You never *have* been just like them, anyway. You've never run your business the way they do—you've been fair and even generous with everybody, even your competitors, and everybody knows it. There's nobody in the world who resents your having this house—your employees love you because they know you've paid them more than you had to and made less profit than you could have and you work harder than any of them and you forgive them for mistakes, and every one of them is glad for you to finally move out of that house that we've stayed in since 1975. Most of them don't understand why it took us so long to move. You can live in this house with a clear conscience. You're *not* like the rest of these people." She looked up and down the street. "For all we know, half of *them* might not be like the rest of these people."

"It's not about them or what anybody else thinks," said Helaman. "I just can't be happy there. It's like what that missionary said. Tom, right?

He said, 'I just can't live in America anymore.' Well, I just can't live in that house."

Lucille stood there in silence, still holding him, but not speaking. Helaman was still full of things to say, but it was always hard for him to talk about things inside himself, and he was worn out with talking, and even though he had stopped weeping now, he was afraid of feelings so strong that they could make him cry. So the silence lasted until Lucille spoke again.

"You can't sell the house," said Lucille. "It won't be a poor person who buys it, anyway."

"You mean I should give it away?"

"I mean we should give it away in our hearts."

He laughed. He remembered the testimony meeting where Sister Mooller, who had more money than General Motors, had gotten up and said that thirty years ago she and her husband had decided to consecrate all they had to the Lord, and so they gave it away "in their hearts," which was why the Lord had blessed them with so much more in the years since then. Whereupon Lucille had leaned over to him and whispered, "I guess the Lord really needed that new Winnebago they bought last month."

"Don't laugh," said Lucille. "I know you're thinking about Sister Mooller, but we could *really* do it. Live in the house as if it weren't our own."

"What, never unpack?"

"Listen to me, I'm being serious. I'm really trying to find a way for you to have all the things that you want—to give this house to us, and yet not be the kind of man who lives in a big fancy house, and still keep the family living under one roof."

"That *is* the problem, isn't it." He felt so foolish to have gotten himself into such a twisted, impossible set of circumstances. No matter what he chose, he'd feel guilty and ashamed and unhappy. It was as if he had deliberately set out to feel unrighteous and unhappy no matter how things turned out.

"Let's consecrate this house to the Lord," said Lucille. "We were going to dedicate it tomorrow, anyway, as part of Christmas. Well let's do it tonight, instead, and when we dedicate it let's make a covenant with the Lord, that we will always treat this house as if others have as much right to use it as we do."

Helaman tried to think of how that would work. "You mean have people over?"

"I mean keep watching, constantly, for anybody who needs a roof over their heads. Newcomers who need a place to stay while they're getting settled. People in trouble who have nowhere else to turn."

"Bums from the street?"

She looked him in the eye. "If that's what it takes for you to feel right about this house, and you'll be here at night to make sure that the family is safe, then yes, bums from the street."

The idea was so strange and audacious that he would have laughed, except that as she spoke there was so much fire in her eyes that he felt himself fill with light as well, a light so hot and sweet that tears came to his eyes again, only this time not tears of despair and remorse but rather tears of love—for Lucille, yes, but more than for her. There were words ringing in his ears, words that no one had said tonight, but still he heard them like the memory of a dear old friend's voice, whispering to him, Whatever you do to help these little ones, these humble, helpless, lonely, frightened children, you're doing it for me.

And yet even as he knew that this was what the Savior wanted him to do, a new objection popped into his mind. "There are zoning laws," he said. "This is a single-family dwelling."

"The zoning laws don't stop us from having visitors, do they?" said Lucille.

"No," said Helaman.

"And if somebody stays very long we can always tell Sister Barnacuse that they're faux relatives."

Helaman laughed. "Right. We can tell her that we've got a lot of brothers and sisters who come and visit."

"And it'll be the truth," said Lucille.

"This can't be one of those resolutions that we make and then forget," he said.

"A solemn covenant with the Lord," she said.

"It isn't fair to you," said Helaman. "Most of the extra work of having visitors in the house would fall to you."

"And to the kids," she said. "And you'll help me."

"It has to be like a contract," said Helaman. "There have to be terms.

So we'll know if we're living up to the covenant. We can't just wait for people in need to just happen along."

"So we'll look for them," said Lucille. "We can talk to the bishop to see who's in need."

"As if anybody in *this* ward is going to need a place to stay!"

"Then we'll ask him to talk to the stake president. There are other wards in this stake. And people you'll hear about at work."

"Someone new every month, unless the house is already full," said Helaman.

"Every month?" said Lucille.

"Yes."

"Like home teaching?" she asked.

It was a sly jab indeed, for she well knew how many times Helaman had come to the end of the month and then would grab one of his sons and run around the ward, trying to catch their home teaching families and teach them his famous end-of-the-month procrastination lesson. "Even when I'm late, I *do* my home teaching."

"If you think you can find somebody every month, then that's the covenant," said Lucille. "But you're the one who'll have to take the responsibility for finding somebody every month, because I don't get out enough."

"That's fine," said Helaman.

"And if we find that we can't do it," said Lucille, "that it's too hard or it's hurting our family, what then?"

"Then we sell all we have and give the money to the poor," said Helaman.

"In other words," said Lucille, "if we can't make this work, then we move."

"Yes."

It was agreed, and it felt right. It was a good thing to do. Hadn't his own parents always had room on the floor for somebody to lay out a sleeping bag if they had no other place to stay? Hadn't there always been a place at his parents' table for the lonely, the hungry, the stranger? With this covenant that he and Lucille were making with the Lord, Helaman could truly go home.

And then, suddenly, he felt fear plunge into his heart like a cold knife.

What in the world was he promising to do? Destroy his privacy, risk his family's safety, keep their lives in constant turmoil, and for what—because some missionary cried over the poverty in Colombia? What, would there be a single person in Colombia who'd sleep better tonight because Helaman Willkie was planning to allow squatters to use his spare bedrooms?

"What's wrong?" asked Lucille.

"Nothing," said Helaman. "Let's get inside and tell the kids before we freeze." Before my heart freezes, he said silently. Before I talk myself out of trying to become a true son of my father and mother.

They opened the door, and for the first time, as he followed Lucille onto the marble floor, he didn't feel ashamed to enter. Because it wasn't his own house anymore.

Joni was all for having Var stay through the whole rest of the Christmas Eve festivities, but Helaman politely told Var that this was a good time for him to go home to be with his family. It only took two repetitions of the hint to get him out the door.

They gathered in the living room and, as was their tradition on Christmas Eve, Helaman read from the scriptures about the birth of the Savior. But then he skipped ahead to the part about Even as ye have done it unto the least of these, and then he and Lucille explained the covenant to their children. None of them was overjoyed.

"Do I have to let them use my computer?" asked Steven.

"They're *family* computers," said Helaman. "But if it becomes a problem, maybe you can keep one computer in your room."

"It sounds like this is going to be a motel," said Trudy. "But I'm going to college after this year and so I don't really care."

"Does this mean I can't ever have my friends over?" asked Ryan.

"Of course you can," said Lucille.

Joni had said nothing so far, but Helaman knew from the stony look on her face that she was taking it worst of all. So he asked her what she was thinking.

"I'm thinking that somehow this is all going to work around so I have to share my bedroom again."

"We have spare bedrooms coming out of our ears, not to mention a whole mother-in-law apartment in the basement," said Helaman. "You will *not* have to share your room with anybody."

"Good," said Joni. "Because if you ever ask me to share my room, I'm moving out."

"We don't make threats to you," said Lucille, "and I'd appreciate it if you'd refrain from making threats to us."

"I mean it," said Joni. "It's not a threat, I'm just telling you what *will* happen. I waited a long time to have a room of my own, and I'll never share my bedroom again."

"We'll be sure to warn your boyfriends that your husband is going to have to sleep in another room," said Trudy.

"You aren't helping, Trudy," said Lucille.

"Joni," said Helaman, "I promise that I'll never ask you to share your room with anybody."

"Then it's OK with me if you want to turn the rest of the house into a circus."

For a moment Helaman hesitated, wondering if this *was,* after all, such a good idea. Then he remembered that Joni had brought home tonight a boy who was attractive to her only because his father was famous and he drove a Jaguar. And he realized that if he let Joni live in this house, in this neighborhood, without doing *something* to teach her better values, he was surely going to lose her. Maybe opening up the house to strangers in need would give her a chance to learn that there was more to people than how much fame and wealth they had. Maybe that's what this was all about in the first place. He had wanted this house to be a blessing to his family— maybe the Lord had shown him and Lucille the way to make that happen.

Or maybe this would cause so much turmoil and contention that the family would fall apart.

No, thought Helaman. Trying to live the gospel might cause some pain from time to time, but it's a sure thing that *not* trying to live the gospel for fear that it *might* hurt my family will *certainly* hurt them, and such an injury would be deep and slow to heal.

As he hesitated, Lucille caught his eye. "The stockings seem to be hanging in front of the fireplace," she said. "All we need to do now is have our family prayer and bring presents downstairs to put them under the tree."

"You aren't going to make us give away our *presents,* are you, Dad?" asked Ryan.

"In fact, that's why we all got lousy presents for you this year, Ryan," said Helaman. "So that when it's time to give them away, you won't mind."

"Da-ad!" said Ryan impatiently. But he was smiling.

Instead of their normal Christmas family prayer, Helaman dedicated the house. In his prayer he consecrated it as the Lord's property, equally open to anyone that the Lord might bring to take shelter there. He set out the terms of the covenant in his prayer, and when he was done, the children all said amen.

"It's not our house anymore," said Helaman. "It's the Lord's house now."

"Yeah," said Steven. "But I'll bet he sticks you with the mortgage payments anyway, Dad."

That night, when the children were asleep and Helaman and Lucille had finished the last-minute wrapping and had laid out all the gifts for the morning, only a few hours away, they climbed into bed together and Lucille held his hand and kissed him and said, "Merry Christmas and welcome home."

"Same to you and doubled," he said, and she smiled at the old joke.

Then she touched his cheek and said, "All the years that I've been praying for another child, and all the years that the Lord has told us no, maybe it was all leading to this night. So that our lives would have room for what we've promised."

"Maybe," said Helaman. He watched as she closed her eyes and fell asleep almost at once. And in the few minutes before he, too, slept, he thought of that Colombian family he had imagined earlier. He pictured them standing at his door, all their possessions in a bag slung over the father's shoulder, the children clinging to their mother's skirts, the youngest sleepy and fussing in her arms. And he imagined himself holding the door wide open and saying, "Come in, come in, the table's set and we've been waiting for you." And Helaman saw his wife and children gather at the table with their visitors, and there was food enough for all, and all were satisfied.

Neighbors

O h, it's so good to sit down and rest!"

"Tell me about it. My joints ache so much all the time that look at me, I can't even stand up straight. But you, you're gallivanting all over the place—"

"Just to the city, you old exaggerator. Just for the holy days."

"The city! I haven't been able to go in years. Not that anything ever changes."

"This time there were changes! I can't believe you haven't heard already—"

"Heard? Who from, will you tell me that? Does anybody ever come to visit? Not the children, you can count on that! Right here in town, too, every one of them, but do they remember me, wasting away here?"

"It's hard being old, I know that. But it's a lot better than not being old, if you get my meaning!"

"I'm not sure about that anymore. I think of old Eph and what he's probably doing right now. Forgot all about me, you can bet, after leaving me all alone here—"

"Well, I can bet you'd rather be Eph's widow than old Joe's!"

"Oh, don't even make me think about that Miriam and her perfect son."

"But that's what the news is, from the city. He's dead!"

"No! No, oh, I bite my tongue that I spoke of him like that—"

"Oh, you didn't know, of course you didn't, no harm done, you silly old dear. You never think ill of anybody, I know that, not really."

"Well it's true, I have only the best wishes in my heart for every living soul. How did he die?"

"Don't make me go into that, please. He was executed. Trumped-up charges, that was obvious."

"But I'm not surprised. He was always so controversial. The government would never let him keep on the way he was going. I said as much to Miriam, and she just smiled that superior little smile of hers and said, 'A son has to continue his father's business,' as if old Joe ever went around stirring up trouble!"

"Joe was always a quiet one, that's true. But when you think about it, so was the boy."

"Well, he didn't have to say much, did he? Not with his mother acting like he was God's gift to the world! Honestly, did you ever have a conversation with her that didn't turn to her wonderful boy and all the marvelous things he was doing?"

"A mother always wants to talk about her children."

"Well, I know a few things she never mentions."

"Really?"

"Now that he's dead, I don't see that it does much harm to talk about it. Can't damage his reputation! Not that the shame should go on the boy himself, mind you. But you were too young when it happened."

"What? I can't believe there are any secrets in that family, after all these years with their son so famous!"

"Let's just say that Joe and Miriam got married in the nick of time."

"Oh, is that all. They were engaged, weren't they? Happens all the time, you silly old dear."

"It didn't then. And besides, you didn't know Joe. The most strait-laced, proper fellow you ever saw. I can promise you he didn't spend so much as five minutes alone with her, even after they were engaged. And then all of a sudden, oops! She's letting out her dresses! Her family tried to put a gloss on it. She's going to visit her cousin Lizzy, that's all. My husband and I escorted her, you know. A young woman can't travel alone, and we were glad to be of help—what are neighbors for? But right there on the road, outside her cousin's house, the girl gives this little 'woop' sound and when I ask her what's wrong, she just smiles at me like it was the most wonderful thing in the world and says, 'The baby moved!' Well, she was only two months married, so excuse me for thinking that if she had any sense of decency she would have kept that little piece of news to herself."

"I've never yet met a woman who didn't feel like the baby she was carrying was the center of the universe."

"There's such a thing as decency, though, don't you think? At least she had the respect not to have the baby here. Or maybe it was Joe, since Miriam never had a sense of propriety—anyway, they found an excuse to go to his hometown to have the baby. Claimed he had to clear up a tax problem but we all knew the truth, they just didn't want anybody here to know the exact birthday, as if it wasn't already common knowledge that the baby was early and it wasn't his."

"It's so hard to believe that none of this ever came out during all the controversy that boy caused. You'd think his enemies would have heard about it and—"

"Well, for heaven's sake, the only people who knew about it were right here in this town. And we don't go around telling tales to strangers!"

"There is such a thing as loyalty."

"And Joe did the right thing. They went off to somewhere else, Cairo I think, until the boy was five or six and ready to start school. He wasn't an in-your-face sort of man, that Joe."

"I wish I'd known him well."

"He was a saint. You never heard him brag about his son. But he was proud of him, as proud as if he really were his, if you know what I mean."

"These things are always so confusing, but good people bear with it."

"We all bore with it. You can't say that a single one of us ever threw it in Miriam's face, even when she was bragging away. And the boy—well, we never treated him differently from any other boy. But I swear, there are limits. When he came back and made some of his most outrageous claims, right here where we knew him! Well, had he no shame?"

"I think events have proven that he did not!"

"Exactly. There were some people angry enough to kill him that day, but we calmed them down. I said to my son Ephie—I mean, my son was so angry he could have thrown him off a cliff, the things Miriam's boy said!—but I told Ephie, You can't blame him, he's grown up with his mother saying that he's God's gift to the world, so you can't be surprised when he starts claiming to be the fulfillment of prophecy. And when Ephie realized that the poor lad was just acting out the destiny his mother charted for him, well, he calmed right down."

"I remember that day. I remember thinking it was a miracle he got away alive."

"I'll tell you what it was. It was neighbors. In the city, nobody knows anybody else. All strangers. But here, we all know each other. We care about each other. Even the crazy people. We understand. We accept."

"He was lucky to grow up in a place like this."

"If he'd just stayed here, even with his strange ideas, why, nothing bad would have happened to him. We would have tolerated him. Protected him, even. But Miriam was always push push push, and so the boy had no chance. She killed him, when you think about it. I know that's an awful thing to say, but it's nothing but the truth. All her fantasies about him, no wonder he ended up like he did. It's fine to have dreams for your children, but you have to keep them in the real world. Their feet planted on the ground."

"Well, Miriam paid for it. She was there watching. She saw him die. The poor thing."

"The poor thing. I wouldn't trade places with her. Oh, I complain that my boys never come to see me, my daughters neither, but at least they're decent people, leading decent lives. Eph and me, we raised them right."

"We should go call on her."

"Miriam? Yes, we must. If I can walk that far."

"She'll be home from the city soon. They buried him there. A rich man's crypt. Can you imagine? Being buried far from home, in a borrowed grave? But it was too far to bring him home."

"He should have stayed here, where we knew him, where we understood him. He should have stayed among friends and neighbors. That's just my opinion, but I'm not afraid to say it."

"That's what everyone says about you, dear. You tell the truth. You see the truth, and you tell it."

"Well isn't that the sweetest thing. You've brightened my whole day."

GOD PLAYS FAIR ONCE TOO OFTEN

My old companion and I met at an embassy party in London. It took us a while to recognize each other, of course—it always does, after so many years. We had no sooner nodded in greeting than we both found ourselves on the fringes of a loud conversation dominated by the most annoying sort of American. He was a Washington lobbyist, one of those people whose career consists of suborning the votes of congressmen, and now, a bit in his cups, he was showing off how well he understood the sordid business of government, going on and on—quite the bore. "Historians are all fools!" he cried. "Same as the politicians and the journalists! They think they have their thumb on the world's pulse, but when something really important comes along—the mere victory of capitalism over communism, for instance!—the only one who wasn't taken by surprise was God."

It was more than my companion could bear. "I'll have you know," said my companion, "that God himself was surprised by that."

The statement was so outrageous—and everyone was so eager to listen to another voice, *any* other voice—that silence fell, and my companion was given a chance to tell the whole tale, which I knew he was dying to do. "All right then," he said. "It doesn't take long to tell, though most of you won't believe it."

"Give us a try," said a lady.

So he shrugged and smiled and launched into it.

It was the tag end of 1841 (he said). God was going incognito in his favorite Manchester pub, looking like any other worn-out workingman getting his pint before going home to a flat full of screaming brats and a wife who had little comfort in her after her own day at the jenny. His hands were dirty, his clothing was sweat-stained, and his sadness showed in his face, which meant that no one was likely to seek out his company. So it should have taken him a bit by surprise when a hale, beefy-handed banker sat down across from him. Only of course God can't be taken by surprise, so he recognized his visitor at once.

"Good evening to you, Lucifer," said God, looking him up and down. "If you insist on possessing the bodies of my children, why do you choose such unhealthy ones?"

"Get used to it," said the devil. "All the best people are going to be fat now. This new machinery thing I've got going has already changed everything. So much money, so much indoor work, so little exercise. I'm going to get people to stuff their bodies so full of sugars and fats that they drop dead all over the place, with their lives half-lived. This little ploy is good for centuries."

"Till the 1970s, more or less," said God. "Then the rich will be the only ones who have enough leisure to exercise, so the middle class will start to imitate their slenderness and musculature."

"Yeah, right," said the devil. "But I'll see to it that it's also in vogue for the rich to be darkly sunburnt, so when the heart attacks let up I'll get them with skin cancer."

"And colitis," murmured God.

"It really spoils my fun, you know, when you flaunt your omniscience that way."

"It'd be better if you remembered it more often, Lucifer. I'm always a step ahead of you."

"Don't I know it. That whole business with Job."

"Still harping on that?" Satan was such a hard loser.

"Because I still think you cheated—you *knew* from the start that he'd never curse you."

"Yes, and I *told* you that I knew it. You just didn't believe me."

"My mistake," said Satan. He grinned. "Buy me a pint?"

"Buy your own," said God.

Satan waved to the publican. "Good sir!" he cried. "Pints for me and my dear friend here."

Oh, the eyes turned toward them *then,* what with a rich man buying for a poor man, and openly, too. What would people think? God knew, of course. Some were thinking: That poor old fellow must have a pretty daughter, and this banker wants to turn her into a whore. It was a measure of just how ugly this world was turning. It made God so depressed sometimes. Give them steam, and they create sweatshops out of it. The idea of cheap energy was to make it easier for everyone to have plenty to eat. I created a world of plenty, and they still manage to manufacture poverty and misery and hopelessness everywhere. Lucifer likes to take credit for it, but maybe that's just what humans want to be.

The pints appeared on the table before them. Lucifer grandly paid the girl who brought them. Of course he overtipped shamelessly. Just like him, the snake—works as hard as he can to make their lives hellish, and then gives a few big tips and they think he's generous.

"Well, I've got to hand it to you," said God, sipping the bitters. "You've really created something ugly here in England. And it'll spread, too, I can see that. As bad as slavery in America, in the long run. It'll take me decades to heal the damage."

"Hmmm," said Lucifer.

"Oh, yes I can," said God. "I can heal it all, and you know I will. This whole miserable thing you have with capitalism. It's so obviously unfair that decent people will rebel against it. I can have it broken up within a century."

"Oh, I'm sure you can," said Lucifer.

"I feel another wager coming," said God.

"We haven't really had a good one since Job. And I came *close,* you have to admit."

"Lucifer, you know that I always know the outcome. Why do you still bet?"

"Ah, but that's one of the terms of the wager," said Lucifer. "You have to close your eyes."

"Close my eyes!"

"You have to promise *not* to know how things will turn out."

"Wouldn't you just love it if I agreed to *that!*"

"Not forever," said Satan. "Just for—a century and a half. Until the beginning of 1992. Then you can be prescient again. What can I do in a hundred and fifty years?"

"Good question. What *can* you do in a hundred and fifty years?"

"I wager that in 1992 I can have things even worse than they are right now, and yet all the best people will think it's better."

"Those are pretty vague terms," said God.

"I'll be more specific," said Lucifer. "I will bet that by 1992, I can have it so that the overwhelming opinion of decent people everywhere is that capitalism is the best and fairest and most wonderful economic system in the world."

"Oh, such nonsense."

"And in the opinion of decent people everywhere, *your* way of doing things, where everybody shares fairly in the world's goods—that will be completely discredited as the most brutal, unfair, terrible economic system in history."

"The only way you could do that is to turn the human race stupider than baboons," said God.

"Do I have a bet, then? No peeking—no fair seeing how things will turn out after you agree to the bet and I start my plans in motion."

"No coercion," said God. "No possessions. You can only do it by your tamer methods."

"Lies," said Lucifer. "And greed. And the lust for power."

"And I can work against you the whole time."

"As long as you keep hands off, too," said Lucifer. "And no peeking into the future."

"You think you're so smart."

"You made me that way," said Lucifer.

"I thought you might make life more interesting."

"I know. That was before you started to actually *care* about these people."

"I always cared about them."

"In fact, my dear God Almighty, I suspect that it's only *because* I make them so ignorant and miserable that you started having compassion for them. Admit it—you were bored with them when they were still back in the garden."

"I was lonely for company," said God.

"And I wasn't good enough for you," said Lucifer.

"You aren't *company*," said God. "You're the competition."

"Is the bet on?"

"What are the stakes?"

"If I win, I get to destroy the world next time."

"Out of the question."

"Come on, old chap, you know that if I win this bet, you'll have to wipe it all out and start over, just like back at the time of Noah."

"I had to suspend all the rules of physics and chemistry to cover the whole earth with water," said God. "You don't have the power."

"See?" said Lucifer. "You've got nothing to worry about."

"I know you've got a trick up your sleeve."

"Yes, and if you *really* wanted to, you could pluck it right out and know all my plans. But you'll play fair, won't you?"

"And you won't."

"But you're God."

"And you want my job."

"No, I just don't want your job to exist."

"Even if we end up destroying all of humanity, Lucifer, I'll still be God."

"Yes," said Lucifer. "But I'll break your heart."

God thought for a while. "I think human beings are smarter and better than you give them credit for. It's a bet."

Lucifer whooped once with joy, then tipped back his pint and drank it to the last drop. "You're such a sport, God, old man! And they say you're a stick-in-the-mud—if only they knew you the way I do!" Then he got up and strolled bold as brass out of the pub.

God smiled. It was such an outrageous idea—to play the next hundred and fifty years without knowing what was coming next. A true contest. Maybe Lucifer would be able to make a contest of it this time.

Anyway, to make a long story short, the century and a half are almost up. And in all that time, God hasn't had a clue from moment to moment what was going to happen next.

The American lobbyist sneered. "So what's the punch line?"

"No punch line," my companion replied. "I just thought you ought to have the facts straight. Not even God knew."

"Right. Like I'm supposed to believe this." The American glowered. "I know when I'm being made fun of."

"Oh do you," said my companion. "But I thought since you were so intimately familiar with the corridors of power, you'd be delighted to have the inside scoop on *real* power."

"You've made your point," said the lobbyist. "Just another snobby Britisher, putting down the American and feeling oh so clever about it."

"But that's not it at all," said my companion. "For one thing, I'm not British. And for another, I admire you greatly. I think you're a swell fellow. It's my friend here who thinks you're a bit of an asshole."

The lobbyist looked at me. "Oh yeah?"

"Never mind him," said my companion. "He isn't British, either. And he's in a bad mood. Just lost a bet, you see."

"Lost a bet?"

"He thought he had it sussed. Thought he understood all my plans. He watched how I got all his ideas about social justice put into an atheist package and called it Communism, and *he* thought it was nothing more than an annoyance. Then he thought he understood what I was doing when I got the Communist Party installed in power in Russia and it became such a horrid place to live, but he never grasped it."

"Oh, I grasped it all right," I said. "Typical of your methods. You set up a system in Russia in the *name* of communism, but you actually had it function like the nastiest sort of monopoly capitalism."

"Don't you think that was a lovely touch?" my companion asked. "They would win converts by *preaching* your theories, but when they governed, what they put in practice was always *mine*. I loved the USSR. It was as if IBM had bought all the other companies in the world, so you couldn't get a job unless you worked for them. Capitalism to *perfection,* and they were all commies!"

"Deception is a cheap trick," I murmured.

"Of course," he said proudly. "And in the meantime, I watched how hard he was working in the U.S. and Europe, trying to get capitalism tamed, to fence it around with laws so that it was fair and the common people could get an even break. Oh, I tried to interfere with him enough that he'd think I was opposed to what he was doing, but he was playing into my hands."

"You're a graceless winner," I pointed out to him.

"Then a few years back, he thinks he's going to beat me. I watch him grooming Gorbachev, and then he makes his move and puts him in power—not very subtle, you know. Killing off three old coots in rapid succession like that—how obvious can you get!"

"Just because you wish *you* could do it," I said.

"He frees eastern Europe, he has the Soviet Union eating out of his hands, and then all of a sudden he realizes the trap I've sprung for him! Just when he thinks he's defeated me, and it turns out that I've used his own actions to defeat *him*!"

"I knew it earlier than that," I said.

"Because when he broke down the system that worked *my* way, it completely discredited the *philosophy* that *he* believes in! And the people who live in those countries where he got the power of capitalism tamed, he's got *them* believing that it was free-market capitalism that accomplished all of that, so they're breaking down all the regulations that kept capitalism in check in the West. So now the victorious capitalists are going to do my work for me! The whole world thinks that capitalism defeated communism, when it was virtually the *opposite* that's the truth. The whole world is *racing* to adopt free-market capitalism. We truly will have Hell on Earth!"

"Oh, shut up," I suggested.

"You leftists are such bad losers," said the lobbyist.

My companion ignored him. "The sweetest irony is that even his own churches are going along with it. I won I won I won!" he crowed.

"Yes," I said. "You did."

"So now I get to do it," said my companion. "I get to destroy the world. Such a simple thing, really. The nuclear weapons in the old Soviet Union—give me a few months and I'll have them in the hands of every group that hates somebody else so badly they're willing to use them."

"But you forget," I said. "Now I get to look ahead into the future."

"Oh, of course," he said. "But there *is* no future to look ahead to."

I let down the barrier that had so long blocked my vision, and despaired.

Lucifer laughed and laughed.

The lobbyist looked from him to me and back again. "Are you guys out of your minds?"

"Enough to make you want to o.d., isn't it!" cackled the devil.

"Maybe I *won't* destroy it," I said. "I don't have to. The wager was that *if* I destroy it, you get to do it."

"Weasel all you want," he answered. "Leave it forever, I don't mind. It's just misery and oppression, poverty and bitter injustice through the world. It'll get worse and worse, until you give up and decide to destroy them after all—and then I get to do it."

I thought of wiping everything clean and starting over yet again, and it just made me tired. No, if I couldn't undo the mess he'd made within a year or two, that would be the end of it. No Noah this time. Just let it all go and find something else to do. Why couldn't these humans, just this *once,* see through his lies? They've spit in my face once too often. Why should I save them again?

Or at least that's how I felt then. I don't feel so depressed today. Maybe by tomorrow I'll get some of my hope back. Maybe then I'll have the heart to set out once again to fight him on every front. Or maybe I'll just take the easy way, and delay him only long enough to find my Noah and get a ship ready for him. It'll have to be a starship this time, and that'll take longer, but I can probably do it. I mean, I *am* omnipotent, when it comes down to that. And I really don't like to lose.

WORTHY TO BE ONE OF US

When the children started moving out of the house and starting their own families, Jared and Rachel couldn't decide whether to be relieved or depressed about it. On the one hand, they would have their own lives back. No more racing home to have a car available for somebody's date. No more sorting through the clean clothes to pick out items that somebody slipped into a batch of the parents' laundry. No more taking endless messages or giving endless reminders. Rachel could actually go with Jared on any of his lectures or conferences that she wanted. Jared could probably do some of his work at home instead of having to flee the house to get peace and quiet in his office up at the university.

On the other hand, the children were in the most exciting phase of life, and for many years their activities had been much more important to Jared and Rachel, emotionally at least, than their own. The house felt empty. "It's too big now," Jared said, several times. And then the suggestion: "A condo closer to campus."

But Rachel didn't want to leave the ward. Jared's life was focused on campus. Rachel's life was centered in the Primary and the ward choir. Jared could leave the ward and still have his friendships at work. For Rachel it would be starting over. She had twenty-five years invested in the Lakeview Third Ward and she wasn't going to throw that all away. One thing about having your career be in the Church: You never vested. There was no pension that you could take with you, eking out long friendships and favorite callings during the lonely years of old age. When Jared finally repeated his remark about moving nearer to campus often enough that Rachel realized he was serious, she answered as clearly as possible. "I'm not going anywhere. When I'm old and decrepit, coming to church with a walker, I intend to be surrounded by children I taught in Primary."

"All the children you taught in Primary will have grown up and moved away, like our kids," said Jared.

"By then I'll be senile and I'll *think* they're the same children," said Rachel. "Don't expect me to be rational about this. If you move, you move alone."

"I can't keep up the yard anymore, not with the boys all gone."

"Hire a kid from the neighborhood," said Rachel.

"And then pay for another sprinkler head every week when it gets chopped up in the lawnmower," said Jared.

"If you keep grumbling I'll make another no-salt dinner."

"If you make another no-salt dinner I'll eat out."

"If you eat out I'll buy a whole new wardrobe for fall."

"If you buy a whole new wardrobe I'll buy a boat and go fishing."

"If you buy a boat and go fishing I'll go out and buy a ten-pound salmon so that we can add it to what you catch and have ten pounds of fish for dinner."

"All right, let's skip all the expensive stuff and have salmon for dinner." Jared laughed and kissed her and went up to the office. He never mentioned the condo idea again.

But they were wrong about having an empty house. They were wrong about needing less space. Because Jared's father died on Halloween, and with him gone there was no one to care for Hazel, Jared's mother, who was severely limited because of her arthritis. "I don't want to be a burden on my daughters-in-law," said Hazel.

"Your daughters live in New Jersey and Rio de Janeiro," said Rachel. "You can't deal with the humidity and pollution in either place. And I liked you even before I decided to fall in love with your little boy. I think we can get along." Inwardly Rachel knew that it would be a severe trial for both of them. But she also knew that there was no better choice. Someday I may need someone to care for me, she thought. I'll treat Mother Hazel exactly as I hope to be treated—plenty of independence, plenty of opportunities for her to help out, and zero tolerance for any interference in the running of the household, not that Mother Hazel has ever tried to meddle.

"I'll do it as long as you understand that I have got to be allowed to help out even if it drives you crazy, because I can't stand to be idle," said Hazel.

"You can help out as long as you fit into the way I do things in my kitchen," said Rachel, "even if you think it's completely boneheaded."

They presented Jared with a fait accompli. "Your mother is taking the girls' bedroom and she's getting exclusive use of the second-floor bathroom," said Rachel.

"How nice," said Jared. "Especially because all the rest homes I've looked into are either resorts or prisons, and none of us can afford the former and I would rather die than put you in the latter."

"You've been looking into rest homes?" asked Hazel darkly.

"I didn't know that Rachel would be willing to let you live here," said Jared. "And you always said that you'd rather be in a rest home than burden any of your children."

"I was lying," said Hazel. "Besides, I refuse to be a burden. An albatross, maybe, but not a burden."

So it was set. By Thanksgiving, Hazel would be in residence, and the house would not be so empty.

In all the busyness of getting things ready for Hazel—they even priced home elevators and stair climbers, until Hazel informed them that she could still climb stairs—it took a while for Rachel to realize that Jared really wasn't taking the death of his father in stride.

"I'm doing fine," said Jared. He had a puzzled look on his face.

"I know you are," said Rachel. "But you get this lost look sometimes. You just stand there, in the middle of some action."

"I'm an absentminded professor. I usually *am* lost."

"Just now, you stood there looking in the mirror, your tie half tied, for five minutes."

"I forgot how to do a double Windsor."

"You don't have to talk about it if you don't want to. But I think it has to do with your father."

"Maybe it does."

"Maybe you need to cry. You didn't, you know."

"He was old. He was in terrible health. Pain all the time. Death came to him as a relief. He was a good man and the Lord will honor him in the next life. What's to cry about?"

"You tell me."

"I still have my mother," said Jared.

"Is that an answer?"

"No," said Jared. "I think it's a question." He laughed mirthlessly. "I'm not sure how to deal with her without Dad."

"Excuse me if I sound judgmental, but I'm not aware of your father ever 'dealing' with her."

"But he did," said Jared. "Quietly, alone, later, patiently, he dealt with her."

"And that's it? That's what you miss about your father? That he won't be here to help with Hazel?"

Jared seemed to be thinking about her question. But then he finished adjusting his clothing and left the room without saying another word. Rachel wrote this up on her mental chalkboard and drew a big thick square around it: Jared is having a very hard time dealing with his father's death. She had no idea what to do about this, or even if she should do anything at all. But she would watch.

At Thanksgiving, everything went perfectly. Hazel had been in residence for two days and had already shed any hint of being a guest. Thanksgiving dinner could have been a nightmare—two women in the kitchen!—but Hazel did only what she was asked, except that she made a batch of candied yams, which Jared and Rachel both loathed but which Hazel needed in order for it to be really Thanksgiving. "My mother made them," she explained. "When I eat them, I see her again. Silly, isn't it? Conjuring the dead with candied yams." It made Rachel think about what she would always carry of her mother, when the time came that she couldn't just fly down to Phoenix to see her. That whipped-cream-and-jello dessert they called "Gone with the Wind"? "All foods have to have a name," Rachel's father had said. "Calling it 'That Green Dessert' could describe half the food in the fridge." So Rachel's younger sister, who was an absolute *Gone with the Wind* groupie, had named it for the sine qua non of American literature. But did that dessert really stand for Rachel's mother, or was it just a family thing? Jared hated it anyway, so Rachel only made it when her parents or a sibling came to visit. Or when Jared was traveling. Maybe it was one of the last remnants of her single life. Who could guess what any of these things really meant? Everybody had their own private mythology, with inexplicably powerful icons arising from the most commonplace things. Candied yams. Gone with the Wind. A double Windsor knot.

Three of their kids lived in Utah, but Lettie (who had finally forgiven them for naming her Letitia after a great-grandmother) and her husband had taken the family to New York to visit his parents. That left Will and his wife Sarah—whom he called, for reasons that probably did not bear examination, "Streak"—and Dawn and her husband Buck. They were all coming to Thanksgiving dinner, with three children among them.

Dawn and Buck only had their three-month-old daughter Pearl, who was, literally, no trouble. Buck bragged that if he looked at her and said, "Sleep now, Pearl," she dropped off immediately. Will and Sarah, however, had the twins, Vanya and Valiant, and at three years old they regarded it as their mission in life to take apart anything that had ever been in an unassembled state. To Will's credit, he did his best to keep them under control, but Sarah was about eleven months pregnant and her idea of discipline consisted of languidly calling out, "Please don't be such naughty-nasters, boys."

Rachel could hardly criticize her for not leaping to her feet and bounding after them, not with her belly that was large enough that Jared was talking about helping them build a stable for the foal she was apparently going to have. But she and Hazel had spent half an hour removing everything breakable from the main floor of the house before they got down to the serious business of fixing Thanksgiving dinner. Thinking of having the twins in the house made her glad that she wasn't starting a new family right now. She just didn't have the energy.

Neither did Sarah, of course. The name "Streak" had to be ironic.

The twins burst into the house screaming "Gamma Ray! Gamma Ray!" at the top of their lungs. Rachel wasn't sure she'd ever forgive Jared for coming up with that grandma nickname for her, but all her grandchildren called her that now, and Rachel had finally decided to regard it as a genial tribute to Jared's career in nuclear physics, even if she *had* always loathed "Ray" as a nickname for Rachel. Then they caught sight of Hazel and screamed—even louder, which Rachel would not have thought possible—"Hazie-Ma! Hazie-Ma!"

"I truly hate that nickname," murmured Hazel as she patted the heads of the two little boys who had attached themselves, remora-like, to her thighs.

"I haven't really forgiven Jared yet for coming up with Gamma Ray," said Rachel.

"He came up with Hazie Maw, too. That's why I cut him out of my will."

They watched through the open front door as Sarah came up the steps, rocking from side to side like an elephant trying to free its feet from clinging mud. "Streak," murmured Hazel. Rachel smiled and patted her mother-in-law's shoulder. For all of Hazel's cantankerousness, for all that she sometimes had to be "handled," she and Rachel had always seen the world through the same amused-but-affectionate eyes. Hazel had been ward drama leader when Rachel was going through Young Women, and Rachel had become like another daughter to her. A kindred spirit. This all happened while Jared was on his mission, and Hazel had written to him in his last month that he'd better not date Rachel when he got home "because I don't want to lose her as a daughter when you decide to break up with her." Naturally, this guaranteed that Rachel was the first person Jared dated when he got home. As Hazel had predicted, they did break up—three times, before they finally got married—but Rachel had made a point of staying close to Hazel through the ups and downs. It drove poor Jared crazy, since, as he often complained, he could never complain to his mother about the wretched way his ex-girlfriend had treated him. "She was always on your side, Rachel," he told her. "If we ever got a divorce, I'm afraid you'd probably go home to *my* mother."

Since those Young Women days and the courting days that followed, Rachel had come to know Hazel much better, and knew more about her difficulties than she had ever suspected before. But it never dimmed her love for Hazel, which was quite independent of her love for Hazel's son.

Now, looking at Sarah coming up the stairs, Rachel wondered if any of her daughters-in-law felt toward her anything like the bond of affection that she felt toward Hazel. Hazel had cast her as Fiona in a ward production of *Brigadoon*. What role did Rachel's daughters-in-law feel that she had cast *them* in? Rachel studied Sarah's face and tried to determine how the girl might feel about her husband's family. As far as Rachel could tell, all Sarah felt was tired.

The twins were already out of the room; poor Will was chasing after them, calling out the words that struck fear into Rachel's heart: "Vanya, Val, put that down! You'll break it!" I will not think of this, Rachel told herself. Possessions are not as important as family, and Will is doing his best.

Hazel pointedly looked Sarah up and down. "Well, is it large twins or small triplets?"

"God, I hope not," Sarah blurted. Then she covered her mouth with her hand and the look of dismay on her face was almost comical. "I'm so sorry," she said.

"For what?" said Hazel. "Sounded like a prayer to me."

Sarah laughed in relief, and so did Rachel. Hazel could do that, put people at ease in a moment. When she wanted to.

Still, it bothered her that taking the name of the Lord in vain came so easily to Sarah's lips. She just hadn't been raised like Rachel's other daughters-in-law. She grew up Mormon, but in a rural family in Draper where the farmers still used the same one-syllable word for manure that the ancient Anglo-Saxons had used. There were junker cars parked on her family's lawn—the back lawn, though, which was probably a mark of the upper class in Draper—and even though Jared used words like "salt of the earth" to describe Sarah and her family, Rachel had often asked herself how a son of hers could even be attracted to people like that, let alone *like* them, which Will seemed to do. Will was a brilliant young lawyer. He would move in elevated circles all his life. He might run for office someday. And this was the woman he would take with him to the Senate or the governor's mansion?

Even as she had these thoughts, Rachel stifled them. She knew it was a flaw in her, not in Sarah. I'm a snob, she realized. I never knew it till Will married Sarah, but I truly am a snob. All those sermonettes I've given about how the Lord is no respecter of persons and the poor and uneducated are more likely to be in tune with the Spirit of God than the rich and "wise"—I meant every word of them, until my son brought home a farm girl who knew what a carburetor was for and how to fix one, "except it's a pretty useless skill these days," Sarah had explained, "what with computerized fuel injection." Rachel had only been able to smile and nod, having no concept what these things were except words in advertisements.

Ever since then, though, it had always been Sarah who had that polite smile on her face, pretending to understand what was going on as Will and Jared launched into long esoteric discussions of arcane Church doctrines or issues in law and ethics or scientific and academic questions. It was the way Jared had always talked to all his children, assuming that as long as you had reasoning behind it you could have an opinion on any subject, but Rachel was pretty sure Sarah felt completely excluded. Rachel had even pointed out to her that she was perfectly welcome to speak up. "I would," Sarah said, smiling. "If I could ever understand what they're talking about."

Poor child! Poor child!

Well, she and Will would be married for a long time—if the twins didn't drive them both into the looney bin. Plenty of chances for Sarah to learn to take part in Will's intellectual life. Rachel had had it easy—she was a professor's daughter and had learned all the social graces from her mother, who was the consummate unaffected hostess, so that without an ounce of pretense she could make anybody feel welcome in her home. Sarah simply hadn't grown up with this—but she would learn. And she was trying to learn, too. Rachel could see how Sarah's eyes were upon her, studying her whenever she came to visit, watching how Rachel did things, learning, learning. Despite all Rachel's misgivings, Sarah was trying to be a good wife and she would become just what Will needed. And one thing was certain: Sarah was already what Will *wanted*.

A couple of times it had occurred to Rachel that perhaps what Will loved about Sarah was precisely that she was nothing at all like Will's mother. But Rachel dismissed that thought from her mind as quickly as possible. She and Will had always gotten along quite well. He couldn't possibly have disliked her enough to try to marry her opposite.

Hunger tamed the twins as no amount of discipline could: When mealtime came, they were perched in duplicate high chairs, cloaked in huge, smocklike bibs that didn't bode well for the condition of the floor after dinner. Oh, well, it's only carpet, Rachel told herself. Jared called on his mother to say the blessing, and to everyone's surprise, she said nothing more than the standard blessing, plus one sentence: "For all thy gracious gifts to us during this year, we give special thanks today." That was it. When everyone looked at her in surprise after the amens, Hazel only laughed and winked. "One of the things I like to be thankful for at Thanksgiving is hot food!"

I hope I get old like her, thought Rachel, not for the first time.

And then she wondered: Was the short blessing really in order to let them eat while the food was still hot, or rather because a mere month after her husband died Hazel wasn't feeling all that grateful? Unlike Jared, Hazel had wept copiously at her husband's funeral. Still, since that cathartic day Hazel had hardly spoken of her husband. It struck Rachel that she and Jared might well be coping with their loss the same way—by avoiding thinking or feeling anything about it at all. Rachel resolved to watch more carefully.

Will was telling everybody about how only a few days ago he had accepted the offer of a law firm in Los Angeles. Dawn and Buck were teasing him about being part of the recently-canceled TV show. "Will you be Arnie Becker?" Dawn asked.

"No divorces," said Will. "And no love affairs."

Everybody laughed. Even Sarah, who then piped up with her own jest: "I'm sorry they canceled that show. I was watching it so I could understand what Will's life was going to be like. But except for the ones who were lawyers themselves, I can't remember ever seeing any of their wives." She laughed, and so did everyone else, but Rachel didn't have to be a genius to detect the fear that lay under the joke.

"Anyway we went to a realtor to see about putting our house on the market," said Will. "And it happened that one of the agents in the firm was looking to buy a . . . how did they put it? . . . a *starter* home . . ."

"A cheap little rental property," said Sarah. "I think those were the exact words."

"Yes, that's it—Streak here always remembers the *exact* words, it's why I don't dare argue with her," said Will. "I can face *anybody* in court, but that's because none of the other lawyers have Streak's steeltrap mind." He laughed, and so did everyone else, but it seemed to Rachel that she wasn't the only one who was unsure whether Will was sincerely complimenting his wife and laughing at the other lawyers, or ironically teasing his wife by praising her for attributes she didn't have. Steeltrap mind? Sarah managed to keep it hidden under her cowlike docility.

"So they already made you an offer on the house?" Buck asked. "Because it really *would* be a good rental, being so close to the university."

"If anyone can ever repair the damage the twins have done," said Sarah, laughing. Again, everyone joined in, but with uncertainty about how much truth lay behind the joke.

"They didn't just offer," said Will. "They bought. The only drawback is we have to be out of the house by December first."

"But your job won't even start in LA until March!" cried Dawn.

Rachel looked up into Jared's eyes. They could both see the handwriting on the wall. Will was planning to move back in with them.

"Will, for a smart guy you are sure dumb," said Dawn, in her patronizing sister voice. "You could have sold it five times over, if you'd just waited, and to somebody who wouldn't take occupancy until after you left. You're going to make Sarah have the baby while you're camping out in some makeshift apartment!"

Dawn was the only one who ever talked to Will as if he were an idiot child. Will didn't seem to mind. "We were hoping," he said mildly, "that all that empty space in the basement here might be available for a few fledglings to return to the nest. It's only till March, but it will save us a lot of money—I think the exactly amount is 'oodles'—if we don't have to move twice. We can just have the moving company pack everything up— at my new firm's expense, I might add—and store it until March. And it would be a great help to us when the baby's born, to be living here where Streak can get plenty of help from Mom. If you don't mind, Mom."

"Fine," said Rachel. "If I get the new baby."

Will looked her in the eye. "You get the twins, Mom. But you raised me. You're tough. And as my work winds down, I'll have more and more time at home. The worst of it would be between now and New Year's. It's a terrible imposition, but where are we going to find a rental for these three months? Nobody in their right mind is moving out between now and New Year's."

"Exactly what I was going to say," Jared said. "You know that with Mother living with us, we—"

"With Mother living with you," said Hazel, "things couldn't be better. I can help with the twins."

"No, Mother," said Jared. "That's too much for somebody your . . ."

"My age?" asked Hazel. "That's rich. I may not be fast, but I'm mean. Nothing wrong with these twins that can't be cured by smacking them around a little." There was a momentary pause. "That was a joke, you beastly children. I never raised a hand to *you,* Jared. You should have leapt to my defense."

Now everyone laughed. But Jared was still reluctant. "Will, you should have asked us before you went ahead and sold your house."

"If you can't do it, we'll work something out," said Will.

"What about Sarah's family?" asked Jared.

It was Sarah who answered. Firmly, loudly. "No."

Everyone looked at her.

"You mean your parents really wouldn't help?" asked Rachel, surprised. "I know they're all alone in that big old farmhouse, and there's plenty of land . . ."

"I mean my children aren't going to have any memories of living *there,*" Sarah said firmly.

"It's really not an option," said Will, his face reddening. He was going to back his wife up on this one, clearly, and he also wasn't going to brook any questions.

"Of course you can stay here," said Rachel. "Your father was only reluctant because he's trying to protect me from overwork. But Mother Hazel's right, she'll be a great help to me. Between the three of us, Sarah, we womenfolk will have those two monsters outnumbered. Just do us a favor and don't have another boy. Smart as the twins are, a solo would probably be born running."

"It's a girl," said Sarah.

This was the first they had heard of the sex of the child. "Ultrasound?" asked Dawn.

Sarah shook her head. "I've known all along."

Another silence.

Will finally spoke up. "Sarah . . . dreams. Sometimes. She knew about the twins before the doctor did."

Rachel had a strange feeling in the pit of her stomach. Why did this bother her? She had always known that some women had visions, true dreams, intuitions that turned out to be true. It was one of the gifts of the Spirit. And it was certain that Sarah didn't boast about it, since this was the first they had heard about her being a visionary woman. Still, there was something faintly awkward about the way Will phrased it. He didn't just say she had a dream about this baby. He said that she dreams "sometimes." He wasn't telling about one experience—he was saying that this sort of thing happens a lot. A very different claim. It made Rachel wonder who really had the upper hand in their marriage. If anyone does, she reminded herself quickly. After all, Rachel and Jared had a perfect balance. There *was* no upper hand.

Even reminding herself of how good her own marriage was didn't make her bad feeling go away. She wondered: Do I feel uncomfortable because I don't really believe in people who regularly get visions? Or do I feel uncomfortable because my son married a woman who is much more closely in touch with spiritual things than I am?

"Well," said Hazel, "that's a *useful* talent, I'd say! Is the baby going to be all right?"

Sarah smiled faintly. "We're going to love her very much."

"We don't talk about this stuff much," said Will. "It's . . . sacred, I'm sure you understand. I don't know why I mentioned it today. I guess if we're going to live here I thought . . . I don't know what I thought. Just till March, can you handle it?"

"What are you going to name her?" asked Hazel.

"We have some ideas," said Sarah. "But nothing is set."

"Just don't name her Hazel. I've always resented my father for giving me that name. It's even more old-fashioned now. She would be teased mercilessly in school."

Buck hooted in laughter. "You can say that again! My parents didn't even have the decency to name me 'Norman,' which would have been bad enough. No, every school year the teacher had to read out my name." He put on an exaggeratedly high teacher's voice: " 'Normal'? Is that right? Is that a name, or an evaluation?"

"I've always wondered that myself," said Will.

Dawn answered. "It's *not* a description," she assured him. "At least not an accurate one."

"What *I've* always wondered," said Jared, "is how you came up with the nickname 'Buck.' I mean, are your folks deer hunters or something?"

"Simple enough story," said Buck. "They call me Buck so they can tell me apart from my little brother."

"Oh, what's *his* name?" asked Hazel.

"Buck," said Buck. Then he took a bite of turkey.

It took a moment for everyone to realize that he was joking. Dawn jabbed him with her elbow. "You didn't have to pull that old joke on my family!"

He shied away from her. "Don't touch me when I'm eating unless you're giving me the Heimlich maneuver."

She started tickling him. "I don't use Heimlich, I just tickle."

"Tickle and *jab!*" Buck cried, holding her hands away from him.

"Children," said Jared sternly. "Try to behave at least as well as the twins."

Well, thought Rachel, that was that. Somehow they had agreed to let Will and Sarah and the twins move into their basement. And Hazel, somehow, was going to help with them. The house was going to be full again. It was just bad luck that it happened to be Rachel's least-favorite grandchildren who were going to be tearing her house apart. Actually, it was bound to be a good thing. When Rachel had a chance to know them better, no doubt she'd find and appreciate the twins' better qualities. The same might even happen with Sarah. Sarah who took the name of the Lord in vain. Sarah whose parents kept dead cars on the lawn. Sarah who had visions.

Strange and mysterious are the ways of God.

The twins weren't as much of a problem as Rachel had feared, in large measure because Sarah went over the house with them, her expert eye spotting everything that the twins might be able to break. For a while, Rachel feared that there'd be nothing left, but as she boxed up every bit of ceramic and her entire clock collection, she reminded herself that it would only be a few months. Apparently Sarah spotted everything. The twins quickly learned that there was nothing to destroy inside the house and so they went outside and worked over the garden. Well, that was all right. A few passes with the rototiller in the spring and there'd be no trace of their massive construction projects in the dirt. The only drawback was bundling them up for the cold weather. But having them out of the house for hours on end was worth the work. Thank heaven the weather was staying dry.

And when the twins were inside the house, Hazel *was* a help. She had infinite patience as a performer, apparently, telling stories to the twins whenever they wanted, which was often. And always with different voices for all the characters and a lot of silliness and wit so the boys were laughing all the time. They actually preferred Hazel to the television. But after a few stories, Rachel could tell that Hazel was exhausted and so she'd bundle the twins into their jackets and herd them outside. In the meantime, Sarah would lie miserably on the couch in the family room and call out, "I can take them in here! Please don't wear yourselves out!" They cheerfully ignored her, except when Hazel went in and plumped up her pillow and gave her hot chocolate or lemonade or milk or whatever Sarah could finally be bullied into expressing a preference for that day. "You are the most *un*demanding, *un*particular pregnant woman I've ever known," Hazel told the girl. "I swear if the baby said, 'Well, Mom, shall I come on my due date?' you'd answer, 'Oh, you just come when you want. This month. Next month. Whatever.'"

"I just don't *have* that much in the way of a preference," said Sarah.

Whereupon Hazel would turn to Rachel. "I swear if Sarah's head was on fire, she'd just say, 'Now, if you're going into the kitchen anyway, and it's not too much trouble, would you mind bringing me back a glass of water to put this pesky fire out? But only if you're already going to the kitchen, don't make a special trip on my account!'" Rachel noticed that Sarah laughed at these jokes, but at the same time she could see that the girl had some kind of pain behind her eyes.

Sarah's due date came and went. December 8th. December 9th. December 10th. "I'm going to start jumping off the bottom step," Sarah told them miserably. "If that doesn't work, I'll try the second step."

"No such thing," said Hazel. "If that baby needs a few extra days to get ripe, don't worry. Besides, the doctors never really know when the true due date is. For all you know, this little girl was conceived late in the cycle."

On the 11th, there was a little false alarm—a sharp pain that Sarah was *sure* wasn't a contraction but she still had to go check. Hazel bravely stayed with the boys while Rachel took Sarah to the doctor's office for an unscheduled checkup. All the way there, Rachel kept assuring Sarah that the doctor would probably make them go right to the hospital and call Will from there. Sarah said little, and her tacit disagreement turned out to be correct. The doctor was as frustrated, it seemed, as Sarah was. "You're not dilated at *all,*" he said. "I really don't want to induce until there's some sign that your body is in birth mode."

"That's all right," Sarah said miserably.

On the ride home, Rachel finally let her curiosity get the better of her manners. "Can I ask you something personal, Sarah?"

"I would hope so," said Sarah. "And I'd also hope that if I don't want to answer, I won't have to."

"Of course," said Rachel. "And it's rude of me even to ask, but the curiosity is killing me. How did Will come to start calling you 'Streak'?"

Sarah laughed sharply and looked out the window for a long time. Just as Rachel was about to say never mind, she spoke. "I'm very shy about my body," she explained. "The first time we went swimming, he dived under the water and snapped my swimsuit. I was mortified, but he assured me that I'd run from the poolhouse into the water so fast that he wasn't sure I was *wearing* a suit. Actually, it was when he did that and I found that I could forgive him for touching me like that, well, that was when I realized that maybe I *could* marry somebody." Sarah laughed nervously. She had said more than she planned to, but less, it seemed, than she wanted to.

Immediately Rachel remembered how, at Thanksgiving, Sarah had been so adamant about her children never having memories of the house she grew up in. "You were molested as a child, weren't you?" Rachel asked.

Sarah nodded. "I knew you guessed when I reacted like I did to living in my parents' house. It wasn't my father, though, I don't want you ever to think that. My father's youngest brother lived with them for a while because of some trouble he was in out in Star Valley, Wyoming. He stayed for a year. I turned eleven that year. He made me do things."

"You don't have to tell me more than that, Sarah, if you don't want to," said Rachel.

"I have some pretty bad memories of that time. Because I felt for the longest time that I was partly at fault. I mean, at first it was almost exciting. I was curious."

"You were a child."

"I know that as a Primary president you have all sorts of training in dealing with this."

"Less than I should," said Rachel. "And more than I was ever required to have."

"Well, they *say* that the child is never at fault. But I was over eight years old and I wasn't stupid. I know that it was mostly him, even though he really was a child himself, only fifteen. But it was partly me, and I couldn't feel right about anything until I was seventeen and I decided that maybe other people could do what the therapist said, but *I* had to repent. Like Enos, you know? I prayed for two days. In the summer. My mother understood a little and she refused to let anyone go searching for me. Out in the far corner of the orchard. It works, you know. I was forgiven."

Rachel had tears in her eyes, but when she glanced over at Sarah she could see that the girl was dry-eyed.

"I don't get emotional about it now," said Sarah. "It's at the very center of my life. Not the molesting, but the forgiveness. That was when I first had a, you know, dream. I don't have a lot of them, if that's what worries you. It's more like going to a movie with a friend who's seen it before, and right before the scary parts she says, 'Don't worry about this, it turns out all right.'"

"But you still can't go home."

"Bad memories."

Rachel had a sudden insight and had to blurt it out. "Did your parents know what kind of trouble this uncle of yours had been in back in Wyoming?"

"They knew it was trouble with a girl. Father told me that it never crossed his mind that it was somebody as young as me, that his brother was messing with *children*. Afterward, Father wanted to get his brother put in jail for what he did to me, but I refused to let him. I knew that Ammaw and Old Man—my grandparents—I knew they'd blame me the way they blamed that evil girl back in Star Valley. *She* was *twelve*. So the way they saw things, I must be even more wicked. It was really ugly. I love my parents, but they come visit us, I don't go visit them. If I was a better Saint I'd forgive them, and I have, in my head. It's just my heart that doesn't know it, when I go home."

"You poor thing," said Rachel.

"Oh, I'm fine. I just wanted you to understand that it's not because my parents wouldn't help me. And I'm not really insane or hateful. I'm still going to be a good mother to your grandchildren."

"Well of course you are," said Rachel. "I never for a moment thought otherwise."

"But you were worried when I reacted like I did about going home."

"I was just afraid that there was some kind of rift in your family. I was worried about *you*. I know you're a great mother."

"Not lately," said Sarah. "I'm just a mountain of flesh piled up on beds and couches made of stone."

"Is that furniture uncomfortable?"

"Air pressure is uncomfortable when you're this far along. I have no navel. But where it used to be, I have this patch of incredibly sensitive skin. And lately it feels like it's spreading. Pretty soon my whole body will be nothing but one huge extruded navel. Touch me and I'll scream."

"I'll remember not to slap you around so much."

They laughed.

As they pulled into the garage, Rachel said, "Don't you worry about what you told me. I won't tell anybody."

"Well, I hope you *will* tell your husband. I was hoping you would. So I won't have to explain it."

"But no one else."

"That's very kind of you."

"Hey, I was going to the kitchen anyway."

That night, when Jared got home from a late night of grading finals with his grad students, Rachel told him about the conversation. She cried in telling it, all the more because Sarah hadn't shed a tear. "Well, it explains one thing that I'd wondered about," said Jared.

"What?" asked Rachel.

"Why Will was drawn to her in the first place."

"Oh, Jared, he couldn't possibly have known about . . ."

"I know that he fell in love with her because she's a great person and all that. But there's a kind of frailty about her. She needs protecting. And Will needs to be a protector."

That was true. They both knew that about Will. Unusual in a youngest child. He should have been the spoiled one. Instead he was always looking out for other people. All through Primary, he was the one who would never let anybody tease or pick on anybody else. What Sarah needed, Will was; what Will needed, Sarah was.

"But it's more than that now," Rachel said.

"I know that," said Jared. "I mean, Will can't be *too* protective if he calls her Streak."

So they figured they knew everything, understood everything. Except Rachel still had a nagging doubt. There was still something wrong. Something in Sarah that made Rachel worry. Was it her spirituality? Hardly that. Rachel was always more, not less, comfortable around spiritual people. No, there was just an awkwardness. Sarah had told Rachel about the most terrible, intimate secret of her life, surely—and yet Sarah still seemed reticent and shy. Something was wrong, still.

On the 16th of December they had their traditional Christmas party for friends in the ward and stake, mostly people who had worked with Rachel in the Primary over the years plus some special neighbors. Everyone made much of Sarah and Will and their kids, and Hazel of course, but then it was time to put the twins to bed and Sarah insisted on doing that herself. "You go help her, Mother Hazel," said Rachel after she was gone. "You know how tired she gets, and she wouldn't ask for help if . . ."

"If her head was on fire, I know," said Hazel with a smile. "Consider it done."

About fifteen minutes later, Rachel realized that she hadn't brought the candy up from the cold room in the basement. She tiptoed down the stairs in case the boys weren't soundly asleep yet. Nobody could possibly have heard her come down. Which was why Hazel didn't stop talking to Sarah when Rachel came within earshot. Surely she would have stopped if she had thought that anyone could overhear her.

"Of course you know that Will's a special boy. They're all special. All of Jared's and Rachel's children. Absolutely brilliant, every one of them. I'm in awe myself. But there's a special burden to being the wife of a man like Will. He's going to be a great man, like his father. The best of a good lot, really. And a woman in your situation really has to keep on her toes just to avoid getting in the way."

Rachel could hardly believe what she was hearing. Surely Hazel wasn't trying to tell Will's wife that she wasn't up to snuff, was she? If she listened just a moment longer, Hazel would say something that would clarify everything and Rachel would see she had been silly to jump to such an awful conclusion.

Suddenly there were hands on her shoulders, sliding down her arms, wrapping around her body from behind. Rachel jumped—but such were her eavesdropping skills that she didn't make a sound. She just turned around and faced Jared and touched her fingers to his lips. "Listen," she whispered.

He seemed to notice his mother's voice for the first time.

"It's a special burden to take this family's name on you," Hazel was saying. "I know it—I wasn't born with it, either. Rachel is a natural, she really was born to be married to a man like Jared, but I wasn't that sort and neither are you. It's just a fact of life."

Sarah murmured something.

"Oh, don't even *think* that you can ever measure up. No matter what you do, Sarah, people are going to look at you with Will and they're going to say, 'What does he see in *her*?' The thing you have to worry about—the *only* thing—is making sure that *Will* never wonders that. I hope you're using this time that you're in Rachel's house to study everything she does and learn from her. She is the perfect wife for a prominent man. But then, she has a real education herself, and she's a professor's daughter."

"I'm going to stop this," whispered Jared. But still he didn't move. This was his mother, after all. One doesn't just interrupt one's mother. Or rather, Jared didn't. Actually, nobody did. Not Hazel. Hazel wasn't good at taking anything that seemed like criticism.

"You just have to cling to your children," said Hazel. "*They* will never know that you aren't really part of this family. For them, you're the heart, even as Will is the head. So you mustn't worry about a thing. When you have one of those awful times when you think everybody must think you're a complete idiot, you just hold these little ones close to you because *they* won't judge you and find you unworthy the way everyone else does."

That was just too much for Jared. He strode into the bedroom where they were talking, and in a fierce whisper he said, "Let's come out of this room right now."

Hazel and Sarah followed him out and he closed the door behind him. "I didn't want to wake the twins," he said.

There were tears in Sarah's eyes. Tears on her cheeks. She didn't cry when she told Rachel about her awful childhood experiences, but she cried listening to Hazel tell her she would never be worthy of her husband. Rachel wanted to slap her mother-in-law. She had never slapped anyone since she grew past that phase in her quarrels with her brother, but apparently she still could conjure up a real lashing-out rage even after all these years as a Primary leader with a permanent smile plastered on her face.

"What's the emergency?" asked Hazel.

"You, Mother," said Jared softly. "You're the emergency. I overheard what you were saying in there, and—"

"You were *eavesdropping*?"

"Yes, Mother, I was. I'll be made a son of perdition for it, I know. Me, Cain, and the devil. But yes, I heard what you were saying to Sarah and I couldn't believe those words were coming out of your mouth."

"I was only reassuring her that—"

"Reassuring her! 'Oh, don't even *think* that you can measure up.' That must have been a real comfort."

"Sarah understood what I meant," said Hazel.

"Is that why she's crying?"

"Watch the way you talk to me, young man," said Hazel. "I may only be an old woman who's good for nothing at all anymore, but I'm still your mother."

"Yes, you *are* my mother. The very same woman who used to weep for days before her mother-in-law came to visit and then weep again for days afterward. And why? Because dear old Mattie was always judging you and you never measured up. That brought you so much joy, of *course* you had to plunge Sarah into—"

"Please," said Sarah. "She didn't make me cry. I was already crying when—"

"No, there's something you have to understand," Jared answered. "You have to know that when I was seven I came in and found my mother sobbing her heart out and I said, 'Why are you crying, Mother?' and she said, 'Because Mattie's right, I should never have married your father, I've ruined his life.' And I knew then and there that this was wrong, it was evil, *no* woman should *ever* make another woman feel unworthy of her place in her own home."

"Are you suggesting that I am anything like my mother-in-law!" Hazel was furious now.

"I'm suggesting that what you were doing in that bedroom was *exactly* what Mattie Maw did to you when you first married Dad. Remember the story you told me? How Mattie called you in and sat you down and explained to you that there was a special burden placed on women who married into that family? Mattie's father, after all, was an apostle, and her husband's father was a great colonizer and his mother was famous in the Church as the general president of the Relief Society—"

"The YWMIA," said Hazel coldly.

"*And,*" said Jared pointedly, "she had always thought that her sons would marry within their social class. Daughters of general authorities, presumably, or people with enough money to move in those lofty circles. Of course that was the 1930s, I'm sure things are different now, but she was full of stories about how her marriage to Grandpa was *the* event of the season in Salt Lake City, and her oldest boy had married the daughter of another apostle but it was beyond her how Dad—she said Alma, of course—could have lost his senses to such a degree as to pick up with a girl whose father was—well, no one even knew *where* he was, and there was certainly no money and less breeding and I think the exact phrase she used was, 'Try as you may, Hazel, you will never be one of us. All you can do is just stay out of Alma's way.' That was a terrible thing for Mattie Maw to say and it caused you more pain than anything else in your marriage and now here you are saying it to Sarah and it—"

"Yes, it caused me pain," said Hazel. "But as you condemn me you're forgetting one tiny little fact." Suddenly she burst into tears. "Every word she said was true!"

"No it wasn't," said Jared.

"Oh, even *you* know it's true. Look at you, Mr. Professor with all the brains, pointing out to the poor daughter of a scrubwoman that once again she's . . . *blown* it!"

"It was never true, Mother. I can't believe you still believe it!"

"I knew it before she ever said it. And so did Sarah! We're just alike, Sarah and I. We both married up. Too far up, and it made us sad all the time. I dragged my husband down. I wanted to help Sarah do better than I did! And she wants to. She asked *me* for advice!"

"She asked *you*?"

"Oh, is that so incredible? Is Mr. Genius-with-Atoms really so stunned that someone might actually ask his poor ignorant non-college-graduate mother for some advice about something besides the best way to get a stain out of wool?"

Rachel could see Jared retreat from his mother's onslaught. Rachel had only caught glimpses of this side of Hazel before. But she was beginning to understand why it was that people had always been careful to "handle" Hazel. "Mother, don't do this," said Jared quietly.

"Oh, is this something *I'm* doing? Is crazy old Hazel having another fit, is that it? You come in here and accuse me of something truly awful, but if I dare to express the tiniest objection suddenly *I'm* doing something bad? Oh, we must calm Mother down. We mustn't let other people see how badly Mother behaves when somebody *hurts* her, when one of her children *stabs* her in the heart in front of her daughter-in-law and her granddaughter-in-law—"

"Mother, listen to me—"

"Oh, I know, I'm busy not measuring up right *now,* aren't I? I'm proving Mattie was right once again, aren't I? Now poor Rachel has to face the fact that she's taken a screaming fishwife into the house with her and—"

Rachel spoke up. "Mother Hazel, I don't think—"

"I'll have you know something, Rachel," Hazel lashed out at her. "I *hate* hearing anyone but my own children call me mother. He can call me mother because his body came out of my body, but you came out of someone else and she's the *only* person on God's green earth who should ever hear the name 'mother' from your lips. And do you know the worst thing about it? It's knowing that since you call me 'Mother Hazel,' *he* must call *your* mother 'Mother Amy.' Or no, it's probably 'Mom Amy,' isn't it? And she has no *right* to hear him call her mother because she didn't bear him and she didn't raise him and cook his meals and clean up his sheets for all those years he was a bedwetter and—"

"Mother!" Jared said.

"Oh, haven't you told her you were a bedwetter?"

"Mother, of course I did, the tendency is hereditary and I told her and all my sons who were bedwetters after me. It's one of many family traditions that we have proudly passed along."

Perhaps they were both aching for release, because this was enough to set them both to laughing. Uncontrollably, for several minutes, while Rachel and Sarah looked on. Rachel had no idea what Sarah was making of all this. For that matter, Rachel had no idea what *she* was making of it. She had heard from Jared about some of the legendary quarrels he had with his mother, but in all their umpty-four years of marriage she had never seen anything like this. Now, at last, she understood what the great secret of Jared's family had been. Hazel had seemed to be the sweetest, most kind and understanding woman in the world when Rachel was growing up. But behind closed doors, she had a temper that must surely be listed in the *Guinness Book of World Records,* at least in the top five.

They stopped laughing. Jared spoke again, more softly. The moment he opened his mouth, Hazel started to speak, but Jared laid his hand on her shoulder and she stopped. The gesture looked familiar. Then Rachel realized: It was the same thing Jared's father had always done, when things were getting tense. A hand on the shoulder, as if there was a button there that when you pressed it, Hazel became calm and quiet, at least for a moment, at least long enough to speak a few words of conciliation.

"Mother," Jared said, "Mattie Maw was wrong. She may have been right about her feeling that you never truly belonged—she was a snob—and she was maybe right about *you* never feeling that you belonged because you're a reverse snob, you've spent your whole life knowing that you were never worthy of associating with the only people that you thought were worth associating with . . ."

Hazel started to interrupt—apparently the hand on the shoulder was only good for a few sentences—but now Jared raised his other hand to signal her to wait. Stage two? How many gestures does he have left, Rachel wondered.

"But I wish you would look at reality. The reality is that Dad's brother who married the apostle's daughter hasn't been in church for thirty years and my cousins are all suntanned men of the world who drive Porsches and have divorces and marry younger women who get older after all but you'd never know it because their faces are stretched so tight you could use them as trampolines . . . but *you,* the one who wasn't worthy to marry the grandson of an apostle and of the general president of whatever, not to *mention* the non-general authority colonizer, *you* were the one who kept your family in the Church and every single one of your children is now a temple-attending Latter-day Saint and frankly I think that counts for something. I think it counts for a hell of a lot more than whose marriage might have been the social event of the season in Salt Lake in 1935."

"I can't have done too well," said Hazel, "because I raised a son who says 'hell' to his mother."

Jared was furious. "You mean that out of all I said, that's the only thing you heard?"

"Jared," said Rachel, patting his arm—*her* calming gesture. "Jared, she was joking."

He looked more closely at his mother, who, despite the tears running down her cheeks, wore a kind of smile.

"Oh. I guess it was funny then. I missed the point."

"Well, I got the point. And yes, having worthy children *is* more important," said Hazel. "But in case you didn't notice, that's exactly what I was telling Sarah. That the children make up for everything. You live in the children. You might get in your husband's way, but if the children make him proud then it's all worth it." She started to cry again. "When your father was lying there in that hospital bed having all those heart attacks in a row do you know what he said to me? He said, You made us some good children, Hazie. That was the last coherent thing he said to me. Talking about *you,* Jared. And your brothers and sisters, of course, but you. And that was my career, my children. You married somebody who could do it all, children *and* being a good public wife. But all I could do was the children, and what I was telling Sarah, before I got interrupted, what I was telling her was that the children are *enough.* Only *you* had to burst in and demonstrate to her that even when you succeed in raising children who are every bit worthy to be part of this *distinguished* lineage, some of those children will still look you in the eye and tell you that you're too stupid to live."

"I didn't say that you were—"

"I may not be college-educated, I may not have graduate degrees and your magma-come-louder—and *yes* I know it's Latin and it's magna cum laude but I also don't care—because I still know when someone has called me stupid and that's what you called me tonight, and I . . . don't . . . have to . . . stand . . . for that."

Hazel pulled away from him and hobbled to the stairs, starting the long climb up two flights to her bedroom.

Rachel started after her. Jared put his hand on her arm and mouthed, barely whispering, "Let her have her dramatic exit."

"I heard that, you smart-alecky brat," said Hazel from the stairs.

"No you didn't, Mother. You always say you heard us, but you never do."

"I should never have come to live here," said Hazel.

"But at least it wasn't your daughter-in-law you fought with," said Jared. "It was your son."

"Don't rub it in," she said. And, as she finally, arthritically, disappeared up the last few steps, she continued to recite, "How sharper than a serpent's tooth it is to have a thankless child."

"Jared, you have to let me go to her," said Rachel. "She's going to move out."

"I'll go to her," said Jared. "But I've got to give her time to start packing. It'll never work if she hasn't got a bag open on her bed."

"Are you serious? Are you taking this so lightly?"

"You forget that I grew up with this," said Jared. "I was always the one she'd listen to. The fact is that she's still acting mad but it's over. She doesn't say 'smart-alecky brat' until the fever's broken." He turned to Sarah. "My mother meant well, Sarah, but she's wrong. You're not just like her."

"Yes I am," said Sarah. "I've known it all along. If you'd only listened to me you wouldn't have had to quarrel with your mother because *I'm* the one who told *her* that I'm not worthy to be part of this family and I've always known it, I knew it when Will asked me to marry him and I should have turned him down and now I have the two brattiest children in the family and I know that everybody looks at me and pities me because I can't produce *good* children like Dawn the writer and Buck the historian or—"

"Sarah," said Jared.

"I'm just so tired all the time and so I started crying as I was putting the boys to bed and Hazel asked me what was wrong and so I told her, I couldn't help it, I've kept it to myself but I finally had to admit it to somebody that I know I'm failing at this and *that's* why she was telling me the things she—"

"Sarah," said Jared, "you're not failing."

"Of course you're going to try to comfort me now and tell me that I'm doing just fine but we both know that it's a—"

"Sarah," said Jared softly, "do I have to fight with you the way I fought with my mother before you shut up and let me talk to you?"

She fell silent.

"I grew up with my mother. I grew up knowing how Mattie Maw judged my mother and how my mother judged herself and you know something? I actually *learned* from the experience. And Rachel was born with a good set of values or else her parents did something right but anyway, we both feel the same about this. Absolutely the same. I'm going to say it this once. And then I'm going to say it again every time you seem to need to hear it, until you finally hear these words echoing in your head when you go to sleep and when you wake up. Are you ready to hear this?"

"Yes, *sir,*" said Sarah, only a little bit snottily. Only pretending to be rebellious.

"All that matters to Rachel and me is that our children be good. That they stay firm in their faith and love the Lord and do good to everyone around them. You know what I'm talking about? It's called the gospel. That's what we care about. And all these years as we've watched our kids growing up, we've been so afraid, what if they find someone who won't keep them strong in the Church? Especially Will. Because he's so brilliant, he relies on his mind for everything, his concept of the gospel was always completely intellectual and he never realized it, he didn't see that anything was missing. So I worried about him. And then he found you, and I thought, well, the boy has his head on straight after all. He didn't go for one of his law school groupies or some high-powered on-the-make colleague. He didn't go for a trophy wife. He married a good woman who is filled with love—so much love that the Lord even trusts her with two impossible children and she's doing *splendidly* with them I might add—and then at Thanksgiving comes the clincher. It turns out that Will, my intellectual son, has chosen a woman who completely fills the hole in his life. He married a woman who has visions sometimes. And he believes in those visions, and honors the goodness in his wife that keeps her that close to the Spirit. Are you listening to me, Sarah?"

"Yes," she murmured.

"What I'm explaining to you is that I'm not an idiot and I wish you wouldn't be one either. I'm smart enough to know that Will found the wife who is the answer to our prayers. I wish you would realize that, too."

She burst into tears again and fell into Jared's arms and hung there, weeping into his shirt. Rachel reached over and patted Sarah's shoulder. "Me, too, Sarah," she murmured. "What he said." Then she looked up at Jared and air-kissed him. "I'm going upstairs before our guests form a search party. And you need to get up and talk to your mother before she calls a cab."

As Rachel left, she could hear Jared saying to Sarah, "Will you be all right? Have we settled this nonsense, for the next couple of days at least?"

"Yes," said Sarah.

"All right, repeat after me, Will is very lucky to have me. And his father and grandmother are *not* strange."

Laughing, she started to repeat it and then cried again and then laughed and then Rachel was upstairs circulating among the guests.

Later than night she watched as Jared undressed wearily. "We have too many friends," he said. "I'm getting too old to host these parties."

"Don't worry," said Rachel. "Our friends are getting older, too. They'll start dying off and then our parties will be smaller and more manageable."

"I can't believe you'd say something so heartless and morbid."

"Jared, it's about time you knew how heartless and morbid I am."

He must have detected from her tone of voice that she wasn't joking now. He turned to face her, gave her his whole attention.

"You gave me too much credit tonight, down there with Sarah. Maybe *you* valued her for what she means in Will's life, but never once did I think of it that way. In fact I always sort of thought that Will married beneath him."

"Do you think that now?" Jared asked seriously.

"Are you kidding? No, I don't think that at all, now. In my heart I always knew better, anyway. Thanksgiving, when she and Will told about her having a dream that their baby was a girl and they both obviously believed it was from the Lord, that dream, I got this really uncomfortable feeling and for days and days I thought it was because there was something wrong with Sarah for having visions. But you know what I realized tonight? It was something wrong with *me*. Because her spirituality, it's something wonderful, just like you said, it's what Will needs. Only *I* was being a snob, I was looking down at her family and their cars on the lawn and—"

"You *are* a dreadful disappointment to me," said Jared. "But you know what? I've decided to overlook this flaw in you and—"

"I'm not joking, you know. That was a very serious confession."

He immediately dropped his teasing manner. "I know you had misgivings about Sarah, and I know you didn't like her having visions. I kind of hoped that when she bared her soul to you about being molested as a child it would break down the barrier but it didn't, not completely. Not till tonight."

"So when you said what you did about how I was born with enough sense not to misjudge Sarah—you were lying?"

"It was future truth," said Jared. "I knew that the moment I said it, it would become true. And it did, didn't it?"

She pulled him down onto the bed beside her.

"I'm really, really tired, Rachel, even though you are still the most beautiful woman in the known universe. At least the most beautiful one with arms and a head—I've always had a soft place in my heart for the Venus de Milo."

"I just want you to hold me for a minute."

"I can do that," he said.

"Your mother and Sarah both think I'm perfect, don't they?"

"So do I," said Jared.

"I'm not, though," said Rachel.

"Close enough."

"But while you're busy understanding everything about me, I understand something about *you*."

"What?" asked Jared.

"Tonight something happened. You're not hung up tonight the way you have been ever since your father died."

"Oh really?"

"I finally understood it," she said. "You felt the burden of dealing with your mother fall onto your shoulders. And until tonight you weren't sure you could handle it."

Jared chuckled. "Well, actually, no," he said. "I've *always* been the one who could jolly Mom out of these moods better than anybody else, which isn't to say I was actually good at it. But what you said about my father—something *did* happen tonight."

"What?" asked Rachel.

"When I was telling Mom that she did a good job and that Mattie Maw was wrong about her? And then when I told Sarah she was just right for Will? All my life, it was my dad who said things like that to me. Good job. You did well. I'm proud of you son. Not that Mom didn't say those things—she said them ten times more, in fact, but I needed it from my dad, you know?"

"Mothers give milk, fathers give approval," said Rachel.

"That's what had me upset. I know Dad was ready to go. His body was so ravaged. But I still needed him. Who would tell me that I was doing a good job? Only tonight I realized—I don't need that anymore. My job now is to tell *other* people they did OK. I'm the father now. I'm the patriarch. I'm the one whose job it is to bless other people. Even my own mother. That's what happened tonight."

Rachel held him close. "Did I do OK?" she asked.

And now, without a trace of jesting in his tone, he said, "Rachel, you are the greatest blessing in my life and in the lives of everyone you touch. When you meet the Lord face to face he will say to you, Well done, my good and faithful servant."

Tears sprang from her eyes and flowed down onto his shoulder.

"Are you crying or drooling?" he asked.

"I'm just happy," she said. "Like you said, you really do have the power to bless now."

It was the week before Christmas when Sarah's baby finally came, ten days overdue. It was actually a rather leisurely process, with plenty of time for Will to get home to take his wife to the hospital. With their mother gone, the twins got so hyper that Hazel and Rachel remarked several times that they would *much* rather be going through labor right now. Of course, they both knew that this was so false that it wasn't even worth saying, "Just kidding." They had just got the boys settled into bed when the phone rang and, against their own better judgment, they told Vanya and Val that they had a new baby sister.

Because Sarah had been so ambiguous about her vision of her daughter—"We'll love her very much"—Rachel had been half afraid that the baby would be born retarded or crippled. But she was fine, a sturdy, healthy baby. Rachel wondered then if the problems would come later; she wondered what piquant burden of foreknowledge Sarah and Will silently bore. But whatever it was the Lord had shown her, it was certainly true that they loved the baby very much.

They blessed the baby in Jared's and Rachel's ward on the first Sunday in February. They named the baby after her great-grandmother Hazel, and in spite of all her protests, they knew the old soul was thrilled. In March Will and Sarah and the twins and little Hazy moved to Los Angeles. They didn't come back until Hazie Maw's funeral the next autumn, a year almost to the day after she had been widowed. Her last words were, "Alma, what kept you?" Sarah gave Rachel a copy of the four-generation picture they had taken: Hazel holding baby Hazy, with Sarah and Will, Jared and Rachel gathered around. "She won't remember her great-grandma," said Sarah. "But she'll have this picture."

"And the stories you tell her," said Rachel.

"I have parties at the house now, you know," said Sarah. "I pretend that I'm you and then I act it out and everything goes fine."

"That's awful. You don't have to pretend to be me or anybody else."

"Well, actually, I don't really have the figure to be you *all* the time," said Sarah. "I just don't rebound to my girlish figure after pregnancy. So when I choose my wardrobe, I pretend to be Barbara Bush."

"That's all right then," said Rachel. "I can handle the role-model business as long as Barbara Bush is carrying half the load."